Mandra

by

S. L. BHYRAPPA

Winner of Saraswati Samman, 2010

Translated from Kannada by Dr. S. Ramaswamy

and

Smt. L.V. Shantakumari

Thanks to Shri Ranganath Prasad

NIYOGI BOOKS

Published by
NIYOGI BOOKS
Block D, Building No. 77,
Okhla Industrial Area, Phase-I,
New Delhi-110 020, INDIA
Tel: 91-11-26816301, 26818960
Email: niyogibooks@gmail.com
Website: www.niyogibooksindia.com

Translated from Kannada by Dr. S. Ramaswamy and Smt. L.V. Shantakumari
Editor: Jyoti Kumari
Design: Shashi Bhushan Prasad

ISBN: 978-93-81523-36-0
Publication: 2012
Reprint: 2020

Printed at: Niyogi Offset Pvt. Ltd., New Delhi, India

Mandra

Mandra

'Looking at art we feel as if we have entered paradise. But it is totally different when entered inside the artist. Why this contradiction?'

Chapter 1

I

'The slut did act so stubbornly, as if she was a great chaste woman.' This one sentence came to his mind again and again. The age-old knowledge when the same musical note is repeated, the harmony of the music gets spoiled, intellect doesn't work and the throat mechanically repeats its function, did not occur to him at that point. She did act stubbornly—like a chaste woman, the slut, like a great chaste woman, great chaste! Mohanlal roared mutely within his throat as if clearing it before beginning to sing.

I will teach her a lesson. When this desire for revenge did rise, a sound which was more like a roar escaped from him. But when he became aware that this decision was only a repetition, a sense of helplessness enveloped him. Teaching her a lesson, what does it mean? What could he do? He could say that he won't stay even a minute longer in her house, pick up his suitcase and leave. She would keep quiet and let him go. Then who is going to be defeated? Me or her? Why didn't I understand that she won't be defeated when she did assert, 'However stubbornly you persist, I will not agree to that one' and closed the door, bolting it from within. He knocked repeatedly and shouted. 'Open the door Madhu, the door, listen, I need to tell you one thing...' Lowering his voice, bringing it to deep bass tone, and still lowering it to whispering mandra. Couldn't she listen to my entreaties at all or was she being cruelly firm and hard? In America, whatever you do, there would be certain tightness. Doors are made in a way that not even air moves from one side to other and sound waves cannot travel from one room to another. Everything is maintained spotlessly clean. Even the bottom of the lake, without dirt or bits of paper, can be seen lucidly just as mandra-shadja to a singer who has mastered the swara-sadhana. The idea of delving deep into that water and setting his voice on those quartz stones and practising shruti filled his mind.

Instead of staying at home and practising mandra I have walked alone for four miles. Again the same thoughts, about her...she had bolted the door of her bedroom from within even after I entreated her with all humility last night. There was no harshness in her words. The same revered address 'Guruji'.

'It is true I was yours before my marriage. I had offered myself to you completely but now I am a married woman. Would it not be cheating and betraying when my husband has gone on a tour of five days leaving just the two of us at home? I am your disciple. I learnt music from you. You are nobody to him. Yet he is completely devoted to you. The moment you begin the shruti, he becomes completely absorbed and devoted. He gets angry with me saying that I am not looking after you properly and treating you like any ordinary guest. You know all this. How can you think of betraying such a person and compel his wife? How can you? You are demeaning me. Tell me. I demand an answer.'

'You were my lover before you became his wife; even now you are my lover. You were the one who married him without my knowledge and ran away to America and now you are condemning your guru.' She had no answer to that. 'Still I will not agree.' She protested when I tried to embrace her by force and said, 'Guruji, you are fifty-nine, nearing sixty. I am thirty. If I free myself you have no strength to force me. You will only lose your self-respect. Please retain your self-respect, please, please...' She said this, went into her bedroom, closed and bolted the door and no matter how many times I knocked and how many times I beseeched, she didn't open it. Fortunately this was Los Gatos, a place surrounded by hills where only rich people live. Her house was built on the shoulder of the hill and there was a thick natural forest above and on both sides of the house. No matter how loudly the door was banged, nobody would hear it. There was no such fear. The entire house was soundproof with not even air flowing about easily. The windows and the doors were shut so tight that no matter how much noise was made within the house, it could not be heard from outside. Yet for how long could I bang on the door? Knocking on the door further and she not opening the door would make me feel small and humiliated. The thought of packing my suitcase and walking out occurred to me. But it is not possible to leave like that in America. Until the host takes the guest out in his car, the house becomes a prison. When I shouted that I would leave the house, I couldn't make out whether she heard it. Even if she did, she didn't open the door.

Feeling drowsy.

Even those who had come early in the morning for walking, jogging and breathing some fresh air in the big park had left. He had not even had a cup of tea or brushed his teeth. If he had to walk back to the house, he will need to climb the hill. He had no money to make a call and ask her to come and fetch him. He could have made a collect-call. He told himself after I go home I should tell her that I would leave your home right away. Just send me away. There are a number of people in the Silicon Valley who want me to stay with them. Such is the fame of Mohanlal? Who do you think I am? There are music lovers here also who will talk to me only after taking the dust of my feet and wearing it on the forehead! Yes I must do that. I must teach this slut a lesson. Or how about going away to New York today itself? This thought also crossed his mind. He told himself, 'I will be a fortnight early. Where am I going to stay? There has been such wide publicity for my visit and very expensive tickets have been sold already. I have heard that one thousand tickets have been sold already. Tickets for no Indian singer have been sold out like this and I believe the sales are still being made. That is Mohanlal's fame!' He felt proud. Another thought crossed his mind. I have heard that in this country if a programme does not meet the expected level, they can sue. Floating in these broodings, he was losing his bearings, the eyes automatically closed and his neck was slanted, without his knowledge. He lay down on the bench he was sitting and stretched his legs. The shade of the maple trees cooled his eyes and sunk him into deep sleep.

2

It was eight in the morning when she woke up. It is always like that. When the mind is agitated you don't get to sleep initially. But after some time deep sleep takes over. After twisting and turning for some time she recalled everything that happened the previous night and was angry. She lifted her neck a little and looked around. The big bolt of the room was still on. She listened. Maria was working in the kitchen. Madhumita had to soon instruct her on that day's course of the menu and other household chores. She suddenly got up, wore her housecoat, brushed her teeth, went down and said, 'Good morning Maria.' Maria who was preparing dough for chapattis replied, 'Good morning' and continued what she was doing. She asked in the midst of her work, 'Hasn't your musician teacher got up yet? I just love to listen to the tune he would be singing to himself which resembles a prayer. I have begun to develop a taste for it. You please go and continue your practice with him. I can manage on my own. Don't worry.' Again the worry recurred. She had not told Maria that Vikram was not in town. Still, this was the time when he would be moving about in the veranda. Or the time when he would get into his car and leave for office. Maria knew about Vikram going on tours quite frequently. Today I got up late and Guruji has not even woken up. Was it possible for Maria to put all this together and guess something? Madhu was suddenly afraid. But I have been seeing her for three years and she is not the kind of a person who was interested in other people's affairs. Her self-confidence returned. She wondered why he was still sleeping. She wanted to go and find out but was not too sure. What if on account of his disappointment of last night he starts shouting. Even if he spoke in Hindi, Maria would understand the feeling behind the words. Madhu felt so and thus kept quiet.

After Maria left, Madhu bolted the door from inside and slowly climbed the stairs and walked towards the guest room. When she touched the handle her heart missed a beat. He would be angry. He would repeat last night's actions and create a scene. Better not to open the door. Let him come out himself. Or...or...she couldn't think further. She tapped on the door with the decision that though he would get angry, she as a disciple must be obedient and behave humbly. With this decision she knocked on the door. When she got no response she entered the room to find it empty. The bed cover was lying on the floor in a bundle. The bed had been crumpled. Obviously he had gone out. Alone. At what time did he leave? Where did he go? She walked up and examined his clothes. He had gone out in his pyjamas, jubba, waistcoat and a shawl. The trousers and the coat were on the hanger. The wallet was in the coat pocket. He had gone without any money. Just in order to hurt me. He wanted to hurt me by hurting himself. She sat on the bed. She felt that he was behaving adamantly, like a naughty child. For a minute she got angry. But immediately the thought where would he have gone occurred. In this town every place is far away. She recounted the places where she had taken him—Stevens's Creek County Park, Santa Theresa County Park, Almaden Lake Park, Vasona Lake Park, San Jose, San Francisco and Sunnyvale Temple. Besides these, the houses of Gupta, Goel, Bhat, Kulkarni, Mishra, Sardesai and Murthy. All of them were music lovers who used to learn from her once a week. She wondered whether she should ask them. If they come to know that he had left home without informing they might come up with their own conclusions. She became aware that she had to let them know that Vikram was not in town. Not knowing what to do, she remembered she had not yet had her morning cup of tea. She felt that at least with a cup of tea in her system her mind would get active. She went down to the kitchen and when she finished drinking half a cup, the phone suddenly rang. She wondered if it was Guruji making a collect call. Or maybe he was carrying some money with him. With this belief she picked up the receiver.

'It is me, from Houston.' It was Vikram's voice. He continued, 'Why is your voice feeble? Finished your morning practice—the swara-sadhana? Don't exert yourself too much suddenly or the voice may sink by the time of the programme. Last night I was in Dallas. You have met Patnekar? The moment he heard that there was a concert by Pandit Mohanlal and you would be supporting him, he immediately said he would also attend. Book him a thirty dollar ticket. He is enthusiastic about listening to you. Today I am going to stay here and will reach DC tomorrow evening. How is Guruji?'

'He must be sitting on the slope of the forest below our house in his musical reverie.' She felt comforted that she thought of some answer.

'Don't take him out of the house in the mornings without a cap or a muffler. You know the weather of Los Gatos.'

After the telephone conversation was over she became aware that Vikram had greater concern and devotion for Guruji than herself and again she became sad. For half an hour she kept sitting in the lounge, by the side of the kitchen. Then she went around the house and checked all the rooms and scrutinised whatever might have been overlooked. She put on her walking shoes and went to the slopes of the house in the forest area. Where exactly could she search? Not knowing what to do, she came to the huge Sitka spruce tree and sat on the stone bench under it.

After a short while she recalled what had happened exactly ten years ago when she was studying in the final year of her bachelor's course at Rooparel College.

For the last three years, in the classical vocal music competition held at the college level, the first prize was always mine. I was going to the music school of Mohanlalji's twice a week in the evenings. Spending the entire day at the college, studying for the exam and classes appeared to be a waste of life and it was pulling me down. My brothers insisted that I should complete my graduation and my mother supported them. After getting my degree, I started devoting my days entirely to music. Mother insisted, 'You are twenty. It is a shame if you remain unmarried. So get married. If your husband agrees, continue your music. We have no objection.' No matter how much I argued that if I marry it is as good as the death of music for me it didn't drive home into mother's head. When I insisted that I would take up a job, leave the house and continue with music, the brothers took my side. My eldest brother liked music. He felt that of late even artists were respected and very well paid. I had said, 'Guruji, I have finished my college. Hereafter my entire life is dedicated to music. I have understood that two classes per week and clearing the Praveen Examination are not enough to master the art of music. I will come every day and will practise at home for hours together. You must receive me as your special student.' There was appreciation in Guruji's eyes. He said, 'Still, think about it for some more time.' To which I said, 'There is nothing to think about. I have decided.' At this he simply nodded his head.

I used to go to West Bandra from Dadar everyday by bus. If he was there in the school, it was all right but sometimes he would not be there and Wadekar Master would take the class. The adjacent flat where Guruji resided would be locked. One day, Wadekar said, 'You see, of late he will not be at home at this time. He goes to meet his friends and play cards with them. You come in the morning.' When I went in the morning, he was awake. Everyone knew that he was living alone. Guruji was married but he did not live with his family. His wife and children were at Kurla in Bombay. He stayed in the flat adjacent to the school. Food would come from a mess. He would teach his special students in the hall of the flat itself. But his style depended on his mood. If he was in the proper mood he would teach the same raga for two hours continuously, step-by-step, in detail. If not, for months together, he would dismiss them by saying, 'Go and practise by yourself. Do you think music is so easy that you will learn it even if I teach?'

After touching his feet and wearing the dust on my head, I said, 'I had come for three evenings. Wadekar Master asked me to come in the morning to meet you.'

'Come, sit down', he said very encouragingly. He enquired after my family background. I narrated, 'It has been five years since father died. We have a business since my grandfather's time which is being managed by my elder brother Anil Mehta who is thirty-two years old. The younger brother also helps him in the business. He is twenty-eight. Both of them are married. My mother is very traditional. We have our own house in Dadar. I have my own room where I can practise. I will give you as much fees as you demand but you must teach me wholeheartedly and every intricacies of the ragas.' I bent down and touched his feet with both my hands.

'I don't teach girls. They learn for two years and then get married and fly away. They forget music in the midst of pregnancy, nursing, and other daily chores. Everything that is taught is a waste. You get married just as your mother asked you to.' How mercilessly he spoke! Was it to strengthen my resolve?

'No Guruji,' I insisted as if I was agreeing with him through opposition.

'Then have you decided not to marry?'

I could not think of an answer. I had not thought about it. Still, I thought I should say something. 'I won't, till I learn music completely.'

'Which means that you won't marry for another ten years? What kind of a husband will you get at that age?'

I became angry because I had not come to discuss my marriage with him. But not knowing what exactly to say I said, 'I have not even thought about it and I won't either. Except learning with devotion whatever you teach me I have no other thought in my head. I swear this by god.'

'Let us see. Take up the tambura and tune it.' He pointed at the wall in front of him with his eyes. There were fourteen tamburas leaning against the wall. I picked up one with a shruti for a female voice and sat in front of him. He asked for Raga Bhairav. I was afraid that if I start the shruti without the suggestion through the harmonium, I could commit a mistake. In a feeble voice I said, 'Black five'. He drew the harmonium which was to his left and started the shruti. My tambura did not set soon. He extended his hand and said, 'Give it here. I will set it right and give it to you. You know it but you are afraid.' He took the instrument from me and within three minutes it was perfect. I started strumming the tambura. As if he was ordering he said, 'Hmmm.' I couldn't articulate my voice. It sank. I started perspiring and just sat there with my head bent. Strumming the strings of the tambura he said, 'Come on, don't be afraid.' He took hold of the harmonium and went into shadja. What power was there in his voice! Just in starting with mandra-dhaivata and passing through nishada and resting on shadja, the emotion of Bhairav was evoked and peace permeated. He slowly demonstrated ascending and descending movement of the raga and then said, 'Yes. You take ascend slowly. Sing as much as you know.' I got encouraged. My voice was settled. Slowly and by degrees I began to reach the upper notes and started elaborating. Within seven or eight minutes of this elaboration I had finished my stock. I indicated with my eyes that this was all I knew. He didn't say anything. He took out the tamburas that were leaning against the wall on both his sides and tuned them. He gave me one and started playing the other. His voice was unique. God had not given it to any other singer. He closed his eyes and dived deep and emanated the shanta rasa sans sound in a happy harmony. The peace of Raga Bhairav did begin to spread in shadja itself. Though the back of the flat was towards the main road and faced the sea from the seventh storey, and that room, which was not able to escape from all external din of Bombay, was now filled with the peace of music within half a minute, the kind of peace which was not found even on the Himalayas. Completely absorbed in the music, he was expatiating and expanding the width of the raga and singing to himself and then returning to the present, he unravelled the swara and started articulating. He demonstrated which subtle swaras he was touching and how he was coming back to his own source without touching any higher note and where he was descending into mandra. Showing and teaching like this, bit-by-bit, but without the use of verbal language and without severing the flow of the emotion he was describing music in the movements themselves. I moved to his fore and started playing the tambura. Explaining with his expressive eyes, where he was moving and to what intricacies with his gesticulations, and finding out with my eyes, what I did not comprehend, he would sing and explain again. When he recognised the shine of understanding in my eyes, he also enjoyed the bliss of music. My fears were gone. He had received me as a pupil and was taking me along with him. He had taken me into his wings of enormous power and was flying with me. He was showing me the moves, the twists and turns, the tremendous speed which I had never seen or imagined and suddenly controlling and he was making me comprehend. What a tremendous texture! These were not tricks which could be mastered by mere learning, but they were the emotional movements born out of genius and power of mantra.

By then I became aware of my surroundings. I had sat in the forest of tall redwoods, big-leaved maple, red alder, dogwood, rhododendron, birch and sedan. My house was built right in the middle of the hill. By the why, what is the time now? In a corner of my mind, the nagging question about where he might have gone was still bothering me. Though this question bothered her, the preoccupation of the Bhairav did not allow perturbation to get the upper hand. The mind was filled with sadness about not singing this marvellous raga recently. She started humming and wondered whether the morning was over and noon setting in? She looked at her wrist and noticed that she had not brought her watch. She recalled that as soon as she got up she had gone to the kitchen. Looking up in the direction of the sky, and the branches with dense leaves, she thought no matter what time it is, if you imagine it is morning, it is. She thought of creating morning by singing Raga Bhairav, and gave a rhythm to her humming. She felt like going back home and picking up the tambura. Realising that there was no possibility of climbing up the steep height of the house panting, opening the door and tuning the tambura, she imagined the shruti by placing it in her own mind and added her voice to shadja. She also simultaneously realised that what she was singing now was not a mature development of the raga but just something to quieten her mind. By the time she had moved to the important movements, a big question crept in her mind as to how this man who could sing in a way that peace would swell in the mind of the listener behave in such a way to create distress, perturbation in her. With this question in her mind she got up and started climbing the stone steps. While Bhairav was still revolving in her mind, she thought she should have been home. He might have made a collect call. She remembered that she had not even switched on the answering machine. When she opened the door and went in, she remembered his nature, then and also now. Then he was fifty and now he is sixty.

He was the one who had taught me Bhairav one morning. It made me decide. He is the 'Guru' I had been looking for. If I learn anything, it must be only from him. Otherwise no music was necessary. Guruji taught fifteen or eighteen girl students once in a while. He had never taught me exclusively like this before, opening the heart of a raga so deeply. Having listened to his concerts and to his programmes on radio, the feeling that this style of music belonged to him had become firm. This was the impression that had firmly embedded itself in me even in those days. It was not hero worship by a young student; this was the power of his music that was being discussed by very senior artists, critics and experts as well. The next morning I went again at the same time, taking fruits and flowers with me.

I placed them at his feet and prostrated. He touched my head and blessed me. Sitting in front of him I said, 'I must learn completely. I am determined to capture the very soul of music. You are my guru. There is no one except you. I will practise every day for as many hours as you stipulate. I will learn with devotion and dedication whatever you teach me. Music is my life. I will not sit for any examination. My only aim is to learn genuine music. You must kindly accept me as your pupil and make me perform the puja. Please let me know what your fee is.'

'I do not take fee from my own students because they are the ones who will keep my name alive but if well-to-do students give anything voluntarily I won't refuse.'

I discussed the fee with my elder brother. He asked, 'Would five hundred rupees per month be all right?' I said, 'My guru is a great artist. It is not possible to evaluate his lessons in terms of money. At least one thousand should be given.' He agreed.

'I told you that I do not take money from students who have the potential to keep my name alive. You are giving one thousand rupees at your own free will.'

There was not a single phone call since morning. What if there has been an accident and he had been taken to a hospital. I felt scared. My heart started pounding. He didn't even carry any kind of identification on him. Shall I take my car out and look for him?

One month had elapsed. Yes, one month. Each day, the lesson had gone on for more than two hours in great detail, the kind of lesson that extended Bhairav in all directions. Through refining it by kneading it, expanding it, developing it, extending it and identifying its pulses and the quintessential details I developed a confidence that I could obtain mastery within five or six years. He would instruct by saying, 'Observe, when the sound of "Aa" is produced the mouth should be opened like this. Otherwise the breath will go out through the nose and the swara will be spoiled.' While saying this he would touch both my cheeks and pronounce Aaa. 'Now, observe the fingers when you are playing the tambura. It should move like this, in this place only.' While showing this he would touch my fingers more often than what was necessary. When I sang well he would approve and pat my shoulder. I wouldn't like it. But I wouldn't get angry. I knew that he was a womaniser. In fact, everybody in the Bombay music world knew it. I believe all the newspapers had reported how he had left Bombay, lived with the dancer Manohari Das for three and half years, quarrelled with her and was thrown out. And then he had returned. I was too young then to read the newspapers. He couldn't get along with his wife. This man had bought two flats in West Bandra, using one of them as music school and the other as his residence. Still, one got an impression by his behaviour that he was not the kind of a man who would force anyone. And nothing was heard to its contrary either, anywhere. After all, there are women who desire artists. How does it matter to me if two consenting adults come together? Otherwise it would be impossible to get into the world of art and with this consolation I tuned the tambura. On the thirty-first day, yes, it was a Monday, he asked. 'Look, Madhumita, how do you like the lessons?'

'You are teaching marvellously. No other teacher teaches his students with such earnestness,' I replied without any exaggeration.

'I am giving everything I have without any reservation, am I not?'

'Truly, Guruji.'

'Then you should also give your guru whatever you have without any reservation, shouldn't you?'

'You just need to ask once.' After I said this enthusiastically, I understood the real meaning of his words and realised I had been trapped.

His face beamed with happiness. I could see desire oozing from his eyes. Though I wanted to make it clear that it did not mean that I would offer him anything he wanted but I asked myself, why I should accept this meaning. I kept silent and thought if there was further discussion, I could clarify that I meant only devotion and obedience to the guru. He said, 'Understand this clearly. I am not compelling you. You are from a rich family. I do not want anybody to say "he spoilt our girl". This is strictly between us. Just as I am teaching you without any reservation if you also offer what you have, I will get further enthused to teach. I can tell you that what I teach you in one month, the so called famous gurus can't teach even in five years. They keep their students at the beginner level even if they turn forty.' Now everything became clear. There was no room for confusion about what he meant. Without wanting to look at him I sat with my head bent down. He continued, 'Nobody will know about this. From ten in morning to four in the evening nobody comes here. Even if somebody does, you will be in the inner room and nobody will know. I will also make sure that you do not get pregnant.'

My whole body was exuding with anger. I wanted to tell him I didn't want him or his lessons and walk out. But I couldn't get the strength. He continued, 'All right. Think about it. I am not forcing you. There is no compulsion. Liking and loving do not grow and develop by force. I swear I am not teaching you for the sake of money. For a person who takes fifty thousand rupees for a three-hour programme, your one thousand does not mean anything. That too, when I am not putting any restrictions on time. I developed a liking for you. I wanted to teach you. I wanted to make you a singer like me and even excel me and become famous. I am doing that. If you also have the same feeling, the same love of music you must be my companion. Doesn't raga mean vadi as well as samvadi? When you and I are together I will not call you Madhumita, I will address you as Samvadi. Yes. Now today's lesson should continue. Start the swara.'

I started playing the tambura. But my voice had sunk. Even when I coughed out, the non-existing clog would not give way. I didn't even look up at him. He started singing himself, elaborating the raga.

'Tomorrow, I will teach you more. I think you know *Jago mohana pyare*. Wasn't it the piece set for your examination? I will teach you how to elaborate it. Also the collocation of the various tanas along with it—five or six different taals in the same raga. It is only when you practise you will understand the notes in the raga. You must practise along with the tabla. In two months after you have perfected Bhairav, I will teach you the variations.'

I was sitting seriously with my head bent which must have embarrassed him. He said, 'All right, come on Thursday. If you feel like it, come even earlier.' He gave permission for me to leave. Just before going out, according to custom I touched his feet but there was absolutely no devotion left in me.

I had to take the stairs as the lift was not working. My entire body burned with rage. I thought what our traditional elders used to say made sense—that girls from good families should not opt for music, dance, drama and other performing arts. I had never looked at this fellow who called himself a guru from the point of physical attraction. Now that I recalled the situation, I was disgusted. He applied black hair-dye above his ears and combed his thick crop of hair backwards. Hair on the top of his head and the part where he coloured never matched. If he didn't shave in the morning his stubble would appear grey. On careful observation one would notice that the nerves on his fingers were prominently visible. His teeth were sooty red as a result of chewing tobacco for years. I felt disgusted. Immediately the decision of wanting neither music nor art became firm. My eyes filled with tears as I waited for the bus.

My daily routine once I got home was to take my food, lie down for half an hour, drink a cup of tea, close the door of room and tune my tambura. That day I didn't feel like eating. But I was worried that mother would ask too many questions if I did not eat, she was not the kind to keep quiet. I decided not to tell anyone about this. I had spoken highly about my guru calling him the personification of all virtues. It was not that I wanted to lie; I had honestly imagined all good qualities in him. I couldn't convince myself that a man like him would make such demands. But if I did not comply, it would mean losing music forever. I was unable to close my eyes when I lay down for rest. I rolled about in the bed for half an hour. I wanted to get up and go to the kitchen and prepare some tea, and start my music practice but my mind refused. The mind did not turn inward at all, and set to shadja. The eyes could not close. Instead of shadja, I could only see the wall in front. The wall where I had hung a photograph of my guru neatly framed so that I could see him while practising. It showed him intensely contemplative, inward-looking with eyes half closed. It was printed in the *Illustrated Weekly*'s special issue for music. This was what inspired me every day. Now I felt that all his inwardness was a hoax and a huge pretence. I closed my eyes and started moving my fingers on the strings. Even the tambura strings would not cooperate, no matter how much I tried to adjust the knobs and the threads. No matter what I did, the tune did not set. I got disgusted, leaned the tambura in a corner and took out the harmonium and started playing it. For the first time my inner personality started unfolding itself. Though I was born in Bombay, mine was a traditional mind. I belonged to a conservative family but my brothers were far modern than my father. They had allowed me to devote myself completely to music without pressuring me to get married. They had great confidence in me. I was never interested in any entertainment that was not serious. I could not suffer film music, light music and modern dance even for five minutes. My love for classical music was not consciously cultivated, it was a part of my being. I had never entertained any thoughts about any kind of relationships. But now for me to submit myself to this fellow seemed like losing my inner ethical strength. How does it matter if I don't learn music? People who don't know music or have no interest in music are perfectly happy. What brings happiness to personal life and makes others happy is moral order, ethics. Not art. What happiness is there in losing one's morality?

Two days passed. I decided to stop learning music. At home my younger sister-in-law, Revathi Bhabhi was fond of reading novels. I borrowed a book suggested by her, a novel. I closed the door of my room and started reading. There was imagination, emotion, story, situations and characterisations. I got interested. I told myself, 'No music and no practice'. When I was bored it was enough to read a novel or a poem. This was what I determined. I couldn't sleep for a long time that night. When I got up in the morning I noticed it was Thursday, the day for the music class. If I did not go, everyone at home would start questioning. I took a quick shower, ate two slices of bread, drank my tea and started out. When I came to the bus stop I could not decide whether I should go there or not. Meanwhile the bus came. When I got in, I decided to go and make him lose face. I mustered up enough courage. Anyways, once I had decided not to pursue music and his teaching why should I feel any kind of obligation? I went up the lift and walked along the long corridor to find the door of the flat open. He was leaning against his cushion and humming. As usual he indicated through his eyes, asking me to sit down. I touched his feet and sat. I did not take up the tambura. I told myself that I had not come for my lesson but to affront him. But immediately I felt sorry and asked myself why did I touch his feet as soon as I came in? I collected my voice and said, 'I want to have a word with you.'

Without articulation he consented only with his eyes. When I asked, 'A pupil is like a daughter, is she not'. My voice was raised to the higher pitch—saptaka.

He was not perturbed. His face showed that it was not a new question for him and his self-confidence shone. The collected crust of the chewed betel leaves was pushed from the tongue to the cheek and then he asked, 'Who said that?'

'When the pupil is equal to a daughter, the guru is naturally equal to the father is he not?'

Now, displeasure appeared on his face. Still, he spoke quietly. 'The world does not move with the notions of equal or unequal. What is the use of emotions born out of false relationships? If you give room to false notes the raga will get spoilt. Keep that in mind. I have already told you. There is no compulsion. If you don't like it, leave it. Have you come to argue with your guru because you come from a rich family? There are only two things in raga—vadi and samvadi. If you start arguing it becomes beraga, without any music or tone. I am telling you again, listen carefully. I have not forced you and I won't.'

I was nonplussed. I couldn't think of saying anything. Many emotions of anger and contempt that could make him ashamed of himself were boiling inside me. But not a word came out. Even without my knowledge I picked up my handbag and stood up suddenly. I looked at him as if to condemn him and walked out. When I entered the lift and pressed the button I couldn't help crying. I cried in spasms. While walking to the bus stop I felt that I had behaved badly. The idea of going back and apologising for having walked out and that too without touching his feet became intense. But when I had left both music and the lessons why should I apologise? I just walked on. To avoid suspiscion I walked to Shivaji Park and sat there for two hours.

After lunch I went to my room for some rest. His words, 'I have not forced you and I am not going to' were echoing in my mind. The other day also he had mentioned that I came from a rich family and he repeated it today as well. He was afraid to misbehave with me. I felt that this was the meaning of his last sentence. Still my decision about not to have anything to do with him did not change. I told my mother and my sisters-in-law that Guruji had said that there was a bit of a problem in my throat and asked me not to practise for two or three days. I asked Revathi Bhabhi to get me another novel. She said this novel was better than yesterday's. But I was bored before I could read even ten pages. The attraction of the tambura and swaras excited me. I felt that the absorption, the melodious tune that tambura creates, the emotional stimulations of swaras, designs of aesthetic relish that are offered by the musical movements, cannot be found in literature. The novel is somebody's story, somebody's situation, somebody's characters, their developing into reaching an aesthetic point was situated somewhere else. The emotions of music come rushing out from within me. In fact they overflow. I closed the book and tuned my tambura. I got immersed in strumming the strings. Immediately the swaras merged into each other and I was enraptured in surrendering my mind to the creation of a whole cycle of swaras. Within a short time, involuntarily shadja burst forth from my throat. I was lost in bliss. Gradually, the morning peace of Bhairav was unravelling its swaras and being manifested itself. I was indulging in alaap for more than an hour even though I was repeating the movements. My anger had subsided. I had reached my comfortable state. By evening I explained to myself that I was wrong in leaving without touching his feet. After all, he was away from his family and that must be the reason why he asked me for companionship. In fact, he had stressed that he won't force me. I felt like going back and apologising but realised he won't be in his flat in the evening. I knew that he liked spending his evening playing cards with his friends if he had no other plans.

I spent the next few days in a state of restlessness. Monday was the day when I had to pay the fee. I decided to go and pay him, and ask for forgiveness. He was sitting on the sofa, drinking tea. I went near him and touched his feet. I took out the money. He took it and put it in his pocket without saying a word. Then I said, 'I left suddenly on Thursday. You must kindly excuse me.' He just smiled as if he knew that I would say this. At least that's what I gathered at that point. I didn't know what to do next and sat in the usual place for the lesson and took up my tambura. Continuing to sit on the sofa he simply said 'hmmm'. I started the swara, developed it and sang. He made few corrections once but didn't sing. He didn't teach anything new. After half an hour he said, 'I have to go out. I will finish shaving and my bath. You keep singing. It will reach my ears', and went inside. After half an hour he came out and said, 'Good, continue like this.' He took out the key and the shoulder bag to leave. I was crest-fallen. While coming back I thought maybe he has some work outside. After all he is a human being, it is not possible to teach with the same enthusiasm every time. I consoled myself.

After that he stopped showing the interest that he had shown earlier. He did not demonstrate by singing. He did not start anything new. But he would always be cordial. 'How is the practice going? Yes, tune the tambura.' He would appreciate me if I got the swaras right. Initially he would ask me to work harder even if I would be singing properly. Afterwards, saying, 'Keep on singing. I will be listening', he would go in. This is what he did for the next classes. There was no progress. Meanwhile two months had elapsed. In the interval he would go to Delhi, Bhopal, Varanasi, Calcutta etc for programmes. He would not teach those lessons, which were missed. One day with hesitation I told him that I get bored of repeating the same thing over and over again.

'Do you know how many years I spent in refining each raga? If the foundation for one raga is firmly established, it is easy to learn the others. What do people think about the art of music? It is a fashionable pastime, you need practice. You need concentrated and continuous practice. I know the level you have reached. After you reach the required level I will teach the next stage myself. Don't worry.' He tapped the top of my head.

I thought of reminding him that two months ago he had discussed far elaborate plans of teaching with me that included getting deeper into the ragas. But I kept silent. Two more months elapsed. No progress at all. What had been taught in the beginning through repetition had become boring and lifeless. One day, I gathered all my courage and asked, 'When cheez and tanas are practised in four or five taals, the pattern of the swaras, their movements, alaaps and the steps become clear, don't they?'

'Oh is that so?' With wide-eyed astonishment he said, 'Very clever method. If this is adopted even a stupid student can be transformed rapidly into a great musician.'

I was very angry with his mocking remark. But I said, 'Four months ago you yourself had said so. I am simply reminding you. I dare not give any suggestions to the guru. If I have erred, I beg your pardon.'

'God forbid, I did not say it was a mistake. What is good must be accepted even if a small child says it. Haven't our elders written so?' He answered very smoothly. I didn't talk again.

The next week even before I began to tune my tambura, he said, 'Miss Madhumita, I have thought a great deal about your progress. You have to go through the foundational exercises for at least two more years. After that it would be easy for you to learn from me and it would be easy for me to teach you. I will tell Wadekar Master about you. I will also tell him what he should teach you and how. Now and then I will be supervising your progress. I will teach after he has brought you to a certain level through training. Anyway, his teaching method is the same as mine. Later on, I will teach you.'

I immediately understood that he was taking revenge. The message was clear. 'You didn't agree, so I am not going to teach.' His words could not be faulted. I wanted to tell him that I have learnt from Wadekar for five years in your own school. Once in a while you have also taught other students of my class. Wadekar Master is not qualified to teach more than that. But I knew that if I said so, this man would become furious. I understood that even though he was speaking gentle words outside, he was reeking vengeance inside, so I kept silent.

When I was waiting for the bus I felt contempt for this fellow. Is he the only music teacher in Bombay? Two lessons a week and one thousand rupees per month is not a small amount. It worked out at one hundred and twenty-five rupees per lesson. Even if it was more, my elder brother would not object to it. I suddenly became aware of my financial status. Apart from the family wealth, I was getting forty thousand rupees in my personal account every month as a result of my father's investments. I suspected that this teacher knew about my financial status and that was the reason why he was constantly repeating that I was from a rich family. I felt disinterested in thinking about what he knew and what he did not, when I did not want to have anything to do with him.

Vinayak Rao Mirajkar was running a music school called Suragandharva Vidyalay from his home in Dadar. All the music lovers across Bombay knew about him. He teaches singing, tabla and harmonium—all three. He was the pupil of Panandikar who was a direct disciple of Abdul Karim Khan. He was a learned teacher and knew the shastra but never gave any concerts. Even well-known singers used to come and discuss shastra with him. He was seventy, and when he taught, his wife accompanied him on the tabla. They were the just two of them—he and his wife. I had seen his house also. In the evening I went alone and told him that I had completed my graduation from Rooparel College and had learnt at Pandit Mohanlal's school for five years. I have come with the intention of learning music at a higher level. He asked, 'Why didn't you continue with that school of Mohanlal?'

'I thought when you are so close to my house, why should I go so far?'

'You are a clever girl. Shall I tell you what is going on in your mind? That teacher Wadekar doesn't have the capacity to teach at the higher level. The musicians who keep travelling from place to place as performing artists giving programmes don't sit firmly in one place and teach properly. The same thing is true about that fellow Mohanlal also. Isn't it?' I just nodded thinking that I had answered him sufficiently. He continued, 'Sing a little and show me what you have learnt. Which raga would you sing? Can you tune the tambura?' I mentioned Bhairav and demonstrated.

'For how many ragas can you do alaap?'

'Only this. I don't know cheez or tana.'

'Then who taught you this?'

'I listened to the cassette of Mohanlal in his concerts and practised myself.' He looked at his wife and said, 'You see, what damage takes place if you follow the Ekalavya method.'

He said, 'Now listen', and started singing Bhairav in detail. I realised that he had the power to analyse the shastra. At that time I did not realise I had exaggerated the ability of Mirajkar Buva on account of my anger with Mohanlal. It was decided. Two lessons a week, one thousand rupees fee per month. I prostrated to both the guru and his wife. He started teaching on the third day. From eleven in the morning till mid-day. I lied at home. I told them Mohanlal is extremely busy this year. He has been booked for the whole year for concerts and would be able to teach regularly from next year onwards. I am going to Mirajkar Buva just to keep up my practice. The innocent family simply said, 'Yes. All performing artists are like that.'

Within a fortnight I understood his limitations. He had the entire history of the music world on his finger tips. He could recollect who sang where and when, which music association was started by whom, how they developed and how they declined, all these details he could mention with dates, months, years and so on.

No matter how much he knew, Buva was just a music teacher. He knew the shastra very well. He also knew the entire history and the particular category and the entire family tree of that raga. He could point out the mistakes that had been committed in the collection edited by Batkhande. He had that ability. But by himself he was not a singer. With the strength of memory he would expatiate upon how to expand a raga and the details of the tanas. Thus he would exhaust his information on how to develop a raga according to shastra he knew very well but he could not show it by his singing. But when a brilliant artist sings, even within the limitation he can show innumerable ways and open up unknown doors and great portals and astonishing lanes and by-lanes unknown earlier. Though he moves fairly fast through only one swara-marga, by making changes in speed, emphasis, density and various emotions he overcomes repetitions. He dissolves the hand posts of metrical calculations and creates them into pillars of melody and moulds into any form he wishes. In that magical moment it becomes music. Madhumita recollected how in her college days, Professor Vaidya who taught poetry would say, 'Only a poet is capable of altering the meaning of the words. A mere scholar would be bound by dictionary.' Without breaking the precepts of the raga a truly artistic singer can create many different emotions in the swaras. Each time they are born differently. I felt that Mohanlal had this infinite power. If a person learnt from Mirajkar Buva this infinity does not manifest itself. I will not develop as a good singer. I can only become another music teacher. I started getting upset by the memory of my earlier teacher's lesson. I reminisced the way he taught Bhairav in the beginning when he accepted me as a pupil. He would show a new flow of an emotional flood in each small step. He would take me through new experiences. He would show the infinite abundance and extent of the exposition and expanse of each vision by lifting the raga to the greatest heights. Though everything he taught did not remain in my memory their radiance would show the path when I walked alone. I would feel as if one day I would leave the ground below me and take off. That was the confidence and emotion he generated. The harsh reality brought a great deal of misery. My mind would often get bogged down in sadness. I lost interest in everything—not merely music but even in day-to-day life. The desire that I should become the medium of transmitting the light of each raga I sing, and the radiance I was finding in his lesson should become a permanent source of light was throbbing in me. On realising that it was a desire which could not be fulfilled, a deep sorrow enveloped me.

The mind started searching. Is he the only musician in the vast sprawling Bombay? Is there no other brilliant musician? There are. But each musician has his own speciality—a gharana. Learning from them can be enjoyed only if you were interested in that particular style. But this fellow would take us directly into the ocean of emotions and immerse us in it. Don't know how he learnt it, whether it was by birth itself or whether he attained it by years of practice. No other musician had his calibre and vitality. With this awareness the sorrow would snub her and increase still deeper.

One day I went to the Rhythm House and asked for some cassettes of Mohanlal. Without reading the details printed on the top indicating the raga, the taal and the tabla and harmonium accompanists, I bought fourteen cassettes. On reaching home, I went straight to my room. The first cassette I picked up happened to be of Raga Bhoopali. I played it immediately. What a voice? As if drenched in rasa and dripping harmony. I experienced such concentration and oneness with the singer that I was not exercising any critical judgement. I listened to eight cassettes and as I went on listening, a decision took shape. No matter how mean he was, I should not refer to him in the singular; but to identify him as Guruji the mind disagreed. I could not call him Mohanlal. It should be Mohanlalji.

One evening, my elder brother said, 'Madhu, next Saturday evening there is a benefit concert at the C J Hall by your guru. A ticket was forced on me. It will be useful to you.' I shivered inside. It was a programme arranged by the Bombay Fort Rotary in aid of the removal of tuberculosis at the Dharavi slum. 'The ticket's price is rupees five thousand and seat number is C-17.' I was excited at the prospect of listening to his concert. But there was a fear inside. I couldn't understand the reason for this fear. Was it because he might see me? Was it because he might ask me why I was not coming for lessons with Wadekar Master? C-17 means the centre chair in the third row. Was it because while singing he might see me? The reason for fear is always vague. But the overwhelming enthusiasm that I would listen to him directly took the upper hand.

Saturday morning my elder brother told me, 'It will be half past ten or eleven by the time the concert gets over. There is a prominent advocate whose name is Gore Saheb. He will come and meet you. Even after the concert is over you just stay in C-17. He will bring you home in his car. He lives close by, in Matunga. Don't take the train alone. Don't get into a taxi. If he is not there, one of us would come and wait for you outside.'

Within ten minutes I had occupied my chair, the person mentioned by my elder brother came and said, 'Aren't you the sister of Anil Mehta—Madhumita? It seems you are learning music from Mohanlalji. Please remain seated right here even after the concert is over. I will come and take you home.' He was about sixty.

I had come early. People were still slowly trickling in. I knew that a benefit programme would always start late. Why did I come this early? I felt embarrassed. I started going through the ticket in my hand. There was one page about the committee for the removal of tuberculosis at Dharavi slums. At the back of the page was an introduction to Fort Rotary mentioning all their philanthropic activities? Two paragraphs in superlative language talked about 'Swara-samrat, Sangeeta-chakravart Mohanlalji. Below it, the details of accompanists were given—Rajaram Tipnis as harmonium sathi, Omkar Prabhu on the tabla, supporting musician Rajani Kaushal, tambura by Jayanth Chandavarkar. Rajaram Tipnis was a very famous harmonium player in Bombay. I had heard him accompanying other artists. Prabhu was an expert tabla player who provided wonderful accompaniment and every singer wanted him to accompany them. Not just from Bombay but even other great singers who came from outside. But who is this Rajani Kaushal? I was curious. Have I seen her? Was she coming to the music school? Was she my senior? Don't remember seeing her. Not even heard her name. I indulged in guess work. The Master of Ceremonies introduced the artist as 'a student of Mohanlalji, Rajani Kaushal is one of the upcoming and fast growing singers who is attracting a great deal of attention.' I felt embarrassed. Twenty-eight or thirty years old, not fair, not dark either. Though she had shapely eyes, nose and mouth, I couldn't see any intelligence in her. Since mine was the central chair of the third row I could see her from quite near.

Mohanlal closed his eyes and tuned his voice to shadja. Not merely because the Master of Ceremonies had mentioned it but in the very first move, the emotion of Shuddha-Kalyan took shape. This was one of my favourite ragas. It was a long time since I had heard it. A feeling of flow fused with the zestful pace of Bhoopali and auspiciousness of Kalyan. This man had a strong voice and yet he brought about the full softness in accordance with the delineation of the raga. It is obvious that he has mastered the emotional details of every raga. I felt that in his rendering the shastra serves the emotion but does not subjugate it. Even without my knowledge I started humming, accompanying his movement. Rhythm was being formed in his singing, as if the calm and cool wind of the evening was spreading the fragrance of flowers and was lowering it at intervals. Of late, listening to his cassettes had become my habit. And also my consciousness had grasped the method of his flow of swaras. It would quite naturally comprehend the places he would pause unexpectedly. I had the vague feeling that he was teaching me and I was following his lesson, I was humming softly. Suddenly I felt somebody's finger on my shoulder. I looked back and the man in the row behind me whispered, 'We have come to listen to the artist on the stage and not to you.' I was embarrassed. I couldn't even say sorry. Consciously I enforced silence on myself. It was impossible to stop the inner movement of the swaras. As the crop of paddy bends and sways to the soft winds, his singing, swinging with delicate harmony around shadja, and then, without a little bit of tiredness, just like air goes across the roots of the crop, the singing swayed, slowly. And then he made a sign to Rajani Kaushal who sat behind him. Immediately she supplemented her voice to the same shadja. With the incursion of soft female voice contrasting the base male voice in the background the listeners were pleased, thrilled and several people intoned, *Wah, Wah*! Even before she completed the avartana, he made a speedy movement of meend from dhaivata and stopped. He was giving her such a lot of opportunity; the attention of the entire audience was diverted to her. Immediately it occurred to me that most of the people in the audience were rich merchants who did not know anything about music but could buy the expensive benefit tickets. After all, what were the patterns of notes of the musical scale she was making? Just repeating when he stopped and making mini movements here and there, that's all. In the background of his full-throated rich voice her voice seems special because it was thin like a wire. Actually, she was not a good singer. There was no melody in her voice. There was no strength. I could support much better than her. There is melody in my voice. How wonderful it was when I repeated what he sang, when he was teaching me! I was angry with this audience. It was obvious he was projecting her, giving her more and more opportunities. She doesn't have the power to cast two cycles of tanas. He knew that if he allowed her a little longer, her defects would become obvious to everybody. How is it fair to give such an opportunity to a woman with so little preparation and practice and push her forward? Was he doing this deliberately? He has seen me sitting in the centre of the third row. He has recognised me. I began to think that is why he is giving her more chances and opportunity and showing to the audience the merit which she does not have. My neighbours said, '*Wah*, how well this girl sings!' They repeated it and then indulged in lewd suggestions like, 'He has given her proper training as his pupil.' His neighbour added, 'How will a singer get his inspiration if he does not prepare his lady pupil?' I was burning with anger. I was angry with these rich uncultured people. I wondered whether I should turn towards him in anger and stare at him, but realised that if I got involved in an interaction with such fellows I would ultimately be defeated. So I kept silent.

Shuddha-Kalyan completely took hold of the audience. Nobody moved during the small interval when it was over and the next raga started. I was happy that his music had the power of bewitching and charming even those who did not know anything about music. Without delay he adjusted the tambura to madhyama-shruti and started a Chota-Khayal in Durga in the Bilaval mode.

de s ss veesbha | jo ss du | ra ga ss bha | vaa s nee s

This was a cheez which I had been taught. Wadekar Master had taught me. I had not heard it in the voice of Mohanlalji. As soon as he started it, my throat started vibrating in accordance. The foot began tapping. My enthusiasm overflowed. When the raga was expanded a little, and he started working on the tanas, my enthusiasm increased still more. In the next cycle the pattern of singing turned to weaving fresh tanas and coming to the saam, the disciple Rajani Kaushal had to sing the first line of the sthayi. This was very entertaining and appealing to the audience. But I felt more and more restless. Primary knowledge of the taals and the place of the saam was enough, a complete command was not necessary for the support she was giving. Still, the audience went on appreciating her as if she was the main singer! The work she was doing did not need even one per cent of that effortless mastery and expertise needed to create the spiral of four, five, six, seven cycles of tanas one after another, and to show saam, so as not to miss even a quarter of maatra. Yet the audience was stupid. I can perform this more melodiously and with more precision. Comparison did begin in me. Why is this man giving publicity to her as his pupil and making her sit on the dais with him? I was furious with Mohanlalji.

Soon it was announced that there would be an interval. After the interval two more ragas were sung before the concert was concluded.

Though all the people had left, I was sitting in my chair. About ten minutes later Gore Saheb came to me with a man of about fifty, who was his driver, and asked me to wait in his car. Even when I was waiting for him, my mind was occupied by Rajani Kaushal. What qualification does she have to give accompaniment to Mohanlalji? I compared myself with her and found that she was not even one quarter as good as I was. Had he seen me? Even if he did, did he recognise me? Now and then he would look at the audience. Since I was sitting in the third row itself, that too in the centre and in the midst of all men he must have noticed the only girl sitting there. Gore Saheb who came bit late, sat next to me. Meanwhile, there was a man of about fifty sitting next to the driver. He had long white hair and looked like a merchant. Gore Saheb enquired after my education and music.

'How does your teacher teach?'

I knew that my elder brother had told him that I was learning from Mohanlal, so I said, 'Very well indeed.' The person in the front seat said, 'He looks like a very sincere artist.' Gore Saheb introduced me to Mr Mathur and talked about Mohanlal.

'Yes, he is a very sincere man. He treats the audience with great respect and concern. Look at today's programme. Everybody knew that there were very few who knew music. He also knew it. Even then he sang with full emotion and nobody was bored. And also he did not make it cheap. He has great aesthetic relish. That is why his music has the ability to reach everybody whether they are learned or slum dwellers. What do you say?'

'Yes', Mr Mathur said.

'As for me, I just love his singing. I have a live tape of his music which lasts fifty hours. I have recorded today's programme as well. Tomorrow evening I will get that copy. I don't believe those artists who say that music is only for the learned. What do you say?'

Mathur said, 'Yes'. Then asked, 'It seems though a contractor once cheated him, Mohanlalji sang without taking any money and gave a concert to the entire town. Is it true?'

He said, 'Yes'.

'Yes, yes. This is only one example to show his commitment to the listeners. This is an incident that happened fifteen years ago.'

'You see, today's was a benefit concert. What does "benefit" mean actually? Whether they are musicians or dancers, they say "You give me my fee, and then the rest is yours. You can sell your tickets at high price and may take the benefit." According to that system Mohanlal had to be given at least fifty thousand today. But you know he didn't touch a single penny. He didn't even take the taxi fare. He merely said, "If I take any money for the benefit concert, how do I acquire punya?" We, the organisers paid only two thousand for the tabla artist and five thousand for the harmonium player.'

I also felt very proud. I wanted to say, 'You were talking about the Nagpur concert.' But it was not proper that a girl of my age should intrude when two elderly gentlemen are talking and I kept silent.

Gore Saheb continued, 'A cheat in Nagpur had arranged his programme. These days, business people have appeared in all fields including the world of art. They continue the cheating which is developed in other areas here also. He, who had arranged the programme had agreed to pay an honorarium of twenty thousand rupees plus local hospitality and had even paid five thousand in advance. Then he arranged a huge publicity canvassing Mohanlal's name and sold tickets for sixty thousand. Wherever Mohanlal went, his wife would accompany him saying she had to take care of her husband. Actually, she went to collect money and secure it. Everything was ready. A college quadrangle was full of people. He had visited Nagpur a few years ago and there was a great demand to listen to him. Mohanlal was tuning the tamburas in the green room when the assistant of the contractor came in and asked him, "Shall we go to the place of concert?" Mohanlal stood up. His wife who was with him asked, "Where is your contractor? We have not seen him since we came here." That fellow cringed. "His mother has had a heart attack. She has been admitted to hospital. He is there. He will come and meet you in a short while." She said, "There is no need for him to see us. You go and get fifteen thousand rupees from him right away, plus two first-class train tickets. Only after that the programme will start." The assistant said, "No madam, he will come himself. My boss is not the one who cheats artists. In Nagpur, people will create trouble if you start the programme late. They are waiting." The wife said, "Will it take half an hour to go by taxi to the hospital and return? You make a call to him and get the information." This woman was very shrewd and expert in dealing with people.'

"Madam, even if I get him on the phone, who carries so much cash to the hospital? In the hospitals of this town, there is no phone facility for patients. Please start the programme, I will get the money from his house and give it to you. Anyway, Mohanlalji will be on the platform. Of course you will be here. I will hand it over to you within half an hour." He begged.

"Why make the people wait? I will start. The tune of the tambura will come down. If I wait my mood also will be spoilt," Mohanlalji said.

But madam did not listen. "You make an announcement that due to unavoidable reasons the programme will start half an hour late, the audience must please cooperate, and you go in a taxi and get the money." She was adamant. The assistant got the announcement made and left. He came back in twenty minutes and said, "Madam, he is not at the hospital. The nurse told me that he had gone in search of a life-saving medicine. God knows which pharmacy he has gone to! I came back because there should be no delay. If you don't believe me, I have two thousand rupees with me. I will give it to you along with my brand new wrist watch." He took it out and held it in front of her. Madam took both the money and the watch and put it in her bag. Then she said, "Come on, let us go in your taxi. I will also come to the hospital. I will enquire about the patient myself." The assistant turned pale. Still, he threatened, "What is this madam, you suspect us. If you don't start the programme immediately these people will turn against you." She turned back and said, "I will tell the audience. The contractor of your town is a cheat. You have bought the tickets from him. You attack him. I am going to lodge a complaint right now with the police." The fellow didn't know what to say, "Please wait, I will go back and find out."

He never came back. Forty-five minutes went by. The audience started making a lot of noise. Some of them came to the room where these people were staying and demanded the cause for the delay. She explained that they had been cheated. Those who had come to enquire were gentlemen. They wanted to know who the contractor was, his name and address. On further enquiry it was discovered that he had vacated his room at the hotel that afternoon. The gentlemen pleaded, "It is already late by an hour and a half. So many people will be disappointed. Please come and sing. Afterwards we will submit a case to the police and catch him wherever he is, get the amount from him and we will see to it that he is jailed." Mohanlal stood up and said, "Come on, I will sing." But she said, "Let the people who lost their money make the complaint and get the money back from him. Why should we suffer a loss?" When she was told, "Madam, if you are adamant like this it will be injustice to music. Anyway, seven thousand rupees have been given. Let the performance go on." She didn't listen. But replied, "Do you think our music is worth only that much?"

An old man asked, "Is it possible to put a price on music? Unfortunately, sometimes such cheating takes place. Disappointing the so many lovers of music because of that is sinful. When you come next time to Nagpur you can yourself ask for ten thousand more." But she intervened, "If you are so conscious of dharma and karma you go home and bring thirteen thousand rupees. Let all the punya accrue to you alone." Now what was there to be done?'

Gore Saheb asked, 'What if you were in the place of Mohanlal? What would you have done?'

I, who was listening to everything and feeling the intensity of the situation thought the question was addressed to me. I couldn't immediately think of an answer. Gore Saheb asked again, 'What would you have done?'

I instantly said, 'I would get on to the platform and sing.' I had said this without being aware of what I was saying. Gore Saheb said, 'Well done! You are a born artist. I will tell your brother not to stop your music lessons, come what may.'

I was thrilled. 'What happened next?'

Turning to Gore Saheb, Mathur said, 'That wife is not the kind to understand the right attitude towards art. Immediately she got hold of her husband and took him to the hotel and picked up the bags.' Since the rent was paid in advance, the hotel manager let them go. She went straight to the railway station with her husband and bought two tickets to Bombay. There was still an hour left for the arrival of the train. Mohanlal was sitting there helplessly like a prisoner. After half an hour he started thinking straight. He told her, 'Today, you have made a mistake. What that old man said was right. It was a sin disappointing so many music lovers. Some loafer has cheated us. But what is the difference between me and that loafer if I disappoint the lovers of art because of money?'

She angrily said, 'Are you calling me, your wife, a loafer. The one who is looking after the entire business of your family.' The argument went on. Usually he would be afraid of her. And she was always threatening him. In the midst of the discussion, a solution appeared to him.

'In front of the art lovers of Nagpur I have taken to heels like a mean coward. I will not get into the train. I am going back and I will sing for them to my heart's content.' She said, 'If you go back, there will be nobody there now.' But he persisted, 'I know that. I am going to make an announcement in the newspaper tomorrow morning that the day after tomorrow evening, I will sing without any fee in the same place. Only after that will I come to Bombay. You also come with me.' She turned around and said, 'You are cheating your family.'

His reply was interesting. 'You have never worn a cheap sari or artificial jewellery. You are wearing diamond earrings. Keep that in mind.' She was ready with a reply. 'It is in order to maintain your respect and dignity that I always wear silk and ornaments of pure gold. You better note that.' It was the railway station, crowded with people. Seeing this quarrel between a man and his wife, people gathered around them to hear and enjoy the fun. Mohanlal, felt even more ashamed. He said, 'Then you go alone to Bombay,' and walked away. In a short while the train arrived. She pushed the others aside and got in. He walked out of the railway station without knowing where to go. There was really no place he could go to. There was no money in his pocket. Finances were in his wife's hands. He walked outside till the train left and then searched the platform for a vacant bench. He found one and lay down. Even in the midst of the light and noise he slept. He had the capacity to sleep in any kind of situation. Got up in the morning, washed his face and asked someone for the way to the college where his programme had been arranged and walked four miles. He went to the principal's home. The principal recognised him and said, 'Somebody said you had gone away to Bombay.'

Mohanlal said, 'No gentleman discusses about his wife with others. I cannot tell you the purpose of my coming to your home without telling you that.' He explained what had happened and continued, 'You please give an announcement in the local newspaper and arrange for my programme tomorrow evening. I will sing without taking any fee. Providing the accompanists would be your responsibility. Please provide for my boarding and lodging for two days—today and tomorrow and a railway ticket for Bombay. I will send the money back from there.'

'Sir, I will earn a great deal of punya if I host a person like you at my home. I will make all arrangements. Right now, have some biscuits and tea, take a bath and I will give you a new pair of dhoti and a jubba.'

He arranged the programme, the second day, in the same quadrangle with the same accompanists. He made phone calls to the local newspapers and asked the representatives to come immediately and publish the announcement in the papers. All India Radio, Nagpur also announced it. The Bombay newspapers also published it as a news item. It was announced that not only the people who had bought tickets for the previous day but anybody could come even without a ticket. The boys and girls of the college also joined the gathering. The vast number of the audience in the concert was the biggest so far in Nagpur. Mohanlal's singing was just marvellous.

It seemed he had never sung so enthusiastically and from such a depth of heart as he sang that evening. It was said that aesthetic emotions and prayerful yearnings did flow like an incessant spring in his singing and it moved the hearts of the audience. Two local newspapers wrote editorials and praised Mohanlal for maintaining the basic dharma of artists.

Since it was half past ten at night and there was not much traffic, the car reached Dadar quite quickly. Everybody was having dinner with the plate set for me as well. The elder brother asked, 'How was the concert?'

I said with enthusiasm, 'Just wonderful music.'

Conversation soon moved towards Gore Saheb. The younger brother said, 'He is the most famous tax consultant in the country. He knows Sanskrit extremely well. In fact, he can even compose impromptu poetry. If he had devoted all his time to his profession he could have made something like one hundred crores. He opens his office at 9 am and closes at 6 pm. The tax consultants and lawyers should work till at least 9 pm, shouldn't they? Isn't it only at that time the customers are free? His opinion is that since the music and dance programmes take place in the evenings, why should he work in the office at that time and miss them? He is confident that the people who come to consult him would come at his convenience. He just loves music. He even helps in arranging music concerts and when they lack money he himself gives money freely. He gets flats at a subsidised rate for musicians when a new building society is formed. He even designs the flats for them so that there is no disturbing noise at either side. He is a patron for music societies. His name does not appear in the newspapers but there is no music society in Bombay which does not take help from him. Do you know how many music cassettes there are in his library? At least five thousand. He has even got an index prepared for the musicians and ragas and taals. The moment he sits in his car he rolls up the windows, switches on the air conditioner and listens to some classical raga. There is a joke that his car does not run on petrol but on music.'

When I went to bed, Shuddha-Kalyan enveloped my ears. Gore Saheb would definitely have arranged for recording the concert and the tape will reach him before tomorrow evening. I decided that through my elder brother I should get a copy made and listen to it twenty or thirty times. I started humming to myself. What a beautiful raga, and what a great rendering by Mohanlalji! His wonderfully resonant voice started making its presence felt. Along with it my humming. An experience that I was actually singing with him and as he moves forward in the movement of raga I follow him. He rests now and then, to help me follow him. He would wait. Sometimes he would ask me to move with him and suggest through his look. Yes, we will sing together the same raga in male and female voice. Again, he moves forward and I would be playing the tambura and support him silently. In the midst of it, he gestures through his hand to come closer and hold the tambura close to his right ear. I play on it so that both our ears can hear simultaneously. He closes his eyes and manifests a subtle spot of the swara and absorbs in meditation. The raga is being sung not for an audience but to teach me. He is singing to demonstrate the minutest subtleties of the radiance of raga to teach me and drive it home to me. Without deviating even a little, I am following him and will master it. Meanwhile I will add my own flourishes and show him, by singing. A dim light of appreciation shines in his eyes.

I don't know when I finally went off to sleep. When I got up, my mind was full of joy. The feeling that I had entered Shuddha-Kalyan the entire night and had realised its secret was filled in me. I didn't feel like getting up, so I continued lying down with my eyes closed. When I finally came out, my brother showed me that morning's newspaper and said, 'Look, the photo of yesterday's concert.' In place of showing Mohanlalji, the newspaper carried a picture of Rajani Kaushal playing the tambura. I was extremely annoyed. I looked steadily at it. The photograph was very sharp. She was not at all good-looking. With her mouth open she looked ugly. She doesn't even know the basics of keeping the expressions natural while singing. She was surely not good-looking. Truly, not at all. She was sitting there with heavy make-up which had melted and was distorted. I drank my tea, came back to my room, closed the door and tuned my tambura and started singing Raga Khamaj, which Mirajkar Buva was teaching me then. But my mind couldn't concentrate on it. It was adamant and was set upon singing only Shuddha-Kalyan. I stopped Khamaj and started Shuddha-Kalyan. I knew the way it was sung last evening. Bhoopali in the ascending movement and Kalyan in the descending movement. When I started singing it was Bhoopali until it touched tara-shadja. Wouldn't the swaras descend anywhere showing Kalyan? It is not possible. Then how and in what way should the change be designed? This question stopped me from continuing further. I was disappointed that music could not be mastered without proper and regular instruction and guidance. The solution occurred to me that if I contact Gore Saheb and get the tape of the programme and listen to it four times, I would understand the secret of that raga. But after some time I realised that even if I listen to the tape, not four times but even for four hundred times, I would not grasp its secret, unless it is taught by a guru and I practise under his supervision. The awareness that the temperament of classical music is such, darkened by mind.

After taking a shower, when I was combing my hair I saw my face in the mirror. How beautiful I was! I had never complimented myself at any time. Yes, I am beautiful. The width of the forehead, the shape of the eyes, the meend-like arches of the eyebrows, a nose which resembled the tender notes. How could Rajani Kaushal get such beauty? But when I compared my looks with hers I felt ashamed. Since last evening I was condemning her voice and ability to sing and now, I was comparing her looks with mine. After seeing her picture in the newspapers my mind slandered her appearance also. I became aware that I was becoming mean.

After lunch when I was taking a nap, Mohanlalji appeared in a different light. Though his house and family were in Kurla, he was staying alone. When I recollected what Gore Saheb said about the Nagpur incident I felt sympathy for him. Poor man, how much he, a sensitive artist must have suffered at the hands of a wife like that! I started to be deeply distressed. Was it perhaps the reason, there was a shade of pain in his singing? This new quality which was unknown to me in his music until now appeared to me and his singing, permeated into the depth of my inner being, which had not been open till now. I got up and played his cassette of Todi. Yes, there was deep-down a sense of suffering in the peaceful morning raga itself. In the afternoon Saranga also there was a pain of tiredness. But in Malhar, the agony has become quite clear. Yes, I felt that in all the ragas he sings the main emotion is pain and sadness. Even in the drita-gati which should put forth enthusiasm, was there only pain? Or was it a state which went beyond pain, reaching fulfilment? Though there was this inquiry, the mind rejected it and determined that it was pain and pain alone.

By midnight my mind was fully occupied by her, his so called wife. What's her name? I didn't know at that time. I was full of hatred towards her. I started cursing her, a demoness, one who had used such a great artist for making money. Shouldn't he have married the woman after examining whether she had any love for music? I knew of the rumour that she was his student. How could a student of music behave the way she did? I was convinced that she was not his student and it was just a rumour. There was no other explanation. This woman had dragged him to the railway station. What a termagant! Her shoulders were like that of a wrestler and the face of a witch. How could he marry such a woman? I felt pity for him and could not sleep the whole night.

I got up late the next morning. When I was brushing my teeth, how mild and gentle did my face look in the mirror? How is it possible for people who are not gentle to love music? Unless a person has a very kind heart unable of hurting anybody, how could he comprehend the subtle harmony of music? These thoughts started moving in my head. I was thrilled to get a new insight about music, the main purpose of music was to melt away all rudeness and coarseness and to create softness and harmony in the world. That was the quality one found in his music. I was moving the brush in vilambit for a long time, observing my own face believing if I had moved the brush in a different tempo, my feeling of softness would melt away.

By afternoon a plan formed itself. Yes, this can be done I thought with enthusiasm that is, to make my brother talk to Gore Saheb. What if Gore Saheb recommends me to Guruji and tells him, 'This is our girl. It is our desire that she must become a great singer. We will help you in whatever way you want but you must teach her with interest and concentration.' If a person like Gore Saheb who supports music, music concerts and musicians so greatly, who is so respected in the commercial and industrial world of Bombay, recommends! Perhaps Guruji also might have been helped by him, may be Guruji himself might have confided in him at some point. All these ideas appeared in my mind, and I was convinced that it was the proper method. I ate with gusto. After resting for about half an hour I thought of calling my brother right away. Why waste time? I wanted to ask him to talk to Gore Saheb on the phone. But could this be settled through a phone call? I doubted. Doesn't it mean that he was not teaching properly till now? I thought it was not proper and lay back again. After rolling about for a long time a plan did flash. Why not call up Gore Saheb requesting for a few tapes of Mohanlal's concerts and leave him to make a selection himself? Fix up a time and confide in him my intense desire to master music, explaining why I had not desired anything else including further studies, and appeal to him that only to learn music did I become Mohanlal's pupil. Yes, he teaches well but he is very emotional. He is moody also. You please tell him to take extra pains to teach me. But please tell him that in such a way that he should not think that I am complaining. I thought this was the correct method. But I shouldn't mention this to anyone at home.

That night I took Gore Saheb's number from elder brother but it was already late. I could sleep only after I decided to call him around 8 am. But I got up at 3 am. After that, no matter how much I tried I couldn't sleep again. Yes, Gore Saheb would surely recommend me and Guruji would forget the past and teach me with total concentration. This hope began to appear like saam. Again, I was drowsy. The same assuring saam. Sleep. In between saams were missed, saam was not found, in that state, sleep was broken. While singing, when the position of the poise itself could not be found, what should happen to the singer! I felt I was perspiring without attaining the beat and without having the control over the movement. I started shivering with the fear of being drowned not knowing in which direction I was being carried by the whirlpool. Within five minutes of waking up I understood everything. Gore Saheb will recommend and Guruji will say, 'Oh is she is your girl? Then I will certainly train her. Don't worry.' Or, what if he says, 'But she has stopped coming at all!' It would be an impediment. I had mentioned at home that I was going to him also. If they knew that I was not, they would know that I was lying. I was afraid. Even if I went back again he would talk nicely and ask me to convey his respect to Gore Saheb. But he would not teach without any reservation. He would say something like, 'Without learning what I have already taught, how can I proceed forward? Your practice is insufficient.' And then he would start right from the beginning exercises of swaras. He would dodge me saying that I still hadn't attained the knowledge of swaras; I still didn't have control over the structure of taal. He would put me off by using only nice words, like saying, let the foundation be strong. Supposing I go back to Gore Saheb and Guruji tells him also the same thing, 'She is the kind of a girl who is ambitious to become a great singer without the proper foundation.' Whose words will Gore Saheb believe? Again and again his condition that I should submit myself completely without any reservation just as I am teaching you sincerely would stand. If I get a recommendation from Gore Saheb, Guruji might decide that I was too big a fish and even take back his condition. He wouldn't teach either. He would use softness and humbleness and circumvent the situation. As soon as this situation appeared, I was surrounded by sorrow. I sobbed profusely. Isn't it possible for a woman to acquire knowledge without sacrificing what was most important for her? I was angry. But I could only cry. The door of the room was shut. The air-conditioner was humming. The only thing that gave some comfort was the assurance that no one at home could hear me crying.

I cried for two days. I simply couldn't think of a way out of this helplessness. It became clear to me that this feeling can be shaken off when the desire of learning the secrets, mysteries and intricacies of music only from him is given up. Is art greater than myself? Let me not have anything to do with it. Let me stop learning even from Mirajkar. So many people live happily without having anything to do with music? Many people do not have even a basic knowledge of it. Most people don't even have a distant interest in it. How many millions of people are there who just listen to film music and think it is great! I developed contempt for music. But it lasted only for a day.

By next afternoon a vacuum encircled me. What happiness was there in life without music?

A week passed. I was assiduously practising a raga when I suddenly recollected the methods of marriage in Indian sociology including the details of the Gandharva-vivaha. This was a secret arrangement of mutual consent between a man and a woman and was not considered sinful. This explanation gave some comfort. There was a flash of new idea in the mind. But beyond this new explanation there was nothing, just a blank. The solution, that he also wanted secrecy occurred by evening, so there was no problem. Music traditionally has been called Gandharva-vidya. The words Gandharva-vidya and Gandharva-vivaha, Gandharva-vivaha and Gandharva-vidya became equated and the question arose whether this kind of a marriage was meant only for artists. Or, was it the name given to the practice of a particular tribe or society called Gandharva and this type of marriage indicated their life was filled with dance and music. Had the two names come down by practice? I thought of consulting one of my professors but decided against it. When I was clear in my mind, why bother about history of sociology?

In two days the decision became clear and firm. Took the 7.30 am bus and went to West Bandra. When I went up the lift and walked towards his flat, I could hear music. It was a female voice. I couldn't summon enough courage. I felt that voice was strangling me by the neck and pushing me out. I stood outside. I could hear Guruji's voice. Ah, this way of demonstrating by actual singing is possible only for a great artist, not for a mere teacher. When I felt this appreciation, the female voice imitated it. I could immediately recognise it. Rajani Kaushal. I felt that she had already trapped him. I was stunned. I was in tears. I hurried towards the lift, took out my handkerchief, covered my mouth and wept. Meanwhile the door of the lift opened. An elderly lady came out and asked, 'Who are you? Who do you want to see?' 'Nobody, really,' I said and in order to escape from her I went into the lift and pressed 'G'. When I came out, I felt I had reached a safe place. Where do I go from here? I didn't know. I couldn't go home. I knew that right behind this building there was the sea. I turned in that direction and stood on the pavement made of hard stones and cement. Just then the sea was waxing. I stood there looking at it and thinking that this was the time Guruji had allotted me. Today it must be her lesson. It is possible that there may not have been any relationship between her and him. She was not beautiful. She had not even one tenth of my beauty. I felt satisfied that he would not have wanted her. I looked at my watch. It was nearly 9 am. Even though the lessons were meant for an hour, he would not stop when he was in the mood. He would go on for an hour and a half and sometimes even two. He would stop teaching and start singing regularly. That was a part of his method. I decided that I should go back and wait till her lesson was over. I went back but was afraid. How to face him? What should I tell him? How should it be phrased? When I was standing undecided, the door of the lift opened and she walked out of it. I was surprised. Yes, she, who sat with him and accompanied him on tambura and sang with him. Yes, her photograph had appeared in the next day's newspaper. She just went away. She didn't even look at me. Before the door closed I rushed into the lift and went straight o the seventh floor. Non-stop, it shot up like a meend from lower shadja to higher shadja. When I came out I was not afraid. I walked straight to his flat. He was intoning in the descending movement of Kafi in Mandra pacing about slowly. He recognised me immediately and his eyes shone. I caught him by the shoulders and said, 'I have come. I have come with my entire mind. I have submitted myself to you completely. You should also teach me absolutely everything. You must teach and train me and make me a great singer'. But before completing my words I started crying and put my head on his left shoulder. I could smell tobacco. I began to sob more. He put his hand over my head and asked, 'Why do you weep?' I replied immediately, 'For having wasted six months.' He didn't talk. But simply asked me to sit down and walked into his room. I waited. Five minutes, eight minutes, ten minutes, fifteen minutes, were over. When I had come on my own fully prepared, where did he go? Why is he delaying? Has he changed his mind? Has he lost his attraction for me? Has some other woman occupied his mind? These questions arose. I got up and entered his room. He was standing near the window and looking at the sea. I started the conversation. 'What are you thinking?' I could see a little hesitation on his face. He came, took hold of both my hands and said, 'You have come by yourself. It's a good thing. Look, I have not forced you. I am not forcing you. You have come to offer yourself to me by your own free will.' When I said 'Yes' his face showed relief.

३

I climbed the steps made out of chiselled stone. I was panting by the time I reached home. Going up and down twice a day would be a good exercise for heart and lungs, for singing too. When I came in, I could see the answering machine had not been switched on. What if he had called from somewhere? I was worried. Suddenly a question cropped up. If this happened in America and had I gone to court, and he had said, 'I haven't forced you. Even now I am not forcing. You have come to offer yourself to me by your own free will. I have told you again and again.' How would the court react? Either you should teach or you should say I won't. Or, if you pay so much fee I will teach. Through the condition that she should sleep with him he has exploited her and has misused her love of art. The court would sentence him with an imprisonment of long period. Or, the court would get her a compensation of a million dollar. The public, the feminists would protest. Perhaps the same thing would have happened in India also. I was a little comforted with this thought. But I realised that in India girls don't go to court out of fear that they would be humiliated in the eyes of the society. The next minute the anxiety that where had this man gone in his anger, possessed her. But he had not simply exploited her. He had taught with complete interest and involvement. He had increased the lessons to thrice a week. At the time of teaching there was no lenience or intimacy as with a beloved, there was no concession in discipline. Everything had to be taught with total concentration. He had explained everything in great detail and had given me complete mastery in five and a half years. One day he had said, 'Listen, you are going to uphold my name in the future. A teacher must be fortunate to get the disciples, who would continue his name and tradition'. This memory filled my eyes with tears. Even when we were in bed together in an embrace we were talking only about music. He would mention the secrets of certain ragas or the inner swirls of the musical world. He gave me much more than what I gave him. I recalled that great musicians teach so well and with such interest only to their children, and tears spilled from my eyes. But then I was unmarried, independent and gave him what he wanted. Now I am married. I am bound to somebody else. Even now to desire me, to insist that I sleep with him and banging on the door when I have closed it, is it fair? I saw this difference. Vikram has absolute trust in me. He thinks of Mohanlal only as Guruji and touches his feet. When, with this trust Vikram has left us alone together in this lonely house in the midst of a forest and gone on his tour, how is it proper to force me? Such a great artist, couldn't he understand this intricacy of dharma? Why didn't he understand the subtlety of this code of conduct? My mind was perturbed. I looked at my watch. Half past eleven. Yes, I must go in search of him. He won't come if I simply wait for him.

She felt he wouldn't even give her a call. She felt hungry and her belly reminded her that she hadn't had her breakfast. She took out the packet of cereal but immediately felt that it would not be right to eat when he had stepped out without eating. Also, she simply couldn't manage to eat. She pushed the packet back in its place, came out, switched on the answering machine, closed the door and got into the car. Running her eyes over the benches that were placed under the thick shaded trees lined on both sides of the roads she slowly moved around the streets of Los Gatos. He might be on one of them. No. She went to all the parks that she had taken him to, parked the car and walked about inside. No. Nowhere to be seen. Finally there was only one park left—Vasona County Park. Thinking that it would complete the search, she looked at the watch. It was half past one. She was really hungry having not eaten anything since morning. If I went out I would feel giddy. And while driving if she didn't have all her reflexes intact there might be an accident. With this awareness she hurriedly poured a little milk on a small amount of crispies which wouldn't take time to consume, gulped it with a cup of tea and started her search once again. Afternoon. There were only five cars in the parking lot. She also parked there and went in looking around. He was not on any of the benches. Where else to look was the question. Just when she started wondering whether he had gone to somebody's house, she saw a figure on the bench under the huge maple tree. Yes, in just a pyjama and a jubba. She hurried up. Yes, it was him. The eyes were open as if he had just got up from sleep. He was staring at the branches of the tree. She went close and asked, 'Why are you lying down here without telling anyone?' expressing worry and anger together. Since he was not expecting anyone, hearing her voice, he was startled. Didn't know what to say. She insisted, 'Answer me'.

Without turning in her direction, and still fixing his sight at the branches he said, 'Why should I tell anyone, that too to a person who would not open the door though I begged in every possible way?'

'You haven't eaten anything since this morning. Haven't had a cup of tea.'

'What happens if I don't eat. Who is there in the world to weep for me if I die?'

She stared at him with burning anger, 'You are saying this just in order to prick and torture me.' Meanwhile, she felt like crying. Her eyes were filled with tears. She sat on her knees on the grass and took his hand and asked, 'Why are you talking like this? You must tell me. I won't leave you alone till you give me a proper answer.' She shook him. He still didn't talk. He didn't even look at her. She insisted, 'Come on, speak.'

Without shifting his gaze from the branches he said slowly, 'You are the one who insisted having me here. After having invited me, you are the one who is making me starve. Now you are showing this fake concern.'

'I have been telling you continuously for five days that I am bound by holy matrimony. Now, being a teacher you answer me.'

'You didn't ask for my permission to marry. You married in stealth and came to America. You were my Gandharva-wife before you married Vikram. I never used the word Gandharva. You were the one who was using it. I was only agreeing with you. If you consider marriage more holy than the union of music, better leave music which means that you should leave me. "Anyway you are coming to New York; we will get you the ticket from there. We have a home on the hill in the midst of a forest. You come and rest here for a month. You must come here and see for yourself what a beautiful atmosphere it is for music and its practice. You may even invent a new raga. Don't hesitate. I will serve you. My husband is your great admirer. He is also asking me to invite you. You come here before the workshop at New York. Anyway, it is summer in India now. There won't be too many programmes either. Come and see the breathtaking beauty of California and our home in the middle of the forest and on top of the mound. Weather here is like tonic," you repeatedly made calls to me and even made your husband talk to me. What is its meaning? And after I come here you are acting like a devoted wife.'

She was silenced. Her mind too. Even then he didn't turn in her direction. He was gazing at the dense roof of the beautifully delicate light green, hand-shaped, swinging tender maple leaves. 'Now, come home. Let us talk.' She put her hand on his shoulder and tried to lift him up.

'There is nothing left to talk. There is no need for you to lift me. I will get up myself.' He sat up abruptly and said staring at her, 'Get me a taxi. I don't want your California contract. You are the one who has arranged the concert? Cancel it. That is your business.'

She lost her patience. 'You just come and sit in the car. Come home, have something to eat immediately, get a shave and bath and have your lunch. Meanwhile, I will think about it. Give me an hour's time. A man who has crossed fifty-nine and stepped into sixty should not talk like a young lover of twenty. You should not mention conditions and decisions. Why do you think that I don't love you?' She bent down and kissed his lips. Immediately his anger vanished. 'In the anxiety of searching for you I couldn't realise that you would be lying down starving. Otherwise I would have brought a sandwich and some juice in a flask.'

They didn't talk while the car was moving. Her mind was immersed in memories. He was teaching me wholeheartedly. In the beginning, in my inexperienced stage I thought that he loved me wholeheartedly as well. Wonderful and abundant teaching twice or thrice a week. There was no surety that on the days of the lessons there would also be love making. There would be some impediment. Mostly his own reasons, excuses. I would not wish for the comfort or pleasure of the body but wanted to just lie down together and dream, and engage in words of mutual love. He was not under compulsion, nor was he especially interested either. Days when he wanted bodily pleasure, he would talk fondly, caressing me and would indulge in pillow talk. Then silence as if there was nothing to say and nothing to share. I was disappointed wondering whether love meant only that. I was learning fast and within three months I realised that I was not the only woman in his life. There were others as well. The music school would function from 4 pm until about 8 pm. By quarter to four the boys and girls of the first year would arrive. Till then nobody would come there or to his flat. If the door had been bolted from inside before we went for physical union, and even if somebody pressed the door bell, if the door was not opened it would be assumed that it had been locked and the visitor would go away. Though there was this advantageous arrangement he would not allow me to stay longer than necessary. He would say something like, 'It will be late for you. No one in your home should suspect anything.' Or 'I am expecting a visitor.' One day when I was in his arms, no, rather when I had taken him in my arms, I had asked, 'I will ask you a question. Will you tell the truth?'

'Ask. I always speak the truth.'

'There is a rumour that you are friendly with many women. Is it true? If it is true then don't you realise that it pains me?'

He answered after a minute, 'If I say no, it will be a lie. Even if I cut off a friendship of many years suddenly, they will be angry. They may even carry on a sinister propaganda about our relationship. Besides, to cut off a relationship suddenly is not fair. Have a little patience. Gradually I will shed off all other relations and will be completely yours. But there is absolutely no relationship between that and the lessons. I will teach you as much as you can learn. If you feel three days are not enough you come for an extra day.' He had shown his love for me by kissing and hugging me with great enthusiasm. Three times a week, two hours of supervised practice each time. That too from Pandit Mohanlalji. How many people can have such good fortune? I was content. I was practising for six to eight hours at home.

I waited for six months patiently. I waited for a year. But the feeling that he was sharing himself with many did not leave me. Knowledge is limitless. It will increase no matter how much you share it with others. But the body, having completed fifty-two and reaching fifty-three, if it is distributed in this diminishing state, how much of it will be left? I became aware of it. I would recognise the look in his eyes when he talked to music-loving women, especially his admirers. He would not encourage anybody else in the slot he had fixed for teaching individual women. But no one was allowed during my class. I would forget this and would be perturbed. One day, I started the conversation and asked, 'Do you remember that it has been one year since we talked about your relationship with others. It was the fifth of November.'

'Is that so? The capacity of women to remember the day, the week, the date and the time is unlimited.' He just laughed.

'You told me to wait patiently for some time. I just want to know if you have given up all that.' I examined his face closely, and asked.

He was not angry. He jocularly said, 'You mad girl,' and dishevelled my hair. Then he continued, 'Instead of reviewing how much progress you have achieved during this one year, you are filling your head with worms of suspicion. Until such emotions are shaken off, there will be no progress in your technique. It is my earnest desire that you should become a great singer. I have decided to make you one. You stop being jealous and envious of other's growth and don't put conditions about not teaching others. If you don't you will never acquire knowledge.'

While driving she swiftly glanced at his face with the corner of her eyes. He sat looking out of the window stubbornly. That day onwards I did not enjoy the bouts of physical union with him. I would not say 'no' either when he desired it. At the height of his excitement he would use musical expressions, comparing my looks and my body to various ragas. It was nice to listen to such words. I would feel like hearing them all the time but his time was limited. I would, however, suppress such thoughts with great effort and immerse myself in practice. I could myself be aware of the progress I was making. No matter which concert it was in Bombay, he would ask only me to accompany him on the tambura. Perhaps to please me, he stopped inviting Rajani Kaushal. He would ask the thirty-year old Mangesh Abhyankar. During the course of the singing though he would give both of us an opportunity, I would get the lion's share because my female voice was more melodious and entertained the audience more than Mangesh's male voice. My voice would provide that dash of colour and variety to Guruji's full voice. Sometimes he would encourage me and I would swell with happiness, satisfaction and pride for I was being elevated to the level of a singer on dais. The shrewd arrangers of concerts had realised that I was specially close to Mohanlalji. While introducing me to the audience they would say, 'A direct student of panditji and tomorrow's star with the cuckoo's golden voice, Kumari Madhumita Mehta will give support and play the tambura.' The audience would clap away as soon as my name was announced. For Mangesh only three or four people would clap in some corner. The knowledge that I was not only the support but the source of panditji's inspiration spread among the music lovers of Bombay. Some of them would even look at me with gratitude for being the inspiration for their favourite musician. I was thirty years younger to him. The clever photographers would take pictures highlighting me, choosing an angle which showed me as an equal. I would be ecstatic. I was floating on the waves like a chain of meends. But one day I met my classmate Rekha Jhunjhunwala of Mahim who said, 'We are all very happy when we see your photograph in the newspaper. We knew even in college that one day you would be a famous musician. But don't show yourself in newspapers as being closely associated with that fellow Mohanlal. It is true that he is a great singer. But he has a reputation of being a philanderer. It seems he had a roaring affair with Manohari Das, the famous dancer and lived with her for three to four years. That was about ten to twelve years ago, and had appeared in all the newspapers as the main story.' Though I was not unaware of the story of Manohari Das, I felt like disappearing.

४

When she recalled this, the car had passed through the main street of Los Gatos and had reached her house at the shoulder of the hill. She shot a glance at him sideways and while she recalled the rumour that such a famous dancer not only romanced with him but had fallen head over heels in love with him. He still held his neck stiff and was looking away from her. She smiled and thought what an obstinate man he was. But she didn't want to show it and kept looking at the road.

She gave him some biscuits and a cup of tea, asked him to take a shower. By the time she heated food, memories invaded her. Five years of music practice without a break. I could see my own development. When compared with the students of other teachers, how systematically and convincingly he taught his students, especially me. I had to learn for another three to four years and then I could shine as a singer and be known all over the country. But striving for this goal, suddenly what weariness did start in me! Meanwhile, mother started pestering me to get married. My sister-in-law suggested that they will find a groom who loves music. My brothers added that men were broad-minded these days and my future husband would not stop me from singing. Suddenly I felt they were right. I have not spent even a single night with Guruji. I have not enjoyed the pleasure of sleeping together, talking and dreaming till morning and getting up with the feeling that we are together. I have never enjoyed this happiness with him. It wasn't possible either. He could never spend his time dreaming with me in a leisurely manner. He never dreams of anything else with me except as a disciple of music. Or, maybe, he never dreams! What satisfaction was there in two bodies coming together hastily at his behest and then hurrying to throw open the front door? I wanted my own home, a husband who was reserved only for me and the family of my own management. He was thirty years my senior, fifty-six years of age and I was simply one of his women. How could I, an attractive twenty-six year old woman, find happiness with this old man? This fire began to burn within me. Yes, my family was right in what they were saying. Also, at this age living in the brothers' house, with their growing children was embarrassing.

My brother soon found a match for me. His name was Vikram Shah, a handsome, computer engineer from IIT and an MBA from

Stanford. He worked in the Silicon Valley and owned a company. He was visiting India on a business trip and my brother had already seen him. He suggested that I should see him as well. I felt nervous inside and said, 'No, I won't marry just yet. I won't regret it even if remain unmarried.' He said, 'I haven't told you the important aspect yet. I have told him that you are a student of Mohanlalji. That is why you have not married so far. He was very happy to hear this and said, 'What, she is a student of Mohanlalji! She must be great.' He is crazy about Hindustani classical music. It seems he has the tapes of all our famous artists. 'I must meet her and talk to her,' he said. What is wrong if you meet him? You may ask him whatever you like without hesitation. Afterwards if you don't like him don't say yes. There is no compulsion.'

The meeting was fixed for the next day in our house. All arrangements were made according to my second brother's suggestions. I had to sing a raga after the evening snacks had been served. Afterwards, we had to meet in the office room to enable us to talk in privacy. Everyone agreed to this. My brother brought the tambura which had been tuned in my room, and placed it in the sitting room. The elder brother came behind him and introduced me, 'Madhumita my sister.' The moment I saw Vikram, I was stunned, and bowled over. In Bombay, especially in my circle, there was no dearth of good-looking men. But this man had combined within himself both the smartness of Bombay and America. He was simply radiant. Not the cheap smartness of a Bollywood actor. And not just the physical agility of a good sportsman. I realised that he was a product of education, culture, self confidence, artistic taste and achievement all combined. In my overwhelming confusion I forgot to greet him, and sat in front of the tambura. I couldn't summon enough courage to look at him again. To start singing immediately seemed to be the only way of protecting myself. I closed my eyes and adjusted the shruti for shadja. My elder brother's voice, '*Areh, areh*, what are you doing?' Vikram said, 'If you sit on a sofa you do not get the mood to listen to Indian music.' Vikram was sitting on the carpet in padmasana. I opened my eyes and I could see his face directly. I got a little courage. My voice became steady. By the time

I did begin, I got enough self confidence and half opened my eyes. I was not used to singing with my eyes completely closed. But I could see even with the half-open eyes that he was certainly absorbed in music. Since the doubt whether the main listener was understanding it or not was solved, I took my time, elaborated it at length and slowly rested on all the subtle points in my singing, pulsating on all the veins of the new zones of the raga without hurrying. It took forty minutes for just alaap. When I stopped, though his look of admiration included me, it was fixed in the mood of raga. He was so struck that he was not in a position to make any comment. My second brother explained, 'We arranged this in a hurry. There was no time to get the accompanists. If there was a harmonium and tabla it would have been more colourful.' Vikram said, 'I like the alaap more sans the sound of accompanying instruments.' My elder brother suggested the closing of the music by saying, 'She could sing one more raga but there will be rahukaala at half past four.' When I sat in front of him in the office room I was anxious and afraid. All the questions I had planned escaped me. He asked, 'What you sang now was madhumasa-saranga wasn't it? Isn't it said, its proper name, is madhyamadi-saranga?' My happiness increased when I saw he could recognise the ragas also. I also got a little courage, I said, 'Yes.' He modestly said, 'I can only recognise them by constant listening. I want to learn music but I am too busy to learn from a guru. And with an enchanting smile he continued, 'If you accept me as a student, I will learn at home.' All my reserve had vanished. He continued, 'Please ask me without hesitation whatever you want to but before that I must tell you something. There is no reason for anxiety that by leaving Bombay and coming to America the continuation and development of music might be hampered. The air of California that too of the Silicon Valley is fully resonating with Indian classical music. Just less than two hours drive from where I stay there is the Ali Akbar School of Music. San Raphael is the name of the town. Ali Akbar himself teaches there. You can go there once or twice a week. Zakir Hussain lives quite close too. So many of our Indian computer engineers learn tabla from him. In fact, Pandit Ravishankar also lives in Southern California. All the famous

Indian musicians are settling down in California, that too around the Silicon Valley. We have music programmes quite regularly and there are a lot of people learning it. You can learn even there. If you like, you can run a school in your own name. In the land where technical experts are all settling down, is it not natural that Indian music also is flowering-forth?'

He was looking at my face while he was speaking. Then he stopped. A minute later he repeated, 'Yes, you can ask without any reservation.' When he was guessing all my questions and answering them even without my asking what was left for me? He said, 'I have started a company with three of my friends. It is running well and growing fast. Marketing responsibility is mine. I have to travel quite constantly. Not just in America but to Europe also. There is also a possibility of extending the export to India. In fact, I am here on a business trip. You must bear with my frequent travelling. In about three or four years when the company is firmly established I may appoint a capable marketing man and lessen my travels. I have built a new house in the midst of a forest half way up the hill. The forest around my house changes according to the season and is very inspiring for music.' That same evening Vikram made a call to his parents at Hyderabad and they reached Santa Cruz at 8.30 am, met me and by 8.45 am, it was decided. They said, 'Our son will be in India just for four more days. If you could arrange the marriage within that time it will be convenient. It would be difficult for him to come again. Make it a simple affair. We don't like any kind of ostentation.' The priest fixed the day and a number of phone calls were made and Hotel Sheraton took charge of everything. My mother and my sisters-in-law went round the sari shops and jewellery marts and the wedding took place. He was emotionally moved and said, 'Madhu, there is an arrangement of issuing visa without delay in the case of industrialists living in the US who marry a girl from some other country. You will join me within a month. Now, I find it difficult to go back alone.' There were tears in my eyes. We could spend only two nights together. I got my visa in twenty days and the tickets were confirmed when I started wondering if I shall go to my guru, touch his feet and tell him, 'I got married. Good bye,' giving him a packet of sweets, a shawl and a gold chain. But somehow I couldn't summon up courage. Was it because I had made a mistake? Was it because I was leaving him in the lurch and deserting him? Or, was it because I had broken my promise that I wouldn't stop till the completion of my education and would not waste all that he had taught by getting into a matrimonial necessity? Or, was it that I was unilaterally cutting off our Gandharva relationship. I felt guilty. I shouldn't have married. I shouldn't have yielded to the pressure of the elders. I shouldn't have been at the very first sight drawn to the magnetic personality of Vikram and succumbed. This was sad. What if he called and asked why I was not going to the class! And my mother, brothers or sisters-in-law asked me, 'Madhu why didn't you invite your guruji to the marriage?' What was I going to say? But I felt that it was not proper for me to leave without getting his blessings. No, it was not auspicious. So I called him and when queried, 'Why haven't you come for the lessons for twenty days?' I replied, 'I will come in about two hours. Right now. You please stay at home.' After his acceptance I went shopping, bought a gold chain, Zari shawl, a packet of sweet and huge bouquet of roses, took a taxi and went to West Bandra. He was wonderstruck looking at my dress and appearance. I had worn a gold coloured silk sari with Zari border, bangles on my wrists, mangalasutra for the neck and vermillion along the line parting of my forelock. 'What is this?' he asked. I bent down touched his feet, gave him the bouquet and then the three packets. He again asked, 'What is special?'

'You must have understood the mangalasutra around my neck and sindoor on my hair. You can see it.' Yes he was looking. But the meaning of it had not penetrated into his head. Or the mind was not prepared to accept it. I said, 'The auspicious moment for marriage had come up. The bridegroom had come from America. His parents asked us to arrange the marriage within two days. There was no way I could invite you. Tomorrow night I am leaving for America. You must kindly bless me.' He said, 'You have come to ask for my blessing after everything is over. After all you belong to the trading community. Did the people at home compel you?'

'No.'

He merely nodded. 'Then what happens to your music?' I said, 'I will continue right there, I will come to Bombay from time to time and learn from you. My husband also loves music very much.' His displeasure seemed to abate a little. Looking at me, two minutes later he asked, 'Are you leaving tomorrow itself?' I said, 'Yes.' He suggested by his look that we go into the bedroom. I showed anger on my face. A minute later he said, 'Don't know when we are going to meet again.' He caught hold of my shoulders and pushed me gently. I said, 'I am married.' He laughed, 'You have forgotten that you were married to me.' 'No, I hadn't. One day I myself suggested it. You had said that it was not possible to get a divorce from your wife. It would not have been difficult to get it if you had tried. I knew that recently the divorce laws had been relaxed. But I didn't want to force you.' He was angry. 'Are you showing your indifference now that you are married? Or will you make love to me at least once before you leave?' I said, 'Look, hereafter I will touch only your feet. What you can touch is only the top of my head. There is no use acting with anger and speaking cruelly.' I just touched his feet and came out.

ड

Though she finished heating the food and setting the table, he had not yet come back from his shower. She looked out of the kitchen window. The leaves of the thick forest on the slope were sparkling in the sunshine. She felt that only a person who loves nature intimately would build a house in such a place. By profession he was an expert in marketing, by inclination a lover of nature, by attitude a person moved by music. When he brought me here from the airport, it was three in the afternoon. He said, 'Madhu, you are very tired. There is a difference of twelve and a half hours. Actually it is travelling from one side of the globe to the other. Have your bath and dinner and lie down for at least twelve hours. Anyway, before you take your bath just take a look at this house. The plan is mine and the place was chosen by me. I am anxious that you should not only like it but you must know where what is in this house. Come, I will show you.' He showed every room, the lounge, everything. How happy he was when I was pleased. 'This is the room for your music practice.

That is why I have not put a chair or a bench here. The tambura, harmonium, tabla and whatever else you need, they are all available at Ali Akbar School. They get it from Calcutta. Now just go and rest. I will take you there the day after tomorrow. We will bring whatever you choose.' The jet lag receded. The feeling that I had come to a new country was forgotten. He had noticed that I had brought the tambura with me. He didn't know that I had carried a harmonium as well. He showed me the single bed. 'In this country even a single bed is enough for two. Purposely, I have not equipped the master bedroom. I had postponed it as I wanted to visit the furniture shop along with my wife and then make choices. I wanted to bring an expert interior decorator to arrange things. Till then we can use this room,' and showed me what was now the guest room.

Guruji has not finished his shower yet. Or, has he filled the tub and gone off to sleep. I felt like calling out to him from outside. But I became aware that if I called at this time it would give rise to excessive familiarity. Let him come whenever he wants.

She went to the music room and sat down. In Bombay if I closed the door of the room it would be hot. If I switched on the fan it would affect the shruti and the voice. If I put on the air-conditioner not only would the shruti be disturbed with the buzzing sound and there would be difference between the sound of the strings and the voice. In this house, in this room there was a comforting atmosphere. Utter silence, which would be the basis for shruti. If I set it once, it would be intact even after two hours. In the beginning when I came here I would just sit listening to the humming tune of the tambura. After a long time when I started the practice, how easily and freely it would open up. There was no fear of my making a mistake as Guruji was not there to correct me. I knew the subtle differences between the ragas myself. Even if I deviated a little in a subtle manner I knew to which raga it would change. When I was in doubt there were the volumes written by Batkhande to refer to. What would I need after regular teaching for five years from Wadekar Master and six-year training given by Guruji? I only needed time to master what I had already learnt and to achieve maturity in it and develop individuality and progress. Meanwhile I was practising hours together and could repeat by consciously making new variations in the movements. When I experimented anew I would suspect whether I was deviating from the main import of the raga. But with whom could I discuss it? Perhaps I needed a guru for another four years. There was no one here in California to guide me. I went twice to Ali Akbar. When I was singing in his presence he would explain the right and the wrong. But the specific characteristic movements were not his special field. Besides, he was such a busy person that he could hardly give me the time I needed. Also, after driving at sixty-five or seventy miles per hour for two hours I would not be in a proper mood to sing and there would be no strength left in my voice. Since I had learnt driving recently, the anxiety would sink the voice still more. Kulkarni would come to accompany on tabla for practising tanas only on Saturdays and Sundays. I felt that this was at best only an amateurish atmosphere. Within six months after coming here the memory of Guruji began to haunt me. In any rhythmic movement, or in any meandering or in whatever different pace did it run, his mastery over the ragas would never allow the pattern of the tanas to transgress from the emotion of the raga. I should have kept my promise that I would not leave in the middle till my training was complete, and sadness began to envelop me. Though I went to Bombay just a year after coming here, I didn't meet him. If I had, he would have certainly taught me but he would ask for his fee. He would say, 'How can I teach with complete attention if you don't give your complete mind?' I felt that to cheat Vikram would be a mean thing. Vikram had said, 'Madhú, since I travel extensively by plane, a lot of mileage points have been accrued to my credit. You can go once in three months to Bombay without our spending even a cent. If you like you can go for two weeks at a time and learn for four hours everyday. What you learn in two weeks there may be enough for practising for three months here. You may call him and find out about his availabilty before going. You have reached the take off point. With a little more special training you will fly to the sky.' How can one deceive such a husband?

Two years without any kind of progress brought boredom in my life. I was not interested in anything. A lonely house in the middle of a forest and a husband who was always travelling provided the perfect ingredients for an attack of depression. After reading about Mohanlal's workshop arranged by the New York Ethnic Art Society, my husband asked me to make a call to Guruji. 'He is coming, anyway. Come a month earlier and stay with us. I will also speak to him. Take lessons from him for a month. Your boredom will be taken care of.' Even when Vikram himself suggested this, I did not immediately agree. 'Why aren't you interested?' When he asked me again what could I tell him? If he comes he will again demand the old relationship. Inspite of knowing all this, I called him. Not once or twice but thrice. It had its effect. It looks as if his bath is over. Yes I can hear his humming. Even through his humming, the raga expresses itself quite clearly.

She went to his door. It was open. She asked, 'Did you have your shower?' He said, 'I wanted you to come and rub my back. But I kept quiet, for service is something which you should not ask for.' She told him, 'The food is served. Come quickly.' As long as he was eating he didn't say anything. But he seemed pleased. He ate with satisfaction as if nothing had happened and he was in a better mood. After the meal he went to his room and sat on the chair. She cleared the table, put the dishes in the sink under the tap, wiped the table clean and went to his room. She must give the hint that she would surrender herself. His anger had not disappeared. She knew that he himself would not make the first move. Even eight and a half years ago it had happened like that. She recalled how earlier also, she went to his flat and said that she had come with her own freewill and she was completely surrendering to him and she had requested him that he should also teach her everything and make her a great singer. She went and sat on his bed. He simply looked at her face. There was not only a question on his face but it also expressed silently why there was delay. She said, 'Come here, why are you sitting on the chair?' He said, 'You should come, and take me by the hand and lead me.' She got up, went and held his hand and pointed towards the bed. He said, 'Not here,' and freed himself. 'Where else?' 'There. In your room. In that huge master bedroom.' She protested. 'This is too much. It is our room. Reserved for me and my husband. I will not agree to take you there and destroy the sanctity completely.' Her voice was firm.

'Which means that you are not offering yourself completely? You have reserved separateness for yourself. What kind of offering is this?' At that moment the thought came to her that she wanted to tell him that neither had he given himself to her completely. Couldn't think of any answer. It seemed weak. She simply stared at him. The fire which had been lit in her eyes turned to vapour and broke out in tears. She said, 'Please, don't force me. I beg you.' When she said this she was weeping profusely. He said, 'I am not forcing you. Just come.' He pushed her gently into the master bedroom. He seized her. She didn't resist. He did not notice the difference whether she accepted him or merely suffered him.

ಕ

He fell asleep. She stayed in his arms without moving. He slept for more than an hour. When he woke up he fondled her like a child and asked gently, 'Did you sleep?' She simply said yes to avoid further questioning. He closed his eyes again. She realised he was not sleepy, but wanted to immerse himself in the enjoyment of post-coital embrace and she caressed him on the top of his head. After a little while when he was fully awake he asked, 'The concert is in the evening isn't it?'

'Yes.'

'Which raga shall we sing?'

'Whichever you like'

'You silly girl. I am not asking you because I want to sing a raga of my liking and go back. In the remaining sixteen days I will teach you two or three ragas completely and perfectly. You will sing these ragas with me in the concert. It is not jugalbandi but it is singing together. Isn't it to learn from me that you have invited me here?'

She did not refuse because that was really her inner desire. Though he had come here seven days earlier he had not even mentioned teaching music. Just demonstrated a bit for enjoyment. Vikram's idea was that a full-fledged concert should be arranged here as well. As soon as the other Indians living in the area came to know, they agreed as well. Madhu remembered how Kulkarni, Gupta, Sardesai and others had got together, formed a committee, given wide publicity to the event, and sold tickets. They had planned to invite him to their house for getting his blessings and they wanted to give him a citation and a bouquet on reaching his sixtieth year before the concert. All this she remembered. Guruji was always after opportunities to satisfy himself and looked forward to Vikram's departure for work. I did not agree. I kept quiet because I knew that if I mentioned about lessons he would impose his usual condition. But after I offered myself, he started taking the initiative. He was also offering an opportunity to sing together. Though I was angry enough to refuse any further lessons and give up practice altogether, I did not show it. My inner conscience told me it was not true that I did not want practice. He got up immediately and said, 'Come on, pick your tambura and tune it. I will join you.' She hurriedly made the bed, went to the bathroom, washed her face, wore a fresh sari, went down into the kitchen, prepared some tea, took the biscuits and tea to the music room and tuned the tambura. He came out looking fresh in his neatly ironed pyjama and jubba and said, 'If you know how to set the shruti it means that you have learnt half of music. Your decision is to start the concert with Kalyan. Won't the audience be bored because every time there is an evening programme it always starts with the same raga?'

'No, that raga has that power and in your voice it becomes something very special.' He said, 'Thank you. It seems in America for everything you have to say thank you. But thank you for admiring my voice' and raising his eyebrows he said, 'Thank you for giving the guru-dakshina even before the lesson.' He leaned against the heavy bolster next to the wall opposite her and said, 'Hmmm, sing'.

She said, 'More than my singing you should sing and show all the details and nuances. I must follow you and practise.'

'I must know first how much you have practised and how much you have forgotten in these two and a half years.'

'I practised for the first six months. After that I gave up.'

'Why? Were you tending donkeys? I didn't see a single one here.'

Though she felt like smiling she tried not to show it. He asked, 'What are you hiding, come on, tell me.'

'You abused calling me a donkey-herder? That means you have accepted me again as your student.'

'I had never left you so the question of me taking you back does not arise. You were the one who ran away. Now let us begin the lesson. Enough of chattering.' He started the shadja incorporating tivra-nishada and tivra-rishabha and closed his eyes. Electrifying waves began to rise in her memory. She felt, this power of voice, this extensiveness is possible only for this man, for this teacher of mine. He stopped and asked, 'Did you understand? Now repeat.' She sang. 'Have you understood to what range and extent the shadow of shadja in Kalyan should spread? Listen again. I will sing once more.' He did. She put the tambura down, ran out, brought the tape recorder and plugged it in and said, 'Please start from beginning.' For an hour and a half he expatiated in detail, and opened the strains of just the mandra-swara, demonstrated and made her repeat. She switched on another cassette. When he descended to gandhara of mandra her voice would lose control. He was really angry. He said, 'You are not performing pranayama.' She bent down her head. He further shouted, 'What kind of music can you learn. You should perform pranayama everyday and practise mandra. Until then how can you see the real form of the raga? Go and tend donkeys.' Then he insisted, 'Though you can't you should follow me exactly, now follow...' That cassette was also full and even after three hours he had not completed mandra and touched panchama of the madhya-saptaka. She put in another cassette. The phone rang at 9 pm. Vikram had purposely not got the line connected to the music room to avoid any kind of disturbance. She ran to the kitchen and picked the receiver.

'Madhu, I rang thrice. Now it is midnight here. Weren't you at home?'

'He is making me practice. He wants me to sing with him at the concert. You will understand how completely he is teaching me, when you see that the mandra portion of Raga Kalyan has taken three hours. I have recorded everything.'

'Very good, I must come and listen. Thank your guru and convey to him my thanks also. Now go back to your lesson. I will call you again tomorrow afternoon which means morning for you.' He put down the receiver.

It was 11 pm when the lesson came to a close. Though he said that they could continue in the morning she was still playing the tambura. She didn't feel like stopping. He also appreciated her absorption. However, he remembered that he had not chewed tobacco all day. He got up to go to his room to get it when she requested him to wait. She touched his feet and said, 'At the beginning of the lesson I had forgotten to touch your feet. Now I will do it.'

He laughed. 'After touching all the parts, what is so special about the feet?' She lowered her head.

She went to the kitchen and put the food in the microwave, when she suddenly remembered. She ran to the music room. The last part of the tape was still running. She stopped it and rewinded it. Again she started. Two minutes later she could hear clearly his laugh and the words, 'After touching all the parts what is so special about the feet.' She stopped the tape recorder, went to his room, brought him to the music room and made him listen to it and said, 'Everything will be recorded clearly. Vikram will listen to it. Make sure that you do not say anything suspicious.' He was also frightened. He said, 'Delete it immediately.' She deleted those two sentences, played the tape again to make sure that it had been deleted. Then she went back to the kitchen.

Even before he expressed his desire she knew that Guruji would expect them to sleep together. Maria would come at seven in the morning. With the key she had with her she would open the front door, and go to the kitchen. What if she comes before he gets up? Vikram was in the habit of getting up before seven. She mentioned this to Guruji.. He assured her, 'Don't worry. I will get up very early and go to that room.' Still, for the sake of being sure she bolted the front door from within. Even after he slept, she was still awake. She invoked her memory and tried to comprehend the inversions that took place in the emotions of the same swaras when the uthaav and chalan of Raga Kalyan descended into mandra. She asked herself why she had forgotten that all the details of a raga could be comprehended while exploring them at mandra. Why did I forget that secret which Guruji kept repeating? 'Truly my mind must have really been tending the donkeys,' she told herself.

He got up at six in the morning and went to his room to sleep some more. She unbolted the additional lock of the front door, had a cup of tea and put on the recording from the previous day. She noticed that her elaboration was very weak compared to Guruji's elaboration of the raga that flowed without limits. By the time Maria left he had finished his shower and came directly to the music room. He took up the tambura and said, 'Sit down. I will see that you get your alaap right.' She put on the tape and started singing. The practice went on till half past twelve. Though it was the same raga and the same method, in the beginning between the steps there was a little difference between yesterday and today, in establishing relationships between steps and in effecting the meend. She had sung more today than the previous day. In the middle he had said, 'Yes, yes, very good.' After lunch he went out and sat on a bench in the middle of the forest and said, 'You go and listen to the tape.' He came back at four and said, 'I will give the ek-taal theka of vilambit and you sing alaap in that structure. There will be discipline to the movement.' This went on till seven in the evening. Even this was recorded. In the beginning stages Wadekar Master had taught the same raga. After that Guruji had taught it in detail. Now he is teaching it at the level of making me a proper singer. I should have learnt for two or three more years. She was remembering Vikram's suggestion of going to Bombay once every three months and staying for two weeks at a time to master a raga. She glanced sideways at him. He was intently following the movement of the swara and playing the tabla. If the present situation had not arisen she thought that she would not have gone there and offered herself. By this analysis the mind wavered and the swara became a little shaky. He noticed it immediately and asked, 'Where is the mind going? Singing is like meditation. Even if there is a little distraction it will be immediately noticed.' She felt guilty. She apologised and decided not to give room for any lack of attention and completely concentrated on the tonal movement.

The next day he continued with the same cheez and tana of the same raga and he took up the tabla. She was surprised that she had not known that Guruji was such an expert on the tabla also. His sense of taal was unbelievable. She only knew that in the matter of rendering a chain of tanas, he could match any great accompanist on the tabla. He had such command. But she had no opportunity so far to hear him playing by himself in so many different ways. As the movement of the tabla quickened, she also started putting together the tanas with enthusiasm.

Four days later when Vikram came back, he was ecstatic listening to the progress his wife had made. He heard all the tapes and confided in Mohanlal, 'You see, I was telling her to go to Bombay once in three months, stay for a couple of weeks at a time and learn from you, four to six hours every day in detail and get the tapes back. You could practise with those tapes and attain mastery for the next three months here. She didn't listen to me. Now you please tell her.' He noticed that her mind was elsewhere, during night. He didn't want to exercise his conjugal rights when she was completely immersed in her own music. So, he didn't force her. When he got up in the morning she was not by his side. It was their habit to stay in each other's arms and talk for about half an hour intimately when they woke up in the morning. He went and saw that she was in the music room alone with her eyes closed practising mandra.

Within a week, Guruji made her perfect in Raga Kalyan and then took up Bihaag. He put her to intense practice in his usual expert method. He revealed the raga layer by layer like cotton, and showed its vision.

The New York Ethnic Society had invited Rajram Tipnis and Omkar Prabhu from Bombay on the recommendation of Mohanlalji, to accompany him on the harmonium and tabla for the workshop. It had been arranged that both of them should arrive two days before the workshop would start. But after the Silicon Valley programme of Mohanlal was arranged, the schedule had been rearranged and now they were to arrive one day earlier in San Francisco and after finishing the concert on Saturday, proceed to New York by the morning flight on Sunday. Madhu knew both of them. Years ago, when she was playing tambura during Gurujii's concerts, they were the supporting accompanists. Besides, whenever Guruji gave concerts in various other towns and cities they used to accompany him. She wanted to ask them to stay in her home but Patil, who was learning tabla insisted on Prabhu staying with him. Garg, who was accompanying on the harmonium wherever there was a concert in the valley, wanted to have Tipnis as his guest. Madhu did not oppose this because she would be close to her guru without any impediment for half a day on Friday and until the time of leaving for the concert on Saturday. Meanwhile Vikram went out on another trip for three more days. When he was in town he would leave home by half past eight in the morning and would be immersed in his office until seven in the evening. So even during the music lessons she and her guru could spend a whole day without any impediment as intimately as a married couple.

7

The concert was absolutely wonderful. The huge auditorium of the Sunnyvale Hindu Temple was absolutely full. There was no arrangement for chairs and everybody sat on the ground and kept making room for the fresh arrivals. More than three hundred people turned up without any prior bookings. Vikram and the other enthusiasts were really surprised to see that more than two thousand people had gathered for pure classical music. He was extremely happy that the fame of his wife's guru had spread so extensively. Two aspects had increased the speciality of the concert. One was the sheer swara-shakti of Mohanlalji, his effortless expertise and endless imaginative prowess. Then the maturity of Madhumita Shah in singing which was fitting for the occasion. They all felt that they had a great artist right in their midst, the wife of a young Indian who had started independent business in the Silicon Valley. What a lustrous appearance, traditional Indian dress and ornaments, the vermillion on the parting of the forelocks, the sparkling diamond earrings and the round large kumkum on the forehead and a shining mangalasutra. Red bangles. Wearing a Cuttack silk sari of a simple design she appeared to be the main focus of the concert. She was not supporting the guru. She had taken over as the main singer. The audience was thrilled that this guru was providing opportunities for his disciple to shine forth, with himself staying in the background.

Some shrewd listeners wondered whether it was the 'inititation programme of the disciple'. Those who knew music remembered that she had sung three times earlier. Yes, she had been trained well, had a good voice but apart from that there was nothing special. But now she was simply electrifying, like lightening. First rate. Equal to her guru. This was not a jugalbandi. It was singing together. The sancharas were pouring forth, once in the male voice and once in female voice. The female voice was shining like a beautiful border to the vitality and expanse of the male voice. She was not only following him but she was independently composing combinations of swaras. She moved about in new directions. Never before had Raga Kalyan been heard in this form. All the nuances were brought out—the shyness of a newly married bride, curiosity, slow movement with the weight of joy, sweetness, *wah*!

> pi yaa s ke | s na ja ri | yaa s jaa s | du bha ri s
> mohali | yo s ss ma s na | pe ss ss ss ma bha ri s

Ah, when this predominant emotion is sung in the male voice, it gives one sort of feeling, and when sung in the female there is another kind of feeling, when both the voices sing together there would be a distinct and expanded dimension. When the same emotion is sung in different musical notations, when its bits are presented one by one in myriad swaras, what a variety of designs do occur! Now, Madhumita had lost her shyness and had risen high. She was complementing the alaap in the background and was singing like a companion. She had now become an equal, challenging, provocating and competing. The man who was playing the table became activised and the harmonium player, Tipnis, got galvanised. The audience straightened their backs and sat attentively. The student could not complete the aavartanas of the guru and finished off just in three or four rounds. When she looked at her guru with a shyness of defeat, the way she looked, was itself a treat. But she herself started the antara.

> kavanaja | tana aba | kariye s | aa s li s |

She overtook her guru. There was a smile on her face. The guru accepted the defeat. He approved of her forward movement and showed it by raising his eyebrows and nodding his head. Yes, a student should be like this. Moving along with the male and female voices mingled together, the swaras of the harmonium which were like that of the flute played at intervals. The words appeared as if they were the expressions of tanas.

Those who did not know music, those who only enjoyed it, those who half understood it, those who had just started learning, those who practised for four or five years and left it, those who knew the shastra—all of them forgot even to clap when the raga ended and were sitting with tightened breath absolutely silent as it happens when a great flood has stopped after a swell. After a couple of minutes of waiting when Mohanlalji said there would be an interval of twenty minutes a few people clapped and then the whole gathering clapped away with a deafening roar with nobody wanting to stop. Though both the singers stood up and took a bow people were still clapping. The secretary, Sardesai's voice was heard on the loud speaker, 'They have sung Raga Kalyan for one hour and fifty-six minutes. You have been clapping for three minutes. Keep it up for one minute more so that it will be exactly two hours.' The clapping continued for another minute.

Though the interval was over, the effect of Raga Kalyan that had filled the emotion of the audience did not decrease. Raga Bihaag took a little time after Mohanlal started it. Gradually it captured the audience. Now Madhumita accompanied and sang with even more self confidence. She had gained courage from the fact that the audience had accepted her singing and it had also realised that she could sing with her guru. She took more liberty and accompanied him in the movement of Bihaag. That lasted an hour and fifteen minutes. Then the secretary came to the platform and informed the gathering that Pandit Mohanlal had completed fifty-nine years and was stepping into the sixtieth and on this occasion the entire Indian community of the Valley was honouring him. He put a shawl around Mohanlal's shoulders and gave him a bouquet. He continued, 'The entire Indian community of America must be grateful to panditji.

Not merely, for creating an artist of Madhumita's calibre but for introducing her here, in our place.' The clapping was so loud that the whole place was filled with a wonderful sound. After the bouquets were given to her and two other accompanists and one more to the tambura player. Finally, the secretary announced, 'Now, Bhairavi'. Guruji turned to his pupil and said, 'You sing this. I am not in the mood.' She felt a bit lacking in courage. 'Me, alone, no.' She said. But even this whispered conversation was heard in the loud speaker. People said, 'You sing alone.' Guruji said, 'Listen to them.' There was no alternative. Though she became red in the face, she asked, 'What shall I sing?' He left it to her and suggested, 'Whatever you have not forgotten, sing that.' Meanwhile, Tipnis on the harmonium played *Mat ja jogi*. Understanding the trail, the audience clapped away. And then everybody joined. Though she had learnt Bhairavi from Wadekar Master as well as from her Guruji, she had not practised it recently. In the last two weeks Guruji had made her perfect in only two ragas Kalyan and Bihaag. But now there was no escape. She started. Tipnis who understood the situation would always go ahead one step further giving her clues. She got immersed and became one with it, and pity, separation, imploration, humility, surrender—all the emotions of the raga came in full force. When the words *prema bhakti ko pedo hi nyaro hamko gaila bata ja jogi* were elaborately presented like a Thumri, taking it layer by layer, the entire audience was floating about in the karuna rasa—the emotion of pathos. When it was made clear that '*jogi*' meant Lord Krishna the feeling of pain, of separation became intensified. She added to this enough alaap, added the tanas, and sharpened the intensity of emotion. In the end she started weeping and this intensity of emotion touched the audience to the extent that there were tears in their eyes too. But Guruji, who was sitting still till then, entered and turned it to madhya-laya and started singing which immediately grasped the listeners. The audience understood the tears of Madhumita Shah and realised how keenly and with what great intensity she was experiencing what she was singing. After singing two rounds in the medium pace, Guruji came to the sthayi and gave an indication to the student to follow him. Meanwhile she had controlled the tears and started singing along. She realised that singing with full concentration was the only means of hiding her embarrassment which had just occurred. She started singing. The guru did not stop. They sang in unison and completed together.

Half the audience surrounded the artists. Some of them were fans of Mohanlal who had heard him in India. The rest were new admirers. Many other admirers wanted to meet the artiste who had just appeared from among their midst and get close to her wishing to be introduced to her. There was a dinner for all those involved with the event. By the time, the dinner was over and they came home, it was 1 am. In the context of the concert, neither Vikram nor Madhu were aware of the intensity of feeling that Guruji would be leaving by the 10 am flight. Even Vikram felt that tomorrow the house would be really empty. Madhu was totally silent. When the door of the bedroom was closed he told her, 'I had not even imagined that your singing would reach the pinnacle of heights it did. You are today's star. I am proud of you. Congratulations.' She could not say anything more except, 'Thank you.' He continued, 'I understood. You wept because Guruji would be leaving. What a lot you have learnt in two weeks. Didn't I tell you? You can go to Bombay once in three months, stay for two weeks at a time and learn two ragas each time and tape the whole thing and bring it back with you. You will take off in three years. You will be a great singer. Let us run a music school in San Jose. Let us call it Madhumita Shah School of Indian Music.'

She felt she had seen a new path. She intoned, 'Thank you, thank you' and held his shoulders.

'I have been meaning to ask you for two days. They have paid five thousand dollars for the concert to Guruji. For the harmonium and tabla accompanists a thousand each plus the air-fare to and from New York. It occurred to me, Guruji has taught you for two weeks on one-on-one basis. We should give him five thousand dollars. You cannot put a price on what he has taught but we have to decide on a fee. Tell me if you think it is too little. We will pay more. I am agreeable to whatever you decide.'

'Thank you, you are always generous.' She said with tearful eyes.

He slept. But she couldn't. Even in his state of sleep he became aware that she was awake. With his eyes still closed, putting his hand round her he said, 'Sleep, we have to get up early in the morning. We should leave home by eight.'

She didn't talk. After a little while she said, 'I won't come to the airport. I may become emotional and start weeping. You can understand. But the fans who come there to send him off and the organisers of the concert may think otherwise. So I will touch his feet right at home and see him into the car.'

He didn't say anything but after a couple of minutes, 'If you break down everybody will think that it is your guru-bhakti. If you don't come to the airport there is a greater possibility of people mistaking you. Anyway, in three months you are going there. You try your best not to break down. I will speak to Guruji in the morning. When you go to Bombay for two weeks he should train you for eight hours a day just as he did here. Every minute has to be recorded. What is the fee he expects? I will tell him, "If you feel embarrassed please leave it to me. I will give you more than what you expect. Not as a fee for what you have taught but as a small token of our respect."'

Chapter 2

1

Women are always like this. Weeping and getting attached. Though he thought like this, he was aware that he was also feeling depressed. If Vikram had not made a reservation for me by United Airlines I could have gone with Tipnis and Prabhu and we could have played cards on the way. That way I wouldn't be bored. Just when he was thinking that six hours of non-stop flight was too much, he remembered how close this girl had got to him. His mind was overflowing with her memory and he felt proud as well. She is from a well-to-do family and married to a successful young man. Still, she was shedding so many tears for me. Along with pride he felt the satisfaction of fulfilment. Let her come once in three months, not only for eight hours, I will teach her for ten hours everyday. When he realised that she looks like the one who can preserve his name if she continues with the same interests and completely devotes herself to music, his interest to teach her was further strengthened. Just thirty years. A very delicate body and the eyes that would reflect the emotions of ragas. The memory of her touch filled his mind and wrung it with a pleasant pain. I must make her a great singer he decided. Though she is thirty, why is it that all the important ragas are not under her control? They have not revealed the extent, depth, the sophistication and their precise pulses to her. Did she commit a mistake in getting married precipitously and coming here? Does music never yield itself to rich people no matter how much they practice? This question stopped his flow of thought. If I was eating just two rotis a day, had a place to live, and spent the rest of the time in learning, may be I would have been a better singer and this made him remember the days of struggle. If you simply practise, music does not yield to you. You must struggle, you must suffer, you must hanker after it, and you must give yourself to it at any cost. You must clamour before and surrender to god, begging him in all humility and must be burnt up to acquire music. Yes, you must burn inside.

Otherwise how do you understand the emotions of the ragas? The mind engaged itself in thinking about how a person who has been brought up in comfort and happiness, who has a husband who looks after her ever experience the intricacies of music? It needs a mother who washed vessels in other people's homes and bringing what little food they had left in the cooking vessels and feeding me who was ten years old. A clever boy who found out that singing bhajans with a one-stringed instrument next to the River Ganga would earn some money. Repeating what was heard on loud speakers and radios. The same emotions but with better singing: it was a boon, a power that had come from birth itself. Earning one and half rupees a day, sometimes two. At that time, fifty years ago there was no naya paise, it was rupees, annas, paisa. The paisa had Queen Victoria's head engraved on it. Yes, eight measures of wheat for one rupee. Four rupees was the pay for a sepoy. But what pride! How my mother did train me, 'Where are you going to sit, my dear? Sit near Har ki Pauri and sing the songs for performing aarati.' She would cleverly save a little, even from this small earning of her son.

I had never seen Omkar Baba. Shining white hair gathered together in a knot at the back of the head. A long beard. A saffron-coloured lungi and a saffron upper cloth. Big kumkum on the forehead. 'Child, god has given you a good voice. I will give you food. I will teach you music. I will teach you how to sing really well,' he said. When I looked at him with suspicion he said, 'Listen to the way small boys like you sing in my ashram. If you feel happy you also learn. Otherwise you can come back here. Are you afraid that if you come now your today's earning will be lost? Take this one rupee.' He held before me a silver rupee. I took it and put it in the small cloth purse which my mother had stitched. Kept it in my pocket, took out my begging bowl, the paisas, and a little bag and started walking. I was taken to the brink of the Vilva Mountain. It was a real ashram. Right on the door there was the saffron flag. Inside, there was an old but big house. Once inside I could see there were several rooms. In one of the rooms, one boy was playing on the tambura, another the harmonium. There were fifteen boys between the age group of ten and twenty. In one corner, two boys were practising the tabla.

All of them were wearing white dhotis and white jubbas. He took me to an inner chamber, sat on the deer skin, and gave me two big pieces of sugar candy. He started playing the harmonium and broke into a song. I was simply stunned by the way he sang. Baba said, 'Sing the song you were singing there and I will accompany on the harmonium.' He said, 'You sing whatever you know and I will play.' He made me sing all the songs. I realised that he knows music; he is not an ordinary baba. I asked, 'Shall I play this?' 'Play. Let me see how you do it.' He pushed the instrument in my direction. When I played it, pushing bellows with left hand and moving the fingers of my right hand on the harmonium, some terribly bad sounds emanated as if somebody was screaming. But when he played, it sounded like my own voice singing. In fact it sounded better than my voice. I asked, 'Babaji, how do you play this?' He replied, 'It must be learnt regularly in a sequence, child. You come here for two hours everyday. I will teach you. I will teach you more songs. Look there, at that collection of books. They are full of songs. Can you read?'

'After father died I stopped going to school. It has been two years now.'

'What does your mother do?'

'She is a charwoman.'

For two months I went there for half an hour for each day's lesson. Practice about two hours, singing various ragas with the harmonium. Learnt Lakshana songs and ten tanas each and whenever I went there, a meal and sugar candy. He said affectionately, 'Child, your voice is given to you by Goddess Sarasvati herself. You are intelligent enough to learn. Just join the ashram. I will make you a better singer than myself. I will give you food and clothes etc. Ask your mother. You bring her here. Tell her that along with music we teach reading and writing also. Sanskrit and Hindi.' When mother came to the ashram and saw Swamiji and the singing of other students, not only did she believe what he had said about learning but she was so overwhelmed by devotion that she put her head on Baba's feet and said, 'I am putting this boy in your care. I will come and do whatever work I can in the ashram. Please teach him.'

'Hello, what would you like to drink?'

He turned his head. American hostess. How tall she was, with a smiling face, there was self confidence mixed with dignity. She gave a packet of peanuts and asked, 'Scotch?' He couldn't decide immediately. She brought a small bottle of Scotch with a half-filled large glass with ice cubes and a straw, went to the next person and asked, 'For you?'

If you look out of the window there would appear rows and rows of hills. Then the plains, again the hills. Looking from the plane, all that was on the ground would look superficial, like bundles of memory. When you come down to earth, it takes weeks or months to open these bundles and reveal the details. Memories are also like that.

Baba firmly believed that music which could express parabrahman through the sound was the means to salvation. Wherever he met boys who were interested in music, he would bring them to the ashram. Not only music, but Sanskrit, Hindi and the *Bhagavadgita* were also taught. Every time a student was admitted, Baba would assign the expenditure incurred by the student for his food and clothing to some prosperous merchant in Hardwar, Meerut, Saharanpur, Barelly and places like that. People would bring enough provisions, clothes and money. Added to this, was the money that Baba would receive by performing at various music concerts. There was no dearth of good food.

I was eleven years old when I joined the ashram. Within five years I was so good that as far as the knowledge of the swara and taal was concerned I was better than the most senior student there, the twenty-two year old Srichand. I became the favourite disciple of Baba and was given the responsibility of supervising other students. Five years had passed, hadn't they? Yes, I was sixteen. Baba took me along with him to Kashi (Varanasi) for a music conference. I was responsible not only for playing the tambura in support but also helping him with his chores. He would show me to the visitors and proudly tell them what a smart student he had in his ashram. However, it was there that the limitation of the music of my guru came to my notice for the first time. Everyone respected him because of the ashram he was running and the impeccably pure life he led.

Singers of his own age would touch his feet. Though all of them were tremendously impressed by the way he sang, during the interval, I overheard some senior singers commenting, 'He is fit only to sing bhajans. If you sit concentrating on god, could music be achieved?' My knowledge of his limitation began to become clear on account of listening to other singers and accompanists at the same conference. Each one had his own individuality and speciality. Every one had his own vocal sophistication. I observed the technique of all those who were considered great—the alaap of a raga, the sudden unexpected twists and turns, sliding from an unforeseen position arriving at the naadi-sthaana and enhancing the richness and augmentation of the emotional presentation etc. For each one of them the swara was everything. They would play with the swaras. They would make the swaras play with them. They would kiss the swara like a lover or a beloved and they would make it elastic by weaving into it various vibrations with the aplomb of a master weaver. They would draw it out like the strands of vermicelli, and form it into whatever they wanted. They would treat it as a leela, a cosmic play, and become poetic artists of that leela. For my guru, swara was just a means for bhakti. He did not see any difference between his music and the flowers, incense and the fruit he offered to god. So his playing with swaras would not last long. There was no variety of enjoyment either. When I asked about these things on the return journey, he answered with another question, 'If you play with swaras treating it as a game, how can it become the means to salvation?' I did not have any concept of salvation, except what I had heard from my guru. I remembered all the lines from the *Bhagavadgita* wherein the attributes and characteristics of a mukta are described by Lord Krishna. I had certain doubts which I did not express to him. Should one earn that state by singing? Are there not many pure and saintly people in Hardwar and Hrishikesh who know nothing about music? Do they not have these characteristics of a mukta? I kept quiet because I was afraid that Guruji would ask another question in reply, and I would not have the power to answer.

Yoga. Pranayama. Extra emphasis and concern for abstinence. Every student would be called to his room and given secret instruction. One day, he asked, 'Have you ever ejaculated in sleep? Does it happen?' Since I had been taught Sanskrit I understood what it meant and so I had to tell the truth. 'Once in a while.' He said, 'I admire your honesty. You should never hide your disease from your doctor. Remember one thing. There are two kinds of energy—storage and release. They are called aadho-retas and oordhva-retas. He who descends to the level of the former becomes weak and loses his strength. Nothing great can be achieved by him. It may be in a dream or it may be in the company of a woman or even artificially. Only he who can sublimate his energy in the upward direction which is the oordhva-mukha can achieve siddhis. All the sages are like that. Is not music also a form of meditation? When you direct and concentrate your mind towards the goal steadily in all the three states—waking state, dream state and deep sleep, then the upper movement of the seminal energy takes place. Remember that. Even if one drop is wasted it is the wasting away of the power of sadhana.'

ऽ

While he was munching peanuts, one at a time, and looking out the window reminiscing the past, he felt no desire for Scotch. It was not forbidden but he did not enjoy drinking without proper company. At least if Tipnis was there, they could sip together gossiping about the Indian music fraternity. What fun it would have been. If both of them were there, they could have played cards as well. He saw the air hostess passing by and told her, 'I don't want this. Please give me a bottle of Coke.' She just smiled and took away the Scotch. His mind again went to Hardwar. He started analysing whether he had left because his mother died or because of the intense desire to learn music from Pandit Rohila.

Mother died first. I was seventeen. One afternoon Mohinder Singh from my neighbourhood came on a cycle and said, 'There are a thousand ashrams in Hardwar. I have been searching since morning. Your mother died of diarrhoea. She wanted to see you once but did not know the name of the ashram.'

Just the memory of that day made me choke. My eyes could hardly see, covered by mist as they were. I was looking at the ground from above, 30,000 feet, I believe. The rows of streets, way down below became indistinct. I remember what Babaji had said, 'No matter how big a man becomes professionally, his mother must be alive to be proud of him. She must feel happy.' When she was alive I would not go to visit her every week. In the beginning she would come to see me once every week. A little later once in a fortnight or twenty days. How far it was for her to walk? Four miles. It seems she would eat only the leftovers in the vessels, and what little pay she received she would put it in a chit fund—private organisations which collect money and repay at the time of emergency—she had lent a little money and with an infinitesimal interest, she wanted to get her son married. One day, Mohinder Singh came to the ashram and told me about the transactions. He asked me to demand the money back. But there was neither a witness nor a deed. Who would return the money? But all of them pretended to speak only the truth and swore on the name of the holy Ganga. Babaji took care of the obsequies. What a saintly person he was. But still I was desirous of leaving the ashram and learn pure music from a really great teacher. In fact, I wanted to ask Babaji to suggest a name. But it would be unmannerly telling him that he was not good enough for me. Meanwhile, Pandit Ram Narain Rohila came with his wife on a pilgrimage to Hardwar and stayed in the ashram. Since I had seen him at the Kashi Sangeet Sammelan, Babaji asked me to look after him. In the evening he sang Bhoopali just for the students. It was like fine twilight dust permeating the height of the Himalayas. Each swara had a silent move as that of a leaf cup of the aarati, with a lighted lamp in it and set afloat on the waters of the Ganga. Though there were only five swaras, there were hundreds different textures. As the singing continued, one wondered if Bhoopali really contains so many moods? So many forms? There is a fickleness of gentle smile, while skirting along seriousness. And the peaceful dignity that sounds in the depth of fickleness. Many friendly forms that are expressed in the depth. We at the ashram were simply singing this beautiful raga by rote. I was even delivering the alaap, perfectly, taught by Guruji.

Rohila, the Gawaai, after staying in Hardwar for three days, went for a pilgrimage via Hrishikesh didn't he? He did not express any idea of coming to the ashram on his way back. Two days after he left, I felt sad. On the third day, there was a strong desire that I must somehow learn from him. I told myself that I had earned my credentials to become his student. With what affection his wife had talked to me! I felt that if I went to Sagar and fell at their feet and begged them, they would teach me with all their heart. What if I asked Babaji himself to send me there? After all, they were both friends. I asked him. He didn't say a word but there was little discontentment which passed through his face. The thought, that his favourite student would discuss about going to some other teacher was enough to make him discontented and unhappy, had not flashed to me. Wasn't it in the evening when he said, 'It is natural, you are attracted to his singing. But it is worldly music, it is without inner enlightenment of spirituality. No matter how perfect the taal and the patterns of the swaras were and the complete knowledge of where he was and reach the saam whenever he wanted, it was like squeezing out the juice by twisting a sugarcane. Was this all that music meant?'

What else? Though the thought that emotions were after all a result of mixing feelings did cross my mind, I did not mention it. Another question was about the spiritual music that he represented. But I did not have the courage to question Baba. How do you question devotion, dedication and gratitude? With what love he had looked after us. How much affection he had for me. Who am I to question or criticise his fundamental faith? Merely because a philosophical song is converted into a cheez and sung, does it become philosophical? Is bhakti the only emotion in music? These questions had been put to Baba by someone at the festival as well and I consoled myself that I was not the only one with doubts. Thinking and cogitating did not become important. The mind was enveloped and attracted by the music of Rohila Gawaai. Yes, if you must learn, you must learn only from teachers like him. I began to feel that all that I had learnt at the ashram was bhajans. Even Baba could, if he wanted, sing Khayal. In fact he even taught us. He had taught me specially to practice swara. But without full freedom, how can a raga develop? When this question had appeared for the first time Baba told me, 'Child, think about the difference between the music of Swamy Haridas and that of Tansen.' Haridas would not yield to any influence by any king and he remained in the temple in the midst of the forest and would sing only for the lord. But Tansen fell victim to fame to be the chief musician of the court of Emperor Akbar. But today there are ragas in the name of Tansen and the variations of ragas he made are available. But what is left of Haridas? This question did not arise then. This was the question asked by Raja Saheb, three, four, eight years after I ran away from the ashram.

When I closed my eyes for a short while and sent my mind back forty-two years, I became aware that I did not have a desire to immerse myself in luxury like Tansen. My desire was only to learn the art of music from the Gawaai. I struggled like this for two months. One day, without telling anyone, I put two dhotis, two shirts and two vests in a bag and went away. When I left the ashram, there was an enthusiasm that this was my first step to achieve something great. I did not have any money. I only had the piece of paper with the address of the Gawaai on it. I did not even know in what direction Sagar was. I was told at the station that I must go to Delhi and then the train would take me there via Agra, Gwalior and Jhansi. I got into the train without a ticket. What to do for food on the way? I could sing bhajans and the passengers in the compartment would give some coins. I was eighteen. The same boy who was singing when he was eight year old was now a youth of eighteen years, adept with proper swara, taal and knowledge of the shastra. I was sure I would be able to sing my way to Sagar but when I opened my mouth, to sing for alms, my throat got parched. My self-respect stopped me from using music for begging. At the same time I knew that if I starved for a day and a half I would not die. Nobody checked my ticket until Delhi. There, when I got into the big train the ticket collector came. I told him the truth.

'I came from Hardwar by the night train to Delhi. Now I am going to Sagar in search of my guru. You please search my pocket and this little bag and then you do what you feel like.'

'I am going to hand you over to the Station Master at the next station. They will decide what to do with you.'

He went on to check the tickets of others. He returned after ten minutes and said, 'You are travelling without a ticket and you are sitting on a seat. Get off and sit on the floor or, stand near the door.' I sat down on the floor obediently. He said, 'I am on duty till Jhansi. After that I don't know what the next TC will do. It is up to him.'

There was a man of about sixty years of age sitting in the same row where I was, before being asked to move to the floor. He beckoned me to him, moved a little giving some room and said, 'Sit here. I have food with me. Let us both eat.'

'It doesn't matter sir. I have decided to fast.'

'What you want to do is all right, if you don't have anything. But I have a lot of food given by my relatives.'

He untied his cloth bundle took out two thick parathas with a vegetable curry, and he also started eating. He asked me if I wanted more but I was full by then.

'From whom did you learn music? From whom are you going to learn in Sagar?'

After I told him everything he said, 'Rohila Gawaai sings very well. I have heard him.' After that he requested, 'Would you please sing a raga. Even a little alaap.' I was moved by gratitude and I was in the mood to sing. I looked out, it was nine in the morning. He asked, 'Can you sing Ramkali?' I prepared my throat and caught on to shadja. I couldn't quite get it. I closed my eyes and searched. The noise of the running train was higher than any human shruti. I said, 'Please forgive me. I am not able to get the shruti in all this noise.' He appreciated it and said, 'Yes, you are a real singer.' He gave me the remaining food, gave me all the details about where to change the train and got off at Gwalior.

Neither the Gawaai nor his wife could recognise me. After all it was two months since they had visited Kashi. I prostrated by touching their feet and introduced myself, 'Mohanlal from the ashram of Omkar Baba at Hardwar.'

'*Areh, areh*, come and sit down.'

I told him about the effect his singing had on me and said, 'I have come to learn from you. You please accept me as your student.' After I had prostrated again he said '*Areh, areh*, what is there in teaching but accepting a student is not child's play. You had mentioned that you had neither father nor mother. Now I remember. Where are you going to stay in this town? What do you do for food and what do you do for the expenses for the initiation ceremony?'

I had never thought about all this. My mind had taken it for granted that the guru would keep the students in his own home, feed them and then teach them. I didn't know what to say.

'You should not have come without taking my permission before coming. Even now you may go back.'

I said, 'If you would recommend me to some merchant in this town telling them that I am an orphan learning music from you, they may arrange for some food in the dharmashala twice a day.' I remembered Baba's arrangement at his ashram. Many saints would come to the ashram once in a while, I would carry the recommendation note given by Baba in my pocket and go to the shop or house of the merchant on a cycle and bring whatever they gave me. If it was rice and such provisions they would themselves pack it in a bundle put it in the cart and send it.

'In Kashi there is a tradition of the merchants accepting the responsibility for the students. Perhaps even in Hardwar but not in this town. I have not given such a recommendation to anyone.'

'Please give me a note saying you have accepted me as your student and now I needed their generosity. Something to this effect. I will myself beg from the merchants.'

'You are a smart boy. How can the student get apprenticed without a ceremony? If I give a letter just like that it will be tantamount to telling a lie. Would you want me to earn sin?'

'Guru Bhagavan, you must yourself kindly show me the way. When I give concerts in the future I will place at your feet your guru-dakshina. You may curse me right away that if I go back on my word let everything you have taught be forgotten. You may add this curse right now.' I fell at his feet with tearful eyes.

At this point Mataji interceded. 'Please give him a note. There is nothing to be lost by it.'

I put the note in my pocket, went into the bazaar, and enquired who among the merchants in this town were generous. I was directed to Bhanvarlalji Sukhmalji's wholesale shop where I prostrated to the owner and placed the note in front of him. Seventy year old, white haired, sandal-paste right across his forehead, white dhoti and white jubba. He said, 'Let the note be. You tell me which shastra says that helping music learners brings punya.'

What I said was not unknown to him. 'Even music is equal to the Vedas.' He smiled and asked, 'What have you learnt so far and from whom. How did you come to this town? How well do you know Rohila Gawaai?' After I answered all these questions and he was satisfied with my answers he turned to Munimji and asked, 'Panditji, have you heard everything this boy is saying?' The fifty year old Munimji who had tied up his hair at the back of the head in a knot said, 'I feel whatever he has been saying is correct. Rohila Gawaai had given a concert during Dussehra three years ago, a great singer.'

The owner said, 'Give this boy two meals a day in our dharmashala at our expense. Arrange for his breakfast and tea. Give him a room to stay. When there is surplus of pilgrims he should vacate the room and adjust. What else?'

'I must get the gandaa-puja done', I said.

'What does it mean panditji?'

'The guru must tie a thread round the wrist of the pupil he had accepted. The guru must be worshipped with turmeric and kumkum and offered almonds, sweets and a fee. These the pupil must bring.'

'All right get all these things and give it to him and get him eleven rupees. Anything else? Take him to the dharmashala and make the arrangements. Go my boy, take your bath and have your meal. Give him two rupees every month for expenses. What did you say your name was? You should not smoke beedies and cigarettes. No bad habits should come near you. We and the people in the dharmashala will be watching you. These are our rules.'

When I went to the Gawaai and told him everything he said, 'You are a very smart boy'. The way he used the word smart brought a little disappointment but I didn't speak. Looking at the eleven rupees, Mataji said, 'What kind of measly sum is this?' Then added, 'You should have told the Sethji that giving such a small sum for such a big singer is disrespect. The least is 1001 rupees according to shastra.' I didn't say anything. 'When I start earning I will pour silver rupees upto the height to the feet of the master. I swear it on the tambura.' Her reply, 'Even your guru does not earn that much. How can you dream of such a sum?' But the Gawaai said, 'Leave it. It is all right. You don't have your own tambura. What will you do there in your room to practice?' The thought had never occurred to me.

None of those who came to learn from the Gawaai had dedicated themselves completely to music. They had a job elsewhere and would come in the evening to learn. Some others came only two or three days a week. Each one had his home, a college to go to or a job. I was the only one who had nothing. They were all paying the fee every month. The next day Mataji said, 'You can pay your fee either in the form of money or by doing some service. If you help me and do the chores, your guru will be pleased.'

'Please tell me Mataji. We were doing all the work in our ashram.'

This is how it all began. Going to the flour mill and getting the wheat ground, bringing vegetables, cleaning and cutting them, washing and ironing clothes. Sweeping the floor, cleaning the vessels and doing other household chores when the maid was absent. The moment Mataji saw me she would remember something for me to do. One day when the guru was not at home she said, 'Don't knot up your face because I give you chores. If I don't approve, your guru will not start a new lesson. There will be no new teaching. He will not reveal to you the secret of our family music. Education for you only if I am pleased. Remember that.' I worked even harder; not because Guruji didn't teach me. But because he did not have any intentions of teaching. Once in a way when he got into the mood to teach, some friends would drop in. He would invite them enthusiastically and start talking endlessly. That day's lesson was over for me. He would tell me, 'Go and practise by yourself.' What could I practise when he had not taught me anything new? Not even once did he teach for an hour without any disturbance. He never taught me any of the inner secrets of music. In fact he was also not practising everyday. At least I could listen to him and learn something if he did. After a year and a half, when Mataji was not at home I told him, 'I have submitted my entire life for music. I have a mind to practise at least for ten hours a day. If you don't teach me the details, how can I do that? Please don't be angry with me.' But I could see from his face that he was very angry. Five minutes later, 'All right, take out your tambura I will teach you Bilaval.' That day he taught for two hours uninterruptedly. If everyday could be like this how the door of my good fortune would open up! The next day he didn't teach. Then I figured out. He was lazy by nature. He loved to take everything easy. What real music he had in him had been taught by his father. He had left it at that. He didn't even have the desire to perform in big concerts and become famous. All his three daughters had been married off and they were happy. So I should not expect anything more from him. I realised that I was impressed by just one raga he sang and came running here like a stupid fellow. Was it not six months before this that I got addicted to cards?

When these thoughts were passing through my mind it occurred to me how nice it would have been if the three of us were travelling together playing cards for six hours. Being alone, all kinds of thoughts assail you. They won't simply come and vanish. They disturb your mind. If one thought is pushed aside it comes back and brings with it fresh memories and fresh feelings.

He blankly stared out of the window.

३

When he was thinking that at the height of 30,000 feet how the earth and the water, the hills and the forests become distant, like memories, a female voice said, 'Your meal sir'.

When I put my plate on the small table in front of me and removed the lid I remembered Jayanarayana. When I was singing to myself with the tambura for company, he would sleep with his wife and child in his room and listen to my music. Though he could not understand it, he had a liking for it. Once he came and asked me if I knew how to play cards. He offered to teach me when he realised that I had no knowledge of cards.

'I will teach you. You can learn it in two days.'

'No. It is a sin to gamble.'

'Who told you so? Haven't you read the ancient texts? The lesson of the *Mahabharata* is that you should not gamble away your kingdom, your brothers and your wife. Nobody says that you should not gamble at all. It is just for recreation.' I couldn't think of an answer. He continued, 'Remember one thing. Life is a gamble. If you make it a habit to play cards or dice you will get the smartness to play the game of life. Otherwise you will be a loser in life.' I did not buy his proposition. Though Sethji was sponsoring the food, the actual people who would cook and serve me food were this fellow and his wife. They were looking after me well. Also, I was bored. One night I got a taste for it, looked at the cards in my hand, guessed the cards in the other fellow's hand. After all, this was the question of intelligence, courage and testing fortune. Within fifteen days I was as good as him. When I understood that just as an unexpected card gives thrill in the card game, the same thrill is experienced in an unexpected twist and turn to a raga, and there was an element of gambling in music also. I was thrilled as though I had invented something new. But nobody should know that the two of us were playing cards otherwise my free meals would be stopped and I would be thrown out. He also would be admonished; his wife would be warned to control her husband. Some days we would play all night. The next day I would be sleepy and not feel like going to the house of the Gawaai. What's the use of going there? I had to work for that old woman, his wife. I would simply make an excuse.

Fortune opens itself out through gambling, no, gambling opens out fortune. Even that is not quiet correct. Anyway, to hell with logic. However, it is because of the connection with cards that I found my true guru. Otherwise, this Mohanlal would have forgotten music.

Jaswanth Bittu is all right. He is interested in music and equally interested in playing cards. Company representative. Though the company would pay him for lodging, he would stay in a dharmashala, save money, and would not even lose it by playing cards. He would make fun of me saying, 'If I play with people like you, fortune doesn't open its door. It will be only a means of killing time. Losing means only one or two rupees.' He understood my situation, he made me sing accompanied by tambura and said, 'You have the making of a great musician. You just need to leave this place and find a proper guru.'

'I may stretch out my hand to the guru but the guru should take hold of it, shouldn't he?'

By next evening, he had a plan for me. 'Do you know Shakapur? Ustad Asad Ali Khan. Yes, his son Bande Ali Khan is the court musician at the Shakapur Darbar. Though he doesn't have his father's genius, his father has taught him everything very carefully, in detail. Though now the kingdom is gone, Maharaja Hukum Singh has not abandoned his retinue—the elephant, horses, the carriers of palanquins, his musicians and the Vedic pandits. He is very kind and generous. He never has said 'no' to anyone who has fallen at his feet. He is of the opinion that to say 'no' is a blemish on his family honour and believes that his ancestors will be thrown out of heaven. You go and fall at his feet and beg him saying, "Oh Lord, you must kindly arrange for me to learn music from your court musician Bande Ali Khan. Otherwise I am going to jump into the River Chitra and die. Before issuing any order to your Ustad, Your Majesty may please examine my voice and listen to my singing." If you plead like this he will definitely consent.' Immediately I got enthused.

'Where is Shakapur?'

'In Malva. You must get off the train at Ujjain and take a bus. Just wait. Now I get it. I know Bhupatram Ojha, who is the tabla guru at the Darbar. We have played cards together. His wife's brother's son sells the product of our company and he is the dealer in Devas. I can take you to Pandit Ojha. He will take you to the Maharaja. If he takes kindly to you and shows mercy, all your problems will be taken care of in a minute.' I got so excited that I was on fire. 'Please show me the way,' saying so, I stood up. He took out his diary and said, 'Just wait a little. Thirteen days from today, on Monday, the twenty-sixth, you must wait on the bench outside the Ujjain Railway Station waiting room. I will come by the train which arrives there at twelve past nine. If I miss it, I will come by the next train. If I miss that also, by the next one to that and also I may even come by bus instead of train. The bus stand is right behind the railway station. Anyway, no matter how I come, you must wait on the bench at the railway station as I said. If by chance you have gone out for a few minutes to answer nature's call, I will wait for you on the same bench. I will bear the train expenses.'

Saying this, he took out twenty-five rupees from the playing cards amount and gave it to me. He knew my financial condition.

'I will wait for a month. If you don't come back within that time I will send your tambura to your guru's house and inform him that you have gone out in search of some other guru and it was not possible to come and take your blessings personally. Don't tell this to anyone yet. If you come back, let not your place for your food be cancelled in the meanwhile.' Jayanarayana warned me and gave me some food to eat on the way. Throughout the journey I was praying to god and the noise of the train sounded like 'Rama, Rama' to the ear. If the Maharaja himself orders, the court musician must teach with all attention, mustn't he? This was the assurance.

Bittu Bhaiya engaged a room for me at a lodge and went to meet Bhupatram. On his return he said, 'I have been asked to take you there at five in the evening. Any further talk will take place only after he listens to your singing. Your work will be done. I have to go to Sadar Bazaar urgently and will come back around quarter to five. You have your food and sleep a little. You need to sleep, else the strength of your voice will decrease.' He left.

In the anxiety about how I was going to sing, whether he was going to accept or reject me, I couldn't get any sleep. But the moment I set eyes upon Bhupatram's face, my anxiety ended. About sixty years old. A shining bald head. Nose like an eagle's. Very sharp eyes. He was wearing a dhoti and a jubba which seemed to have been worn for the last two days but were clean and ironed. A fairly big house. The wood that had been used for the doors and the rafters were made of teak. I thought the house had been built by the royal family. When I put the dust off his feet on my head I could feel that he had blessed me with his own hand. He asked about my welfare and gave me refreshments. He asked me where I had learnt and why I left that place. Without attributing any blame on the previous guru, I told him that on account of his age he could not demonstrate singing and added a lie that the Baba of Hardwar ashram himself had sent me to the Gawaai at Sagar. He believed me and asked me to take up the tambura and tune it. I noticed spider's web on the edges of the tambura. This person was a tabla master and was obviously not using the tambura everyday. 'Do you need harmonium or will you tune without it?' I said, 'I will just tune'. His admiration could be seen. My ability to bring that tambura to shruti so quickly increased his approval. He said, 'Sing any raga which you like. Show me everything you have learnt.' It was six in the evening. I thought not of Kalyan and suggested Pooriya. 'For two hours you must sing whatever you like. No matter which raga. Now wait a minute.' He drew the tabla to his side and adjusted the shruti. I started the alaap in vilambit ek-taal. Smiling encouragingly he built up the outline of my taal. After my alaap for half an hour, I started singing.

chinaa chinaa| baa s tata| katahoo s| mai to s ri|

I had sung without inhibitions, as if a friend was accompanying me on the tabla. When I finished he was immersed in thought. I didn't ask him if I should begin another. He did not come out of his deep meditation. I continued playing the tambura. After a while, he observed my face and said, 'I feel that in your case the yogaayoga or the coincidence will happen. Understand what I am saying. If you act accordingly, your fortune will really unfold itself. You will be a great musician.' I bent down my head along with my body treating it as a salutation. 'If the darbar had heard your singing, you would meet with praise and the court singer would be ordered to accept you according to your request. But he would not teach you with full interest. He would simply spend years teaching you superficial things. Though I belong to the same court I should not tell tales against others. You promise me that you will never mention this to anybody ever.' He stretched his hand. I touched his right hand and made that promise. He looked at Bittu Bhaiya. He also swore. Then 'I used the expression yogaayoga. You listen to this. Twenty miles from this place there is a Raja Thakur. No professional guru or ustad knows as much about music or has achieved the control over swara and laya as he does. But he never gives concerts outside because he is a king. He has his own forest, in the confluence area where rivers Chitra and Narmada join. The extent of the forest is 1,000 acres. On the banks of the river there is a Mahadev temple that was built by his ancestors for their family deity. He sings only sitting inside that temple. He has been doing it for forty years. I will take you to him. You sing in his presence just like you sang to me. If he agrees, that's it. The big door of your fortune will open.' It was nice to hear all this. I remembered that even among kings there were great musicians. The forest. The banks of the river. The Mahadev temple. Sadhana. These words generated the memories of the ashram at Hardwar. The memory of Omkar Baba, who took a beggar boy from the banks of the Ganga and taught him so much, came rushing through. I felt like seeing him. But the way I had absconded without learning one hundredth of what I could have, made me feel utterly ashamed. How could I show my face there again?

Bittu Bhaiya asked, 'Panditji, I must reach Ujjain tonight. Would you please accommodate this boy and permit me to leave.'

'All right, where is this boy's bag? Bring it. Tomorrow I will take him to Chittarpur.'

I went to the lodge to bring my bag. Shakapur is a city of times. It has a fort. A main palace. Large mansions where the relatives of the Raja lived. Though the streets were arranged neatly in squares because of the denseness of the population it was like Kishkinda. When the lorries and the buses moved through the roads, even a cycle rickshaw, a car or a tonga could not negotiate its way and there would be a traffic jam. Bittu Bhaiya said, 'Isn't what I said about gambling true? If you don't gamble at all how do you know whether you are lucky or not?' I understood that what I had done by leaving the comfort of the dharmashala with food and shelter was also a gamble.

In the morning Bhupatram asked, 'Do you know cycling?'

'Yes.'

'Can you ride if I sit at the back?'

'I used to. For two and half years but I have lost practice. They say you won't forget once you learn it.'

'Why I asked you is because Chittarpur where we have to go is twenty miles away. There is a road but no buses. I can ride on the bicycle alone. But with a twenty-one year old boy sitting at the back I can't. I hope it won't be difficult for you to take me.'

I hung my bag on the bicycle handle and began to pedal with Bhupatramji at the back. It took me a few feet to gain balance but then I started enjoying myself. There were cultivated dry lands and paddy fields on both side of the road for the next five miles. After that we had to pass through a mango grove which was followed by a forest full of hillocks. I could cycle up the hillocks without feeling tired. There was a river after fourteen miles, this was River Chitra, I was told by Bhupatramji. There was a bridge at low level but it was obvious that it would be submerged in the rainy season. Now, a shallow strip of water was running under the arches. Bhupatramji told me that Narmada was just three miles away. Chittarpur was not a city like Shakapur. It could be called a town. But since it had been built in the style of a capital, the roads were formed in squares. There was a big door for the fort. Rows of houses. Electric streetlights. The palace of the Raja Saheb was situated on top of the mound outside the town. Around it and at the back were huge trees. The palace was grand and prominent from all around. At that time I had not seen many palaces. Though not very huge, this was definitely a palace. Anybody could see that. We parked the cycle outside and came to the gate. It was obvious from the way the watchman saluted and informed that the king was inside, that Bhupatramji was a highly respected man in that place. Another man in uniform saluted Bhupatramji and took us to the waiting room and seated us on the sofa. Bhupatramji whispered in my ear, 'I had forgotten to tell you, when you speak to Raja Saheb you must use a different grammar. You should not say "You told me". You should say, "Raja Saheb has ordered that way". You should not say, "I am telling you". Instead say, "This is my humble request to the Highness". When he is speaking don't say things like "Yes". You must say "Hukum, hukum". The other items of etiquette you will yourself understand gradually. This particular Raja Saheb doesn't stand on formality. But we must follow the etiquette. He is so immersed in music that nothing else enters his head. No matter what you say, always remember that he is a king. He was born a king. We must obey the customs and rules.'

Meanwhile, the man in uniform called us in. There was a huge courtyard, and another small room which had to be crossed before reaching the main receiving room of the Raja. A very handsome, dignified figure of an old man of sixty was sitting on a shining gold-polished chair of old royal style with upholstered cushion of blue satin. A very thick crop of shining white hair on his head. A proper moustache unmistakably becoming to a king. He had not coloured his hair to hide his age. Though he was wearing only pyjamas and jubba they had been beautifully stitched to measure by an expert tailor. A shining one-string gold chain around his neck. The ring finger of the right hand had a sparkling white diamond ring. For the left wrist, a watch with a gold chain. Bhupatramji bowed. I prostrated. It was clear by the way the king stood up and held Bhupatramji's shoulders that they were close friends. Introducing me, Bhupatramji said, 'This man is greatly interested in music. Has also been trained to an extent.' Immediately the king welcomed me by making kind enquiries and said, 'You have travelled in the hot sun. Have you had your bath? Please go and have a wash. Have your meal and then we can talk.' The uniformed man came close to me and said, 'Please come. I will take you to the bathroom and then to the dining table.'

There was a huge, beautifully polished black wooden dining table. Around it about twenty regal-looking chairs. They placed a big plate with five bowls in front of me. Three types of vegetables, dal, kadi, pickle, kheer, sweets, curd, roti and chutney. Looking at the first serving itself I was happy. I thought this is really what is meant by a royal dinner. I asked the server, 'The dinner for the tabla pandit?'

'He will dine with Raja Saheb.'

I understood that Raja Saheb wanted to discuss the situation with him alone before meeting me. I began to wonder if it wouldn't be difficult for me to work for such an intelligent man. I felt heavy with the food. Again the uniformed man came and said, 'Let me show you the room where you can rest for some time.' He took me there. A small room with a bed and a clean sheet to cover myself, and an attached bath. I slept immediately. After all, I had pedalled the bicycle with a pillion twenty miles in the hot sun.

At around 4 pm Bhupatramji called out and woke me up and asked, 'Shall we go to the place where you should sing? It's two miles from here. We will go in Raja Saheb's car.' I went to the bathroom to wash my face and by the time I came back, there was tea waiting for me. I drank it and followed the uniformed man to the back of the palace where a huge car was waiting. Within a couple of minutes, Raja Saheb and Bhupatramji came. They made me sit at the back while Raja Saheb drove. From the palace to the forest, the way was smooth without any pits and inundations. The first gate gave entrance to the fence surrounding the forest. The watchman, even when the car was at a distance, saw and opened the gate. There was a thick forest on either side. One had to raise one's neck in order to see the tall trees like teak, honne and matti. Neem, peepul and banyan, surrounded us. At some places, the dense tree-clusters made us wonder if the sun's rays ever penetrated the ground. The road in the forested area resembled those from the hills, with curves and regular ups and downs. We felt that we had come to the Himalayas at Hardwar. Suddenly, there was a downward slope. The car stopped behind a stone temple that faced a river flowing in the precipice. By looking at the size of the river I knew it was Narmada. The river shining in the light red colour of the evening filled my heart with the emotion of mandra-shadja and I felt that an unknown raga was being invented. It was a Mahadev temple. Even in the partial darkness of the evening, the lingam which was shining black seemed like Shiva absorbed within the shruti. Wonderstruck I stood there unmoving, as if my eyes were fixed. I didn't even notice Raja Saheb switching on the light. After a little while I looked all around. Next to the wall in the courtyard where we were standing, there were three iron almirahs in a row. Bhupatramji opened the door of one of them. There were three tamburas, lined against the back. He took out two of them and placed them on the soft mat that Raja Saheb had placed on the floor by then. In the lowest rung of another almirah there were two pairs of tablas, daggas and a harmonium. In the upper rung there were books. The third almirah had a glass door and the books inside could be seen. Bhupatramji said, 'This is the place where Raja Saheb practises. The tabla, the tambura boxes have been kept in the iron almirah because the rats and the bandicoots could damage them. Now you tune the tambura and sing a raga. Even if it is what you sung yesterday, it's all right.' After going around Mahadev in a pradakshina and prostrating, I tuned the tambura. Raja Saheb sat leaning against the wall. Bhupatramji prepared the shruti for his tabla. Though I knew that this was the examination for accepting a pupil, I was not afraid. I had a feeling that I would be accepted. I sang as I did the previous day. Raja Saheb slightly bowed his head a couple of times. However, there was in his eyes, a feeling of dissatisfaction. Though I noticed it I continued unperturbed.

After I finished, Raja Saheb said, 'Shall I sing? Would you listen to me?' I was embarrassed as he had addressed me in the respectful plural using the word 'aap'. Bhupatramji, the moment he met me yesterday quite naturally addressed me in the singular as 'tu'. I wondered why this man who would be my guru was behaving like this. I said, 'I would play the tambura.' He lifted his left hand signalling it was not necessary, closed his eyes and started playing on the tambura. For quite some time he played the tambura without articulating. No, no, I was mistaken. He was already one with shadja and there was advaita between his voice and the shadja. In order to comprehend this subtlety and minuteness one needs tremendous concentration. I understood that one should be accustomed to his style of singing. When I sat listening spellbound I wondered whether his throat was pronouncing 'Ummm' or 'Om.' Very slowly his voice began to swell like milk spilling from a large vessel on a low fire. The spiritual emotion of how minutely the manifest emerges from the unmanifest began to flow around. My mind got absorbed in that sound. It was not mere minuteness. It was precision. The shadja that we express was only an approximation, whereas his was of the very source and essence. I could see that he had mastered the moolanaadi-sthaana defined in yoga. After a long time his shadja started becoming audible even to my external ears. Yes, this was not the voice of any approximation. But the power of naada-brahma itself flowing out of the most minute point. Even while listening to shadja it was clear that he was singing Raga Pooriya. I suspected that he was singing this to show me the correct way of singing. But those with swara-shuddhi do not descend to the level of competition. I felt that the raga that I sang had suggested what he should sing. Yes, gradually he is descending to mandra-saptaka *Ni, Dha, Ni, Ma, Dha*. Oh, what purity of swara even in the mandra! This voice was not his. He was not the one who was singing. The raga to manifest itself in its purest form had chosen his voice. Sitting with closed eyes, he had surrendered himself completely to the raga. His own role was nothing more than that of a medium. The person who was sitting opposite me was not a king but a sage of musical notes. With this feeling I just sat looking at him. Even when he was groping, patting and awakening each and every swara of mandra and even when he was constructing the impenetrable magic circle of swaras, his eyes remained closed. Again, when they awoke in the madhya-saptaka, they were half open. The complete mastery of his voice in all the three saptakas, his competency to delve deep and rise effortlessly from lower mandra to taara-taara from taara-taara to mandra-mandra without losing the precision and the accuracy of the swara reminded me of the Matsyavatara. I got the picture of that divine fish which could delve into any depth of the ocean and shoot up all the way to the surface as if targeted, and enjoy itself. I did not notice the chronometrical time. When he was engaged in alaap I never noticed it. I did not even have a wrist watch. But the time of the movement of the swaras had created infinity. Finally, he looked at Bhupatramji and began in madhya-laya tri-kaal.

tha na | naa dhirr dhirr dee | s mtha na na |
tha daa s re | tha na de re |

I realised that he was showing me how the time beat works. Bhupatramji was an expert tabla player. A student of Ahmed Jan Thirakhva, who was a great guru and who taught his students without any reservation. Raja Saheb was adjusting the taranas to the playing of Bhupatramji and Bhupatramji was adjusting and creating bols without any sense of unaesthetic competition. It was a harmonious play of sounds.

After the tarana, Raja Saheb closed his eyes and came back to the movement of the swaras of Pooriya. After augmenting the pulse of the raga, he settled down in the aarambha-shadja. His voice slowly merged into the shruti of the tambura until it became one with it and gradually only the tambura could be heard. When he opened his eyes he didn't look at me. He didn't ask me what I thought even through look or gesture. He just pressed the tambura to his eyes and leaned it against the wall. Bhupatramji looked at me. My eyes were shining in admiration. Raja Saheb said, 'Shall we go for dinner? It's time.'

I couldn't sleep that night. I was thinking of only one thing. If I learn I must learn only from him. But will he accept me? Even the personality of the Raja Saheb was awe-inspiring. Every inch a king. I felt that it was not possible to be persistent with him. He had addressed me in the respectful plural as 'Aap' purposely to keep me at a distance. If he decided that I was not fit to be his student, further persuasion was impossible. I began to feel that he sang the same raga that I had sung, for demonstrating, 'You know only this much. You are not good enough to be my student'. Even if I went back to Sagar I could get food but no knowledge. Though Rohila Gawaai may teach with interest I didn't want to be taught by him any more. After listening to the singing of the Raja Saheb no one else's teaching was acceptable. I kept rolling about in the bed without realising when I went to sleep.

At sunrise, Bhupatramji came to my room and said, 'Raja Saheb gets up late. Let us go and get some fresh air in the forest.' We took the bicycle till the main gate and went inside, leaving the bicycle leaning against a tree. It was like entering a new world. It was not a penance grove meant for meditation, it was simply a dense forest. The trees were growing very close to each other, rubbing against each other, and touching the sky. Little pathways paved with forest rocks had been laid around for walking. Bhupatram was familiar with all the paths. Inside, there was the sound of various kinds of birds chirping continuously, including the musical notes of the cuckoos. There were a lot of peacocks and deer. Bhupatramji said, 'There is not a single dangerous animal here. However, you might find some serpents. So be careful when you walk.' He continued, 'This forest is spread over 1,000 acres and Raja Saheb himself has planted several trees here. He comes here for strolls everyday. It is believed that when he walks here he sees before his mind's eye the form of the various ragas and raginis. Have you noticed another thing? He has planted huge trees immediately around the palace. Not a garden. Do you know why? Flowering plants are artificial species. They are nurtured using artificial manure. They don't follow the seasons of the year properly. Gigantic trees are not like that. You can tell what season, what month it is just by looking at them. Isn't there an immediate connection between the season and the raga we sing? He believes that if we are friendly with the trees we will understand the ragas more easily.' After a little while he continued, 'Around 10 am after being milked, all the palace cows are left in this forest to graze. When Raja Saheb comes here to walk, each cow approaches him and moos and licks his hand.' By then we came to the spot where River Chitra merges with Narmada. There was not much water in Chitra. Still, when you looked at that confluence from a distance, it was a breathtaking sight. To our left was the Mahadev temple. Last evening when I looked at the Narmada from the temple, I had not noticed this spot of the confluence. I stood there looking at it for sometime. Since, Bhupatramji did not have the key for the temple both of us sat outside on the stone slab and he told me, 'I used the word yogaayoga. The yoga has come to you. Raja Saheb has agreed to accept you as a student.'

'Is that so? Is that really so?' My heart swelled.

'Do you consent to learn from him?'

'Why this question?'

'He told me to ask you. After you completed your song yesterday, you remember he sang as well. This was to show his method of singing. Singing is a very serious art, more serious than meditation. You get admitted only if you fully desire it. There is no compulsion. Remember one thing. He has never taught anyone so far. Even now he will not teach anybody else except you. This means that he will use all his time to mould you and bring out your full potential. You must practise at least ten to twelve hours a day. There will be supervision and lesson every day. There will be the duty of showing that you have understood the previous lesson. And if you commit mistakes you may even have to bear his anger. It is just like if there is only one son, there will be more love, but he has to bear all the responsibility as well.'

'I will bear the responsibility. This is my lot.' I agreed and held both his hands tightly.

I went to the palace, had my bath and while I was eating biscuits and sipping tea, Raja Saheb came there. I immediately got up and touched his feet. He lifted me up by my shoulders and said, 'Don't ever do this again. I am not your guru. It is Lord Mahadevji in the temple. That is where you practise. He is the one who teaches. It is to Him that you are accountable. Come and sit here.' He showed me to the chair where I was sitting earlier. He sat in front of me and said, 'Why the temple is meant to be the place of practice is that the shape of the Shivalinga is the shape of the naada-brahma. The spherical form of the Shivalinga is like that of the humming melody of the tambura which rises spherically, creates and permeates the space and descends into the space of the room and absorbs itself in the strings. You should meditate on that. While going to the temple, on the way to the right there is a small cottage. Have you seen it?'

'No.'

'You will see it. It is small but enough for one person. There is a parlour, a room to sleep, bathroom and a toilet. That is where you are going to stay. You will also have a bicycle to help you travel around. You may come into the town also. Two meals a day and refreshments will be brought to your hut. You may prepare tea if you like, right there. There is no fear of wild animals. No thieves. This forest is protected by Lord Mahadevji. Still, there is a watchman who will be going round all through the night. Are you afraid to stay alone in the forest, that too during the night?'

'I have no experience of staying alone but most probably I will not be afraid.' I said.

'If you are afraid then get rid of it in three or four days. The reason for living right there is, that trees, birds, cattle, the sky, the stars, the moon, the river, the temple, day, night, evenings and evening brightness all these are related to our ragas and swaras. Unless a person lives amongst them, the essence of the ragas and swaras is not realised. There is another principle, if the ragas are practised at the prescribed time, they will be easily under your control. The tanas may be practised at any time but the alaap must be practised at the prescribed time. So, you have to stay close to the temple. I also practised in the same way. I will teach you only during those times.' He poured tea for all of us and continued, 'Once a week you should cycle up to Shakapur and learn all the taals and their bols of the tabla from Bhupatramji and practise at least for two hours after that. When the bols of the tabla are mastered, the tanas will settle properly.'

I was heartily saying 'Hukum, hukum' for everything.

Next Thursday. In the morning along with the puja, the beginning of the teaching had been fixed. 'Isn't it customary that the expense of the puja must be borne by the pupil? Should he not be given a nominal fee?' I asked Bhupatramji. He said, 'You just keep quiet. If you mention any such thing it will be like disrespecting Raja Saheb. The very characteristic of the Raja is not to make others spend.' That was what happened. In a large plate full of fruits, flowers and sweets, 101 rupees of dakshina were sent by the palace to the temple. The next day, the Rajpurohit performed the puja. A brand new tambura which had been brought by the palace was placed in my hands and the benediction was pronounced. I prostrated to Lord Mahadevji. The priest applied kumkum on the foreheads of Raja Saheb and Bhupatramji, put garlands round their necks and gave them sweets. Raja Saheb said, 'You require seven to eight years training, may be ten. You must promise in the presence of the Lord that until I give you permission you will not give up your training.' I did likewise. He said, 'Tune your tambura to panchama.' I sat on the soft mattress and started. The priest left along with all puja utensils, dakshina and fruits. I was filling my inner being with the shruti. Raja Saheb leaned against the wall and said, 'You know all the shastras of main ragas. If you have any doubt, you see there, the almirah is full of the books. You have to understand and start from here. There are twenty-two shrutis. You know roughly where they are situated. And you also know the area and extent of each shruti. Each one of them has a narrow area. Even if you deviate slightly from it, you will be entering the area of another shruti. You must practise how to master and expand each area in your mind and understand everything about it, just as the scientist when he looks into the microscope sees each nerve as if it is a big tube. When you say komala-rishabha, it is not a small zone. Within it there are tens of inner zones recognisable by you. If you practise further, you will be able to find fifteen or twenty. Each eye sees some eight or ten types of green. But a great painter can recognise a hundred varieties of green and create further. The singer must have the ability to recognise within the twenty-two shrutis, very minute differences and have the power to create further. I am going to start teaching you those. Come on; let me see your shadja.' The tambura which had been given in Lord Mahadevji's name started vibrating in my ears.

४

The memory of the forest filled my mind. I was afraid for two nights but gradually I got used to the forest. Soon the sounds of the jungle changed into swaras. The little flutter made by the wings of a butterfly, the crowing of the crow, the chirping of the sparrow, bleat of the little calf to its mother, the ripples of water—all these sounds made me think about the various aspects of music. This was my only thought. Though it was a bit boring in the beginning, gradually I started enjoying it. I could see each shruti as a cluster and within it the several nerve centres would be woven intricately. I began to feel that when prodded separately, the special individual character of each nerve would be experienced.

Though Raja Saheb never talked to me about anything except music, we became close. We would often have tea together and when he sat with me he wouldn't get up for at least two hours at a time and there was no question of missing even a single day's lesson. Many times when I was practising inside the temple, he would sit outside, listening. Once in a while, singers from all parts of India would come to his palace for concerts. Music lovers from Chittarpur and surrounding villages would be invited. I would normally play the tambura but sometimes accompany with the harmonium as well. If it was an important singer, Bhupatramji would be invited for accompanying with the tabla. But Raja Saheb never sang. Once when a famous singer from Bihar insisted that he wanted him to sing for the gathering, Raja Saheb agreed saying, 'Let it be tomorrow.' But the next day he sang only to the singer and that too in the temple. Bhupatramji was also there. Only five connoisseurs from his state were present. I was playing the tambura. When Ramsharan asked, 'I have heard that Raja Saheb does not sing in the auditorium but only in the temple. May I know the reason?' The answer from Raja Saheb was, 'Lord Mahadev has ordered me in my dream that I should not sing outside the temple. I must follow the order of the family deity.' Ramsharanji bent down his head in the direction of the lingam and folded his hands in namaskar. I was curious. Why did the family deity give such an order? Was he using music for an ulterior motive? I had heard that usually, rajas, sultans, nawabs and badshahs were doing it. But in my mind, I knew that for Raja Saheb, music was the most sacred.

Once a week, I would cycle upto Shakapur to Bhupatramji's house. He was an extremely strict and disciplined teacher, just like Raja Saheb. He used to say that not only the technical pattern of beats but the very primeval sound of the letters of the alphabets was most important. Whether for a vocalist or instrumentalist, no matter how delicate the meend was, he would play and show it with the shade of the raga. I was not interested in learning tabla primarily but he showed me all the intricate secrets.

'Coffee or tea?'

'Tea please.'

It seems in this country you must add 'please' to everything just as we add 'ji'. A good practice. But these people don't know how to prepare strong tea as we do. They remove the tea leaves too soon. What is the use of drinking that kind of light tea? Madhu used to prepare excellent tea. The perfect tea can lift your spirit and make you soar like an eagle. Just at that moment I became aware of the fact that I never taught the secrets of swaras to anybody as thoroughly as Raja Saheb taught me. In Bombay where do you find that kind of peace, quietness, the chirping of the birds, the sound of bamboo touching each other, the ripples of flowing water? Madhu's house is right in the middle of a forest inhabited with birds, butterflies and crickets. She has the opportunity and the means of getting such training. Still, the two weeks I had trained her, it was only with the intention that she should sing equal to me and capture the audience. But then Raja Saheb never trained me for any public appearance or for attaining fame. Not even once did he talk about pleasing the audience. He would always explain what happens in a particular swara and what affect a particular laya has and he would sing and demonstrate what he meant. During that time I also never thought about performing for an audience.

My chain of memories was broken when the airhostess noisily kept the plate in front of me and poured tea into the cup. Outside the window, only clouds were visible. Dark clouds. Not even a bit of earth could be seen. Was it raining? The plane flies above the clouds in the space where there were no clouds and no Malhar. What kind of travel is this, I felt? There is no pleasure in it.

Suddenly it started raining and that too for more than two hours without a break. The tabla would not sound sonorously, no matter how much you tighten it. Bhupatramji said, 'Give it here. I will do it.' But even he didn't succeed. He said, 'It is completely cold. The air is damp. It is better to leave it alone for some time.' Though the rain stopped, it continued to drizzle. Bhupatramji went out, looked at the sky and said, 'It is raining from the west, it won't stop now. When there is such a heavy rain, the River Chitra which you have to cross starts overflowing on the bridge. Stay here tonight.' His concern was a result of two years of acquaintance and friendship.

After dinner just the two of us sat in the room talking. I asked, 'Guruji, a question has been bothering me for many days. Whether you answer me or not, but you should not mention to anyone that I asked you.'

'Ask.'

'Raja Saheb doesn't sing anywhere except in the temple. Why?'

Bhupatramji started, 'When the family deity appeared in his dream...' I could see in his face that he was not telling the truth and he himself knew it. After a minute he explained, 'Since it is you who is asking I cannot hide it. You put your hand on mine and promise that you will not tell anyone.' After he extracted this promise he said, 'Even though, the kingship is gone, me and Bande Khan are both his vassals. If this matter spreads from one person to another it will be an irritating problem. Remember you have promised. Shall I tell you?'

'Shall I swear on my tambura?'

'No, I trust you...Bande Khan's father Ustad Asad Ali Khan Saheb was the court musician of Shakapur. He was considered absolutely extraordinary in both—melody of swaras and rhythmic beats. Aspiring musicians would come from far away places just to learn from him. His admirers would compare him with great artistes like Fayaz Khan and Abdul Karim Khan. Though I felt this praise was excessive, knowledge of this court musician was certainly of the first order. I had the chance to hear his music often as I accompanied him on the tabla when I was young. Anyways, that is a different story. Our Raja Saheb was a lover of music from his young age. Pandit Haricharan Upadhyay, the court musician that he had employed was not a great musician. Raja Saheb's father, Jagjit Singh, was not that interested in music to get a musician of high calibre for the court. Meanwhile our country got independence and the income for this kingdom was drastically reduced. Haricharan Upadhyay taught our Raja Saheb as much as he knew. After that he left Chittarpur and went to Indore where his son was employed. Raja Saheb was anxious to learn from Ustad Asad Ali Khan. He told his father and the father sent for the Ustad and engaged him. The king would send his car to bring the Ustad and send him back after a day. Ustad taught for two days in a week and would return the next evening. The fee was one thousand rupees per month. Remember, forty years ago one thousand meant today's twenty-five thousand. For two rupees you could get twenty kilos of wheat. Raja Jagjit Singh was neither zealous nor whimsical to pay that kind of money. Isn't it only when there is that zeal the fancy takes shape? But the son persisted saying that if that amount was not given to such a great musician the honour of the palace would be discounted. So he was employed. The lesson started. Thus three years passed. Meanwhile the king died and the son was enthroned. Though the kingdoms were abolished, the paraphernalia still continued. In addition to the Privy Purse that had been fixed by the government for the king, the zamindari of hundred towns was his. Though our Raja Saheb has spent all his life with music he did not neglect his business. The old minister, Ambalal Naagar continued. A perfectly honest man. All the day-to-day affairs of the zamindari would be conducted through him and Raja Saheb would only supervise. He was spending all his time in the practice of music and in the study of books about art, history, literature. Have you seen the Palace Library?'

'Yes.'

'What a variety of books it has! Remember there must be a library in a palace. Even Raja Jagjit Singh was a scholar. The library was collected over a number of years, and was handed down through generations. In addition, he also kept on adding books and studying them. The lessons with Ustad Asad Ali Khan had gone on for four years. Raja Saheb had a feeling that he was not teaching everything full heartedly. There must be more firm foundation of the swaras. If a building is built without a strong foundation it will collapse. The ustad would compliment him about his progress. He would tell Raja Saheb that they learnt from their teacher for at least twenty years practising strictly in ustad's house. Music is not like the other arts. The ustad was always smiling. He would caress his long beard and his speech was smooth. One day Raja Saheb came on some errand to Shakapur. He told himself that since he had come this far he could look up his guru and went to his house. The ustad was not at home. His wife could not speak to any visitors. The servant could not recognise him immediately. In the inside room the ustad's son, Bande Ali was practising. Raja Saheb told the servant not to disturb anyone and he simply sat in the drawing room. The teacher's son was practising. His voice was not very impressive but his training must have been excellent. In how many different ways he was weaving the sounds! He was marking the saam by a pat on his lap. Even after four or five aavartanas of tanas he would stand exactly on the required swara, without omitting a single sound. Raja Saheb knew that the son of his guru was four years younger to him. The guru has taught him so much. He has cheated me. One thousand rupees a month plus and other sundry benefits in the intervals. He sat there listening for about an hour, then without telling anyone he left. He got into his car and came home. To whom should he convey his raging anger?

He could not sleep the whole night. In the morning he sent for the minister and confided in him.

'The minister said, "These people are always like that. The goldsmith never teaches the secrets of the work to anyone else except his son. Music is also a hereditary profession. I always felt that the thousand rupees that were being given to him were too much. I did not intervene because when the king has decided something I should not interfere. Besides, this was a decision that was taken during your father's time." "What can we do to set this right?" "If your Majesty gives me a day's time I will think about it and try to solve this problem." The minister assured.

'The next morning the minister submitted: "Tomorrow is the day on which the ustad has to come. Your Majesty should not show even the slightest displeasure. You should behave as if you do not know anything at all about this. I know the ustad is tight-fisted. He doesn't give his son even a single pie. That young man has a fancy for eating out. We must approach him with a trick and tell him that once a week he should come to Chittarpur in the car that will be sent to him and teach Your Majesty. He will be given a hundred rupees, a month. He must be told that he must teach you what his father teaches him and assure him that it will be kept a complete secret. It will not be known to his father. Get him to agree and through him you must learn everything new but should not sing those things in front of the ustad. That's all." After all, it was the brains of a minister. Raja Saheb nodded in approval and even said, "Let us give him hundred and fifty." The Diwan intervened. "You should not be that generous. If he gets a lot of money and makes merry his father will get to know about it. A hundred is quite enough. If Your Majesty says 'Yes' I will look after the rest." Do you see the inner working and tricks of learning music?' Bhupatramji looked at my face. Though I had heard stories about the gurus hiding the secrets I was touched by the way Raja Saheb was being cheated.

'A year and a half passed this way. Bande Ali would teach everything that he learnt. Whatever he learnt during each week from his father he would transfer it to the Raja Saheb. Lest his coming to the palace was known to the servants and they blabbered about it to the ustad, the house where you are living now in the forest was built. The car would go straight there. After the lesson it would take him back. The driver had been ordered not to mention this to anyone. After this other music lessons started in the cottage of the forest, the Raja Saheb felt it was better to practise right there. Gradually he started practising in the temple itself. Who was his real teacher? Though the ustad sold himself for money, he was a cheat in the delivery of the goods. Though the son was not a cheat he was the sort to sell himself. The feeling that Lord Mahadevji himself was his guru strengthened. While sitting in the temple and singing, he felt that the ragas opened up their inner secrets to him. Besides, Mahadevji was his family deity.

'It was 10 am. The priest had gone after completing the puja. Raja Saheb was sitting in the temple and practising the alaap of Todi all by himself. He had practised all the methods that Bande Ali had taught and was mastering the technique. Suddenly there was a shadow at the door. The ustad was standing there. Raja Saheb immediately understood that the ustad had come here after finding out about the secret classes being conducted by his son and he became a bit nervous. Though he was the king he had a feeling that he was learning through stealthy means. He welcomed the ustad courteously. The ustad, sitting in front of the student said, 'I am in great trouble. I have come to ask for guru-dakshina from Your Worship. I know the practice that asking for and giving guru-dakshina is at the end of the education. But being the king you can give it right now.'

'Tell me how much do you want?'

'Not money. You must promise me something.'

'Without knowing what it is how can I say yes?'

'I am not asking for any wealth. It is a word related to music.'

'Then all right. I promise.'

'You have given your word.'

'Yes, I have.'

'Your Majesty is a devotee of god. You are practising for the sake of that god in His presence. It is enough if you promise that you will not sing anywhere else expect in the temple.'

'Without comprehending the full implications of that word, he said, "Yes."

"The promise has been given not to me but to your family deity Lord Mahadev. This also must be added in the promise."

"All right. I have promised this to Lord Mahadevji."

"I am happy. I will not ask for guru-dakshina again. I am going now. I have engaged a horse cart. Your Majesty should continue the practise. Anyway, I am coming the day after tomorrow," he said and left immediately.'

'Why did the Ustad insist on this promise? Why this emergency? Raja Saheb kept wondering. He couldn't understand the meaning of this promise. He couldn't continue singing. He got into his car, went to the palace and sent for his minister. When he told him what had happened the minister said, "Your Majesty should not have given this word of honour. The ustad came to know that we were learning the secrets of the art from his son. He had come here in anger and worry. He knows that Your Majesty has a very sharp mind and is a firm achiever and his son stands no chance. He knows that you are completely dedicated. He realised that Your Majesty will achieve greater fame than his son and even teach it to others. Then what happens to the secrets and property of their family? If singing is confined only to Mahadevji's temple there will be no concert given anywhere else. He has stymied your chances of shining in the presence of the music connoisseurs across various platforms. What he has done is, even before Your Majesty is recognised in the music world, your talent has been buried, there."

'Raja Saheb never had any intention of giving concerts in various places. Neither had he any necessity to use music as a profession for a livelihood. Still he felt he had sunk to the ground. He was very sad that he had fallen into a trap. When he saw unhappiness on the face of the king, the minister said, "For every mistake there is a remedy. Your Majesty need not be unnecessarily unhappy."

'When he tried to console him in that way Raja Saheb persisted that he had said, "I am not giving the promise to you. I have made it quite clear in so many words that it is a word given to Lord

Mahadevji. Such being the case how can there be any solution?" The king showed his utter helplessness.

'The minister advised, "If god is adorned with the garland of deceit, does that garland become holy? This needs to be pondered over carefully. Now please have your meals."

'I think that Raja Saheb had not thought deeply and specifically about his belief in god and at what level it was. The family deity was being worshipped by the family purohit. His father had complete faith and devotion. There is a big puja room in the palace as well. Now Raja Saheb started rethinking: Was it not my responsibility to think about the pros and the cons before making promises? I am the culprit. Though I have sworn in the name of god, the sanctity of that promise does rest on me also. For whatever reason, if I transgress that promise, I will be destroying my own self-respect. It is like denigrating god's ethical order. No matter how much did he think the decision would stop there. He could not take a final decision by himself and he went to his mother and asked her. Her reply was "Son, ours is the Suryavamsha. Your name also is Raghuveera Singh. This is the lineage of Lord Sri Ramachandra. If he had even slightly changed the meaning of what his father had said he could have occupied the throne after his father died. But Lord Sri Rama didn't do so. What do you gain by wandering from place to place, giving concerts and entertaining thousands of people? You sing as much as you like in the temple itself. I will also come and listen there. "The king's decision became firm. He went to the temple and prostrated. The second day the car driver was instructed to bring the car with the ustad directly to the temple. When the ustad came and sat in his place, the king said, "It is the dharma of the guru to desire that his student should excel the guru himself. You have lost your place as a guru by crumpling away the student's fame even before it flowered. You were never my guru. After receiving so much money you have cheated in your teaching. Otherwise there was no need to pay your son separately and learn by stealth? You are not my guru. Only Lord Mahadevji is. You are a broker selling education. So, for the money you have enjoyed so far, you must continue to teach honestly in accordance with the pay you get every month hereafter also. If you continue your deceit I know how to deal with you. Your king is related to me. I will tell him to send you out of the city. But I am not going to do that. I will get you killed. Though the kingdom is lost, our orders still carry weight. Nobody will question if your corpse is found lying around. We know how to do that. See here," he said and removed the cover of the tambura and pointed out the revolver which was resting there.

'The Ustad was shivering. He started perspiring and said, "I take back the promise and I am saying this in front of your deity. I have released you from your promise,' he mumbled. "Merely because you took back your word out of fear of the gun, I cannot change my promise to my god. All that I am asking is that you should teach me without hiding anything. If you play tricks, I will get to know. You come here two days in the week and you must teach for seven to eight hours, must sing and explain the minute details. You should demonstrate and answer all my questions by singing, and explaining. If you do that much you will live. If you run away with your family from Shakapur you will be shot wherever you are by my people. You start the lesson right now."

'From the next day, the driver would go and bring the ustad. He was made to stay in the newly built hut in the forest, the same hut which you are occupying now. Same place. Food would be supplied right there and a servant would always be present to keep an eye on him. He was not taken to the palace even once. He was not invited. He would get to see Raja Saheb's face only in the temple. There would not even be a word other than what was related to music. Not even polite enquiries. A new raga would be taught each day and practised the next evening. For the rest of the week, Raja Saheb would practise on his own. The ustad would correct and demonstrate by singing along with him on his next visit. Like this, one raga would be taught in two week's and over the next two years, Raja Saheb mastered forty ragas. One day the clerk who had come to pay the ustad told him, "Your lessons are over and your account has been settled. From next week onwards our car will not come to your house."

The manner of the kindly dignity in which the ustad was punished by Raja Saheb pleased me. Whether the ustad had understood the subtleness of the punishment or he was happy about the thousand rupees per month which continued for two years, as extra benefit, I did not understand then.' Bhupatramji continued. 'After the music lessons were over, Raja Saheb's independent practice started. He would sing each raga for hours together. Sometimes for days together, making all the clarifications, thinking about the alaap of each raga day and night. He would not come to the palace for days. His meals would be sent to that small hut. He would even take his bath there and sit in the temple, and sing through the night or play the tambura without singing. Watching the leaves and trees, he would meditate upon the form and get the essence of the raga. He would also sleep in the temple. Actually, what the ustad had taught was only raw material. Raja Saheb was practising with the purpose, that, if he had to own that raga he should realise its form and that raga must be his creation. By this time he was thirty.

'I was a student of Ustad Ahmed Jan Tirakhva and had been employed in the court of the Maharaja of Shakapur. Raja Saheb employed me to teach him the tabla and the tabla lesson had to be given only in the temple. Once a week the car would come to fetch me. The next morning it would bring me back. My training was just like yours. Bombay, Vadodara, Jaipur, Delhi, Gwalior, Varanasi, Calcutta, wherever there was a music festival he would go there. He would take me along as well. Sometimes the organisers would invite me as an accompanist to other singers. Listening to excellent music and enjoying it, understanding the various ways in which the singers would present the ragas, he would experiment in his practice. If I was asked to accompany any well-known artists in a different place, he would come for those concerts also. He did this for ten years. By this time he was far above the so-called great musicians. He left going out altogether and completely engaged himself in his own personal sadhana.'

I asked Bhupatramji, 'Raja Saheb could not give an independent concert. He couldn't demonstrate his singing. Where was the inspiration for him?'

'True. He could not give concerts. Still many great artists have been wonderstruck listening to his singing. When famous musicians came to Shakapur, Raja Saheb would invite them to his palace and arrange a festival. They would say, "We had heard that Raja Saheb himself was a great singer and would they have their good fortune of listening to him." He would take them to the temple and sing there. I was the tabla accompanist. If anyone asked, "If Your Majesty comes out and sings in conferences, the entire country would recognise him as a great singer. Why don't you sing?' His smiling reply would always be that he had been ordered by the family deity not to sing outside. Now the question of inspiration. It is true that the main source of inspiration are the listeners. Still even self-satisfaction is also an inspiration, isn't it? Raja Saheb developed only this argument. Gradually it became a habit.'

The rain seemed to have stopped. We listened. Yes, it had stopped. The peace that follows heavy rain was heard. Outside the hut it seemed to be very cold. After taking out a bit of tobacco, putting it in the palm of his left hand, he powdered it until it became soft and put it in his mouth. He said, 'There is another secret. Since I have said all this already, I will tell you that also. Promise you won't tell anyone.'

'I swear on my tambura.'

'This happened four years before you arrived. Raja Saheb had developed a worry. "I have learnt this art with a lot of devotion, dedicating my whole life to it. I am already fifty-six. If I die without giving it to some deserving pupil it will be a disservice to music itself. Can't I get a deserving student?" This was his thought. Have you heard that if a scholar does not give his knowledge to anybody and dies, his soul does not get peace and keeps wandering? Normally Raja Saheb doesn't believe in such things. But when the sixtieth year was approaching he began to be really anxious that he might die without getting a chance to share his knowledge with anybody. Good student means, not someone who leaves after four years but one who will receive the entire training and education of the guru, and absorb and develop it. That pupil must dedicate himself entirely to music alone and give himself to the art just as Raja Saheb had done. He must have a good strong voice in addition to quick grasp. If he was a famous singer, students would come in search of him. Who would come to him, who has no fame outside? It is a tremendous attraction for a student to boast that he was a pupil of a famous singer. He must, in order to gain fame and recognition mention the name of the guru. When such a thought occurred to Raja Saheb, the evil intention of the ustad began to pierce his mind and heart. Of late Jaswant Bittu—isn't that his name—hasn't come this side. The travelling agents change the companies they represent. Or the company itself transfers them. Many employees give it up and start their own business. His remembering me was what made me bring you here. Isn't it called yogaayoga. How did it happen this way?'

ऽ

Not time yet, not yet. The watch has to be put forward by three hours and the local time had to be subtracted from that to get the correct time. There is a bit of fun in this difference in time. The arrival in New York was at six. But still two and half hours more away. Tired of looking out of the window. The neck had also started paining.

He pushed back his chair, leaned in and closed his eyes. Nobody could sing to this shruti of the steady sound of the plane which was flying very high. He couldn't sleep. Still he tried. After what seemed a long time he felt a little bit sleepy. A feeling of comfort filled in followed by some inexplicable dream.

Suddenly I woke up. When I tried to recall, it was a dream about sex. I was surprised. Also bored. There is no regularity or order of time in sex. It suddenly appears and haunts. Many times when it is desired it never comes. Only the day before yesterday, on Friday I had sumptuously gratified the urge with Madhu. I knew that this opportunity would not come again. It was to my full satisfaction. Saturday was a holiday for Vikram. It was also the day of the programme. I was adorned with a shawl for having reached sixty, congratulated, given a beautiful bouquet and applauded. When will this sexual urge dry up? How independent and free man would be without its trouble! He can use all his time for achieving whatever he wants. He can be a higher being if he saves all the time, when he is free from lies, envy, anger, appeasement and all that unnecessary time is saved.

When the eyes were closed again, the memories of how that mad fountain of sexual desire did rise from within while practising in the Mahadev temple filled the mind. Day and night, while wandering in the forest, while standing on the banks of the river and looking at it, and while sleeping. It is an exulting power that tramples down the raga which permeates and expands all over the space, into the netherworlds, and reins the earth and the sky as if it is the sovereign. The mind thought of fasting. But Raja Saheb's rule was clear. For vocal music you need extra energy. It is not the feminine art of a delicate touch of fingers on wires of a string instrument. The voice is different. If the voice has to thunder in full force and strength, everyday you must mix almonds, pistachios, dates and sugar candy into milk and drink it. You should have ghee along with rice.

Why is the strength which should be collected in the throat, haunting me as sexual desire? In whom should I confide this? In the first two years, along with the self-confidence that I was learning properly and mastering music, the power of sex was also breaching its bounds. Should I tell Raja Saheb? I was ashamed and also afraid. Even Bhupatramji was my guru. I felt ashamed to tell him either. I was going mad. The cattle and even buffalos that came to the forest to graze started appearing like women. When I saw copulating dogs, I would gaze at them. I didn't care if others were looking at me. No, matter which woman I looked at, I didn't care about her age. She was only an instrument to satisfying me, my urge. I totally abandoned my inner warning that it was my utter downfall. When the front door of the temple was open and I was practising the midnight ragas, my mind would engross itself not in the raga but in anuraga. The Mahadev lingam, with its pedestal and its pout, turned inwards, absorbed in penance, and instigating mandra-naada, began to appear like phallus immersed in vagina. Fie, fie, there was not any other downfall lower than this, alas, sin, sin. I rushed out of the temple, locked the door and was suddenly struck with fear that Raja Saheb might have come to observe me and had sat somewhere silently, unknown to me. I believe he would choose to sing a raga suitable only to the proper time. At nights he would sit in the temple and would visualise the form of ragas in his mind's eye. I felt sorry that I had deteriorated because of my obsession with sex. Even after three or four months, ragas were caught in the whirlpool of disgusting emotions. Nothing doing. I must give up music and run away. At least I can be a coolie and earn enough to go to a prostitute to get comfort. Or should get married. But I was bound by my word to the guru that I would not leave without his permission. There is really no other knowledge except music. Who will give his daughter to an unemployed man? I was caught in a dilemma. When I was suffering in this constricted situation, I noticed Chunni. Instead of Bansi who usually brought food, his wife Chunni came that day. She placed the food respectfully in front of me and said, 'Gawaaiji, here is your meal'. She took out a big plate which had been covered and there was rice, dal and curd which were kept in separate small bowls. After I finished, she took the plate away, cleaned the floor very neatly and went out. For the first time, I became aware of how good looking she was. Though she used to come to the forest everyday, I had not realised that at all. Her full skirt, the nose ring, the glass bangles on her wrists, another metal bangle which looked like it was made of gold, rings for the toes, kumkum on the forehead. She was dark but had an attractive appearance. About thirty. Five or six years elder to me. I was trying to tell her, 'Chunni, hereafter you bring the food yourself'. The whole day my imagination did not take the form of any cattle, plants, the trees and the clouds, but I kept remembering Chunni. When she brought the food next day I was extremely happy. 'Oh, you have yourself come. Very good. Where is Bansi?' She replied, 'He has gone to the fields to work near the canal' and asked, 'Will you be unhappy if I bring the food?' I was about to say I will be happy if only you bring the food but resisted the temptation. Chunni asked, 'Has the food become cold? My husband had told me that hot food is good for the throat of the singers.' He felt close to her because of her kind words and said, 'No, no, you have to walk two miles to get here'. However, he wanted to make sure that hereafter only she would bring food everyday and she replied, 'Looks like it. I have to tend the cattle to bring them here. Do you know how good the cattle are? Even if I put my basket on my head and walk, the cows do not run away but come straight to the forest through the gate.' After thinking the whole day I came to the conclusion that if I backed out now I would not be freed from my obsession. The next day, after she put down her basket and I addressed her as 'Chunni' my voice was trembling and so was I, as if a cold wave had struck me. Suddenly she said, 'Master, why are your hands and legs shivering?'

'Chunni, I want to ask you something.'

'Please do.'

'Will you promise that you will not be angry?'

'Why would I be angry? Please ask.'

'You promise me holding my hand.' I went close to her and took her hand. 'I cannot ask. You please understand yourself. How much I am suffering. You must save me. It is difficult for me even to continue living.' Tears came rushing forth from me and I sobbed profusely embracing her neck. 'You are my only hope. Please understand.' When her neck became wet with my tears she replied, 'Master, I understand. You are an esteemed person. Why use such big words? You first have your food.' She caressed me, wiped my eyes and I said, 'I don't want food. Please don't delay,' I requested and held her hands. What a kind soul she was. What compassion and what anxiety to allay the pain of another and how protecting. She steadied my body, encouraged me and became a guru, adjusted, and prodded the fountain of peace. The whole day it was like the peace that permeates after the first showers of monsoon. Infusing life, in a trice into plants and trees that were almost dying, making them radiant, causing green to sprout from the earth, which had turned to ash, spreading coolness into the burning sky, swelling up the river that had touched the bottom and causing it to flow, oh, I was surrounded by cleanliness, purity and delight. A comfort, as if summer prickles that appeared on the back and the chest, and hurting, were dried up as soon as drenched in the first showers and the skin did become soft and smooth. That night the raga came without interruption. How the dedication, the peace hidden in that pattern did open up! 'Chunni, you are my tambura.' This was my gratitude. The next day when she brought food I told her that she should bring food herself everyday. 'You will come won't you? I have been waiting since the morning.' What a pleasant smile she had! When the lesson was delivered to the guru! When the door had been bolted from inside, what if Raja Saheb called? Anxiety. He had never entered this hut, he would meet me only in the temple. Even if he came here, he would call out my name from outside. He had never set foot inside this hut. Chunni comforted him. 'This is time for Raja Saheb's meals, master. Isn't it? He takes a bit of rest after food, doesn't he?' Yes, yes. She is right. If he comes, he comes only when I finish practising a raga, otherwise never. Now what was being taught was Bageshree which was a midnight raga. Raja Saheb would not come every night. He was confident that his pupil had reached a level of practising by himself. Two days later Chunni asked, 'Master, do I please you?' I realised that she also desired me. What greater happiness was there than this! 'Doesn't Bansi suspect something?' She said, 'Leave it to me. I will see that he doesn't suspect anything.' 'Chunni, what assurance you have given me. What a good person you are.' A boy would bring the food on days when she could not come herself and one day Bansi brought the food. I had seen him a month and a half ago. Before that he was bringing food everyday. When I saw him I was stung. I thought how stupid he was. When talking about him, Chunni would call him an idiot. It had never entered my thought whether Bansi was intelligent, idiotic or simply dumb until I became friendly with Chunni. The mind had never thought in that direction. Now when I compared myself with him I began to feel proud about my own bright personality. Chunni was a smart woman. Bansi was not equal to her. But I was. I enjoyed this feeling. But I would not allow such thoughts to dwell in my mind for long and I would immediately return to my practice. My meetings with Chunni would go on uninterrupted everyday. There was no anxiety about somebody finding out but she was careful and would not stay for long. She would say, 'We must be on our guard'. I wanted to give her some present. A sari, glass bangles, something like that. I couldn't even think of gold and silver as I hardly had any money. 'Chunni, I haven't visited Shakapur in a year. I don't have enough money to get you a sari. I am ashamed'. But she said, 'Masterji, I don't want anything. You are still a student. After you become a famous singer and start giving concerts in the Darbar of the Maharaja and earn diamonds and pearls, then you get me a present. Until then if you need I can give you some money.' She became my friend and lover. But there was no time to talk at leisure while in bed. We had to be so careful, both of us.

Didn't this go on for four months? Everything was moving peacefully like the fine tune of tambura. One day she put down her basket on the ground and said, 'Master, I think I am pregnant.' It was like a bomb exploding inside me. But she was calm. There was a sort of mirth and victory on her face. So far we had kept our meetings secret. Is it possible to conceal pregnancy? The question of by who is bound to arise. I am stupid. I had never thought about it. In an alarm I asked, 'What do I do now?'

'Why are you perturbed, master? God has been kind.'

'How can our relationship be kept secret?' I saw Raja Saheb in my mind. He will kick me out. Or may be he will give me some other severe punishment. I began to feel that I had molested one of the women of the raja's retinue and deserved any sort of punishment.

'My husband is happy. I told him, "You were always taunting me that I could not give you a child. Look now, everything happens at the proper time. Didn't I tell you that you should take a religious vow to god?" Bansi thinks it is his child.' She said as if there was no problem.

'How can you be sure that it is not his child?'

'If the child was his why didn't it arrive in fourteen years? You told me one day that you could not give me a new sari or necklace or something. There is nothing better that you could have given me?' She made love with gratitude.

Two days later I got suspicious. Did she consort with me because she wanted a child? I wanted to ask her. But she might be hurt and even get angry so I kept quiet. After a few days two emotions started appearing simultaneously. Though it was my child I have no right over it. After the child was born Chunni might stop coming here and send Bansi instead. Even now she has continued to come and copulates with me for my satisfaction. But she does not have as much desire as she had earlier. Does the desire decrease the moment a woman is pregnant? I don't know. Neither did she, though she had been married for fourteen years and was six years elder to me.

६

The mechanical droning of the plane was unvaried. A sleepy sensation took over and he drew the curtain of the window and closed his eyes. He slept. For an indefinite time. There was a dream. Chunni's full belly. Even with this full stomach she was coming with the basket on her head. Couldn't ask her for lovemaking. She might agree if I insisted! Suppose something happens to the child! Her stomach looks like the rounded hollow of the tambura. But how attractive her face had become. She would say, 'Master, walking two miles one way tires me out. I stopped on the way a couple of times for rest. Hereafter somebody else or Bansi will bring food.' One day Ganeshi Lal brought the basket and that continued for seven or eight days. Bansi came with the basket after that. I asked, 'How is Chunni?' He happily announced, 'They say she will deliver in another week's time.'

She gave birth to a boy but I couldn't go and see. Again I felt I was sleeping. Immediately there was a dream, then woke up to the same old droning noise of the plane. When he opened his eyes he saw that everyone was sleeping.

One day Chunni came with a three-month old baby and the food basket on her head and said, 'Master I wanted to show the child to you. Mayavati asked why you take such a small child so far. I told her that I would roll the child in front of Lord Mahadevji three times. From tomorrow I will come alone. Look, does he look like you?' and put the child into my hands. Like a young doll nothing could be inferred by looking at the face. While putting the child against my chest it was ever so soft that it would permeate into the heart. 'You tell me does he look like you? Is it obviously so? Do you know what Mayavati said? Look how the child opens his eyes wide and enjoys when you sing. He will be a musician in future.' I began to be worried if she had suspected. I was silent. She also didn't say anything more. 'What if he does become a musician? You tell me. Now you come with me and open the door of the temple, I want to roll this child at the feet of the Lord Mahadevji together—you and I.' When I lay him down on the threshold of the sanctum sanctorum I was full of love. 'We have named him Giridhar. You also call him by his name.' From the next day onwards Chunni started coming alone with the basket, to tend the cattle. No, she was not coming only for the sake of the child. She wanted me. Now that the thirst of five months which was full of heat was satisfied, my mind came under my control.

It was at this time, wasn't it, that Chunni said, 'When I come here I must be a bit careful. The prince has come for his vacation. Once in a while he comes into the forest alone to wander about. He drives the car himself. What if he sits somewhere close and observes me coming here and our closing the door from inside and opening it after some time! When I suspect something I will tell you. I will just put your food here and go. I believe that he will stay here for two months.'

Raja Saheb had two daughters. Both of them were married and living with their husbands. The son was born after many years, I heard. I did not know what was happening in the palace as I was living in the forest. There was no one to inform me. I wouldn't go there either. Raja Saheb never spoke about anything else except things connected with music. I didn't have the courage to broach any other topic. It was not proper either. What little information there was could be gathered only from the casual bits of conversation with Bhupatramji. Though Chunni would give some information about the palace there was no time for leisurely talk when we met. When I came here, I had heard that Raja Saheb's son, the prince, Dilip Singh was studying at Mayo College in Ajmer and after finishing studies there, the prince went abroad for higher education. That's all I heard. Though I had the curiosity to see him, there was no opportunity. Now one afternoon, at about half past four, when I was practising in the temple there was the sound of a gun going off. I thought it must be the prince. Raja Saheb never brought his gun to the forest. Even if one shot is fired, the sound makes all the cows and the calves, the peacocks and the deer run about helter skelter and the birds start screaming with fear. Raja Saheb was so sensitive that he thought that, after the gunfire the birds would take three days to get their natural sweet voices back. While teaching once he had said, 'You can tune the tambura to a proper shruti in the midst of a forest. You can start with mandra and slowly you can build it up to taara and sing with a pure voice. The birds, the peacocks and the deer respond to this music.

They come close. They lie down listening to music. When the drita-laya is reached they start dancing. If there is the purity of swara that can reach their life also, and if you catch panchama in pure swara they will respond to you and we can test our swara-shuddhi and mastery of the swara in this way.' In fact I have done it. Starting from mandra when I reached the taara it was so gradual that even the birds had not been frightened. The peacocks and the deer had not run away. They had come close after listening for some time. Now, though I was sure that it was the prince's gun I had a desire to go and see him. A little away from the front of the temple, he was standing with a gun in his hand. A sepoy was holding a dead white crane in his hand. It was clear that the prince had aimed and shot it when it was flying in the sky. The birds of the forest were still crying out in fear and flying about wildly. The prince, who was wearing a white shirt of foreign make, grey pants and a black tie with red dots saw me and asked, 'Did I disturb your singing?' He had used the respectful plural 'Aap'. 'No, Prince,' I replied politely. But he said, 'If I didn't why did you stop singing and come out?' He said, 'Sorry'. I repeated, 'No. It really doesn't matter'. Meanwhile the sepoy approached with the bird in his hand. The prince did not touch it. But just looked at it and said, 'Yes, it has been hit right in the stomach.' The sepoy meekly cringed and said, 'It is after all the pointed aim of the Darbar.' Both of them went into the forest. I could immediately see that he and Raja Saheb were very different from each other. Chunni was right. We must be very careful as long as he is here. He might be wandering about in the forest even without a gun. However, I did not get to see him again during his visit. The next year, during his vacation Raja Saheb, the queen, their two daughters with their husbands, all went to Europe taking the prince with them. The year after that was when I saw the prince again. He had to perform the funeral rites of Raja Saheb.

When he thought of Raja Saheb he was full of tears and had a choking sensation in his throat. It had been thirty-three years.

I was filled with the same pain that I felt when mother had died. The pain that I experienced when Raja Saheb died was the pain at the death of a person who was a bestower of education and had converted a lump of mud like me into a live idol. I knew his worth.

The more I tried to suppress the sorrow, the deeper it was trampling me down. I sobbed profusely. The passenger on the adjacent seat looked at me questioningly.

Mohanlal lifted the curtain of the window. He remembered that the memory of his mother had not made him cry like this. Even in his death Raja Saheb had maintained his independence. He was sitting in his easy-chair reading when he put the book on the teapoy next to him and closed his eyes and did not open them again. I didn't know anything. Bhupatramji said, 'I also don't have any part in the obsequies. Let both of us sit in the Mahadev temple and perform the service that offers satisfaction to his soul. I will stay with you in your cottage.' I sang all the ragas he had taught me one after the other indicating morning, midday, afternoon, evening, night and midnight and thus singing seven ragas day and night. Bhupatram played the tabla. Though he had the idea of inviting great musicians to the palace and get them to sing in the auditorium, he did not mention it to the prince, the queen or the daughters. None of them thought about it either. When I said that he could suggest it to the queen, Bhupatramji said, 'You don't know. The queen does not like music. The rule of Raja Saheb was that the ragas should be sung only at the prescribed proper time. He would suddenly get up from his bed at night and go away to the temple. The queen thought of music as her husband's other wife. He would invite the queen to come to the temple. He even offered to teach her, tried to persuade her. She did not have the taste for music. She didn't go. She even poisoned the minds of the children by telling them that the other kings had improved their property by investing it in industry, luxury hotels and other enterprises and earned crores of rupees whereas this man didn't do any such thing and wasted his property in the cause of music.'

'Raja Saheb must have experienced a great deal of the pain of loneliness as he bound himself to the promise he made of not singing in front of others.'

'You guessed correctly.'

The next day he asked, 'What are you going to do next?'

'I haven't thought about it. I was under the impression that I still had to learn for a couple of years. Meanwhile, this happened.'

'Tomorrow I am going to my place. You have no work here either. After the obsequies are over, your meals may also stop. Or, they may send you back saying you have no work here. You also come with me. Stay in my house. Let us think of something.'

I also thought this was right. Even if they gave me food and shelter, staying there without my guru was of no use. I felt that when the palace had passed on into the hands of people who had no respect for music, staying here was showing disrespect to the memory of the guru. I decided that before leaving I must see Chunni at least once, talk to her, so I told Bhupatramji, 'You please go ahead. I will join you in a couple of days.' After the twelfth day of the obsequies, he left.

The next day I had thought of sending for Chunni through a message with the boy who was bringing food. But she came herself with the basket of food. With Raja Saheb's death she had become dull and lacklustre. It was thirteen days since I had seen her. She said, 'There was a lot of work. The relatives, people from the same caste, people of this town, the landlords of the surrounding areas—too much activity. I was expecting you to come. When I realised you are not coming, I wanted to bring food for you myself but I came to know that the tabla master from Shakapur would be staying with you. So to avoid any suspicion I sent the food with the boy. I will come from today onwards.' She thought that our meetings would continue as before. It was difficult for me to speak about our separation. Leaving her and getting away became even more difficult. With the awareness that if I gave room for her touch and talk it would be difficult for me even to converse with her, I said immediately, 'I can't stay here after my guru is dead. If I stay here, the queen may ask me to leave. Leaving before I am asked to is a respectable way. I myself don't know where I am going and where I am going to stay. I have to leave you and go away.' When I said this I couldn't say any more and I simply embraced her. She wept profusely. Embracing each other, we sat at the edge of the bed for a long time. She agreed, 'It is correct that you should leave before they ask you to. I have five acres of agricultural land which is my own. When I and Bansi work we have enough to live on. A small house can be built in a corner. I will cook hot meals twice a day for you. You please stay there.' I was filled with a feeling of gratitude with her invitation. I felt like crying. I could merely say, 'Chunni, I want to stay with you till I die. But I am a musician. The kind of music that I practise cannot be sung in the corner of some village field. I have to go.'

Who should I inform before leaving? I didn't feel like meeting the queen or the prince. I was apprehensive about how they would look at me, with what feeling. This anxiety was also there. The supervision of all the property was vested with the minister. It would be all right if I tell him. I reached this decision by five in the evening and immediately got on my bicycle and paddled up. He was still in the office and invited me affectionately. I told him, 'Sir, I am vacating the place tomorrow morning. The bed, the chairs and the table are all in the hut. In the temple all the books, two tamburas, harmonium, tabla, they are all in the almirah. Also the floor mat and the pillows. Please send a servant to whom I can hand over the two keys. I have only taken my clothes and the tambura which was given by Raja Saheb on the day of ganda-puja.'

'So, you are leaving, are you?' When the Diwan asked this question the present situation was quite clear. Both of us understood it and after I simply smiled he asked, 'Where are you going tomorrow morning?'

'Shakapur.'

'I will send a horse-cart. It is difficult to walk twenty miles with your bundle of clothes and the tambura.' The bundle was fairly big, what with the three pairs of clothes I would receive at every Dassehra from the Diwan's office, three pairs of underwear, my dhotis and towels. Though they were old they were not torn.

'In a short time our flight would land at the J.F.K. International Airport. Please fasten your seat belt.'

When I looked out of the window the altitude of the plane had already been lowered. 'I was thinking of you when you were performing propitiatory rite of music to Raja Saheb in the Mahadev temple. The day before yesterday while returning I saw a way out. Your education is complete. No guru can teach you more than what you have learnt. Hereafter you should make it perfect by constant practice through continuous singing. I have a student in Bombay. His name is Brij Narayan Nattu. I had mentioned his name to you earlier. When I go to Bombay for programmes I stay with him. He has a small house in Borivali which is the last stop for Bombay train service for the Western Railway. It's a bit far. It's a quiet place without much noise. Wherever there are the medium level singers' programmes he is invited. They give fifty, seventy-five and sometimes even a hundred rupees. He is not very bright. But he is a good accompanist, closely following the beat, and plays apt bols to the tanas. His fingers are made to play the tabla. But his achievement is not sufficient for accompanying sitar or sarod. These days I believe he gets a chance to play for famous musicians also. I will call him and tell him to host you for two months. He knows all the Sangeet Sabhas in Bombay. If you get a chance, you accept, because in the beginning you have to make your name though they don't pay even a penny. But you must be seen by the people and after recognition, gradually your fame will spread out of Bombay also. Shall I call him?'

Was there any other option? 'How could Raja Saheb know that he would die suddenly? It is true he had never discussed your future with me. But that is because he wanted you to continue here for two more years. After that he would himself, at his own expense create an opportunity for you to sing in a conference and would have made you famous on a national level. You are not lucky. But what you have learnt is of a very high order. You will certainly be an all India figure. Only it may take a little time.'

I felt what Raja Saheb would have done if he was alive was being done by Bhupatramji by showing me a way in Bombay. 'Raja Saheb helped me for thirty years. He gave me money for the wedding of my daughters. He helped for the education of my son. When he came to Shakapur he would even sanctify my home with his presence at my house. He would discuss personal things with me which he would not discuss with anybody else.' When Bhupatramji said this he lifted his head towards heaven and folded his palms. With this memory I got a bit drowsy.

Chapter 3

I

The arrangement for the workshop had been made at a theatre which could accommodate two hundred people, and was located opposite the Central Park on the ground floor of a thirty-storey building in Manhattan. Since the place had to be rented out for other programmes in the evening these people had to finish by 5 pm and vacate. Though the programme sheet said that it would start at 9 am, the watchman had been instructed to open it earlier for use. In addition to the main stage there were four extra rooms as well. The programme was about imparting training in music for six weeks to those who had already finished the primary level in Hindustani classical music and who were between the ages of twenty-six to sixty. There were fifty such to be trained at the advanced level and at the end, a day had been fixed when all the participants had to sing from morning till evening. Out of the trainees, twenty-two were Whites. Among them, twenty had learnt a bit of sitar and sarod. They were capable of recognising all the important ragas with their characteristics. Six had come to receive advanced training in tabla and three to learn the harmonium. On the first day everyone had to sing for five minutes to show the extent of their learning. In the afternoon for half an hour, there would be Rajaram Tipnis' harmonium and Omkar Prabhu's tabla solos followed by two hours of concert by Mohanlal. They all became his devotee after listening to him sing. Without being instructed by anybody to do so, they all started calling him Guruji. Among the group, sixteen White people had gone to India and had learnt some amount of India classical music. The ones with Indian origin knew about the tradition. Everyone began to give Mohanlal special respect. The Indians started serving him in various ways—bringing coffee and lunch wherever he was sitting, carrying a huge pillow for him to rest on and the first thing in the morning as well as just before leaving in the evening they would touch his feet respectfully. Out of the fifty, eighteen were women and among them sixteen were less than thirty years of age. Women showing special affection and excitement towards him was not new to Mohanlal. But he was pleased by the way the White women and even among them those who could be called just girls showed the same interest.

One of the girls filled his heart. He guessed that she was between twenty-five and twenty-eight. She was absolutely white. Her physical features were stunning. Fairly longish face, the brightness emerging out like the flame of a lighted lamp from her shining blue eyes, the nose in the shape of the flame of a lamp! In the emotion of Raga Bhoopali which she did sing, her figure appeared like a series of tufts of lights in the twilight, placed one behind the other and placed step by step, each one a little higher than the other. Was she describing herself when she was performing the aroha and avaroha of Bhoopali or was it to concretise *Sa re ga pa dha sa*, her body and face were created? Her red thick hair was the flame of shadja and she was like the maid of five soft shining lamps. She was wearing a soft, thin light-green silk sari with a border of rose colour and a blouse with the same coloured border. Red glass bangles. When she told him in Hindi that she had learnt from Acharya Shritisagar Pandey of Varanasi, he felt at home and at peace. Though there was no perfection or purity in the swarasthaanas and though the time beat was going on its own way, Mohanlal thought how much could be learnt in two years? She was still Bhoopali. She mentioned some name.

How to remember so many names? Fortunately for me when I sang she sat cross-legged right opposite me, playing the tambura as if she was also singing with me. I could see only her when I half opened my eyes as only she would fill up my mind. Those blue eyes, how minutely and brightly they were reflecting the emotion of each swara! When I reached saam how subtly her body would be swinging and would appear even more attractive. Bhoopali, if you were not sitting there I would not have been able to sing with such absorption. Do you know? I sang Kalyani. Yet the manner in which your body was responding to the patterns of drita did seem as though the flames of five lamps, in the Ganga at Hardwar, were following one behind the other at different heights rapidly and were creating a circle. Do you know that?

Though it was the second night in New York, I was still not used to the local time. I kept rolling about in the bed sleeplessly. If Tipnis and Prabhu were in the same hotel, we could have played cards. But those two were all for saving money and decided to stay with their relatives. Out of the seventy-five dollars per diem they would spend two or three dollars for the bus ticket. Tipnis had even brought a packet of chapattis and said that he was staying at the house of his wife's maternal aunt's daughter's daughter. Both of them were completely keen on saving money. I believe the house where Tipnis was staying was in Staten Island from where tens of thousands of people come to Manhattan daily for work by boat and return. I was the only one who had no relative in the whole world. The breakfast was bread and cereal and meal of sandwich and pizza. If you went to an Indian restaurant you would be ruthlessly exploited. What a good cook Madhu was and how well she had served for three weeks. Today is Monday. 8 pm there. Vikram would have just come back. He might be having his dinner. They might be quite at peace. Even this thought was like a dagger in my heart. It gives pleasure if you know that the female companion is remembering you and feeling sorry you are not there. But if she becomes extremely sorry and feeling sorry and is weeping for you, you feel uneasy. Everything should be within limits. I wanted to call her up. I hadn't even informed that I had arrived safely. She doesn't know my phone number. Poor thing. I felt sorry for her. I was affectionate towards her. I felt pity. He switched on the light, opened the telephone index and pressed the buttons.

'Guruji, great, you know how hard we tried to find your number?' It was Vikram's voice. 'Now, give your number and put down the phone. I will call you back.' I was full of admiration for Vikram. He saw the difference between here and India. No one in India offers to ring up. Within half a minute the phone rang.

'Before you left I forgot to give you a phone-card. Please give me your address. We will send it. You can ring up anybody anywhere using it. Just say "collect call". That's enough. Even if you are using the street phone, you don't need a coin. Please ring us up. After you left we are feeling very dull. The house looks empty. The newspapers here carried big photographs of your programmes. They have said that tomorrow there will be a detailed review. I will send you a copy. Madhu is really dull. If she had known earlier she would have also joined the New York workshop. Please speak to her. I will give her the phone.'

'Look here my dear girl, if you had come to the workshop you could have done the work of a guru. What did you practise yesterday and today?' What could she say when Vikram was at home? What could even I say? He would be holding the other receiver. With this thought it was just a courtesy call and after that he felt sleepy.

At half past six in the morning after my shave and shower, when I was starting out for breakfast, the phone rang. I thought it was Madhu. There it would still be 4 am. Vikram would be sleeping. She would have come to the music room to call me. Mad girl. He picked up the receiver and deriding her lack of discretion, not even aware of the possibility of Vikram holding the other receiver. 'Guruji, my name is Lauren. Can you recognise me?' English with an American accent. Female voice. How could I remember a name out of eighteen women?

'Can't recognise by the mere name.'

'I have come to meet you. I am speaking from the lobby of the hotel.'

I had a mind to invite her into the room but may one do so in this country? 'I will be there in two minutes' and went down. The moment she saw me, she bent down and touched my feet. Now she was wearing a shirt and jeans. A jerkin for the cold. Bhoopali. Does desire have the strength to attract? How could I know if she says Lauren? She should have said Bhoopali. In her blue eyes the brightness of dhaivata of madhya-saptaka, and tara-shadja shone forth. The lips parted.

'I am sorry for troubling you at this time. I thought that if you came there at exactly nine there will be no time to speak to you.'

'Shall we sit here and talk? Or shall we go to my room?'

'As you like.'

He touched her shoulder and walked her to the lift. After sitting in the chair opposite him she said, 'I heard such a lot about your singing. During the two years I spent in Varanasi your programme was not arranged even once. My guruji himself had said that your purity of swara, clarity of expression, sense of timing, the emotional completeness of swara, knowledge of the subtleties of movement were not found in any other maestro. After I listened to you yesterday, I got this intense desire that I must learn from you. I am a music teacher in a school in the state of New Jersey. You might have heard about Atlantic City, the famous gambling centre in the entire States. It is a place quite close to it called Pleasantville. I registered for this workshop six months ago and paid the fee. I could not get the money I was expecting which would suffice for staying here for six weeks. I had asked for a loan from a friend. He also could not get the expected amount of money. At best I can stay here only for two days. Besides, Manhattan is an extremely expensive place. If you recommend my name to the organiser of the workshop and if he helps me out financially I can stay for all the six weeks. Or, even if some arrangement is made for my stay, I can somehow look after my food expenses.'

He looked at her face. He felt sorry. 'Look, there are two beds in this room. I am alone. They are charging three fourths of the rent. You can stay for just paying a quarter of it. I will pay that amount. I am also sorry to lose a student like you.' Immediately after saying this he felt that he made this offer too soon with too little acquaintance. Supposing this girl thinks it is an insult! He was also worried.

She said, 'Guruji, we have not been introduced properly. How can we say that we can adjust ourselves to stay together for six weeks?' He felt relieved.

'How much will it cost for food and lodging for six weeks?' He asked.

'There is no need for such a comfortable hotel as this. I can stay in the cheapest lodge. Two thousand dollars should be sufficient.'

He got up, opened the door of the almirah and unlocked the inner cabinet and out of the money that Vikram had given him, he counted the money and held it in front of her. 'I am giving this as a special scholarship. Please take it. Don't leave the workshop.'

She thought for a minute. Then she extended her hand, received the money and said, 'I will treat this as a loan. I will return this one day or the other. It won't be embarrassing to receive financial help from an institution. But it will be so taking it from an individual. Please don't feel bad about it. The organisers may give you a helper from the workshop. If you suggest my name I will get a little remuneration. I can return your money in Manhattan itself.'

He felt happy about the self dependent attitude and self-respect that was shown by this girl. There was no mention about any helper from the workshop. Lauren was sharp in understanding. When he tried to explain in English and found it difficult and used Hindi, she would immediately translate that into correct English. Not only that; she would also mention any similarity of usage in Western music. She was experienced as a music teacher. After explaining the various facets of a raga, once in two days, he would sing that raga as it would be sung in a concert in the evening to demonstrate his lesson. Then she would sit next to him with the tambura. She would catch on to the swara where he had stopped when he indicated. Or, she would accompany him a little. With the experience of two years at Kashi and having seen the role of the pupils, she was ahead of the others. One day, by the time Lauren arrived, another had started playing the tambura. There was no place close to him in the semi-circular space to fill his observation with half-closed eyes. She went and sat in a corner. That day the guru did not get the proper mood to sing. Ted who was holding the tambura did not have the knowledge that he should follow the swara of the guru. The programme was over in just forty minutes.

When everyone was leaving, he signalled her to stay back. She followed him into the office of the workshop. He asked, 'Did you observe how bad my singing was today?' She didn't reply. Looking steadily at her when he asked her in an angry tone, 'Whose fault is it?' She met his gaze for half a minute and then she asked, 'Really Guruji?' He didn't reply. She came forward, put her arms round his neck and said, 'Sorry, sorry. I am sorry Guruji.' She kissed his lips and kissed again for a long time.

'Let us go to my hotel.' He said. When she said yes there were tears in her eyes.

The next morning she vacated her room at the lodge and came to his hotel. They shifted to a room with a double bed as his room had two separate beds. They decided not to tell anybody that they were staying in the same room but if anybody got to know, it really didn't matter. He knew that in this country there was no objection on people staying in the same room together. But in this workshop there were twenty-two people of Indian origin. Besides, on the intervening breaks, the Indian associations of Washington, Boston and Chicago would ask him about arranging his concerts. He could not stay alone without Bhoopali and ask her to meet him only when he had a physical need though he was aware that everybody would know about his affair if they stayed in the same room. He remembered the days when he was in love with the dancer Manohari Das twenty years ago. Then he had experienced what was excessive infatuation in love for the first time in his life. He remembered how love had risen to the level of devotion and he had engaged himself in serving her after giving up his good name, his profession, his income and his wife and children and had gone away to Delhi. Since then such a deep, intense love had never happened. No other relationship came up to that level. He became aware that it had not touched even one tenth of that intensity. Such relationships happen only once in a life time. It happened at the age of forty. Now it is not possible. 'I am approaching sixty.' He had thought about it several times. Now, in the year of my having attained sixty, it had happened with a twenty-nine year old White girl. It was not just physical. It was not even because she was White. She also loves with the same intensity. What a physique, oh that toughness and softness was possible only in a dancer's body. It was a body which was tough like that of a working woman—a coolie. But combined with that of the delicacy of a dancer. The body had not become lose or sagging like that of woman without exercise. Each square inch was like a cluster of swaras emanating emotions of a dancer. The mind was not satisfied of simply looking at that body with a worshipful admiration. The realisation that touch was worship and not just a means to happiness had not been realised at that level afterwards. But now it had happened. It is foolish to compare one love with another. It was like comparing one raga with another and saying that one was lesser or better than the other. This is like half-baked would-be artists. But why is it that this kind of intensity is not experienced with all women? The logic of comparison became confused. Leaving it just at that he looked at Bhoopali who was sleeping next to him. Whatever you say it is very rare for Indians to have this kind of a body. She had said that the mother was a Canadian with French origin. The father was English. She herself had mentioned that she looked like her mother. Every morning she would do her daily exercise without fail. If one looks at the conglomeration of proportions, one gets an idea of how a raga can be developed in harmony and in a complete manner. Tightness without roughness. Ups and downs without folds. Without the slightest fat but without being bony. How effortlessly she opens up without any fuss. How poetically she expresses her intensity. Even I, who doesn't know English well, can understand that poetic quality. 'Guruji, don't struggle with your English. Speak Hindi. I can understand the emotion behind it. The part played by language is only secondary in love.' Just her deep blue eyes were enough to express the emotion as vast as the ocean, and to inspire the heavenly imagination as immense as the sky. Within each eye if the tears are layered it is like a raga which had become a reservoir of emotion. 'Bhoopali, you have made me twenty-nine again, like yourself.' In gratitude I kissed her eyes which were closed in sleep.

From the next weekend every Saturday and Sunday there were concerts in various other places. Go to Chicago on Friday evening, stay there on Saturday, go to Detroit on Sunday and the next Saturday drive up to Baltimore, go to Washington DC on Sunday, and the Saturday after that and the Sunday go to Los Angeles. On the final Saturday evening, a public performance arranged by the workshop organisers themselves. 'Panditji, it isn't important how much we pay for each concert. Let the people know that you visit America. A situation may be created where every summer you may come and go round the country. Even those who are not equal to you come here every year and make twenty to thirty thousand dollars. Being such a great artist why haven't you got that publicity? You leave it to me.' The words of Patel who arranged the programme were true. I can make at least fifty thousand dollars. They will arrange for flight by economy class for the singer, tabla and harmonium accompanists. If you say I will bring someone for tambura and singing along, it will be expensive.

We will get them locally. How to remain without Bhoopali even for two days in a week? These management bastards want programmes but they are tight-fisted about provide travelling expenses for the inspiration of the main artist. 'You deduct the amount for her ticket in my remuneration. She is my student. You arrange for a room for us together.' Though the eyebrows of the organisers went up, they really did not question his suggestion and made the required arrangement. Bhoopali was really an inspiration. The audience also agreed that she was an inspiring student. An Indian sari and the blouse, glass bangles, the hair parted in the middle and also a red-haired braid tied in the Indian style. The tilak on the forehead like the flame of a lighted lamp and shining white earrings in traditional Indian designs. Sitting on the floor, the posture of playing on the tambura, the support to the guru by giving him a minute's rest in between and the lightening frills which would intercede in and out of the tanas gave a boost to the singing. The white Americans who had developed a taste for Indian music also appreciated her role. Many young Indian art lovers admired the artistic brilliance of the singer who had captured such a student in a short time. In Los Angeles when the morning concert ended at half past one and the young man proposing the vote of thanks took a liberty and said, 'We also thank the consort of the main artist who heightened the mood of the concert,' the audience admired this pun and clapped loudly. Mohanlal who did not know the meaning of the word consort simply said, 'Thank you, thank you.' Even this was heard by everybody in the mike. After the programme a meal was arranged immediately and all four were rushed to the airport. Six hours journey. Three hours ahead. Tipnis and Prabhu were purposely taking seats in different places. They knew that Pandit Mohanlal wanted to be alone and undisturbed with Lauren Smith.

When both of them sat together, Bhoopali asked, 'You said thank you, thank you, did you understand what he said?'

'Who? When?' When she explained it, he confessed that he didn't.

'Consort means the wife of the king or the husband of a queen or two people who were physically united—a couple. That fellow has used a pun while using consort and concert. Who gave him the liberty to speak like that? You also without understanding showed your acceptance by saying "Thank you". The audience clapped.'

Now he understood the words of the secretary were unwarranted and he had taken liberty. But even in that there was a kind of comfort. The entire audience had given their consent to this relationship. After the take off when the flight settled to a steady balance, Bhoopali got sleepy. She leaned towards him and putting her head on his left shoulder slept. She hadn't changed. She was still wearing the same sari and the kumkum on the forehead was still shining like the flame of a lamp. The shine of the earrings matched the glint in his eyes. She was sitting to his left like Goddess Lakshmi beside Lord Narayana, like Goddess Parvati beside Lord Shiva. Even in the concert she was sitting to his left, a little behind. 'She was really my concert. No. No. What was that? Consort.' When he was thinking like this he remembered that a goddess is the bringer of fortune. He was filled with the sense of satisfaction that all the concerts in America were so successful only because of her and the fortune that she brought. The sculptor should have this woman as a model for carving the images of Goddess Lakshmi, Parvati and Radha. She was in deep sleep. Since she was sitting next to the window he could not look out. To kill time he picked up the newspaper in the pocket attached to the seat in front of him. *Los Angeles Times.* In the first page itself there was a bit of news in a 'box'. A fortunate man by name Jim Armit of Huntington Beach flew for 3,000 miles to Atlantic City just to gamble. In the first round itself he got one million dollars. He immediately put the money in the bank asked them to transfer it to his town branch and took the next flight back home. He did not play the second game. This man, who had been going to Las Vegas in the past, went to Atlantic City for the first time just to test his fortune. This had been mentioned as reported in a television interview. Mohanlal got excited. This is what is meant by fortune, he thought. He read the news in the box again and again. He remembered all that he had heard about Atlantic City. There is a direct bus from New York. Free return tickets will be provided by the coach service. There are huge casinos facing the sea. Millions of dollars are won and lost everyday there. Food and drinks are supplied wherever you are seated. People who want to test their fortune go there not only from America but from every corner of the world. He remembered that he had heard from several people in Bombay that if you return without visiting Atlantic City your trip to America is incomplete. The concerts had been fixed for distant cities for every Saturday and Sunday. Now he began to wonder how he could go to Atlantic City. In a short while he felt sleepy. Bhoopali was still sleeping with her head on his shoulder. He pulled up the hand rest between the seats very quietly, moved her head on to his thigh and put his head on her neck and slept. It was a very pleasant sleep. He had a dream. He was winning in Atlantic City. The hundred-dollar currency notes were simply pouring down the machine. One thousand dollars, one million dollars. His name in the newspaper. He woke up. Not wanting to wake up, repeating the same thoughts of tanas and he noticed Bhoopali sighing deeply in her sleep.

ऽ

When I woke up in the morning she had finished her shower and was ready. 'You go ahead. I will come a little late. Let them practise the harmonium and the tabla,' he said and closed his eyes. He got up immediately after she left and in a hurry, took a shower, had his breakfast, opened his box and put a bundle of currency notes in a bag and went to the bus station. He went to the counter marked 'Atlantic City – Free Coach Service,' got the return ticket and sat in the coach. There was joy and enthusiasm of gambling on the faces of all the fellow passengers. Yes, he admired these happy faces and thought of the dull and lack lustre Indian faces. 'Good morning,' he greeted the fellow who was sitting next to him. They reached their destination by mid-day. The driver announced, 'Ladies and Gentleman, the return free coaches will start right from this place every hour. The last coach is at the ten in the night. Good luck,' and pressed the button to open the door. Mohanlal went all the way along the road next to the sea and came back. There were casinos, in a row, one next to the other all along. Right opposite was the Atlantic Ocean with continuous waves reaching the shore like the beat of the tana in the madhya-laya. Which centre should he go to? Was there anything special at each place? There was no one to tell. Everywhere there were machines where you drop money, press some keys and pull the handle. If the number you guessed matched with the winning number, money would drop into the container attached to the machine otherwise nothing. In each casino hundreds of people were playing with tremendous concentration. Here and there, in the middle of the huge halls were counters where one could exchange currency notes for metal coins. What sort of a game is this? There is no pleasure in this. There were no real players, you were simply playing with a machine. He felt like going back. But once he went inside there were lots and lots of tables where people were sitting opposite each other and playing. He was satisfied. He felt like playing every kind of game for having come there. He went to the counter and got coins for hundred dollars. He lost them all in no time and staked some more. He won, he lost, won and lost and then won and won again; and then he was losing. Five times he won. Twelve times he lost. Yes, he got ten. The stupid thing once more. He got change for another hundred. Yes, this time he will be lucky. He got angry with the machine and cursed it saying 'You son of a bitch, shell out money. Otherwise I will kick you.' Again he got some money and went back. Tried once more and then cursed all machines. You should play with human beings. Not with stupid machines. He had won against such proficient cards-players in Bombay, he told himself. When he went in he couldn't understand the game they were playing. He knew rummy and the game of twenty-eight. He just stood there for half an hour and watched them. Then he told himself, 'Ah, I understand. This is very easy. I can play too.' He got encouraged and sat on a chair at the table. During the game, he began to understand the game just the way you master the art of floating when you start swimming. He gained confidence and was sure that he could swim even in the Atlantic Ocean. He played with self-confidence with four Americans. The extremely expensive and well-dressed employee of the company who was acting as the umpire would show his approval by uttering words like 'Well played'. He was also saying how winning or losing was not important but the clever way in which the game was played. There was a lot of fun. There was determination. There was jealousy. He was also goaded into it. He got so enthusiastic that he wanted to stake everything and see what happens. Finally, when he put his hand in his bag it was empty. The man in charge said, 'Finished. Best wishes next time' in a friendly manner and moved his chair for someone else to occupy. 'Thirteen thousand dollars', Mohanlal uttered to himself. Nobody asked him to leave. Everybody's attention was fixed on the newcomer. The central focus was changed. He thought it was humiliating to watch others playing when he himself had lost everything. With his empty bag in his hand and coming out of that glass enclosure he found on looking around that there were countless number of such enclosures.

He came out of the main door and looked at his watch. It was quarter past eight in the night. All along the road, the streets were decorated with lights of different colours; white, green, red, yellow, all glittering. On the opposite side was the ocean, which was now black and making the splashing sound of 'dhap, dhap' of the waves as in vilambit and reminding its existence, through these waves. He went and sat next to the wall on the shore. Suddenly he felt like jumping into the sea, jumping off the four-feet wall. What is the use of living? What is the use of not living? This emptiness pressed from within. Thirteen thousand. Three lakh and ninety thousand rupees. He started cursing himself profusely. He asked himself, 'What a mad thing have I done in coming here by a bus? Again the fellow players are strangers, not known to me. Perhaps those players who beat me might have been employed by the company.' He abused himself quite loudly, 'the fool that I am, I have behaved like Dharmaraja in the *Mahabharata*.'

After abusing himself for quite sometime he lost interest in jumping into the sea. He just felt tired. Oh, for a cup of tea! Now it is time for dinner. He remembered he had not eaten since morning, not even his lunch. He put his hand in his pocket. Not a single dollar. Not even ten cents. Again, he abused himself, 'You deserve it'.

'The free coach service to Manhattan starts at 9 pm,' he heard a voice from behind. It was the security man of the casino. It looked as if the security was telling him directly. No use staying here any more. The coach was ready. There was no other way. What could he do if he stayed back? He walked fast and sat in the bus. The faces of the others in the bus were like his, resembling those of corpses. Just a few of them looked like they had eaten and drank to their heart's content and had actually enjoyed themselves. Four old couples were looking happy. All of them had gambled. Just for fun. They had also taken the advantage of the free coach service. I am a fool he thought. When he counted the corpse-like faces of the people in the bus there were nine others like him, he felt a bit satisfied. Within a short time he fell asleep.

3

At midnight, when I came out of the coach station, it was biting cold. I walked in the cold to the hotel. When I rang the bell, Lauren opened the door getting up from her sleep. She touched me and asked, 'Where had you gone the whole day? Your body is cold. Aren't you well?'

'To Atlantic City. I didn't have the money to pay the taxi from the coach station.'

'My God. How much did you lose?'

'Thirteen.'

'Hundred?'

'Thousand.'

'My God. Whoever takes so much of money there? Did you have the plan to go there this morning and is that why you said that you wanted to sleep a little more. I thought you would come late. Darling, when a person has lost money you should not criticise. Your face itself indicates that you haven't eaten anything. Now it is 1 am. At this time you don't find anything anywhere.' She continued, 'I have a few cookies. Just wait, I will bring them.' She searched and held a few cookies in front of him.

'Don't worry, I am not the least bit sorry that I lost money. Man earns money. Money doesn't earn man. I don't care.' He put on a brave face. But meanwhile he was on the point of weeping. 'My darling Guruji,' she said and embraced him. Then he wept. Then in a controlled way he said, 'It doesn't matter. What I earned in this country I lost here. I want to take a hot shower. Afterwards I will eat the cookies.'

After the shower, when he was putting on his clothes he asked, 'Do you have some change with you? I don't have a single cent.'

'I have plenty.' She unlocked her suitcase and took out the whole wad of bills and put it in front of him. 'This is one thousand four hundred. You remember I came away from there to your room. So, there is still some money left. I wanted to return it'. And smiling she added, 'If I had given it earlier, this also would have gone.'

'Take this for your afternoon meal. When you go to town you need some money for expenses until you get the pay.' Saying so he gave her back four hundred dollars.'

'I will get you a little more cereal and some toast. If you eat only what you usually eat everyday you will be hungry within half an hour.' When both of them sat for breakfast she said, 'You are not the only one who has lost in the Atlantic City. I had gone twice. When I was desperate for money. Borrowing from friends. With the great hope of winning. Every time I returned after losing a hundred dollars.'

He looked at her with steady eyes. Then he said, 'Thank you.' After half a minute added, 'I did not go because of financial problems.'

'You might have had the desire to convert the money you had into a million.' Then he mentioned the news item in the paper which he had read the day before on the plane, she explained, 'The gambling centres invent such stories. Even if a person gets a million accidentally they give it wide publicity by making it a newspaper advertisement. Do you know this?' He nodded his head in admiration.

When he went to the workshop he took Tipnis aside and told him about his adventure of the previous day. He wouldn't be satisfied until he confessed to him. He said, 'If you had given me the money for safe keeping, I would have brought it to Bombay safely.'

'Rajaram, I blame you for my losing there. You should have come every evening to my room and played cards. Then I wouldn't have gone there.' He accused him. 'You stayed away at a great distance in some relative's house and would run away as soon as the work was over here just like the people of Bombay would run to the local train as soon as the office is closed.'

'Even if I had gone home a couple of hours late my relatives would not have objected.' He counter accused. 'You are the one who ran away to your room with your partner in the evening. Now you are trying to accuse me.' When he answered half seriously and half teasingly with a smile, Mohanlal became quiet.

Chapter 4

I

Since Prabhu had planned to stay with his uncle's son for a week at Buffalo before returning to India, Tipnis and Mohanlal started off together. The pangs of separation from Bhoopali augmented because the likelihood of meeting her again was very little and a chance of living with her for more than a month at a stretch may not come again. At the airport, the area leading to his flight, both of them embraced each other tightly and kissed for a long time. The Indian admirers who had appreciated his singing in New York and had come to the airport, raised their eyebrows. After the plane reached a steady height, Tipnis took out a pack of cards from his pocket and smiled. Mohanlal grabbed it immediately as that was the best way to forget his separation. They didn't ask each other how much it was for a point. Whether in Mumbai or on tour, their accounts were specific. One paisa per point. The winner would pay for tea and snacks which meant that a part of the money lost would reach the stomach of the loser. Even losing the whole day would not exceed twenty or thirty rupees. Now, though they didn't mention money by the time they had played for an hour, food was served. Both of them were satisfied. Mohanlal asked, 'How much are you taking home?'

'Whatever it is, it is less than yours,' Tipnis answered.

'I say, what is it they call it? Per diem. It was three thousand and thirty dollars. Since you stayed with your relatives, you saved the entire amount. Take out five dollars per day for transport,' Mohanlal started calculating.

Though it was not unusual for them to talk like this, Tipnis was not unhappy. 'How much did you spend on that girl?'

'Why do you say that girl? Doesn't she have a name?'

'Lauren Smith.'

'Hey, I have given her a code name. Can you guess? If you win, ten paise bet.'

'Spending dollars on her and you want to bet in Indian money with me?'

'Let it be, old chap. You tell me the name I have given her. No matter how much you try, you won't be able to guess. I will tell you myself, "Bhoopali."'

'Ah! Indicating the enthusiasm which takes you up from dhaivata to shadja?'

'*Wah*, only an artist can understand the secret.'

Mohanlal did not discuss all his women with Tipnis. He would only refer to affairs casually which Tipnis had come to know by himself, that too only superficially. Tipnis was not a fellow who would talk to others about these things. Though he himself had no relationship with any other woman he would not condemn Mohanlal's affairs. But he didn't approve of them either. He knew that if he joked about it when they were alone, Mohanlal would be pleased. These jokes were not taken beyond a certain limit. 'I haven't spent much on her. Well, the lodging and food for four and a half weeks with me, that's all. What kind of an artist am I if I can't spend even that much for a person interested in art!'

'But why do these kind of candidates always come in search of you? Why don't they come to me?'

'The lovers of art are attracted only to creative artists. Aren't they?'

'Isn't it your meaning that only singers are artists and harmonium accompanists who help the singer don't have any creativity?'

'What applies to other harmonium accompanists doesn't apply to you. You know that without you I can't sing at all.'

With these words Rajaram Tipnis was happy and said, 'I am not envious no matter how much inspiration you get from Bhoopali. Because I am not a competitor at all. But if I don't tell you something that reached my ears it will be doing injustice to a friend: Everywhere in America, people are crazy about your singing. They are also enthusiastic enough to arrange a tour of America every year. This time itself there were so many music lovers who were ready to be your students. In this country, a concert is possible only on Saturdays and Sundays. If on the other five days you stay in the same city, music lovers will come to you for lessons in the evenings for four hours at a time. More than learning music they feel pride in advertising that they are Mohanlalji's students. They will keep you in their homes and treat you royally. They will create an association of your admirers and pay you a grand fee in dollars. They will arrange for a programme in their own cities. During the summer, in two and half months, you can make fifty thousand dollars. This is how our Indian artists are making money by coming here. Ordinary artists earn fifteen to twenty thousand dollars. When it is summers in India, there is pleasant weather here. The seed for all this might have been sown this time itself. But wherever you went you brought Bhoopali along and stayed in a hotel. Under such circumstances nobody likes to disturb the privacy of the love birds. In all places the music lovers hinted this to me.'

Mohanlal was a bit sad. Within the four and a half weeks he gets, how could he be separated from her for three days in a week? Besides, I get the inspiration to sing when she sits next to me with a tambura. This became the excuse. Rajaram Tipnis cannot understand this. If he had understood, why would he be only the accompanist? He would also be a main artist like me, he thought. He said, 'All right, let us come next summer. You write to your acquaintances. You must, of course, come along with me.' He told himself that this was the main point.

The meal arrived. While opening the packet of knife and the forks Tipnis asked, 'When did you learn to play cards?'

'Why?'

'Oh, I just asked. Tell me.'

'I had learnt when I was in Sagar. The manager of the dharmashala taught me when I was in the discipleship, I had not known it at all. I have told you all this. When I came to Bombay I stayed for two months in the house of Brij Narayan, the tabla accompanist. Did I tell you that? At Borivali.'

'Yes, I remember.'

'Nattu was addicted to cards. It all started there. Not much money. The same rummy, one paisa for five points.'

'I asked you this because you see, please don't misunderstand me and think that I am carrying tales against another artist. For me you and he are the same. But you are a famous singer with a great name. If someone makes false allegations on you how can I keep quiet? At least I must listen to your side of the story. No one will dare come to an important person like you and question you. People derive pleasure by whispering scandals about great people.'

'Tell me, what is it,' Mohanlal asked with interest.

'This has to do with an incident that happened thirty years ago. It is said that you went to Junnarkar Senior begging him to get you a programme. Junnarkar Junior claims that it was his father who arranged for your programme and made you famous. He was the one who introduced you to many musicians in Bombay, arranged for the harmonium accompanists and launched you in the world of music. Let it be. It seems your fascination for playing cards was so great that you pawned your tambura and took a loan of twenty-five rupees and still haven't gone back for your instrument. The Junior is proud that his father knows the inner secrets of all so-called great artists.'

'Did he talk about my addiction of cards?'

'Yes, that is why I asked you, when did you learn to play cards because my own estimate is that thirty years ago, as he mentioned you didn't know how to play cards.'

'Doesn't a man undergo happiness as well as sorrow? During that period in Bombay I was very poor with no money to even buy food. Junnarkar Senior had a good name all over Bombay as a good harmonium player. He also knew various Sangeet Sabhas. It is true that I begged him to get me a programme. Every artist has to do this in the beginning. Do you know why we quarrelled? He was a very proud man who thought that there was no harmonium player equal to him and he was the only direct student of Govindarao Tembe. He would claim that great singers would come to his home to know, and grasp the theory of music and sit with arms clasped. It is true that he knew the shastra very well. But in the concerts instead of accompanying he had the urge to take lead. The singer rests for as much as time as he likes on a single swara. He gives the impression that he is going to the next swara but doesn't go actually. He will do so after quite some time. Instead of going up, he might even come down. It all depends upon each singer's capacity, mood, doesn't it? The accompanist, if he is capable must go along or follow him. If he himself leads, what would happen to the idea of the singer? Senior Junnarkar would always give the impression that the singer was his student and he was the pathfinder...'

'Yes, yes. I know. He was a total egoist.'

'You know my method. The subtleties of the swaras that my teacher has dinned into me are beyond the harmonium. Isn't it so?'

'That is why it is very difficult to accompany you. Others can't do it.'

'One day, in a crowded concert I said, "You follow me. Don't go forward. I am the main artist." Everybody heard it on the mike. Since that day he started spreading rumours about me saying that his own student had insulted him.'

'Even the Junior has this same quality. He keeps boasting that nobody in the entire country has achieved such mastery of harmonium as his family members. The secretaries of many cultural associations believe this.'

'Let them. All of them know that I will not give a concert if Junnarkar's name is mentioned. I will tell you about my tambura. If I hadn't pawned my instrument, I would have died of hunger. His house was close by. I went and said, "Vittal Kaka, please give me a loan of twenty-five rupees. I will return it in the very next programme or if I get any money through the lessons I give I will pay even earlier." I didn't mention that I was starving. Even a starving fellow has self-respect, hasn't he?'

'Yes, he must,' Tipnis replied firmly.

'He grieved that he didn't have a single pie. I said, "If you don't believe me I will pawn my tambura with you. You must kindly borrow money from someone else if you don't have it" and I went to my room, brought the tambura and placed it in front of him. "Look here, I didn't have any money. Since you asked me, I went to somebody else's home and I have borrowed it. I will take this tambura and put it in his house and come back. When you pawn something, there is a time limit on it. When will you redeem it?" I said, "One month," and put the money in my pocket. Afterwards for one year I could not get enough money. At that time, thirty-three years ago, even twenty-five rupees was a big amount. After a year I went to Junnarkar's house and told him that I had brought the money and would pay him the interest as well and asked him to return my tambura. He said, "I will ask those people with whom I have deposited your instrument. You come tomorrow." The next day he was not in town. Then he said, "Come after a week." Meanwhile the money I had saved was spent. Three months elapsed. Again I collected enough money and when I went to him, he said that those people would not return what had been pawned, since the stipulated time was over. I believed him. After about four or six years when my name was well-known and I was famous, that fellow continued to tell people that my tambura was in his possession. By then I had quarrelled with him. I had already told you know, that by saying that it was wrong to become a teacher instead of accompanying, I had shamed him in a full gathering, do you know what he said? "Yes, your tambura is with me. If an article cannot be redeemed within the stipulated time you cannot to get it back according to law." In my anger I said, "You can keep it and go to hell." But in reality I had fallen in love with it. That was the tambura which my guru had given to me with his blessings. Somehow, I wanted to redeem it. Swallowing my pride I went to his house and asked him for it. Do you know what that eighty year-old man said? "I am glad you have remembered your tambura now. I have kept it safe for twenty-five years. What will you give?" I told him, "If I had put money in the bank and calculated the compound interest, in five years it would be double. Now, twenty-five rupees for twenty-five years, how much will it be? Calculate." I calculated on my fingers and said, "It will be eight hundred rupees. I will add two hundred and give you a thousand. Take it and give me back my tambura." The old fellow said, "I don't run a bank to calculate your compound interest. I will tell you something finally. You just do accordingly and take back what you have pawned."

"Tell me," I said.

"Look, the day on which you pawned, you were taking twenty-five rupees per programme. That was your fee. Today, I hear you take one lakh per programme. I got to know through Jayant Matrani that he gave you one lakh for the concert which he had arranged. Which means your value today is one lakh rupees per programme. You give that much of money and take your instrument. Is it acceptable, you tell me.'

Tipnis intoned, 'Unjust, unjust. Scoundrel.'

'I went up to ten thousand rupees. He didn't agree. Why should I accept defeat and fall a prey to his avarice? I was firm. You tell me whether what I did was right or wrong.'

'You should have told him that he will go to hell for this.' But the only thing that was playing on my mind was that this was the same tambura that was given by my guru on the day of the gandaa-puja along with his blessings.

'You put it correctly. This is something which only an artist can understand. But because of it can I give him one lakh?'

Tipnis was yawning when he said, '*Che, che*,' indicating that Mohanlal was right. The air-hostess picked up the plates, put them in her push cart and left. Within a short time all the lights were put off. Passengers pushed back their chairs and relaxed. Tipnis started snoring softly.

Ƨ

Mohanlal also pushed the back support of the chair, leaned and closed his eyes. But he couldn't sleep. What a tremendous force sex is. It destroys all knowledge of former and latter experiences and the sense of right and wrong. Unable to be separated from Bhoopali even for two days in the week. Taking her along might look a little excessive but without her, how would he have spent five weeks? This was his self justification. If this urge can trouble so powerfully at the age of sixty, imagine what it was at thirty, no even earlier, at twenty-eight. The force pulling this way and that from within. Senior Junnarkar thinks that the tambura was pawned in order to gamble. Fortunately, he has not guessed the real reason.

There was a sense of restlessness. Couldn't sit still, couldn't stand steadily, it was a maddening feeling. One should not go to Suklaji Galli again and again. It is a bad place. One can get disease or some acquaintance might recognise you. It might even result in a quarrel if the money matters were not satisfactorily solved. He knew all this but still could not stop himself from going there. This was the situation. Who will advance the money? Who will trust a newly-arrived singer? How could anybody trust a man living in the chawl with coolies? The only man who knows my worth is Junnarkar Vittal Kaka. He didn't ask why I pawned the tambura? But apart from Junnarkar who would give me a loan on an instrument knowing its value? How horrible of me that the instrument which had been bestowed upon me by my guru with the blessings of god, on which I had practised my music, such an instrument should not be used for a sinful act. Why didn't I have even a bit of discrimination? When I was going forward I heard, 'Hey, come here. Where are you looking? Who are you going to meet who is more beautiful than me? Come on.' In the midst of many women with bizarre dresses, shouting like this I couldn't choose any one of them and then I heard the sound of a harmonium from somewhere.

sa ma ma pa ga sss sa ss ga ma pa s ma
pa sss ra si yaa sssss ho ss na jaa

I stopped suddenly. What reached my years in the midst of the clamour were the swaras of Raga Marubihag. She was also singing along. Which house, which floor and where the steps were. I figured and started climbing. Yes, these were the old steps. I wanted to sleep with this woman who was singing. As I entered the room on the second floor, the singer turned towards me and with a salaam and a happy face asked, 'Have you come to listen to music?'

'Not just to listen.'

'Only if you listen to my music. I am not just a prostitute.'

'I also like someone like you. But how much should I pay?'

'Whatever you feel like. Do you understand music?'

'Why did you use *Ni Re Ga* in Maarubihaag. Doesn't it become Kalyan?'

She jumped up with joy and came running, touched my feet and said, 'Sethji, I have not come across such a knowledgeable customer in this lane.' She made me sit on a bed. She was dark. The body was withering. She must have been thirty or thirty-five. She was wearing a salwar kameez and her hands and the neck were adorned by glittering artificial jewellery.

'What is your order sir?'

'The same you were singing now. Maarubihaag.'

'But you found fault with it.'

'Doesn't matter, sing the same.'

She went out and called Bhaijaan. A thin withered man of about fifty came in. He was the very personification of poverty. He took out tabla daggas from under the cot and tuned them. She didn't have a tambura. She used the harmonium for shruti and indulged in alaap and then she sang along with the tabla. Her singing too lacked subtlety as that of the harmonium. I was intervening. She asked, 'Sethji, will you listen to another one?'

'Let us do it another day. Now I have to take a little rest.' The tabla man understood the implication and went out. When Mohanlal took out twenty rupees and said, 'This is all I have today.'

'If you think it is not enough you can give me next time when you come. Long time has passed since I sang in front of a real musician like you,' and she prepared the bed. She gave herself with a free mind. When I had come to this lane four times earlier those women had created a great clamour about it and complained that the Madam would object if I stayed for a little more time. She went to the bathroom and returning a little later she caught hold of both my feet and asked, 'Have you come to examine me Master? Why didn't you tell me you were a singer yourself? A fortnight ago you sang at a concert, I believe. Bhaijaan who played on the tabla heard you and said that no one in Bombay was equal to you. And he had told me that you would be a very great singer one day. It seems he recognised you after he played tabla. Please take back your money. If you could please sing one song for me I will consider myself a fortunate woman.' Again she touched my feet and returned the twenty rupee note, placing it on my thigh. In what a place had I been recognised! I was so ashamed that I thought I had lost my life. I wanted to run away but she had requested with such humility. Besides, no matter how crudely she had learnt, she was herself a singer. I was embarrassed to see Bhaijaan who had recognised me and said, 'No need for tabla. You should be alone here. And the door of the room should be closed. Take up the harmonium and sound the shruti.' Like an obedient student she got the right shruti and sat down. I put her folded sari on the pins and reduced the sound of the harmonium. I slowly showed the places of the movement through the gesture of fingers and then I sang for more than an hour. 'Look here, you can use komala-nishada as vivadi-swara after you have developed the raga only to show the expertise of the artist.' Her eyes filled with tears in gratitude and were looking at heaven. Five minutes after I had stopped she said, 'Guruji, I can't call you anything else except Guruji. The twenty rupees that I had returned to you, please give it back. I have thirty with me I will add and make it fifty and give it to Madam as commission. Without giving her the rent she won't keep quiet if you stay here. I will get the meal from a hotel. Please stay the whole night. You can yourself see how well this slave of yours will serve you. What else can this poor woman give to the one who made her listen to such wonderful music?'

I had not enjoyed such a service till then. I understood that Chunni, though she had given herself to me, was only a village charwoman who did not know any art. We were talking for a long time into the night. She was from Udaipur. Her mother worked in the Darbar of Udaipur. With the cessation of kingship, her employment was also lost. The daughter didn't know any other means of livelihood except music. Realising that the time to live with that profession had come to an end, she had come to Bombay. But in Bombay the flesh trade goes on like a village fair. Nobody wants to listen to music. She was not desirous of joining the profession. She did not have either an attractive body or the youth required for that trade. The thought of going back to Udaipur kept recurring. Though she could not make enough money there, at least the city had a few connoisseurs who appreciated music.

In the morning, after she got me tea she said, 'Guruji, I will tell you something. Only if you act accordingly it will be good for you. Nobody can conquer the desire for sex. If it is true that Lord Shiva with his eye on the forehead burnt and reduced the lord of love to ashes, why did Shiva marry Parvati afterwards? You also get married. If there is a wife at home, your mind will be under control. Don't come to these places hereafter. You can get a disease. Besides, you are going to be a famous singer in future. How proper it would be if you are recognised here and by word of mouth the news spreads?'

I was scared. I thought what she said was true. Even when I was told that Bhaijaan had recognised me I was mortified with shame. I came out without showing my face to him. I did not go to the red-light area again. But what to do with this sex urge? Within three days it shot up again though it had been satisfied three days ago. One day it had receded. Then it augmented. And what an augmentation. An inner compulsion made me think of barging into some house in the afternoon when the husbands go to work and rape some woman. Whenever I was going upstairs or coming down, no matter what woman I saw, I began to assess her sexually and tell myself, "Not bad. She will do," and trying to find out the house number where she lived was the only thought. But at the same time I was afraid that I would be jailed or if any of the men folk who were mill workers found out. They would beat me to death. My room was a small place between two pillars, and half of it had been divided into kitchen, bath and toilet. I felt like closing the door and practising music there. But I had pawned my tambura though I borrowed another from the house of Sethi Sab where I was going to teach. The upsurge of sexual desire would rise up like a tornado and it would blow away all my swaras. I remembered Chunni. Shall I go there and spend some time? But where will I stay? She wouldn't have built her own house so soon. If I go as a guest to her house who was doing a charwoman's work at the palace, everybody would recognise me. It would be a scandal. Would she give room for such a scandal? When I was in this turmoil, Daulat Chand, father of Kanshi Ram who occupied the last room in my row and used to listen to my music, sitting outside my door asked, 'What is the matter? You stop singing suddenly. Isn't your throat all right?' I had imagined this old man's daughter-in-law also as a means of sexual satisfaction. But this old man would always be sitting or sleeping outside on a mat. Even during the night he slept outside his door coughing non-stop. I replied, 'No Kaka, I have to think in the middle. Can't sing continuously.' He was satisfied with the answer. Since that day he started coming into my house without invitation and enquired about my life. He had no one to talk to during the whole day. When I heard that he was from Amroha near Moradabad, I also felt happy that he was from my area. When he heard that I was from Hardwar, he felt so happy that I was his neighbour. He started becoming friendly and often said, 'Whatever you say, this city is not a nice place. The milk from Bombay is not even as good as the water from our area. What do you say? After all ours is the pure water from the Ganga.' When he said this in pride, I also felt that he was speaking the same language as me. I remembered the Sanskrit saying *Janani Janma Bhoomishcha Swargaadapi Gariyasi*. Within a week after entering my room for the first time, he put before me a proposal. When I was cooking on my noisy stove, he said, 'No man should cook. You get married. Why should you stay alone?'

'It is difficult for me to earn a living even for myself. How can I feed a wife?'

'You get a girl from our side. No problem. My friend has a daughter at Amroha. Do you know what a nice girl she is? In her looks as well as in her character. You know the women from our area, they feed their husband and children with whatever they have, drink only water and spend their time smiling. If the husband has no work, they themselves will do odd jobs and take care of their families. Not like these social butterflies of Bombay.'

The words about working as charwoman and feeding the husband brought back memories of my own mother. Amroha is quite close to Hardwar. Chunni had said, 'I will work on my land and feed you hot meals twice a day. You please attend to your singing.' When I was contemplating catching hold of his daughter-in-law he himself had said that she was also a good girl. 'Talks very little. Doesn't brazenly talk to her father-in-law directly out of respect. But she cooks whatever is available.' What is the name of that woman who had told me that when the madness of sexual desire rises, if there is a wife at home, the mind will be under control? I hadn't even asked her name and she hadn't mentioned on her own. The next day when Daulat Chand made the proposal I said the girl should be good looking and he replied, 'You see for yourself. If you don't like, say no. There is no compulsion. I will get them here. She is the daughter of a close friend of mine. From my own place. Tell me which girl won't be good looking in our parts?' On the twelfth day along with the girl, her parents also came. Kanshi Ram, the son of Daulat Chand went to the station and brought them. Arrangement had been made to see the girl in their house. She was eighteen. Not yet in full blossom but just stepping into youth like Raga Kalyan. The face of a village belle which had become wet with shyness could be clearly visible even through the thin veil. She didn't even glance at me. Afterwards she herself told me that she didn't see me that day. Kanshi Ram introduced me saying, 'This man came to this room a year ago. He doesn't smoke, doesn't drink alcohol and has no bad habits.' The parents immediately agreed. They didn't have any money to spend. Neither did I. In the Amba-Bhavani temple, the priest uttered the mantras and the girl was sent to my room the same night. When she touched my feet and stood there with her head bent I removed her veil and looked at her face fully, smeared with turmeric, kumkum and sindoor. Being conscious of the fact that she was eleven years younger to me and her childhood had not completely gone, and her fear-filled face and not knowing anything about her future instead of erotic thoughts I only saw in that young girl the sway of shyness of Raga Kalyan.

Rajaram was snoring. An English film of adventurous lovers was playing on the screen. Except a person here and a person there who were watching the film with ear phones on, the rest of them had drawn the black patches on their eyes and gone to sleep.

The girl would cook whatever was available. Served her husband and though she was starving she would silently hide it. She would clean the floor, wash the vessels and the clothes and iron them and since it was only a single room, when I was singing she would silently sit leaning against the wall in the corner of the kitchen. I had instructed her once not to start the noisy pump stove when I was singing. She never did it. We didn't have enough but we were not starving either. A music programme in Shivaji Mandir would fetch fifty rupees. One programme during the festival of Lord Ganesha in Dadar got me fifty rupees. I could not succeed in any of my attempts to sing in concerts. The wife, Ramkumari asked, 'Instead of just sitting at home shall I work in one or two homes?' When I said that it was below my dignity, I remembered that my mother had brought me up the same way. My love for my mother increased. After marriage why should I send this girl also for such a job? For this girl I had only tender feelings. Chunni was elder to me. This girl was eleven years younger. Her only way was to submit herself to my wishes and fancies. A pefect wife for me, I used to think. I didn't have any money to get her a new sari, a couple of glass bangles or ribbons though I wanted to. It was difficult running a family without wheat flour, potato, onions and the kerosene for the stove. After enjoying great happiness with me for four months she got pregnant. I didn't have the income or the means of welcoming a child. She also couldn't think of anything. When it was certain that she was pregnant she suggested that it was fine to send for her mother at the time of the delivery. I knew by then that her family was incapable of taking care of her. A pregnant woman should not be made to eat only dry roti and chillies. There must be plenty of milk, at least a tumbler full. When I was worrying about how will I manage, I got to sing in a programme arranged by the Bombay Fort Association and got seventy five rupees. I gave it to my wife and asked her not to spend this money on any other item. 'You must drink at least a quarter litre of milk everyday.' When I said this her face was full of gratitude!

Bakula, right from her mother's womb, grew listening to the soft tranquilising sound of the tambura. Even when she was just a child of three months if she was left in front of me on the mat, she would never weep but stay still, listening to music. Even when she started to cry, the moment she heard the sound of the tambura she would fall silent. In fact it was after she was born that my fortune started shining. But the child's good fortune came to a stop. When I remembered this I wondered how she might be looking now! The neighbours said that she had my nose, eyes and the forehead.

When he remembered that though in the same city it was twenty years since he had seen her, he let out a long breath. Tipnis changed his position and resumed his snoring in the same rhythm. It was then that I got the assignment to teach at the house of the Desais of Malad. It was twice a week and for two sisters together. A hundred and fifty rupees per month. When Bakula wore the long zari skirt for the first time how lovely she looked! It was when she was a year and a half that I got the assignment of Champa's house through Desai Saheb. A hundred rupees per month. Even when the girl was alone at home, with both her parents gone out for work, the music master was free to go there and teach. She had a brother who was studying in college and practising cricket. The sister was twenty-four years old. She was of a slightly bigger build. Eyes full of self confidence. A true Bombay girl. She had learnt music upto the primary level. She had been to the concerts of big musicians and could recognise all the important ragas and mention their characteristics. I was attracted the very first day I started teaching her. The difference between her and my wife was clearly visible. The shortcomings of Ramkumari which were vaguely appearing in the inner mind, began to appear clearly: No education, no knowledge of music. Even when I sang the same raga for ten days and asked her on the eleventh what raga it was, she would only smile innocently and say, 'How should I know?' I used to get annoyed and think that her innocent smile was a proof of stupidity. She was fit for washing vessels and the floor and ironing clothes and preparing food. That's all. When I lay down at night she started to bore me and I began to think of Champa in her place. At times the memory of that songster from Udaipur, of lying down talking about the secrets of the various ragas and raginis would haunt me. How pleasant it was! I longed for it. What a fountain of enthusiasm sprang up when I realised that Champa was also attracted towards me and it was revealed in the bending of her eyebrows and the shine in her eyes. When I showed her how something had to be played by leaning on the harmonium and when my fingers touched hers, there were pleasant feelings on her face. She didn't oppose when our fingers would touch and neither did she withdraw them. There was a silent acceptance. How soft were the fingers. There was not a spot of dirt and the finger nails were cut in a shapely manner, and painted red. I would get the feeling of having started the shruti even when I looked at her full face, and the thick hair that was parted to the left. It was only in Bombay that I saw parting the hair to the left. How nice it was! I felt that the women of Hardwar, Sagar and Chittarpur didn't even know how to part their hair. This girl was intelligent. Quick in understanding but little practice. Her father, Prataprao Nayak was an officer in the Information and Broadcasting. Her mother was employed in a bank. One day when I had gone to teach, her father heard my alaap and asked me, 'Master, you sing so well. I have not heard anywhere the expansion of swara as you do. Why don't you give concerts?'

'Who will give me an opportunity, sir?'

He merely intoned 'Hmmm' and said, 'Sing the alaap in another raga.' The daughter took up the tambura. I sang in great detail emphasising on the fine aspects and revealing layer by layer, the subtleties of the swaras. 'Usually, the pupil is respected on the strength of the guru's name. You say that your guru has not given a concert anywhere. Maybe that is the reason why no established organisation has invited you. Wait. I will do something.' The next week, during the class, Paranjape came. Just thirty-five. Four years elder to me. It seems Prataprao Nayak himself was responsible for his coming up as a journalist. He made me sing and observed. Only for ten minutes. Then he interviewed me. My birth place, the ashram of Omkar Baba, Sagar, Raja Saheb. He liked the personality of Raja Saheb. There was no time for asking the details. The next question would come immediately and then he would go to the next step. He asked me if I had the photograph of Raja Saheb. 'I don't have.' He listened to my description of the forest, the River Narmada and the Mahadev temple. What is the speciality of music of Raja Saheb? What is your speciality? You tell me in your own words. What I described in Hindi was translated into correct English with Champa's help. She gave the Marathi version also. A gold chain was put around my neck and a zari shawl on the left shoulder and he clicked some seven or eight photographs of me singing in absorption, holding the tambura. The second Sunday after that there was a big write-up in the magazine section. The story of the great singer, a Rajarshi. King Raghuveera Simha's story which was discovered by doing a great amount of research at Chittarpur of Malva where Dharmaananda Paranjape went solely with this purpose. The cheating on the part of the guru forty years ago who took one thousand rupees a month as fees. In his last days in order not to die without giving away his knowledge, he trained a student after searching a great deal and for eight years taught him in the midst of the forest. There was an introductory description of me as the only representative of what might be called Chittarpur Gharana. My special way of singing. Two photographs of mine. I didn't fully understand English so Mr Nayak explained it to me. The father's knowledge of Hindi was better than that of his daughter. The next week the same story came out in the other newspapers like the *Indian Express*, *Free Press Journal*, *Loksattaa* and *Kesari*. Wasn't it after a month that the Swami Haridas Sammelan was arranged in the grounds of Poddar College by Brij Narayan? I was given the opportunity to perform on the second night of the three night's programme. I was to perform at half past ten. Paranjape, Nayak and Champa, all of them suggested that I sing Raga Darbari. Since it was half past ten nobody else would have sung it earlier. For the people of Bombay, Darbari meant bhakti. They were mad about it. A singer who can immerse them deeply in its depth and majesty and transport them slowly into sublimity is considered great by them. If by chance there was no opportunity for Darbari, then it would be Bageshree. This suggestion that I should be prepared for both came from Champa. My introduction was written out by Nayak himself in the folder of the programme. Champa decided my outfit for the concert. White pyjama, rose-coloured silk jubba, black waist coat. She spent her own money, took me to the tailor and told him that the fit should be exact. A gold-coloured chain for the watch on the left wrist and for the right hand, a shining ring with a red stone. A gold necklace. She had decided on what hair style I should have, with long hair. She had given a powder box with a puff which she said I should smear on my face before the concert. A bit of lipstick. The gold chain and the watch were from her own house. I knew by then that to succeed in public you needed all these things. But I was feeling embarrassed about the make-up and the costume I had to wear as if in a play. What costume was necessary to sit in front of Lord Mahadev and sing in the temple? Even Raja Saheb would come there dressed in a pyjama and jubba; a dhoti once in a while. During the summer even the jubba was taken off and he would sit in his thin vest. But I understood that Champa is insisting on these cosmetics for I must succeed in Bombay.

That day's Darbari was marvellous and I felt that even when I was singing. It was a raga which suited Raja Saheb's style of singing. Thought, which other raga would be more suitable than Darbari to reveal effectively the distinctiveness caused by time, even while pausing on each swara and yet suspending its nature of movement? I could have sung two ragas in the two-hour time given to me. But when I sang the alaap of Darbari for an hour and forty-five minutes and exhibited adana for half an hour and stopped, the entire audience proclaimed through their deafening clapping that I was the king of the entire concert. When I got down from the platform the Secretary came close and said, 'We didn't know your strength. The profound impression that you have created makes it impossible for the next artist to establish himself.' The lovers of music came and surrounded me. When I went to the first row where Mr. Nayak was sitting with his wife and daughter, he stood up and embraced me. Champa's eyes were showing admiration and wonder. As a chair near her was empty, the Secretary asked me to sit there. After a quarter of an hour when the next artist started on his sitar and the eyes of the audience turned in his direction, my side glances caught the side glances of Champa directed towards me. The next evening she found an opportunity to be alone with me and asked, 'Now you are a famous artist. Can a person like me talk to you?' When I said, 'You are the manager of a famous artist,' her face broke out in smiles.

Two days later when I went to her home for the lesson she put a file in front of me asked me to look at it. She opened it for me. It had newspaper write-ups of my performance. The heading of *Times* was, 'A new sun rises in the Indian music skies.' The *Indian Express* started with the sentence, 'The only pupil of a Rajarshi.' *Free Press Journal* said, 'If Tansen was alive and he had sung in the Khayal style, he would create the sublime majesty of Raga Darbari in the same way in which the new artist Mohanlal did on the second night of the Haridas Sammelan.' Champa read all those and told me what they meant. The Marathi newspapers had also praised my performance. Since it was in the Devanagari script I read it myself. By then I had been in a position to understand Marathi. When Champa said, 'I thought you would come on Monday itself,' though I said, 'Isn't your lesson on Wednesday and Thursday and bit my tongue in regret, she had already stared at me. I blabbered, 'I wondered how much time you had.' When she said, 'You could have called and asked. You know that I don't leave home and go anywhere.' I felt guilty. A minute later

I said, 'Champa, you are responsible for all this success. If you had not arranged everything who would have cared for me in this city?' Though she said, 'It is really not so. These words are too kind,' her eyes were receiving my words of gratitude. She said, 'You know what I gained? You wouldn't have been able to sing such a profound Darbari here in the house. I felt like dancing. Will you teach me that raga?'

'Certainly. But I don't know how to express my gratitude.' Getting close to her, I embraced and kissed her. By this time embracing and kissing had become a daily routine. When I took her in my arms and felt her body close to mine, my gratitude broke its bounds. If her father and she had not planned and put it into action, I would never have got such an opportunity. They were the people who created me as a concert singer. Realising that she was more responsible for the success than him, my feelings for her increased. How could I express this gratitude? Immediately I felt like making love to her. Not that this feeling had not occurred earlier. But I didn't have the courage to proceed. The bodily necessity also had not arisen. Now as soon as I realised that it is only through physical union that I could express this feeling, I tightened my arms around her in the embrace. The whole body was imparting more words to her. I whispered, 'Champa, now we must unite.' Though her tongue said, 'No, no.' Her body did not recede, her arms did not loosen.

'You will become a great singer. You are already a great singer. You will forget me in the future.'

'I swear by you that I will never forget. I swear by god. I swear by music.'

'But you are a married man. You have a wife and a child. I will be supportless.' When she said this her arms were tightening around me.

'It is not possible. I cannot remain a musician without you. You are my wife.' These words were uttered by my tongue automatically. She lifted her face and asked, 'Really?' I said, 'Yes, really'. I remembered that this was her method, even when excited she would keep holding a fibre of intellect firmly in her hand, controlling the situation. Mine was promising in a hurry even before she asks.

After I was physically united with her, the wife at home didn't hold any interest. Champa's arms meant protection. An assuring protection. She elevated the man, who was giving lessons in four houses and living in a rented dump, to new levels. Not just that, she knew music. She said, 'As soon as I heard your Darbari my mind was totally absorbed in you.' She said again when we were together, 'That tabla accompanist was not good enough for the kind of nuances that you brought out!' She was the protector, companion. What is there in that village wife? Companionship? Knowledge of music? Self confidence? Ability to fulfil one self? Though Champa looked a little fat, she was full bodied with a powerful personality. She was better than that dry stick of a wife. Not only music but she knew English, Hindi and Marathi. She knew the inner soul of Bombay.

Wasn't it a month after Swami Haridas Sammelan that the Trinity Club of Girgaon arranged my concert? As my address was not known to them, they contacted the secretary who directed them to Prataprao Nayak who in turn sent for me. The person who made the contract was Champa. The secretary had been given to understand that he should say that I have been paid five hundred rupees. Champa suggested that since it was a service to Swami Haridas he accepted five hundred. It was not possible to make him agree for less than seven hundred and fifty. She had stipulated that they should pick me up in a taxi. If the secretary came to my dwelling place with the taxi, how could I maintain my dignity? So it was agreed that I would come to Nayak's place earlier, the secretary should pick me up from there and drop me to the same place. In those days when even the famous singers were not paid more than a thousand rupees, my beginning with seven hundred and fifty was not a small feat. A competition to invite me was generated among the other music associations. Each performace was followed by a newspaper write up. In four months I became one of the most prominent singers of the city. From then onwards invitations from outside began to pour. Pune, Sholapur, Kolhapur, Miraj, Belgaum, Dharwad, Hubli, Nasik, Aurangabad, Vadodara, Ahmedabad—non-stop engagements. Not less than rupees seven hundred and fifty. Besides train fare, stay in a good hotel, the address of the house of Nayak, his telephone number and Champa as my secretary. Telephone and business enquiries, everything was hers. My gratitude overflowed. Money started flowing in. I didn't even know how to open an account in the bank. She herself gave the address of her house and made me open an account in a branch which was quite close to their house.

They had stopped the movie on the screen. All the passengers were sleeping. Here and there some three or four people, no, five people were reading with their overhead lights swtiched on.

Memory is spoiling my sleep. Memory is like the flow of water. When it starts, it doesn't recede even if you trample it down. One shouldn't remember the past. Though a great deal of effort was made to look forward and not look back, the past would come rushing forth. I had not even once thought that if I married this woman, I would have had to give up my wife and child. Realising that he is married and has a child as well, she would agree to adjust to two houses. There would be enough income to run both the families. When I suggested that I would spend most of time with her, keeping my musical instruments here and would visit the old house once or twice a week to meet the first wife, so that she was not unjustly treated, how she blew up in anger! 'All that is not possible. You have to divorce that family. You have to marry me according to the law. I did not agree to be your concubine.' She didn't pay any heed to my conscience that divorcing Ramkumari would be unjust. 'You should have thought about all this before you ruined the girl from a good family. I didn't ask you to marry me. That proposal came from you.' When I said that men marry twice or thrice and what is wrong with it, the answer was, 'You are talking of the times of Maharajas. Now the law has changed. Would you agree if a woman marries two or three men at the same time? Either you stay with her or stay with me. But you have ruined me. Nobody knows about this. I am from a good family. Do you know what happens if father gets to know about it?' I was scared. Prataprao Nayak was an officer who had influence on all the Bombay newspapers. Even the All India Radio people give heed to his advice. It was because of his influence that I was given a chance to audition there. I was giving regular programmes now. Jyothindra Ghosh, the Station Director had said that in six months time I would be an artist and he would recommend me for the Saturday night national broadcast. If Nayak was displeased with me, everybody would abandon me. There were people who were saying that my singing was balderdash and unclassical. What if their ideas and view were broadcasted. I would be ruined. This was my fear.

After I started my clandestine affair with Champa, even though I was sleeping at home next to Ramkumari, any kind of physical contact had completely ceased. I couldn't think about it. Ever since, I became familiar with condoms, there was no fear in making love to Champa. Now the position of my dilapidated house had improved. When I was not in town I could give her some fifty or hundred rupees for the expenses. She believed that my prosperity was related to Bakula's good fortune. She would often take the child to the temple of Amba Bhavani for puja. After she started wearing good saris and applying powder to her face, even she began to look bright. But she was illiterate with absolutely no knowledge of music. I broached the subject stage by stage. I told her, 'The programme I am getting now is with the help of someone. In a year or two we can leave this old house and move to a flat with three rooms. You can buy gold bangles for yourself and new gold chains for the child. He is helping me so that I can marry his daughter. If I say no, I won't get any programme. Starvation and wandering will start again. Let alone a cup of milk for the child, there won't be any food to eat. Think about it.' I said that in the bed. She didn't say a word. She became so silent that she didn't even seem to be breathing. I didn't talk again. After a little while when I put my hand on her and asked, 'What do you say?' She said, 'So that is why you haven't touched me in six months isn't it?' She started weeping. I realised my mistake. I said something absurd, 'It's not like that. I must prepare for my programmes. I don't have physical contacts with anybody else'. The liking for her asserted itself and desire made its presence felt. She also agreed. For the first time she co-operated actively while the two-year old Bakula was sleeping.

४

The next night, after the light was put off and the child slept, she embraced me and said, 'I don't want any ornaments. Not even new saris. Let us stay here. I will work in four houses as a charwoman and earn enough to run this house. Don't marry again.' I also didn't think that she would agree. It was again confirmed that she couldn't think of anything beyond just the three of us, our food and shelter.

Even in Champa's house there was opposition for this proposal. I may be the famous artist who had won the hearts of the audience in his first concert and had become famous all over Western India and was on the way to being crowned the king of music in other parts of the country. But I was uneducated. Didn't belong to the educated class of Bombay. The circle of Nayak was not confined only to music, he was in constant touch with ministers, politicians, lawyers, managers and other dignitaries. Though I had learnt Sanskrit and Hindi in Hardwar and I had read all the works on music in the Mahadev temple I was not considered educated. Besides, I was a married man with a child. It was not easy to get a divorce. Even if it was obtained it would be unjust. Nayak told his daughter that my mind would still be harping on that part of my life. It seems he even said that it was a mistake taking me into their household and helping me. He sent for me and talked to me separately. 'Do you really love Champa?' What could I say? I said, 'Yes'. 'Why did you love her though you have a wife and a child?' I said what occurred to me as truth. I praised Champa's good qualities and strength. Her mother was also opposed to this relation. She took her daughter to task and told her, 'You two, stop meeting each other. You will be all right in two months. Let him arrange for his programmes from his own house. After learning music is it difficult to arrange for one's own programmes?' Champa didn't agree. If she had, I would be out of this muddle. Meanwhile I came to know that her nature was that of a stubborn woman. But I didn't apply it to our situation. I believed that she had been stubborn because of her great love for me. She was good at her studies but she dropped out of her graduation course. Though the parents tried to persuade her to get at least a degree, she didn't listen. She went to a typing institute and even learnt accountancy for a year. If she had continued for one more year she would have got the diploma. It seems she gave up that as well. She didn't even practise music properly either. Later her father arranged for her to write music reviews for an English newspaper called *New Age* but he used to correct and rewrite her columns. Though there was no money in it, there would be publicity but she gave up that as well. How could a girl who wouldn't do anything and who had no job get a good husband? All this was narrated to me by her mother herself.

But I had not understood her real personality. I hardly knew anything about city life and English education. Besides, she was using the secret of the physical relationship between us, blackmailing me by saying who will marry a ruined girl. On account of this guilt, I agreed. We went to the advocate, Chaman Lal of Goregaon whom she had fixed up. After listening to everything he said, 'These things happen. In the world of art and cinema and in some other places these things keep happening. They all come to me for consultation. None of my clients have ever faced a complication. If you ask for a divorce, the first wife will not give it. If you get her signature on a blank sheet of paper it won't be considered a divorce. Consider yourself as unmarried and get your second marriage registered. Keep paying compensation to your wife every month for her livelihood. Let there be no injustice. Your second marriage will be an official marriage. You say that the first marriage took place in the temple of Amba Bhavani. And you mention that the priest got the two of you married. Believe me, she will not go to court. She doesn't have the resource or the education. Even if she does, we will make sure that there is no evidence of that marriage. If she is paid enough for her livelihood she will never oppose you. Even the neighbours will ask her to reconcile herself and keep quiet. Your second marriage will be your only legal one.'

Champa had made up her mind. And once she had decided, I did not have the courage to oppose? Nayak didn't agree. 'What you are doing is against the law. I am a government employee. I might lose my job if it is discovered that I knew about all that was happening. You should not give my home address. I won't be a part of this in anyway. We are going to say that our daughter quarrelled with us and left home and we don't know what she did afterwards. I have made my position clear.'

When I asked Champa what would be gained by earning the displeasure of the parents, not able to tell her directly that I didn't want this marriage, she merely said, 'Where will they go? After a few days they will come looking for us. You don't know the way the entrails of the parents work.' She found a two-room flat for two hundred rupees by paying five thousand rupees 'goodwill amount' and started living with me even before the marriage. She used this address to get the marriage registered. She even arranged a party, inviting all the people of the music circle. Nobody except Paranjape knew it was my second marriage. She met him and spoke to him, 'Look, my father has sent me with a message. Mohan was married to a village girl. You know about it. That was a stealthy marriage. Still, he paid twenty-five thousand and settled it. She gave it in writing that she and he were not in anyway connected and that she had no objection for him to marry another. She gave this in writing, took the money and went back to from where she had came. Still, this news should not reach anybody's ears. People who dislike us might write in the papers. So my father has asked me to tell you to take care of that possibility.' She knew how obedient Paranjape would be if the word came from her father.

I asked how much money I had to give to Ramkumari per month. Champa opposed. 'Should you really give? What did the lawyer say? It is not necessary to do everything that the lawyer asks you to do? If you get into the habit of paying now, they will extract money from you till their death. They will never stand on their own feet. And its not easy for you to spare money, you make money only after making long train journeys and singing yourself hoarse. Where will we get the money from?'

'The lawyer said, didn't he, to give compensation at least for four years and said that by that time her anger would have subsided.'

'Let's give. What does she have to do in this city? In Bombay everything is expensive. Isn't it wise to tell her that you would give a lump sum amount and ask her to go to her place? She atleast has her parents and relatives there. There is nobody to take care of her in this metropolis? You send her away telling her this.'

This suggestion brought some peace to me. But I knew that these days all the villagers come to the cities, looking for jobs. I didn't tell her that. I only said that I would talk about this. Now, how much should she be paid for the first month was discussed. She said fifty rupees was enough. I said the rent for the room itself was thirty rupees. After a long discussion, she agreed to give two hundred rupees. Since she had taken the entire money matters into her hands, I couldn't do anything independently. She gave me two hundred rupees for her and one rupee for the return train fare. And then she gave another five rupee note for tea and other expenses.

It had been fifteen days since I had gone to the house in Borivali. Bakula simply stood at the door as if she had forgotten me and stared at me with her large antelope eyes. I had bought peppermints for one rupee out of the five rupees Champa had given me. A smile finally broke on he face when I offered those peppermints to her. I lifted her up and made her sit on my lap. She called out 'father' loudly to let her mother know about my arrival. The mother was standing near the kitchen door with her head bent. She had stopped wearing a veil after living in Bombay for such a long time. After my income had improved and there was enough to eat, her face had filled up but now it looked worn out again. I guessed that she was worried whether I would ever come home as I had been away for so long. I took out the currency notes from my pocket and said, 'Take this. It is two hundred rupees. I will bring the same amount every month. Use this money to pay the rent and running the house. I will bring more money and also keep visting from time to time. I won't leave you.' She didn't say anything. She didn't even extend her hand. I asked her, 'Did you hear?'

'I don't want anything from you. I was planning to start working as a charwoman after talking to you. Anyways now that you are here please give me your permission,' she said.

I got up from the steel chair I was sitting on, went to her, took her by the shoulders and embraced her. She freed herself and went into the kitchen. I followed her and said, 'Look, my stars are not favourable. Even though I did not want it personally but it is said in the shastra that the second marriage is inevitable for me. Who can change what is written in the destiny? It seems my earnings will improve as a result of this marriage. Then I will buy a house for you. Or I will give you ten to fifteen thousand rupees. I won't abandon you. If you like, you can visit your parents for some time.' She didn't say anything and started weeping. Not knowing how to console her, I put the currency notes in the niche of the kitchen wall and came out. I told the child that I will come back and walked out. Before descending the steps when I looked back and saw Bakula, the memory of Giridhar, the child born to Chunni came back. I had no contact with that child. I thought that even if I went there, the child would not recognise me as the father and I felt sorry at this loss. Bakula couldn't recognise me only after fifteen days. What if she forgets me altogether? It made me very sad to even think about it. How to retain Ramkumari and Bakula as mine? This thought began to trouble me.

When I went again next month, Bakula was not at home. I had the permission to go there only once a month. The rest of the time Champa would ask where I was going, what I was doing and such details. She would know. She would control. Her control over me began to spread gradually even without my realising it. She was the manager of all my activities and programmes. I couldn't go to Borivali in the midst of the schedule she would plan for me. It would take a very long time to go to Borivali in those days when it was the end of Bombay. From Kurla one had to go to Dadar and then change the train. And from the station it was half a mile's walk to the house. The return journey would be equally complicated. If the trains were not caught on time, it would take two and a half hours to three hours for the journey. When I saw Ramkumari a month later, there was happiness and a look of welcome on her face. I asked, 'Where is the child.'

'There are two children of her age in the house on the lower lane. She has gone there to play with them.'

I said, 'Come here.' She came close. Taking hold of her shoulder with my left hand, I asked 'Are you angry?' She didn't reply. 'Tell me.' With the right hand I drew her face towards me.

'I asked the priest at the temple. The one who married us. He looked at my palm. He identified the stars on the basis of my name and made calculations. Your stars are malignant. Shani is in control. Come to the temple everyday. Light a gingilly oil lamp to Lord Shani. I started last Saturday. Today you have come.'

'Lord Shani has caught hold your husband also. You pray to Him to release your husband.'

'I am praying.'

I felt pity for her. My eyes blurred with sorrow and tenderness for her. The feeling that she was my wife took hold of me. I looked at the open door. I went, closed it and drew the bolt from inside. She didn't say no. I wondered where else I could find such childlike softness, dedication and submissiveness. After I opened the door I asked her to bring the child. Since she brought her by telling her that Pitaji had come, Bakula came straight to me.

३

It happened just the way Champa had predicted. Two months later, her parents came to our home and invited us. They prepared a lavish meal and gifted a silk sari to the daughter and a safari suit piece to the son-in-law. Everything went smoothly. Champa asked me gleefully, 'Didn't I tell you, it would happen this way only?' I didn't know any alternative. I felt that she was thinking of my welfare in everything she did. I got a phone for the house, a letter-head with an address and phone number and our own envelopes. She was looking after all the correspondence and telephone conversations. 'An artist should have a secretary. If you carry out business through the secretary, there will be firmness and control. You tell everybody that whatever you want should be discussed with Champa Mohan. You don't understand business tactics, anyways.' She would record it all in writing; things like fixing up engagements, taking the full amount in advance and filing all the newspaper write-ups. She would even write down which ragas were sung at which place with the intention of avoiding repetition. She would tell me, 'Artists would not have any discipline. You must have acquired the goodwill of seven births in order to get a disciplined wife like me.' No matter how much money the organisers gave, I would sing on the platform for four to five hours abundantly. I would get involved with the audience as I was young, strong and enthusiastic to sing. Even after the show was officially over, I would continue singing whatever they requested. Once in Pune when I was about to conclude the concert with Bhairavi, an old member of the audience stood up and requested to sing Lalit and then conclude with Bhairavi. It was a concert of the Indian style, people sitting on the floor. Champa who was sitting next to me with the tambura drew the mike to her said, 'Next time.' The old man asked when the next time would be and when they could listen to it. She answered, 'It could be next week if you invite us. Our diary has a blank that time.' I didn't think this was the right answer. Is it proper that while eating if you ask for one more morsel to say next time? I just started Lalit. The audience clapped. The fact that Champa was upset could be seen in the rough and uneven way her fingers were striking the strings of the tambura. It was diffcult for me to sing a delicate raga like the Lalit in the rough shruti being used by her. I looked at her. She stared back at me, meaning she didn't care. I didn't have the courage to shout at her. Any other singer would have sent her away and appointed someone else to play the tambura. But I knew her nature. I somehow managed the nuances of the raga with great difficulty. When I looked at the face of the old man who had requested this raga, the lines of pain on his face indicated that he knew what was going on. Within fifteen minutes I completed Lalit and started Bhairavi. And even for that raga, she played with the same roughness. On our way to Bombay, she said, 'You insulted me.'

'Doesn't next time mean that the same amount of money should be paid again? It is humiliating for an artist to talk like that,' I said.

'Then you give free concerts. Why do you take money?'

I got angry. 'When once a prostitute takes money she must give the satisfaction that her customer demands. When he asks for another kiss, does he leave her alone, if she says next time?' I blurted without realising the impropriety of the comparison.

'What a comparison you are giving. These words must have been spoken by your own experience.' She spat out.

In fact, it was something from my own experience. Before I met the musician in the Bombay whorehouse, what's her name? I didn't ask her. She didn't tell me either. The one from Udaipur. Before her, I had been with others, and one of them had shouted, 'For the five rupees which you have given you cannot make so many demands. Just get up and go.' The comparison became quite clear immediately and I felt that the comparison was not inaccurate. But for her records I told her. 'Is experience an absolute necessity? I only said that to make the point that singing and serving music should not be reduced to calculations of a prostitute.' She was silenced.

But it was not her nature to accept defeat. Five minutes later she said, 'Then we will have two rates. Full programme for one thousand rupees. Half programme seven hundred and fifty rupees. Half programme means it will be over within three hours.'

'Recently in the hotels they have thought of what they call full meal and limited meal. I hate it. When once you sit down to eat they should serve you till your stomach is full. They must serve again and again until you say enough and then they should serve curds and sugar,' I said.

'How can an artist live if he does as you say?' She said.

'What are we lacking now?' I asked back.

'We are staying in a rented flat. Aren't you ashamed? Should we not buy a big flat of our own with four bedrooms?' She replied.

Gradually, she implemented another method. She ensured that the anouncer at the time of the programme should mention that they could not be grateful enough to Smt Champa Mohan, the wife and the inspiration of his music for making him available for the programme. She would write down these instructions. They were completely involved in taking good care of her, leaving out no service and civility though it didn't matter whether my comfort who was the actual artist was taken care of or not. The local connoisseurs who wanted to listen to certain ragas from me had to send her the list and I could sing only if she permitted. The news spread in the music world that nobody had the right to ask me directly. All these were changes that had taken place without my knowledge. I used to keep silent, not knowing anything. Saying that the artists are delicate like flowers with soft temperament, and unless they are protected from the mad rush of people towards them, art would not survive, she took the position of a saviour and a protector and having created a position superior to that of mine, she clung to it tightly.

After mastering the music programmes of Bombay and Western India, it was not difficult to conquer other parts of the country. By then my fame had spread to Delhi as well. Nayak got in touch with the organisers of the Delhi Shankarlal Music Festival, through some locals and suggested my name. He saw to it that I got the time of midnight. The Bageshree that I sang there won over not only

Delhi but the entire North India. With Nayak's contacts, the music critics of Delhi newspapers wrote ecstatically and put me on a high pedestal. After that, the requests started coming from Calcutta, Lucknow, Allahabad, Varanasi, Patna, Bhuvaneswar, Cuttack and even from Bhopal, Gwalior and Hyderabad etc. With each concert the rates kept increasing. One thousand, one and a half thousand, two thousand rupees, the amount was increased by Champa. The music associations agreed. What was given in one place became the standard amount for the next. In Kurla the newly formed Goodwill Co-operative Housing Society was paid half the amount in advance and a four bed room flat was bought. The other half would be paid in instalments. I also began to ask myself whether I, by myself would have done all this. Her dictum that an artist needs a protector became mine also and took the form of 'Yes, it is absolutely necessary'.

ၒ

Champa got pregnant after three years of marriage. It could have happened earlier. But it was her decision that her child would be born in her own house. Only after we had moved into the flat with two balconies, did she cohabit without any contraceptives. Her pregnancy was a great celebration for her. She got immersed in it. Her mother visited, took her daughter to her home, preparing all kinds of dishes that the daughter was fond of, and taking her to the specialist doctor, indulging in guesswork whether it would be a boy or girl, deciding on the principle that if there was discomfort in the left side a girl or a boy if there was discomfort in the right side. A lovely sari which would suit a pregnant woman. Buying new ornaments. She entered a new world that had opened itself to her.

I was not unhappy with her pregnancy. I was perturbed. Ramkumari had also got pregnant at the same time. I was afraid. I was making love to her only once a month and that too only once. I had not taken any precaution. I didn't want that she should get pregnant. I was not afraid that she might. That possibility never occurred to me. This is another example of my irresponsibility. The next month when I went to pay her the money, she herself revealed the news and I drew a deep breath. What to do? When she said, 'Bakula is alone.

God Shani, because of lighting gingilly oil lamp had granted a brother to her.' There was satisfaction on her face. She caught hold of both my hands. 'You have not given me up though you have married someone else.' In her grasp, she made it clear that they were man and wife. I couldn't think of anything to say. I didn't feel like closing the door of the room. She also didn't ask anything. She didn't reveal any greater expectation. She said, 'We should go to the temple and light the lamp together, perform puja and receive the prasadam.'

'Yes,' I said.

She didn't specify when and I also didn't mention anything. I asked her to bring Bakula. She came running. I made her sit on my lap and gave her the peppermint packet and started out. She was five years old. Not yet admitted to school. Which school should she be admitted to, who should take her there and bring her back, these thoughts had not occurred. Ramkumari was assured that God Shani had opened his eyes and when they were fully open and looked at her, everything would be fine. I kissed Bakula on the forehead fondled the tresses of Ramkumari and came out. Even after a week, her pregnancy was bothering me. When she delivered what should be written in the column for father's name? This was bothersome. Shall I take her to the doctor and get the pregnancy terminated? This thought occurred. Champa now trusted me enough to let me go out by myself for a short while. She would give me ten or twenty rupees pocket money from time to time. I was confident that I could take out a loan in secret and there were people who would give it to me.

Two days later I went to Borivali. Bakula was not at home. Happiness showed itself on Ramkumari's face, who saw me just after ten days. I took her on my lap and caressed her. I felt happy when I had her sit on my lap because of her thin and light body. Champa's body was so big that I couldn't even imagine making her sit on my lap. After talking about this and that and the trials and happiness of life and the education of Bakula, I said, 'Look, it is difficult to bring up many children. How about we get this accidentally acquired pregnancy removed by a doctor?'

She looked at me with fear and wonder and said, 'We should have taken care earlier and avoided the pregnancy. Getting the foetus removed after it has occurred is a sin. I will not come. I would rather starve and feed that child or work somewhere and bring the child up. I am not working anywhere only because you asked me not to.'

The next morning when I was practising in the music chamber when the solution occurred suddenly. Even if I hide it now, one day or the other Champa will find out. If I say that the child is not mine, it is as good as saying that Ramkumari is a whore. If I tell her myself, Champa will shout. Let her. For the first time I had the courage to face her. If I delay it might vanish. She had made it a rule that during the morning practice not only should the door of the music room, but even the door of the bedroom should be closed. Sleep at that time was necessary for a pregnant woman was her wise thinking. I blurted out, 'Are you listening? I must tell you a bit of news. Ramkumari too is pregnant. I suggest that it should be terminated but she refused.'

She was awake. She asked, 'Who is Ramkumari?'

'My wife.'

'Who is your wife?'

With the onslaught on her voice I realised the reality.

'My first wife.'

'Come here.' I went up close. 'Sit here.' I sat next to the bed. 'You have only one wife. The one whom you married. The one who has been registered. You have no connection with any other woman. What is your responsibility if she has slept with some other man? Why did you tell me that, ruining my morning sleep?'

Though I understood that she was suggesting that I could slip away by saying that it is not my child, I got another wave of courage and said, 'She is not the kind of a woman who sleeps with any other man. I used to make love to her everytime I would visit her to deliver the money.'

She didn't reply. She was hissing and fuming inside. Then, 'You betrayed me though I was giving the money out of pity. That child will not live. Her first child also will not live. This is a curse. This is my curse. I have a prophetic tongue. So the curse will definitely come true.' She joined the fingers of both her hands and bent them noisily. Then she started weeping aloud. Then in the midst of her spasms she said, 'One should not weep with a three-month baby in the womb. If something happens to it, you would have committed a sin. This is the child who will carry on the name of the Mohanlal family. Not a child born to some concubine.'

I was perturbed. When I realised that the child in her womb was also mine, all my courage vanished. Not being able to reply I just sat there with my head bent.

She didn't talk about this subject again that day. When we went to bed together that night she playfully caressed my hair and said, 'I am worried about the reporters. I was keeping silent because I didn't want to disturb your peace of mind and create problems to your practice by letting you know that musicians like Gulati, Vyas, Jaffer and others are so envious of your great success at such a young age, that they are spitting poison. Those who cannot surpass in your superiority in music will be waiting for an opportunity with this kind of news to harm you. It is even possible that they have already employed a secret agents to watch you. What will happen if the print media give a big news item that you have a bastard child? All newspapermen don't listen to the words of my father. If it is known that you have done such things, will my father continue to respect you? If no respect is left he may even stop speaking about you to the newspaper people? Newspapers might stop writing a critique of your concerts. Or, they may write a bad critique.'

I was frightened. What if my name is trampled on the ground! The thought itself made me shiver. She was moving her hand through my hair—sort of touch therapy—as if to give me a secured feeling. In a short while though she slept, I couldn't. What a blunder I had committed. Though I was cohabiting with Ramkumari, why didn't I take any precaution? I criticised myself. In the morning while sipping tea she said, 'I will give one thousand rupees. Meet some doctor in Borivali and tell him that you are a coolie, that your wife has become pregnant, that you have no means of bringing it up and that she won't listen to you. You tell him that you would bring her to him under the pretext of some checkup, and request the doctor to remove the foetus secretly. You put one thousand rupees in front of him, he will agree. You do this.'

I saw a way out. I put one thousand rupees in my inner pocket. While travelling by local train to Borivali, I remembered Ramkumari's words, 'Care must have been taken earlier. Getting an abortion is a sin. I will feed it by staying hungry myself. Otherwise I will work somewhere else and bring up the child.' I felt that getting her aborted without her knowledge, when she wanted to retain the child was a bigger sin. Let another child come. It's enough if care is taken hereafter. I got comforted. Which newspaper fellow is going to write about such things? People come to listen to my music. Nobody will give up the pleasure of music, filling their minds with such gossip. It doesn't matter if no programmes are obtained in Bombay or Delhi, Calcutta and Varanasi. How vast this country is! I got courage. I got off in Borivali and walked about for two hours, sat in a tea shop drinking tea. I didn't see Ramkumari. I felt embarrassed to go in and see her. I was a bit afraid. I boarded the train and returned.

'I consulted four doctors. They said that a law had been passed that her signature should be obtained, giving her consent, and without it we cannot proceed.'

When he said this, Champa reacted, 'You should have frightened her by telling her that the pregnancy was shaky and it was dangerous both for her and the child.'

'I said even that. The doctor said, "Are you asking us to tell lies? We will hand you over to the police."' I put the money in front of her. She couldn't think of any other means. Or, at least immediately. Her eyes filled with tears. Thinking that it was accepting defeat if she wept in front of me, she turned her face and went to another room.

Next morning after she performed the puja for the idol of Lord Ganesh as usual, she told me, 'Come here.' I went. She said, 'Bring the tambura and repeat what I say.'

I realised that it was a word of promise I was giving before god. I also realised that it was something to do with Ramkumari. I said, 'You tell me first what it is. Before making a promise one must understand its full text and meaning.'

She got angry, 'Then you are not going to stop seeing her?'

'When did I say that?'

'Then promise. You should never see her again. If you see her, her child will die in her belly itself. Sankalpa Ganapati has given me this boon. It has been informed to my inner self.'

'Then when it has given you the promise, why should I give the promise again? You have told me. You leave it at that.'

She pulled me, caught hold my right hand and placing it on her belly said, 'This child will die. That also Ganapati has said. Do you want to save my child or do you want to kill it?' She started weeping aloud.

The size and shape of her belly looked like the round hollow of the Miraj tambura which I was holding in my left hand and my mind was perturbed. I began to ask myself a number of things. Is her swelled stomach equal to the size of the tambura? Was it Lord Ganesh speaking to me through this message? Was it equal to a symbol? In addition, her crying with her shaking belly. Without knowing what to do I said, 'All right, I won't see her.' I did not realise the truth at that time that she was telling a lie in the name of Lord Ganesh. I realised it a week later.

When I recalled that my word of promise, that I would not see her again sank into my consciousness, Tipnis changed sides. What a lucky fellow to be able to sleep peacefully as if he was on his bed. Now he is fifty-five, then thirty. Along with the memory that twenty-five years had passed, the explanation also occurred, that perhaps I wanted relief from looking after the pregnant woman and caring her and shouldering the responsibility afterwards. My mind had used a lie. A fat woman with a big stomach. When pregnancy was added it was natural that it looked like the hollow of a tambura. What an idiot I was not to realise even this much. Shall I wake up Tipnis, I thought. If you have to escape from memories you should talk to somebody or sleep. But the memory of this fellow persisted, the trust and friendship of twenty-five years. Though three years earlier that he was my accompanist, friendship really established itself twenty-five years ago. Without an opportunity to trust, how can friendship strengthen itself? I could tell him anything, he would keep it to himself and never squeal on me. Otherwise how would I be attached to him? How many harmonium accompanists in Bombay wanted to accompany me permanently and how much they tried!

The programme of South Delhi Music Circle was arranged. Six-months pregnant Champa could not travel that far by train. How nice it is to travel without her! I am free! I could just sit next to the window of my first class compartment and without any interference by anybody I could look at the trees and the vegetation, the hills and the rivers, the bridges and the cattle, the fields and forests. How elaborately the ragas would open themselves! In each swara these trees, the cattle, the deer would appear in different shapes and in that absorption, passing of hours of time was unnoticed. God, give me an opportunity to travel alone without her hereafter. Then, Tipnis would have a third class sleeper coach ticket but he would come and talk to me.

After the programme of the music circle at Kailash Extension, was it Srivastava who requested, 'Panditji, my mind has decided that you should sing at my place and sanctify it. It seems your reservation is for the night train tomorrow. I will get it changed for the day after or any other day that you suggest. We must have a chamber baithak at my home, tomorrow evening. Twenty of my friends. All of them are aficionados. Not just amateurs.' How pleasant the private baithak was, bringing about the experience for the first time, how nice it would be if this woman was not there who thought that she was the boss. What freedom, what respect! For the first time I experienced this.

It was during the return journey that a place was reserved in first class for Tipnis also and while sitting together, after crossing the Faridabad border, my heart opened itself out for the first time and I talked to him.

'Rajaram Rao, I will tell you something which I have not told anybody. Will you keep it a secret?'

Rajaram caught hold of my hand and said, 'Nurse no doubts about my integrity.'

'You may know about my family problem.'

'Just a little.'

'What are the things that you know?'

Hesitantly he said, 'You were married and had a girl child and then you married a second time.'

'How do you know?'

'Everybody in the music world knows. Nobody speaks in your presence.'

'Oh, is that so!' I was surprised. I was ashamed but I was also relieved. 'Do you know that I don't have any freedom?'

'The music audience of the entire country knows it.'

'Yes, isn't it so!' I became aware of the stupidity of my question. 'Rajaramrao, I will give you the one thousand rupees that I got from yesterday's chamber baithak. I will give you the address of the Borivali house and the landmark. You must take the money to her. You should not mention about the private performance to anybody. Champabai will call you up asking you why there was a delay in returning. You should simply say that there was a mistake in the reservation. This should not be known to anybody. Not even to your wife.'

Saying, 'Don't worry,' he again put his right hand on my hand and said, 'These are the fingers I use to accompany you.' He has kept his trust for twenty-five years.

In these days how many people are there who have such principles! While thinking this, I remember how good it was that Champa was pregnant. She was fixing up telephone, correspondence etc., by sitting at home and deciding on my programme and monetary details, but while travelling outside I could come to an understanding with the organising secretary and get five hundred or a thousand without her knowledge about the private sittings also. Rajaram himself said, 'Panditji, I don't know if Ramkumari has the knowledge to look after the financial affairs by herself if you pay in such lump sum. You will also not get the proper account. There is a bank near my house. You open an account giving the address of my house. I will deposit the money you give in that account. When there is a need, you sign the cheque which I will prepare. You will have control and if you give a fixed amount to Ramkumari nobody will know.' Yes, a real gentleman. I can keep an account of the money given to him but whether it was given to Ramkumari his word was the only proof.

'Good morning. It is light outside. In an hour our flight will land at Frankfurt. Breakfast will be served in five minutes. Please straighten your chairs.'

He looked at his watch. It is still showing New York time. Was it a difference of seven hours between New York and Frankfurt? I must ask the air-hostess. Yes, seven hours forward. Didn't realise when the sun came out. He remembered, he had sat with his eyes closed, and without removing the curtain of the window. He woke up Tipnis and both of them went to the toilet in a hurry and came back.

One must wait for four hours in Frankfurt. When he was washing his face vigorously, he felt like singing something. There was no tambura. Tipnis's harmonium box had been deposited along with the luggage. Also, he was afraid. If classical Indian music was sung in swara and alaap at this airport of White people, would they tolerate it? But the mind was full of dullness. There was a feeling of sadness. If I do not sing at least a little, the sadness will augment. He confided in Tipnis. Saying, 'Come, I will take you to a place,' he made me walk for a furlong and took me to a lonely corner. This airport was covered by transparent glass walls and ceilings. We sat next to each other on chairs. There were around forty-five planes in two rows. It was cold outside and warm inside. Though the passengers were moving about, since it was a corner, there was not much noise. 'Don't sing aloud. Just give it a soft expression. I can understand. You imagine that I am accompanying you.'

'What shall I sing?'

'It is so cold outside and it is morning. Intone Aahir-Bhairav. It is suitable.'

Mohanlal started intoning softly. The shruti was pure. The concentrated gaze of the eyes of Tipnis was holding the shruti like a pair of tamburas. His pointing fingers were indicating through their movement, the taal. The singing which started in a low tone continued in the same pitch and voice. Though there was tiredness after having travelled all night without sleep, he could easily find the mandra-shadja. Within a short time he got a feeling that he was singing without any inhibition. The singing went on with the safe assurance that there was the support of the harmonium and the beat of Tipnis. Even the madhya and drita-laya tanas emanated. His mind was at peace. When he looked back he found some seven or eight white people who were standing silently and listening. One of them said, 'Great!' in English. Another said, 'Cabello'. Yet another said, 'Quelle Belle Musique'.

Chapter 5

I

It was a week since his return from New York. In addition to telephone and electricity bills, the tax objection had also arrived. Twenty thousand rupees had to be arranged immedietly. But there was no music programme scheduled in near future. Had been away for two and a half months and now there would be no performances in the rainy season. There was no other way except asking for a loan from Tipnis. He may not express it in so many words that he had lost thirteen thousand dollars i.e., three lakh and ninety thousand rupees in gambling but he would think so, and this saddened me. Let him. He can be thinking so many similar things. Is it new to him that this Mohanlal is an irresponsible singer without any restrains? He consoled himself.

I have not kept back even a single rupee I have borrowed. Then why this obligation? Also, I always offer to pay an interest which he had refused. I am not at fault. He is increasing his income by not wasting a single pie on frivolous things and investing everything in compound interest. What does it matter if I borrow a little money now and then? Have I not been getting him programmes, no matter where I was performing, by insisting that only he should accompany me. This feeling of having helped him also came to my rescue. Just when I was about to pick up the receiver to dial his number, the phone rang. Could it be Rajaram? When I picked up the phone it was him.

'Hey! Rajaram, you will live to be a hundred. I was just about to dial your number when you called.'

'Will you be home? I am coming over.'

'Don't say home. Say flat. For you it is home.'

Mohanlal's pointing out this difference was not new to Tipnis. Having heard it for many years, its pain also had been blunted. He said, 'For everything there will be its own freedom and its own happiness!' Mohanlal was mollified. 'If there is someone else it will be a bit awkward. It's a private conversation.'

For these words of Tipnis, he replied, 'You know that there are three separate rooms in addition to the hall. Don't you?'

Sometimes Tipnis used to come to this West Bandra flat to play cards. Never would he come without calling in advance. Though it is a common practice in all big cities to call up the person earlier, making sure that he will be at home and free and desirous of meeting, Tipnis's special care was his awareness of the delicate situation at Mohanlal's place. Usually, he would walk all the way from his home in Mahim. But today he had taken the train for the first half and walked the other half. After the customary polite exchange and tea and biscuits, Tipnis said rather hesitantly, 'Bakula had come. It seems she is getting married.'

Softly he uttered, 'Is that so?'

Tipnis noticed that Mohanlal's face had withered. He had expected this reaction.

'It seems she was waiting to fix up the date after your return.'

'Isn't she married yet?' After he said this inadvertently he thought he had put his foot in his mouth. Though the question that if she had married wouldn't he have known about it, he could only be ignorant about it, for how and who should have informed? The fact that all these years he had not tried to find out about Bakula made him feel guilty. Tipnis was sitting silently. How old is she? She was born when I was thirty. She is marrying at thirty. Why hadn't she married all these years? Rajaram would know but he wouldn't speak. He might if I asked him. Who would take the initiative? How could it happen if someone did not take the responsibility? That was the reason why she had not been married till then. He felt a little more depressed inside. It was twenty-four years since he had seen her though they were staying in the same city. The ninth station from there. It was ten to fifteen years since he had got into a local train. If you get used to travelling by taxi even the memory of the local train brings fear and disgust. She was six years old. She used to play in the lower lane. She would come running if she heard that her father had come. Not for the love of peppermint but for the love of her father. Her eyes would reveal this. My own eyes, nose, eyebrows and forehead. Champa had me swear on Sankalpa Ganapati, on the tambura and her pregnant belly which was like the hollow of the tambura. And more than anything else on the foetus that was still in Ramkumari's womb. Later, I found out through Rajaram that she had a baby boy. I didn't even go to see the child. If I had, I was afraid that the child's life itself would be blighted. I did not go to see in the child's own interest. Bakula also blurred out of my mind. Having left Bombay and pure music for three and a half years and settling in Delhi had caused forgetfulness. After having come back, I had distanced myself both from her and from Champa. This woman Champa, was collecting money for daily livelihood every month and she was still doing so. That woman didn't even ask for her basic right. I also didn't send anything. How is the boy? He must be twenty-four years old? Rajaram would know but he wouldn't speak unless asked. Why didn't I ask him? Mohanlal asked, 'Is the date fixed?' and then said, 'Me?'

Tipnis did not understand the meaning of this question. 'Me?' What does it mean? Could it be, 'I should decide the date?' This hazy explanation occurred. He said, 'Is it not the father who has to take the responsibility and decide. Shouldn't the invitation be printed in the father's name?'

Mohanlal became excited. He felt as if his throat was choking, when he thought that the six-year old girl had still retained the same affection. Not only the wedding invitation but the father himself performing the kanyadaan was ideal. He thought that she was a girl following the tradition.

'Tell her to come and meet me here. Does she have a telephone?'

'Not at home. The office has a phone. She is employed in the administration office of the Century Mill. Secretary. She has completed her graduation.'

He was happy. 'Oh! Then she must be intelligent. Who has fixed up the bridegroom?'

'It seems they are colleagues. They have decided themselves.'

'Even better.'

Tipnis couldn't say anything more. He was aware that if he said anything more he would have to enter into private matters. With the satisfaction that he had achieved more than he had expected, he diverted the conversation. His wife's uncle's son lives in Surat. They plan to start a music association under his leadership. If it is inaugurated by Pandit Mohanlalji, they will get good publicity. Many people will become members. But right now, they don't have enough money. You must kindly receive a small token. I have agreed to accompany you on the harmonium without any money. When the association grows economically they will requite this help in a big way.

'Rajaram, I had stretched out my hand to call you to ask you for a loan of twenty thousand rupees when you called me.'

'They can't afford to pay twenty thousand.'

'I did not say twenty thousand. I only mentioned my problem. You know, don't you, that my present rate is one lakh rupees?'

'One lakh is not enough for you. Putting a price on your music is a fool's job. But in Surat there are really some artistic-minded listeners.' Tipnis knew by experience that this transaction could not be decided just at one stretch. Saying, 'Think about it. We will talk again,' he got up. He was confident that this man would agree.

5

Mohanlal was excited by the sudden news of his daughter's wedding. She has completed her graduation. She is a secretary in a private company. Not bad. If she is waiting for my return for fixing her marriage date, she must feel some kind of love towards her father. Will I be able to recognise her if I invite her to come? She might recognise me. She might have seen my photograph in the newspapers. She would definitely have seen me on television. Is she even interested in music? When she was a little baby, her mother would lay her down in front of me when I tuned the tambura. She would listen to the strum of the tambura for hours without crying and her eyes would open wide when the crescendo was reached. One day, when I cast tanas in six aavartas of drita-gati, she started crying thinking I was scolding her. Her mother came and took her away, embracing her lovingly. Had she grown up with me, she would perhaps have learnt music. I felt sad. So many girls come to learn but none of them has the ability to reach perfection and carry on the name of the guru, even though I taught without any reservation. When I realised that the other musicians started training their children at an early age and mastered them with the family knowledge of music by the time they were twenty or twenty-four. I realised that I had nobody, and this saddened me more. But after about an hour of being depressed I told myself that such musicians would not teach their secrets to others and I had never done such a mean thing. When I teach, I lay bare all the secrets in great detail. What can I do about their learning capacity? With this self-justification sadness was abated but I was not happy. I was sixty. Not one disciple to take my name. Then I thought that Madhu might grow as a student. Coming once every three months, spending two weeks at a time and along with that she had the effective method of taking the whole thing, every movement, its explanatory aspect of theory and the possible mistakes on tape. I believe that Vikram sends fifty cassettes from there every time. A good husband. That's the way to encourage the wife. For many husbands there is an inner suspicion if the wife goes to learn music. All kinds of restrictions. How can she learn with so many restrictions? How can she grow? Madhu is a fortunate girl. It seems her husband has released her from the responsibility of child-bearing also. He has a greater guru-bhakti towards me than a student. He touched my feet with fervour when he performed the namaskar. In her case, one week was enough for each raga as the practice would be for seven to eight hours and the telephone connection was also unplugged. Each time when she comes, why only two weeks, she should stay for four. If I have a programme during that time I could attend the programme and come back. Let her keep practising. Or, let her come to the programme as well. By listening to a live concerts, the methods and nuances of music would be understood. By singing the same ragas in the concerts, they would settle firmly. Her name also would be better known. In the whole of America the only pupil who is worthy of perpetuating the name of Mohanlal is Madhumita Shah. When the thought occurred that she was his first important pupil, he wondered why she had not yet called him. He thought at least Vikram should have called. He felt like calling her. Now it would be midnight there. Why should I spoil their sleep? I will call tonight he thought. Suddenly Madhu filled his mind. It was as though she was singing with him. He imagined that when she was struggling to produce the most intricate structures, he was expatiating and unfolding the swaras involved. Her knowledge of the swara was very subtle. Mad girl. Suddenly she got the crazy idea of marrying and left. Had she stayed right here, by now she would have been completely trained. When he thought that, he consoled himself thinking that it was a good thing to find a husband like Vikram. Madhu filled his mind. No other woman would offer herself so completely. Not like Bhairavi. No, like Kalyan. In Bhairavi the pull of separation and pity are more. The line between devotion and love is a very thin one. As in the case of Meerabai. There are many sides to Madhu, the softness of a newly married girl, shyness, fear, expectation, the desire to dedicate herself to her lover and the wish that the lover too should dedicate himself to her...Madhu has them all! In addition there was the basic quality of living in peace and supporting family life. Training her in Raga Kalyan and making her sing along with me was not an accident. It was a choice in keeping with her inner nature. It had happened without my conscious knowledge. While lying down, memory of her strong and delicate body was winding around me. What beauty, what tenderness, the embrace of the lovely arm raising from nishada to rishabha and delicately descending to shadja! In spite of the intensity of the swaras a delicacy and a tenderness. Bhairavi does not have the strength to give a firm support. While not only the organs, the nerves and the veins, but even the bone structure is delicate, how can support be obtained? Kalyan is all right.

'Madhu, hereafter your name is Kalyan. No, the name is not all right. Kalyani as it is called in Karnataki. Kalyani, when you are there, it is Kalyan in your embrace. There is auspiciousness in being united with you. The feeling of marriage in the evening. Moving my fingers in your thick hair there is the taraf of minute strings fixed below the main strings of sitar resonating Raga Kalyan. The sparkle in your eyes revealing shyness. Come quickly. Not for two weeks but for two months. Let us just stay together. Not just staying but I will teach you. I will give you practice. The mere pleasure of the body that is not inspired as music is for ordinary mortals. Not for artists. You are also an artist. One who gets inspired by my speech after understanding the words, female swara that inspires.

Let it be night. There it must be morning, and you will be alone at home, I will call you. I will call you by the name I have given you and explain all the nuances. The entire evening he couldn't think of anything else. Couldn't even remember that Bakula was waiting for his return regarding her marriage.

At ten in the evening the phone was dead. Though I meddled with it in a number of ways there was only silence. Not a single call had been received since afternoon. I had also not called anyone. I don't know when it died! These Indian phones. I believe in America it never conks out. Not even for a single day. Even if I lodge a complaint, they would not be able to do it before tomorrow. This made me feel disappointed. I could go out and speak from the telephone booth but she couldn't reply to that number. Supposing I called from here and took some time, let alone speaking for a long time, even speaking for a minute would cost me more money than I had in my pocket. If Rajaram brought twenty thousand rupees I could spend one thousand and speak to her for fifteen minutes. Anyway, he realised that if he went to the booth and lodged a complaint right now, he might get his phone fixed early next morning. He put on his sandals and went out to make the complain but found out that his phone had been disconnected due to non-payment of bill. He gritted his teeth and cursed them. Even if I paid the bill, they would not restore the connection the next day. They would put it into their list, give it to the communication section and those people would move very slowly. If I said I was Pandit Mohanlal, nobody would care. These people don't know anything about music. This Wadekar Master should have made sure that my bills were taken care of when I was out of town. I decided that hereafter before going abroad I will personally settle everything.

He went to bed with the conviction that calling Rajaram the next morning at seven was the only way out. Again, Madhu occupied his mind. Out of the blue, he remembered something. Why hadn't she called me at New York after two weeks? Was she angry because I had said that I would myself call her when I was free and asked her not to call me? Besides, what else could I say? Bhoopali would be with me. She could understand Hindi. At that time Madhu's call would be a problem. I should have called her myself. I didn't. My mind was occupied by Bhoopali. I felt so irritated that the appearance of any other swara would spoil the purity of the raga. While singing Bhoopali, we should completely be dedicated to the movement of the swara. When singing Kalyani, we should offer ourselves to it completely without drifting into another raga. Specific mantras should be chanted while worshipping the specific deity. One should not mix up one mantra with another. With this comparison it occurred to him that he had completely offered himself to only two women: Manohari and Bhoopali. It was fifteen years since Manohari's turn was finished. Yet, what an intense offering it was! I had never given myself to Madhu the same way. Since this afternoon she has occupied me intensely. She has ignited the fire of separation. She has become a raga by herself. She has seen to it that Raga Kalyan could never be sung without her memory. He realised that she has personified all the aspects and moods of that raga. Madhu, you are greater than all these. You are the one who has to perpetuate my name. See to it that it lives. Not just as a pupil of Mohanlal but you should give publicity to a whole method which could be known as Mohanlal Gharana. If the name of the place is required, call it Hardwar Gharana, no Chittarpur Gharana. Madhu, you are my tambura. If I am with you the happiness greater than the comfort of shruti would emanate.

३

By the time I finished my shower, the door bell of the flat rang. When I looked through the wire mesh from the top of the door, I saw him waiting outside for payment. Twenty-four years old. Week-long stubble. Crop cut with fairly long hair. The large build of the mother. Jeans and a white shirt. A hat like the one worn by cricket players. Mohanlal opened the door. That youth came in and said, 'Hi, Daddy.' The son addressing the father like this upset Mohanlal. According to him, who was in the music world, touching the feet was the only way of greeting. But this fellow would not listen to his words. Besides, Mohanlal also did not feel a compulsion to teach him proper behaviour. Right from the beginning, his behaviour was strange. When he was six years old I got separated from his mother.

Had she brought him up by speaking well of me instead of spoiling his mind against me? She would send the son only to collect money. No money had been paid for three months. Oh, I have forgotten. Borrowing twenty thousand from Rajaram was not enough. Three months payment for these people was in balance. Thirty thousand rupees. When I remembered this, it occurred to me that when both the children had finished their education and had reached majority, wasn't it enough to pay only the wife? For how long should these children also be paid?

He came inside wearing his sports shoes and sat on the sofa without taking them off. He started the conversation, 'Mother had called twenty times yesterday. This morning also, after trying twice, she sent me here.'

'It has been disconnected for not having paid the bill.'

'Couldn't you have made some arrangement before going abroad?'

'If money was available, there are twenty people right here who could have remitted. The question is having the money...' he gave a straight answer.

'It is a week since you returned, isn't it? Why do you need so many days to get the dollars converted?'

'The American president did not give me any dollars. Did your mother tell you to ask this question?'

'Why should mother say anything? It is commonsense.'

He looked at his wrist watch. 'I must go to Brabourne Stadium now. I was ready to go there when I was sent here with the instruction: "It is one week since your father came back. For three months, money has not been paid. Whether the phone is dead or it has been put aside to avoid my call, there is not a pie at home. Go and get the money." Give it quickly, it's getting late for me.'

When Mohanlal said, 'I am figuring out how to pay the telephone bill...' he felt ashamed.

'How should we have been managing for three months?' He asked.

'When you say "we" you mean you and your sister, don't you? You are twenty-four years old. You have completed your B.E. It is six years since you attained majority. Get a job somewhere. Your sister is twenty-two. Four years since she became an adult. She has got her

M.A. She must also get a job. For the upkeep of your mother there is the interest on the fixed deposit.'

'Dad, I also have some self respect. I don't wish to be under your obligation. But a father should act with responsibility. Any respectable father would not say you have turned eighteen now I don't have any obligation towards you. Merely finishing B.E., and getting a job immediately does not raise a person to a high level. A post graduate degree is a must. You also know that if you don't have a foreign degree it has no value. I have to study in England for two years. Getting a seat is my responsibility. But seeing me through the course is your responsibility. All the musicians, when they go on a foreign tour, earn in dollars and put their children there to study. Am I not your son? Now, give the money which you have brought from America. I am going to England this year itself. You go on a tour every year. How does it bring you credit if people say that Pandit Mohanlalji's son is working in some company. You think about it. Be reasonable.'

Mohanlal understood that he was putting forth this proposition only after consultation with his mother. Though he thought he could have arranged the money, he didn't want to succumb to his son's demand. He became firm. This fellow says England. All the people who do engineering are running to America. When he asked him, his son replied, 'America is a country without culture. I prefer England.'

'What is culture?'

'In that country there is no cricket. Only games that ruffians play like soccer and basketball. England is all right. I am good enough to become a university captain there. It is not difficult to convert the dollars you give into pounds sterling.' He stood up and said, 'It is getting late for me. Will you pay now? Or, like every month send it by messenger? I have no time to come again and again.'

'You ask your mother what happened to the bank interest. There is no need for you to come.' When he said this, not knowing what to say his son left.

When he looked at him from behind, he remembered that he had the build of his mother. The height, the breadth, the size, everything. Mohanlal felt, how can this fellow play cricket? Was it not during the pregnancy of this one that Champa had make him swear on her round belly that he would never see his first wife again and if he did this child would die but also the child Ramkumari was carrying and her daughter too. The question arose whether these oaths would ever be effective, or true. Every time you get into a bus or train or even walking in the bazaar, how many times does one hear the swearing in the name of god, the mother, the speaker's own name and the name of the person to whom one has spoken. Do they all keep their word? Are they all dead? Anyway at that time I believed and followed it. But did I really believe? Or did that belief come to my aid to cover fear? I gave Ramkumari up. But not completely. Every month I would be send enough money through Rajaram. For how many years? Till I went to Delhi, five years. Still, I did not visit them. I did not see the children on account of the fear that they might die. Here, Champa was busy with the celebrations and rituals related to the birth of the baby. Compliments such as, this child, like the father will be a great singer and this girl will surpass her father. Even her crying is like music! Flattering words like these and the names that she herself thought of Swarmohan, Shrutimohini. Even I got enamoured by the activities; singing and rocking the cradle myself. Amidst this, the memory of Bakula who would just be rolling on the floor without the comfort of a cradle listening to my daily practice. Ramkumari had named her son Kishan. This is what I had heard from Rajaram. I didn't go to see the child's face. Hadn't seen him either. By the time I remembered that I stopped sending money after going to Delhi, I saw two gentlemen coming in, who looked like someone coming to schedule a programme. They stopped at the door and asked, 'Is your phone out of order Panditji. We have been ringing since yesterday. Got tired and came to meet you personally.' He decided to accept without bargaining no matter what the amount was. But the very next moment it occurred that if he accepted a lower sum, then everybody would offer only that amount. Anyway, Rajaram would surely give me the money. Besides him I have plenty of people who can give me a loan of twenty to thirty thousand rupees. So I got wary of not giving in to outsiders and for a lesser sum. But those who came in after touching the feet kept standing with great respect and said, 'We have started a small music association. We will invite great singers like you in the future. Now please give us a message for the inauguration. We will write it down.'

I felt as if a bucket of cold water had been poured on my head. But without giving up good manners I dictated a message of congratulations and good wishes and sending them away locked the door, got down in the lift and went to the phone booth. Tipnis answered and said, 'I have been trying since yesterday evening, your phone is out of order. Bakula had called again. It seems the invitations have to be given for printing today itself. There is another thing, very urgent.'

'You remember I had asked you for twenty thousand yesterday. Now please bring thirty thousand. They have cut off the connection for not paying the bill. We will talk in person. If you don't have cash at home, please bring it from the bank. I will pay the interest.'

'No, no interest from you? It's out of the question.'

'I won't give you the interest. But I will pay the interest that the bank charges. You see, business is business. Friendship is friendship. Come quickly,' he said.

Now, after Tipnis agrees I will send her only ten thousand rupees. I will tell Champa to consider this as payment for all three months. How long can I support you when both the children have grown up and completed their education.

At the most, Rajaram might come in an hour. The necessity that within that time the details of the invitation must be settled did appear. Let them use my name, what is the problem there? I wanted to say yes. It seemed that it was like lending of my name for the good wishes for printing by the visitors who had come just then, but it occurred that this was not so easy. If the invitation was printed in my name I must go personally to give away the bride. I felt that I had lost the right to perform this religious duty, standing with her mother. Not only that. I also felt a bit afraid to face her. It was twenty-four years since I had seen her. She had brough up her daughter well, and all by herself. Now, not only can't I stand next to her to perform the ritual but how could I even meet her gaze and say that I was her husband? Not just shame but cowardice. Was it my daughter's wish or her mother's that the invitation should be in my name? Or was it just a way of looking respectable in the eyes of the bridegroom's parents! I realised for the first time that it was easier to face Champa than Ramkumari. Now, she is forty-nine. I wonder how she is. She must be still as lean as before. There was no way of her putting on weight. It was natural to put on weight if like Champa she was getting ten thousand rupees a month, plus the bank interest, a four-bedroom flat and it seems she was also teaching music at home. Ramkumari's life was not like that. The skin would have become rough and black. Perhaps grey hair might have started appearing and not knowing how to dye it, and perhaps unable to afford for such things, her age would be prominently visible. Who else knew better than me, how many different ways rich women use to look young? It is only after they reached middle age that women get the courage to deal with men, breaking the social hesitation and shyness. A woman like Ramkumari wouldn't be aware of any such things. He asked himself for the first time whether she had remained pure. One couldn't say. Though the experience of life told him that, after all when I got away from her she was only twenty-four. This thought was perturbing to the mind to accept. What did she do for money and what did she do for her physical desire? Though these precise questions occurred, it was not possible to continue with imagination and, were left at that, and he took up the question of Kishan and what he was doing. Anything but playing cricket, he thought. Didn't know where and what type of wedding had been arranged. Or had they desired to print the invitation in my name so that I could bear the complete responsibility and the total expenditure! Another thought flashed. If I had not lost three lakh and ninety thousand rupees in the gambling, I could have performed the marriage in a magnificent manner and lessened my sense of inadequacies of all these years. Though it was not the season of concerts if I had not gone to America and stayed in India, in three or four programmes I could earn that much money.

४

Tipnis came holding a bag which looked as if there were vegetables or old clothes in it. When he travelled by train this was the sort of bag he used to carry to protect himself from pickpockets. As soon as he came in, he took out three bundles of hundred rupee notes and putting them in front of Mohanlal said, 'Please take this thirty thousand rupees which you asked for. Another important thing is look here' and saying so he took out a packet from a bag. Meanwhile Mohanlal said, 'That's all right. I have thought about this thing. Let there be no invitation in my name. I will give one lakh for the wedding expenses. If I had more money I would have certainly given it. As far as money is concerned you are the saviour. You are the one who has a deposit in the bank. If you agree to be my guarantee, I can get a loan of one lakh from the bank. As soon as I get a programme I will return the money. I don't have a deposit of even a single pie. So I don't want to lose face by asking the bank.'

Tipnis turned in his direction. There was a question about his decision. 'It is true that I have a responsibility. It is also true that I have deviated from it. If I go to the engagement ceremony, as it is a part of a religious ritual I will be embarrassed. They will also be embarrassed. You please take the money and give it to her mother.'

'Bakula is desirous that you should perform kanyadaan with your blessing.'

He said, 'Tell her to come here with her husband after the wedding. My blessings are always there.'

Mohanlal understood from the expression on Tipnis's face that he was not happy. Without allowing room for further talk he said, 'You said there was another important thing. What is that packet?'

Tipnis loosened the tight rubber band and opened it. There were six cassettes of Mohanlal's singing and a beautiful photograph of an expression of absorption in music, shot between twin tamburas. Another picture of his casting tans like a hurricane with his hair flowing about wildly. Another one with his right hand lifted to the sky and showing the extent of the emanating sound. And all the six photographs in various poses. He took each cassette and looked at the back of it.

The name of the raga had been mentioned on the wrapper at the back. Below it, it said 'Harmonium accompaniment - Rajaram Tipnis. Tabla - Omkar Prabhu, Editing - Smt Champa Mohan, Production and Distribution-Mohan Melodies, Bombay.' Very attractive printing. Below it price. Sixty rupees.

After he had examined all the six cassettes, Tipnis said, 'Do you know why I have brought this? My name is mentioned as harmonium accompaniment. It is true that I have played the harmonium. So has Omkar on the tabla. I talked to Omkar also. He was also surprised. These production and distribution people have not taken our permission. They have not paid any royalty to us. We have not signed any agreement. Yours is a different case. It is a husband and wife affair.'

Mohanlal was speechless. Though he understood what had happened he didn't know how to react to it. Tipnis himself continued, 'Mohan Melodies, Bombay means only Champabai. I listened to them. I can recollect from memory what ragas you sang and where. You never sing any important raga for less than an hour and a half. She has edited it to twenty five minutes and has put down her own name as the editor. She has cut off the hands, legs, ears and nose of the ragas and shortened them. Have you given permission for this? And second thing. Similarly, how many cassettes has she released, what is the sales income from it, what is the amount due to me and what is the penalty for having brought them out without my permission? I have decided to go to court. Who is going to bear the expenses if one goes to court, for all the wasted time spent, the court charges, the trouble to be taken to prove that the opposition is telling lies, who is to bear all these expenses?'

Automatically certain words came out of Mohanlal, 'I must also go to court against this shameless woman. Or, break her legs.' His dumbness broke. And the second sentence also took shape. He got up, went to the telephone directory and searched for the number. Even that number was in his own name. He noted it down on a piece of paper went down the lift to the phone booth in the street and pressed the buttons. It was her own voice. In a gasping voice he said 'I am Pandit Mohanlal speaking.'

The reply came quite quietly, 'I am Mrs Mohanlal speaking.'

He was confused. He didn't know why he had to wait for a minute. She reminded, 'Did you hear?' He brought out certain words 'Since when are you doing this stealthy job? How much money have you stolen so far?'

'Pandit Mohanlal's wife has never done a stealthy job. Never will. Say what you want to.' She asked quite calmly.

'What are these Mohan Melodies cassettes? Whom did you ask to bring out the cassettes? Where is the agreement for it?'

'What agreement is necessary to do that? In our marriage itself all these agreements are already incorporated. I searched for them and produced them lest some people might copy them unauthorised and sell them privately. If I hadn't done it, would you have done it? If it was to be done why wasn't it done all this time? It seems a mad husband demanded from his wife as to why she washed his dirty clothes and ironed them without his permission. Your talk is like that. I know that in the past you gave some cassettes to sell. Do you know how many cassettes they sold and for how many they gave an account? Tell me when did the phone get repaired?'

'Don't change the subject. The permission of the harmonium and tabla accompanists has not been obtained. They have not been paid.'

'You do that. You talk it over with them about the amount. Do you think it is possible to discuss these things over the phone? Come home, let us talk. When I have done something with devotion to preserve your music for future generations, you are talking about agreement and all. It is early in the morning. Have you learnt to get drunk right in the morning?'

'No, I don't drink like that.'

'Then why are you talking like that? Come home and talk.'

He couldn't think of saying anything. Just put the phone down. Walked in the street and went up to the flat by lift and relayed the conversation to Tipnis and added, 'You see, she always makes me feel I am in the wrong. If somebody else listened to us they will get the impression that I am the culprit and behaving madly and she is a noble wife. That's the way she turns around any conversation.'

Tipnis knew the background. Mohanlal would mention sometimes the circumstances under which he married her and the aftermath. After thinking for a minute Tipnis said, 'Mohanji, I will tell you something very clearly. Will you please not misunderstand me!'

'Come on tell me, tell me.'

'She can prove that according to law she has not made any mistake. Even the telephone is in your name. Which means that you live there? It is as if you have accepted the fact. The telephone bill has been paid in your name. In front of the flat, the sign board says, Mohan School of Music. Which means that you are running it? Her marriage to you has been registered. If something happens to you, both the flats will go to her. Now, the flat she has in Kurla is in her name. She has told everybody that it is a flat built for her by her father. She has seen to it that according to law Ramkumari and her children get nothing. You also don't attach your name to your daughter's wedding invitation. You have decided to give her one lakh and wash your hands.'

'Hey, how is it possible? I have married by tying the mangalasutra in the temple of Amba-Bhavani. She is my lawful wedded wife. After knowing everything please don't hurt my feelings.' Mohanlal's voice sunk and there was helplessness in his eyes.

Tipnis was aware that he was speaking to a famous musician whose concerts were greatly admired by the music lovers and as his accompanist he should not indulge in more cruel criticism, so merely said, 'I spoke about only how Champabai might argue according to law. Not only I believe it. If need arises, I am ready to speak for you and give witness in whatever way you want me to. But the law does not consider just or unjust and will not bother about the actuality. So, what you should do is to get hold of a good lawyer and strengthen your own position. You have to make it clear that you have two flats in Bandra which in today's market will cost at least forty-five lakhs. You are sixty. Who knows how many years of life a man has? Have you got your horoscope? There is an astrologer in Mahim whose name is Suryaprasad Shastry, who has a very good reputation. If you show him your horoscope, he will tell you exactly what will happen in which year. He will tell you when your life stops. He will give in writing that his calculation does not cross the particular year.'

'How can I get my horoscope? You know about my childhood.'

'Then, show your hand to a palmist. There is a man called Ksheerasagar in Mahalaxmi. What he told me twenty years ago has come true. Then he was sixty-five. We don't know whether he is alive or not. We should go there and find out.'

Mohanlal said, 'Yes, yes. Please do it immediately. I feel my stars are not right.' He felt he had seen a way out.

ड

After Tipnis left, the thought to show his palm to a palmist was haunting on his mind. In each area, there will be ten people announcing themselves as palmists. But one who can forecast accurately is rare. Long time ago, he was in the habit of showing his hand to palmists. In Calcutta one palmist had said specifically, 'You are a musician. You have the luck of women's company.' It happened like that and it is still happening. When I was thinking if a person who could predict so accurately could be consulted, even a thousand rupees may be given for his prediction. When I was entering his shop, I was humming a tune to myself. I was also wearing a laced jubba of a musician. I had long hair. Was it possible that he had made a guess on the basis of this? Then is all palmistry a hoax? My mind did not want to reject this as hoax completely. Let Tipnis make enquiries. What's his name at Mahalaxmi? Ksheerasagar. If he is alive I will go and show him my palm. I will go alone by finding out his address. A person who goes to show his palm should not take anyone with him.

Next afternoon, the phone rang at 3 pm. As soon as I picked up the phone a woman's voice said, 'Your connection has been restored.' Though I cursed them as bastards, it occurred to me that if they did not do it how many people would pay the bill on time and I forgave them. Then I called Tipnis. The answer came, 'I had called seven or eight times. When did the line get connected? It must be just now. I enquired with the bank. Lending the money to someone else on my standing as guarantee and before that you should open an account, all this is something that cannot be done in a hurry. Don't I trust you? I will take the loan in my own name. You said, didn't you, that I must deliver the money to Ramkumari?'

'Yes, yes, my friend. It has helped me a lot. One lakh and thirty thousand. I will repay it as I keep getting money, including the bank interest.' He was filled with gratitude. That whole day it was the memory of Ramkumari. Twice during the pregnancy and the aftercare, staying in Champa's house and without her knowledge, my earnings from private concerts would be deposited by Tipnis and given to Ramkumari regularly. He was a truly trustworthy man. Friendship of how many years? He also went to accompany other singers. He was an accompanist capable of playing with a singer belonging to any style. But he is completely devoted to me. No matter how friendly, he would never cease to be polite. When he was thinking about the trustworthy qualities of Tipnis, Mohanlal remembered that after he returned from Delhi and started living by himself, he had never invited him home. He also remembered that earlier he would invite him home often. On the day on which he opened an account in the bank he had compelled me to take food in his home. His wife, an innocent girl who had just been married to him at that time, had prepared puris and served him with great aplomb and devotion. He had bought srikhand from Vadilal. He had also invited me for the naming ceremony of his child. Now and then, he would invite during feast and festivals. It became clear that after I came back from Delhi and started my free relationships with many women he had not invited me even once. My mind pricked me. He trusts me in all programmes, involving money matters and all other things. That's all. I felt sad that he did not have the confidence that this Mohanlal never even looked at the wives of his accompanists and friends who trusted him. I felt angry. He is very correct and meticulous in business. But he has kept me at a distance, feline fellow. All night it was bothering him. I couldn't even sleep properly. By the morning certain other parameters suggested themselves. He speaks admiringly of my good fortune with women, saying, 'Where is the attraction of a mere harmonium accompanist compared to that of a main singer. Who comes in search of me asking me to teach them harmonium as they do come to you to teach music?' I remembered this playful envy and his ragging me. Don't know why he has not invited me. Who knows really what household problems he may have! Mohanlal consoled himself.

At 8 am, Tipnis called, 'I thought the whole of yesterday. It is good if you meet a good lawyer and make secure arrangements for everything. Do you know anyone?'

'Don't know personally. There are some music lovers.'

'They won't do. It must be someone who knows the law perfectly. They must also work with conviction. The best is Gore Saheb. He also loves your music. When you built the two flats wasn't it him who gave instructions to the builder and helped you?'

'Yes, yes.'

'Meet him and tell him everything. You must see that Champabai doesn't bring out any more cassettes. For the cassettes which she has already done, she must give an account and she must pay me and Prabhu. Isn't what I am saying lawful?'

'Yes, it's perfectly legal. She must also shell out my share of the money. These two flats and all these must be properly secured. I will see him. I know his office. Kalbadevi.'

'When you tell him everything you have to tell him about Ramkumari also. I don't know if you know. She has been a cook at the house of Gore Saheb for the past seventeen-eighteen years.'

'Is that so? Did you know about it? Why didn't you tell me?'

'How could I take the initiative and tell you? I thought you might have known about it through some other source and you were keeping silent because you didn't want to talk about it. Now I will tell you. Then you had given me the assignment to go to Borivali every month and give her the money. I did it for five years and then suddenly you left Bombay and went away to Delhi. How could she make a living then? Where could she get money to feed her children? She told me that she could work as a charwoman but it was not enough to survive and asked me to fix her up somewhere with a job. You had one and half thousand rupees in your account but there was no cheque with your signature. Even if there was, it would be enough for three or four months. She is not educated. She doesn't know anything except how to write her name. What job would she get? Thinking that if I approached Gore Saheb, he might show a way out, I met him. He himself said, "It seems Mohanlal has left Bombay. The news is that he is in Delhi. To what level a great musician like him has sunk his music, by being a mere accompanist to a Kathak girl." Since he started this conversation it was easy for me. I asked if he knew about both your marriages. Yes he did. I said, you must kindly find a way out for the livelihood of the first wife. She is a village girl with no education. A good girl. She works honestly, I told him. He asked me to bring her there. I took her. Two children. An eleven year old girl and a five year old boy. If it was the job in a mill it was a duty of eight hours. Three to four hours to go there and get back. What would happen to the children? Gore Saheb himself thought about it and asked her, "Can you cook?" I answered, "She prepares very tasty food. I have tasted food prepared by her." "North Indian dal roti may be all right but how about our Marathi cuisine?" "Where is the difficulty for her to learn? She learns very fast," I replied in Marathi. Meanwhile Ramkumari added in Marathi, "Batata Pohe, Pitla, Amti, Poli, Aluchi Bhaji and Srikhand. I have learnt it from my neighbour." It meant going there at eight in the morning and returning at three in the afternoon. She adjusted herself to Mrs. Gore also. It was five hundred rupees in those days. Now, it may have been increased. Hello, are you listening?'

His throat had sunk to such an extent that he couldn't speak clearly. 'Yes, I am listening.'

'Without his help how would it be possible for Bakula to study and get a job? How could Kishan get a job?'

Mohanlal felt that he knew nothing at all about this. Nobody had told him. Gore Saheb had helped even after knowing about him. He had suggested my name to programmes. He had admired my music. When he remembered he had even once advised him, he felt that he had not been unjustly treated. But he had not been treated intimately also. It seems he invited so many musicians home for tea. I had not been invited even once. Was it because my wife works there and it may be embarrassing if we met face to face? Was it the attitude that 'I respect his art but not him?' Tipnis concluded, 'Gore Saheb knows everything. He has a soft corner for artists.'

Let everything go to the dogs. He thought about not going to see Gore Saheb, he who knows everything about me, if I mention one thing, he might remember a lot of other things. He might not speak harshly to me but he will judge me. Mohanlal was afraid, that Gore

Saheb who had placed him on a pedestal after listening to his music might bring him down. But if it is left just like that, Champa might swallow everything. 'Will she hesitate to do anything at all when she had shut my mouth with just one point that everything had been incorporated in the agreement called marriage?'

ნ

One day passed. The decision took shape. It is right to see Gore Saheb. At least the account of Tipnis and Prabhu must be settled; otherwise I will lose face. Knowing everything, I was still being treated with respect. Even a month before I went to America when I met him at N.C.P.A, what polite enquiries he had made! His fears receded. When he called Gore Saheb he told Mohanlal to come to the office at 5 pm. He had never gone to his office even once. What a big place it was! Four rooms. All air-conditioned. Piles and piles of books. The peon took him to his chambers. He himself stood up, welcomed me and asked me to sit in the chair opposite and kept standing till I sat down and said, 'Yes, please tell me Panditji.'

'Sir, I have heard that your time is very precious. For us sometimes even to find the shruti on the tambura it will take half an hour and after that to show shadja it depends on our ability. Delaying is our profession.'

'That is why I asked you to come at five. I don't have any other engagement this evening. No other client is waiting for me. How did your American trip go? A friend of mine has sent me the cassette of your concert at Chicago—the cassette of Jayajayavanti.'

'What did you think of it, sir?' My embarrassment was gone.

'That voice which sounded like a foreign-woman's and gave support to swara doesn't fit in. She doesn't know the feeling of the raga. The rest is nice. You had sung the same raga three years ago in the Gujarat Stree Mandal Hall arranged by the Santa Cruz Suburban Music Circle. I have that cassette also with me. The life-force that is in that cassette is not found in the Chicago cassette. I felt it was mechanical. I compared the two by listening to them one after the other. Anyway, every time the same vivacity, the same exuberance will not be there. How much did you earn and bring from America?

I am asking because I wanted to tell you how exactly you should invest it, keeping the long term benefit in view. Because hereafter you may go again and again to Western countries on music concert programmes. If you don't keep a proper account and not submit your income tax correctly to the government you will be in trouble. I am telling you because I am a tax lawyer.'

He felt like telling the truth. 'Sir, I had thirteen thousand dollars in my hands. I lost my head, went to Atlantic City and gambled away everything.'

'*Wah*! Great. You are a true artist.' He laughed with abandon.

With Gore Saheb's laughter Mohanlal lost all reserve and confessed, 'Sir, I have a very strange problem. There is nothing you don't know. You must yourself solve this problem.' It was not possible to talk about the second part without mentioning his first marriage and the children. Besides, the first one, since she was working in his own place, Gore Saheb would know about it more than he himself did. By the time he narrated the whole story of his estrangement with Manohari Das and coming away to Bombay and staying by himself, Champa asking for expenses immediately after that, the amount of ten thousand rupees per month for the past five years and her recent business transaction of making Mohan Melodies, by this time it got to be half past six.

'Will you have some tea?' Gore asked.

'If it is available close by.'

'There is an electric kettle. I have sugar, tea bag, milk in the fridge, everything. Our office closes at five. Everybody has left. I will prepare tea.' He got up.

'Then please don't bother sir.' He also got up with embarrassment.

'No, I also need it. It's very easy. Have some biscuits meanwhile.' He went to the next room and came back with two cups of tea. 'Now that you have told me everything, tell me what do you want and what I should do.'

'Champa says that in the marriage all other agreements are incorporated. I am afraid. My music and my two flats in Bandra should not go to her. I have the letter from her that states that the Kurla flat was also bought with my earnings.'

'If you decide to divorce her, all these calculations will arise. Otherwise you can deal with it by making a will. Since the Kurla flat is in her name, it cannot be included in your will. If you divorce and give compensation you can prove that the Kurla flat was bought with your own money. You say that there is a document for it. Or, it can be extracted in the cross examination. Now you decide what you want. I will introduce you to a reliable and able lawyer. This is not my kind of case. I am a tax lawyer. If you don't decide anything and keep silent you cannot prevent her from indulging in any kind of business. If you die, your two Bandra flats, your music earnings, your good name will all belong to Champabai. So it is best to decide and settle everything.' He looked at his face. There was confusion writ large on it. Gore continued, 'Even if your marriage with Ramkumari is not finally settled, those two children have the same right as these two. Do you accept that those are your children?'

Some more confusion on his face. 'Even if you don't agree, they can prove that they are your children. But the best thing is that you should mention it yourself. You should not leave it to the decision of the court.'

'If I accept that they are my children then I have to accept that she is my wife, won't I? If I do that I will be jailed won't I?' His face registered fear.

'You can accept that those two are your children even if she is not your wife. Since all your property is your own earning, even without accepting her as your wife, you can still give her a part of your property. Indeed, the whole property. The law is one thing. Your moral freedom is another. You first determine about the second. How to bring it into effect will be told by your lawyer. I will fix it up.'

All details were clear. He didn't think of asking any further details. After looking at his face for a couple of minutes Gore Saheb asked 'What's all the news about America? What is this thing called workshop? What did you do there?'

Chapter 6

I

After Mohanlal left, Gore Saheb closed all the rooms and locked the front main door with inner and outer locks. Since he had sent away the driver he had to drive the car. It was his practice to close all the windows, switch on the air-conditioner and put on a cassete of classical music. But he would not do so when he was driving. Now it was half past seven. It was difficult to drive at night. He was seventy. At his age though his limbs and eyes and blood pressure were healthy but the lights piercing from all directions like flood would trouble the eyes. Though he had been using this route for forty years, sometimes at night there would be perturbance. He felt that no matter how late it would be, the driver should not be sent away. He had not stopped thinking about Mohanlal. He thought that most artists were like this, without a clear thinking pattern. Some of them, though they were smart in their professional dealings, were confused in their emotional relationships. Should he have told Mohanlal that he had done injustice to Ramkumari and her children and he should mend the situation? He hesitated. In his long professional life he had never insisted on any client to do anything in a particular way. He remembered that he had always said, 'If you do this, this is what happens. The decision is yours.' But he became aware of the fact that this was not a matter only about the injustice done to the wife of a client. It was now eighteen years. She was a woman of thirty or thirty-one. A grey complexion which was neither black or white. There was more bone than flesh. Even in the face, the bones were prominent. There was not enough nourishment. But the eyes were shining. Will power. It was not just the will power of animal level. It was a strength of culture accumulated from thousands of years. That fellow gave up such a girl and married again. Then he left both of them and ran away with a dancer. Then, Gore Saheb didn't know the story of a second wife. Would he have employed her if she was not the wife of such a great artist? She was from the north. Didn't know our way of cooking. Suneeti said, 'No matter how much she learns, a non-Maharastrian does not learn to cook tasty Maharastrian food.' And so Suneeti had said no. He had told her that she would learn gradually. And what was needed was a trustworthy person, and had fixed up five hundred rupees though it was a bit more than usual. She was a woman who did not even know how much should she ask for. Then Suneeti had said, 'Why did you say five hundred suddenly? Isn't it too much?' He had consoled her by saying, 'She has to bring up two children. Poor thing, she is the wife of a musician.' What a mild-natured woman! No matter how much work there was she never complained. Within a year I had developed respect and affection along with pity towards this woman who was in such a difficulty, working so hard and bringing up her children and being so tranquil and calm. After she started working in our home her thin body filled up a bit. Even Suneeti's old saris looked nice on her as she had not developed a paunch. I started feeling like seeing her once just before I left for the office. If she was late, I would get restless. Why did this attraction start? I still don't know. I was never a womaniser. If I wanted, it would not have been impossible for me to be friendly with several good-looking and rich women. Moving about as I did in the world of women who had invested crores of rupees, and were coming in for tax consultation, and my acquaintance with the music world, but I never did. Why this attraction in my fifty-second year? Would I be attracted to her if she was not an unjustly treated wife of a musician? This question appeared. After struggling for a couple of minutes, it occurred that these were all matters of conjecture; questions of ifs and buts. More than her being an artist's wife she had a special appeal by herself, a dynamism, will power which was capable of attracting my respect. For me who had been born and bred in Bombay, her simplicity was attractive. Not just that the self-confidence that was reflected in her eyes and the assurance that she was totally trustworthy, were these the reasons for my attraction? At this time Suneeti went to Chicago to look after our daughter who had given birth to a child and I was alone at home. She had trusted Ramkumari and had given her an extra key to get into the house even when I was not there, cook and send me the lunch box and keep my night meal in the referigerator. But she started coming an hour early. When I asked her whether it wouldn't be difficult for her, she said, 'Madam is not in town. Who would prepare breakfast for you?' One day I asked her. My voice was shivering. She was kneading the wheat flour. I called out 'Ramkumari' and she lifted up her head waiting for my orders. 'I will ask you something. Will you promise me that you will not feel bad?' 'Please tell me master.' 'If what I say is acceptable to you, please accept, otherwise there is no compulsion. Don't stop coming here telling yourself what bad people these are. Promise that and then I will tell you.' 'I won't stop, my master. If I am responsible for your not having food, what hell will I go to!' For a minute when she looked at me. What a lustre on her face! 'That is why I am telling you beforehand that if you don't like it there is no compulsion. Don't think that I am taking advantage of my wife's absence and I have an evil mind. I am not that kind of a man. But still in your case my heart is very very...I don't know what to say. This is not going to be a relationship only until the wife returns. I will give you my office address and I will take you there once and show you the place. Once a week, in the evening you come there after half past five. Nobody will know about it. The salary that you get here from the mistress is separate. I will give enough to maintain and educate your children. Nobody would know about it. Your happiness and sorrow is mine. Think about it and tell me. You won't get pregnant. Don't be afraid. I am repeating this again. I am not a bad fellow.' By the time I said this, my throat was dry. If I continued standing there without giving her any time to think it would be putting pressure on her and so I came out of the kitchen and went to my room. That day I started late for the office. I didn't see her again. I didn't talk to her. The whole day I was wondering whether I should have broached the subject. Though there was a sexual urge, it was not only that. A kind of mental attraction which exceeded even the caution of why I needed it at my age. The next morning she didn't come at the usual time. I waited for ten minutes. Fifteen minutes. Half an hour. No, she won't come again. I was filled with the sadness that I had done an improper thing. She will tell Tipnis. He will decide that this Gore is also like the others. He will give it publicity in the entire music world of Bombay. Why did I get this evil thought? A kind of justification followed when I told myself that I have stressed that there is no compulsion and what I wanted was a long-term friendship not the satisfaction of temporary bodily need. No matter how much I thought about it, I couldn't understand what attraction this woman did have, the education, the complexion, the facial expression or any of those things which were not there in Suneeti. Though I sat in the car listening to music, I was filled with the feeling of defeat. She had condemned me by indicating that she would accept her own poverty and not cross the threshold of a mean fellow like me. In the office, I had no interest in work. That afternoon the lunch box did not arrive. Yes, she had rejected me. After Suneeti returned if she asked me why Ramkumari had left, what could I say? What if one day when I was not at home Ramkumari came and told her what sort of a fellow her husband was. The mind was perturbed. Though I was sad that I had done an unbecoming thing, I was not angry with her. Had I just tried to misuse her difficult situation? Indulging in self-criticism till the evening and denouncing myself at night, one part of my mind was justifying that I had not stooped to a mean endeavour. She didn't come the next day also. Nor the day after that. Supposing I concocted a lie to tell Suneeti that Ramkumari had stolen my watch with a gold chain and I had dismissed her and had not complained to the police as she was a poor woman. Tut! What a mean thing to do. I should not descend to that low level. When I was cursing myself like this, on the fourth morning she came at eight, with a bag of vegetables in her hand. With her head bent she went straight to the kitchen and came out with breakfast and a cup of tea. Placing them on the table she stood behind me when I was reading my paper and said 'Saheb, the breakfast will get cold.' Then she left, closed the front door, stood behind me at a little distance and said, 'Saheb, the bad woman that I am, I have made you go without food for three days. Please forgive me.' When I looked back I saw that both her eyes were filmed with tears and her voice was wet. I had got back my life. I asked intimately, 'Were you upset?' She simply addressed me as Saheb and wept profusely. Then she came up to me and touching both my feet said, 'A great person like you asking for my friendship, truly I am lucky. I know that you don't flirt with all kinds of women. I thought about it for three days. I went to the temple where I was married and prayed. That fellow has done this to me. Though I am here with his children, he married again. He even left the town. What is wrong if I married secretly? Last night the goddess appeared in my dream and told me 'each person's paapa and punya is that person's only. You don't do anything bad. Your boss is a good man. Tell him. You serve him with devotion.' If I make a mistake you please correct me. If you feel like taking me please do so. I am a village girl with no education.'

'I will tell you tomorrow. Be calm.' I told her touching her left shoulder. That first touch was very pleasant. I thought about it the whole day. She had not left the job. There is no need to tell a lie when Suneeti comes back. There is no lacuna to trouble me from inside. It was clear that she would accept it if I told her that what the goddess had told her in her dream was only what she thought about during the day. There is nothing wrong with it. If I told her the next day, she would offer herself tomorrow itself. I could start for the office a little late. Or, I can tell her tomorrow and wait till the day after. By then she would have fully reconciled. Her belief was natural, considering her background. It seemed a satisfactory plan to give her four day's time when she would come out of her belief. But when I went to bed I asked myself for what intention and why I should uproot her belief. To make her offer herself to me? I thought it was mean on my part. It was not new to me that the concept of god was a deceit or fraud, created to keep the poor in the state of sleep and ignorance. I had read it in college. I had also heard it in the study circles outside the college. I don't know whether god exists or not. Even if he does, does he say that we should not have a secret relationship without harming anyone? Is it god's duty to watch our secret meeting in the office and punish us? This question arose. For a long time I couldn't sleep. No answer did flash. The next morning she came a bit early. She didn't take the initiative to talk. She prepared a special shira with plenty of dry raisins and cashew for breakfast. Even the food—curry and aamti—which had been prepared for the night was very tasty. He could have talked to her after the breakfast telling her that what she had experienced in the dream was not the voice of the goddess but just her own mind. But a greater responsibility appeared. If I tell her what I am thinking, that is, destroying her god who is giving her strength and establishing myself in that place. Do I have that capacity to give comfort to her external and internal problems? I may pay her a lot of money without anybody's knowledge. Once a week I can give bodily pleasure. She has not become mad because of her craving for her bodily comfort. Somehow she has controlled it. I am luring her into it and creating a necessity in her. I felt that I was the sort of fellow who was converting a good family woman who was earning her livelihood with honest work, into a secret prostitute. What nobility is there in this relationship? This was another question. I did not utter a single word. She started churning out really tasty dishes. I began to love my food. I got a feeling that she was getting close to me. From that day onwards even when I listened to good music I could only see a noble emotion. The thought of not using Ramkumari for an improper relationship began to gain strength. In the same circumstance Gore Saheb listened to the tapes of Mohanlal sung in various concerts. All the ragas reflected only noble emotions. A feeling of elevation. When a relationship takes place with a woman, it should be noble in nature. What harmony exists in the relation with a poor woman who is used by promise of economic support? This thought started getting stronger. A fortnight elapsed. Meanwhile, I was also not in town. I had already given up this proposal. But I had forgotten to mention this to her. One morning when I was having breakfast, she asked, 'Sir, do you like my cooking?' I turned in her direction and there was an intimacy in those eyes. I said, 'It's very good. I have started eating more because of the good taste. At my age, too much eating is not good for the body.' I could see confusion on her face. She asked, 'You are not displeased, are you?' I couldn't immediately understand the implication of the question. Was she trying to ask me why I had kept quiet after my proposal. Did it mean that her desire also had been awakened and she had been subjected to neglect? I did not at that time realise that a woman never says anything directly. I said, 'No displeasure, when goddess herself has told you in the dream, we should not get displeased, should we?' There was no clear indication about what she was thinking.

From that day another question started bothering me. I had mentioned that I would help with the education of her children by paying separately every month if she agreed to this relationship. Wouldn't it bother her and make her sad to think about how separate help would have been forthcoming if she had agreed? Whether the actual relationship took place or not, even a proposal is a relationship in itself. In a week, my mind was made up. The decision matured. I called her, 'Kumari, come here.' She came from the kitchen and stood near the dining table. 'Here, this is five hundred rupees. Keep it safe. You open an account in a bank near your house. I will give you money like this every month. After Suneeti comes I will tell her to increase your pay. Whatever you can save after household expenses, deposit in the bank for compound interest. Come to my office once a month after five in the evening, I will give you money there. Let us talk about our daily problems. Let there be no relationship that is not approved by Amba-Bhavani. Let your problems be mine.' She didn't touch the bundle of currency notes on the table. With tears in her eyes, she said, 'When you are there to look after my problems, why do I need money?'

'Yes, I am here but it doesn't look nice to pay you in the presence of my wife. You just do as I say.' When she came to the office she would talk about her problems—children, their education, the husband who deserted her. Before she left, she would remove my shoes and socks. She would put her cheeks one after the other on my feet. It was not pure surrender, but intense devotion, and love. She would establish a contact of touch between my feet and her cheeks. The door of the office would be half open. It would not be difficult for me to close it completely, and touch other parts of her body. But my mind would not agree. There was the hidden consciousness, if the relation is reduced to the level of the body, the sublime emotion of Bhairavi would degenerate into ignoble abyss. Even the awareness would be an indivisible swara of Bhairavi. She doesn't know music. She doesn't know devotional literature. She had only heard of the name of Meera Bai in the bhajans in the temples. But the experience of the touching of the cheeks and the feet was a kind of experience of surreal for both of us. It is a feeling, a feeling of being mutually melted and becoming one.

Where am I? I have not yet reached Dadar. Broadway Shopping Centre. On so many days he had taken her in his car, dropped her at Dadar station and while getting off from the car, she would touch his feet and when he was wondering what kind of relationship this was, the question arose whether Mohanlal who creates such noble emotion in ragas had ever experienced such a noble feeling in real life. The ways of the artists were not new to Gore. Where do these feelings come from? Where do they dry up? What is the relationship between the life of the artist and these? Does the life of the artist resemble a mound of sand which is dry in a minute after the rain stops? Questions after questions followed. Suddenly the car in front stopped. The car in front of that also. The scream of horns of the outside vehicles were audible even inside the air-conditioned car. May be it's a stupid traffic jam. When he was thinking this he thought what a careful girl she was, not creating the slightest suspicion. How carefully she has conducted herself. One day when I brought her a gold chain, she had great happiness on her face. Though I was feeling romantic and wanted to put it around her neck myself, I resisted the temptation. She was so happy, as if her dream had come true. The next day when she came home with empty neck except for the black-beaded mangalasutra. She came quietly to me when I was reading my paper and whispered, 'The mistress has gone to take her bath. Please don't feel unhappy as I am not wearing your gold chain. If I wear it, she might ask where I got it from, how much I paid for it etc. The neighbours also will ask. Why do I need a gold chain? I have hidden it away to give it to Bakula when she grows up.' When I remembered this, the car in front moved a bit.

Chapter 7

I

When Tipnis went to Borivali, he couldn't recognise the place. The place was known not only as the end but was not even considered a part of Bombay at all. Now, it is as crowded as Dadar and Parel. It was difficult to locate the house of Ramkumari after sixteen or seventeen years. He thought that he should have asked Bakula for the directions from the station. Finally, he found the place. Yes, this is the place. When he climbed up the second floor he saw the nameplate outside, Bakula Lal and Kishan Lal. There was a calling bell. 'Behenji, can you recognise me?' The hair near the ears had turned white. The face was not withered as it was before.

She could immediately recognise him and said, 'Tipnis Saheb. Today is an auspicious day. The dust of your feet has sanctified our house. Please come in.' There was enthusiasm on the face. Gratitude. The inside door had been painted with emulsion. A sofa which could be converted into a bed at night to sleep. A tambura in the corner. Opposite there is a kitchen. On the side a door leading to what looked like a room. On the upper portion of the wall on all four sides, longish cupboards. In another corner a Godrej almirah. Next to it an ironing board. All the facilities adjustable in a small place, typical of Bombay could be seen. Ramkumari who knew what he was thinking said, 'The children have done all this.'

After the formalities were over Tipnis said, 'It seems Bakula is getting married. Mohanlalji has sent this for the expenses.' He opened the small box, unlocked it and raised the lid. Inside there was a folded white towel. When it was moved aside there were ten bundles of currency notes. Hundreds. He took them out, put them on the teapoy and said, 'One lakh.' There was confusion and surprise on Ramkumari's face.

'Saheb, who told you that Bakula is getting married?'

'She had called me.'

'Had she?' Not knowing what to say, Ramkumari became silent. It looked as though her face was perspiring. 'What had she said on the phone?'

Tipnis immediately understood that there was some problem here. He felt he shouldn't have got entangled in it. But having come so far and having even brought the money if he didn't say anything it could be covering up. And if anything else was said it would be like lying. He understood this and said, 'Mohanlalji had gone to America. It seems Bakula waited for him to come back to take care of the wedding invitation. She may be shy to meet her father directly and tell him. She called me and asked me to. She even met me. Asked me to get her father's consent. He has sent this money for the marriage expenses.'

It was painful for Ramkumari to understand the situation. After a little while she asked, 'Is he going to be associated with the wedding invitation?'

Tipnis found it difficult to give a direct answer. He said, 'I don't know. He didn't discuss it with me. He asked me to deliver this money.'

'Saheb, you are afraid to speak the truth. That is why you are saying you don't know, isn't it?' He looked at her face silently. It would be embarrassing for him to say anything more and get entangled on either side.

A minute later Ramkumari herself solved the embarrassing situation. 'Tipnis Saheb, your name is Rajaram bhaiyya, isn't it? You are really my brother. You came every month for five years and gave me money for my livelihood. Afterwards you showed me a way for livelihood by introducing me to Gore Saheb. Now the children can be on their own. Afterwards, I don't know why you stopped coming home. Now, please put back this bundle in your box and lock it. If the children come home and they see it, they may object to my sending it back. How can the children have the self-respect of a person who has struggled hard? I have saved money for the wedding expenses. Look at that almirah. I have even got gold and silver jewellery from time to time for the girl.' He sat quietly. A minute later, she bent down, took that box in her hand arranged the currency notes inside, covered it with a towel, closed the lid and said, 'Please lock it. If accidentally in the rush in the local train the box opens, you won't even find one bundle.' He locked the box on both sides.

He made polite enquiries 'At what time do you return home everyday? How is the work in Gore Saheb's place?'

'Please sit here and keep talking. I will cook quickly while talking with you. You must have your dinner here.'

'I will come another day just for dinner. I am expecting someone to come today.'

'Why will you come another day to a poor woman's house? Afterwards I also didn't ask the children to call you up. Now, I know how to call. I will prepare pohe at least. Just five minutes.' She got up and went to the kitchen.

'Does the tambura belongs to Bakula? Is she learning?'

'There is a person close by. His name is Bijapure. If she feels like she goes on Sundays. She doesn't practise regularly.' He liked the pohe prepared by her. He said that he had not eaten such delicious pohe and asked her for a second serving. She said, 'I learnt all the cooking at Gore Saheb's home. Both the husband and wife are very good people. No problem of any kind. They never interfere.' She expressed her admiration and gratitude. When he left she took leave of him by saying, 'Please keep coming. No matter how late it gets, I will be back around half past three.'

Ƨ

The anger which had been suppressed till Tipnis left came back in five minutes. She thought that after working so hard in other people's homes to bring up her children, the result is still the same. The invitation has to be in his name. Though I had firmly told her that, even kanyadaan should not be performed by him, this idiotic daughter of mine has contacted Tipnis Saheb. She thought of asking Bakula to get out of the house immediately. They say that only daughters understand the difficulty that mothers face. It is all false, false. She brooded again and again that the daughter herself was the enemy of the mother. Let her go to hell. Let Kishan get married and bring a daughter-in-law. I will treat her as my own daughter. A daughter should be like Pratibha Bai, Suneeti Tai's daughter. Though she has come from America she herself stitches the falls on her mother's saris, repairs her blouses and teaches me how to prepare new kind of soups for her father. Has this Bakula ever cooked, even on a single day? Her clever way of escape is, 'Mom, I don't know how to cook as well as you.' Now, how is she going to cook for her husband when she sets up her family? With these thoughts she started cutting the beans very fast with the knife that Pratibha had brought from America. This horrible girl, even without telling me has approached Tipnis Saheb to recommend her to her father. That fellow sent one lakh and a word that he would not come to the engagement ceremony. Wasn't I right in sending the money back? How much is one lakh anyway? She calculated. It is one hundred thousand rupees! One thousand rupees interest per month. She thought of a way out. After my death from whom are you going to beg? Three thousand rupees interest per month. If you have a roof over your head, the son and the daughter-in-law have to give you food. Don't ever spend the principal. Don't tell the children about the bank account. Now, if I take it out of that amount will one lakh be enough? Supposing I told her you have been working for so many years. You take care of the marriage expenses out of that amount. Where can I get it from? How much I worry about her. Bakula moves only towards her father. Let her look after the expenses. Why should I spend for this also? Was it the right thing to send the money back? Should I have kept quiet as it was her father who had sent the money? Would her doggedness stop going to her father thinking that her mother had spent so much for marriage, Ramkumari wondered. One lakh. It was not a small amount. One thousand rupees interest per month. It flashed that she should tell Gore Saheb and ask him whether what she did was right. She went to the hall and looked at the clock. It was 7 pm. She remembered that he had mentioned that on some days he would stay in the office even after seven. She told herself that if her stars were good Gore Saheb would be still in his office. She came to the hall, took a little change, locked up the house, got down the steps and thought of calling up from the shop of Bhai Kaka. No, someone might recognise her there. She didn't know anyone in Bapat Road. She walked a furlong on the road behind, turned left again and entered the glass telephone booth, closed the door and pressed the buttons. It was Gore Sahab. 'You are lucky. I was at the door. In half a minute I would have left. What is the matter?'

When she addressed him as 'Master,' she couldn't help crying. She cried profusely. 'Kumari, tell me. You were all right this morning when I saw you.'

Consoling herself she said, 'I came to tell you. This evening the harmonium master Tipnis Saheb had come. Mohanlal had sent him. It seems this girl had asked him.' And she narrated everything. 'Was I right or wrong in sending back one lakh rupees? Please tell me.'

'You did a good thing. I know that you always do the honourable thing. You did the right thing in not touching his money who says that he will not come to the engagement, not even to the wedding and wants to terminate his responsibility by simply paying money.'

'Even if he comes to the wedding and performs the ceremony of giving away the bride, I will not stand with him. He may be the father of this girl but he is not my husband.'

'Still, on such occasions you have to stand with him for half an hour. You must understand the feelings of the girl.'

'You also say this?' She was angry. She started weeping. Her voice became feeble.

'Come to the office tomorrow evening. Let us talk. Be calm till then. Don't touch the deposit in the bank. That is for emergency. I will pay for the marriage. Don't use the money which your daughter has earned. This is your final responsibility. These days, children spend recklessly. Don't give room to it and perform the marriage economically. Tell them that it's all you can afford.'

'Please don't pay again and again yourself.'

'Where is the question of again and again? It is only once that a daughter gets married. A son's wedding is not your responsibility. Let him spend from his own savings and get married.' Meanwhile, somebody tapped on the glass door of the telephone booth. There were three people waiting. She said, 'I'll come tomorrow,' and put down the receiver. She felt relieved. Tomorrow when I put my cheeks on his feet all my sorrow will be over and I will know what to do. She asked someone in the street what time it was. He said quarter to eight. She would have to go home by now. She became aware that Bakula might ask where she had gone at that time. She went to a vegetable vendor and bought lemon, coriander leaves, curry leaves and took them home.

Bakula had just come home. She had brought five or six cassettes and had put them on the teapoy. As soon as the mother came, she piled them up so that her mother could not see them. After the mother went to the kitchen, she took those and went to her room. 'Room' meant seven foot long, four foot wide partition in plywood. She had got it painted to look like a wall. She had insisted that a girl should have a separate room to herself. It had a cot measuring five and a half feet long and two and three quarters feet wide. In the upper part of the wall a series of compartments had been made. There were some boxes under the cot. Though the mother grumbled when it was being done, now she has accepted that it was a good thing. By the time the cassettes were hidden, Bakula changed her clothes and came out, mother was ready with food. She asked, 'Shall I serve you or are you going to wait for your brother?' She replied, 'I am hungry.' After she took the plate in her hand and sat on the sofa, Ramkumari said, 'Had you gone to him without telling me to recommend you to the Gawaai?' For half a minute she didn't understand and then did—completely. Mother always referred to father as Gawaai. She will not refer to him as your father. Ramkumari never called him her husband. Bakula understood that after she met Tipnis and called up there was some development and this question was a preparation to talk about that. Though she wanted to ask her just to tell her what the important matter was, she would get more angry. Realising that she who had said this much would continue further, she was silent. Mother came out of the kitchen and asked, 'Do you have any self-respect? Is it a lie that I brought you up? Hadn't I told you that I would get you married according to my means?'

'All this you have said several times before. Tell me what happened now.'

Meanwhile Kishan came home. He understood that some exchange of words was going on between his mother and sister. He felt he shouldn't have come at that time. But how would he know that this would be the situation? He had grown six inches taller than the elder sister and had long hair. Jeans. Loose fitting shirt. Sports shoes for the feet. A leather bag in his hand. He had thought that mother would be comfortable if this girl got married and left home. The mother thought of stopping the conversation since the son had come. But he should also know what the matter was. She thought that it was good to tell them both at the same time. 'You take out your shoes and wash your hands and feet. Food is ready.' He did likewise. He put the clothes on the hanger and hung it on the wire which had been tied from wall to wall high above their heads. He went to the bathroom, quickly had a cold water bath, wore a lungi and by the time he came back the food was ready on the teapoy. He took it out, sat on the floor, leaning against the wall. He felt happy only if he sat on the floor. His mother narrated how Tipnis Saheb had come, what he said and how she returned one lakh of rupees—all this. She asked him, 'Is it right that this girl sent for the Gawaai without my knowledge?' She wanted justice.

The son was angry. 'It is true that he didn't look after us and bring us up. But now when he voluntarily sends not five thousand, not ten thousand but one lakh rupees, with what discretion did you send it back?' Now the mother understood the son's mind. If he had come earlier, she wouldn't have reported everything in such a straight forward manner. He didn't finish college. Still Gore Saheb had got him a job. A job which involves a great deal of running around. The pay was not bad. I believe that the Seth has told him that if he works honestly, his pay would be doubled in two years. But he is grumbling that he wants to give up this job and do business independently with one of his friends and complains that he has no capital. He doesn't save any money from his salary. Doesn't give anything for household expenses. She guessed that he was thinking that if that same one lakh had been given to him, he would have invested it in business and would became a millionaire.

'What else did Tipnis Saheb say?'

'Nothing. The Gawaai has given money. He doesn't know whether he will come to the engagement. I feel that he won't come.' Saying this she turned to her daughter and asked, 'Why did you go and beg him?'

'Why did you send back the money that father had sent for my wedding?' The daughter asked.

The son came to the rescue of the mother. He asked, 'If the money had been sent to you, why did Tipnis Saheb come to give it to mother? He could have called you directly and asked you to take the money.' But he turned on the mother all the same, 'You returned money which had been sent voluntarily. Now where will you get the money?'

The mother had the last word and said conclusively, 'I will spend what I have saved by cooking in other people's house. I am not going to ask her to spend the money that she has saved through her earnings. Nobody should say that what I did was wrong.'

३

Bakula went to her room, put on the light and closed the door. Though she switched on the table fan on the stool near her head, it was very hot in the room. Though a quarter of the window opening outside was a part of this room, there was no scope for cross ventilation of air. If I say that I will sleep outside, Chotu was ready to occupy this place. She remembered this was a room which she had designed for herself. The anger against her mother was increasing. Why did Tipnis Kaka come when I was not at home? She remembered that he had asked her at what time mother would be back home. He did not want to give me that one lakh directly. By 'he' I mean father, he must have instructed Tipnis Kaka to give it to the head of the family. When the money itself had been rejected how could he come to the engagement? How could he come for kanyadaan? Had she returned money so that he should not come? She got angry. This woman is stubborn. Did he leave her not being able to cope with this stubbornness and marry another one? She had newspaper cuttings. She took out a box from under the cot, opened the file and looked at each photograph. What moods. What an arresting expression. When she looked steadily at them her opinion was more confirmed that he had left this woman only because she never had the ability and the power to understand a great artist. She closed the file and put it back in its place and took out the cassettes that Avinash had given her. The seal had been opened. So he has heard them all. She understood that he had asked her not to open the bundle till she reached home because he wanted her to be surprised by her own father's cassettes. She took them out and looked. Each cover had a picture of him singing. She saw the inward look, concentration, the celebration welling forth at the hitting of a tana. And the look of a maestro expatiating on the emotion of the relevant raga. Rare pictures indeed. Each picture was good enough to be enlarged, glass-framed and hung on the wall. She looked at the rear side. The name of the raga, the name of the accompanists. Oh, Tipnis Kaka. Music editing: Champa Mohan. For a minute it stopped her breath. His second wife. She thought of her as a great lady who had searched, arranged, edited and recorded bits of music which would have been otherwise lost. She remembered how her mother was abusing Champa, the second wife in bad language until the daughter had asked her not to go on any more. She turned all the six cassettes which had twelve ragas and picked Raga Kedar. She wore the earphones so that nobody else would be disturbed and she started the small cassette player and lay down. Oh, what a beautiful voice. Just with the starting of shadja, the emotion of kedar would well swell up and envelop the entire atmosphere. Which other singer has this strength? Avinash, what other gift is there better than this in this world! It's great having agreed to marry you. You are the pefect husband for me. I love you, I love you, I love you. What an elevating emotion father generates when suddenly he rises from shadja to madhyama. Though the other singers follow the same principle, why is it that they can never generate this elevating experience. When she was thinking this, the alaap continued. She couldn't make out the intricacies of which swaras he was moving on. She remembered what her guru Bijapure had taught her and tried to recognise them.

> saa ma mapa dhapa nidha saa | saa nidha pa ma pa dha
> pa ma gamaresaa saa ma mapa dhapama pama re saa.

But she couldn't. It will be possible by constant practice in course of time. His statement that it was only after four or five years of constant practice that the knowledge of swaras became clear was true. In this job of a secretary of a private company, they squeeze the life out of you. Added to that the travel by local train. If she came home and sat down for practice, the silent antagonism of the mother. Even when she had to listen to the cassette, she would have to use earphones and the clarity would be lost and the ears would be tortured as if listening to a drum. When she was thinking this, the tri-taal Madhya-laya began.

s kaa s nhaa | re s ss ss | s nan s da s | nan s dana
pa ra ma ni | ran s ja na | he s du kha | bhan s jana

Just like what my guru had taught me, the Kana-swaras. Couldn't get the meend. Drowning kana-swara to meend like this was not possible for mere teachers. It required only great singers. Great singers like father. She sat up in bed and adjusted the earphone. *Wah*!

Along with remembering the swaras, she imagined that she was singing along with tabla and kept time by snapping her fingers and thumb. During this, the movement of the swaras of tana was not comprehensible. Still, as if she was accompanying the music without leaving out even a single swara, imagining this and following it up, involuntarily complimenting herself aloud by intoning *wah*! She became aware of her mother's shouting. She was also angry with mother. Stopping to accompany the music she started merely listening. She thought, what a precise and clear sound pattern even while singing in drita-laya! Remembering her guru's words that for those who had not perfected practice, if the speed increased, the places of the swaras would be jumbled up and she wondered how many years it would take her to achieve this precision. She was thirty. No daily practice. Though she practiced on Sundays, within an hour the throat would get weak. She remembered that her father used to practice for ten to twelve hours a day in the middle of the forest on the banks of a river. Silently she pulled out the box from under the bed and searched looking at the file of paper cuttings. Yes, here it is. In the article in *Dharmayug.* She read the entire article once again. What an achievement! What complete dedication. The photograph printed in the middle of the page may be old. But how handsome he was. What lustre in his eyes. She started staring at it with admiration. After a long time, she put back the file in the box and pushed the box under the cot silently. She felt like rewinding the cassette and listening to it again. Couldn't sleep when she started listening.

But I couldn't sleep. My head was full of Kedar. Want to listen to the same cassette once more. Whenever Pitaji sang a raga it was for not less an hour and a half. Even for oudava-shaadava raga like Kedar he would take not less than an hour. I asked myself why in this cassette, it had been reduced to twenty five-twenty six minutes and that too only on one side. They should have recorded it on both sides. I felt like opening the door, taking out the tambura, tuning it and singing Kedar. But I did not have the knowledge to expound it for more than five minutes. I was not sure whether I could do it even that long. How many months had it been since I tuned and strung the tambura! After I got involved with Avinash, I was coming home late every day. In the mornings I had to start early. Now, if I start playing the tambura, mother would scream. Even the neighbours. Mother hates music from the bottom of her heart. She didn't allow me to learn music till I started working and earning. Her fixed opinion was that all those who learnt music would get ruined. Starting to learn at the age of twenty-four, how much could one learn? The knowledge of swaras, knowledge of ragas and knowledge of taal must be achieved at a tender age. Just like a fish which starts swimming the moment it is born. Mother said, when Pitaji was practising on the tambura she would leave me around him and I would listen very quietly. Shouldn't he have had a desire to teach music, knowing that his daughter just loved it. Though he got married again shouldn't he have sent for me and taught me? He runs a music school in Bandra. Shouldn't he have said, 'Come and join the school?' Shouldn't he have at least sent for me? Suddenly she was angry with her father. She remembered that it was not for the first time either, she was getting angry. When I was in college I had gone to his concerts twice with Shakuntalaben Dave. She said, 'Your life is wasted if you don't listen to Mohanlalji. I will arrange for the ticket. You come with me. After that I will put you on the train.' I was also anxious to see him perform. I wanted to listen to him in person though I had heard him on the radio. I had told my mother that there was a function in the college and I would be late in returning and my friend would be with me. For Shankuntalaben, Pitaji was a big hero. No film actor could compete with him. Not even a cricket player. All along she was praising his music to the skies. How could she know that I was his daughter? How could I even boast about it? If I did, I would be humiliated. Father, whom she worshipped would also be humiliated. I was uncomfortable and wanted to tell her that I had a stomach ache and would go home. The entire gathering was worshipping him. The melody of his swaras, the richness of his voice, and art which captures those who do not know the shastra of music, with the intense emotion. I was just looking at his face. Are his nose, eyes and forehead like mine? I was angry enough to leave but the power of music kept me glued to my seat. The words of Shakuntala were right. No one else's music could equal his. I went only to two of his concerts. Didn't go again as that would have made the inner agony unbearable. One day Shakuntala herself said, 'Do you know that Pandit Mohanlalji had a wife? He left her and married a student of his. After two children, he left her also and ran away with Manohari Das. After three or four years he left her also and came back to Bombay alone.'

'Alone?'

'Alone doesn't mean he is any short of lovers. His very name is Mohanlal. Is Krishna not Mohan?' I had also heard a little, just a little, vaguely. Even knowing about this aspect of him, how are people head over heals in love with his singing! I half uttered it and half muttered to myself. She said, 'What is wrong with it? Artists means, they will be connoisseurs. The more the romantic stories, the more is the attraction, do you know?' I was angry with her. I got scared that if I was in her company I may also be spoiled. Not only about him but she talked about so many singers, instrumentalists, tabla experts and many present-day artists, in the same way in which the other girls talked about the private matters of film stars. When I asked her who told her all these things, she replied, 'I go to the music class, don't I? Before the class starts, the girls share such gossip.' I thought I was the only stupid one. I was also ashamed that my father was this sort of a fellow. But Shakuntala described, that what I was ashamed of, as a great qualification! I was surprised. I was also angry with her.

She invited me, 'If you want to really learn music, come with me. The Gandharva Mahavidyalay runs classes near our college. I will help you get admitted to the first year. You will be admitted I am sure. It's enough if you learn for two years. You can enjoy music by understanding it.' When she did ask me, I got excited about joining. I could tell mother that the college time table had changed and go home late three days a week. But at the same time, I was afraid that if I listen to the things that they were saying about my father I might be unhappy. If some girl accidentally knew that his first wife was in Borivali, and knowing that I was also coming from Borivali she might put two and two together, take a clue and come to her conclusion that I was his daughter! This was the fear. I felt, it was safe if I was a little distant from Shakuntala also. The fact that my name was Bakula Lal and his name was Mohanlal did not make her curious. There are millions of people in Bombay and in the whole of Hindustan with the name of 'Lal'. What if I joined the music class and Pitaji came accidentally and the teacher, while introducing the students mentioned my name as Bakula Lal. What if he recognised me. This was mortifying. It is best to remain incognito like this. Otherwise it is not safe to me.

४

Though the board meeting was at 3 pm, the M.D. was very active since the morning. He might send for anyone at any time. Not even for a minute could anybody be away from his seat. The same thing for Avinash. He couldn't budge from his room to come this way. The personal assistant of the Marketing Manager would be discussing about marketing as it was the main topic in the board meeting. Until the meeting was over and all the members got into their cars to go for dinner, no one would be free. Avinash also had to go to the Sheraton. The arrangement for food always rested with the marketing people. Avinash says, that all the important decisions are taken only at the dining table after the foreign liquor gets into their veins. Today nothing else was registering. He sent the money and said he wouldn't come to the engagement. Which meant that he wouldn't take part in the wedding ceremony. What to tell Avinash? How to say it? If she had told him the whole truth earlier itself, this problem would not be there. Why didn't I tell him the truth? I commited a mistake. A sadness filled my mind. I also got angry with that man who was supposed to be my father. God knows what else he has done! That is why mother was so harsh in sending him back the bundle of one lakh rupees. My friendship with Avinash grew because of our interest in music. He doesn't have training in classical music. But he knows on which raga a particular tune is based. Many a time I can't recognise it. It was because of me that he developed the patience of listening to pure classical music. The emotion of raga must immediately be wrung and pour forth drop by drop. He started enjoying the pure swaras which would take shape slowly without dependence on poetry. He cultivated the taste when both of us went to the concerts together, and when I whispered in his ear, the characteristics of the theory of the concerned raga. He had a hobby of buying cassettes. Now, he was buying classical music records when formerly he would buy cassettes of only film songs and ghazals. With his mellifluous rich voice, if he had learnt music right from childhood he would have been a famous classical music singer. One day he went to the concert of Pitaji. He came to know about the concert when he left office on his way home. Straight away he went to father's concert and luckily he got a ticket. He immediately became his admirer. 'Bakula, if Pandit Mohanlal starts singing for films, our playback singers would have to pack up and go home. Even without the dependence on words with just the variations of the swaras he creates the effect of poetry. Great, great, great.'

I was elated. I just called out his name, 'Avinash!' After that I didn't know what to say. My eyes became moist. I held his hands and sobbed profusely. Without even bothering about what other people who sat on the chairs and who were waiting for a place in the restaurant might think. Had I already fallen in love with him? Because he praised my father so much did the friendship transform itself into love immediately? He was surprised that I wept holding his hands in front of so many people. There was confusion. His watery eyes met mine. They got transfixed with my tears. 'Avinash, the person about whom you said, "Great, great, great" is my father. I am his daughter,' I uttered.

'Is that so? Why hadn't you told me all these days?'

'I will tell you later. This is lunch time. The hotel people expect us to leave as soon as we have finished our food. The others who are waiting are also staring at us.' We finished soon and came out. For him curiosity to find out; for me inner compulsion to tell him. 'Neither did you ask me nor did I tell you. When I was a six year-old girl, Pitaji married one of his students. He stays with her most of the time. My mother's dissatisfaction hasn't completely melted. She doesn't take the attitude of consoling herself that artists and men are like that. Father's attitude is very generous.' Without telling him the whole truth, I talked about using up a part of my father's fame.

Avinash consoled, 'After all, he is an artist, Isn't he? You should not be ashamed of it. But why did you weep?'

'Because you admired my father's music so much.' He pressed my hand. It was getting late for the office. Both of us walked quickly.

The next day when we saw each other there was shyness in our eyes. He came near me at midday when I was sitting in front of the computer and said in a shaky voice. 'There is a lot to tell you during lunch break. As vast as an ocean.' When I looked at him there was adoration in his eyes. I couldn't lower my gaze. In this stupid Bombay is there any place where lovers can talk intimately? Right there in the office corridor we stood in a corner and he said in a soft voice inaudible to others, 'The whole night I dreamt. I realised the form of the Raga Malkauns which your father sang the day before yesterday. I have heard that raga so many times in the films. I have even sung it. The film people use only its outline. Your Pitaji opened up infinite possibilities of that raga. Expanded it like an ocean. He made it swell up like huge waves of the ocean. Since last evening I began to see the real shape of Malkauns. Bakula, you are Malkauns. Though I was with you all these days I was stupid not to recognise it. Don't you know its chalan? Would you sing a little of it? Not aloud. Just croon it.' I also felt like it.

ma ga ma dha ni dha ma ga saa
ni sa ga ma dha ma ga ma
ni dha ma ga ma saa ni dha ma ga ma.

When I joined the swaras and intoned, I saw great love in his eyes. What an adoration! A surrender inexpressible in words. When I stopped and told him that it was all I knew, he looked around making sure that nobody was watching, he bent down and kissed my lips. When I melted and bent down my head he caught hold of my right hand and squeezing it said, 'I love you. You are mine.' The next day he used 'Tum' instead of 'Aap' thus changing from respectful plural to familiar singular. He said, 'Come to think of it, the resemblance between your face and your father's is clear. Even your voices are similar. Why did you give up music and come to this secretary's job? The great loss to the music world became my gain. Otherwise there would never be any possibility of our meeting.'

'I also love music a great deal. To the extent that I want to give up this job and give myself to music. But in this job I met you. I want nothing else now. Not even music.' When I said that, my eyes became blurred and voice feeble and the hand extended by itself automatically and took hold of his even without thinking about whether anybody from our office might observe it.

I never told him the truth that there was absolutely no contact between my father and the family. Was I afraid that he might become distant if I did? One day I told him, 'He has lots of programmes, if he is in town for a day he is absent for a fortnight.' Another day I told him, 'If he meets us frequently, the second wife would make it hell for him.' That was the reason I gave. He responded, 'This is the fate of all those who commit themselves to second marriage. It is enough if he puts your hand in mine with his blessings.'

I said, 'Certainly. He is very fond of his daughter.' My mind basked in the sunshine of my imagination. Without bridging the gap between reality and imagination, I described that when I was in college he would give me money stealthily without my mother's knowledge. One day, he took me to the Joys Parlour and made me eat five big scoops of ice-cream. He also wanted to teach me music but his second wife opposed that. Even when his parents came to our house, I had instructed mother and brother to not give any indication that we had no contact with father at all and concocted a lie that father had to suddenly gone to Bhopal. Why did I nurture this lie?

The entire office was silent. Nobody was making any sound. The board meeting was on. I felt like calling up Tipnis Kaka and finding out from him exactly what discussion took place between him and Pitaji. When the board meeting was in progress, there was no rule that no one should call someone outside. Even if accidentally anyone called who would know about it, anyway? The intercom connection was different and she pressed the buttons. It was his voice. She lowered her voice so that it may not be heard by anybody else and said, 'Kaka, me Bakula. It seems you had come yesterday. What did Pitaji say exactly? Mother is still angry. She cannot understand calmly what you told her and tell me. I will come and see you. Please tell me what Pitaji said.'

'He sent me by asking me to get a loan of rupees one lakh for the wedding expenses and deliver it. When I told him that Bakula didn't ask for money and what she wants is for you to attend the wedding and giving her your blessing, he replied that the blessing was always there."Ask her to bring her husband after the wedding to my place."'

'Why doesn't he take the lead and perform both the engagement and the wedding?'

'How can I tell you daughter? I do not have either the familiarity or the status to question him.'

'What, if I myself meet him personally and ask him?'

'How can I answer you? Though you meet him accidentally, you should not tell him that you discussed this with me. Because I am his dependent. He is my benefactor. I should not do anything to upset him, should I?'

'Does it mean that he will be upset if I meet him?'

'My dear girl, you are very intelligent. How can I answer the question whether your father will be upset or not if you meet him? What authority do I have? This is something which you should decide?'

'Kaka, I did not want to get you entangled in this affair. I can't think of anything. I am in a helpless situation. This matter cannot be discussed with anybody else.'

'Father does not want to join the wedding celebration. Mother doesn't want to involve him. She has even rejected his money. I have already mentioned this to your father. He would certainly have been upset. Meanwhile, why do you want to be so stubborn? All these years you have been looked after by your mother. Now you are on your own feet. You have arranged for your marriage yourself. After the wedding if you go and see your father he will certainly bless you. He is generous by nature. When you touch his feet he might even give you one lakh and ask you to use it for setting up the family. I can also put it to him that the money that was set apart for her wedding should be given to herself with his blessing.'

She didn't think of anything further to say. If she asked anything more it might be putting too much pressure on Kaka. I thought what he has done already is too much. She finished the conversation by saying, 'Kaka, I am very grateful to you. Please excuse me for giving all this trouble to you. I have nobody except you. My boss is calling me. Bye, bye.'

ऽ

She knew that she couldn't meet Avinash in the evening. At half past six as soon as the meeting was over, all the board members got into their cars and went to the Sheraton. All the people waiting in the office ran out to catch their buses and trains. Bakula couldn't sleep that night either. Tipnis Kaka's talk implied that sending one lakh was in lieu of not attending the wedding. She began to feel that mother's rejecting it was in keeping with maintaining self respect. Chotu who was lying on the sofa outside was arguing with mother, 'Any how he gave the money. You didn't want to use it for Bakula's marriage. You should have given it to me. You are not keen on my coming up in life, are you?'

'Your argument doesn't make sense. You shameless fellow, you wouldn't have said this if you had any concern for your mother's respect.' Mother was shouting. What she had done was correct from her point of view. I also started feeling the same. But how to tell Avinash? Suppose I said that he won't be in town for two months and so won't be able to come to the wedding. We should just get the wedding invitation in the names of Smt. Ramkumari Lal and Pandit Mohanlal. But he should be present at least on the day of the engagement. Her head started hurting after thinking so much. In spite of her best efforts to keep the mind quiet, it was rushing forth without control in all sorts of by-ways in every direction. This is perhaps the reason why big executives take sleeping tablets at night. I had never taken one—not even once. I didn't even know its name. You must have it at home but you shouldn't take it. Keep it for an emergency like the present one. This middle path flashed. Thinking let this night be over she shut her eyes and brought all the nervous systems to an immobile state. She thought she almost got sleep. A lot of time seemed to elapse. Still no indication of sleep. Cursing angrily she threw her legs about and changed sides. After a long time a thought crossed her mind. There is no use trusting anyone. The so-called father didn't even seem to be aware of the existence of a daughter. The mother can't understand the delicate details. The brother was always cranky. Though Gore Saheb himself had called him home and told him that nothing else was useful except Engineering or B.Com degree with computers, he didn't listen. He didn't even get a degree. What sort of a good job could he be given? Instead of applying himself to the job on hand, it seems he wants to go into business! How can such a fellow understand the intricacies of the mind of an elder sister! Only my Avinash is all right. She thought of burying her face in his chest and telling him, 'My dear, I was telling you fibs, being ashamed to tell you the truth. We have absolutely no contact with father for nineteen years. Now I had sent a word myself. He may be ashamed to come to the engagement ceremony or the wedding. He had sent one lakh rupees. Mother rejected and sent it back. He has said, 'Let her come with her husband after the marriage and I will give my blessings.' He is not even living with his second wife. He is staying in a flat next to his music school at Bandra. I am telling you so that you may know everything beforehand. You shouldn't have mistaken notions and wrong expectations. I am the one who is going to be your life-partner. Look at me. Believe me.'

When she thought of this intimate confiding in him, her eyes were wet. I will wet his bosom with my tears and tell him. He will melt. He will understand. She consoled herself by thinking, 'If my Avinash understands, I don't need anybody's name, nor anybody's blessings.' She felt that was the way; that was the right thing to do. When she decided, it should be done that evening itself, she realised, in this stupid city, there was not a single solitary spot where one could have an intimate heart to heart talk. No matter where. Next to the ocean, people, people, people everywhere. Lovers like us. The police. Wasn't it in search of privacy that she had told her mother that there was special duty at the office, had got up early on Sundays went to Dadar West where he would be waiting with a suitcase, met him and took up a room at a hotel and stayed till the evening, being assured by him, 'Don't be afraid Bakula, all lovers do this.' His assurance. My desire but fear too. Four times. Every time her heart would be pounding. 'My dear, let's not indulge in this clandestine activity. I am perturbed. Let us get married. Then we can spend the night together, come to the office in the morning and go back together in the evening.' He also agreed. Let us go to the Juhu beach this evening. I won't be able to speak to you unless I bury my face in your bosom. This is not something that can be said standing in a corner of the local train station. She thought she must tell him.

Avinash immediately accepted Bakula's proposal. He thought... I love her. She loves me. What more is necessary? Let her father be present or not at her engagement. Let the bride be given away by him or her mother. All these conventions last half an hour. When the person who is going to be a partner for a whole life time is accepted, what else is necessary? He thought. But his father did not consent immediately. He tightened his hold. 'She said in the beginning that the father himself would take the initiative in the printing of invitations and giving away the bride. Now she is saying this. It is not wise to get entangled without making proper enquiries.'

The mother said, 'The girl is on the same level of employment as yourself. Except that she brings home her salary, there is no speciality about family status. Living in a rented house. You said she is thirty. If a woman is thirty, it is old age, remember that. Isn't there anyone who wants to propose his daughter to you?' She also didn't show much enthusiasm in this alliance.

The father again continued, 'Is it difficult to make enquiries about the kind of relationship between this girl's family and Pandit Mohanlal when everyone is in Bombay itself and you are also here in the same city?' Avinash had never agreed with his mother's disagreement. But he had never talked back to his father. His father also never spoke without the worldly experience of long-term consideration of consequences. The father asked, 'Shall I make enquiries or will you do it yourself?' The son who knew that his father's knowledge of art and music circles was rather limited said that he would himself do it. One day Avinash felt that his father had his son's good at heart so he is telling me to enquire. He thought about it for a whole day. The thought of approaching a private detective agency. But the problem was that they would extract too much money. Another day, a way out suggested itself. He was acquainted with Kapadia who owned the shop where he had bought the cassettes of Mohanlal. He had been buying cassettes only from him for the last seven, eight years. That evening after taking leave of Bakula he went straight in Sane Guruji Street to Melody House situated on the first floor. Kapadia enquired in a friendly manner, 'How are the six cassettes I gave you?' When he talked to him about random things to start with and veered the conversation to his purpose, he found out that the maker and distributor of Mohan Melodies was none other than the wife of Mohanlal, Champa Lal who was the compiler of music. Along with the information that her residence was at Kurla, he could also get the address and the phone number.

'Is it true that Panditji has two wives?' he continued his inquiry.

'Your question is like how many wives did Lord Krishna have. He is an artist. As far as I know his official wife is Champabai. A very nice woman. Straight dealings. No hanky-panky. No bargaining. . Commission as per purchase of material. Do you know how many cassettes of Mohan Melodies I have sold? Thirty thousand rupees worth. If I call, she will get the product delivered in two hours. No other company does such brisk business in Bombay. No H.M.V. No Link House.'

Avinash who was working in the marketing division felt an admiration for the woman who would deliver the goods within two hours. 'Is she herself a musician? She has printed music compilation also under her name?'

'The name-plate on her flat says Mohan Sangeet Mahavidyalaya. Whenever her husband is away for a programme, she herself conducts the classes.'

Meanwhile three customers came. Kapadia stopped talking and turned to them. Since it was a small room there was not enough space even to stand. Kapadia signalled 'Thank you' with his eyes and said, 'Come next week. Some new cassettes would have arrived.' When he was crossing the threshold as he understood it was a good-bye to him, Kapadia said, 'Look here. Mohan Melodies don't sell retail to individuals. The rebate is only for shops. I am telling you because you took the address.'

Avinash thought for one more day. He perceived a plan. He called the number that Kapadia had given and said, 'I want to speak to Madam Champa.' The answer was 'Speaking.' He said, 'My name is Vinayachandra Prasad. Journalist. A big fan of Mohanlalji. I am writing an article in the context of the release of his cassettes. My editor asked me to write after interviewing you. Even more than the artists, the words of their life-partners are of greater importance. May I come?'

'Which newspaper?'

'It gets published from Delhi. It has a nation-wide circulation. It is published in Hindi, Bengali, Oriya and Assamese. The name is *Bhasha*.'

'Come.'

'This evening at five. Would you please give me the location of your flat?'

'Come at four. Our class starts at five.'

He noted down what she said and left the office early. He put a shorthand notebook and a pencil into his leather bag. He removed the visiting card of his company and inserted a card, typed on the computer—V.C. Prasad. Journalist. Bhasha. New Delhi. From the taxi itself he could see a prominent signboard on the third floor, east side of a big building—Mohan Music Academy. Professor Pandit Mohanlal. A watchman at the gate itself. Lift. A corpulent lady past fifty-five opened the door. Diamond ear-rings. A round bindi on the forehead.

Next to the shining gold chain, a mangalasutra. A Cuttack silk sari. A soft-skinned delicate face, arms and elbows softened by living in the shade and smoothened by expensive creams. 'I think you are Madam Champa Lal. I am Vinayachandra Prasad.' He bowed a little. She said, 'Have a seat please.' It was a big hall. Four tamburas leaned against the wall—two harmoniums on the floor. A pair of tablas. Except for a sofa alongside a wall, a carpet spread out on the floor from end to end. Mohanlal's photographs in various poses and in different occasions decorated the room. In the middle a very recent big photograph of Mohanlal with this lady. She went in and brought biscuits and tea. After asking some questions about Mohanlal's music, his early training, etc. and writing down the answers he started, 'I have heard in several places that you are the inspiration for his art. How many years since you have married him? How many children? Please give me, if you have some photographs of the wedding, and some others taken after your married life. I will certainly return the originals.' After this he put down his book and the pencil and asked, 'Madam, people indulge in a lot of loose talk. It is my duty as a journalist to correct the mistakes. Only if you give the permission to print what you say will I write them down. Otherwise I won't. Is it true that Panditji stays in Bandra itself but doesn't come home?'

'Nonsense. You have seen this house. All these are residential flats. As it is not possible to admit a lot of students here, we have opened a branch in Bandra.'

'You see, now I know the truth. There is a rumour that Panditji is already married—rather, was. Is this true?'

'Totally false. It's a pure lie.' She refuted straightforwardly.

'His family is in Borivali. Some say that he has a thirty year-old daughter and twenty-four year-old son. What do you say?'

'I told you, it is a complete lie.'

'It seems those children are named "Lal". How can they call themselves that unless they are born to him? It seems he was married to someone before he married you?'

'Mr. Prasad,' she spoke intimately. 'Don't you know the government rules that marrying more than one at the same time is illegal? Shall I show you the entry in the marriage register?'

'Oh, no. The whole world knows that you are his wife. I also know. But I need to know about the earlier marriage and about the two children. I won't write about it if you ask me not to.'

'Will you swear by me that you will never tell anyone?' She extended her hand.

He administered a slap on her right palm.

'I also don't know exactly. Anything is possible with an artist. As far as I know my husband doesn't have this inclination. It is possible that before marriage he might have paid some money to some woman and had got his physical satisfaction. I have heard that charwomen and the cooks earn secret money that way. I believe many important gentlemen have a contact with such women. Sometimes such women somehow get pregnant and name their children after these famous people. I believe a girl of twenty-five who comes to the street behind ours boasts that the film actor Vijaykumar got enamoured of her and had got her over. What do you do with such people? My husband is a very innocent man. He doesn't know anything. Otherwise would it have been possible for him to become such a great artist. No matter where he is, he will come by half past nine. Once in a way, when he is very tired he takes some drinks. That's all.'

By that time some three girls of about twenty appeared near the door. Smt Champa Lal signalled them with her hand to stay out there. Avinash couldn't think of asking her any further question. Two more girls joined those standing outside. Understanding that the class was about to begin, saying, 'Thank you very much madam,' he put his shorthand note book and pencil in his leather bag. He forgot the photos which she said she would give. She also forgot.

Chapter 8

1

He woke up early in the morning. Fifteen minutes past five. When he slept the previous night it was past one. He closed his eyes but could not get a wink of sleep. A musician must have the capacity to go without sleep at least for twelve hours and sleep for twelve hours when he felt like it. Otherwise how to carry out the programmes? He recalled how he had adjusted the twelve hours difference when he went to California! Remembering this he decided that he should sleep in a couple of minutes and filled darkness into his eyes. Just when he was about to fall asleep, he remembered the matter which had kept him from sleeping, so far. Whenever there is any worry, it prevents sleep and it also wakes you up early. Otherwise he wouldn't have woken up so soon. It seems she returned one lakh saying that she didn't want it. That the father should be present for the engagement and perform kanyadaan, was only the daughter's wish. The mother doesn't want anything. This was the feeling since morning when Rajaram called. Why should he involve himself? It was twenty-four years since he left her and nineteen since he cut off all contact. I had remained unattached. Yielding to the pressure of Rajaram and agreeing to pay for the wedding expenses. What arrogance! Thinking this he tried to force darkness into his eyes. He remembered that if a thought like this enters the mind, it would be haunting him for two to three days. Suddenly he sat up. Took a cold shower. Didn't shave. Switched on the kettle, prepared a cup of tea, drank it, tuned the tambura and engaged in practice of mandra. This was a panacea for all worries. By immersing oneself for an hour in mandra all the impurities of the mind will be washed away. And then he could sleep immediately. This was his experience. The medicine is known but to take it at the moment the disease appears, doesn't flash forth. He thought philosophically, this is what is meant by Prarabdha. This philosophical thought suitably related itself to the mandra level of Bairagi-Bhairav. It also receded from the mind. The mind was occupied only by the movements of the mandra and its moods and feelings.

Though it was eight, he was still singing Bairagi-Bhairav. After passing mandra he would go up and down upto madhya and tara-saptakas. He was in a good mood. He felt the need of supporting instruments but knew that they would decrease the inwardness, how long it would be possible to sing by mere turning inwards? Is it possible to live with only meditation all the time? Though it begins with meditation without worldly adjuncts, can it be called life? From the external into the internal from the internal to the external. If it doesn't flow in both the directions how can raga get its nourishment? These thoughts arose. His mind felt at ease. He thought he should write down all these things. So many thoughts on so many occasions have flashed which deserve to be recorded. But he wouldn't write them down. Without wanting to complete the raga he was changing the tanas from drita to madhya, from madhya to drita and again to vilambit. Meanwhile the phone rang. He looked at the wall, the clock showed quarter past eight. This was the time for people to call. He put away the tambura got up and picked up the receiver.

'Is Pandit Mohanlalji there? I am Mahaveer Prasad from Delhi. I have come to Bombay. I want to see you. I have to fix up a programme. Can I come in an hour?'

'I am Mohanlal speaking. Come.'

Feeling of happiness. For last two years, I was being paid one lakh per show in Delhi. Flight. Stay in at least a four star hotel. Rajaram's thirty thousand should be returned. The rest I must keep. What's the meaning in borrowing such small amounts for a musician of my status? These thoughts occurred in a fraction of a second. He shaved, ate bread with jam and a banana, drank a glass of milk. Enough until midday when the meals carrier would come from the mess. If he felt like it he would prepare a cup of tea for himself. This was his routine. What's the day today? Revathi had to come. After he returned from America he was not teaching anyone regularly. He had no mood. He yawned. Told himself that this was a result of not sleeping properly. He sat on the sofa and thought , he could have gone to sleep if someone from Delhi was not coming, and began looking at the wall clock running silently. He just closed his eyes. With the front door opened two inches wide, he dozed off. The door bell rang. When he said, 'Who is it? Come in please' The person who came in, confused and stunned him so much that he stared in surprise. He couldn't believe his own eyes. Manohari. Manohari Das. She came inside and bowing a little, extended her hand asking, 'Panditji, may I come in?' Salwar kameez and a dupatta. On the left shoulder a vanity bag. Pencilled eyebrows. Dark shining hair cascading down. Rouge for the cheeks. Lipstick for the lips. Kajal for the eyes. He was too surprised to speak, so she herself started. 'Please don't think I cheated. I was scared that if I had myself called, you may not give an interview. So, I hesitated. Please give vent to your anger. You can hit me if you like or even kick me. After you are satisfied I will talk. *Uuufff*! How hot is Bombay, Delhi is hot but you don't sweat like this. Where is the switch for the fan?' She looked around and switched it on. She came close to him and sat next to him on the sofa and taking his right hand in hers said, 'Pandit Mohanlalji, at least please tell me how I should address you. It is fifteen years since you left me and came here. I wrote to you afterwards. I begged you to forgive me. You didn't. An artist, that too a great connoisseur like you being so cruel. Have you seen at least one performance by me in these fifteen years? No, but wherever there is a programme by you in Delhi I have attended. Do you know that? Not only in Delhi but at Tansen Samaaroh in Gwalior and Savaai Gandharva at Pune and right here in Bombay at the Maharashtra celebrations. Shall I tell you what raga you sang where? Your anger is not just with me, but on my dance itself. I am not angry either with you or with your music. I still worship your music just I used to earlier. Do you know?'

He felt embarrassed. He felt small. He suspected that through her clever talk she is making him small. But he remembered. Once on the occasion of the death anniversary of Savaai Gandharva, my programme was there. Her's too. But mine was the last item on the first day. Her's was the third item on the third day. The same thing in Gwalior. Everybody in the music world knew of our separation. The organisers would put us on different days. She might have come on the first day and listened to the singing of everybody. Or, she might have made enquiries about when Pandit Mohanlalji sang. No, she is interested in listening to music. She knows music. Not just surface knowledge like other dancers. She herself can sing. I would come away from there a day before her programme. 'Didn't you sing just the alaap for two and a quarter hours at ITC Yaman celebrations in Calcutta? Wasn't it since that time that Bengalis started praising you as India's number one? Shall I tell you what colour jubba you were wearing on that occasion?' Now, his doubts were cleared and his face registered happiness.

'Mohan, I know that you are also alone like me. If you show me the kitchen I will make some tea for us.' He felt it was a bit too much when she used the familiar singular intimately.

'The tea can wait. You just tell me why you came,' he demanded angrily.

'You have yourself shown that yours is a pretended anger.' She tapped gently on his hand and laughed in exultation. 'Those who are angry don't use the familiar singular.'

'All right, kindly favour me by enlightening me the wonderful purpose of your visit,' he corrected himself.

'When once the truth has come out, Panditji, understand, that however much one tries, it can never be hidden. I am on my way to the airport. The car is waiting downstairs. I can call and tell them to put me on the next flight and not on this one. Or, give it to me tomorrow. I can pay the difference. But I have a programme in Delhi this evening. The German Embassy has arranged an Indo-German Cultural Meet. I have my dance item. I have to go. I will come to the point directly. An International Dance Festival is arranged in Paris. One day I have to give a lecture-demonstration. The same evening I have to give a public performance. Do you know the subject? The internal relationship between Indian music and dance. I did not choose the subject. It is given by the organisers of the festival. Is it possible for anyone except you, to execute this and do justice to the subject? What I have thought of is, let us choose three ragas. One for each phase of the day. You should sing quite elaborately bringing forth the mood of those times of the day. And I would dance the same raga. I show the appropriate action expressive of sentiments. The dance part is less. The same thing in the evening raga also. For the midday or the midnight the dance part of it, is more. The tarana of the same raga has to be sung. If we rehearse together it would bring out an integrated show. It is my desire that the best music and dance of India should come together. It is enough if you come to Delhi for eight days for the rehearsal.

'Madam, I don't sing playback for mere dancers,' he shot out immediately.

'This is not just hopping or jumping about. When a person is angry the old feeling will still erupt. The mind will not be ready to accept new suggestions. You will be in the forefront. I have to only illustrate what you sing. The items will have only the names of the ragas. Now, tell me which is the main thing? Think about it. I will give you a call tomorrow. I will talk for one whole hour if you like, till your doubts are cleared. Or, I can come here again. Now it is getting late for me. Please give up all your anger. Artists should not retain anger.' So saying she came close, caught hold of his face and kissed him on the lips tightly and said 'Goodbye.' Her eyes were ordering that there should be no more room for further talk. She got up and left hurriedly.

ऽ

He was happy that she came looking for him after fifteen years, and for having retained such great admiration for his music and calling him the number one singer of India. A girl with great ambition. She wouldn't leave undone whatever came to her mind. She was number one in the world of dance. She had kept her body fit and in addition to dance she would practise yoga everyday and whatever new ideas came to her she would adopt them to the acting and dancing aspects with resoluteness. No matter whoever objected, she had the tenacity to achieve it either by compulsion, or by beseeching. She would perforce carry out her resolution and had an effective way of bringing into her talk, the gestures she had achieved in her dancing. Number one. She wouldn't wait till the next morning. She would call up tonight itself as soon as she returned home from her performance at the German Embassy. He told himself that he should have his answer ready by then.

The mind went back and remembered how they had come together. The performance without tickets at the enclosure of Nagpur college. The organiser who was a cheat. How Champa had not allowed him to perform. Mohanlal recalled, when he had asked her how he could disappoint the thousands of music lovers who had come to listen to him. She had pushed him out of the hotel and had led him to the railway station with the luggage. When he had tried to argue with her by saying that though the organiser was a cheat he also should not be one and had said, we should not disappoint the music lovers, she did not heed to and pushed him, at the last moment, he had said, he would give a free concert, after the next day in the enclosure of the same college and oblige the music lovers, she could return to Bombay. He remembered, then, how she had accused him of cheating his wife and children...

There should be no monetary transaction between the artist and the art lovers. The best thing was to sing free in the temple. Anybody could come and listen, as I had sung on that day in the college enclosure. Three or four thousand people, that agony, singing at the level of supplicating the god. And the god that exists in the heart of the audience and listens and all the audience becoming the collective form of god himself who listens to my supplication, and it was an act of contrition for disregarding them who had sat and waited day before yesterday. The next day Manohari Das had come to the Principal's house, touched my feet and introduced herself. 'My name is Manohari Das. Dancer. I have come from Delhi. This evening I have my programme here. I will consider it my good fortune if you can come and watch it. It was a great opportunity that I got yesterday by chance. I heard your music. I have no other way of showing my appreciation except by touching your feet. Please come to the hotel where I am staying. I will get you a room. There are lots of things I want to tell you regarding music and dance.' Manohari Das. I had heard the name, a talented dancer, famous everywhere. Haven't had an opportunity to see her dance. Eighteen years ago, she was in her mid-thirties but looked twenty-two. Not a line on the cheeks or forehead or the edge of the eyes. Last evening when she sat in the room and acting out the chalans of the various ragas I had sang and had asked, 'Mohanji, your concentration, the emotional intensity to lift music from the terrestrial to the celestial, I had not heard anywhere. It is enough if you just sit and sing in front of me, my dance will reach new heights.' She showed the feeling of a pupil. During that evening's programme, when I was sitting in the middle seat of the front row in the auditorium that was full. Before performing the invocatory Ganesha Vandana, when she stood in front of the mike and announced, 'I heartily welcome the great singer Pandit Mohanlalji who has come to see this evening's dance programme. His presence has given a great dignity not only to me but to the entire gathering,' the entire audience clapped. I was filled with gratitude. She had the ability to recognise and encourage another person's greatness. I had not really seen a dance performance. I had a sneaking feeling that it was only an art of shaking the body. The kind of lame music they used in dance would make me angry. But that day when I saw her performance I felt that it was a visual art which would exhibit the feeling of music in a concrete form. One should not expect the complete form of the music here. I realised that one should only observe the exhibited feel of it. There was a hypnotic attraction here, not found in music. The entire body became the expression of the movement of taal, time. In the movement of the limbs, in the stance of the neck, the look in the eyes, there is the beat of the movement, there is the structure of time. When our meaning springs forth in the throat, this girl's emotion is expressed in the entire body. I had never realised that there was so much elegance in the human body. When I looked steadily, a new meaning began to emerge in the background music and the movements of the tabla. I felt that it was not possible to bring about this in mere music. What details. I had not heard this kind of structural strategy in tabla solos. Sitting stiff I felt that there was a natural beat in her feet.

She was this evening's star. After the programme, the fans rushed to the platform and surrounded her. I was sitting quietly in my chair. She and her three accompanists went to the greenroom to change. After informing the organiser I engaged an auto, came to the hotel, finished dinner and lay down in my room. The mind was aglow palpitating to the movement of the dance. But one side of it was filled with the thought that she would go to Delhi the next day. I had to go in another direction to Bombay. This feeling of loneliness had caused depression. Quite some time elapsed. The sound of knocking on the door. I felt it was her. Yes. When I opened the door, it was actually her. 'How is it you have left early, were you bored with the dance?' She had removed her dancer's make up. She had washed her face. A bindi on her forehead. A thin sari which highlighted her beautiful body.

'Please come in. I came away thinking it would be embarrassing if I stayed on after the programme when you were in the midst of fans. I didn't even wait for you. Did you have your dinner?

'I was informed that you had your dinner. So I also dined with my fellow artists. Tell me what did you think? We can talk the whole night.' She came in, sat on the chair and I sat on the bed.

'To tell you the truth I don't understand all the aspects of dance. If I say it was good, it was incomparable, it was wonderful, they will only be well-known words. I could discover through the human body, a variety of feelings can be expressed and what a range of structure of taals can be created through the feet. I feel like just looking at your feet.'

'Really?'

'I don't have the poetic ability to give expression to it in words. Look at my face. You will yourself understand whether I am speaking the truth or I am merely being polite.'

Her look pierced my eyes with an examining sharpness and descended to the depth and to the origin of her appraisal. Her look had that power. I submitted myself to her gaze without moving my eyes this way or that. Otherwise it would mean that I was giving her false praise. After she evaluated my look she said, 'Yes, you are telling the truth.'

'Manohari, I feel like seeing your dance again and again. Your depiction of the emotion. The charm of the movement of your feet. The brightness of our eyes like the sprinkling of lightning when the saam is reached. The sculptural form of the lustre your whole body moulds into, in that one moment.'

Her eyes expanded. They expressed a feeling of gratitude. 'Manohari, your dance is more concrete than my singing. It is like touching and embracing emotions. It possesses the attributes that embodies and makes the emotion visible. But music has the invisible quality that raises emotion beyond control and beyond measure and then disappears. Your body, face, eyes, eyebrows and the curve of your shoulders have a greater power of concretisation than my voice.'

Her eyes had surrendered to me. At that moment I felt both of us are unique individuals immersed in some complete ripeness of aesthetic emotion. I started looking at her eyes. I tried to enter them. She cooperated by making way. My gaze was touching and knowing the basic root of her perception. In a trembling voice, without any thought I said, 'Manohari, stay here tonight.' Her eyes were still open. After a silence for the duration of three beats, as if to show saam I repeated, 'Please stay.'

'If I sleep I get up late. It's not good if the companions in the party get to know about it,' she whispered.

'You have come after locking your room, haven't you?'

She showed the key in her right palm.

'It was not possible for me earlier to imagine that a woman's body was an aesthetic garland strung together. So many fleeting and transient emotions into a predominant rasa. What symmetry! The palm, the fingers, the elbow, the arms, the shoulders, the chest, the midriff, the thighs, the knees—there was no sagging flesh anywhere. But no hardness either. I understood that this kind of symmetrical and artistic build and grace of the body was possible only for dancers. They tune up every inch of their body in order to express emotion. From the toe to the hair on top of the head, from the fingers to the nerves in the neck, each step will be a minute spot of swara for emotional expression. To touch it, itself is a yoga. If you touch it with a finger and close the eyes, you experience the essence of swara being cognised in the sky. An artist does not play an instrument; he worships it. If I say Manohari I love you, it will be an incomplete expression, insipid and devoid of meaning. It is closer to say I adore you. Please favour me, be kind, be merciful, only such words are acceptable in this sphere of feelings. You are wise. You are an expert artist who knows the minute differences of swaras and experiments and practices them. You have such knowledge of music and you can converse in the language of music. When the basic pulse of the raga throbs, you are encouraging the acme of pleasurable pain. Your quality is such that you transform the transient moment into infinity with your absorption, while immersed in the quest of swara in such a way that this quest alone is the ultimate object of life and there is no step beyond it. Though you are a dancer, you have the quality of trampling down the tendency of time to be ended, you fix yourself in the infinity of meditation. She said, 'Mohan there are two kinds in dance. Laasya and Tandava. Tandava expresses power, vitality. Laasya plays and amuses itself gracefully in emotion. In your music emotion, grace are prominent. That is my quality also. That is why I love your music.'

'Wah, Manohari.'

'Wah, Mohan.'

'Both our names have been decided earlier by fate.'

'True. Very true.'

'I hope you don't feel that I am some cheap woman who agreed as soon as the suggestion was implied! I surrendered to your artistic excellence. All kinds of people follow and send propositions to a dancer. I never allow anyone even to touch the dust of my feet. You haven't lessened your respect for me, have you?' She asked suddenly looking at me with her piercing eyes which were capable of finding out any lies when uttered.

'Certainly not, I swear. You also don't think that I am a singer who goes behind all kinds of women. You are the only one who entered my inner being. You are my Rati.' When he intertwined his fingers with hers, she had a look of happiness.

'My organisers told me that your wife dragged you to the railway station because the organiser cheated you. And you pleaded, that because you had been cheated you should not cheat your listeners. Finally, you ran away from the station and came to give the concert. Mohan, yesterday's singing was such that even gods came down to listen to it. It was my good fortune that I was there. Even while I was listening, my mind had surrendered itself to you. Do you suspect that I am saying this as I want to get something out of you? Or you believe me thinking what will she gain by telling lies?'

My eyes became misty. Her right cheek became wet. She pressed my face to her bosom and consoled me. Love turned to affection. Manliness began to search for refuge. Her firm breasts which were so far provoking the sexual instinct, now took the place of a mother's bosom and were anointed with my tears. I wanted to confess everything to her. I started telling, reviewing my past in wave after wave. Without mentioning Ramkumari it was not possible to talk about Champa and marrying her. I had to mention in what circumstances I married Ramkumari. I mentioned only the physical urge that I had. I hid my visit to the whorehouse. Similarly, I went farther back and described my birth, the ashram at Hardwar, Sagar and the training I got in Chittarpur from Raja Saheb and my achievement. That she was listening with rapt attention was clear by the look in her eyes. When I finished narrating her everything I wanted to, the crows were crowing outside. 'Mohan, I must talk more with you. I feel like listening more from you. This is the time when people get up. I will leave. Sleep a little. I will come again. Don't be distraught.' She kissed me a number of times. Then got up, wore her blouse and sari, asked for the comb, combed her hair, took out her key, opened the door silently and left without making the least sound though she was wearing her footwear. I lay down and slept.

When the door bell rang, I woke up. It was quarter past nine. When I opened the door it was her again, having taken a shower, combed her hair neatly, wearing kumkum on her forehead and in a different sari. She was looking like a celestial nymph. She came in, closed the door and sat on the bed. 'I slept for three hours. You must have slept for four. Brush your teeth and come quickly. I will tell you something important.' I finished my shower and came. She held my hand and said, 'Why should you stay in Bombay? Entire India is your field. What's the difference between Bombay and Delhi? Delhi is closer than Bombay to the centres of Indian music like Kashi, Bihar and Bengal. You just come away. Start your life again afresh. My associates travelled this morning by Janatha Express. There was AC or first class in that train. I have my reservation in the 3 pm train. If I tell the organisers they will get you a berth also. Just come with me. In my music school there is a guest room. You stay there till you get a flat close by. It is not as difficult in Delhi to get a house as in Bombay. You can find one in a day. I will be there for you. You be there for me. Your earnings are yours. My earnings are mine. Let us stay together without marriage, authority or any other kind of restriction. Once in a while you sing for my dance. I will accompany your song.'

'Why not?' It occurred to me. There was no need to go to Bombay again and witness her jargon. Music is not born where she is present. The presence and the affectionate gaze of this heavenly damsel is enough to create new areas of ragas and concepts of swara. Even when she is sitting quietly by the side of the bed she has assumed a posture of an artistic statue that spills emotion. No matter in what posture she sits or stands or in what direction her eyes move, how her hands gesticulate, there will be emotions in it. There will be movement of swaras. When such a person is inviting me herself, what more I need? It was like finding freedom. I said, 'I don't even have a sinlge penny for my train ticket.'

'Don't say mine and yours. This is yours.' She said put her hand in her handbag, took out the purse which was full and placed it on my thigh.

३

The vast expanse of the sea can be seen from the bedroom window. A large fishermen boat was sailing in the middle. A sail tied in the height establishing the connection between the water and the sky, like the sound which emanates from the throat would involve the sky. Whenever a boat is seen, the notion of freedom comes to mind. Moving about in the wind, sailing in whatever direction. Yes, I shouldn't have married, that too the second time. Caught up in the idea of freedom; leaving Bombay behind, the train was running. The sight of the plants and trees, hillocks and boulders and houses silently moving behind from the air-conditioned compartment, fingers intertwined with Manohari's, what a sense of freedom! There will be no bondage of marriage between us. She won't ask for my earnings.

I won't ask about hers. No burden of children. She is a devotee of my music, I am a devotee of her dance. There is no burden of any kind of worldly relationship. I am free. I am becoming a real artist. Like the boat sailing in the vast ocean. Her eyes which are looking at the window are dreaming. It is my dream. I can see by looking at her eyes that she is seeing my dream. It won't do to disturb her concentration by talking in the middle. Once in a while she tightens her grip. She has told me everything about her honestly. It seems she had married her own guru. He is seventy-eight. They have been married for fifteen years. Then she was twenty-two. 'Why did you marry an old man?'

'His wife was dead. He was sixty-two. His married daughter was in Lakimpur. Nobody to cook for him. His earning was not enough. The times were changing. The programmes for him were rare as he would not compromise even slightly in the purity of shastra. He decided to leave Delhi and go to his daughter's house. I liked the discipline of his lessons and his commitment to the pure form. There was no one who could teach with such complete dedication. I did not want to lose him. I was twenty-two. I wanted to marry him and make him and his learning my own. In the beginning he did not agree. Later he also got interested in my proposal. We got married. What sort of marriage was that? The good fortune of serving one's guru. What was the present he gave the bride? Without holding back anything from his vast knowledge, in three years he made me learn all the remaining portion of his knowledge. He made me master every aspect of acting and gesture, the dance movement of the limbs by unfolding the inner secrets, by a detailed demonstration and constant practice. He himself pronounced clearly the complex structural variations of taal and by wearing the dancing bells and dancing, made me practise many times and perfected me. His training was so efficient that when I was made to enter the stage in my twenty-fifth year for the first performance, several newspapers wrote that a top-class dancer had arisen on the Indian horizon. If it was one fourth of what he taught in the first eight years, what he taught in these years was three fourths. He was not physically strong enough to demonstrate everything. He would be short of breath. He danced a little, the physical aspect of the dance movement and made me perform the rest with a tabla player for hours on end. In the facial expression, and part of acting he is still like an ocean, even in his seventy-eighth year. No matter how much a person gets from him, his knowledge is immense, irreducible and his imagination is fertile.'

'What's his name?'

'Sohan Guru.'

'Ah, I have heard the name. I have heard that he is well-versed in music as well.' I was surprised.

'Well versed! He has the title of Maharaj. Maharaj means he must have trained one hundred pupils. He must have composed independent oratorial compositions. He must have total mastery over music. In the All India Dance Conference he was given the title of Nritya Guru, higher than that of Maharaj.'

I felt like learning new structures of taal. I remembered that the musicians, especially the vocal singers do not have the skill of the dancers, that too the Kathak artists in the matter of weaving webs of taals. Manohari asked, 'Do you know Delhi well?'

'Just a little.'

'My house is in South Extension. Guruji doesn't leave home. My school is in Green Park. Three kilometres. As soon as you reach, you will be staying in a room in the school. Let us search for a rented house close to it. I started the school myself. I own that building. There is a big businessman by the name Ramcharan Mittal. Transport business. People say it is the biggest for the entire North India. I believe he has 1,500 trucks. He is fond of fine arts, especially dance. He is the chief patron for my school. It was only with his help that I could get the site and the money for the building. When he is free he comes to the school and makes enquiries. He always comes for my programmes in Delhi. He is the supporting pillar of my school. '

With our fingers intertwined and both of us looking out of the window silently, my mind was contemplating the details of what she had said. I had told her all the main aspects of my life the previous night itself. Though I felt that she was telling these things so that when I got off in Delhi I should not be totally ignorant of her background, I somehow felt that there was a special relationship between her and

Ramcharan Mittal, the chief patron of the school. I understood that she had mentioned it so that I was properly informed. I asked 'Do you have the letterhead of the school with you?'

She, who was looking out of the window silently, asked, 'Why?'

'Oh, I just asked.'

She got up, took out the small box placed on the upper berth, opened the lid and gave me her letter pad. In large letters the title 'Manohari Das School of Indian Classical Dance' below it the address and the phone number. On the left side President and Director: Manohari Das. That was all. I said, 'The name of the patron is not mentioned here?'

'I told you that's all. He doesn't like it to be mentioned. He has clearly said that he doesn't want any publicity.' Saying so, she looked at me sharply. 'What exactly is your question?'

'I just asked that's all.'

She put the pad back in the small box and sat holding my hand as before. Since the two others in the berth in front of us were playing cards with their friends who were four rows away, we had privacy. After a little while she brought her face close to mine and whispered, 'Get one thing straight, true affection and love can exist only between artists. The rest are worldly affairs, gratitude. Staying with the husband is a duty, devotion to the guru and worshipping at the feet. Let your mind be at peace.'

I felt ashamed. I understood that she had a very sharp mind. Affection also began.

४

I couldn't even imagine that the Manohari Das School of Indian Classical Dance would be so big. She was the owner of the entire building. The two-storied edifice of ivory white colour was in the middle of the huge compound quite close to the shopping complex. At the lower floor there was a dance auditorium thirty-five feet long and twenty-feet wide. Besides, there were four rooms for teaching, apart from other basic facilities like a pantry, toilets etc. Upstairs there were rooms of the same dimensions and design. For my room there was an attached bath, a boiler for the hot water for bathing, a cot, a sofa and an air-conditioner. Inside, there was total silence, cut off from all outside noises and a courtyard which was full of greenery. Though I did not know about the rates in Delhi, this building alone must be worth more than a crore. Maintaining this and appointing a staff was a big business indeed. I felt I should be proud that an artist was the owner of such a place.

Manohari, after finishing her breakfast would come to the dance school at eight in the morning and stay till night. In the afternoon a servant would bring lunch for both of us. In order to teach the beginners in the morning as well as in the evening, fifty year-old Jaisukhlalji would come. In the morning there would be thirty-two boys and girls and forty in the evening. Manohari taught in a small room, just to one or two senior students. From morning half past ten to four in the afternoon, there would be no one else in the entire school. There was nothing to disturb our privacy. After drawing the bolt from inside and coming up, she would descend the steps only when the lunch box carrier pressed the door bell. The rest of the time we would be lying on the bed and no matter how much we spoke and in what manner we were, nobody was there to enquire. There would be a phone call occasionally. Around half past ten in the morning and half past six in the evening again, there would be a call from Ramcharan Mittal. He would make polite enquiries about her and the school. When she speaks with him, she holds my hand with her right hand or she puts her hand round my neck, embracing me. Or, she invites me by gesture to come close and sits on my lap while talking on the phone. By doing so, my intimacy with her increases. I feel like I am protecting her from him and giving her inner strength. After the telephone conversation she embraces me tightly and kisses me without fail. If it is in the morning and there is nobody around, she drags me to the bed. That phone call becomes an instigator and infuses enthusiasm in us. Addressing me as a dear one and saying that I was her refuge she would tighten her embrace. She groans from misery, happiness and by mixing both happiness and misery. I feel like her chief protector. My manliness is stimulated by this and I get strength and inspiration to sing untiringly to my heart's content. On the phone she calls him Charan. She exhibits false anger by telling him, 'Yes, yes, isn't so? If you take hold of my hand all problems are solved. What would be my future if in your busy schedule you forget me? It is three weeks since your lordship extended the favour of crossing the threshold of this haveli. Keep in mind I won't speak to you at all when you come next time.' She exhibits this lover's erotic anger once in every ten or twelve days. After such a conversation is over she would pat her forehead gently as if to indicate that was her fate. That day my sense of protectiveness would overflow. He never comes without informing her, and enquiring about her convenience. Even if he comes, it would be half past seven in the evening. He would stay with her for about an hour alone and go.

One evening she told me, 'In half an hour Mittal Saheb is coming. You stay in your room upstairs. I will be practising downstairs with my tinkle bells on, to taped music. After he arrives I will come up and call you. You come down. I will tell him that you came day before yesterday from Bombay and were searching for a house. After introduction and polite conversation you leave saying that you will be going to a friend's house for dinner right here in Green Park. He doesn't stay for more than an hour. You look out for a white Benz car from a distance at quarter to nine. If it is still there you go for another small round or wait at the corner tea shop.'

'I will go right away if you like.'

'No, it is best if I tell him that you are here. It is not good for him to find out through some other source. He is not a mean person. Very dignified. Still we must be careful. Anyway in the future you and I will be close, so it is best if I have already introduced you. I am an artist who visits so many places to give performances and he knows that I dance with many male dancers. All this he knows. He has no objection about these things. You just do as I tell you.'

I was surprised when I saw Mittal. I had imagined him as a fat, khadi-wearing, pot-bellied seth. But the person who stood in front of me and shook my hand was trendy. He had a thick crop of hair, dyed shining black, fair complexion, and rose coloured frame for his spectacles and a wrist watch with a leather strap. Since Manohari herself had mentioned that he was sixty-five there was no problem about knowing his age. Otherwise his physique said fifty-five to sixty. He smiled with a winning charm and said, 'I have heard your name.

A great artist. Otherwise Manohariji would not have such great respect. Welcome to Delhi. There is a lot of encouragement for music here.' He showed the sofa and said, 'Please sit down.' I sat. I praised his generosity in promoting art. I got up saying that, 'I have to go to a friend's house for dinner. He has invited several people. They will all be waiting.' I excused myself. He said, 'I will tell the driver to drop you there.' I responded, 'No, no, the house is in the next street. Not even five minutes walk. Manohariji, I may be late in coming back. Anyway, the guard will be here.' She replied, 'It doesn't matter how late it gets' and walked upto the door and sent me off.

Though I performed my acting role before Mittal extremely well as indicated by her, my mind withered. She has married her guru. It seems he is seventy-eight. I have not met him. This person is a patron. When she has to meet him I have to give room and disappear pretending to be a casual guest. What a fate. I was walking in front of the market. By then I was familiar with that place. Hauz Khas, Yusuf Sarai, Safdarjang hospital, all these I knew. When I looked at the watch fifteen minutes had passed since I started walking. I felt disgusted when I imagined her lying naked with that Seth. I got angry. I was filled with sorrow, blaming myself for having come away to this place by believing a woman like this, without weighing the pros and cons. On the same road I walked slowly towards the Indian Institute of Technology. This city was not like Bombay. One could walk in the streets, and I felt happy. It was also pleasant walking at eight in the evening. When I looked at the watch and returned by quarter to nine, the car was not there. The guard had not yet come. I rang the door bell and waited. There was light inside. When Manohari opened the door her hair was wet. She had just finished her bath and had washed her hair. Even the sari which she had worn round without lingerie in a hurry was wet here and there. There was no kumkum on her forehead and no makeup on her face. No wrist watch. After I came in she closed the door and said, 'You went away for so long. He left at quarter past eight. I thought that you would be in the corner tea shop watching his car leave.'

I didn't talk. I didn't know what to say. The intimacy which I had felt with her earlier had decreased. She seemed to understand my thoughts by just looking at my face and eyes. 'Mohan, I feel ashamed to tell you but I must. Immediately after he left I felt that I had become impure. I felt like taking a shower immediately. I applied shampoo and soap twice. I thought I should give those clothes to the washer man and not touch them with my hand. Still, I don't feel like touching you. At least till one night passes and a new day dawns.' I stared at her. She lowered her eyes to the ground. The lower teeth clutched the upper lip, the head bowed, silence pervaded. After a little while, still with her head bent she said, 'I had never felt like this before. After all he is my patron. Without him this building and this dwelling house would not have happened. This institution would not have developed to this level. I have friendship towards him. Also I am full of gratitude. After all what is it I am giving him in return? Now and then my company. This was the feeling I had. But today, do you know how miserable I felt? I had to question myself about the very root of the relationship with him.' After saying this she lifted her face. Both her eyes were watery. I put a step forward to console her with my hand outstretched. She receded saying, 'No, no, don't touch me. At least till this night is over and a new day dawns.'

After she left, I opened the lunch box and dined. The sorrow had disappeared. Anger and disgust had come to an end and my mind was light. I felt comfortable.

The next morning after the class was over and everybody had left, she came to my room sat on the cot and sat next to me holding my hand. I also held her hand. No erotic overtures were made. After talking about this and that expressing shyness on her face and lowering her head she said, 'I feel shy to tell you. Do you know how I feel? Though it is a bit troublesome for the mind, we must unite and if there are any traces of stains these must be wiped away.' I also felt it was right. She said this was a new day. We made love.

After we rested in each other's arms she said, 'There is so much place vacant here. I was thinking why should you pay the rent for a separate house. Do you know what he said yesterday? He always speaks in a delicate suggestive manner. Never says anything directly. 'You are a famous artist. He is also a famous singer. If he stays here, people might concoct stories. Why should we give room to them?

Think about it.' That is what he said. Which means that he has started feeling jealous. You are an artist and I have favoured you. Let us look for a house close by. You may come here for the entire day. I may come there when I want. In a way that is more convenient for us. Let him learn about our intimacy gradually. Not all of a sudden.'

I also thought it was right. Let there not be demeaning feeling of my leaving for an hour on the day on which he comes. Why should the boys and girls who come here to learn dance, see me everyday? Also the sound of the dance taking place uninterruptedly both in the morning and in the evening were not supportive of my mood for music. She took me to a shop close by who performed the 'To Let' service. I got a place just six minutes walk from the dance academy within two hours. A quiet remote place, unimaginable in Bombay. The entire roof top was mine. A single private place where no matter how loudly I sang, nobody could hear. Lying down on top of the roof facing upwards, I could get a feeling of proximity with the sky. Plenty of wardrobes and almirahs. Even the rent was unbelievably low, unimaginable for the people of Bombay. One and a half thousand rupees per month. Manohari wrote out a cheque covering ten months' rent there and then. She said, 'I will arrange air-conditioning for a room. I have it with me. I also have a carpet, a cot and chairs. She also brought a tambura from the music school.'

ƾ

Three weeks after I came to Delhi, a week after I had my own rented house she took me to her house. I was also curious to see her guru, Sohan Guru. My mind always used to recognise him as her guru and never as a husband. Though she was going home every night and there was a suggestion in some words or reference that she went to bed with him, I could never have a low opinion of their relationship. She had hung many of his large dancing photographs on the walls of the music school. Many of her pictures were also hung there. There were three photographs of them dancing together. There was a resplendence on his face. When both of us reached home at 8 pm in her car, he was sitting on a sofa, watching a tennis match on the television. He seemed older than I had imagined. Though the eyes were shining they were droopy. It could be immediately seen that this was the result of liquor. As soon as he saw Manohari he asked, 'Why so late?' I remembered that she had told me that it was his custom to ask her why she was late no matter how early she went back. When she introduced me, he asked, 'Why did you come here leaving Bombay? In this city there is no encouragement for art. All that you have here is the intrigues and corruption of the government, which loots money from anybody and everybody.' Since I already knew this quality of Delhi, I did not make any comment. I touched his feet in the traditional manner. He stood up and embraced me.

Though the house was not large, it had been built with artistic taste. There was a hall where a small gathering could witness a music or dance performance. There was no carpet on the floor. Not even mosaic. Just hard cement. It was clear that mosaic could not sustain the swiftness of the dance movement. Apart from that, there were two rooms. A kitchen and bath. Upstairs, there was a small hall and two rooms and there was an open space exposed to the sun. To start with, he enquired after my guru and my training. Manohari poured a peg of whisky into a glass, added cold water and ice cubes and gave it to him. I was given Coke. Sohan Guru asked, 'Why, am I the only sinner?'

'No, you are the only saint. He won't have any,' she answered.

'You see, I don't transgress my word. I wait till she returns and gives it to me. I don't drink by myself. You see, look at this stingy woman. I am not supposed to ask for a second helping. I have followed this honestly,' he laughed. He lifted his glass looking at me and said, 'Cheers.' Manohari went in to heat up the food. After three sips he said, 'Manohari had told me that you like only very profound ragas. Would you sing Bageshree?'

'Certainly, if you wish. But I am out of practice for three weeks.'

'So what? Manohari,' he called out loudly. After she came he said 'He is going to sing Bageshree now. Food afterwards. If the stomach is full, it affects the breath and singing will not be easy. Don't drink that cold Coke. Take either hot tea or very hot milk. Bring the tambura here. Bring me the tabla. I will tune it. You accompany him. I want to listen.'

I drank hot milk, tuned the tambura and by the time he tuned the tabla, his glass was empty. He turned to her saying, 'Now, I must hear music. You have said that he is a great singer. That too Bageshree. Pour me another glass leaving aside your stinginess.' She got up and prepared another peg. She spread a carpet on the ground, seated him leaning against the wall and put a large pillow behind his back. Four feet away I sat and opposite me she, with her tabla.

'It is disrespectful if I sit on the sofa when you sing sitting on the floor. Though you are younger to me, music must be given its proper respect,' saying so he leaned against the pillow. Before I intoned the shadja my eyes naturally turned towards him. A man of seventy-eight, he looked like Dronacharya. It was clear that he had dentures. Broad forehead. A sharp nose. Since he had been constantly practising abhinaya, his eyes were completely under his control. A bald head. A lustrous face. I was diffident in front of this great guru. I thought that if my guru, Raja Saheb was alive now, he would look like this. I felt that his soul had taken this shape, sitting in front of me and telling me 'let me see how you are going to sing this great raga.' But I conquered this feeling and told myself that no matter what a great artist Sohan Guru was, he was basically a dancer. I am a singer. And I have also done a great deal of sadhana. It took me more than five minutes to get this self confidence.

By the time I came to *saa ni dha saa* his face registered the feeling of comprehension of the mood of the raga. He started directing himself with his index finger. The raga caught hold of me and all the anxiety and secondary feelings were got rid of. There were just the elaborate proceedings of loving worship. No matter how the movement was depicted, they were all aspects of worship, devotion, action, leisure, assurance, confidence and disappointment. The strange grace arising out of *dha ma pa dha ma ga*. I was singing to myself. After quite some time my eyes recognised that the emotions that I was singing were being enacted on his face. The movement of his hand and fingers were not just the reaction of a mere listener absorbed in music. He was accompanying my singing with his acting. After I understood it I kept looking at him continuously and started singing for him. I began to receive inspiration from him. If it was a harmonium accompanist, the movement of his swara would follow the movement of my singing and remind me, and would help in imagining and creating the next swara. But Sohan Guru's accompaniment was following the emotion of the movement of the swara. I must repeat that same emotion, or invent another emotion or mood. But all this had to be done only through the movement of the swaras. The new confidence of managing the swaras, keeping alive the consciousness of emotion, seemed a little difficult in the beginning, but after the path was found, I followed it as it seemed to be the new method of propounding a raga. I derived an unusual happiness hitherto not experienced by identifying that my singing was not merely a movement of swaras and bhavas but was taking shape visually through the medium of abhinaya. A complete companionship between me and him was achieved. I, who did not know anything else except the admiration of the harmonium accompanist, found in him not just equality but companionship of emotions. Not quite knowing whether he was following me or I was following him, we were flowing as if two different modes of expression of the movement of one raga. He was leaning forward from his pillow at the back, straightening his backbone, sitting in partial Padmaasana, was expressing the essence of the raga through both his hands, chest, shoulders, face and eyes.

Manohari who was playing the tabla must have found it difficult to move in vilambit rhythm continuously. Once she slipped into madhya-laya even before I noticed it, there was displeasure on her guru's face. His eyes flashed at her in a punishing gaze. Her face expressed her mistake and confession. Though she did not change the rhythm again, she put four letters in each time unit. Only then the guru interceded, 'This is not dance but music.' She melted with shame. She didn't commit such a mistake again. Though I realised that it was a punishment for her, to give form to the variety of the innumerable beats at the vilambit movement, used as she was to dancing with two hundred little bells, it was quite clear to me she was very much interested in the swara and the raga.

After performing the alaap for more than an hour in the madhya-laya of ek-taal, I thought of starting in the madhya-laya tr-itaal the cheez kou s na ka | ra ta to ri | bi na ti pi | ya ra vaa s

But instead of starting the cheez I suddenly changed my mind and in the same tri-taal of madhya-laya I started the tarana

u da ta na | de re s naa | s s ta na | de re naa s a ta ta na |
de re naa ta | daa re daa ni | naa dir dir ta

I realised it was a mistake, after starting that. I felt that I lost the sublimity of emotions, that emerges from the confluence of feelings, along with the meaning of poetry and melody, and the emotions that could be created in a cheez. With a secondary reason of giving her a chance in playing tabla, I had sacrificed nurturing and developing the raga. But by then, Sohan Guru by his hand movement had caught the taal and given it the beat. As if Manohari was waiting just for that, she began to downpour the bols incessantly. Her accompaniment, I felt was relevant for dance but not for music and an unexpected feeling started in me. The movement of the hand beat of the guru was directed towards her. Correspondence began between them and the vibrating movements of the taal had started. The guru who was sitting got up and started dancing. She expanded the beat with great happiness. I stopped singing. The guru ordered, 'No, no. You shouldn't stop. You bring in the lehara in your tarana.' Showing the beat with my fingers I started singing the lehara. The dancing went on for five minutes. When I was anxious whether he had the strength to withstand the tiredness of dancing, he commanded, 'Tie the bells to my feet.' Giving the indication for me to continue, she got up and opening the door of a almirah in the same hall, she took out a pair of belts of bells and tied them quickly to his feet, came back and started playing the tabla. My lehara was continuing in Bageshree itself. He started dancing to that raga. What a structure of beats! What a variety of taal! With this astonishment I was continuing the lehara.

ma ga ni saa ga ma | ni dhaa s ma | ga s ma ga | re saa ni dha

Leaving the tarana I turned to the swara. The emotion of Bageshree gave a clear frame work. Again, for a little while her beat of the tabla and the sound of the bells was mingled. By then he was getting short of breath. He, who was dancing, stood still and showing the beat with his right foot, started taking a bit of rest. She got up, went to him and took hold of him saying, 'You please come here. I will dance.' Though he protested, she held him by his shoulders, brought him to the place where she was sitting and removed the bells from his feet. She went quickly to the cupboard, opened the door, took out her bells, which had more bells, put them in the hands of the guru, knelt at his feet, took them back, tied them round both her feet and tied a tight belt round her waist. He played the tabla. She danced. He took up a simple beat without too many complexities. She started dancing intoning aloud the bols of rich structure and more complex. I was continuing to utter the lehara of the swara. She was immersed in the pure dance. Her entire body became a medium for the variety of devotional worship of Raga Bageshree. The bells for the feet, simple salwar kameez and the cloth belt she was wearing round her waist. No decoration. No makeup. No ornaments. But she looked like the very incarnation of Vageeshwari, the earlier name of Bageshree. There was no literary meaning of words, no verbal poetry. Just the beat. With the movement of her body and of the feet, with only the pure beat, she had made my singing take a concrete shape. I felt that hers was not just a body of flesh and blood, born in this world but an incarnation which had descended in order to reveal the divine force. She danced, and danced with complete involvement. No matter how much she danced, there was no tiredness and no disruption in the evenness of her breath. Even the sweat on her face and armpits added lustre to her beauty. I couldn't get at the formation of that beat. I had not heard those bols. But I was showing the saam without break. Guruji also stopped playing the tabla and started indicating the saam by clapping. For the saama, ateeta and anaagata she was performing, the indication of the hand beat was necessary. My lehara was not enough.

After dancing for a long time, she stood still and drew in her breath. I was still singing. The guru turned to me and said, 'Sing a cheez in madhya-laya.' I was surprised. I felt that he had understood that I wanted to sing a cheez but had changed my mind and started a tarana. Immediately I started singing.

kou s na ka | ra ta to ri | bi na ti pi | ya ra vaa s

She started acting that. Dancing the tanas I was working in, she enacted the literary part of it.

She danced so expertly that I felt she had known this piece and had practised it earlier. This was more difficult than accompanying on the harmonium. I became aware that the poetry part must be understood and then it had to be expressed in abhinaya. The abhinaya was not equal to that of the guru but the footwork was surpassing. I could imagine that in youth, the guru must have been much superior to her. After singing the cheez in madhya-laya for ten minutes, I ascended to the drita-laya for five minutes and concluded. As I had seen her representation of atee-drita and anu-drita in the dance part of it I felt that my drita-laya was weak and feeble.

After the singing and dancing were over and Manohari was untying her waist band and removing the anklets of bells, Sohan Guru got up from the floor and sat on the sofa. I sat on the sofa opposite. He said, 'You are a good singer. You have a sound foundation. Your power of imagination is also good. We should get singers like this to dance properly. But to sing only for dance, you need a slightly different sort of practice.' Manohari went to the kitchen and started warming up the dinner. I felt sad that her body which was the vehicle of such great art was engaged in doing kitchen work. When she invited us for dinner her teacher-husband said, 'I am tired after dancing. Give me just one more peg. I won't ask for more.'

'I am not saying that you aren't tired. But you have already had two pegs. No more, no matter whatever you say,' she answered.

'You are also tired. You have danced very well. You have earned the right to have a peg yourself. I won't say don't,' he argued.

'If I have earned it I will have it. But that doesn't increase your entitlement,' she replied firmly.

'This person here is our guest. He has sung extremely well. If he hadn't, I wouldn't have danced. Neither would you. It is etiquette to offer him a peg. What do you say, Mohanlalji? If you say no even after such an enthusiastic representation of art, it would be showing discourtesy to an elder like me. How old are you? Forty, forty-two? How much younger to me are you?'

She smiled at his clever mode of speech. All three of us had a peg each. I was not particularly appreciative of the taste of liquor. By the time we finished dinner, it was one hour past midnight. Sohan Guru was nodding with slumber. I understood that since he was also tired after dancing, three pegs were excessive at his age. Though a single peg had not affected her enough not to be able to drive the car, she decided not to give me a ride at that time of night. I accepted her suggestion, 'I will arrange your bed in the upstairs room. You may leave in the morning.' After helping Sohan Guru and taking him to their bedroom, she accompanied me to the room upstairs. The bedspread was quite clean. She embraced me tightly and sighed, 'My inspiration, I want to hold you tight just like this all night and sleep. But sometimes he wakes up at intervals.' Sleeping together was a pleasant prospect for me too. Though we were enjoying undisturbed pleasure of company during the day, the joy of sleeping together the whole night hadn't been obtained. Besides, just now, her dancing body had reflected my singing. It had become the celestial body and shone like lightning inspired by magical power. What greater fulfilment would be possible than to press that body to my bosom and sleep? This feeling filled me. At the same time I was worried about her husband waking up.

Saying, 'I will go only if you ask me to,' she lifted her face, looked at my face seeking consent. 'We have both imbibed a little. It's also a bit late. If I ask myself whether I would go down after lying in your arms for a little while, what can I do if sleep overtakes me?'

'No, leave right now,' I consented.

I couldn't get any sleep. I remembered Manohari telling me a number of times that though he was seventy-eight, no one could match him in acting and gestures. The thought occurred to me that I should practise to expand the raga, supporting on the emotion also, along with my method of supporting it on the swaras. The question arose that if it is accomplished wouldn't it be subjugating the raga to literature and music to Thumri? Raja Saheb was always against Thumri. Pure music meant depiction of pure aesthetic emotion. It was his opinion that Thumri moved about in the realm of sentimental feeling and depiction of rasa was artistically more complete and fulfilling. I also used to feel that it was true. Doesn't acting mean depiction of emotions? This question was whirling in my head. Along with this word Bhramari, the memory of the dance just performed by Manohari came to mind and even when she performed Chakkaradar Paran, it would shine forth only if it was accompanied by tabla. I became aware of this shortcoming. Though Guruji could play on the tabla, he was not a tabla maestro. Also, I remembered that at his age it wasn't possible for him to have the strength in his fingers to play for the tatkaara of a vibrant dancer like Manohari. These were the thoughts interspersed by remembering her. A feeling of loneliness. While turning and twisting like this in the bed, there was the soft sound of footsteps. When I opened my eyes, Manohari was standing next to the bed. She bent down and whispered in my ear, 'I felt that you too weren't able to get sleep.' I extended my hand. Though the window curtains were drawn, her figure was visible in the dim street light that had wriggled into the room. She shut the door silently, lay down by my side and said, 'I have switched on the light in the kitchen. Even if he wakes up it would be all right if he thinks that I am working in the kitchen. If he wakes up, he makes a sound; doesn't get up and come. He certainly won't climb the stairs. Don't be anxious.' She embraced me tightly. I made love to her. She whispered, 'I experienced how difficult it is for us to sleep separately in the same house. We make love in the afternoon interval itself. But the peace of sleeping together at night is quite different.'

I blurted out what came to my mind at that time, 'Manu, shall we get married?'

'You are a married man, aren't you, with your wife and children in Bombay?'

'When I have left Bombay itself, how do they matter? I will divorce.'

She embraced me with even greater fervour. Her breath was intermittent. She took my head in her hands and pressed it to her bosom. A minute later she said, 'The welfare of Guruji is my duty as long as he is alive. I have married him. But he has never objected to anything I do. He never enquires about money, earning, spending etc. If I marry you he won't touch what is earned by me and starve himself. Who should suffer that sin?'

I had understood that she was not only grateful to him but worshipped him lovingly. I now realised that it was a firm commitment. 'No matter what I do. I can never do anything to hurt him. In a manner of speaking, I worship him like god. When I am in town, I begin my daily routine only after prostrating and touching my head to his feet,' she said and fell silent. I also didn't utter a word. The mind was immersed in wonder, measuring the depth of her feeling.

After a little while, she asked, 'Are you upset?'

'Why?'

'Listening to me. Will she really love me as she is so faithful to him? You might have suspected. Speak the truth.' I was silent. 'Your silence is the answer. But understand one thing. He is my husband and you are my loving Lord Krishna. Who is the lord of the loving heart of Radha? The husband or Krishna? You would understand the meaning of my words if you were a dancer. Musicians don't understand anything beyond *sa ri ga ma pa da ni*. Isn't it through the understanding of the emotional content that the true nature of love is understood?' She began to make love. My inner conscience immediately accepted that what she was saying was not acting but reality. I also responded.

Embracing me more intimately she whispered. 'I told you earlier. He doesn't wake up. If he wakes up accidentally he would call out "Where are you?" It is fine if I go to the kitchen from here and go to him from that side. Don't be anxious in the least. The lady-love has come into your arms. You enjoy your Radha to your heart's content on this sand-bed on the banks of the River Yamuna. Until morning all the time is your own.' I was enthused under the canopy of silence. The love-making was endless in the cover of silence. Even after the hot perspirations of both of them mingled and gradually the cool calmness spread, the arms did not disengage themselves. After a long time she gasped, 'Hereafter, once every few days I will say that I have a programme somewhere else, mentioning the name of some place and

I won't be back in the night. There is your house. No matter how much leisure there is during the day, the peace and unbroken tranquillity will not be there.' I immediately comprehended that was the reason why they arranged music concerts at night in the olden times.

ಆ

I got cards printed with the address of the Manohari Das Dance Academy, and posted them to all the music and dance art establishments that we could remember. A concert was soon arranged in Delhi itself. '*Who has come from Bombay and settled in Delhi*' was printed on the invitation. It was publicised everywhere. Delhi and Bombay newspapers made this a news item. A local newspaper reported the Nagpur incident in detail and the main aspects of it appeared in the Bombay newspapers as well. Paranjape sent the cuttings, accompanied with a letter. 'Some people are commenting that due to the anti-art attitude of your wife, you left Bombay. Please let me know the truth without hesitation.' Paranjape was the one who had rested his confidence in me. Though he came to know me through Champa, he had developed a regard for my musical accomplishment. I replied that his guess was correct and it was not proper to write everything in a letter and invited him to meet me when he was in Delhi so that we could talk. A couple of weeks later he sent me a cutting from a Marathi newspaper. 'After seeing the dance programme of Manohari Das in Nagpur, Mohanlal shifted from the Principal's house to the hotel where she was staying and left with her for Delhi. This was the information gleaned by our Nagpur correspondent. This is an instance of music attracted by dance. If dance itself had been attracted by music and had come to Bombay, it would have been a feather in Bombay's cap. As a result of this incident it has become a matter of discussion among art critics whether music was greater or dance.' The article had been written with a combination of romance, humour and sarcasm. I did not reply to Paranjape either on having received the cutting or regarding its veracity. It was clear that in the art circle of Bombay, it had become an entertaining bit of news. I realised my stupidity. I had mentioned the address of the Dance School on the cards which must have given rise to this story. It was awkward for a week. Then indifference took over. It is a fact. How does it matter if people think the way they do. Gradually there was disregard about this. Not only that, it even seemed to be a matter of pride. A sense of achievement for her that she had attracted a musician of his stature. The feeling took shape in me that I was the companion of as famous a dancer as herself and it would be construed as such in the circles of the art connoisseurs. She herself laughed, 'Mohan, isn't this a greater recognition than tying the sacred knot, the mangalasutra?'

7

One morning, sitting in my apartment, I was practising to the accompaniment of the tambura. It was 9 am when the doorbell rang. Though the door of my room was open, I had bolted the door at the entrance to the building. I never had visitors of this sort and it wasn't Manohari's usual time either. We had agreed that on that day I would join her for lunch at the dance school. When I got up and opened the door, it was Champa standing. I was confused. I fet somewhat afraid, the reason for which I couldn't understand. I didn't talk to her. Didn't invite her in. I didn't ask her to leave either. I climbed the stairs and sat in my place. She followed me, came and sat on the sofa next to the wall as she was too big to sit on the floor. I started strumming the tambura. I had realised that the mood for singing in this situation was impossible. I didn't lift my face or look at her but for how long could I keep looking down? She was sitting in front of me, just ten feet away. Shall I get up and go to another room? Or, shall I say I have work outside. The fingers were moving on the recumbent tambura. After a long time, realising that there was no other option except talking, I lifted my head and asked, 'Why have you come? Tell me quickly. I have to leave by the afternoon train.'

'Why did you do this?' She asked with a defeated look.

'What do you mean by "this"? There is no point in going through what we both know. I am not going to give you any answer.'

'Hereafter, you decide the details of your programme yourself. Bargaining, fixing, collecting the money, all on your own. I won't interfere in anything, all right?'

'I am now arranging my programmes myself anyways. There is no need to ask anybody about anything.'

'What will be the plight of your family? What should I say to the children when they ask where is father?'

'Go to Borivali and meet Ramkumari, find out what she tells her children when they ask where their father is. You tell your children the same thing.'

Her face went pale. I experienced a triumph on having found the correct answer. But it was not her nature to accept defeat. 'You are saying "your children". Are they not yours?'

'Ramkumari's children are also mine. Are you saying they are not?' I hit back. Now she was silenced. My eyes were spitting fire on her. Her eyes were passing flinters on me. Her lips were trembling in a state of not knowing what to say.

A minute later she said, 'If you like, you sing aartis everyday at the temple. I won't object.'

'No one has the right to question me, no matter what I sing.'

'How should my life and the life of my children go on?'

'The flat at Kurla has been built with my money. You will get ten thousand rupees a month if you rent it out. You can rent a flat for a thousand in Kalyan or Dombivali. Or take a rented house in Borivali. You can get it for a thousand and five hundred rupees. The remaining money is enough to make a living. What is the amount of interest on the money saved so far? I can get it checked.'

She challenged, 'When you say you are going to get it audited, are you implying an attorney?'

'Have you come here without consulting an attorney?' I countered.

Again her lips started trembling not knowing what to say. After half a minute. 'I am from a respectable family who wants to carry on the family tradition. You are the one talking about courts and attorneys,' she said.

I asked, 'Who is the one who consulted a lawyer and lured me into the net of registered marriage?' She had no answer.

A minute later, in a weeping voice she said, 'Just accept the truth. The dancer has become more alluring. Even the name is Manohari. I have become less attractive after having borne you two children.'

She really started weeping. My mind was perturbed. I began to feel sorry for her. With tears in her eyes, she came to me, sat on the floor and embraced me. Embracing me tightly, she took my face in her hands and started kissing my lips, intoning, 'You are a good man, good man.' I became aware that it was an attempt to win over me or to triumph by exciting me sexually. I felt disgust. That stout body, that expressionless face, those dreamless eyes... In stark contrast, the shapely angelic body of Manohari, which pulsated with rhythm even in unconscious state and spread swaras, and sparkled with quick wit and agile with the power of a doe surfaced in memory. I got up, walked away and sat on the sofa. She started fuming. Wiped her tears. Her eyes started spitting fire that could melt iron. She bit her lips with her teeth and tightened her mouth. Not to be defeated in the war of looks, I kept staring at her.

'Who is she? I am going to beat her with my slippers,' she said.

'Her legs are strong by dancing for a long time. If she kicks you once, your waist will be broken and you will have to crawl till you die. Beware. This is Delhi. If she informs the police and gets you into jail, you won't be able to escape even after six years,' I replied.

I wanted to put an end to this situation of verbal warfare. I got up and moved into another room. I put some clothes into my travel suitcase, closed and locked it. Wore a freshly ironed pyjama and jubba, combed my hair, tied my wrist-watch, took my suitcase in my left hand, two locks and keys in my right, came to the room in which she was sitting and said, 'I will be late for my train. Just leave.'

'Where is your programme?'

I realised that only she could ask such a question even after an altercation. 'How are your concerned with that?'

'I won't go. I'll stay right here.'

'Should I call the police?' She got up with some difficulty. I locked the house and the entrance door, descended the steps quickly and came out. When I came to the dance school, the gardener said that a stout lady had come and he had directed her to my place.

Observing the suitcase Manohari looked at me quizzically. Narrating what had happened, I told her that Champa might come here. She said, 'The gardener has left. I have shut the front door.

Let's not answer the doorbell to anyone other than the attendant who brings the meal. Even if she comes here accidentally I'll tell her that you're not here. 'If she says anything else I will threaten to call the police.' I found refuge from Champa. I narrated every word she had spoken and the answers I had given. It was my habit to return to my place by 4 pm, even when I came here. By quarter past four the students would start arriving. That was the time when Master Jaisukhalalji would also come. Not that he wasn't aware of our relationship. But I would go back, exercising caution, not wanting to make it obvious unnecessarily. Should I go home at four? If she did come again, how could I explain my coming out saying that I had a programme elsewhere? Would it not amount to giving an impression that I had walked out in fear? The thought arose. Manohari suggested, 'Don't go out at all till eight. Just stay in the room upstairs.' I lay down listening to the sound of the tapping feet down below.

Champa didn't come that night. Not even the next day. The day after Manohari said, 'She has gone back. She is not the kind of woman who would sit quiet. She may take recourse to legal procedure. Once you get into litigation it is like getting entrapped in a net. I will introduce you to an advocate. You tell him everything. By everything, I don't mean our relationship. But about her nature, the fact that she entrapped you into marrying her though you were married, etc. You tell him that you came to Delhi, disgusted with her. He will advise you about the precautionary course of action.'

Advocate Ramoo Walia asked, 'How much money do you have now?'

'Maybe, fifty or sixty thousand.'

You appreciate it to one lakh. You write an account payee cheque for her. An accompanying letter saying I am sending this cheque according to the decision we took when you had come here the other day. I am providing this after taking a loan since I didn't have the money. The income of a musician will not be constant. The family has to be maintained with the interest from the deposits I made in your name when my income was good in Bombay and the flat I bought in your name. Education of the children must be taken care of with that. I have come to Delhi, as you know, because my income was meagre and I came here in search of new markets. If my income increases, I will send some more money now and then. Add this one lakh to the already existing deposit. Anyway, you will get twelve to fourteen per cent interest. With that you can live and get your children educated. There is a possibility of good times here. Both of us must trust god.' I didn't understand the trickery of this suggestion. Firstly, it is difficult to get together fifty thousand. Even if I do why should I part with one lakh?

'Panditji, you are a great man in music. You don't understand management. It is a cheque for one lakh. The moment she sees the tenor of the letter and the aspect of placing trust in god, she will immediately sign the cheque and credit it to the bank which amounts to accepting that the flat and all the money in the deposit in her name were earned by you. Don't you send even a single pie again. If she goes to the court we can get hold of the deposit and the interest it has yielded and details like that. We can shut her up in a way in which she won't be able to ask for anything again.'

Manohari got together fifty thousand. She had only thirty thousand cash. She arranged a bank loan for the remaining twenty thousand. Though such an intelligent woman, Champa fell into the trap. She wrote back, 'I have deposited the one lakh that you sent to the Finance Deposit Fund. It fetches fourteen per cent interest. They have added this to the twelve lakh already with them. Still the interest money will not be enough for the education of the children in future. Keep sending me money as and when you earn through your programmes. Don't deposit money anywhere else in Delhi...' I didn't write again. I didn't send any money again either. The advocate suggested that I should keep this letter as well as a copy of my letter safe.

ड

The sail suggests the relationship between the sea and the sky. A lone boat always engenders the image of freedom. I recalled that Ramoo Walia got me freedom from Champa for one lakh rupees. But, why did I not give some money to Ramkumari? Why didn't I send a little money every month? Didn't I remember her at all? I did. I desired to be free from her as well. If money is sent regularly, where is the question of freedom? Just a thought. Justification. Duty towards children. I had assuaged my responsibility towards Champa's children by giving money. The children of Ramkumari had faded from memory. After all, it had been six years. How free Manohari is without children! Yes, I should be free like her. The weight of responsibility pulls down an artist and sinks him. It does not allow him to fly. I speculated that the children born to Ramkumari became even more indistinct. 'Give a lakh to Bakula not to Ramkumari,' I should have said. How could he have guessed that she would reject the money? Even Rajaram couldn't have thought about this. While ruminating thus, the curiosity arose whether in that boat there was one person or two. You can't see it with the naked eye. You have to see through binoculars. I should also have bought one and brought it with me. I could have even seen how many people were there on the boat; if two, whether it was a couple, a man and a woman or both men.

It is a fortunate accident, a rare phenomenon to get the suitable companionship. As I got Manohari. And she got me, she herself confessed. What poetry would ensure with this companionship! The lightning of melody, the conspiracy of rhythm. It seems even in my sleep I would be murmuring the tune. It was she who told me that first. She in her sleep, makes movements through her legs. The feet vibrate more according to beat, they move, they collide, keeping time. I have experienced it, sleeping by her side. I have observed it. Even during her talk in sleep, she doesn't miss a beat, the feet move rhythmically. She is a born rhythmist. One day, she said, 'Mohan, I want to dance to your Bageshree on the stage. I am desirous of creating a new dance-drama. I will request the help of my Guruji, you sing full-heartedly. I will understand all its nuances and sophistication and dance. Guruji will teach me. Let us invite a tabla accompanist and practise together.

I felt happy. Not that I didn't know that no great musician sings as an accompaniment to a dancer. If by chance he does sing, it is considered a blessing for the dancer and danseuse. Or, it is accepted that the dancer is a greater artist. I decided that there should never occur any feelings of superiority or inferiority between me and Manohari. Besides, what we are doing is not the usual performance of dance. It is basically a raga, melody, created by the singer. She is only showing it through dance form. Along with this justification, the feeling that this work was a contribution of our love, sprung forth. I agreed immediately. The rehearsals started. I am not fond of Thumri, nor have any respect for it. I also shared the view of Raja Saheb that singing at the level of poetry and sentiments was not pure music. But now I had to do the alaap which was accessible to acting. What would she do if I stayed on, elaborating the subtleties of the raga? It became a form of poetic feeling. I compromised. Because what we set out to do was to show the visual version of Bageshree. He changed the cheez of madhya-laya, from the gat of singing into the gati of dancing. I had to agree to that too. How is it possible to transgress the rules of dance, while a raga is being revealed in the form of dance? They are not demanding that the design, frame and definition of the raga should be abandoned. This was an experiment involving two arts and in an experiment, each art form has to accept the discipline of the other and adjust to it. In the final stage, the dance part, the bols would be spoken by the dancer. I didn't have the knowledge of that beat. But when she was uttering the bols, my accompanying lehara would be in Bageshree and so it would be nritta of the raga. Thus I accepted the notion that it would be an expansion of my singing.

The organisation Abhinaya came forward to sponsor the show. Manohari arranged the publicity. *Artistic Conception: Pandit Mohanlalji and Guru Sohanlalji*, with my name coming first. She also added ten sentences explaining the technicality of the creation from the point of view of the raga. Bageshree would take an hour and twenty minutes. Thinking that one particular item alone would not be sufficient for a full programme, she added two items which she was usually performing and designed the whole programme with the main performance at the end. For the first part as usual Durgaa Prasad sang.

Not only were all the chairs of the Kamani Auditorium occupied, people were standing on both the sides. They had put additional plastic chairs in front and in the aisle. Everybody said that so many people turning up for a dance programme was quite unprecedented in Delhi. This was an event which had attracted both music and dance lovers. Not only that, the publicity in the brochure that Mohanlal himself would sing was the star attraction. *Bageshree* witnessed a tremendous success. All the newspapers sang its praises. In the *Hindustan Times*, Braj Bhushan wrote, 'It is a well-known fact that when new experiments are done in Indian music, new styles are born in dance as well. Similarly, the new experiments in dance have made the signers, especially the instrumentalists, adopt new beats and rhythms, experimented and invented by dance. Following the basic principle that creating a new rhythm without the foundation of a raga or, singing the alaap of a raga without the beat of the dance is not possible, Mohanlal and Sohanlal have created the *Bageshree* musical dance drama and have shown the new possibilities of both the arts. This work has catapulted the talent of Manohari Das to new heights. The immeasurable emotional impact of the singing by Mohanlal, mingling with the enormous talent of acting and dance movement of Manohari Das, *Bageshree* gives an unforgettable art experience...' The other newspapers also praised the performance in a similar tone. Five performances followed in Delhi itself. Within two months, performances were arranged in Jaipur, Gwalior, Bhopal, Nagpur, Varanasi, Lucknow, Cuttack and Calcutta. In every place, connoisseurs and local newspapers appreciated it with one voice. My singing was an important aspect of attraction. Until Nagpur, Durgaa Prasad sang for the first part. He couldn't travel to the programmes at Varanasi, Lucknow, Cuttack and Calcutta. He had other commitments. It was not easy to find other singers.

'Mohan, I know that you think that singing for a dance is demeaning. With just Bageshree there can't be a complete programme. The programme can take place only if you sing for the first three small items also. Otherwise the engagements have to be cancelled. Do you feel that singing for my dance is demeaning?' When Manohari requested this, we were both lying down with arms around each other. By that time our pairing had become so well publicised that during the tours we were staying in the same room. Just for the sake of appearances, two adjacent rooms would be booked. Anyway, the accompanying artists would be booked into less expensive hotels. It wouldn't be possible to sleep in separate rooms after the performance. Besides, both of us would be happy at the newly created opportunity of being together in peace during the night. How could I say I wouldn't sing? I had seen the items that Durgaa Prasad was singing. No preparation was necessary to sing. Still she trained me once.

Thanks to *Bageshree*, I also got new publicity. The romantic notion that I was the inspiration of a dancer of Manohari Das's stature, created in the minds of the connoisseurs augmented my star value. For my personal solo performances, I increased the fee from twenty to thirty thousand. The music associations and the organisers accepted. I felt happy. She was also happy. She contemplated about designing another musical dance-extravaganza. It would be monotonous if she was the only dancer. She thought of adding at least three more girls and bring about variety in the choreography. I agreed.

The friction started with this. I had my programmes and she had hers.Though *Bageshree* started a new wave of attraction for her spectators, her old wave had not receded. Whatever her programme, when she entered the stage, there would be an electrifying response from the audience. The days for my programme had to be planned. They shouldn't clash with her engagements. The venues were not of my choice, I had to make my choice from the days when it would be convenient for the audience and the organisers, when the halls would be available, on holidays and on days when the next day would be a holiday, etc. When once the choice was made the schedule had to be stuck to. Meanwhile she would get an invitation, which had to be readjusted to the particular day as it was a festival or a special occasion and the dance programme must be run on that day only. Mine would have been already fixed somewhere in Calcutta. She would get an invitation for the same day or the previous or the next day from some place like Baroda or Ahmedabad. It would be impossible for me to reach this place from there. She would put the responsibility on me by saying, 'The music programme is yours alone. The dance belongs to both of us. You decide which is more important.' Mine was a moral problem. The problem of my loyalty of love for her. Meanwhile Durgaa Prasad had left her and I had become her sole singer. We had shown our togetherness to the organisers of other places and to the audience by staying in the same room. Everyone had accepted silently that we were a unique artist couple. No one anywhere had talked about it scandalously. No yellow newspaper had written about it. There was a belief in many places that we were a married couple. I developed a feeling that when we were together the feeling of me and mine was sheer selfishness. I started giving up the music programmes. Gradually I became a singer for dance. That too, what kind of music? Bageshree was a rare thing. Though I was singing songs, poems, bhajans and Thumris written exclusively for dance, my rich voice vibrated with vocal resplendence, the reputation that Mohanlal was the best dance-accompanying singer grew. Gradually, the fact that I was a pure, classical, singer was forgotten. Now and then, in the reader's letters column of newspapers some letters would appear to the effect, 'What has happened to the pure musician Mohanlal? He is doing a disservice to his art by reducing it to the level of dance.' However, I had not given up giving music concerts intentionally. It was difficult to adjust dates for such programmes. Though I continued with the performances, the prolongation of the period of laya as much as possible and immersing myself in swara had decreased. It would be difficult to descend into mandra-gandhara. I had stopped getting up early and practising. I had given room to the notion that music was just a background for dance. Within three years my stature and value in the music world had gone down.

The earning also got reduced—reduced drastically. How different from just going without even a tambura, sing for four hours, earn thirty thousand rupees and if accidentally a private sitting was obtained, another five or ten thousand extra, and, now going along with a whole troupe, getting forty or fifty thousand and sharing it with the instrumentalists, other dancers, for costumes and rehearsal expenses and sometimes even spending for travel—when all this was there, how could I ask for a separate share for myself? If I asked for a share after all, what was my contribution compared to that of the principal dancer? Of course she would say, 'Your singing is really my inspiration.' But that compliment had lost its meaning within two years. I myself knew the truth that I was not singing with inspiration. How could she not know it? I felt embarrassed to calculate in terms of yours and mine. She started looking after me—my house rent, meals and apparel. I wouldn't ask anything extra. One day, she asked, 'Why should separate rent be paid for the house? The owner is talking about increasing the rent. There is so much place upstairs. Is it possible that Mr. Mittal doesn't know that you and I are very intimate? You just stay in a separate room. Of late, his visits are becoming rarer. Once in three or four weeks. Then isn't it all right if you go out for a walk for an hour or so?' It is true that there would be a saving of two thousand. But my going out for a walk when he came seemed demeaning. I just said, 'No, no.'

In the begining, the notion that love was constant, it was eternal, had filled my mind. Somehow it had entered my head that constant meant permanent and eternal. In every raga there is the concept of constant, transitory emotions. That mood or emotion which suggests and runs from the beginning to the end of the raga is the constant. But it is not suggested by itself. It must be nurtured only by the transitory emotions. In order to keep and develop the constant emotion, music must keep running. I was not aware that with the cessation of the act of music, the mood too would come to an end. Constant emotion called love will be alive and oozing only with unceasing togetherness, companionship and involvement in the life activities. When there is no act, from where can the mood flow? This subtle truth had not been understood by me. Recently my attraction for her was receding. Her dancing, the designful jingling melody of each of the two hundred tinkle-bells attached to the dancing belt, the rhythmic movement, the expression of emotion through her neck, eyes and proportionate body which I got used to, had lost the flash of novelty that I had experienced in the beginning six months. After I got to know the secrets of what bol she would use for which saam, the style of her udaans, what kind of paran, where she would give what kind of tihaai—after knowing these secrets, where and how I should adjust my music became easy. The magical effect, her dance would create on me also began to decrease. The same happened to the physical attraction. In the early days, the love-making would rise to the level of enjoying the celestial nymphs like Rambha or Urvashi. It would be the fulfilment of a dream. Every single time it was the worship of the goddess of love. Now it was just a bodily act. Not that there was no love. But there was no dream. She was busy with her work. Still she would make time to be with me. I cogitated as to what was lacking in me. What happened to the constancy of love?

Even before I understood these things, gradually, other chores had fallen on me. Chores like going to the tailor's shop to get new costumes made, booking train tickets, and not only for accompanists on the instruments like sitar and tabla but for her fellow dancers also. Usually these fellow dancers would be senior boys and girls studying in her school. How to say no when she implored, 'Mohan, there is so much work pending. These girls, you know, no matter how much you make them rehearse, still commit mistakes. I must perfect their acting and choreography today. Would you please go and get the reservation done? Om Prakash is not available at this time.' How could I say no to such an emotional appeal? How could I refuse when she kissed my lips and said, 'who else is there to communicate with the organisers?' When she requested thus showing her helplessness in her eyes, eye-brows and face, how could I refuse? 'Don't feel bad that I am giving you jobs to do. I am telling you because it will give you something to do in your free time. I don't have the time to breathe.' She began to travel by plane to save time. 'Don't get me wrong. I am scared about leaving these girls in the company of boys and the accompanying instrumentalists. What if something untoward happens. Who would be responsible? If you come with them, there will be some supervision. Please.' I would end up travelling without air-conditioning as I had to accompany the girls even if she was in the same train. She would be in the upper class by herself. What would the organisers think if such a famous dancer travelled by the ordinary class and got off the train when the welcoming party came to the station to receive her? Why did I agree to all this? The question that confronted me was why I didn't tell her, 'Look, I am a greater artist than you are. I am not a dance-accompanying singer, but a pure, classical, independent music maestro. There is no comparison between us.' Love too turned into a whimper. The reason was that I did not have yet the knowledge of severing the connection and coming out of it. Can't a binocular be bought in Bombay if I want to? May be not the best, but I should write to Madhu to bring one with her.

ʒ

Love is not eternal. It is like the essence of a raga. No matter how much you extend it, it comes to an end on its own. Did she know this inner truth? It had come to an end with her. In me it was still there. Like the ignorance which is the result of previous births. In spite of the advent of Kartikaram, I hadn't understood fully. How can the trade of any visual art progress unless new items are presented and novel choreography is experimented with? She was constantly searching for new items and new choreography, like the previously prepared *Bageshree*. It was also in her nature to do new experiments. She works very hard at it. She worries about it. Kartikaram was from Bhopal and belonged to the Jaipur Gharana, the essence of which was Laya and Tandava. She was from Lucknow Gharana which emphasised emotion and acting, and it maintained that even the pure dance tatkaar also should be an expression of emotion. She intended to make Kartikaram, Krishna in whom action should be more prominent than emotion and she should be Radha who would be the river of emotion. Her anguish of separation from Krishna should express the meaning that it is the form of sorrow of an emotional woman who cannot possess and control the man in whom action is prominent. Manohari pondered about adapting select Ashta-padis from *Geetagovinda* to concretise her concept in dance form. At one end of the stage there is Radha, suffering the pangs of separation. On the other, Krishna. Hers' is the pure and total laasya. His is tandava. For her laasya, each word and cluster of words of the Ashta-padi had to be split up meaningfully and should be sung analytically in the Thumri style. It has to start in madhya-laya and should reach the bols of drita and he himself has to continue in the Jaipur style.

She had invited Kartikaram from Bhopal. He was happy with the prospect that if he danced with her, his name would receive a boost. They had to rehearse together. She accommodated him in the guest room of the dance school. I had to be present for her practice. They would rehearse even when I wasn't there. If I stayed on, she wouldn't object. I had cut down my visits there as I was apprehensive that she would assign additional duties to me as an assistant. I didn't have the courage to decline the work that was assigned to me. I used to be afraid of a sharp look from her. Apprehensive that she would deny me something, or she would punish my disobedience silently. When I came back to my lodge and lay down I would suspect whether she was attracted to Kartikaram. Just as we would be together in the guest room, before I got my residence and even in afternoons after that, now she would be there with him. After his arrival, she never came here voluntarily. I felt that she would do her duty without enthusiasm when I called. Shall I go and find out? Will she know if I do so? The front door would have been locked from inside. If I ring the doorbell, she would come and open it. Supposing she asks, 'What is the matter', what will I say? From that day onwards, I started observing unnoticed by them, their facial expressions very discreetly, their eyes, the secret messages that were being sent to each other. I told myself, yes she had softened towards him. Even when he made a mistake by not following her instructions during practice sessions, though she orally corrected him, her eyes expressed admiration. I asked myself whether it was not possible to hide love even for a consummate actress like her. Or, was it just a common appreciation shown by one artist to another? Was her love for him the reason for her reluctance to meet me? Or was it the immersion while devising new choreography? There was the same concentration even while planning *Bageshree*. But then her love for me was intense. Remembering the night at her home, how she was unable to sleep, leaving her husband-guru, she came up the stairs silently and slept in my arms till morning, is it not possible that she entertains towards her Krishna the same kind of emotion now as she was his Radha? I doubted. Turmoil, torture. There was an emotional upsurge wanting to get the door opened, shake her shoulders and take her to task and charge her of deceiving him and demand to know the truth. But self-respect came in the way. Love and affection should arise by themselves. They should grow and survive by themselves. There was the pride that they cannot be retained by anger, begging or claim and quarrel. I used to just roll about not knowing what to do. Getting bored I would get up and go out wandering. I would walk up to Safdarjang Hospital, sit there amidst the waiting people who had come to see the patients. The neighbours would ask me who the patient was, an acquaintance or relative and what the problem was. I would be enveloped by a feeling of emptiness. Another day I would walk up to the campus of the Indian Institute of Technology and walk about there, all over the place. Loneliness even there. One day I tuned the tambura. I started singing to myself. Without prior decision the voice sounded the Darbari-shadja. Immersing myself in it, I went on singing it for a long time. I knew from experience that one can dispense with time but without connotation of rhythm no swara would develop. But it was not the rhythm that cooperated with the bells attached to the dancing belts. But they were only minute the latent outlines, self-determining, and self directing their own horizon. This is enough, I felt; a further movement was not proper. To go after movement consciously, I felt was a mean thing. Gradually I descended to the mandra, causing each swara to transcend its limit and making it rest in its expansion, when finally reached the shadja, there was the state of omkara, which completely suspended the movement. Though I had neglected music, it has not deserted me. I have found mandra. The bliss of having attained mandra-shadja intertwined itself with the bliss of mandra-shadja itself. There were tears in my eyes. The turmoil subsided a great deal. From the next day, I got up in the morning and engaged myself in practice. I felt I had attained peace of mind. A sort of royal disinterest took over and I told myself, what did it matter who slept with whom. There was a satisfaction that though it was royal, disinterest had taken place. I did not tell her what was happening inside me. She didn't ask me either. She too had neither the delicacy nor the patience.

The first opportunity of experimenting with this ashta-padi was in Patna. As usual in the publicity pamphlet Manohari's name was printed prominently. Below that was Kartikaram's. My name appeared afterwards. Already my name as a singer had receded. I had given a place commensurate with that of dance-accompanist. I had travelled with the entire group by ordinary sleeper-class after reserving seats for all of them. Kartikaram was also with us. She was to come the next morning by flight. For some reason Kartikaram was not speaking to me normally. I also kept my distance. The other boys and girls and the tabla and sitar accompanists used to address me as Masterji. The appellation Guruji was deserved only for the dance teacher, Manohari.

Before the beginning of the programme I was sitting in the centre of the orchestra. To my right the tabla player Jaswal, to my left was Sheela, to her left the saarangi player Sirajuddin and to his left was the sitarist Sarfraz. There were five minutes remaining for the programme to begin. An old man sitting in the front row gestured a namaskar in our direction. I couldn't make out which of the five of us he was greeting. Thinking that it really didn't matter, after half-a-minute I reciprocated. He who was sitting got up, came up the stage, stood bowing in front of me and said, 'My name is Fiyaz Ahmed. I sing Drupad.' I had heard his name. Remembered listening to his singing in the Calcutta Festival. Long hair. Dark complexion. Pyjamas, jubba and a waist coat. I stood up, took hold of both his hands and bowed. He said, 'I am saying this as a singer. Why did you give up pure classical singing and descend to the level of a dance accompanist? Nobody can equal your alaap and the mandra delineation at the Yaman Utsav at Calcutta. What a voice! What an elaboration of emotional upsurge! I feel like listening to it again.' The indication was given then for the commencement of the programme. Fayaz Ahmed said, 'Let's meet later.' Descended the steps and went and sat in his chair.

The Ganesha Vandanam was performed by Manohari. Then the important composition was Ashta-padi. The first one selected was

Nindati chandanamindukiranamanuvindati khedamadheeram
Vyaalanilaya milanena garalamiva kalayati malayasameeram

After singing it wholly in Raga Darbari, I started splitting each word in detail and began to expand it in vilambit. Without being conscious of it myself I descended to mandra and went interior and doing aandolan I forgot myself.

In the same aandolan and extending the vilambit into further vilambit, enjoying the pleasure of the suspended movement of Darbari I closed my eyes. When I half opened my eyelids, my face was turned in the direction of the audience in the first row. Fayaz was looking at me with admiring eyes and holding forth the right forefinger, was moving it in conjunction with the movement of my swara. I got inspiration. I further slowed it down. I just stopped reaching the vadi-rishabha. Though it was mandra, the peace of the swara didn't ruffle. The face of Fayaz was emanating wonder. When he, who was the master of Drupad, was so full of admiration, I got further inspired. His finger stood still as if to say, 'Don't change. Augment further the emotion of rishabha. Meanwhile the girl sitting to my left the accompanist Sheela bent towards me and whispered, 'Panditji, Panditji' as if to warm me. I stared at her and again half closed my eyes telling myself that I was singing correctly, the swara hadn't been affected, not exceeded its limits and hadn't digressed into another raga and asked myself why she should unnecessarily interfere. Then Fayaz was moving his hand as if a misfortune had happened and was pointing his finger towards Manohari. I didn't understand. After he repeated the gesture I turned my face towards Manohari. She was just standing still. Her face was burning with anger. She approached Sheela and asked her to draw the mike towards her and sing. Sheela quickly snatched the mike and placing it in front of her started singing to the proper rhythm of the dance movement. Manohari started abhinaya. Then I became aware of the damage done. As one descends deep inside, the movement slows down, if one goes down further, it approaches the state of stasis. In fact the secret of Darbari aandolan lies in that. That is the stance which superior music should reach. It is like the stillness of the solidified ice on the surface of the water though there are currents moving underneath, and arresting both the kinesis and stasis of time. It is the state of yoga in music. Dance which is based on movement only has no place there. Even abhinaya which is an integral part of dance if gets arrested becomes statuesque. The dance ceases. It took three to four minutes for me to understand this. Sheela didn't have the ability to sing this ashta-padi. She was struggling, attempting to do something which was beyond her capacity. She was there only to fill in certain bols of dancing. She was a dancer. A senior student of Manohari. Like all dancers, what she had learnt was also elementary music. She was struggling, unable to express the sophisticated details of word and meaning and different layers of multiplicity. Manohari had lost her direction without the support of music. A man in the third row of the audience shouted, 'Mohanlalji, you please sing. That girl can't.' Fayaz stood up and said, 'You must sing.' I started singing. Sheela moved the mike towards me and the dance continued uninterruptedly. But Manohari's mood had been spoilt. She was acting by strength of sheer practice. Her usual talent was not in evidence. I was also singing poems consciously to co-operate with the abhinaya. The mind was contemplating the vilambit movement of the mandra-saptaka of the raga. No matter how much time it took, there was no adjustment to the swift movement of dance. The connoisseurs were aware of this defect. The ordinary audience was being entertained. The common people in the auditorium felt happy when Kartikaram started dancing. Sensing this Manohari also turned to entertaining dance. All in all, not only was her original concept not realised, all the artists in our troupe felt that the performance did not reach the expected level.

The curtain came down after the performance. Fayaz climbed the steps and came to where I was. Offering me the traditional paan, he said, 'Dance cannot come up to the level of pure music.' He expressed my own view. He asked, 'Why did you stop giving classical music concerts altogether? It seems our Magadh Association of Patna had invited you last year, and there was no response at all from you.' What could I tell him? How could I explain the situation? I started making polite enquiries. I said that I would certainly come if invited this year. Meantime, Sheela came and said, 'Guruji wants to see you.' I understood immediately that Manohari had summoned me to take me to task. Purposely I ignored it and continued my conversation with Fayaz. Natvarlal, the senior student was searching for any stray bells that might have fallen away on the stage. Sheela came again. She said anxiously, 'Masterji, Guruji is calling you. You must come quickly.' I took leave of Fayaz and went backstage. The boys and girls who were not inclined to remove their make-up were standing in a side. Manohari who was on the right hand side of the greenroom, still in make-up seemed to be waiting only for me. I was also angry for not allowing me to talk to Fayaz and for sending for me twice.

Controlling her anger she asked, 'Had you come determined to ruin the programme?'

'I don't understand to whom you are saying this.'

'If you had told me that you didn't want to sing for dancing and that you would do only music concerts, I would have employed someone else. You had pretended all these days and you had planned it all, hadn't you?'

'If you get a hold on your tongue and speak sense, it may be possible to give you a reply.' She had never been openly angry like this before. I hadn't replied like this either.

'No one all these days had told the owner of the group to hold her tongue.'

'I am not your employee. You are not my boss. Shut up.'

'Shut up, rascal!' She shouted in English.

Saying, 'Are you calling me a rascal?' I went close to her. I stared at her in anger. The fire that had lit in me, because of shame and anger, hadn't come under control. I lifted my hand and slapped her on left cheek. Her cry must have been heard by the girls. Meanwhile Sheela and a couple of other girls came to the door. They saw me slapping her. She saw them seeing it. In a fraction of a second she lifted her hand and slapped hard on my left cheek. It was unexpected for me. I stood still not knowing what to do. I felt that my prestige would be at stake if I did not hit back. I lifted my hand. At once, she took hold of my shoulders by both her hands and pushed me. I was pinned to the wall. She lunged forward and caught hold of my arms and pushed me towards the door. The girls gave way. She kicked me out of the door and fumed, 'Get out, rascal.' The boys who were in make-up, the tabla player Jasraj, the saarangi player Sirajuddin, the sitarist Sarfraz—all of them saw it. I felt giddy. Since the boss herself had done it, none of them had the courage to come to me for help or console me. After a minute I sat up. She had gone into the greenroom and had shut the door. I had understood that pushing the door open, barging in and hitting her was not possible. Not because others would stop me. She was a dancer, and had a physically strong body. In addition to it, in order to keep it beautiful, she would exercise and perform yoga everyday. Except singing, my body did not have any practice at all. I became aware that when she pushed me I didn't have the strength to resist. The students of dance and music and the instrumental accompanists were all standing there, looking. I felt ashamed to stand there. But what could I do, standing there? I moved away quickly and walked out of the door of the auditorium. Got into a cycle-rickshaw which was close by and mentioned the name of the hotel. Went to my room, picked up my suitcase, went to the registration counter, said, 'I am from the dance party, I am leaving alone', got into the same cycle-rickshaw and went to the railway station. They said the Howrah-Delhi Express would arrive in half an hour.

The memory of being beaten by my mother when I was a very little boy came flooding in. But soon after, she would embrace me. Massage my back. I used to get pushed around by the rowdy boys of the neighbourhood but after joining the ashram, there was no such experience of roughness. It is true that I was the first one to hit her. But when being accused persistently that I had come determined to ruin the programme, how was it possible not to get angry? I felt fortunate that I could find a place to sit in this compartment. All the others had their reservation in the next day's train leaving at 8 am. Her flight was at half past one in the afternoon. When I remembered that, I recollected that she herself would have flights, first class AC and gradually the rascal had brought me down from flight to first AC and then to ordinary sleeper class travel. Anger filled me. There was no sorrow that the relationship had broken.

Long before the train would reach the New Delhi railway station, my mind had been made up. I went to my flat, packed the clothes. Looked into the bank pass book. A hundred and twenty one rupees. Six thousand in my jubba pocket at Patna. After the train fare, the remaining amount was in my pocket itself. Decided not to return it to her. Thirty thousand for each programme. She had ruined the prospect of my income of at least eight to ten lakhs per year. Why should I go like a beggar without even a train fare? Gave the key to the owner of the house downstairs telling him, 'Manohariji will come. Give it to her.' Got into an auto and reached the railway station. The Bombay train was on the platform. Twenty rupees for the ticket collector for a sleeping berth.

But after the train started, the question whether I was running away like a coward started tormenting me. Whether this train would stop at Nizamuddin or not, if it didn't, get off at Mathura and go back. She would have just arrived from the airport. Stand before her and telling her, 'The relationship between us has ended. I am going. Goodbye.' It would take an hour. Suppose she says, 'Just go.' She will certainly say so. This possibility flashed forth. I got consoled, and felt, after all, why this drama of goodbye again, as Mathura was approaching.

१၆

The doorbell rang. It was time for the lunch box. It's nineteen years, isn't it since these box meals started, including the Delhi sojourn. The cook from her home also used to send meals by carrier. A good meal meant what was cooked by Champa. Ramkumari's too. If you want home cooked food, you should marry again. While eating, thinking that all the hotel food were the same. He felt sick at the monotony of the taste. He remembered that even when he went to give concerts, it was hotel meals, only big hotels. The Prashanti at Dadar was a Gujarati mess run at home. Eating, sitting on the floor. It wasn't available anywhere else. Arriving from Delhi, checking into Vithoba Lodge at Dadar at fifty rupees per day. Food at Prashanti, a place behind two narrow lanes for eight, no, ten days. Returning after three years and a half, everything had to be re-discovered—the music organisations, the organisers. First to get in touch with Tipnis, not only his, but all telephone numbers had been changed in Bombay. Went walking to Mahim. Thank god he hadn't changed the house. Informed that I had come back to Bombay and was staying at Room No.16 in Vithoba Lodge and asked to send Rajaram Rao as soon as he came back. Good fellow, he came first thing in the morning. After listening to my whole story he said, 'It won't be difficult for you to re-establish yourself. Still, out of sight is out of mind. There has also been an anti-propaganda that your standard had been only enough to provide background-music for dance. Now nobody even mentions your name.' He thought for a while and added, 'It would be good to have a talk with Paranjape.'

'He is on Champa's side. Her father established him in his profession. There may be trouble for me from him.'

'Not really. Not much love is left after her father died. Once he himself had told me, 'If the wife was mean, he should have kicked her out. Why did he have to leave Bombay and demote himself to be a dance-accompanist? What singing! What great voice control! I have his telephone number. Wait just a minute. I will ring him up.' When Paranjape heard the news, his reply was 'not to pull his leg.'

'I will hand over the phone to him. Speak to him yourself.'

The next day, while cogitating what to tell him and what to hide, I thought that though he was a journalist, he wouldn't write everything, and I felt confident. 'Panditji, please don't think that I am asking you an unwelcome question. Tell me if you consent to live with Champa Bai again. I will speak to her, make her swear that she will never act again as in the past. But I am not insisting.'

'To escape from the clutches of this woman, I fell into the stranglehold of that woman. Now having escaped from her shall I be caught in this woman's trap? I will never again fall into the clutches of any other woman as long as I live. I will live like a monk.'

'You can never be that. You are an artist.'

'So what? Wasn't Swami Haridas a sanyasi? Only being like that can one achieve greatness in the musical field. I have decided.'

'His music is also a sanyasi's music. I know the attitude and approach of your music. Don't tell anyone that you will lead an ascetic life and get caught. You are now in a depressive mood. If you don't want the company of Champa Bai, then don't.'

Though, I felt that he was more worldly-wise than me, my feeling seemed more true. 'Let it be. Are you comfortable in your lodge? Just rest for a week. I will do something. Don't meet anyone else, don't mention your present predicament to anybody. If the news that you are in trouble spreads, it would be difficult for you to establish yourself again.'

I thought he was right. I wasn't meeting anyone else except Rajaram. He also agreed that my condition shouldn't be revealed to anyone else. On the sixth day I received a phone call from Paranjape. 'Panditji, you agree to my plan. There is a village near Devalali called Koregoan. There is a well to do Desai there. A lover of music. One of your former fans. He has a big farm a mile away from the township. You stay in that farmhouse for a few days. It seems he has kept three tamburas for the use of children. You select one of them. You don't need anything else. You practise your own pure classical music. For three and half years you haven't had the practice of mastering mandra. Not in touch with pure music. How can you give a performance? For a couple of months you forget everything else and immerse yourself in practice. I will arrange to establish you back in the musical world.'

His words made sense. Rajaram also agreed. He said, 'In the course of three and a half years, the sophisticated theatrical subtleties of many a raga would have been forgotten. I will give you the books by Batkhande for your keeping. You can refer them when necessary.'

The garden of Desai was reminiscent of the forest of Rajasaheb, and the River Narmada flowing beside it. The only thing lacking was the temple. A comfortable farmhouse. A hundred and fifty acre garden with mango, guava, sapota trees etc. Modern method of cultivation. Jayavant Desai also had knowledge of music. Though he was not a connoisseur of technical details, by constant listening he had cultivated the ability to recognise good music in a minute. When I was practising he would be silently lying down in the next room. I would get up early in the morning and practise mandra. Another sitting at ten. Siesta after food. Again from four in the afternoon till dusk, another practice session. Healthy food from home. The kind that was being sent from Raja Saheb's palace. At night hot milk with the ground powder of dates, dry grapes, badam and kesari. Gradually the power of my old music was regained. Not just the strength of voice but the imaginative ability and the subtleties of ragas. All this came back. Looking into the book was a rare occurrence.

Paranjape was right. Mine was not the blood of Swami Haridas. Within a fortnight sexual urge showed itself. The sort of thing that would surface in Raja Saheb's forest. The kind that would impede the concentration and immersion in music, the current that would start inside and would fill the interior. Should not the sex-urge recede? How about giving some excuse and going to a brothel... no, it's disgusting. After enjoying Manohari, even touching any other woman is an artistic degradation. Though anger against her hadn't subsided totally, the mere memory of her great love-making, brought the realisation that it wouldn't be possible to think of any other woman. While sauntering about in the gardens, after a spell of singing, while looking at the well built just-blossoming eighteen year old girls or staring at the twenty-two or twenty-four year old buxom wenches who were ripe and ready for it, the memory persisted that none of them could have the enchanting beautiful body of that exquisite dancer. But why did our amorous affair turn sour! The mind would begin to cogitate. In the beginning she also made love passionately just like me. Otherwise how was that ecstasy of love possible? This train of thought would occur. The interest in ogling the women tending the garden would recede. A couple of months of intense practice. An optimistic feeling that something would turn up after that would assert itself. Again, I would go back and take up the tambura.

One day at 9 pm Desai's driver brought me a note. 'Please come. Paranjape from Bombay wants to talk to you.' I went with him. Desai himself connected the phone and gave it to me. 'It seems you have completely immersed yourself in music. Desai says that you have got back your old form. I have made a plan. A benefit performance for the Press Club of Bombay from you. You don't get a single paisa. Tell Tipnis. He will get nothing either. You must get hold of a tabla accompanist who will work for no payment. We have determined to sell tickets and collect at least ten lakh rupees. Since it is for the benefit of the Press Club all the newspapers will give it an enthusiastic publicity. Articles will be published about you. They will print your photographs and interviews. There is a group which is carrying on propaganda against you that you were fit to be only an accompanist for dance and you were never good enough as a pure classical maestro. You must sing in an impeccably classical style to shut their mouth for good. Afterwards there will be reports and critical comments. If this concert is successful it means that you have re-established yourself. What do you say?'

I was already thrilled. 'Dharmaananda Rao, who knows better than you what is good for me? You needn't worry about my singing that day. Be assured that I will sing better than before.'

'Journalists are mischievous people. You will be asked all kinds of cheap questions about your relationship with that dancer. You should not utter a single angry word. What you should say is that you went because you thought that dance would give a concrete shape to the emotion of raga but that you returned to music as you realised that music is needed to dance, but music can stand independently as a basic art form. That is what you should say, you shouldn't utter a single angry word against her. Some people may come to interview you even at the place where you are staying.'

I was angry enough to say that she had reduced me to the level of a servant but felt that Paranjape's worldly wisdom was better.

I hit the headlines in the English, Marathi and Hindi newspapers of Bombay. Photographs of the garden where I was practising now. The details of my sadhana that I had attained near the temple at Raja Saheb's forest. Though I didn't utter a word, a hush-hush conspiratorial gossip about the relationship between dance and the dancer, music and the musician, were cleverly interwoven as an undertone in the write-ups. Desai took me to the concert in his air-conditioned car. Stay at a five-star hotel. Desai himself said, 'Your performance was not just better in quality from earlier times but much above what you had achieved so far. Life dances about animatedly in the rhythm of your singing. The emotional upsurge has become more dignified. You have gained from dance. Remember at one time music had acquired colour from its association with stage singing?'

Some people from the audience had sent notes requesting that I sing a dance tune before ending the concert. I replied, 'I won't. I have given that up completely and have returned to pure classical music.' Two cheap rags had quoted this and had added within brackets, 'Nobody should infer that Pandit Mohanlal was hinting that an unbridgeable gap had taken place between him and the dancer.' It seems there were reports in Delhi newspapers too regarding the great success of the benefit performance. I believe one of the newspapers had published a report with the heading 'A singer who returned to his own art.' I felt very happy. Derived a satisfaction that she would have read it.

Three weeks later I received another phone call from Paranjape. 'The Swar-Vilas Music Association' of the Fort has asked for your address having decided on arranging a concert by you. In these three years and a half, other musicians have raised their fees. The national-level sitar and sarod players particularly are demanding fancy amounts. You must say that your fee is not less than fifty thousand. If one organisation pays, the others will follow the precedent. If you have to maintain your status as the 'Number One' singer, you must charge number one fees.'

The next day, Samarchand Kapoor, the Secretary of the Association came to the farmhouse where I was staying, signed a contract for fifty thousand, paid an advance of ten thousand and went.

Dinner over. Lay down. Couldn't get sleep. Without the after-dinner siesta, the evening will be dull. If some thought enters the mind, sleep escapes. At ten she will definitely call. What to tell her? No news of her at all. She came wihtout notice and said, 'You sing, I will dance.' Without coming to any decision, he turned to the other side.

Chapter 9

I

I couldn't sleep the entire night. I felt I shouldn't have slapped and kicked him out. Why did he hit me first? Shouldn't I have asked why did he spoil the show? Without discipline how can the business carry on? What other reason was there? Jealousy. There has been occasional silent anger after the entry of Karthik. I thought that gradually he would adjust but the rascal had plotted secretly. He should have spoken out openly, if he had the courage. Couldn't sleep no matter how much I rolled about. Yes, I was alone. In order to make sure that nobody got suspicious, I have accommodated Karthik in that hotel along with others. I have made him travel in the sleeper class along with the others. I have balanced in such a way as not to arouse any suspicion in him. Still, why did he do this? Anyway he is only a singer, sitting on the side with three others. Karthik is a dancer who shines on the stage. He is the one who dances in close proximity with me and extracts applause from the audience. He is Krishna who attracts love from Radha. I thought that the musicians are always envious. They always suffer from inferiority complex. I felt mollified. But I shouldn't have gone to the extent of hitting him and throwing him out. But it was he who provoked me to do it. In the morning, no, it wouldn't be possible in the morning, after going to Delhi, explain his mistake to him patiently but firmly and he must be brought round so that he won't repeat it. I thought that he should be dealt firmly. A peg of whisky after the show would have helped in leveling all these ups and downs and I could get sleep. One peg is enough for me. I never exceeded it. Now it is 2 am. The hotel bar would be closed. Karthik would be sleeping. No, he will also be rolling about sleeplessly. What charming love he expresses in his eyes! He had confessed, 'Manohariji, I learnt abhinaya of shringar, from you. I was only mechanically going about manipulating my eyes and my eyebrows.' It seems, never in his life had he experienced such passionate love. His expressive, poetic words would spontaneously spring forth when love had reached a climax. He is truly immersed in love. Yes, the love pair of Manoharidas-Karthikram should become unparalleled in the entire dance world of India. His Krishna and my Radha should become unprecedented. Yes, I will train him. I will make him the personification of aesthetic figure by mixing his expertise in footwork of the Jaipur School with my emotional finesse of the Lucknow School. It is the quality of love which elevates positively. Karthik, don't be shy because you are young. Radha is much older than Krishna who is very young, by how many years? At least ten years as in our case—between you and I. Still, Krishna, not embarrassed by his young age, without being hindered by ignorance would he not take the initiative and make passionate love, defeat and tire out Radha in the coital duel? You should drop your shyness further and exult. Are you afraid that Mohanlal will come interrupting? No, you and I should go away somewhere else for a couple of days. Or, stay in a hotel in Delhi itself. This fellow Mohanlal has no place of his own, he has no home. He doesn't go anywhere. In an unimpeded atmosphere you will be constantly exulting as an erotic hero. I will be your slave with as much devotion as Radha had for Krishna. My dear Karthik, though I am the boss of the company, though you do as I tell you in the group, in the privacy of our lovelife I am your slave. Not a slave like Meera but a slave like Radha.

When she became aware that in the humming tune of the air-conditioner from behind the thick black window curtains, that the cawing of the crows and the chirping of the birds will not be audible and that light will not penetrate, she slided her blanket, pressed the bed-switch. The silently moving wallclock was showing half past six. 'My God!' She suddenly sat up. All the others in the company must leave by the half past eight train. I must enquire if all of them caught the train and she started brushing her teeth hastily. Yes, they must all get ready, pack up. Sheela is so lazy and forgetful. After a wash, wearing her clothes and taking her handbag, coming out of the lift, she found the secretary waiting for her. In another half an hour, they will reach the station. If you like I can take you to that hotel, he said. While going in the car, her mind was at work. Thousands of Gopis were loving Krishna. Indeed, were worshipping him—though there was the heat of anger that he is playing with another neglecting me, there was no monopolistic angst that he shouldn't love anyone else. Were there not husbands with two, three, four wives? Should not there be two lovers to one woman? If both of them could be satisfied physically as well as emotionally, why can't both men live together in harmony? Why can't his singing and this man's dancing be both my accompaniments? The thought occurred. It dominated my mind. Yes, I hit him. Because he hit me. It is only a reflex reaction. Even this indicates love. I love him too. Won't neglect him. I haven't stopped visiting him at his place. My love is still flowing peacefully though it lacks the exultation of earlier weeks and months. I must explain this to him. I must take him by the hand in front of everyone and apologise. As soon as he arrives in Delhi in the morning I must shut the door of the lodge, arrest him in my arms and beg him to receive Karthik as a friend.

Everyone was standing at the door of the lodge with their luggage packed. Her eyes quickly surveyed the scene. He was not there. She thought maybe he is taking cover, being ashamed or maybe he has gone to the railway station. Sheela approached her, saying, 'Didi come here for a minute', took her a little away and said, 'It seems Masterji left the lodge last night with his bag even before we came back. The receptionist at the counter told us just this morning.'

A shiver went through Manohari. She thought, when I come here with the generous intention of holding his hand and apologising publicly, in front of everyone, he has done this mean thing. She simply intoned 'hmm'. But realising that she had been denounced, she added a couple of minutes later, 'He might have gone elsewhere. His reservation is for this train. He will have come to the station. Where else could he have gone?' Four girls and four men. Sirajuddin the Saarangi player, Sarfraz of sitar—both around twenty-four. Though Karthik was thirty he had the looks of Krishna. Among them only Jaswal, the tabla-player was the senior most at thirty-eight. She called him aside and told him, 'Mohanlalji might join you at the station. If he doesn't, you must take the responsibility of looking after everything. They are all very young. You must leave after seeing all of them to their homes. He said, 'Certainly, Madam. The organisers have left all the tickets with me.'

She didn't go to the station, she went back to her hotel. She must also get ready and start for the airport at half past eleven. The thought that he was ashamed filled her head. Is it the transitory emotion of the combination of shame and anger, she cogitated. When the thought occurred that he might have left by some night train, she remembered that he had six thousand rupees with him. Thinking that she would have reached there herself by the time he would, she went to take her shower.

When she arrived at the airport she came to know the flight had been delayed by two hours on account of unavoidable circumstances. She who was anxious to reach Delhi early, get hold of him and make love to him and console him and get some consolation herself, felt that it was like slipping and falling while trying to hurry up. But there was no alternative. She remembered that the Patna flight was always like this. She sat there making a mental calculation, constructing sentences with specific words to please him and cajole him back to her fold. In a little while there was another announcement over the communication system: There is a possibility of a further one-hour delay. One hour... practically means indefinite. She became angry. With every bit of delay, his anger will get hardened. What a setback to her who was intending to rush to him the moment he reached his place, surrounding him with her shoulders like flower-garlands, shower kisses and cool his anger off with wet lovelorn looks! These airline fellows should be hanged.

The flight scheduled to depart at half past one left at half past five. Throwing her suitcase at her place in a hurry, driving the car to Green Park and ringing the doorbell of the flat. There was no answer. Coming into the street and looking up, she saw that there was no light in the flat. Though the thought occurred that he might have gone out for dinner, whatever it may be, she came down where the owners lived and rang the doorbell. The lady opened the door, invited her, went in, brought the key and said, 'He left asking me to hand over the key to you.'

'Where did he go?'

'He didn't say.'

She went up the stairs quickly and looked. He has vacated, along with his clothes. Only the bed, the sofa, the drinking glass and the container and the tambura which she had brought for him remained there. He had six thousand rupees with him. He has absconded with it. She got angry when she realised that he had knocked off six thousand. But there was also a peculiar satisfaction which she herself couldn't understand. Why should she feel sorry for such a fellow? She felt he was a thief, a cheat. However the curiosity about where he had gone didn't stop. Could it be someone he had gone in search of? She cogitated. She couldn't think of any such acquaintance. He didn't have close friends outside her own dance circle. Has he gone back to Bombay, into the fold of his wife, telling her, 'Look, I have brought six thousand. There is no more connection between me and that dancer. It is cut off for ever. I will do as you say.' Has he gone back to fall at her feet? Her mind was agitated. Let him do whatever he wants. Let him keep the money. But the very thought that he has surrendered himself to a woman, that too the very woman whom he had left to surrender to me was like dagger piercing her heart. He has decided to distance himself in anger. He has no money apart from what he has taken. She also felt sorry for him. She spoke to him, within herself. 'If you don't fall into the hands of that wife again, I will write off the money. If you want I can give you six thousand more. Just call me that you want money.' While driving back, she remembered that she must settle the account of the flat, since it was being vacated without giving three months' notice, they will collect rent for three months. How about keeping it for myself? Another plan occurred. How about keeping Karthik there? Now that the jealous man is not here, what does it matter if Karthik is in the school or stays separately? Though this thought occurred, it was followed by the idea that instead of paying rent gratis, just keep the house myself and enjoy complete privacy with Karthik there for at least three months.

When the daily quota of a peg was handed over to the Guruji, he asked, 'How did the programme go?'

'The mood was spoilt right at the beginning. Mohanlal, instead of singing nindati chandanamindukiranamanuvindati khedamadheeram in the madhya-laya of Raga Darbari, started the vilambit alaap and descended to mandra. What abhinaya, what emotion could I show?'

'Why did he do that?'

After having blurted out 'jealousy' she realised that if he asked, 'What is the reason for jealousy she would have to give the background of Karthik which was unnecessary and added, 'You know how greedy musicians are. If you don't pay them as much money as they demand they ruin the programme.' He didn't speak. He started imbibing the liquor. She went in, changed, heated the dinner, put it on the table and called him. While dining he himself said, 'He doesn't look like the sort who spoils a programme for the sake of money.'

'How do you say so, taking his side?'

'It is not a question of taking sides. I said so on the basis of my understanding of his nature. That is what happens if you appoint pure, classical singers. Their preference and inclination is always in the direction of alaap and the expansion of swara. They slow down the laya and make the taal non-functional.'

She didn't talk. If more was said, she would have to give details, she thought she shouldn't give away any information about Karthik. When he went to bed he fell asleep. He started snoring with his misshapen toothless lips and discordant sound. Though it was an impediment to which she was accustomed, this day it was a big obstacle. After turning sides for a long time she felt like shaking his shoulders and asking him to stop snoring. But she didn't feel like disturbing his sleep. She got off the bed, went upstairs and lay down in that room. There was silence. Just when she felt she was falling asleep the memory of the first day on which Mohanlal had sung Bageshree, the night when she and Guruji danced together and Guruji had three pegs and sank into sleep, she remembered coming up here to this same room to this same bed and making love to him. It was three and half years ago, wasn't it? What happened to all that intensity and passion? She searched her mind. Did it recede after Karthik came? No, it was getting cold even before that. After Karthik came, it heated up again. She felt it became really hot. Karthik, you should have been here now. In my arms. Consoling my desperation. I am alone here. You are alone there. What does this loneliness achieve? It is eight days since

I was alone with you. Mornings and afternoons spent in rehearsals. Lessons in the evening. After seven in the evening, the anxiety that the owner of the flat might come. Tomorrow afternoon must be entirely ours. When she was consoling herself that the house-rent need not be paid for nothing she ruminated, 'Did he really get the mood for the vilambit alaap. Instead of watching me dance, he was watching that old man in the front row of the gathering who was gesticulating with his hand, guiding him to descend to the depth of mandra! She remembered. She felt a bit consoled when she thought that he did not ruin the programme purposely. Then he is not jealous of Karthik! Is it possible to engender friendship between them? This ray of hope appeared. But he has left. Has run away. Where to find him? She felt sad for having exhibited her anger in front of the students.

The next afternoon when she was lying down with Karthik in the rented barsaati after prolonged love-making, she told him about the leaving of Mohanlal. She didn't tell him about their relationship. When there was no possibility of bringing about friendship between them, where was the necessity of revealing it, she thought. She only let him know that he was a pure, strict, classical singer. 'Right from the beginning he was looking down on accompanying dance.'

He was beginning to say something, addressing her 'Manohariji.' She said, 'Haven't I told you to drop that ji?' In the beginning he was addressing her 'didi'. After the love-relationship started he discontinued that and addressed her Manohariji. She wondered if it was the impediment of not being able to forget that she was ten years older than him. She said, 'Look what happens if you address me as ji,' and gave him a slap playfully and then kissed his cheek where she had slapped and whispered, 'Oh, are you hurt, oh my dear' and intoned intimately, 'We are both equal. You are the bigger one. Look here.' She measured her body against his and pointed out that he was half a foot taller.

His face blossomed. 'Is he the only singer in the world? Actually, employing strict a classical singer is more of an impediment. One who doesn't know the beat of the dance shouldn't be allowed anywhere near us. Only the dancer, male or female is the primary person. The singer is only subservient, accompanist, that's all. Get another singer. Let us prepare within a week and give a stellar performance.' She was happy. Yes, it should be done in just a week. There should be a great publicity. All the newspapers should write rave reviews. He should get to know about it and his pride should be deflated, she felt.

Durga Prasad, who used to provide accompaniment for her was located. 'Panditji, it is only natural that you are displeased. I employed him for *Bageshree* as he was a big name. The theme itself was like that. You couldn't sing that. But he insisted on singing other items as well. I never wanted to let you go. But what to do? Sometimes you fall prey to the stubbornness of some persons. Hereafter, you are our permanent singer.'

'Didi, what knowledge of swara do you think Mohanlal had? Does it become music if there is a voice that could fit film music?'

'What you say is true. I also realised it. That is why I sent him away.'

This was enough for Durga Prasad to rejoin.

Nupur group of Delhi organised this programme. The performance was to take place in a month. Kamani Auditorium was available. There was good publicity as well. A short preview of this was published in two English and three Hindi newspapers. Manohari vowed to herself that this performance should put her reputation up by at least three or four steps.

5

One afternoon she received a phone call. 'Madam, my name is D L Guha, Dhanik Lal Guha. A journalist, I want to interview you regarding the *Parikrama* show organised by Nupur. I want to take photos of your rehearsal. Would you grant an interview?'

She was happy. Excited. If pre-performance publicity photographs are printed as they do in the case of films, the tickets will be sold out in two days. She remembered that so far such publicity had not been accorded to any dance performance or dancers. 'Please do come. The rehearsal starts at five. Have you seen my school?'

'Is it possible for any journalist to work in Delhi without having seen the Manohari Das School?' She was further pleased.

He came at half past six. About thirty. A manicured beard. Was wearing jeans and a sports shirts. Long hair. A watch on the right wrist. A camera on the left shoulder. He bowed politely. For ten minutes he watched the rehearsal with seeming concentration and then clicked some seven or eight shots. He also took a photograph of the front view of the school. He said, 'Manohariji, I must interview you privately.' She told Karthik to rehearse, took him to a separate room and offered him tea and biscuits. She also held a cup of tea in her hand and sat in front of him. Since the door was closed, the beat of the dance was faintly audible. He asked some questions about the genesis of this work, its artistic uniqueness and wrote it down. Then he asked in an innocent, intimate tone, 'Is it true that Mohanlalji, the singer who was with you left you?'

She became a little nervous. She simply said, 'Yes.'

'Why did he leave?'

'He is a pure classical musician. He went to pursue his own calling.' Her mind approved, that was the right answer.

'But he was with you for three and a half years, to the extent that he and you were intimate, inseparable, I mean, his singing and your dancing were just one single act.'

'In art, it takes time to find one's own attitude.'

'That's true. It is rumoured, in Patna you slapped him, took him by his shoulders and threw him out by the scruff of his neck. That is why he left you. Is it true?'

She lost her cool by this unexpected direct question. Her eyes betrayed the truth. 'It is a lie. Who told you this?'

'A lie, is it really a lie?' He asked staring into her eyes. Those eyes which could express any emotion in acting had lost their direction and confusion reigned. The mind got busy in speculating who might have told him and had lost the nerve to confront him. 'Please tell me why this misunderstanding set in?'

'Why are you bothered about all that. You are interested in my art. You sought an interview regarding my composition.' She strongly asserted herself.

'Sorry Madam. It isn't my intention to poke my nose in your personal affair. But everyone knows that you slapped him and threw him out. Rumour is rampant everywhere. It is my duty as a journalist to proclaim the truth. Should I or shouldn't I, as an honest admirer of your art publish something in your favour and see to it that the wrong opinion that has arisen in people's minds regarding you is set right?'

She trusted him. But the very next moment she became alert that he might be deceiving her. 'Who told you all this?'

'How can I say who told me when the news has spread everywhere? It was not wrong of you to have slapped him and kicked him out. The leader of the troupe always has that right. But tell me, why did you do that?'

She felt like denying the whole thing and escaping. But was apprehensive that he might put forward some other witness and allege that she was telling a lie. 'Guhaji, enough of this. If you like, write a few lines about my new composition. Otherwise, be quiet. All these are not public affairs.' But the next minute she became suspicious whether Mohanlal himself had informed the newsmen. But then she felt that he wouldn't advertise this shameful incident. She ruminated whether it was possible that someone from the group itself had squealed. Yes, she should have immediately ordered that none of them should reveal this to anyone. She was thinking why it had not occurred to her then and there. She became aware that he was noticing her absentmindedness.

'So, it is true that the incident took place.' He didn't swerve from that point.

'I must look at my schedule of rehearsal. The date of performance is nearing.' She got up.

'Sorry, Madam, I troubled you.' He also got up. The smile on his face gave her a feeling that he was not a scoundrel.

The article he had written in the Sunday cultural supplement of the English newspaper *Horizon* was just the opposite. The title 'End of a Romance'. 'An Experiment in Art' was the sub-title. He had written a couple of appreciative paragraphs on the uniqueness of her new choreographic creation based on *Geetagovinda*. But he had continued that the experience of life that was to be noticed in this art experiment was the entrance of the dancer Karthikaram and as if it was a consequence, the exit of the singer Mohanlal from Manohari's art life. The vagaries in the life of artists raise eyebrows when one contemplates that three and a half years ago, Mohanlal who had earned the reputation of enhancing the talent of this dancer had to exit in very ignominious circumstances. After the show this dancer called her former inspiration to the greenroom, slapped him and threw him out by the scruff of his neck in such a way that he fell on his face. The news, that poor singer has disappeared, ashamed to show his face, is circulating in art circles. When this journalist met her face to face and questioned her, though she tried to be evasive in not giving a straight answer, her trained, beautiful expressive eyes became the true screen exhibiting the truth! That was what Guha had written. There was an old photograph of Mohanlal singing with concentration with half-closed eyes resembling the inward-looking expression on Buddha's face with the caption: The departed singer. There was a big photograph of Kartikaram in the pose of the summation of a whirling stance come to a stop with uplifted hands in unison, smiling triumphantly with the caption under it: The entrance of new inspiration. Right next to it Manohari's photographs in gorgeous costume with an expression of erotic shyness lifting her veil a little on her face, taken at some earlier performance.

She came to know about it only when the secretary of Nupur called her and asked, 'Manohariji, did you give an interview to the newspaper *Horizon*? A rascal called DL Guha has written all kinds of things.'

When she read the article, her anger erupted. She felt like hitting him. Guha is the name. He didn't give his visiting card when he came. She also didn't ask him. She swore that no matter where and when she met him next, she would pull him by his hair and hit him with her slippers. After fretting for about five minutes, she picked up the telephone directory and searched. She got the number. She insisted, 'I must speak to your editor.' 'Mr. Editor Sir, I am the Director of the Manohari School of Indian Dance. In your yesterday's paper a scoundrel by the name of Guha has written a pack of lies. He must apologise to me. Otherwise I won't keep silent.'

The editor spoke calmly, 'Madam, if you would write a letter about what aspects he has written are wrong, we will certainly publish it in the next Sunday supplement in the same column. Let your letter be as brief as possible. Please post it today itself because the Sunday edition goes to the press three days in advance.'

She thought he was a decent fellow. She took out her letterpad immediately and wrote, 'The article written by your reporter is full of lies. It has done the abominable thing of interfering in the private life of artists. If he doesn't apologise through your newspaper column, I will file a defamation case against him.' She put it in an envelop, sealed it and posted it at once. After posting it she wondered whether what she had written was right. Should she have written something more? She felt she should have consulted Karthikaram. He was returning the next day from Bhopal where he had gone to see his wife and children. She consoled herself that she couldn't wait till the next day. She felt what she had written was enough to make the rascal get the jitters and write an apology.

Next Sunday her letter had been published with the heading in large letters 'Manohari Das's clarification'. A photograph of her in an angry expression on her face had been printed. But when she saw beneath it in equally large letters 'The reporter Guha's Answer' she was perturbed. 'Through the condemnation of the interference in the personal lives of the artists, Mrs. Manohari Das has admitted herself the truth of my article. Once again, I assert that there is not even a single lie in what I have written.' This was what had been printed. She was burning with such anger that anybody who touched her would be reduced to ashes. She called the newspaper again. She got the answer. 'Today is Sunday. The editor won't be available. She felt impelled to talk to someone. She thought of going upstairs and showing it to Karthik. He couldn't understand clearly this question-answer correspondence in English. When she was thinking that she must translate, the phone rang. The Secretary of Nupur said, 'Madam, four Hindi newspapers have made a feast out of what Guha had written last week. I will give you the names of those newspapers. Please note down. Otherwise I will send you the cuttings. I saw in today's *Horizon* your letter and his answer. Why did you write an answer? The newspaper has made itself more popular and salacious. It is better you ignore such things and keep quiet. Why couldn't you have at least called me before writing?'

'I will teach him and his newspaper a lesson in the court.'

'Don't act in haste. If you do, you will be asked all kinds of provocative salacious questions in the cross-examination. They will print all that in the newspaper to increase its circulation. There is no certainty of winning the case. Please keep your cool. I will come and have a talk with you.'

It was not possible for her to be quiet. The secretary also didn't come. All the boys and girls—the students who come to her school—would have read about this scandalous episode. But no one would speak about it in her presence. She felt that she had gone down in their esteem. Even Karthik does not have the strength to give her courage in this matter. He has lost his courage. It seems his wife is a she-devil when angry. She doesn't read newspapers. He is bothered about her reaction, if someone gives her the news. He doesn't seem to have the manliness to tell her to shut up or it would be the end of their marriage. It is true, he loves me. To what extent could he give up his other relationships hadn't been tested. When she became aware of it she got angry. Controlled it. She ruminated, 'Why should these people harass me like this? For what sin and against whom? Shouldn't these people have at least the gratitude that I am serving the world of art?' Wasn't even feeling like making love to Karthik. It was the same with him. Afraid and anxious about who would know about the affair and who was spying. There is no one else, what will these two be doing all the afternoons behind closed doors of the school? If someone investigates! She would get fidgety about his not having the strength to stand shoulder to shoulder in support of her.

The secretary came on Thursday. 'I came to enquire how the rehearsals are going. They have agreed to give us the hall for rehearsals for three hours on Saturday morning. It must be a grand success. I ran into that fellow Guha. I took him to task. But do you know what he said? "You two should be grateful to me. I have made her a celebrity and stirred public curiosity in the show without making any direct allegations. That woman is not intelligent. She frets as if she is Queen Padmini of Chittor." You know he seems to be right. Do you know how fast the tickets were sold out after this salacious news got out? It became houseful. We have accommodated three hundred extra chairs and got more tickets printed and sold them. It is a packed house. Though we have told them that the extra chairs are narrow, they have still queued up and bought the tickets. This is the first time that so many tickets have been sold for a dance programme in the history of Delhi. And there is demand for more. We can't get a bigger auditorium than this. People want us to arrange another show next week.'

She was confused. Three hundred extra chairs after houseful. Another show next week. Her anger abated. The Secretary said, 'Guha also said, "The film people pay money and get the gossip column written. This woman doesn't understand the help I am extending."'

After the Secretary left, she went upstairs. She told Karthik everything and added, 'Our own well-wishers get such news items printed in the newspapers. The news items about film stars are also concocted. You tell your wife that you call me Didi and regard me as your guru and that you touch my feet. When we go to Bhopal for the performance bring your wife to the hotel. Or, better still, you take me to your home and in the presence of your neighbours, touch my feet and get your wife also to do it.'

'Excellent. It is a good plan.'

The show was a great success. The newspapers also reported with care. Only the *Hindustan Times* and *The Statesman* critics wrote that it was an unsatisfactory experiment as there was no agreement between the abhinaya of Radha in the Lucknow Gharana and the footwork of Krishna of the Jaipur Gharana. But this was no impediment for the appreciation of the ordinary spectators. Invitations poured in from places like Agra, Jaipur, Jodhpur, Lucknow, Allahabad and Gwalior.

3

One morning around 10 am, Guha went to Manohari's house in South Extension. Manohari had gone to Jaipur and Jodhpur with her troupe. As expected Guru Sohanlal was alone. The cook opened the door. Introducing himself as a journalist, Guha appreciated the guru's fame, the purity of his art, the dedication and discipline of the tradition of his times. The guru's face beamed and he started expatiating upon the pristine purity of the tradition of his times. His head was totally bald. Though the eyes were bright, they had sagged. The beautiful row of teeth proclaimed that they were new dentures. Directing his talk to his purpose, Guha asked, 'Guruji, aren't you eighty-two?'

'Yes, completed eighty-one and have stepped into eight-two.'

'What do you say about many young male and female dancers mixing the Lucknow and Jaipur gharanas?'

'What do I say? It is pollution, prostitution. To be drawn to the footwork of the Jaipur style is like Lord Krishna abandoning his chariot and riding away noisily on a motorbike.'

'Guruji, what a comparison you gave! It is possible only to Kalidasa. Your disciple and wife Manohariji, retaining the Lucknow style for Radha has made Karthikaram of Jaipur style as Krishna dance to that style. What do you say about that?'

'Did she do it? Is it true?'

'There were two shows in Delhi. May be she hasn't told you because you would object and even scold her with your authority of the guru.'

'Is that so? I will throw her out of the house. Who is this fellow Karthikaram? These Jaipur fellows proudly say that they alone are genuine and we are naive and are polluted by the Muslim influence. Do you know with what contempt they treat us? Is it dance, merely skipping rapidly and jumping about vigorously like a horse? If the emotion of poetry doesn't show itself and spill even in the footwork, what sort of dance is it...'

He stopped the guru in his flow of words and asked, 'What is your opinion about Karthikaram?'

'Who is he?'

'You mean, you don't know him at all? He is a dancer of the Jaipur tradition. The one who was given the role of Krishna by your wife.'

'I haven't seen his dance. What is there to see in it?'

Guha took four photographs of the guru when he was speaking with anger. He also recorded in his camera the wedding photograph of him with Manohari, hanging on the wall. He also took some photographs of the front view and the first floor of the house, told the guru, 'Thank you Guruji. I will come again. I need to learn a lot from you. I must have the great good fortune of seeing your dance abhinaya.' He touched his feet in the traditional manner and left.

In the next Sunday edition three days later, his article was published. The heading was 'Prostitution of Art: Guru Sohanlalji'. Below it, his photograph looking like Dronacharya.

The eighty-two year-old dance guru has called the dance experiment of his forty-one year old disciple-wife which she is exhibiting with Karthikaram, ten years her junior as prostitution of art. He doesn't even know who Karthikaram is. He doesn't know what experiments she is conducting with him not able to go out of the house. He, who is spending his ripe old age, nostalgically meditating on his glorious past art-life in the house built by his wife in South Extension, has great anger about his wife for polluting the pure art taught by him.

He had published the information he had collected, designed in mischievous language using puns suggesting double meanings. In addition, four photographs. The face of the guru, burning with anger. The face of Manohari, exuding shy eroticism in the role of Radha, dancing with Karthikaram. The photograph of the sixty-three year-old Sohanlal and twenty-two year-old Manohari taken soon after their marriage and a smiling photograph of Karthikaram with the caption: Ten years younger than Manohari. A big scandal started in the art-world of dance. Sunday evening there was the programme of Manohari and Company at Jodhpur. That same morning she got a copy of the *Horizon*. Curious to know the mischievous news item that had appeared in that newspaper after her reply and the answer they had published to that, she had developed a curiosity to read the Sunday's supplement. In the room of the hotel where she was staying, they had dropped a copy of that day's *Horizon*. She wasn't interested in the daily news. When she glanced at the supplement, three-fourth of the second page, God Almighty! Four photographs! Heading containing the word 'Prostitution!' She read it twice, though her understanding of English wasn't very good, she understood the mischief of the double-meaning. This fellow has gone to my house. Why did Guruji talk like this? She got angry with him. I am looking after him so well without the least discomfort for him to the extent of arranging for the cook staying at home even during nights, in her absence. Shouldn't he have any gratitude? That son-of-a-bitch Guha, why is he taking it out on me like this? Is it because he wants me to invite him and bribe him? She suspected. Her mind was clouded. After the shower, when she was having breakfast, the question how can the attraction of the people increase with this sort of negative publicity, bothered her.

Till the evening, her mind was depressed. During make-up, she determined that no matter how many such things happened, the show must not be affected. Karthik doesn't know about this news article. It seems nobody else in the company knows about this. She decided if she was strong, that would be enough. The programme was very successful. At the end of it, she got a standing ovation. She was inspired. As the leader of the troupe she introduced the fellow artists and addressed the audience. 'You have all enjoyed the show. There is no greater success than that. Some people may concoct envious reactions by bringing in things like this gharana or that, their mixture and such spurious distinctions for their own pleasure. All the gharanas and traditions are only the different vehicles of the basic Indian tradition of dance. I have adopted the creative aspect of the Jaipur Gharana for Krishna's role. I have adopted the feeling, emotion, grace and acting of the Lucknow Gharana for Radha's role. It is enough if this has brought lustre to the creation. Anyway, haven't you all appreciated this or not?' She asked and stopped. The entire audience clapped vigorously once again. Some of them shouted to give another show of the same. She got confidence. She told herself, 'I don't care what any bastard writes.'

4

When she came home from the airport, it was past four in the afternoon. Guruji who had got up from his siesta came and opened the door immediately after the doorbell rang. Just as she was angry with him, it was clearly evident that he too was angry with her, and it was visible in the irate expression on his face. As soon as she dumped the suitcase in the bedroom, she came to the living room.

Sitting on the sofa, he was looking at her. 'Merely because some evil newspaperman came and asked something, how could you say all that came into your mind?' she asked fuming with anger.

'What newspaperman? What did I say?'

'Look here', she opened the newspaper wide and said, 'Look at these photographs. He has written with a punning innuendo that I am prostituting. Has he written this without your saying so?'

'Oh, that! Yes, I am also waiting to ask you. What else is it but prostitution, your including that Jaipur fellow in your choreography and contaminating it with mixing his style? Knowing that I will not like it if I come to know about it, you are stealthily performing with him, aren't you?'

'Where is the question of stealth or concealing? The whole country knows.'

'Does the country know what Guru Sohanlal's wife is doing?'

'What have I done that I shouldn't have?'

'Haven't you done what you shouldn't have?' She found it difficult to meet the sharpness of his eagle-like, piercing, penetrating eyes. She couldn't immediately think of an answer. She had come prepared to take him to task having carefully rehearsed the words she would use. Art will not survive if minor rules of different gharanas, different styles were upheld. Isn't Hindustani music taking the ragas from Karnatak music? Haven't all the styles of dance emanated from the original *Naatya-shaastra* of Bharata-muni? She had prepared a whole set of arguments regarding the theory of dance. But his straight question 'Haven't you done what you shouldn't have' had collapsed the whole logical structure she had built and caused it to take a different shape. Unable to face him, she walked away to the kitchen. Since she had to do something after coming there, she started preparing tea. She drew the teapoy close to the sofa where he was sitting, placed the tray with biscuits and tea, returned to the kitchen and drank her tea there, sitting on a stool.

Even when she was lying next to him on the large bed his question 'Haven't you done what you shouldn't have' was piercing her. Though she tried to justify her stand to herself, the sharpness of his question didn't lose its power. The hot food after the customary one peg had induced sound sleep in him and the hollow mouth and the lips devoid of the artificial dentures were emanating snores in shapeless sound. This indeterminate shapeless snoring had always upset her. But now it became insufferable. When she thought, why only totally hollow toothless mouths made such discordant sounds, the question occurred why I wasn't sleeping by myself in a separate room. Not just the snoring. Not now but even fifteen years ago when his manhood had completely ceased, then itself I should have started sleeping in a separate bed. Why did I continue to sleep by his side out of devotion? Without understanding the value of this devotion he asked, 'Haven't you done what you shouldn't have?' When I thought that this was a man without gratitude, I realised that his question had a double meaning as in the case of that bastard Guha. It is possible that he means only the mixing of the two styles by prostitution. It is possible that he doesn't know about the relationship between Karthik and me. Or, is it possible that Guha has implanted it in his mind? This doubt occurred. Now he is travelling. The train will arrive at seven in the morning and he will come to the dance school. I have not brought him home. I have not introduced him to this man. Had I done so, not only would he have cross-examined him by asking to what gharana he belonged, who his guru was and such things, but he would have condemned his style right to his face. After that he would have been asked what he was doing here and I would have to reveal that I was partnering him in my composition. This man wouldn't have allowed this. This train of thought began to unfold itself.

The shapeless snoring hasn't at all ceased. Remembering that it was like this all the time, she turned over to the left. Even in the darkness of the night, his face was visible, or assumed a shape. A shapeless mouth sans the dentures. A forehead with bulging nerves. Twenty years ago, it wasn't like this. He was sixty-two. Old age had just set in, not invaded itself. I couldn't see much difference. How much can one understand at twenty-two? Though I was looking at old men around, how could I understand that in just half a dozen years, geriatry would totally envelop, dry up and fossilise this man, especially when I was thirsting for insatiable desire for knowledge, accomplishment in art? He fell ill. I did everything. Comforted and cleaned the small house, cooked for him, got him medicine from the doctor, washed the clothes, and cleaned the vessels. The fever raged for a week. He became insecure. 'How long can I stay alone? Who will look after me if I fall ill? My daughter is constantly remonstrating, "Enough of Delhi. Come and stay with me." I will go away. After all, what do I have in Delhi?' When he made this decision I was enveloped by a void. Who is there to teach me? There may be a host of Kathak teachers in Delhi, may be a hundred. But there is no artist like Guru Sohanlal. After being taught by him, how can anyone else be even thought of? Who else has his ability, the skill and imagination to interpret a single line of a poem in twenty or thirty different ways? Others may exhibit physical skills and tricks in the movement of their footwork but who else is there who can create visual poetry in taal? What future is there if this kind of guru is lost? In this anxiety, unable to get proper sleep in the night, lamenting silently and beseeching 'Guruji, please don't go, don't leave Delhi, don't forsake me' and dreaming as if I am the grieving Radha when Shyam who was ready to leave Brindavan and go to Mathura. When I woke up, in the dim light coming from the window of the small room of the fifth floor apartment, this old man did appear like the sixteen year old Shyam dancing ecstatically on the sounds of Yamuna with agile feet and I stretching my hands and saying sorrowfully no, I am not going to leave you...this imagination of dancing began.

In about a week's time, what a strange thought! No, not a mere thought but a strong decision. Yes, there's no one to cook for him. He has no companion. Doesn't such a great artist need support? A companion? I have not seen his wife. It seems she died seven or eight years ago. She was not a dancer. Just a housewife. So she was not a companion. How will it be if, for the first time in his life he found a proper companion and could dance with great enthusiasm, teach dance and create fresh and new compositions! What if I am that companion! He is sixty-three. He has never concealed it. So what? When he starts acting out in dance, he becomes the sixteen year-old Shyam. He becomes the mature Radha too. *Yadbhavah tadbhavati* as the Sanskrit saying goes. What a man desires or yearns for, he becomes that. 'Reality follows the Intention.' The emotional identification is the important thing. Art means emotion. When these thoughts took a firm form, telling herself, 'No I will not let go my guru, my Shyam'. I locked my flat and when I took the bus and went to Turkman Gate, he was cleaning the rice to ready it for cooking. 'Manohari, why have you come at this time?'

'Have you written to your daughter to come and take you to her place?'

'Posted the letter just before you came. Why?'

I couldn't speak. The mind was clouded. After a little while, he himself asked, 'Did you come at this hour to ask me that? Tell me.'

'What is my fate if you go?'

'Your thinking is also right. You dance in your very pulse. You also have the right body and looks. You have dedication. But I can't stay here alone. And Lakimpur is not near enough for you to commute. Such is life.'

'Guruji, please listen to me. Don't leave Delhi. I will cook for you, wash your clothes and serve you in every way. I will stay with you.'

He thought for a moment. 'What are you saying? If a girl of a marriageable age stays with me, will the neighbours keep quiet? Will your mother keep quiet?'

'I will marry you to make everybody shut up'

He was stunned. A minute later, 'Are you mad? What's my age and what's yours? You are younger to me by forty-one years.'

'So what? I have decided to marry your art. Not your age. Does art have any age? Has it geriatry? Don't you become a sixteen-year-old Krishna in just a minute!'

I didn't know I could speak so eloquently with my guru. 'Don't talk like an imbecile, you have come in the hot sun. It is obvious that you haven't had anything to eat. I was just going to prepare some rice and dal as I was not feeling upto preparing vegetables. Go and get some vegetables. You know the place where I keep petty cash. There isn't even wheat flour at home. I haven't brought it to avoid the bother of kneading, rolling and baking.'

He had his meal, praising my cooking, the dish I prepared, entering the tiny suffocating kitchen by igniting the kerosene stove. I had really cooked well so that he might admire it and accept my proposal.

He didn't raise the topic at all though a week passed by. Twice a week my lessons continued. I felt shy to ask again. All these things must be initiated by men. I had spoken that day in an excited mood. Something within me was coming in the way of my re-iterating it. Was it reticence? Was it shyness? I was praying to god, 'Let him not leave Delhi, no, let him not leave me and go to his daughter's house.' Wasn't it on the eighth day that after the lesson that he told me, 'Stay on a little. There is something I want to talk to you about.' Yes, it was a Friday. He made me sit in front of him and asked, 'You had spoken about something the other day—is it still on your mind?'

Immediately I felt shy. I bent my head. He said, 'If yours is a firm decision, I will talk further.' Even now I didn't know what to say. 'If it was a momentary feeling and hasn't lasted, tell me. I am not forcing you. Because my daughter and son-in-law have written that they will come and take me. I have to write to them before they leave and inform them not to come.' I understood that he had decided to marry me. There was warmth surging in my heart, out of fear. It flashed through my mind to say, that thought wasn't in me any more. But I didn't have the courage to say so. If I said so and if he left, what would happen to my learning. Not just learning. But I felt how could I live if he, who had taken the shape of a companion within a week left me? 'You aren't saying anything. Which means you don't like it. All kinds of things appear and disappear in the minds of twenty-two year-old girls. You also had that experience, didn't you? Tell me so, clearly. I do not insist. I am not asking you to marry me and stay with me. You are the one who proposed. Only if it is a firm decision will I venture on my next move. I am asking this question to find out whether your idea is true or false.'

I felt I have been caught in a cage from which there was no escape. I didn't understand then whether it was a cage of words constructed by me or whether he had built it by using my words. A minute later I said, 'Once uttered, my word is always firm.'

'With you I have no reservations. I earn five hundred rupees a month. I must live within that means. Since I have been staying here for a long time, my rent is forty rupees. If I leave, there are people prepared to pay seven or eight hundred. The owner is trying to get me to leave somehow. There is no assurance that this earning will continue the same way. If you work hard in the manner in which I teach you, I can make you a dancer of the national level in three to three and a half years. After that we can live comfortably.'

'I will dedicate myself completely no matter how rigorous your training is,' I was enthusiastic when I said that.

'You should know this also,' he continued, 'Don't think, what will I get by marrying this old man. Though I am aged, I am not old. Through continuous dancing this body has protected its vigour. Even now if I tie my dancing tinkle-bells and dance in the role of Krishna who in entire India can keep pace with me? Which expert tabla player can keep pace with the swiftness of my footwork?' I felt that was true too. I had also seen the programme of my guru. Even Bindu Maharaj of Varanasi found it difficult to keep up with the swiftness of his footwork and had complimented him. How could I understand then the bodily youthfulness and real old age? I was inexperienced though I was twenty-two. His forearms with swelled nerves looked like the hands of sixteen-year-old Krishna who was dancing with lightning speed, holding a flute in his hand.

How could I convey to my mother about this marriage? She had the ambition of making me a science graduate and seeing me as a teacher. I never could comprehend science. Algebra was a fast knot. If it was the arithmetic of dance, calculation would flash easily. I could immediately understand the calculation of the dance beat—whether it was one, two, three, four, five, six or tat-tat-teegada, deeg, deeg, teegada, or teegada, teegada, teegada, tat, tat, thaii. I could comprehend any change that was made in the rhythm. It seems even in sleep my feet would move with unerring accuracy. I was going to college but I knew that I wouldn't pass in the final examination. Mother was also thinking that instead of Mathematics and Science, if I was admitted to any Humanities I would at least have a Bachelor of Arts degree. But she had put me in the Science course because it was easier to get a job as a teacher with a Science degree than with Arts. This she knew from personal experience as a teacher herself. If at least a diploma was obtained in dance, there was a possibility of getting employed as a dance teacher in some big school. But not all schools have such a post. Also, she was worried that the dance and music teachers would find the last priority not only in pay but in prestige. As a woman who was widowed at the age of twenty-three with two children, mother had definite aims regarding the education and employment of her children. The son had got admission in engineering. Mine was a hopeless situation. She would blame herself for admitting me to the dance class. But for me dance was not merely a means to get a job. It was the very breath of my life. I had to practise what the guru had taught with anklets, nupura bells tied to my feet everyday. But in the fifth floor of the small flat, if I started practising the footwork of Kathak, the people in the lower flat would come up and bang on our doors. 'You girlie! Do you need a police complaint?' They would complain to my mother too when she returned. Had I not become friends with Jayanti, it wouldn't be possible at all to practise. She lived in an independent building with both ground floor as well as upstairs. We would keep the time beat for each other. How much better I was than her!

I knew that mother would not approve. I was afraid to tell her my decision. How could I have the patience to think from her point of view? How could she who had lost her husband at a young age and brought me with such difficulty consent to my marrying my guru who was my grandfather's age? She objected and threatened me. She said she would break my legs so I could never dance. She came to Guruji's house and abused him loudly. 'You have spoilt my daughter's mind. I will lodge a police complaint and get you arrested,' she shouted. She called him a scoundrel for all the neighbours to hear. My decision hardened. I replied to her in the presence of the neighbours, 'Go to the police. I am twenty-two. The police can't do anything.' She left in anger and didn't see me for three years. After my debut in the Delhi stage and reading the praises of my performances in the newspapers, she herself came. The anger against her daughter had receded. But she could never accept a man her father's age as her son-in-law.

On his retorting, 'I didn't ask your daughter to marry me. She was the one who asked me to marry her. If you are angry, take it out on her. Why do you vent your anger against me, having come to my house?' She left shamefaced. After that she didn't come. It became a habit for me to visit her now and then. She never forgave me. After she retired she went away to Hyderabad to stay with her son. But I did not go to see her. She didn't write any letters. Now, how many years is it since I saw her? Manohari cogitated. She ruminated, 'Mother, the house in which I am living is mine—earned by me. Come and stay at least for a month.' I must go to Hyderabad and invite her. Tell her, 'If you can't stand the face of this old man, there is plenty of space in the dance school.' Does this man remember that I diverted mother's frustration and anger on him to myself and protected him? She turned aside. He is lying down with his back towards me. The sound of breathing is audible. Not snoring. As he directed, three and a half years of grinding. How many different kinds of bols, what ingenious chakkars, how many different kinds of movements! The secrets of abhinaya. The imaginative unfolding of the compositions, layer by layer. He playing on the tabla showing them in practice. Instilling enthusiasm with words, 'Don't think you are tired. You should get rid of tiredness by incessant practice.' Instructing, 'This is not enough. Perform yogasanas, learn pranayama. These are essential to retain the shape of the body and to keep the breath under control. Those who have mastered this, though sixty can prance about like an antelope. Understand this.' He taught me that as well till I felt the lightness of the weight of my body and experienced wonder. Dancing is as easy as floating in the air. Taught me such control that in spite of four hundred jingle bells tied to the feet, they could produce one single tinkling sound. I remembered, what intensely absorbed learning and what profound loyalty in teaching! Before going to bed, he would apply oil to my feet and massage them expertly and if I protested that he shouldn't touch my feet, he would console me by saying, 'Each day's pain must be alleviated that very day. You have to practise more rigorously tomorrow. When you wear your nupur, the dancing bells, there won't be the feeling that you are my wife, my student. You are Parvati, goddess of the art of dance—devi of laasya.' Massaging my feet everyday, putting back into its place if a straying bell fell off, tying it up properly with the concentration of a sculptor carving a statue—whether it was love or affection or devotion or the desire that I would perpetuate his name in future.

Whatever it was, if he had not taught with that kind of involved concentration, how would I be a dancer? Along with this memory, came the thought that whatever may be the purpose it could even be worldly wisdom on his part in escaping from the obligation of depending on a daughter at this old age when a young girl had come voluntarily to take care of him enabling him to continue his life-long love of a congenital dancer. What mattered was that he taught with such single mindedness! With this host of memories suddenly gratitude asserted itself.

What wonderful days they were—those three and a half years! New taals, new footwork, new command over the old movements. What bliss in the achievement, in expounding time bit-by-bit by splitting it, as a web adjusting the timing of the footwork to the flow of time, creating the grid taal itself through the movement of the feet. What joy it was! The thrill of expounding new and newer emotions and feelings while practicing the movement of the eyes, sitting before a mirror, and watching the changing expressions. Except the enthusiasm of achieving the unity of meaning by coordinating the footwork, hand gestures, the meaning of the designs of eyes, brows and lips to the bending and swaying of the body nothing else did exist. Nothing else was needed. No, there was not even the consciousness that anything else existed. Not even the awareness of the difference that he had completed sixty-two and I was twenty-two. Though he would fulfil his sexual desire once in a while, I was not aware of the limitations of his old age. I had the contemptuous feeling why people made so much ado about this! Dancing all morning. A siesta in the afternoon. Dancing again, learning music in the evening. Dance again. Deep sleep after dinner. Even in the dream the accompaniment of the feet to the bols of tabla words of the song in the mouth. Even the Krishna of Brindavan would manifest himself only through striking of the feet, conduct of the feet and as thousand petals of time movement, and not as a companion instilling sweet and pleasing emotion of love. Right in the middle of all this penance, when there were the intimations of pregnancy I didn't even have the knowledge of understanding it. When the doctor mentioned it, I was upset. Pregnancy. Child. What will happen to the practice? I was angry with him for not lying down quietly but having done this to me. The doctor who examined me, noticing my stupidity asked me if I didn't have a mother. All these things are taught by the mother. Instead of her, you have come with this grandpa. He is not my grandfather but my husband. On hearing this the lady doctor burst out, 'Husband! Did your parents, because of their poverty dispose of you to such an old man?' 'No doctor, I myself married him. He is my guru. I am learning dance.'

What an angry look on her face. Not with me but with my husband who was sitting out of the examination room. 'It is not for me to criticise what you do with each other. But there is no guarantee that a child born of the semen of a sixty-three year-old man will be healthy and strong. Yours is a fertile strong womb of a twenty-two year-old young woman. But his seed is a weak.'

'Abort this, doctor. I had decided to get rid of this even before you told me. He has also agreed. It comes in the way of dedicated commitment.'

'Really, is it a definite decision?' She looked at me steadily as if to test me.

'Yes'

'Then come next Wednesday, on an empty stomach. Along with him.'

When I emerged out of the doctor's room, I felt relieved. But an indefinable sadness enveloped me. A feeling of having lost something, deceived of something, of having lost without being aware of being robbed of not only the suitcase, handbag and purse but even of the bangles on the wrists and necklace while travelling on a pleasure trip. I didn't at all have the idea that pregnancy had such a powerful root of happiness. I hadn't enjoyed while being impregnated. I had only endured his whim and fancy. But now, when I took the decision of getting rid of it, how much it began to bother me! It didn't matter even if it was a weak child, I felt a desire to retain it. I could practise dancing keeping the child in front of me. I didn't discuss it with him. He also never brought up the issue again. I couldn't go home to my mother's place and share my feelings with her. After going through the turmoil, weeping alone, on the morning of Wednesday, I went to the nursing home and standing in front of the doctor, said, 'Doctor, in addition to performing this abortion, please operate me in such a way that I never will be pregnant again.'

Looking at my face she asked, 'At such a young age?'

'As time passes, the age of my husband will be advancing. If the present pregnancy is weak, those of the following years will be weaker. Why should it be necessary for me to come again for another abortion?'

She didn't say anything. After a minute she said, 'In that case, sign this form. Get your husband's signature as well.'

This man is sleeping soundly and comfortably. He has forgotten the sacrifice that I had made. Not only did he talk about prostitution, to the journalist, but mentioned it to my face. Even if it was not just the mixing of different gharanas of dance but the mixing of two bodies, is it a greater sin than severing the fertility chord of a twenty-three year-old girl and cheating her of the possibility of becoming a mother ever? I felt like asking him. I must wake him, make him sit up by hauling him up by his shoulders and ask him, the way of cross-examination of a culprit in a court of law. The left hand moved in that direction. Meanwhile the thought occurred, 'What is the use of taking the old man to task?' If I insisted on questioning him he might say, 'You wanted your art. It was your decision. I didn't say anything.' Or, he might say, 'Yes, you wouldn't get a healthy baby with my semen. You didn't want such a baby. Would you give birth to a baby by inviting a strong young man to impregnate you?' What answer could I give if he asked that question? She remembered that if he was cornered, he was the kind of man who wouldn't hesitate to say anything. The result was that the fertility chord was cut. That was all. After that his desire abated. Gradually that also stopped. He trained a wife who would maintain him in old age. He didn't think about her fate. Her anger again heated up that he had now talked about prostitution in a devious way.

ड

How the desire which had been suppressed till the training was over did sprout again! The one and only disciple of Guru Sohanlal. What with the tremendous success achieved as soon as the gandaa-puja was performed as the successor of his art, and the money pouring in, along with the thrill of the completion of training, that desire too began to appear and it was maddening. Age twenty-seven. Health exulting. Radiant looks, shining eyes that effortlessly expressed inner emotions. The grace and beauty, the confrontation which would make any man lower his eyes in confusion and defeat. But there was this old man's serpent vigilance establishing his overlordship though he himself was without cravings. Isn't it a sin to betray a husband who was also her guru? Along with the fear that if I commit the sin of betraying, he might curse me and whatever he had taught would be perished. There was another anxiety that men who exhibited desire for me would remain only at that level caused frustration and it made me suffer in another way also. It was then that Mr. Mittal appeared on the scene. I didn't know that he was fifty-six till he himself mentioned it. Even then I couldn't believe it. The hair colour that had been applied to his profuse crop of hair was so natural that I couldn't make out. No trace of wrinkles on the face or body. I thought he was forty. My dance programme of one hour was arranged at the annual celebrations of the Transport Operators Associations of India. At the conclusion when the President, Ramcharan Mittal handed over the memento and put the rose garland round my neck and shook my hand, he sent forth a silent message of touch. There was no agitation in his eyes. Like the bridegroom who holds the hand of the bride after garlanding her, his self-confidence proclaimed that he was her de-facto husband. When my hand which had been extended for a handshake was squeezed firmly causing slight pain, there was a feeling that he was imparting an additional message. After that, at dinner he invited me to sit next to him. Guruji, tabla and sarod players were in various places. A banquet for about two hundred people. How expertly he engaged himself in polite conversation in order to extract the information he wanted! How many years of training? What about the parents? What is your telephone number? On saying that I didn't have a telephone, 'Please take my card. Won't you please call me yourself? If you give me the number of some neighbour of yours, I can get you to the phone, can't I? I have something to say to you privately. You consent, won't you?' I, who had learnt acting was stupid. How precisely he was comprehending every emotional change that was taking place within me from every question! How could I understand then that he was a veteran? But his powers of comprehension were very sharp as a result of managing such a huge business. He was the sole boss of the Mittal Transport Corporation. He owned one and a half thousand lorries. He has been the president of the All India Transport Association for two years. After the dinner, at the time of saying goodbye, he squeezed my hand tightly and said, 'Please do ring me up. I will be waiting. From ten to one in the morning and four to seven in the evening is my prime time', a message flashed forth from his eyes. He called his private chauffer and instructed, 'Take Madam and her fellow artists to their place. Take note of the house.' Then his intentions became pleasantly clearer to me. I had never sat in such a posh air-conditioned car earlier. Guruji said, 'So many people! We had to sit for dinner wherever we could get place.'

He has made everything clear. He has put the responsibility on me. Since I don't have a phone at home, it is me who has to call. I couldn't sleep that night. The pain in the right palm which he had squeezed had a pleasant association. The imagination of his firm grip began to occupy my mind. What self-confident eyes! Looked forty. What style in dining, talking and congratulating someone! The modes that were explained and illustrated by Guruji were surpassed in his style of expression. I didn't know this. I must learn this sophistication. His was a sophistication that did not come from learning. I couldn't sleep till the wee hours of the morning. When I got up late in the morning, Guruji brought the newspaper, saying, 'Look, there is your photo here.' The picture of Mr. Mittal shaking my hand. He is four inches taller than me. 'The President of the function Ram Charan Mittal felicitating Miss Manohari Das who enraptured the audience with her scintillating dance' was the caption under it. Below it a report of the problems of transport workers. The cameraman has focused on my face. Only his profile is visible. What a bad photographer. She was angry.

While having a wash and performing yoga, rumination she kept thinking, 'All this is wrong. He is a millionaire. God knows how many people like me he has bought and enjoyed. Why should I fall into his trap? I have married art. I felt I should derive pleasure and happiness only in it. No matter wherever and however the mind wandered, at least bodily purity must be maintained. No matter if he is old or decrepit, I have myself asked and got my mangalasutra tied by him. I got married in the presence of the holy fire. He has taught me very sincerely without any reserve. He is still teaching me. At least physically I will be faithful to him. When the mind wanders, I get up and immerse myself in dance to my heart's content in front of the picture of Lord Krishna on the wall. If I spend my energy till I get exhausted, I sleep being tired and the mind is consoled. If I maintain my celibacy this way, my dance gets dedicated to god and I will become a great artist. Isn't it for this purpose that I married this man! This train of thought gained ground. 'That my body has attained a sophisticated power of bending and swaying, by yoga practices—more than any other dancer I knew. I have attained complete breath control, no matter how much I dance and how many twists I perform I don't feel short of breath. There is no yoga without celibacy. Dance is also a form of yoga. I decided to attain the highest achievement in dance through celibacy. I immersed myself totally in dancing and through the sound of my anklet bells and through the manner of the calculation of taal drew applause from Guruji himself. Dancing and dancing like that, I immersed myself in dance. While dancing with absorption in pure dance, which transcends the barrier of music and language of poetry, the new structures of taal, new and newer calculations and new choreographic compositions flashing forth in the mind and when they are difficult to be expressed in the language of bols and to be articulated by the tongue, the feet engrossed in the bliss of effortlessly expressing to themselves. Oh, is not it the state of calm that the yogis do attain! With this awareness, sharpening more and more the pace of the rhythm and descending in the middle to vilambit laasya, I was becoming the Parvati and the Shiva as well. Guruji not having the physical strength to accompany on the tabla confessed, 'You danced superbly. You have gone beyond what I have taught you. Let us teach this item to Jaswal the tabla player. Let us see to it that there is no one equal to you in this city.' This, from a man who had never praised so freely.

After cooking and finishing lunch, a slumber. Even in that slumber the feeling of samadhi. I understood the meaning of the devotees of Lord Krishna resorting to dance playing cymbals as a part of worship. I must spend my entire life this way. I must tear up the card of that Mittal and throw it away.

The next morning, while practising yoga, the memory of Lord Krishna who was a dance teacher too. Like a yogi, he had not eschewed all company. Even while enjoying the company of Radha and other women, he encouraged them to dance and himself danced with them. Shiva who performed the Tandava needed a Parvati for the Laasya. Such comparisons. Yesterday I just danced like mad, only the nritta. I didn't do abhinaya—after all, what is abhinaya that I know? Just book-learning and what Guruji has taught. I have not experienced love, or shyness or pangs of separation. I haven't experienced even a single type of the traditional eight types of heroines. I have never really experienced the ecstasy of copulation. What sort of dancer am I going to be? Is mine the achievement of an ascetic? The thought process continued. The picture of Lord Krishna took on the shape of Mittal. He is not Ram Charan Mittal but Krishna Charan Mittal. No, not even that. It is Mittal in Krishna's form, the mind corrected.

I spent the whole week like this, swinging between the two walls of righteous behaviour and the pressure of action. I felt that if I should remain a healthy artist, and not lose my mind, I should see Mittal. The next morning at half past ten I started out from the house saying that I would go shopping, and called up his number from the telephone at the corner of the street. Though it was the first time, I could recognise his voice. When I said, 'It's me. Do you recognise?' my voice was shaking. He said, 'Please hold on a minute. I will speak to you from the inner chamber.' The noise from the office was in the background. A minute later when I heard his voice, a totally silent zone. When he said, 'Manohariji, why did you make me wait for so many days?' There was the pang of separation which was reaching me.

'Are you upset? I needed time to take a decision.'

'You saved my life by making the decision. When can I meet you? Tell me where should I pick you up?'

'I can't think of a way of coming out of the house'

'Don't you have a friend? Say that tomorrow is her birthday and you have been invited for dinner.'

Immediately I remembered Premalata, my classmate in high school. It was four years since I had seen her. After I married this old man and came away she was not only displeased but angry. After that she hadn't contacted me. I also hadn't gone in search of her. I thought I could easily use the excuse of going to her birthday party without any trepidation.'

'Then tomorrow morning exactly at half past ten I will be waiting at the bus stop opposite the Krishi Bhavan on Rafi Marg. Note down my car number. Benz. Ivory colour. Number... Do you have a paper and pencil? I will come there sharp at half past ten. You shouldn't be late. It is not proper to come there by car, to park and wait or to loiter about. It doesn't matter if I am late by five minutes. You come there five minutes earlier. Don't wear heavy make up. But dress decently.'

'I am afraid.' My voice was shaky.

'There is no reason for fear. Trust me completely. When you are with me no one will interfere. I will look after your safety. Inform that you will come home in the evening.'

I couldn't think of anything more to say. 'Did you hear?' he asked.

'Yes.'

'Shall I put the phone down?'

'Yes.'

I also put the phone down. When I went home with the provisions, I was afraid, looking at Guruji's face. I have promised Mr. Mittal. How to broach the subject of the birthday? I spoke while serving him delicious hot food. I will go, after preparing the food for you. Please serve yourself. He asked the details about who she was, where she lived and why I hadn't spoken of her all these days. I understood that day that telling lies came naturally to a lover.

I had heard the name of the Hotel Meridien. There is a well-equipped auditorium in it. I had heard that dance and music programmes are arranged there for important foreign guests. I had entertained the hope that some day, I would be invited to perform there. But I hadn't imagined that now I would pass through the lobby, get into the lift and enter a room on the fourth floor with

Mr. Mittal. After closing the door and bolting it from within, he said, ‘Manohari, don’t be apprehensive in the least. Nobody comes into this room. Nobody knocks on the door. This place and this time is completely ours. Now tell me shall I address you as aap or tum,’ he asked holding my hand and pressing it gently. This brought tears to my eyes.

‘Should you ask for my permission,’ was my inner voice. Love not expressed through the body has no meaning. Without love, complete physical satisfaction is not possible. Without the emergence of mutual trust, none of these will be fruitful. I understood this truth that day. It seems he is fifty-five. Twenty-eight years older than me. I never got that feeling. I felt he was of my age, nay, even younger as Krishna was to Radha. I didn’t feel that he was a rich man and had brought me to a posh hotel spending a lot of money. When he said, ‘Hey, if I have to address you as tum, you also have to address me as tum. As soon as he said this I called him tu. I patted him on the cheek. Punched him softly. Familiarity sprang forth like a fountain. I said, ‘I am very jealous. Tell me the truth. I won’t tolerate it if you have another girlfriend.’

‘I swear. There is no one else. There were. Not at the same time. One at a time. There were two. One of them was a secretary in my office itself. Affection developed. It didn’t seem proper that when she was an employee, and I her boss, such a relationship should be carried on. I got her employed in another company. We would meet for four or five hours once a week. We used to have telephone conversation. She got married. After that she said, ‘My mind doesn’t approve. Don’t force me.’ I respected her feeling. I helped her husband get a good job in another company. I haven’t met her for five years. Twenty-five years ago I had another relationship. She started extracting a lot of money. I would have been pleased to help her. But her mental attitude made me feel that loving her wasn’t possible. So I discontinued. You tell me about yourself. How did you come to marry Guru Sohanlal?’

I confessed everything honestly—the suggestion that he should marry me, which I did myself in order to retain him in Delhi, my attraction for him, later my training under him, I described both the sides. I had never shared this with anyone. He listened with deep sympathy. He expressed his great regard for Guruji. He said, 'Manohari, we must meet this way at least once a week.'

I was in tears. 'I hope I am not cheating Guruji. If you support me that I am not I will come to you.' I buried my face in his chest.

'You have cheated only yourself. You haven't cheated anyone else. Nor are you doing so now.' He gently caressed my back.

'You must swear that you will not abandon me under any circumstances', I said.

He put his palm on my head and said, 'You just trust. I have believed that trust is love.'

While taking leave he said, 'I will drop you at the same place. Do you have money for an auto? Next Wednesday, meet me at the same place at the same time. You should have money for that day also. Do you know why I am asking? I can give you four or five thousand rupees right now. But after such a great happiness, if I pay you, it is lowering the level of our relationship—yours and mine. Do you understand what I am saying?'

It took a minute for me to understand. My respect for him increased further. I said, 'After I start giving programmes, I will have money. I am the one who buys the provisions for home. I don't need it even if you give me.' His face beamed with joy.

While going home, I bought a packet of jalebi. I said my friend has sent some sweets. All the friends had got together. They have decided that we should meet at least once a week, I said. I mentioned several incidents remembered during the party and some jokes too. I myself didn't know that I had such a fertile imagination.

When we were in bed together, while making love, I used to call him tum. But at other times, no matter how much I tried I couldn't use that endearing pronoun. I would automatically address him as aap. He would ask me, 'My friend, why do you do this?' I said, 'I can't do otherwise. Don't insist.' He said, 'Please yourself.'

We met like this at various hotels over the next six months. He would take charge of the room in advance and get it ready. Till entering the hotel, getting into the room and closing the door, I would be anxious. Also while coming out. I am a dancer. One who gives public performances. I get my photograph in the newspapers.

Won't someone recognise me? Hasn't someone already done so? I was afraid. But it was not possible to stop our meeting or making it less frequent. One day Mr. Mittal said, 'Look, I have an idea. Engaging rooms like this in various hotels continuously is not safe. I am in the business circle. Yours, of course, is a public field. We must have a place of our own. Not just for the two of us to meet. Also from the point of view of the development of your art. Let us build a building of your own. Name it Manohari School of Indian Dance and start a school. Let us build a big building. If there is a private establishment of one's own, it will have a special prestige in the performing world. You conduct classes there in the mornings or evenings or at both times. We can meet there itself in the afternoons whenever we feel like it. If we so desire, even after the classes are over, we can meet there. 'Keep one thing in mind. The building as well as the school, both of them should be totally in your own name only. Your Guruji should not have any authority of any kind over it. He should not come there even to engage a class. Right from the beginning, this must be managed only in this manner and be accepted as such. Do you understand?'

It took me ten minutes to understand. 'How much money is required to build such a building in Delhi?' I asked.

'Don't you worry about it. I love not only you but your art also,' saying so, he added, 'You have to bear another thing in your mind. Right from obtaining the site from the Delhi Development Authority or buying from some other source, to raising the building, everything will be transacted in your name. Even if someone asks where the money came from you should say you have taken a loan. My name shouldn't appear anywhere. I will tell you the real reason. Among my three sons, I have established two of them in different business. They must work hard and develop those. I have trained my eldest in my transport business. If it is known that I have helped you, some journalist might make a news story about it. My wife may get to know about it. Naturally she will develop anger and jealousy. She will antagonise my children against me. This building is a very small part of my earnings. But she will poison the minds of the children by instilling hatred towards me. I have tightened my hold on them by subjecting them to a rigorous discipline. My two younger sons have a feeling that I hold a dictatorial authority over them. They will have this feeling till they establish themselves in their own business. It is easy for my wife to turn them against me at this juncture. She won't have either the discretion or forethought to realise that she will be destroying their future. Why give room to all this? It is natural for you to express your gratitude before some people, for the help I have rendered. But bear the consequences in your mind.'

How soundly this man is sleeping! Has he ever struggled like me, not being able to sleep? 'How is it you are building your school there? So far and not somewhere near here? How did you get so much money?' He demurred.

'I have taken a bank loan.'

'How will you pay it back?'

'I will repay by earning through my performances.'

'When you named it Manohari Das Dance School, did you become independent, without adding my name the name of your Guru and husband?' Again he grumbled.

'Your name is there anyway in connection with the home. If it is known that it is a school run by a woman, rich people will send their daughters there. There are a lot of rich people in that area. I am going to appoint only women to teach tabla and sarod. There is no entry for any man there.'

'For me either?'

'Yes, for you too.'

'All right. I will never step in there in my whole life,' he swore.

A wonderful privacy from morning ten to evening four without any hassle of checking-in and checking-out. A separate telephone for the school. Conversation with him at a time convenient for him. Six months passed. 'My dear, Mana, there is a house for sale in the South Extension. I have decided to register it in your name. I will buy you a car. You learn driving. How can you park a car in the congested narrow lane where you are? The new house is about three and a half to four kilometres away. Not the present twelve kilometres. Both in clean New Delhi.'

He has got this school built which is itself so large. In addition to that a new house. How much he is spending for me! The thought of saying, 'This school is enough. I don't want a house' was on my mind. But worldly wisdom warned that when he himself was volunteering why object to it? 'Thank you. Thank you, dear,' I embraced and kissed him. Guruji said he wouldn't come to the new house. This is a familiar place. I have been here for thirty years. I have run my school here. I won't leave and come to some extension in New Delhi. You go alone, he insisted. I understood that this was the expression of his anger for the non-inclusion of his association and name and forbidding his entry to the school. Then I will stay in the new house. You stay here. If your earning is not sufficient I will give you. Is it all right? He screamed, 'I know what you are becoming these days.' 'What is it that you know? When you are capable of earning, you should. In the English speaking extensions they give whatever money you demand. It is enough if you can teach them in English. Leaving that why should you rot in this foul smelling little lane? You have a dirty mind. You said you knew. What exactly is it that you know? If you ever again say it, your reputation will be at stake. Be careful.' With my outburst he became submissive. I decorated and equipped my house the way I wanted. I learnt driving. I got the license. Once a week I would go and look him up in the tiny house. I didn't invite him to come and live there. He didn't ask to. In a way it was easy. The advantage of Mr. Mittal's possibility of coming to the new house appeared. But it was painful to see the husband cooking rice, dal and roti for himself. The guilt that I was not doing my duty was bothering me. However, there was also the decision to keep him under control. I found the solution, let him cook for himself and get tired and then let him beg me to tell me that he would come and ask me to take him there. Then he will be under control. He fell ill in a fortnight. Half of it was genuine, half pretence and acting. I understood immediately. If you stay here it won't be possible to come and see you everyday. Will you come if I take you there? Do as you like, he moaned. I took him in my car, the doctor prescribed medicine. He would have recovered even without it.

Another six months had passed. One day Mr. Mittal came at half past ten in the morning and said, 'My dear, Mana, your bank is close by, isn't it? Here, take this suitcase. It is not necessary for me to come. There are ten lakh rupees in it. Put it in the fixed deposit. You will get an interest of ten thousand rupees a month. Of late you are getting programmes. I know that your earnings aren't bad. But if there is an assurance that there is no problem of livelihood even without programmes, artists can work with greater dignity and self-respect. Then the income also will increase.'

I didn't know what to say. I certainly couldn't refuse. All this was just an atom in his earnings. Is he denying anything to his wife? How much happiness is she giving him? If she had pleased him completely why would he come in search of me? I hadn't seen her even once. When I had asked, he himself had brought and showed her photograph. An idle, rich, fat woman. Gold and diamond ornaments to hide the fifty past age. I was angry with her. Jealousy, of course, was always there. It seems just her earrings cost ten lakhs. What extra merit has she more than I? Isn't she and aren't her children those that enjoy the crores of rupees he earns? What does it matter if he gives me ten lakhs? But exuding gratitude, I encircled his neck with my arms and kissed him. After returning from the bank, I took the amorous initiative and without tiring him, set him afloat on waves of bliss. I asked myself, isn't gratitude also a transitory emotion of love? I lovingly remonstrated, 'My lord, by giving so much, please don't make me small. What can I give you in return except the spontaneously springing forth, heartfelt pouring of love? Hereafter, not only me, but my art itself is dedicated to you. Don't be afraid. Please come to every programme of mine in Delhi. I will bring the tabla and sarod accompanists to this very place and give a private performance for you only. There will be no one else. I won't tell even the accompanists who you are. Why should you be so scared? May not your companion dance for you? Shouldn't you see it? If you say so there will be no accompanists. I will dance playing the cassette. You must kindly see it.' I could see in his eyes how fulfilled he felt.

The happiness that he enjoyed that day became a benchmark for me. I decided to give him that much happiness, even more, every time I met him. I had understood clearly by then. That ornament-laden fat woman past fifty could never have the power to give such pleasure. She certainly doesn't have the art. That is why he comes to me. But never does he utter a single word either about her beauty or her erotic proficiency. What is the meaning of this silence? Isn't it dissatisfaction? Shouldn't he mention it to me? My mind was perturbed. I felt she was the only rival I had in the world. No other dancer. Even if a young talented dancer, with classical beauty by birth and had attained the complete blessing of her Guru in an adolescent age had arisen on the scene, I won't be competitive to the extent to which I was with this lady. Not just competition but jealousy. This man never mentions her, he only praises me. But he has not spoken even a single sentence saying that I am better than her. Is he doing this deliberately only to make me boil inside and die? In my sleep, she, that woman in the photograph appeared and started parodying me. You are worth only two buildings, a car and ten lakh rupees in cash. How can you have my status, she asked me one night. Yes, I don't have her position and status. I am just a concubine. A prostitute. But she is a married spouse. A legal wife. A householder. This sorrow filled me. Couldn't sleep the whole night. Why is this man teasing me like this! Mana dear, let us not meet stealthily like this. I will divorce her. Let us get married. The children are grown up, standing on their own feet. I don't have any other binding. Why doesn't he say these things? This question began to bother me. He needs a reason to divorce her, doesn't he? The trend of thought continued. If she has an affair with another man, if he gets to know about it, if he finds a letter written by her to her lover. He sending her away saying that he wouldn't see her face again and get out, taking an alimony, he coming in search of me, marrying me in the foyer of our school, or her getting killed in an accident...Or, dying of cancer...Somehow, for some reason, if she dies, she who is my impediment for everything... he saying, 'My dear, the impediment is removed. Come, let me marry you. I will hold your hand and introduce you, 'Meet my wife, Mrs. Manohari Mittal' everywhere, in the meeting of the various parties—together. In dreamful, half-wakeful state, and while being fully awake...One day this picture too came before my mind. I, disguising myself, wearing rubber gloves, stabbing her again and again in the chest and stomach with a sharp dagger, escaping, and the police reporting that it was a murder motivated by robbery...

ಽ

One day he had free time. He said he would stay till four. I made him a raft and floated him on the waves of pleasure. I caused him to swing into the depths and raise to the heights as he had experienced never before. Total fulfilment was dripping from his face. Intoning, '*Badiya, bahut bahut badiya*' he embraced me tightly. After a brief silence I whispered in his ears, 'I will ask a question, if you say you don't mind',

'Ask. Please ask, my Ratidevi,' he also whispered.

'Have you ever experienced such happiness with your wife?'

'Why are you asking this question?'

'You never speak about it.' I looked steadily at his face. He became silent. Though his eyes had met mine, his inner being had receded. I was afraid. 'Are you upset by my question?' I asked in the tone of begging his pardon, remembering that he was the big boss. He didn't speak even then. Realising that it was immature to persist in talking when he was immersed in deep thought, I fell silent.

After a while he fondled the top of my head. I understood as I was closely observing his face that a secret smile passed through his being. I didn't ask about the why and the wherefore. He himself said, 'We have all read in our school text-book that the Buddha discovered the venerable truth that desire is the root-cause of sorrow. If I were the Buddha I would have told a deeper truth that comparison is the root cause of sorrow. What a lot of competition there is in business. Pushing the others back, even trampling upon them. I have never competed with other transport businessmen. I have conducted my business honestly and I have developed it to this extent. I am happy.'

I felt as if I had been slapped. I felt giddy. The strength to meet his eyes was shrunk and my eyes closed. I felt that from my question he had understood my entire inner being and I felt helpless having been caught. I didn't say so. I couldn't think of putting forth any excuses or lame explanations and had to accept my state. I became aware that if I said, 'I am sorry, it was a mistake,' it was tantamount to accepting my mistake directly. Finding it difficult to stay in the same room, I got up and went to the toilet. Since it became difficult to come out and meet his gaze, I stayed there for a long time. Since that day her picture began to bother me less. However, there remained a dormant discomfort, about the form of relationship between us.

A month after this incident, no, after three weeks, the Transports Traders Association met and elected Mr. Mittal, as president for the third time. I read in the newspaper that the Delhi Transporters Association had organised a felicitation function. At the end of the celebration they had arranged a dance programme by Chitra Vyas. I felt uneasy. In fact, I had met Mittal because my programme had been arranged in the conference of the transport companies. Why have they invited Chitra now? Though it was the decision of the organisers, wouldn't they have consulted him? Or, he himself could have told them that Manohari Das was a better dancer than Chitra, couldn't he? Was he displeased with me? He had come here after that incident. He was quite happy as if it hadn't bothered him at all. When he paid a visit next, I myself asked him. 'I am not envious of Chitra Vyas. But it is proper that I should dance free, without fee on the occasion of your felicitation. I wouldn't have told others that I would dance gratis, as it would make them indulge in speculation as to the reason. But you could have told them to invite me, couldn't you? I feel sad that I couldn't dance in the presence of god in the temple.'

For a minute he was silent. Then, seeming to have come to a decision he said, 'I will tell you the truth if you promise not to get upset.'

'Please do.'

'I also wanted that you should dance. When Chitra was dancing, I was seeing you in her. The organisers had insisted that I should attend the function accompanied by my wife. They had brought presents of a silk sari and a silver plate for my wife. I didn't suggest you because I thought it would be difficult for you to dance, looking at me sitting next to my wife.'

Though I understood his good intention of avoiding embarrassment to me, he had pierced the secret of my conscience for the second time. I was angry. I felt that if I kept silent it would be akin to admitting to guilt. Acting out the acme of anger, I said, 'Do you think I am so mean? I would have danced happily considering your wife my elder sister.'

'If another occasion arises, I will certainly suggest your name,' he said. My mind was hankering not to prolong the conversation.

7

Don't know at what time I slept. When I woke up, it was quarter past nine. I felt relieved that I got at least this much sleep. Though I remembered that I should have gone to school an hour ago I didn't feel lively. When I shook my body and turned I remembered his admonition, 'Haven't you done something which you shouldn't have?' His piercing eyes of an eagle. She listened. He had finished breakfast and was sitting on the sofa. She quickly finished her bath and breakfast in five minutes. Deciding that if she didn't punish him with at least two day's silence, he would go out of control, she didn't talk to him, took her handbag and car keys asking Raji the servant to close the garage door. The morning classes had been over at the school. The teacher Om Prakash was waiting for her. He informed that Karthik had said that the Jaipur and Jodhpur shows were a grand success and handed over a registered envelope. It was a small cover. It felt like it had a lot of papers in it. At the designated 'From' space, there was the printed address 'Jayant Desai, Landlord, Koregaon, Devalali Road, Maharashtra.' It must be some invitation. She thought it must be a record of the old programmes they had conducted and without opening it, put it in her handbag. After Om Prakash left, bolting the front door, she ascended the stairs. Karthik was packing his suitcase. There was a look of worry on his face. As soon as he saw her he held up the telegram which was on the table: 'Mother is seriously ill. Come immediately.'

'This came half an hour after I arrived. I was waiting for you. If you hadn't come I would have called you. There is a train at 1 pm.' There was no time for much talk. She was disappointed as she was planning to be alone with him and refreshing her body and mind. It was six days since they had made love. She looked at her watch. It was quarter to eleven. He must start immediately. He must get an autorickshaw, reach the station, stand in the queue for buying the ticket, secure a seat in the compartment. She asked, 'Can't you go by the night train?' His speech faltered when he said that they had written that her condition was serious. Without uttering another word she opened her purse, gave him two thousand rupees and asked him to go. After sending him away in an auto and she went into her office, sat down and opened the envelope. There was another cover in it which had been firmly packed. On carefully cutting the edge of the envelope and shaking it she found a bundle of currency notes neatly secured by a rubber band. There was no covering letter. She unbound it. Counted. Sixty. Who is this Desai who had sent six thousand without any mention of why and wherefore? She just couldn't remember no matter how much she tried. No landlord by the name of Desai had met her so far. Had not talked to her. Let alone Koregaon. She had never gone to Devalali even once. While thinking this she remembered it was a railway station near Nasik. This person was not even from Devalali. Koregaon, on the way to Devalali. A landlord. There was no other indication except the printed address on the outer cover. Then it flashed forth. Six thousand. Sent by him. She turned to the other side of the cover. The postal stamp of Koregaon. If it was a cheque his name would be revealed. His address also would be found. Thinking of the possibility of my rejecting it, he has sent the currency notes affixing some one else's name. It is mandatory that a registered material must have the address of the sender. The address is not in his handwriting. It was superscribed Registered A.D. So the receipt would have gone back for having received. It is tantamount to receiving the money once, the cover is opened. The same envelope cannot be returned. He is the guest of this landlord or there was a private concert at his place. He has shown his nonchalance in saying take back your money. All these implications were apparent. But ten minutes later it occurred. He has rejected and denounced me. I had taken your money by mistake or I didn't have money at that time. She thought that he had suggested he could earn a hundred times more. I shouldn't have hit back. I shouldn't have thrown him out. These mischievous media fellows had made news out of it. He would have read it too. He has sent back the money only to hurt me and had sent the money with the contempt that it was equal to his discarded footwear. There is no letter, not even a line. Not written even abusively. She thought that he has meant that I am not worth even to his contempt, and so has sent just the currency notes. She began to feel that a mood of pure classical music must have possessed him and so he must have descended to mandra in vilambit. She also started humming that musical note softly. It got stuck in the throat, blocking it from within. She felt like crying. She cried in fits and bouts. She remembered that it was three months since that incident at Patna and his departure. She sat slumped in the chair. His memory filled her. He was more warm and emotional than Karthik and a man of hot and intense love. He had come forsaking his family completely. She remembered that he had sacrificed his own musical career and she had been puffed up. The doorbell rang. She looked at her watch. Half past twelve. The lunch box. She opened the door. The boy has brought it from home. Lunch for two. Karthik has left. She thought she should have called home asking to send lunch for only one person. She put the plate on the table, and started to eat. She began to ruminate. Did I neglect him in my intoxication of having found a dancer ten years my junior, dancing as my Krishna? After lunch, she washed the plate and looked at the wrist watch. It was 1 pm. The train to Bhopal would have departed. While thinking that he would have found a place to sit, she felt that the telegram was a bogus one. Getting upstairs and entering his room, she found it lying on the bed. The sender was signed 'brother.' No name. It had been sent last night at eight. The supplement of the *Horizon* newspaper of the day before yesterday would have reached there too. Though they are not the sort of people who read English newspapers, someone who does, must have read and translated for them. Or, it is possible that some local Hindi newspaper would have translated some salacious details and printed Sunday evening or Monday morning. These people would have read it yesterday morning. It seems his wife is a termagant. He would be afraid even if anything was mentioned regarding her. She herself has invented the story of his mother's serious condition and got the telegram sent. This flashed forth in a jiffy. She felt she shouldn't have sent him at all, felt sad that it didn't occur to her when he started. The train would have started.

No matter how fast the car was driven—Nizamuddin, Faridabad—does it stop at these places? On to Mathura—how is it possible to search for him in such a big train? When she realised that it wasn't possible to overtake the train, her inner voice forecast the future that he would not return. She had his address. She remembered he didn't have a telephone. He will reach Bhopal by midnight. She thought, he might call by tomorrow afternoon. When I am giving special training to the senior student Rajat separately, he will certainly call. She consoled herself.

But there was no phone call even by the next afternoon. Not even at night. He might have left without noting down the phone number. His memory might have failed. The explanation flashed that he was the kind of man who didn't have either the education or the training to note down everything in a book. She consoled herself that it would take a couple of days for the letter to reach. Though Guruji was lying next to her she didn't talk. She turned to the other side deciding not to talk to him till he himself begged her pardon. Though she felt like going upstairs she resolved that she would teach him a lesson by continuing to sleep next to him and torture him by being silent. The anger due to the frustration of not having heard from Karthik was intensifying her anger against Guruji.

On the sixth day she received a phone call from Calcutta. 'I am Dr. Amit Ghosh, the secretary of the Arts Association of South Calcutta. We have decided to show your recent dance composition *Parikrama* to our members. Please give us a date. If it is a Saturday evening, it is convenient. Otherwise, Sunday. Please let us know the total number of members in your troupe. We will give the sleeper coach train fare for everyone. We will arrange for shared accommodation in an ordinary hotel. Please inform about your total fee.'

'Airfare for me. Accommodation in at least a three-star hotel.'

'OK. What is the total remuneration?'

'In other places they have paid fifty thousand rupees. If you pay more, we won't say no,' she laughed.

'We would pay more if we could afford. Air ticket and three-star hotel alone will cost seven to eight thousand more. So please agree for thirty thousand.'

'I would accept if it was a solo performance by me. But we are two principal dancers. The other five are supporting dancers. How much do we get after distribution?'

'OK, make it thirty-five thousand. I will place it before the committee to pay more. However, even if the committee agrees, it is a question of getting hold of the money, isn't it?'

'Please think about it. My partner-artist has gone to his native place. After getting to know when he is returning I will call you regarding the date. Please give me your number.'

There is a programme in Lucknow on the twenty-sixth. If I make it en route to Calcutta, some travel expense may be saved. It is six days since he left. Has he forgotten about this Lucknow programme? In the evening an idea flashed. Why not go to Bhopal and return? Immediately she called her travel agent. 'I was wondering why Madam hadn't phoned. To Bhopal? Reach in the morning and return in the evening? Yes, certainly, madam. If you leave Palam Airport at seven in the morning, you are in Bhopal at eight. If you leave there at six in the evening, you are back by seven. For tomorrow? Please wait for five minutes. If there is room, I will confirm right away.' In just five minutes he called back and said, 'Would you be in the school? I will send the ticket in ten minutes with my servant.'

ន

The address that Karthik had given turned out to be Sarasvati Vidya Mandir, a small music school. There were four old harmoniums and four tamburas. There were five boys from fifteen to eighteen years. When she asked them, 'Children, are there no elders, your teachers?' They said that the teacher had gone out for tea. She requested, 'Please one of you go and fetch him. I have to meet him urgently.' One of them left. After about fifteen minutes he returned with a man about forty, wearing dirty pyjamas, a washed but unpressed jubba and a congress cap. When she enquired he said, 'It is true that Kartikaramji was conducting dance classes here. But now he is in Delhi, a famous dancer, the dance classes are not taking place.'

'I must find his house.'

'I don't know. Suklaji would know'

'Where can one find him?'

'I will give direction to his house. You can go.'

'I have come from Delhi. I don't know this place. I have a taxi. Please come and show me. I will drop you back.' After this appeal, he agreed and sat in the taxi. After wandering in several streets, Suklaji's home was reached. He also said that he would give directions. After begging him the way I had requested the music master, he came and sat in the taxi. Again the taxi started moving on the meandering roads and tiny streets. In order to avoid answering the prying questions of Suklaji like, 'Who are you, why have you come from Delhi? What is your relationship with Kartik?' She asked, 'How is the health of Kartikji's mother?'

'The health of Kartik's mother?' He was surprised and said, 'Look here, madam. Why this affair for me? Why this misunderstanding? I won't show you the house. Please stop the car. We will get off.'

'Don't be afraid. I swear by god that I will not mention that you showed me the house. Show me from a distance and both of you can get off. Take this for the auto fare. She held out a hundred rupee note.

Suklaji's countenance changed. His eyes communicated with those of the music master. Then he said, 'Oh, you don't know the auto rates in Bhopal. We have to go to two different places. Please give another hundred rupees.' After she gave the money without another word, they directed the driver. After circumambulating a bit, they told the driver at a dirty little street, 'Stop. Stop at once' and pointed, 'Look, over there. You see that old woman sitting there, washing vessels? That is Kartik's mother. We will get off. You shouldn't mention our names. You have sworn.' They got off in a hurry and disappeared.

The old woman was washing vessels next to the drain. An old, tiny house. Stairs right in front of the house. When she asked her where Kartikaramji was, she replied 'upstairs' but immediately, as if waking up she asked, 'Who are you?'

'I have come to fix up a programme. I am right from this town.' She started climbing the stairs. Karthik was staying in a tiny house. As soon as he saw her, exhilaration, confusion and fear, all appeared simultaneously on his face. He stood still, not even being able to invite her to come in and ask her to sit. After a minute he stammered, 'Please sit. How did you find the house?' She understood that the woman who came out of the kitchen after hearing him was his wife. A round-faced, strong, country woman not afraid of anything in the world. A broad, wide-bodied wench quite incapable of dance. Red complexion, oozing out oily sweat. Karthik who felt impelled to give her an explanation said, 'This is Manohari didi. She has come from Delhi.' Saying, 'Please sit down didiji.' He brought a stool and he himself kept standing.

Uttering, 'Have you come from Delhi?' the woman went out and shouted, 'Hey Sajan, where are you? Tell your father that she has come from Delhi, bring him here quickly. Run.' She came in and stood leaning firmly against the wall as if to say that she wouldn't talk until Sajan's father came.

Karthik himself, in a vain attempt to get over the embarrassment, started to talk. 'Didiji, Have you had your breakfast? All well in Delhi? How is Guruji?' Meanwhile a man of about thirty-five, clad in blue pants with oil stains on it and a half-shirt in a similar condition, came up the stairs. A spanner in hand. It was clear that he was a mechanic and had come in the midst of his work in a hurry. Right behind him came up Kartik's mother. Karthik said, 'Didiji, this is my elder brother. He owns a scooter-repair shop. Nobody in entire Bhopal knows more about scooters than my brother. Even from distant parts of the city, people come in search of him to get their vehicles repaired. They even wait for three days saying, "Dasharathji, only your handiwork is required. No one else can repair as you do," they beg.'

Dasharathram said, 'Please introduce the lady.'

'This is my didi, Manohariji. The greatest dancer in the country.'

Immediately Kartik's wife cut in. 'I have been counting your saying didiji five times. Do you think we will be deceived if you say didi?' Manohari stopped short of breath at the vehemence with which she shouted. Karthik also stood dumbfounded. The wife said, 'She has come from Delhi in a car to kidnap him. That is why I sent for you. Do what should be done. Otherwise I will do it myself.' She thumped her way into the kitchen, the old wooden floor shook.

Dasharatharam spoke, 'Madam, one should not speak ill. Why should we be bothered about what relationship is there between this fellow and you? If it has been published in the newspapers, can we live in this town with dignity? I myself sent the telegram to him. We don't have to make a living only by dancing. Let him get trained by me for two years. I have told him that I would commission an automobile service centre and establish him in that trade. If this fellow comes to you stealthily, we will all come and create a scene in front of your school. Along with the children. It is not as if I don't know your Green Park area. You know the Yusuf Sarai Kapoor Auto Garage, the best place in Delhi for repairs of scooters, motorbikes and rikshaws? That is where I learnt my job for three years. You understand this.'

'Dasharathji, the newspaper fellows write lies to blackmail. Make it juicy to sell. Can you believe all such stuff?' By the time she said it, a number of people had already come—ten, twelve, fifteen. Dasharathram shouted at them. 'What do you want here? Can this old loft bear the weight?' The street was full of people.

'Whether it is true or false, we have lost face in our locality. You see how people have gathered?' The aged mother of Karthik screamed gesturing her right hand at Manohari.

'I am not saying that your son should stay in Delhi. The programmes will be in different places. If he comes to Delhi for a week for rehearsals it is enough. Would the organisers who have arranged the programmes keep quiet when they have paid advance money if we suddenly say we can't come?' she asked.

The brother Dasharathram understood this. He didn't look as if he had an answer. Meanwhile, the wife who came rushing out of the kitchen told her brother-in-law. 'Is that so? Let him go to Delhi. Let him go to the programme. I will also be with him. As soon as the programme is over let him remove his make up and the dancing bell-belt and come away with me. Ask her if she agrees to this.'

Manohari felt insulted. Her anger was scorching her, thinking what has this village woman thought of her. She looked around. Karthik was gazing at the ground as if he was guilty. Not a word. He didn't have the courage to ask his wife to shut up. She was disgusted.

She said, 'Dasharathji, I have signed the contract. Your brother who received two thousand rupees and came away hasn't even called. Neither has he returned. I can collect the damages claimed by the organisers of the programme from your brother by going to court. Understand this. It is insulting to me to sit here listening to the talk by people like this.' She got up and proceeded to leave.

Dasharathram asked the people to make way for Madamji. When she was at the doorstep Karthik stepped forward, 'Didi, I will see you out.' She looked back. Immediately his wife caught hold of his left arm firmly and shouted, 'Where are you going to send her off? Are you planning to disappear with her just like that? I am not going to let you go.' She pulled him. Sweat broke out on his face and started trickling down. Manohari's eyes were afire, spitting contempt. But his eyes, unable to meet hers were glued to the ground. The spectators gave way. She got down the steps, found her way to the taxi, sat down and said, 'Direct to the airport.'

The taxi was meandering its way through the small lanes. Her mind was telling her that she had never undergone such humiliation in her whole life. She knew that he was afraid of his wife. But she hadn't imagined that he would shiver like this in her presence. My God, those narrow lanes, those people! Before she came to the new house in South Extension she was also staying in the lane at Turkman Gate. It was a Delhi lane. Not a Bhopal lane. She saw the difference. What a lot of people gathered as if it was a free show! In their eyes I became a hungry husband-stealer! She felt that she should have slapped her hard. She remembered, that woman's shoulders were made for a fight. But consoled herself that it was good that she came away quietly rather than quarrel with such mean and dirty people. Meanwhile the taxi had come to the main road. She looked at the wrist watch. It was still quarter to eleven. The flight was at six in the evening. What could she do till then? When the taxi was moving fast she was about to burst into sobs. But thinking that weeping was a sign of weakness she controlled it. When she was sitting in the airport swatting flies, she got curious. Couldn't he have guessed that the telegram he had received was a hoax? Even I could see it. Couldn't he, who knew those people and had grown up amidst them?

Or even knowing it as such, did he lack the courage to not go? While pondering, she remembered Mohanlal. He was a courageous one. He left Nagpur immediately. Though the wife came to Delhi and tried to influence him, he sent her out. Such love, such loyalty. What kind of dancer can this fellow be, who was attached to a village termagant? Except the skill in footwork what else did he have? She thought the lack of skill in abhinaya was not a fault of any particular gharana or tradition. After a couple of hours, going to the canteen, grabbing a sandwich and a tasteless cup of tea and returning to the waiting hall, she fondly hoped he might come there. He knows that I travel only by flight. She looked around hoping that he might have escaped from home under some pretext and had come there. She looked again and again. Then she adjusted the chair to face the entrance and sat for another two hours. Then feeling ashamed about her expectation she turned the chair back to face the counters.

While driving back from Palam she thought, how about training Rajat for Krishna's role? Am I not running the show with the singing of Durga Prasad after Mohanlal left? I am the chief artist. I am the one who sponsors and promotes the others. I promoted this coward as his footwork was good. He himself lost the opportunity. She felt proud. If I train Rajat for a month and teach him the footwork of Krishna and accompany the acting with nritta myself, the show can be made colourful. But he is a student. Abandoning his engineering classes if he comes for dance classes morning and evening—his parents would not agree. They won't send him out for outstation programmes even if he is taken by flight. She felt a challenge that she should find someone, and a great programme of the same design should be given with a lot of publicity in Bhopal itself.

On going to bed after dinner, Guruji as usual started snoring inexorably from his open shapeless mouth. The question bothered her as to why she was sleeping there with an eighty-two year old man when they had drifted apart mentally as well. She thought of the solution of going to the upstairs room and lie down so that she could at least relax. She couldn't sleep here. It is not necessary to sleep there. She went up just to lie down there for a while. When she switched on the fan and lay down on the large double bed she felt relaxed. She felt independent. She remembered the intensity of the union when one day Mohan was sleeping here, she had come up the steps silently and slept with him. Suddenly desire rose like a wave. It became stormy. She remembered it was thirteen days since she had made love to Karthik. He will never come again. He is a coward. I myself lost Mohan. The visits of Mr. Mittal have become few and far between. Not much enthusiasm even when he does come. He is getting to be sixty-nine. He has discontinued even dyeing his hair. She remembered he had started talking philosophically that one should accept one's age. The old man Guruji was always old. When I volunteered to wed him, I was immature and lacked understanding. He who was mature in understanding, why did he agree? Why did he talk in a way to incriminate myself? He has brought me to a pitch where there is no one even if I want to make love. She began to pant with anger.

೨

There was a phone call at half past nine in the morning. Voice of a woman. 'Madam, I called several times yesterday. No one picked it up. I am the Assistant Secretary of the organisation Bhagini. My name is Sarala Srivastav. We wanted an interview with you.'

'I don't give interviews for any newspapers', she replied immediately.

'We are not newspaper people. Ours is an institution to help needy women and enlighten people about the injustice that is being meted out to them. We work silently. If you don't want to be interviewed, it is all right. I will come and meet you anyway. I will show you the work we are doing. If you believe in what we are doing then you may talk. Otherwise don't.'

She agreed. That lady said she would visit in an hour. She was about thirty. Was wearing a simple sari and blouse. Except a wrist watch for the left hand, she had no ornaments. The moment she saw her, Manohari thought she was a widow. Face with ordinary features, complexion and build. There was absolutely no make-up for the face, not even lipstick. Black, bobbed hair. She had a carry bag in addition to her own handbag. After Manohari took her to her office, she described the activities of her organisation. Women were being treated unjustly everywhere. Even at home the mother herself neglects the girl and prefers boys. The teasing and torture in schools and colleges that girls have to face, the problem of dowry, the pinpricks from the mother-in-law, a husband with bad habits, etc. Our job is to bring this to the notice of women. She took out half a dozen selected issues of the magazine, placed them on the table and said, 'These are not provocative articles like the newspaper ones. These describe and portray the problems of women in a serious manner. Their circulation is also limited. They are not available at newspaper stands. It is not important for us that you are a dancer and a glamorous figure. But we think that you have been unjustly treated. How did you come to marry a man forty years your elder? Has he not exploited you by saying that he will not teach if you didn't marry him? It is not only your experience. How many girls interested in arts are exploited this way? In the fields of music, literature, dance and also in many other fields. After that the newspapermen make a salacious story about it and put the blame on the girl. One can marry a man forty years older. But why should they make a story about dancing with a man ten years younger? If you keep quiet because the press misrepresents things, how can the truth be known? Please read these issues. Or at least glance through them. If you are satisfied, please tell me the truth. After I write, it won't be printed without showing it first to you. This is my promise.'

She introduced herself further. She has got her PhD. A lecturer in Lady Sri Ram college. Manohari glanced through the issues of the magazine. Not even a single picture. No provocative titles. A dignified style. She believed her. She said she would talk to her and she could take down. The reporter took out her paper and pen. She talked about her mother, brother, her background and her decision to dedicate her life for dance. She also mentioned how she nursed her guru back to health when he took ill, her mental torture when he decided to go away to his daughter's place and how she herself proposed marriage but withheld giving details about the consequences of marrying an old man when she was only twenty-two. She blurted out how he said that he was still youthful.

'The relation between you and your mother after that?'

'My widowed mother had the determination to bring up her children and give them a good life. She was upset by my stubbornness. She would perhaps have accepted if he was of her age, but did not accept a son-in-law of her father's age. Our relationship cooled down. Became remote. Now not even a letter once a year. No phone calls either. All her love and concern was concentrated on my younger brother. She is now retired from her job. Brother is an engineer in Hyderabad, married, with a family. Mother is staying with him.'

'How did you build such a big building?'

'I pledged this building itself and raised a loan. I paid it back by giving programmes all over the country. There is still a little left.'

'Did you never feel like becoming a mother?'

She hesitated. The reporter egged her on. 'Why should you hesitate to share the truth with a sister?' She mentioned how she got pregnant and then got an abortion with the fear the child born of an old man's semen might turn out to be weak.

Dr. Sarala Srivastav left and the very next day returned with a typed copy of the interview. 'There should be no discrepancy between what you said and what we print. Please read the typescript and make corrections, if any. We won't print a single sentence without your consent.'

Manohari thought for a moment why all this should be printed. But she had found a bit of a mental relief since yesterday because of unburdening her mind about the raw deal she had in life. She had no one to confess to. Mother had distanced herself. At least these people call themselves a circle of sisters. She has shown the honesty of saying that not a word will be printed without her consent. She has a Ph.D. Not married and says that she doesn't want to. She says that a women's fulfilment need not be only through marriage. She felt friendly towards her. She said, 'Everything is all right. You may print it.'

After a week, the issue with her interview arrived by mail. There were two other articles. She didn't read them. When she read her interview again, she felt why all this had to be printed. She felt she had announced her own story to the world. However, she felt that this was the kind of paper which would be read only by a few educated women like Sarala Srivastava and kept aside. But on the third day the same news had been published in a sizzling set up. One newspaper had given the caption: The slap that Manohari has given to her old husband. Another newspaper said: Taking up arms against the exploitation of women in the field of fine arts. Another said: Sad story of an impediment to motherhood. These had searched all the important aspects published in *Bhagini* and had salaciously publicised. A couple of newspapers had announced, 'Please see our Sunday section for more details.' She received a continuous stream of phone calls. One of them said, 'We will pay five hundred rupees for an interview.' When she asked, 'How could you use what is printed in *Bhagini*, the answer was, 'When something is published once, we have the right to make use of it. We have not reproduced it verbatim.' She was angry with *Bhagini*. She telephoned Dr. Sarala Srivastava. She got the reply, 'Madam, the newspaper people are like that. They don't protect the dignity of anything. They throw it to the streets.' Still the interview in our paper has its own sanctity. Your interview will be the basis for serious thinking.' Then she added, 'You shouldn't be so sensitive to such things. Every newspaper has quoted the source. It means that serious intellectuals subscribe to our newspaper. You should ignore such commentaries, you must be strong.'

ꝏ

A week had passed. She was in the school in the afternoon. She received a phone call from home. The call was from Raji the cook. 'Didi, the daughter of Guruji has come to take him with her. She is asking me to call you.'

She couldn't understand, for a minute. Guruji's daughter is from Lakhimpur. She is of my mother's age. Sixty. She has been hating me since my marriage. She had confronted me, accusing me of appropriating the knowledge of her father by ensnaring him with the web of infatuation. She has visited five or six times in these twenty years. Every time accusing that I am not looking after her father properly and my own publicity has been important for me. Manohari understood that she must have come after reading the newspapers.

She said, 'Give the phone to Guruji.' She heard Raji asking him to speak. Then she said he is asking for you to come. She felt that the daughter and father were going to carry out a cross-examination of her. She decided, let things take their own course and saying that she was coming, put the phone down.

As soon as she parked the car and entered the house, the daughter shouted, 'What, ye, my father's keep. You have acted like a prostitute. Would any devoted wife scandalise her husband in a newspaper?'

She immediately asked, 'Would any husband call his wife a prostitute?'

'Is not what you are doing what a prostitute does?' She enacted the word prostitute with a gesture.

She was disgusted. She felt it was below her dignity to descend to her level, she said, 'Just tell me why you have come.'

'I am taking my father home. I can afford to take care of my father's food.'

She turned to Guruji and asked, 'What do you say?'

'If I eat your food, may I go to hell. I am going. I will go cursing you. May what I have taught you perish,' he screamed.

'Screaming and shouting are not allowed in my home. Those who go must just shut up and go. Raji, bundle up this man's clothes and give it to him.' The cook was standing silently. She herself went into the room, gathered some clothes like dhoti and jubba threw them in front of the daughter and said, 'If you want to go, just get out. I have work to attend to.'

The daughter too was stunned. Guruji was also stunned. 'I am capable of getting some clothes stitched for my father. These rags are not good enough even to be used as a mop to wipe the floor.'

'Then without further talk, just get the hell out with your father. Not a word more.' Manohari stood staring at her.

The daughter picked up her small suitcase and moved holding the hand of her father. Just before crossing the threshold Guruji cursed. 'You are throwing me out into the street. May what I have taught you get obliterated. Let it be perished, let it be perished, let it be perished. This curse of the tihaai will come true. Even if you come and fall at my feet, I won't come back. I won't come back. I certainly won't.' He started descending the steps, following his daughter. Manohari stood watching. She was just standing there, gazing, even after they were out of sight.

She felt a load off her chest. She had not been sleeping with him for the past twenty days. She was sleeping upstairs. He had also not asked why she was doing this. She had also not given any reason. They did not even speak to each other. She felt it was a good thing he had left. She didn't even feel concerned that his curse may come true. She thought, 'I am not a Karna. Neither is he a Parashurama.' She bundled up his clothes threw them into an almirah and shut the door. Cleaned up the downstairs room and changed the bed-clothes. She felt she could sleep anywhere she wanted in her own house. When she returned home at night she felt lonely. Mohan left. The coward Karthik went away, became unacceptable. The old man had done a favour by leaving. When she became aware that she was alone, both in the school and at home she experienced a sense of being deserted. When she dined and went to bed she remembered Mr. Mittal. His visits were becoming rare. She calculated that it was a month and a half since he came. She remembered that it was him who was the master of this house and thought of calling him the next day, telling him that he could come to the house and he need not have any anxiety about his being observed and watched. She thought of telling him that she would cook him a hot, delicious meal. He had insisted on getting the school building as well as the house registered in her name. She became aware that otherwise the old man would have given it away to his daughter. She felt that he was her protector, her Krishna. She looked at the watch. It was half past ten at night. Tomorrow morning she must call him. She must inform him about the departure of the old man and invite him home. A fond wish arose that she must have his company for the whole night in this bed.

The patron picked up the phone and said that he also wanted to meet her and talk to her. Though she wanted to mischievously ask him whether it was only to talk, she was cautious that there may be someone listening on a parallel line. Informing about the departure of the old man she said, 'Please come to the house. If you ring up, I will be there. Can you recognise the place? How many years since you came there!' He asked for the address and noted it down.

He came to the house. There was no sign of baldness but his hair was snow-white. Somehow he looked like a man without desires. She shut the door and embraced him. She unbuttoned his jacket and put it away. He didn't embrace and kiss her. She herself put her arms round his neck and kissed on the lips. He didn't say 'no' or push her away. But he didn't kiss back. Saying, 'Come, let us sit' and made her sit next to him on the sofa. Didn't lead her to the bedroom. She understood that since it was home and there was plenty of time, he was not hurrying. He squeezed her palm and asked, 'Manohari, how did you become a victim to these newspapermen?' She felt comfortable that she had found someone in whom she could confide. She started with the time that the young man Guha interviewed her. But she felt impeded while doing so. It was embarrassing telling him about her relationship with Mohan without arousing suspicion. In the same way she had to gloss over Kartik's affair also. Mr. Mittal's was a very shrewd mind. He never says anything openly. She was aware that if he got hold of a tiny thread he could fill out the entire piece of cloth with its price, warp and woof. Still she played down that part and it was difficult managing the details. He was also listening silently as if completely in sympathy. Finally he spoke.

'I will speak if you don't feel hurt.'

'Please do. Only your words must give me strength,' she pressed his hand.

'There is an age difference of twenty-eight years between us. Age has its own logic. Both of us should accept it.'

'Our love for each other is not confined only to the physical aspect. Even if another twenty years pass, I am yours. You are my Krishna,' she embraced and kissed him.

Fondling the top of her head, he said, 'It is not as natural for an artiste to fall in love with an ordinary man as it is for her to love a fellow male artist or vice versa. The others wishing for the love of an artist, I understand, is transgression.'

'What are you saying?' Contradicting his comprehension, Manohari adding intensity of gesticulation to her protest asked.

'The newspaper people have no right to write about your personal affairs. In my opinion there must be a proper legislation and they must be imprisoned. But there is no smoke without fire. Weren't you romantically involved with Mohanlal? Speak the truth. After that weren't you involved with Karthikaram? I am not asking this question to criticise you. It is natural for you. That is your world. An outsider like me should have no entry into it. But the way of the world is different. You get caught by moneyed people.'

In spite of her trying she was not able to contradict his words spoken with a searching, steady gaze. She caught hold of both his hands and remonstrated, 'Nothing will suffice for the help you have given. Why should you say there should be no entry?'

'If they want to help, they should help, enjoy your art from a distance. But it is not possible to anybody to be uninvolved. The attraction towards an artist exceeds the original, primeval attraction. That is why many people give away their money and property to the artists and become beggars. Women also would get enamoured if they had both money and freedom and succumb to artists. But you never asked me. What little I gave you was of my own freewill. It is just an insignificant fraction of my earnings. You are not avaricious. You don't have the worldly ways of ensnaring men by using your art. That is why I respect you.'

She felt at ease. She kissed him saying that he was the only one who had understood her. Her eyes filled with tears. Wiping them with his fingers, he said, 'That is why I want to continue our friendship for ever. Call me whenever you have any problem. I will help you as long as I am alive. Not merely because you have surrendered your body to your artist friends but because your mind and inner being has moved away in that direction, I have no love left for you. Without love, desiring carnal satisfaction is animal instinct. For me who is approaching seventy, physical pleasure is not possible, neither is it necessary. The time when you were entirely mine, that period I consider the best time of my good fortune.' He pressed her right hand. She did not find the strength either to contradict or accept his words. She didn't even have sufficient strength to confront his gaze. She started looking at his right hand with the swelling nerves. She remembered how fifteen years ago he had held her hand with the same firmness and the way their love had sprouted and grown.

She must say something. Though she felt like explaining that her attraction for Mohanlal and Karthik was of a different kind and it shouldn't be compared with the love between them, words would not come up from within.

II

Loneliness began to bother her. At school she had to maintain her dignified distance as a guru. This was no one when she came home. How did this situation come to pass? These mind-boggling questions were doing their unceasing rounds in her head. The mind used to warn that she shouldn't have any conversation with journalists. But her worldly wisdom used to warn her that cutting them off altogether would result in getting out of circulation and it would not be possible to be in the foremost position of the dancing world. She dismissed Karthik completely from her mind. But the memory of Mohanlal began to trouble her. The memory of the intense and keen love with him would fill her mind. The words of Mittal were true. She began to feel that the intensity of love of an artist with another artist does not happen with any common person. If he has to send six thousand rupees, he must have secured some programme. She even thought of visiting Koregaon via Devalali. But she was filled with consternation that he might take accumulated revenge on her for the shame inflicted on him.

One day she received by mail a printed announcement of 'Shruti Sangeeta Sabha.' It was printed on the envelope 'For favour of publication.' A concert by Mohanlal had been arranged in Delhi. In addition to giving details about price of tickets, place of sale and the phone number, there was a detailed introduction of the artist. We have given some excerpts from the opinions of Bombay newspapers:

'Mohanlal has demonstrated convincingly in the benefit programme given for the Bombay Press Club, his definite re-incarnation as a pure classical singer, he who had been lost to this world as a dance-accompanist in these three and a half years. He has firmly established himself in the tradition of the very root of music which is the mother-root for different types of singing like singing for dance, Thumri etc.'

'No matter what the cheap yellow papers might have written, the return of Mohanlal to the world of pure music is a happy news.'

'Though Mohanlal has returned to pure classical music, he has gained experience which is an added attraction to his original emotional richness. Speaking from the point of view of the artist, instead of dividing the experiences as good and bad, it must be observed from the point of view of whether the other experiences have been beneficial for the artist's knowledge of emotions, their clarity of emotion and emotional sophistication. Even the desertion and decamping of Mohanlal from his own place and position for three and half a year have helped in making his music more mature. From this point of view the world of music must be grateful to the world of dance!'

There were such excerpts of a page and a half.

She didn't feel that the newspapermen had sent the announcement to her out of mischief. She thought that the sending of information about the activities of an organisation to others was common practice. Yes! He has resurrected. She thought that if the Press Club had arranged a benefit show he had certainly established himself very well. The next day's newspapers also carried the announcement of Shruti as a news item which means that the Delhi newspapers also had a good opinion of him. She thought that if a favourable wave started, the newspapers would toe the line. She suddenly wanted to hear this concert. She noticed the places where tickets were available. She decided not to contact the Shruti office. She herself drove up to Karol Bagh and bought a ticket from the counter. It was just the way the cashier had sold a packet of sweets and received the money. She felt relieved that he couldn't recognise her. She found a place in the middle of the auditorium. She thought it was a good thing. But still, there would be people in the audience who would recognise her. Many of the music lovers are also dance lovers. She was worried that the newspapermen would definitely be there. After worrying for a day she felt defiant. What kind of dancer was she if she didn't defy the journalists. She went to a readymade clothes shop and bought a burkha. Before going to the concert she applied make-up to her face and added a black spot one on the left cheek and one below her right eye. She applied collyrium so heavily that when she looked into the mirror she couldn't recognise herself. She arrived five minutes before the concert started and sat in her place. She didn't remove the lid of the veil until the lights were dimmed and the attention of the audience was fixed on the stage.

Yes, he is radiant with his original power. He has mastered not only purity of melody but the emotional peace also. The moment he entered the shadja the emotional tranquillity spread out. It felt, not thin like water, no, not even viscous, but a peace that spreads itself like moonlight. There is no room for noise. The egotism of the tabla player had no chance to lift its head. Indeed there was no external concentration. It was wholly a slow movement, difficult to identify and preparing itself to capture the very centre of the psyche. Not just the audience but the entire auditorium has become like a cave, immersed in meditation. In a short while she herself was experiencing peace. He was her lover. Now he has left her. He is exulting as her rival. All such adverse thoughts subsided and only the peace of the swara that is beyond understanding was the reality. The eyes became moist with tears. He, who was sitting at a distance on the centre of the stage, with half-closed eyes engaged in exploring the swara became invisible. She sat with her eyes closed thinking, where was the need to see him. He presented the alaap alone for an hour and stopped. He didn't sing the cheez. He didn't at all give a chance to the tabla player except for the thekas. This was not just singing a raga. It was sheer act of magic, mantra-kriya. The audience sat spell-bound even after he stopped, not even feeling that it was concluded.

Then he expatiated on Raga Khamaj at length and gave an interval. Most people went out for a cup of tea. She didn't stir from where she was sitting. She covered the veil on her head. Two people sitting in front of her didn't go out either. They started conversing, 'It's a good thing he left her,' one of them said. 'Not just because his music survived. It seems he was just eating the food she gave him and surviving, without any pocket money. Do you know what his fee is now? Within five months since he left her? Fifty thousand. Air fare. Accommodation at Imperial Hotel. The treasurer of Shruti is my colleague. He told me.'

After the interval he started the Raga Shahana. It was a rare unprecedented raga for the Delhi listeners. It gave a sort of support to her. She began to experience the mood of forbearance incorporating the enthusiasm of adhana, the seriousness of Darbari and the pain of Malhar, giving out the message that pain is not the end but there is life if there is patience. By the movement of her right hand to the pattern and the places of swaras, *ni dha ni pa dha ma pa*, she began to realise in her soul that emotion, without being aware that her apparel was ill-fitted to these gestures and without bothering what people around her might think. When the transitory emotions developed to a stream and became a full-fledged flowing river of the raga, she felt that he was her only refuge. Such a great singer was at my command. He was completely mine. Though he was there, I desired Karthik, accepted and appropriated. She felt that is why he punished her and left. Mohan, I deserve the punishment you inflicted. The mistake is not yours. You are not cruel. You are noble. The punishment must have a limit. It must be commensurate with the mistakes. You never transgress your evenness not even by one per cent. Accept me. Don't sing at my dance performances. Don't come to my programmes. Now the house is completely empty. You just stay there. You practise to perfection your music. I will listen to it staying outside your room and derive my strength. Accept concerts as you like. Earn as much fee as you want. I don't need a single pie. I will be responsible for your food, lodging and will serve you, who else do I have? I will find satisfaction in offering myself to you, and serving you. What Mittal Saheb said was true. An artiste can love only another artist. There is none else who can flood the mighty river of emotion.

Ah, ah! In your anger you have not gone and fallen into the clutches of that wife of yours, have you? An hour after your concert is over, I will come to the Imperial Hotel. I am not afraid even if the Secretary of Shruti and others are present there. I will remove this burkha and throw it in the car itself and come. Why fear others when we become one? Let any newspaperman write anything. At an auspicious moment when lovers unite, the sound of shehnai is auspicious, the sound of a dog barking is aversion of evil.

When sitting in the car she became a bit cautious. I am in a mood of pushing forward. But who knows how he is going to behave! If he rejects me contemptuously in the presence of others? She sat silently for ten minutes without starting the car. She started the car thinking of going home and telephoning after an hour. But after she opened the door of the house, she felt that a call from a distance will not build a bridge of emotional understanding. One must meet physically, personally. Uniting the eye with the eye one must plunge down and enter into the depths of the inner being. One must hold the shoulder by the left hand, bend down, touch the feet with the right hand and dissolve the difference at the beginning itself and then talk. Even now, shall I go there? By the time I reach there one and a quarter hours would have elapsed. She looked at her watch. Visitors are not allowed after ten. Besides, it is the procedure at that hotel to inform by intercom who had come. The impediment occurred that on hearing the name he might reject the interview. Not able to see anyway out she took out the dinner from the fridge and even without heating it up, she ate and went to bed. How easily we got together in Nagpur! There was no impediment. Didn't even occur to the mind. He said, 'Manohari, please stay the night here' and I did. We had such a glorious union with an emotional intensity which no other lovers had experienced and no chemistry could explain or decipher. She thought, but now, once the relationship is broken, how many hurdles have cropped up even to make a contact! She looked at the watch. Should she ask the receptionist to connect the line. But the reply would be, 'Sorry, the guest is resting.' There was a snag.

Two weeks had passed. No way had suggested itself. One morning while she was at school, there was a phone call. 'Didi, do you remember me? Aditi Agarwal, your student. You used to make fun of me, calling me AA. You had also come to my wedding and blessed me. I have come to my parents' home. Feel like seeing you.'

'You married a Bombay boy, didn't you?'

'Thank you, Didi. You still remember.'

'Come over. I will be free in half an hour.' She decided to enquire about him without any embarrassment. She remembered that Aditi was also interested in music.

The classes were over and even Om Prakash had left. She felt all alone in such a big building. From ten in the morning to four in the afternoon, completely empty. She remembered that even when Mr. Mittal was visiting once a month for an hour it hadn't been able to avert this emptiness. As for Mohan, he didn't even stay here for a full month. Only Karthik did. Still, she couldn't dismiss it from her mind that this was Mittal's. She thought, how if I rent out that house and stay here itself? It fetches at least eight to ten thousand rupees. I can save on the electricity bill. The petrol expense will be less, when she realised that the entire upstairs was empty, it seemed wise.

As soon as she opened the door she remembered Aditi had been married six years ago. When she bent down and touched the feet of her guru, Manohari noticed that peeping out of the sides of her blouse there was a bulge. 'Did you give up dancing?'

'I thought you would scold me. You haven't put on even an ounce of weight. I am very strict in my diet. Still… smiling, she touched her bobbed head with the fingers that had touched the feet. She talked about her family, sitting in the office opposite Manohari on the sofa. She has two children—a girl and a boy. It seems she was told that after delivery, she should not dance, that too, Kathak. So she has given up.

'Who told you that?'

'All the relatives say so.'

'What do they know about dance? If one who was dancing gives it up, won't the weight increase?'

'Didi, to tell you the truth, my interest in music has increased. I go to all the concerts in Bombay. In Maharashtra there is a better atmosphere for music than for dance. Recently, I have been going twice a week to learn. I approached Pandit Mohanlalji himself.' Immediately, as if she had remembered something she stopped abruptly. After she herself asked, 'Did he consent?' Aditi said, 'I didn't know how stupid I was. He said, "Sing, let us listen." I was out of practice. He said, "You see, we people who give concerts are always travelling. After a certain level is reached, if you come, I can teach, time permitting. But before that, get trained by a good teacher and then come," he said.'

'Where is he staying? His wife also teaches, doesn't she?' She got an opportunity to ask the question she wanted to.

'Don't know about his wife. He is not staying with her. He stays in a small rented flat at Khar. He moved there recently. Until he got it, he was staying in a farmhouse near Devalali.'

She was relieved on remembering that he had sent the money with the address Devalali Marg. After leaving here, he has not fallen into the clutches of his wife. He is independent. Hope did shine. It is possible to get hold of the address if she asked Aditi herself. Even the phone number. She thought of asking her that even if she didn't have it here, with her, to write or telephone after returning to Bombay. But this person also knows about her relationship with him. If she asked her, it would be arousing her curiosity. She thought no, there are a hundred ways of finding out.

After Aditi left, the matter of giving the house for rent and shifting to the school came up again. But she stamped it out. Her inner voice started saying that it was easy to bring Mohan back to Delhi. Don't married people quarrel? Don't they hit each other? Don't people who fight come together again? I will go myself. I will fall at his feet; tell him I have sent Guruji to his daughter's place in order to get you back. The Delhi weather is better than that of Bombay. It is close to the North India, to Calcutta, Punjab, Haryana and Rajasthan. It is the country's capital. Come there, I will serve you, you don't sing for my dance performance. I adore your music. If I say all this, why won't he come? She made sure of this to herself.

12

It was as if she had shed a load after Guruji left. At the same time, a sort of listlessness. The regularity in food was lost. There was an order in routine because of him and his age. Now the regularity had to be maintained because the cook was being paid. She felt lazy even to perform the yogasanas every morning. A lethargy was setting in. Especially after the departure of Mittal Saheb, the aimlessness became more persistent. After Karthik dropped out, no new programmes could be devised and even the invitations of programmes had to be given up. The enthusiasm for regular dance practice waned and she began to feel that the lightness of her body was lessened. But after coming back from the concert of Mohan there was a sudden awakening. It was not a competitive spirit that he who had totally lost touch given up practice, had regained the mastery over pure classical singing of ragas. She felt that his music was an inspiration to her and she must regain in dance the peace and expertise that Mohanlal had achieved in music, absorption he obtains in the contemplativeness of naada, she must attain in tatkaar. One morning she got up early and started performing the yogasanas. The inertness that had already set in resisted. She felt it a challenge and performed a score of suryanamaskars slowly. She decided to perform the difficult aasanas in three days time. When she turned around a few times and observed her own sides in the tall mirror, she was surprised to see how soon the suppleness of the body will be lost and stiffness would set in, if one becomes careless. Yes, I will send for Jayaswal. If I don't dance for an hour every evening to the accompaniment of the tabla, this body will become useless. The utter necessity to keep his body agile and in shape is not there for the singer. Mohan used to do pranayama in the beginning when he came here but not the aasanas, she remembered.

She got his address, she telephoned the secretary of Shruti. She introduced herself as the secretary of a transport association and there was a proposal of inviting Pandit Mohanlal for a concert. She asked for his address and phone number. She got it. She thought she would write a letter rather than call him up. What to write and how to do it was the problem. She remembered the love-letters in novels which she had rarely read and in special editions of the magazines. She became aware that what she had to write wasn't a love-letter but a letter of reconciliation to a lover, to placate him. After struggling for three days she found a way. She took out her pen and the writing automatically followed.

No one has conquered anger. It brought down even the saints and sages. I have fallen in the fire of contrition for having hit you back. Everyday I am burning in it. I am waiting for a phone call from you telling me that you have forgiven me.

She wrote but was afraid to post it. She kept it with her.

I had come to your 'Shruti' concert. Though I was sitting in front of you I was in disguise, wearing a burkha not to be recognised by you. I had taken care to see that neither you nor I would be food for mischievous newspapermen.

After describing, *'You are my guru, your singing is really the power station of inspiration for my dance,'* she invited him to come back. Guruji has gone away to his daughter's home. *Mr. Mittal has taken leave of me, for good. You stay in the house. It is enough if I listen to you practising in your room. I will be inspired. Don't sing for my dance. I will never ask you to do so.* She wrote another lengthy letter after a week. She remembered she had not posted the first letter. She cursed herself, what is the use of writing without posting it? She took courage, put the two letters together, got them weighed, affixed the stamp and posted it. It will reach him tomorrow. With the hope that he would call immediately, she waited near the phone the whole day. Nothing. She imagined the explanations that there might have been a postal delay, that he might not be in town, that he was busy with programmes etc. She waited for a day, two days—a week. Then she told herself that the postal department would have mistakenly sent it to the wrong address. In a delayed realisation she felt she should have given the address of an imaginary music organisation as he had done and got it registered. She thought of calling him and asking him if he hadn't received her letter. The mind opposed, if he had decided not to answer, why should she demean herself.

Gradually, she tried to develop indifference towards him. After all, he was the one who hit out first. I only returned the blow. Could he spoil the whole programme? The longing which was hiding in a corner everyday when she opened the mailbox gradually diminished. After sometime, before opening the mailbox, she would bet to herself that there would be no letter from him. After sorting through the mail she would tell herself that she had won the bet! After some time the betting and the gloating over winning, both stopped. She decided that she shouldn't simply remain the director of a dance school but without depending on anyone else she should create new items with her at the centre of the performance. She should do it involving only her students, her senior students.

13

An invitation arrived. The news had been published in the papers too. The Delhi Thumri Organisation had arranged a programme of five famous male and female singers of the country. In addition to Siddheshwari Devi and Girija Devi there were others who were famous Khayal singers.

What was surprising to Manohari was the third item Bhaav-batana by Guru Sohanlal. In addition to being a surprise, his being invited to Delhi and his agreeing to come was a matter of embarrassment to her. She remembered after some time that when he left her, he had not said that he would never come back to Delhi. She also realised that though he could not dance any more, there was no impediment for his abhinaya by sitting on the ground. She thought she could have attended if his item wasn't present. More than the pure music, Thumri has influenced the abhinaya part of Kathak. She knew that the nuances of acting cannot be understood until each line of a poem, then each word and sometimes each letter is separated, its meaning, change of meaning, made clear, the implications explored, the various meanings and innuendos explicated and the puns brought out and all these brought to the fore through the variations of the exposition and unless without knowing the secret of the art of singing and bringing it out to the emotional cognizance through the delineation of musical tone. She remembered that her guru was an expert in it. Recently she hadn't heard Thumri at all. She felt that she shouldn't miss this programme with Siddheshwari Devi and Girija Devi. If only there was no item by Guruji right in the centre of it! Bhaav-batana programme must be seen sitting close by, sitting in the front row. She was worried that some scandal-mongering journalists might photograph her and create a story. After a day she felt courageous. Why should she miss the programme, being afraid of some bastards? When she remembered the burkha with her, she felt confident.

After Guruji left, when she came home, though she felt lonely, she didn't feel sad. Her home completely belonged to her and she had thought that Mittal Saheb could come there and spend a lot of time without any disturbance. Her mind wasn't perturbed about remembering Guruji as it had been, by desiring Mohanlal. She did not feel the fear, the excitement and inner turmoil, she had felt while going to Mohanlal's programme. She wore the burkha and sat at the centre of the third row. All the Delhi connoisseurs of Thumri had gathered. The hall was full and they had put folding chairs in the side aisles. She was sitting without any anxiety, that anyone could recognise her. Her mind was filled with curiosity to see Guruji. After leaving, he had not written to her. Hadn't got one written by others either. Hadn't called. She hadn't written either. His daughter had come to show her anger and taunt me. She exhibited her bravado by offering to take her father back. Her bravado and taunts had recoiled on her. God knows how she is looking after him! She felt she should have sent some money once a month. Another voice spoke, but why should she have done it voluntarily for someone who had called her a prostitute? Meanwhile the Secretary began his introductory speech. He talked about the uniqueness of Thumri and the intention of encouraging it through the programme and introduced the first singer Brajnarayan. Then the concert began. Her mind started getting immersed in the emotion of the raga. Every time the singer made a variation, the audience was showing its appreciation with intoning *wah, wah*. She felt it was not possible to escape from this kind of involvement. Every time the singer expressed an emotional pattern, she started imagining how she would act it out and started making hand movements within her burkha. The eyes and eyebrows moved accordingly. The fear that someone might recognise her vanished. After half an hour, the second singer came onstage. Bindeshwar Prasad from Varanasi. He was introduced as the pupil of Siddheshwari Devi. She felt that he was also singing well. Music means Thumri. How is it possible to find its abundance of a hundred varieties of emotion, in classical music of pure rasa? She felt that it was an ascetic art. That is why that fellow hadn't replied though she had written such a lengthy letter. Hadn't called. The classical musicians love themselves. She felt that they were egoists without compassion or conscience who don't love others, don't partake of their pleasures and pains in their vanity.

When the third artist, Guru Sohanlal came to the stage, the audience welcomed him with a prolonged applause. Her heart began to beat fast. He had become thinner than when he left her house. She felt that the legs and thighs had dried up. Even the bones of the face were protruding. The waist-coat he was wearing on his jubba was an old one. The one she had got stitched. He sat centre-stage with his legs crossed. The artist who sat to sing for him was Saheb Singh Kajariwal. A veteran artist. Guruji's friend. The accompanists were a tabla player and saarangi player. Sohanlalji spread his red shawl on his shoulder over his legs to cover the feet and thighs. The secretary introduced, 'After leaving Delhi and going to his daughter's place, Guru Sohanlalji is setting foot in Delhi for the first time. It is no exaggeration to say that there isn't another dancer who can express emotion and feeling so expertly through abhinaya. He has very kindly deigned to come to Delhi so that the connoisseurs here can directly experience his power of expressing meaning and patterns even at his advanced age.' Meanwhile the star performers of the post-interval period Girija Devi and Siddheshwari Devi arrived, came to the front row, sat in the centre and greeted Guruji with a namaskar. He acknowledged it and returned the gesture. Manohari's heart beat quickened. Saheb Singh sang. Guruji started performing.

Ghira Ghira Ayi Baadara

It was a composition known to her. Had been taught by Guruji himself. How emotionally Saheb Singh was singing in spite of his advanced age! She felt impelled to act inside her burkha. The face of Guruji with prominent bones, sunken eyes, the drooping skin beneath the eyes and bald head on top, had begun to express emotions appropriately. The feeling was created that he was dancing where he had sat. How naturally it was expressed through his abhinaya! The meaning of the clouds of Raga Megh that gather in the sky, assuring the returning of the power of life to the earth exhausted and parched, by the summer heat and where the sap of life had reached to its lowest ebb—oh how natural! Both Girija Devi and Siddheshwari Devi intoned *wah* in unison and lifted their hands in a roof-like arch as if in support of his acting. Megh became Malhar, and became Megh-malhar. The rapport was so perfect that it was difficult to know, whether Guruji was enacting according to the changed ragas of the voice of the singer or the singer was following the change of emotions of the abhinaya of the Guruji. It looked as though Guruji was also singing along with acting, in the microphone put before him. She remembered the old tradition of bhaav-batana in which the dancer himself was singing too. In how many different ways was a single short line *Ghira ghira ayi baadara* being enacted! He brought it all into existence. He caused the feeling to be emanated that cloud means the luxurious tresses of hair on head, by creating with his gesticulations, the waves of meaning one after the other, which suggested, the dark clouds gathering threateningly, incessantly, consternating the mind with thunder and lightning, floating from the cool wind bringing comfort and suggesting that cruelty of heat is ended and grief and agony are warded off. Then it turned into the emotion of Bhairavi and the gathering clouds were transformed into the emotion of doubts that siege and harass the heart of the lover. How many different moving moods of lovers' separation! The abhinaya that the rain dropped by the clouds was not only to assuage the heat of the parched earth but they were teardrops squeezed out of the heart of the separated lover. How many different meanings for a single line! She didn't count. If the subtle emotions and feelings had been counted, they would have exceeded twenty. God knows how many more subtleties he had hidden away in his abhinaya as secrets. He had taught me. I had not understood fully. These things cannot be taught entirely. These are to be created on the spur of the moment by individual talent. Through his eighty-three year-old bald head with sunken eyes and a beak-nose, how he has created and brought out the youthful face of Radha at the banks of River Yamuna, caught in a storm and being affrighted! Manohari beheld a marvel within her. The devotion to the guru flowed forth.

When he concluded his presentation the audience was sitting dumb founded. Girija Devi and Siddheshwari Devi stood up and said, 'Wonderful, Marvellous.' Manohari had lost control. She stood up and ran rapidly towards the stage. While climbing the steps, she removed the burkha and threw it away. Everybody recognised her. She rushed on to the stage, bent low, held his feet and blabbered, 'Guruji, please pardon this nobody. Please pardon this good-for-nothing non-entity. I will not let you out of Delhi. If you are angry, my learning will all be destroyed.' These words filled the entire gathering through the mike. Dozens of cameras clicked and flashlights shone. The mike broadcast her fitful weeping.

14

Three years had elapsed. Now pushing forty-five. No problem about spending time. Classes, rehearsals, travel, the time passes. On certain nights sleep eludes for no reason at all. Though the body is tired but sleep eludes. If the mind is engaged in planning some dance choreography it is not difficult to bear it. But if the mind follows the track of tracing the joys and sorrows of life and contemplates on what use all this effort is, the feeling that sleep is teasing intensifies and pain of loneliness begins to trouble. Though she had brought Guruji home she would sleep by herself in the room upstairs. Let alone the physical aspect. When there isn't even affection, why undergo the torture of sleeping together? It was the same with him. Not even a single day did he ask her to sleep with him so that they could talk things over till falling asleep. She remembered that from the day she brought him home, he had accepted the situation as if it was perfectly natural, perhaps he was waiting to be invited by me this way! The daughter also never came even once to invite him back. Not on a single day had he said anything about how he had been looked after at his daughter's place. Why should I ask? It was as though this house had been kept without renting it out only for him. When the account of ten thousand rupees a month rent, the maintenance and electricity charges came to her mind, she would think that she had acted rashly in an emotional moment. The journalists, as if just waiting for it, made a scoop of it. As if expecting it, Guha had made a story out of it under the heading: Mad Girl. When she took him to task on the phone, he had said, 'Madam, trust me. What I write becomes the role model for Delhi artist groups. Just wait for a week.' The Hindi newspapermen christened her Mad Girl. Guha himself called up and came to the school. He said, 'You haven't understood the secret of this. In the expression Mad Girl, the word 'girl' is important. Your asset is the wiry, supple body you have maintained through the practice of yoga. Everyone has believed that you are just a girl. They believe that madness is a genuine qualification for an artist. Even after another twenty years you will remain an evergreen dancer. I will make a pictorial article on you. Listen to me. I will make you the number one dancer of this country.

'No more being a victim of your double pun of your pen!'

'That stage is over. Even with that, some good happened to you. Trust me. Just do as I say.' He made me consent. He took photographs of me giving an oil massage to the feet of Guruji, me sitting on the floor, of me serving him food, depositing him gently on the sofa, and posing as if following his instructions in dance. He prepared a write-up entitled 'The inner private life of a Mad Girl steeped in traditional roots.' He wrote about the yoga practice in the morning, the dance routine, serving the guru, teaching dance at school etc and said that I was the only dancer who had elevated dance to philosophical heights. His research article became the source material for other journalists and the Indian audiences began to see a spiritual dimension in my dance. My name was noticed by high government officials and I got opportunities in national events. The State Governments extended invitations. Manohari Das was transformed into a VIP artist and was invited by consulates, the well-known newspapers printing articles with photographs, including house magazines of various airline companies etc. She thought, what a metamorphosis in three years? Still, this loneliness. No love remained between her and Guruji. No sense of intimacy either. But still, why did I become a mad girl? Why did I convert a transitory passion of art into an enduring passion and brought it on to me? Perhaps as far as I am concerned the emotion of art is the truth! If not which sane and balanced girl would become mad by marrying this old man for the sake of learning and get distanced from her family. This sadness enveloped her.

१५

The next morning at eleven, she was sitting in her office looking through the mail. Guha telephoned. If he called, it was usually at this time. Besides, now she felt instinctively it was him. 'Good morning, Manohari, sorry, Manohariji, are you free?' He used to address me as 'Madam'. Now, calling her by name and nervously adding the honorific 'ji' as an afterthought with an unsteady voice made her suspect some ulterior motive about his intentions. Still, she said calmly, 'Please come.'

'You are not angry, are you?'

'Angry with you? What madness!' she said.

'I want to ask you something. You must assure me beforehand that you won't be angry after listening to it.'

'Enough of your "interview" questions.'

'Not an interview. Personal talk.'

'Come. You are intriguing over the phone itself.'

She guessed his mental state. But was also aware that she might be mistaken. There was confusion in her too. Remembering that she had been alone for four years she felt like inviting him. But again she was cautious lest she was mistaken. Coming in, Guha was avoiding her gaze. As if totally innocent of the situation she invited him quite normally to her office. When she proceeded to sit on her chair behind the table, he said, 'Please come here. It is easy to talk about intimate matters while sitting close to each other.'

She came and sat next to him. At once he took hold of her right hand. She tightened the grip like a handshake and said, 'How is it you have become English, all of a sudden?'

He was confused. Embarrassed. Couldn't think of words. He struggled to lift up his head. When she herself asked, you said there was something you wanted to talk about, he said, 'I want your friendship.'

'Don't you have it now?' she asked naturally.

'I mean...'

'I have always been friends with you. Otherwise I wouldn't have believed you at all.'

'No round-about talk. I love you. You must consent.'

Immediately she felt pleased. Though Guha was not handsome, he was a healthy well-built young man. She was also inclined to have a go. After Karthik left, I have been leading a dry life. She became aware that nobody had proposed like this. But somehow her heart wasn't responding. 'Guhaji, you are ten years younger to me', she said.

'No, you are ten years younger to me. I swear that you are twenty-five.' He spoke looking straight at her. It was not possible for him to take a step back when once he had advanced. Justifying his word he said, 'I know that Guruji is just Guruji and no more. I will marry you.'

'Really?' she said straightening her chest and with a provoking side glance like a coquette. She saw by his looks that he was confused and said, 'Let alone marrying. Even just friendship with a younger man is not proper.'

'Don't lie. Wasn't Karthikaram ten years younger to you?' He shot out suddenly.

'I didn't have any friendship with him. You did an injustice by writing in your newspaper that I did.'

He was nonplussed. 'Is it true?' he said.

'I will swear on you.' She put her right hand on his head and pressed it. 'You are my brother. You are alone. If you agree I will search a suitable girl for you and get you married. I will bear the expenses of the wedding sari.'

'I don't believe in the difference in age.'

'You don't believe. But nobody can transcend it. Time and rhythm are the same. You haven't understood. You join my dance class. I will teach you,' saying so she slapped him gently in jest.

He blushed. Confusion spread all over. 'You have accepted that I have the right to punish you. Because you have said "I love you". Love means affection. Affection means filial feeling. Do you know that Yashoda would slap Krishna this way for indulging in mischief outside?'

He fell silent. Five minutes later he said, 'Sorry.'

'Hey, would Krishna say sorry, in English? Say that in Braj language. Or, in Sanskrit.'

He didn't know what to say. He was feeling embarrassed to sit in front of her. Looking at his watch, he got up saying that he had to go to a press conference. 'When will you come again? I have written an article, in English. You should correct it. Hereafter, I will speak to you only in the familiar single you have agreed.' She slapped him on the back.

After he left she felt she was saved. Her mind said that friendly relationship with this man, this journalist was improper. She remembered the words of Mittal Saheb that love for an artist was possible only with another artist. I must deal with tact with this disappointed man. She decided to make him accept her as a sister, an elder sister.

Chapter 10

I

He was fast asleep. The phone rang and woke him up. Thinking that it was her call, he picked it up and switched on the light. 'Hi, Mohanji, please forgive me for disturbing your sleep at this hour. Do you know what happened? I had forgotten that after the dance programme, there was dinner, the ambassador and his wife had come. The French ambassador and the Italian ambassador with their wives. There were five in all. You see, there is a possibility of invitation from those countries. I am sorry. You see, I have taken a swig, still, it has become not only difficult, but impossible to address you in the respectful plural. If you like you can address me with the formal plural. Call me "Madam". Call me "Madame" which is the correct pronunciation. I am the kind of person who will address you only in the familiar singular. My inner voice is telling me that you have agreed to come to the Paris Festival. It has never failed, I am sending up the acceptance to them tomorrow, suggesting your name, OK?'

She has dined with five ambassadors. His mind had contemplated it when he heard Manohari's proposal. A visit to Paris will facilitate the visit of other European countries. Why miss it? He said, 'I am not a singer for your dance. For the first half hour I will sing a raga. When I give it life and motion you must dance. My name should appear first. I am not new to being abroad. I have returned just now after staying there for two and a half months.'

'All right, my man. I will get your name printed first—even use big letters. At least for one week before leaving, we must practise together. All the accompanists are from my group. You must teach them the secret of your alaap in slow motion. Thank you, Mohan, thank you. I apologise again for disturbing your sleep. Shall I put down the phone? Good night.'

The memory of his having performed *Bageshree* eighteen years ago recurred. He yawned. Muttering to himself what she would have lost if she had made the same phone call in the morning, he switched off. If one stays in Delhi the transactions will be only with embassies, ambassadors, cultural attaches and government councils, unlike Bombay. Here the programmes are held by public contributions. If the artist proves unsuccessful, the members will be bored. The organisations don't invite. Making this comparison, he closed his eyes.

5

Manohari got agitated asking herself what had happened to her for spending twelve years without any soft feelings like love and affection. The moment he agreed to come to the Paris programme, she was confident that the relationship between Mohanlal and herself might rejuvenate. This was not a programme designed by me. It was a show planned and arranged by the Arts Council of Paris. They were the people who requested a three-hour presentation showing the essentials of Indian music and its dance forms. How is it possible to select a musician other than him? Isn't it necessary to choose the very best while presenting it to the other countries? Did they choose this theme so that she might contact him? There seemed to be something providential in this. He has also agreed. The confidence that he would again be my friend, my companion, was strengthening. She must suggest it, sound it, express it in body language but not openly put it in so many words. When she called, 'Mohan, where shall I arrange your stay in Delhi? The French people will put you up in a five-star hotel, of course. But I can get the guest room at my school cleaned and decorated. If you stay in the dance school, it will be convenient to rehearse for as long as we like. What shall I do?'

He merely replied, 'Those who pay for the hotel will also pay the taxi-fare, don't they?'

'Certainly they will. But why should you take a taxi when there is my car?' She lightened her embarrassment.

He was on friendly terms. He co-operated with the instrumental helpers. He also received her suggestions with a helpful attitude. He mentioned new concepts and improved the artistic quality of the compositions. He remained friendly when she put her hand on his thigh while driving. That's all. He would get off at his hotel and say, 'Why do you drive up in the mornings all the way? I can take a taxi and come myself.' He never invited her to come in and come to his room. How could she invite herself and put out? Has he come only on contract? Has he not forgiven me? Or, has he lost his manhood? Different kinds of doubts started assailing her. She had heard in the music circles of Bombay as well as in other cities that he had young women admirers and he stays alone in a flat in Bombay. She had also heard the light-hearted explanation that the secret of his musical brilliance was due to the inspiration he got from so many women. She noticed with irritation whether she wasn't lowering herself to the level of those women in trying to regain her friendship with him. She was perturbed the whole night. It was only when she gained the self-confidence that, once she possessed him she would see to it that he wouldn't be interested in any other woman, she could sleep. She shared with him all her problems after he was separated from her. She mentioned Karthikaram leaving her. She described his cowardice. But she never even told him suggestively of her bodily relationship with him. She described the circumstances of her distancing from Mittal Saheb. She mentioned Guruji's departure and her bringing him back in an emotional moment. But she didn't say how she was longing for Mohanlal. Should this be mentioned in so many words? She stopped with the dignity that he himself should understand. He was listening with sympathy. He never said anything further indicating attachment, or affection.

The accompanying musicians had economy class tickets on the plane. For these two it was the executive class. While occupying the wide, sofa-like soft push-back seats and stretching out their legs, she put out her hand into the soft rug and held his right hand. He also held hers. But there was no warmth in it. Still she didn't let go. She slept like that. He sat looking out at the darkness of the night from the window to his left. Then he slept.

3

The performance was very successful. The connoisseurs admired and praised the way she described the moods of morning Todi, evening Bhoopali and the midnight Malkauns ragas and the way she demonstrated by adapting them to dance. Music had the upper hand in the presentation. Mohan was the main artist. So he was happy. She was also happy. The rest of the five days were spent in listening to the discussions among other artists in the morning and seeing the performances of dance and music of other traditions. They wandered together and saw things and places. Though they were in adjoining rooms in the same hotel, he didn't invite her to join him. She didn't go on her own. He was getting into his room like a gentleman. She would also return to hers to guard her proper behaviour. The day before their departure there was no performance. Both of them went for a boat ride on the river. They sauntered about on the promenade on the park beside the river. She asked, 'Mohan, do you know that people who come to Paris are either lovers or honeymooning couples?'

He commented, 'It means that honeymooners are not lovers?'

She was sad that her barb didn't hit the target. She also wondered if he was purposely evading the implication. She told herself I am not going to leave this fellow today, I should not allow him to escape and accept defeat. 'Lovers come to Paris. Or they become lovers after coming here. Or, they revive their old love. Have you heard this?' she said.

'Poets may have written that,' his stubbornness increased.

In the evening, on returning to the hotel, when he opened the door of his room, she also followed him. 'Look, after coming to Paris, if you don't taste their drink, what is the use? They say that one who doesn't understand the subtlety of this, is no artist at all. If I don't make you taste it, my bringing you here is itself a waste. That is why I came to your room. I know you don't know much about the taste of drinks. I will initiate you. There is only one day, today. Tomorrow we are leaving anyway.' She made him sit on the sofa next to her. Then she got up, opened the door of the fridge and took out two medium-sized bottles from a whole row of them arranged in a line. She placed the glasses and the ice cubes outside. 'Look, this is a special French wine. It is not intoxicating. But this other one is a mildly inebriating. I will also drink. Don't worry. Friends drinking together is not an improper thing. It is a means of augmenting friendship. It is a method of mental relaxation and opening up the mind and sharing.' She poured the drink and offered it to him.

Saying, 'I am not an addict, but don't think I don't know,' he said, 'cheers.'

After some time his hesitation and embarrassment started to recede. She kissed him. He also kissed her in return. She was happy that he was responding. She got enthused. 'Mohan, tell me the truth. Have you forgiven me? Speak with your inner conscience.'

'Ah, that! Your hitting me and throwing me out. If you hadn't done so, I wouldn't have left you. I wouldn't have risen to this level by giving pure music concerts. I am grateful to you, dear.' He embraced and kissed her.

'It means that you haven't forgiven me completely.'

'Isn't gratitude superior to forgiveness?'

'Then why aren't you accepting me as before?' She stretched her hand to remove his jacket. He co-operated in disrobing himself. He tried to remove her clothes too. She completed his efforts. He said, 'Come,' and took her to the bed nearby. Since they felt it was a bit chilly, they drew the folded blankets over them. He kissed her with ardour. She started exciting him. No matter how long it took, he still remained in the same state. Didn't rise to the occasion. She didn't show displeasure. As if it was natural, she lovingly started to increase his self-confidence. 'Don't worry if it isn't possible. What I want is your heart. The body sometimes betrays us. Next time it will be all right.' She whispered consolation in his ears. After a long time she said, 'I will ask you a question. Don't feel dejected. I have heard that you have relationships with a lot of women. Is it true? I am not objecting that you are indulging yourself. After I committed an indiscretion in a senseless moment, how could you even remain a pure celibate? Besides, you are an artist. I am asking because I have heard that men who indulge in too much sex lose their manhood. Have you spent away everything at sixty itself?' There was no condemnation in her voice. Only pain.

Now he spoke, 'Look, I will tell you the truth. I feel love for you. But you have aged. That day when you came to my flat in Bombay, you held my face in your hands and kissed me, didn't you, on my lips tightly? After that you left. I remembered the touch of your lips fifteen years earlier. I thought, what a lot of difference between then and now. Eyes and ears are not the only media of knowing an individual; touch is an invaluable medium. The touch with the cheeks, lips and tongue is far more communicative than the touch with fingers and hands. Just as the memory of the look in the eye or the voice in the ear, the communication through the touch also remains in the memory. Otherwise your touch of that day, how could I feel the difference of fifteen years ago in a rush?'

'What difference?' she asked with curiosity.

'Listen. The touch of one woman is not like that of another. The quality of each person's touch is unique. Like the voice, like the thumb-impression, it is unique. In fifteen years, between forty-two and fifty-seven, such a lot of appeal in the feel of the lips, lacking in taste, lacking in softness, and the texture of the skin deteriorating to the level of getting the feel of soft rubber, I thought. I felt it was the way of the body. You have maintained the shape of your neck. You have not discontinued your yoga practice. Your body has not put on weight. Your strength has not decreased. You had dyed your hair jet black like that of a twenty year-old, not neglecting even a stray hair, you had arranged it in such a way that your forelocks looked quiet thickset. Though you have kept under control your shape and agility of body through the practice of yoga and dance exercises, can you control or stop the natural change in the body as it ages? All such thoughts passed through my mind.'

'Are you saying that I am an old woman?' She was shocked.

'That's not what I am saying. You were saying that people who came to Paris would become lovers. I was also thinking that it was true. Even now I think so. What a shapely figure these French women have! An erect posture. The shapely eyebrows and nose. Not just the actresses, the dancers and singers. Even when you are walking on the street when you see a woman you can always tell whether she is a native French woman or of mixed blood. But no matter what woman I saw here, I would remember Bhoopali. Her ancestry was also French. The father was English by name Smith. On her mother's side they were all totally French.'

'Who do you mean by Bhoopali?'

'It was a name I gave her. My pupil. We stayed in the same room for four weeks in America. She has all the happy combination of that raga. I remembered you when I made love to her for the first time. In the physical build, the shapely limbs and in the love abandon. But when I had sex with you, you were thirty-seven. She is now twenty-nine. Do you know what happened...?' He was still talking. She became totally silent. 'That day you ran away to catch the plane, you called at midnight, around quarter past twelve. The next morning I got a letter from her. The Arts Council of America had given her a student scholarship to stay in India and learn music traditionally from a guru. I had to send a letter of consent immediately that I would teach her. The scholarship is for two years to start with. If I send a recommendation that her progress was good and that the training should continue for some more time, they would continue it for one more year. It seemed she had called several times. I was not in town. Do you know what happened? After I returned from America I was not inclined to ask any student to call and come to my flat, and didn't feel like asking her to stay back after the lesson was over. I used to ponder why it was so. I understood after I got her letter. I didn't feel like desiring anyone after my involvement with her and enjoying her. What would have happened to me if the American government hadn't given her a scholarship! I would have bought a flight ticket from Paris to New York.'

He fell silent. She was also totally silent and still. After a little while she felt sleepy. He put his hand round her neck, drew her face to his chest and said with an inebriated look, 'Darling, why aren't you saying anything? I love you. You should lie down like this, with your head buried in my bosom so that I get good sleep.' He slided away into sleep.

She quietly loosened his left arm and got free. She put on her clothes, opened the door of the room, closed it and went to her room next door.

It was only when the receptionist rang him up that he awoke. He became conscious that they should leave now. The body and mind were still lethargic. He got up quickly and took a shower. There was no response when he knocked on her door. He went alone to the breakfast parlour. She had already finished hers. She was just drinking tea as if she hadn't seen him though she had. Without making an effort to understand why, he went to the counter, picked up a plate and started selecting the items of his choice. By the time he came back with his plate she had already left. Thinking that women are like that, imbalanced, he started eating. Even when they went to the airport in the hotel limousine, she didn't talk to him. She was looking the other way through the window. He himself put his hand on her left hand. She was sitting still like a rubber doll. After they put their luggage into the push carts, she opened her bag and said, 'Here, this is your ticket. You can check in and choose the seat you want.'

'Why, you take care of the checking in yourself for both of us as you did while coming. We can sit and talk...'

'No, I will travel by myself.'

He didn't understand. 'Why suddenly like this?'

She looked at him as if she would burn him alive. Putting her hand into another compartment of her bag, she said, 'This is the ticket from Delhi to Bombay. There will be a free coach service from the International Terminal to the Domestic. Otherwise, take a taxi and go.'

He also got angry. 'You could have got a direct ticket from Paris to Bombay. What is this nuisance of changing airports?' he said.

Saying, 'I was not in my right senses when I booked the tickets, sorry,' she walked away swiftly pushing her push cart.

He who was staring at her back, thought, 'Women don't have a steady mind. If they did, why would they be women!'

Chapter 11

1

When he was about to go for his bath the phone rang. 'Hi, Guruji, I am Bhoopali speaking. I am arriving on Wednesday night, at half past nine. Please note the flight number. Please book a room for me in an inexpensive hotel near your place. I will ring you up again in the evening. Please let me know the name of the hotel, the address and the phone number.'

'Hi, Bhoopali, in another month, your own flat will be ready. Till then, stay with me. Why a hotel?' He was excited.

'Won't you be inconvenienced?'

'If you come, all problems will solve themselves. I will get inspiration not only for music but for life itself.'

'Thank you Guruji, thank you.'

'I will come to the airport. Arriving alone in the night, and searching for my flat in a taxi is not advisable.'

'Thank you Guruji, thank you very much.'

After putting the phone down and while taking a shower, he began to wonder if he had spoken in haste indiscreetly. Anyway, she was staying for three years. Her own flat. I have my flat anyway. Staying together for a month means giving room to unnecessary rumour. I will also lose my freedom. He thought if she had checked into a hotel as she suggested, had rested the night and had come in the morning here by eleven, we would have a wonderful time till the evening without interruption. I had succumbed to an impulse. The thought recurred, 'Shall I call and tell her that I will book a hotel for her?' But he hadn't taken her number. By now she would have vacated her room in Pleasantville. He became aware that there was no use calling there. He remembered what Rajaram had said. That staying in the same room in New York and staying together wherever they went on tour was not a wise thing. Why stay together in Bombay and give room for scandal? The other girls might also get angry if he allowed Bhoopali to stay with him. Now everything is private. It should be so. He decided against undue publicity. Actually it was Bhoopali whom he loved deeply at present—only Bhoopali. Though it was five months he returned from America, he had no affair with anyone. He remembered, the idea hadn't occurred to him. Such intensity and devotion to one person was not good. He cautioned himself if love becomes loyalty towards a single person it might draw the mind towards marriage. He remembered that many people in America stay together without marriage though there is intense love. She was also an American. She may agree to this arrangement. But, who knows her attitude? Was she attracted only to my music or to me also? Difficult to decipher. Still, he thought there was a difference between the two. After finishing the shower, lighting incense sticks and worshipping the picture of Goddess Sarasvati and the tambura and before meditating, he decided to book a room in a nearby hotel and meeting her at the airport, to tell her that there was a problem which he couldn't remember earlier and that he had reserved a room for her in a hotel. Tell her to rest the night and that he himself would pick her up the next morning around eleven. There was also the feeling that there were still two more days in case there was any afterthought. He closed his eyes and contemplated on Goddess Sarasvati, the patron deity of the sapta-swaras to brighten, sharpen the knowledge of the musical tones and begged her to give him the power that articulates the sharp notes spontaneously in his voice. He incanted it thrice as he did everyday. The face of Goddess Sarasvati in the photograph, with the light of knowledge and the affection of the mother combined, flashed forth clearly to his inner mind. He wouldn't stop praying till this picture emanated within himself. Now he stopped, circumambulated thrice and went into the kitchen for breakfast. After pouring milk on the cornflakes and switching on the tea kettle he went to the bedroom and while putting on fresh pyjamas and jubba, he heard the doorbell. Who could it be? Whom had I invited for a lesson today? When he went and opened the door, what a wonderful surprise! Not even without a phone call—Madhu!

As soon as he saw her his mind was transfixed in her. The offering of a new bride. An expression-assuring a lifelong companionship and desiring one. A shy and blushing demeanour looking down firmly though desirous of looking straight with a full vision. *ni dha ni re ga re ni re ssaa s.* Kalyani. The mind forgot everything and got immersed in her. 'Hey, you are standing at the door itself. Please come in. When did you arrive? Why didn't you call earlier? If I was away on tour you would have had to wait at the door.' He led her in holding her hand. A plastic paper bag in her right hand. Her handbag in the left. As soon as she came in, she put down both the bags, sat on the floor and holding both his legs, pressed her forehead on his feet. That surrender and devotion was pleasing. Madhu's devotion was such. He became aware that such was dedication and devotion were not found in any other student. He stood still until she herself lifted her head and then lifted her up holding her shoulders and embraced her tightly. He remembered the warm embraces. He felt it was unique. He was possessed. He lifted her downcast face and kissed her lips ardently. She didn't respond. Her neck was sagging down as if under a weight. She was always a new bride. Shy. Every time he met her it was the same. Her transitory swaras were as such. Her bhavasthayi-bhava itself was just that, he thought. The nomenclature 'Kalyani-yaman' has no meaning. Kalyan itself is the original name. In Karnatak music it is called Kalyani. It is a still better form. 'Hereafter, I will call you Kalyani. It is what I taught you for a week. And then sang together. You are the personification of the mood of that raga. A new bride,' he whispered in her ear. Her neck was still hanging down heavy, like iron.

'Have you had your breakfast? I am reminded of the breakfast you used to prepare in Los Gatos. Only you don't get all those things here.'

She took up both the bags and came to the kitchen. The bag on the right hand was full of fruits. She took them out and cut the apples and grapes and put them into the bowl of cornflakes that he had kept ready. She sprinkled the raisins into the bowl from a packet. She mixed them up, placed a spoon and placed the bowl in front of him and asked him where the toaster was kept so that she could prepare toast. She had come unexpectedly. Though it would be heavy, he felt like eating. He showed where he had kept the toaster. He said,

'You have given me all the cornflakes. Have some yourself. Join me. Let's eat together. Saying she had finished her breakfast she started placing the slices of bread in the toaster. When he put the fruit-mixed cornflakes into his mouth and started enjoying it, his mind which was contemplating that there was no equal and substitute to Bhoopali, the moment he saw Kalyani, it engaged itself in analysing the experience of having immersed in her. Though there was a momentary surprise, the experience came to the rescue and the explanation became clear. When the mood of Bhoopali fills the mind, it doesn't allow any other raga to come anywhere near. But even when the mood of Kalyani is full, it keeps its distance from others. That is how it should be. Otherwise, the purity of the raga doesn't survive. When the tambura is tuned differently and shadja is commenced, it is a different shadja altogether. He felt that the explanation, that it was a different movement and a different delineation of emotions was convincing. It is best that she should be accommodated in a hotel room. I must meet her there. Once she finds her own flat, there will be no problem. She should come here only for her lessons. Since she is an American she keeps her appointment punctually and leaves. However, this girl, once she comes, stays for two to three weeks, from morning till evening. He saw that there would be no problem if he asked Bhoopali to come from eight to nine in the mornings thrice a week.

He looked at her face. 'Kalyani, after I left your place and particularly, after leaving America, do you know how often I have remembered you? You are the only student who will bring credit to my name and continue the tradition. Learn with devotion. I will also teach you with all my heart. How is it you have not brought your cassettes and the recording machine?'

'I will bring them.'

'So today, it is only preamble of raga.' Uttering so he looked at her amorously. She didn't meet his gaze. Just bent down her head. He got up, embracing and kissing her, he led her to the bedroom. He closed the window-curtains, switched on the air-conditioner and sat her next to him on the bed. 'Don't compare this to your feather-soft bed of royal comfort. In this hot country if you sleep in a bed like that, it will be hotter still.' She didn't say a word. He watched her closely.

He understood for the first time that ever since she came, let alone the animated shy look of a newly-wedded bride, there was not even an ordinary interest. He saw that it was the attitude of an unworldly, disinterested sage. He examined attentively. In her eyes that were gazing at the wall opposite, he saw a detached, unconcerned vacant and pensive look which had been summoned with determination. He felt bad. He turned her face to him and asked, 'Kalyani, why are you like this? Is everyone all right? Is Vikram all right?'

'Yes,' she replied unemotionally.

'Then why are you like this. Tell me.'

She went into the kitchen and brought her bag. She took out a bundle of papers of some twenty-five, thirty pages, put it in front of him and said, 'I will say what I want to after you read it.'

'You read it to me. Have you written this? What is it about? Is it about music? As for me, I can't even write four sentences.'

'You must read it yourself. No, you must read it for yourself, by yourself. Don't show it to anyone. Now I am going home. After you read it, you call me. I will come. Let's talk. Look, here is the number. Placing a card on the bundle, she took her bag and left. When he realised that she had left, by hearing the sound of the door closing, she was already gone. He became curious. Had Vikram come to know about the affair and had they quarrelled? In addition to this suspicion there was concern. He took up the bundle. White, Xeroxed sheets. He went to his room, wore his spectacles and started to read. Her own handwriting. Written in Hindi.

2

Is this what is known as viraha? Vipralambha also means the same. If it is so, then why is it called Shringara? This pain, this inner fire which silently reduces one to ashes. Why did they call it 'Vipralambha Sringara' and not 'Vipralambha Angara?' It is like being lifted to sky-high bliss and thrown down into hell suddenly. It is like a flight sailing smoothly in the sky at thirty-thousand feet suddenly is broken in two and hits the earth with a bang and a thud. God, I had never experienced such pain. Not even when I left home and went to America. I experienced only sorrow. For three weeks, especially for two weeks.

It was not mere totality of musical notes. But I had become an integral part of a great artist. I was flowing along in the same stream joining my swara to his. That flood was making me flow. Effortlessly without loss of my strength I was being floated along. The acme of that bliss, of that flowing was when I sang with you, nay, when you graciously permitted me to sing with you in the presence of an audience, exceeding two thousand. I wasn't even aware that you would leave the very next morning. I simply didn't remember it in practising with you, and the tremendous expectation of singing with you as an accompanist in a full house. I felt that this companionship, this musical harmony would continue for ever. This harmony of singing together was causing to fill and spill the feeling of eternity. While singing Jot me jot mila ja jogi *the intensity of the rasa of pathos of Bhairavi was not simply rasa only, but it was bursting out of the dam of my personal inner being... Guruji, didn't you understand? Still, why did you leave by the morning flight? Didn't you remember the whole-hearted, unlimited love of a fortnight and my total offering to you, body and soul? Is your love so limited that it can be contained in the time-table of an air-flight? The car in which you were sitting descended the slope from the house. My intense sorrow flowed down too. Vikram couldn't look back as he was driving downhill on the woody zig-zag road. But why didn't you look back even once at my face? Was it the caution that you shouldn't give rise to suspicion in Vikram about your feelings for me? It is possible only for men to be so cautious in such an emotional situation. I don't know about other women. But for me it is impossible. It was a good thing that I didn't come to the airport. Supposing I had broken down as I did at home, what would people think? Looking at my crying if you had also started weeping uncontrollably the secret would be out. At least to that extent, your Madhu is wise, isn't she? Vikram said, it seems thirty-six people had come to the airport to send you off. Only Indians have this quality. Coming to the airport, felicitating with a garland and bouquet and making an occasion of it. Your music of that evening has conquered all of them. Panditji, none of us wished to send you away. We want to have a private concert in the homes of each one of us and listen to you everyday. It seems, they said, why did you accept that six week engagement in New York? Indeed you conquered the entire Silicon Valley. You win like this wherever you go, that's why you are proud. You didn't condescend to look at this Madhu once you were in the car. Eight women also had come to the airport who didn't know any music but who had become your fans by just listening to you last evening and they looked around for me asking whether Madhumita Shaw hadn't come. When Vikram told them, 'She is not feeling well' they said, 'She must be tired after singing as magnificently as her guru.' Vikram said, 'Don't feel low. Listen to the tapes of the two ragas you practised everyday. Practise further in the same direction. Let us ask him to come back here after six weeks at New York and teach you two more ragas. If it isn't possible, you can yourself go to Bombay.' Do you know what a great devotee of yours Vikram has become? To the extent that if anyone says your music is not good he tells them they don't know music. If anyone repeats he would almost assault them!*

As he kept on reading he felt elated as if he was floating in the sky. So far he had not received a love letter. He hadn't written one either. Even a couple of his favourite students, after they got married were sending him only greetings for Diwali and New Year and not letters expressing such intense feeling. Madhu's love was not the kind to be extinguished soon. He felt no one had loved him so deeply. He proceeded to read further.

Today is Wednesday, you left on Sunday morning. I am still alive. Did you think I died? Why didn't you call me on the phone? Don't you know even the elementary courtesy that people who leave must inform that they have reached safely and that it is not just a courtesy but a duty? In the rush of music, I forgot to note down your address and phone number in New York. Or, may be you also didn't know. After waiting for your call on Monday, do you know how hard I tried and how many numbers I rang up? Until your call in the evening when we were having dinner and Vikram noted down the number. You also know that since Vikram was there I couldn't talk freely. Why didn't you call me the whole of today? If it is a collect call, you can call even from a roadside booth. Hadn't I and Vikram told you to do so? 'Guruji, you are taking away my whole life' is what I said. Is it possible to be more explicit in the presence of Vikram? Still, why didn't you call the whole of today? Stupid New York is earlier for three hours from here. It is 11 am for you when Vikram leaves for his office. Now even after three calls, the hotel receptionist is saying that you have not returned. Why didn't you give at least the number of your workshop? Have the organisers themselves forbidden it as it may interrupt the lessons in progress?

Guruji, no, my jogi, my life-companion, can't you understand why I am struggling so much just to speak to you? In whom can I confide this inflammation within me and find appeasement? I don't have any such confidante. If I do confess to someone, unable to control myself, they will comment perversely that a music student is having an affair with her teacher. How can anybody else understand the purity of my feelings? I can confide only in you. Aren't you also feeling sorrow, nay, the torture that I am undergoing? You too must, mustn't you? For you also, this is something which you cannot confide in others, isn't it? In whom do you find a confidante? If the lovers confide in each other, it is alleviating, bearable and gets deeper. Don't you know the primary principle that mutual dependence strengthens the bond? I have found a way out with the fear that my feelings may burst forth in front of others, in the presence of Vikram too. I am putting down my feelings on paper, writing, sitting alone, with the belief that you are present and listening to me. With the inner thought that after writing continuously, I will write your address too and put it in the post-box. You, of course are a stone god. An idol who doesn't even make a phone call, no matter how much I am longing.

Yesterday I thought you were a fixed idol—a stone god. As if to prove that eulogy through blame is more effective than eulogy though devotion, you telephoned today. Since you were calling from a roadside booth you weren't able to hear properly. Though it was true you were not able to speak properly, still it wasn't the emotion that I expected. How honestly I used to blabber away my feelings. You were listening with caution and circumspection. You never said, 'Madhu, I am also equally, no, even more perturbed than you are. I remember you everyday at least a hundred times.' You only said, 'Be calm. One shouldn't be carried away by emotion. You are coming to Bombay anyway in three months. After returning, depending on the programmes, I will give you the dates.' You never said you were being *consumed by the pangs of separation. You are older than me. It is true that your experience is also greater. Even after knowing that you were very 'experienced' I gave myself to you completely. Therefore have I become inconsequential?*

He stopped reading. Even if she has written ironically, she is right, I am 'experienced.' If something like 'I remember you a hundred times everyday' is spoken, women may consider it to be true and jump to madness? Their words like 'deathless, eternal, of many lives' it must be listened to, shouldn't be spoken. The relationship should be maintained only at that level. I have learnt from experience that only as much as is necessary at the moment, must be said. When once a total relationship is established, it lasts till their learning is completed or till they get married or some impatience occurs, they will certainly keep meeting. However, this writing of Madhu is very pleasant and full of melody. He felt that it was so emotional that he should surrender himself. He continued to read.

My companion of life, companion of music, I was very angry with you an hour ago. Actually there may have been someone close by when you were talking on the telephone. You said that half the students were Indian. It didn't occur at all to my stupid head that someone might have been there and so you couldn't speak in Hindi. You can make a collect call even from your hotel room in the evening. Vikram never comes home before seven in the evening. Even if you call at half past nine from there we can talk for at least half an hour. Hereafter I will try to ring you up. Another thought. It isn't possible this weekend. The top-brass of Vikram's company have arranged a picnic. They have said that everyone must bring the spouse along. How about my coming to New York next weekend? We can be together for two days. If I say, 'I must see Guruji. I must learn the first round of an alaap,' Vikram will agree. Is it stretching his credibility too far? Supposing he says that he will also come along! Not because of suspicion, but his inclination to meet you. If he also comes along, the New York trip will be a waste.

Early this morning I did a courageous thing. I couldn't simply help it. The intense desire to see you, to be with you was, striking me from within and driving my sleep away from me. Around 4 am Vikram was in deep sleep. I silently got off the bed opened the door silently, closed it equally silently, came down the steps and entered the music room. Even if he wakes up and comes down, I could say I came down to practise mandra, I closed the door of the music room and called you from there. Though there is phone in our bedroom, it doesn't make even beep, unless he picks it up to call someone. But he is in deep sleep. Besides he has not called anyone, till now, at this time. I remembered that if one doesn't take any risks nothing can be achieved in life and I called you. Then it was 7 am for you. But the answer came from a female voice in American English, 'Guruji is in the bathroom. Any message?' 'No, I will call later' and disconnected. I perspired, if it was evening, it could be some student of the workshop. In this country nobody visits another in their hotel room at seven in the morning. Is he with another woman? There are many white women who are attracted by Indian music. Half an hour later I felt like calling again and asking who she was. Supposing she asks what does it matter who she is? There was this fear. When Vikram left for his office at 8 am, I thought of a plan. I called again. After ten seconds, the operator said, 'No response.' I said, 'There are two people in that room. The other person must be there.' She repeated, 'No response' and didn't mention how many there were in the room. That is the training in this country. They never reveal anything strictly beyond their jurisdiction. I called again when it was 9 am for you. You yourself picked it up. You spoke in Hindi. After enquiring about my health and well being you said, 'I will myself call you. You please don't.' Will your room be full of students?

He remembered. Bhoopali might have answered like that. After I read these papers she may ask about this. There were many students at the same hotel—men and women. On many days they would come early to my room. On some evenings they would stay till late. He could say, 'How can I remember who said what on which day?' He got over this problem and continued to read:

Guruji, my life breath, yesterday you said that you would yourself call when you were free. You didn't, I had called you to confess something which I could confess only to you without any reservation. You didn't call. Even today, until now you haven't called. Therefore I am expurgating myself through writing this letter. I want to post it directly to you. But I am afraid it may fall into wrong hands. The day on which you left by flight, on Sunday, the whole day I was dull. My eyes had swollen. In the afternoon Vikram was sitting in his room attending to office work. After dinner when he asked me, 'Shall we go to bed early' with a suggestive look, I was hurt. Though we were going to bed together for the last three weeks, he hadn't insisted on having sex. He had sent out signals, made mischievous remarks. Then he would say concessionally you are in a mood for music and slept by himself. But the night on the day you left and it was Sunday too, when a husband wants his wife, what excuse can be given for not obliging? If it is denied will the conjugal concord continue? Is it proper conduct? But that large bed was not Vikram's. It was yours, I felt that if I gave myself to him it was like prostitution. Still I didn't deny him. With the awareness that if I was totally non-responsive, he might feel hurt, I satisfied him with my body by suppressing my mind. I suffered internally. The happiness that we were enjoying since our marriage, for the first time resulted in a feeling of torture, impropriety and schism. I felt that only my union with you was free from all duality and it was the experience of religiously pure bliss. When you were actually there, that was not the feeling. Anxiety might have been the reason. But now it is the only dharma, giving myself to Vikram is sin. In whom can I confide this?

Mohanlal was pleased to read these sentences. He felt proud. He derived a sense of fulfilment that she was completely his. He blessed her within himself that he would teach her every minute detail of music and he would stay with her only to teach her, without any other engagements for two to three months. He remembered the king-size bed. He felt that only by being united on that bed there would be total fulfilment. He promised her silently, 'I will come, Madhu, I certainly will.' Then he also told himself not to displease Vikram as he was a good boy. Besides he doesn't come in the way of our privacy and being united. Such a husband was very rare indeed, such generosity. For some time he sat there just watching the revolving fan. He felt friendly with Vikram. He read on.

You have done something more unbearable, don't you know that in American calculation Los Angeles and the place where we live are very close. Don't you even know that Los Angeles is in California itself? Should I get to know by reading the newspapers that you are giving two concerts there? Couldn't you think of the fact that the music lovers here would call me and ask me, 'It seems there are two programmes of your Guruji in LA? Didn't he call you to tell you?' If you neglect and disregard me this way, what should happen to my good stature? All these people think that I am Pandit Mohanlal's music representative in America. Tell me, which other pupils of yours are there in this country? Doesn't anybody feel that way who listened to the marvellous concert when you made me sing with you? Supposing you had commanded me, 'Madhu, there is a concert of mine in Los Angeles, you must give me support in signing and accompany me on the tambura,' to what heights would my reputation would have risen! If you had informed me earlier what ragas you would sing, I would practise and come prepared. Or, if you would come a week earlier, stay with us and trained me! Why did you forget? I won't come. I won't listen to your concert at Los Angeles. An entire group is starting off from here. Mishra, Sardesai, Goyal, Gupta, Murthy, Kulkarni and some seven or eight more with their families. When a coach has been engaged, it isn't right that we fly and saying so Vikram has given our names too. After listening to your concert, the people around this place, though they don't understand classical music, the numbers who listen have augmented. They say that they will listen only to classical music hereafter. They are saying we want to listen. You give a concert, sing the same Yaman and Bihaag ragas that you sang with your Guruji...No, I won't come. I will say I am not feeling well. I am angry enough to ring you up and take you to task. You asked me not to call you but you yourself would. After that you had rung up only twice. And then there was silence. I didn't call myself. So you know why? Not out of fear that you might get angry. I also have self-respect.

With whom can I confide your disregard for me and the pain you have caused me? And how? I told Vikram, 'He hasn't informed nor has he invited us, that he is coming to Los Angeles and giving a concert there. I won't come; you can go in the coach.' Vikram said, 'A workshop means that the people will be busy from morning till evening. Artists are moody people. Great artists will have tremendous moods. Are you not moody yourself? Do I get angry because of that? After all, he is your guru. You are a disciple. Don't behave stupidly. Besides, it is even possible that he doesn't know that San Jose and Los Angeles are so close and that they are in the same state. Has he ever taken note of geographical spaces leaving out the positions of musical swaras?' Vikram has become your devotee. He takes your side. Still, the fact remains that you have disregarded me. You shouldn't do this.

Though tired after a seven-hour journey, as soon as I did see you coming on the stage, there was lightning which passed through my body. Since we made our booking late, we had obtained only balcony seats. I who sat by you playing the tambura had to see you sitting at the back of that big auditorium. Who is that White girl, more or less of my age? From where have they brought her, after searching, these people from Los Angeles? The parting hair, the braid, bindi, the earrings, sari and choli, glass bangles, made up like hundred per cent Indian. After all, Los Angeles contains Hollywood, doesn't it? The welcome introduction said tambura support given by Lauren Smith, a disciple of Mohanlalji. I pondered, when did she become a disciple? You started with Maarva—a raga that is very soft but equally difficult. You haven't taught me. Not even in Bombay. With what dignified delicacy did you move without the meend ma dha ni dha saa wah dha ma ga re ga ma ga, re saa... *How simple and equally difficult. Only you can achieve it. Even if I was accompanying you, I wouldn't be supporting the swara. You haven't taught me at all. That girl is not bad. She was playing the tambura very steadily. How soon you captured the audience though it is a very subtle raga and not familiar to the audiences. Guruji, you are great. Really great. No musician I have heard has this mastery. An hour of spellbinding, magical melody. When you next announced Bhoopali with what happiness the audience welcomed it! Now, I should have been accompanying you. I would have caught the swaras. I would also add tanas. However, Lauren Smith too caught the swaras. She accompanied you faultlessly though not in keeping with your greatness. A simple raga. Simple swaras. You are purposely giving her an opportunity, in order to give her publicity. She strikes one tana. You wait for her to complete the round. Where did she learn? When did she become your disciple? I am getting angry that you are deceiving me. I was feeling that I had heard her voice somewhere. I couldn't place it. Bhoopali became very dear to the audience. There was no interval. It was a good thing. It is just a waste of time. Also a distraction of mood. The final piece, Jaladhara-kedar is also not a very familiar raga with audience. Still, the moment you started singing the mood of fatigue, of tiredness, tender excitement, and blessedness of complete union of Kedar and Malhar filled the minds. You had taught me Kedar. Not the jaladhara form. When you came to this raga, Lauren Smith just shut herself up. Perhaps Bhoopali was the only raga she knew. You gave her a great deal of opportunity because of your natural generosity. She has plotted to shine as your student by learning from someone somewhere and then meeting you. As soon as the concert was over, people surrounded you. We had arrived by coach. Hadn't checked into hotels. We couldn't find accommodation in the same hotel. So we had to rush from the auditorium. Our coach reached the other auditorium five minutes late where the morning programme was held. We Indians don't start punctually, exactly on time. Your Shivamata-Bhairav had already started. A raga not very much known. Many people in our coach had taken a bet that you would sing Todi. They had tried to involve me in the betting by asking, 'What do you say? Which is your guru's favourite?' I had said, 'Nobody can guess what he draws out of his limitless repertoire.' After we took our seats in the auditorium, several people in our group asked me what raga it was, silently by an interrogatory gesture. Guruji, you hadn't taught me this raga either. You had taught me only Bhairav and Aahir-Bhairav. I won't leave you till you teach me everything in your collection. Just as yesterday, today also she is sitting clad in a sari and choli with kumkum on her forehead. She is not adding her voice anywhere. Bhoopali is the only raga she knows. Your singing has already created the peace of the morning. If I had not come out of anger with you, what a loss I would have suffered! After that, you started Jogiya. After singing Shivamat Bhairav why did you choose another raga of the same type? Was it because the peace of Sivamat wasn't enough but philosophical detachment was also necessary? The Saranga which followed initiated jollity. It created an atmosphere of bright light, and the morning shedding off its coldness and emanating the warmth of the afternoon. Guruji, it is true that you choose the ragas according to the time of the day. But when you begin to sing, the raga itself creates the time of the day. If you sing Darbari in the heat of midday, it creates the peace of tranquil, midnight. If you sing Saranga in the cool midnight, the activity of the midday sun is created. Your art has the power of creating time. You are great. Yes, you are great. I would have accompanied you for Jogiya. For Saranga too. Why didn't you give me a call and invite me? Why did you make that girl in whose veins our music doesn't flow, sit with you to play the tambura? I am not saying this out of envy. No. How can a White girl not born as an Indian and somebody who has not grown up digesting our life pattern and emotional culture, understand the sources of our ragas. Her fingers are moving monotonously on the strings. But a simple machine which moves as regularly could have been placed there. Why did you make her sit there? She added her voice at the time of the brief alaap of Bhairavi. She seems to be familiar with that raga. Is there a student who is not familiar with Bhairavi? Ah, you started* Mat ja jogi. *Even now on hearing it I feel like sobbing profusely. My Jogi, my Krishna, don't go. Don't leave this Meera, your slave, and go away. I will build a funeral pyre of sandalwood and lie on it. You light the fire with your own hand and go. Jogi, don't go. Guruji, why did you choose this song? You know that I have come here. Otherwise you would have sung a different song. Don't I know how many songs you know in Raga Bhairavi. I feel like crying. Vikram is sitting on my right side on the left Mrs. Mishra. If I weep uncontrollably, what would they think? All these people have seen me weep singing this song in Sunnyvale Concert. That girl is also accompanying by repeating* mat ja *refrain from time to time. No, you don't know the essence of Bhairavi. The depth of feeling of Meera is quite beyond your comprehension. The pressing sorrow is abating now.*

Wonderful concert. The audience is giving you a standing ovation. There are some ten to fifteen per cent White people also. The Secretary is standing there to propose a vote of thanks. How is it possible for anyone to comment on such a marvellous concert and thank in fitting language. After thanking Rajaram Tipnis the harmonium accompanist and Omkar Prabhu of tabla, he said, 'We also thank the consort of the main artist who heightened the mood of the concert.' The mischievous rascal. A novice who doesn't know the English language. It was a mistake of the Managing Committee to have asked him to propose the vote of thanks! I felt like going there and slapping the fellow. But Guruji, for his mischievous innuendo you said, 'Thank you, thank you.' Why can't you learn a bit of English?

I started out wanting to meet you. But you were surrounded by your fans. Then the organisers led you away to the car and saw you off. The accompanist on the tambura, she also sat with you. It seems you had to go to the airport directly. We also started off. We had checked out in the morning and had deposited the bags in the coach. A journey of four hundred miles. Barging into a wayside McDonald we had got takeaway packets of burgers and sandwiches we wanted and immediately the coach started. Everyone was in a musical mood. Even those who didn't know music were humming to themselves. Some others were performing the actions of the hand like Guruji and striking tanas. Mishra who has learning music from me once a week stood up and said, 'Everyone is in a mood for music. It will be satisfied only if we listen to the same ragas that we heard last evening and this morning. Let Madhumitaji, the direct disciple of Mohanlalji sing those ragas. There are no accompanying instrument—harmonium and tabla. We don't need them. It is enough if she just sings them.' Everyone clapped. 'Yes, yes', they intoned. A person at the back said Piya ke nazaria. *But Mishra said, 'It can wait. First let's hear the ragas we listened to yesterday and today.' Everyone approved with a single voice. I was embarrassed. I felt myself blushing. The nerves on the neck seemed to bulge. I said, 'The outside noise doesn't penetrate into the moving bus. It is airtight. But the running engine has a different tune. It is difficult to sing.' Everyone persisted, 'It doesn't matter if it is different. Please, you must sing.' Vikram also insisted. I sang last evening's Bhoopali and this morning's Saranga quite elaborately. People were satisfied. They didn't ask for anything more. Some were sleepy. Some others slept. Some others indulged in casual talk. I was sitting in the middle. By my side was Mrs. Sardesai. Vikram sitting in front started conversing with some four or five others. Sitting two rows behind me, Kulkarni was telling Bhonsle next to him, 'You remember the Secretary who proposed the vote of thanks made a pun on consort and concert.' It seems it was not just to show off his knowledge of English. It was done deliberately to prick Mohanlal. Mohanlal had asked that the accompanying tambura artist should also be paid airfare. A hundred people are available in Los Angeles itself who can play the tambura. Why should we get someone from three thousand miles? The association doesn't have that kind of money. That was what they said. To that Mohanlal replied that he himself would pay for her ticket, that they need to stay together and asked them to reserve a double room. Where will the organisations have money to lodge the artists in hotels? Isn't it the practice everywhere that the artists are lodged in some host's house and it is for him to look after the hospitality and travels etc. But to mention it in so many words, it is embarrassing to both the guest and host, besides lack of privacy. He is a big artist. He cannot be accommodated in a small lodge. In a star hotel, food and other things are also expensive. All in all, for two days the expenses are four to five hundred dollars. They had lodged the harmonium and tabla artists in somebody's house. This White girl was his catch in New York. That is why the Secretary said "consort". The pun that was made in fun couldn't be understood by Mohanlal. You yourself heard him say, thank you, thank you. I heard every word clearly and distinctly that was spoken in Marathi by Kulkarni. 'Before coming to the coach I had gone to the comfort room. Then I met Raikar. You know him?' 'Yes, I know him. Goa, Software, Deccan Engineering College. He is also a member of the organising committee. He told me.'*

I felt giddy. The coach bore the silence of a cave. It was like I was sinking into the cave. And as if there was no one to support me from collapsing. The eyes closed on their own accord. It seemed as though a lot of time had passed. By the time I came to my senses I had felt that what Kulkarni had said was hundred per cent true. It became certain that I knew the innate nature of Guruji. The answer to a question that had been nagging since last evening flashed forth. The call made to New York at seven, local time, the voice which had answered that Guruji was in the bath and asked if there was any message, was hers. This means that within a week after taking leave of me he has been living with her. I am felt like I was slipping deeper into the depths of the cave. Utter silence in the coach. As time gets slower and slower between one prosodic unit to another, it seems the interval never ends and the next prosodic unit would never come. After a long time, the voice of Bhonsle in Marathi, 'When you experience art you feel you are entering heaven. But when you enter inside the artist, it will be very different. Why this contradiction?' 'This question has troubled me too,' Kulkarni answered.

When the coach reached San Jose coach station at half past nine and everyone was moving towards the parking lot, some people said, 'Madhumitaji, thanks for your excellent music.' Not even thanking them in return, I walked behind Vikram. Within five minutes I heated up the food. Since Vikram had to leave for work early in the morning, he slept at once. I, who lay down next to him was rolling about, unable to sleep.

Mohanlal remembered both the concerts of Los Angeles. He also remembered what Rajaram had said about them. Because of his taking Bhoopali with him not only did the organisers incurre unnecessary expenditure, the proximity of his fans and admirers stopped. Besides, for most Indians this doesn't seem to be proper conduct. Since he remembered that he had decided not to do this in future, the turmoil in his mind ended. Actually I didn't know that Los Angeles and Madhu's place were so close to each other. Los Angeles and Los Gatos both have the prefix 'Los'. He felt sad that the proximity didn't strike him even from this. But at that time the feeling for Bhoopali was so intense that it was difficult to be without her even for a couple of days. Otherwise, would I spend money for her ticket from my own pocket? Perhaps, had I known that Madhu's place was so close and that she and others from there would come to the concert, I wouldn't have taken her! Even that was not certain. There was the clarification perhaps when one is totally immersed in a raga, no matter how densely emotional the other raga is, it will be obliterated from the mind! But now seeing Kalyani a couple of hours ago, Bhoopali was erased from memory. Must be, my love for Kalyani is deeper. She is angry. How can I explain this in detail? He got embroiled in this difficulty. She is an American. Within the limited time available, I took her along and kept her with me. I was explaining the ragas. I hadn't asked for a double bed. They hadn't given me. Kalyani will accept when I say, 'Who is that bastard who added the innuendo?' What else can she do except accepting? This thought brought some comfort. Such situations have arisen in the past also with several women. They have all accepted when I swore that I had not touched any other woman except her. Is there any alternative? Kalyani also will accept it and keep silent. He gained this confidence. He continued to read.

Guruji, looking at it objectively there is nothing surprising in your behaviour. Doing this sort of thing is natural for you. After knowing this perfectly well, submitting to you again was my mistake. I offered myself to you in the beginning because you wouldn't teach if I didn't. After six years I wanted to have my own family. I wouldn't get any friendship, love or companionship from you except learning music. I got a husband who could give me complete protection and encouragement to practise music. In three years I felt that it was not enough and wanted music lessons. Your memory became an attraction. I myself put out and invited you. Didn't I know that you wouldn't leave me alone? I did. But it was covered up in the attraction of your music. Though it was an open book, I couldn't fathom all the implications of actuality. You didn't leave me alone. You acted according to your true nature. Not just me but you invaded my conjugal bed itself. I was also a victim of infatuation. You destroyed the sanctity of the nuptial bed. Still, I wasn't aware of it as long as you were there. I would avoid Vikram. Thinking that I was tired because of my practice of music, he also left me alone. After you left, when I gave myself to him out of purely a sense of duty, I felt that I belonged only to you and I was committing adultery with Vikram, my husband. I was pushing my days, suffering this torture of the bed. Though I did not receive a phone call from you and though you have forbidden me from calling you, after I came to know last week that you had demanded that Lauren Smith should also be given the airfare, their refusing it, that they should arrange a room with a double bed and you staying in such a room, after knowing all this, I am angry with myself. I have realised that I have no right to be angry with you. I am blaming myself everyday, that I was an adulteress, a prostitute who has deceived such a good husband. Vikram is asking me to go to Bombay every three months and get intense music training from you uninterrupted. He has even been chiding me that I am becoming lazy and asking me to get up in the early morning and practise pranayama and pursue mandra. He has decided to make me a first grade artist in three years. The day before yesterday I got up at 4 am, had a shower and a cup of tea, closed the door of the music room and tuned the tambura and adjusted the shruti. The shadja gave me peace. Forgetting to descend to the depth, I was immersed in that bliss. After a long time, remembering the purpose of my sitting there, I started to descend, step by step. As I kept descending I became perturbed. Began to experience agony, the strings of my sin started reverberating. Every syllable that emanated from me began to sound like adulteress, adulteress and began to prick my conscience. Whenever I touched mandra-shadja, hell was found inside. I experienced lethal pain. The mandra-shadja of Raga Kalyan that you specially taught me here. I was perturbed. Does that gentle raga emanating the shyness of a young bride have this quality of creating hell? I stopped singing. Sending off Vikram to the office, I again sat in the same place with the tambura and started entering into the same mandra. The same sense of sin. The feeling of punishment for sin. Not just a feeling, the pain that emerges out of all the sensory nerves of the body. The kind of pain that is described as a result of blood cancer. A wringing pain in all the organs where the blood circulates. I stopped the practice of swara and singing and placed the tambura in a recumbent posture on the rug. Mandra means introversion. Not just the depth of a raga. It is an experience of descending into the depth of soul. It had been my experience even as a little girl beginning to utter the notes sa pa sa *that the essence of the raga was in the mandra. You had also said that touching the mandra was like reaching the moolaadhaara in yoga. Now I have realised intensely that it is an experience of groping in our innermost being. As far as I remember I haven't done any other evil deed. Knowingly I haven't hurt anyone. Except that I hadn't told Vikram before marriage that I had surrendered my virginity to my guru. I haven't cheated anyone in any way. He trusted me. He still does. Worships me. Is still doing so. Promising before marriage even without my asking that my development in music will not be hampered in any way. He has been acting accordingly. He has trusted me to the extent of leaving you and me alone in this house surrounded by a forest and going away on tours. It is he who has arranged for sending me to Bombay once in three months and to pay you a substantial fee. He has even shown me the generosity of not raising a family to save me from the obligations of pregnancy and postnatal care since I mentioned that it would impede my progress in music. It appears to me, he is the mandra-shadja and its moral fibre. I am afraid to approach it. The pain of fear augments. You remember our Silicon Valley programme was captured on video. Vikram saw it everyday for a week. He distributed copies of it to his friends. You remembered I taped everything you taught me. He listened to it all. Now he himself supervises my practice. From the mood and movement he can recognise the raga but doesn't have the technical knowledge of identifying the position of swaras. Still the suggestion he makes are useful in practice. He has learnt enough to recognise whether there has been any improvement when he listens once a week. I am even concerned, if I don't show any progress what might he think. Not just a moral fibre, but he is becoming my guru in my vocation.*

I haven't written for two weeks. The circumstance of writing to a guru is passé. My mind has decided that there is no bond between him and me. It is three weeks since he went to Bombay from New York. I am writing as a therapy to save myself from turmoil. I have stopped the practice of mandra for a week. It is as good as stopping the practice of other parts of music. I am not even listening to the tapes. An idea is taking shape. Not everyone lives by music alone. In most of the Indian women who come here, there is neither the love of music nor knowledge of it. Aren't they happy? Shall I just remain a housewife? The truth is that looking after such a large house, it is not physically possible for me. Not used to it. I haven't grown up that way. Maria can be relieved of her duties. But that also becomes monotonous. How about joining computer classes? So many educated wives who have come from India have got computer training and are in good jobs. After all, this is the Silicon Valley. That is the only means of employment in this region. I don't need a job. How about trying something in Vikram's own company? No. Staying at home I can help him in his job. Without knowing computers and the way they work, it isn't possible to do anything in this country.

When I put forward the suggestion, Vikram didn't show any enthusiasm. He said, 'There are a million people who work on computers. You are the only one who has the training and ability to sing the way you do. Why do you give this up? He accepted my argument— 'I am not giving this up. I need a change. If it is music all the time while walking or sleeping or dreaming, won't it be boring? If there is some change, even music can be comprehended in a new light. Don't many aspects of music which do not flash to me, occur to you?' 'You don't have to go to attend classes in the beginning. The elementary things can be learnt at home. I will teach you. Pay the fee for the guru and perform gandaa-puja and get initiated.' He laughed. Again, since it was put in musical language itself, I was irritated. But couldn't show it. I hadn't even learnt typing. He brought a small machine and taught the basics. 'You play the harmonium, don't you? Just as when you play it in whatever manner with eyes closed, the fingers find the right keys, here also with practice the fingers automatically press the right buttons. Learn by following this book.' Vikram is a computer engineer. The firm he has founded and is developing is such a company. His wife entering his own business world was pleasing to him. But he was not willing to lose the unique individuality his wife had. 'There are millions learning computers. Are you continuing the practice of music?' he keeps asking.

Now I can type without committing too many mistakes. I can correct the mistakes I commit. I can manipulate the computer to perform the magical things it does. It seems to be an amazing world. Even the computer games. There is an intoxicating dimension. 'It is remarkable the progress you have made in three months. But you have given up music completely. Why this philosophical disinterestedness suddenly?' Vikram asked. If I tell a lie that I am practising, he will know it. Besides, telling a lie is a sort of prostitution. Actually the act of prostitution must be made known. Mishra and Sardesai also keep calling, 'Madam, when are you starting the music classes? If there is an hour's training per week, there will be an obligation to practise ourselves. Otherwise, we will forget what we have learnt.' The other day Mishra had come. 'Vikram has mentioned that you go to Bombay once in three months and learn two ragas thoroughly, tape them and come. The next three months you practise intensely and make it your own. Then again you go to Bombay and learn two other ragas. You have given up music itself. You are not teaching us. You have started on computers. Does Vikram need you to work? Sorry. My question may appear rude.' It was 10 am on a Saturday. Mishra had come without calling. Vikram was not at home. He had gone to the company office though it was a Saturday, saying that he would come home for lunch. Mishra was a man of strong moods. Fifty years old. Hair turning white around ear-lobes and in the middle of a thick crop of black hair, a tiny tuft knotted concealed which could be noticed only if carefully observed. Only those who knew that he was a Brahmin from Kashi would notice it. The rest, that too, the White people's attention would not be drawn to it. He was one of the people coming to learn music from me. He has no melody in his voice but has strength. The voice emanates deep within from the region of the navel. There is an intense emotional upsurge breaking the bounds. He knows the style of every raga but he doesn't know the elaboration or the extension of a raga and arranging of tana. Teaching him enhances my knowledge of the raga still more. No one in this valley has heard as much music as he has, saying, 'Madam, what's the use of sitting here? Please move to the music room. I am going mad. Please teach me the alaap of any raga for at least two hours, please do it yourself. Otherwise, I will take the next flight available and go away to my native Kashi. The company here may dismiss me.' Saying so, he proceeded right away to the music room. It was two months since I had entered it. Maria's son came once a week and hoovered and dusted the walls. He took up two tamburas and started tuning. 'Why are the strings so stiff? Have lost the suppleness? The knobs won't turn. Seems many days since they have been used. You please tune them yourself.' He leaned them towards me. I wanted to say, 'I have no desire to sing or to teach. I don't like to sit in this room. Let's go to the lounge.' But noticing his earnestness, I tuned both the tamburas. 'It is immaterial whether it is morning, noon or night. Begin any alaap. If you leave the choice to me, it is komala-rishabha-asavari. It has been urging me on for three days.' He started right away saare mapa dha sa. *Expanding on what he knew he descended into mandra. Though his theoretical knowledge isn't much, he knows what he knows precisely. Doesn't commit mistakes. If a mistake is made it will be straining the emotional mood. Such subtle knowledge. I also got involved in his emotional strength of pulsating to the roots of the raga at madhyama-shadja itself. I started teaching the slow descent into mandra. Teaching him sitting in front of me I began to discover new and newer nuances. His throat didn't have the strength to create and show every variation I demonstrated. He would look up at me with mixed feelings of sadness and pleasure whenever he fell short. Then I would find new ways. I felt inspired. In the middle, he himself would intone* accha, bahut accha, *and ask me to continue. When we tried to descend from gandhaara into komala-rishabha, he, unable to follow, gave up and made a sign for me to proceed. My throat also became stiff and I started coughing. After all it was two months since I had given up practice. The twinkle in his eye looked like a challenge to me. I thought he was chiding me. I didn't give up. I started again with madhya-shadja. Gradually I descended. Finally, I did touch mandra-shadja. He commented, 'You jumped down from komala-rishabha as if you wanted to win a race. In the process the emotion got muffled up.' I felt embarrassed. I felt like asking for pardon saying that I was out of practice for two months. But feeling shy, I tried again. Now Mishra had become my guru. I had become a pupil showing that I had learnt the lesson taught. Finally, he showed his approval by shaking his head in such a way that even the little tuft that had been entangled in the crop shook with approval. Since he was also supporting by singing I was moving slowly with pauses. During the pauses new and newer naadi-granthis would open up. Finally, when I took up the cheez in teen-taal* | to tu mha ro | daa ss sa | ja nu ma ja | nu ma ki, mai | *he joined in showing the time scale with his right hand. Then suddenly he got up, went to the box by the wall, took out the harmonium and started accompanying. Though he was not playing all the subtle nuances of my singing, and of tanas he was showing the saam correctly with his left hand. When he found it was difficult to follow he stopped playing and was just indicating the framework and the saam of the taal and was thus encouraging me. Interspersed with exclamations of approval,* 'wah, kyaa baat hai.' *The entire room was filled with music. Though the door was not closed the sound would not escape. Though there was repetition in the tanas, I didn't feel like stopping. His face was also beaming continuation. No tabla. No support of harmonium. I sang it again and again in rondo. When I finally concluded* | ja nu ma ja | nu ma ki, mai | *with a tihaai there was not only appreciation but satisfaction on his face.*

When he was saying wah, *I felt satisfied. Vikram came into the room. 'It was very good. I came even when the alaap was in uttaraanga of madhya-saptaka. If I barged in, the mood would shift, I was sitting outside the room.' It was 1 pm. I told Vikram, 'Please call Mishraji's home and inform that he will be having his lunch here.'*

The next day, when I sat down at the computer, I thought that it was a meaningless, futile endeavour, not an art by which I could absorb myself within my inner being. I felt like going away to the music room and taking up the tambura. I went and started the shruti. Unknown to myself I thought of the komala-rishabha asavari. I started singing to myself. The karuna-rasa, pathos, filled me. The more I descended, the greater the depth of compassion for life's vicissitudes increased. When descended further down, there was repentance. Reaching the shadja from the rishabha was not as difficult as it was yesterday. After attaining mandra-shadja and resting there, I experienced a feeling of accepting all the rights and wrongs of life without any fear and adjusting it to the basic shruti of life. I remained in that state for a long time like a yogini performing tapas. Meanwhile I felt Vikram coming and sitting outside the door of the room. He doesn't enter when I am practising. He doesn't create the slightest distraction to the prevalent mood. Still, my attention moved in that direction. It included him. I felt I was actually standing in front of his physical form and confessing all my virtues and sins. There was no impediment for singing. I came out of the waters gradually having immersed myself in the depths of mandra for a long time. Passing through madhya-saptaka too slowly, digesting it, I reached the crescendo of begging forgiveness. After a prolonged prayer, the anguish seemed to abate. Without being aware I began:

| to tu mha ro | daa, ss sa | ja nu ma ja | nu ma ki, mai |
| s sa s ki | i s cchaa s | pu s ss ra na | ka ra ho daa | sa

Shedding all sense of heaviness, a lightness of feeling and sense of surrender was generated by it. Strumming the strings of the tambura with the right hand and defining the time beat with the left, when I started singing, an emotion, that there is a state which transcended guilt, contrition, confession and retribution began to swell in my mind. I went on singing to myself for a long time. I didn't pay attention to refrains and repetitions of tanas. There was no frame of mind to think and plan new variations and calculate their beat. There were no supporting accompaniments either. There emerged a self confidence which disregarded the instruments, and there was the realisation that I was alone and must make the journey alone.

Though the singing stopped, the moving fingers on the strings of the tambura didn't stop. The mind which had immersed itself in the tranquilising humming sound was contemplating the meaning of the movement of the emotion it did experience till then. A strange state which seemed to be understood but yet not being known what it was. I had never before seriously contemplated on the meaning of the mood of raga. There used to be a vague feeling that emotion should not be subjected to reason and tortured. Emotion meant emotion. What is there to think about it? Such an idea. But now it appeared that there was a profound thought, palpable to grasp, now in this Asavari.

I have been singing the Asavari of komala-rishabha for a month. I have taught this same raga to Mishraji for four Saturdays. Sardesai is also coming. The day before yesterday, Vikram went to Germany. He will take four more days to return. I feel that it is easy to take the most important decision when he is not in town. Everything has been decided. The question that remains is whether to tell everything to Vikram in person or to write a letter after leaving and informing him. It is enough to leave these sheets for him written over the last five months and he will understand. Every detail cannot be remembered if you sit and talk face to face. Even if you can, it may be embarrassing. Besides, it is painful to me. And, painful to him. But writing a letter to reach him after I leave is a cowardly act of not being able to face him. But my being a coward is not a lie. What is important is to tell the truth to such a noble person. Not how it is done. Whether to confess face to face or inform through a letter. This kind of confession of guilt face to face becomes an act of brazenness.

Vikram, please forgive me is a meaningless polite phrase. If you can find peace of mind by forgiving, please pardon. You got deceived. I deceived you. It is not possible to live with you continuing the deceit and having conceded my deceit perpetrated earlier. I am not leaving with only the single purpose of ending this deceit. I will dedicate my whole life only to pursue music as my goal. The desire for freedom, not to be in the position of deceiving others, though I have committed a mistake is also included in my decision. I won't come back from Bombay. You can get a divorce by showing this letter itself to an attorney. Or you can ask the attorney himself to send the papers to me directly. I will sign and return it. I do not expect any compensation from you. Actually, I must give you compensation for having deceived you, for marrying by concealing my past, for making you a divorcee at this middle age, for ruining the chances of your finding another girl who is satisfactory in every way. This is not a compensation which can be settled by money but by putting my forehead firmly on your feet and begging forgiveness. I will not mention this episode to anyone. I have decided to tell my mother, brothers and sisters-in-law in Bombay—I have returned with the sole purpose of pursuing music. Vikram is a god-like person. It is not possible to continue music in that country. However, you have the authority to tell the truth to anyone you like.

3

Has she come away, leaving her husband? Mohanlal was perturbed. He had a sinking feeling. That is why there was no liveliness on the face. Mad girl. Why couldn't she consult me, even give me a call? This is a Xerox copy. He understood that she had given the original to him. Such a co-operating husband. Why should she have told him? After all, what's there to tell? The relationship between the teacher and the taught will always be intimate. Not just a student but a close pupil. How is it possible to teach everything, without any reservation to an ordinary pupil, to make her perpetuate his fame and name? The pupil must be one's own son or daughter. Nobody reveals the secrets of art for nothing. He justified himself by telling himself that he had never asked her to transgress her chastity and asked her not to love her husband. He derived a complementary justification that he was always quite friendly with Vikram. She was always like that. A girl of moods, she plunges into madness when impelled from within. The doorbell rang. The watch indicated that it was time for the arrival of the tiffin. The moment he opened the door the savoury smell of food entered. Though the tiffin-box had been put on the table, he didn't feel hungry. He remembered that she had made him eat a heavy breakfast that day. It is true she has written all this. She has even given me a Xerox copy. Has she really given the original to the husband? Or has she reserved it till knowing my reaction? He told himself not to believe her immediately because god knows what wiles women are capable of. But his mind asserted at once that she was not a tricky girl. He drew the window curtains. The sea was unoccupied, deserted. Not a single boat. After looking at the empty sea, an emptiness appeared in his mind. The sea means that it must have boats. Yes ships too. At least one. Otherwise it is terrifying, he thought. To block out the light he drew the curtains as before, came back to bed holding the sheets of paper she had given and lay down. He tried to compose himself by telling himself that merely because some insane girl had done something, why should he bother? Did she consult me before doing it? He decided to ring her up and give her a piece of his mind, upbraid her and tell her that he had no part in the mess she had created for herself. He turned over to the other side in order to strengthen the resolution. He felt like having a cup of tea. He went to the kitchen, prepared tea, sipped a couple of times and put the cup on the teapoy. Is it possible that she has informed her family by now? She has written in the letter that she wasn't going to tell anyone. Still, in a mad moment, if she might have poured forth her turmoil to her mother. When he thought this, he remembered that she came from a prosperous business family with two of her brothers managing it. He saw the possibility of the brothers taking it out on him for having ruined their sister's life. But he saw the solution—what can they do to me after all? She has joined me with happiness; she has herself written this in her own handwriting—look at this. He felt at ease remembering that decent, respectable families don't make a rumpus about such things.

He felt hungry at 2 pm. He ate the meal that had gone cold and lay down. Couldn't sleep. Even after closing the curtains and switching on the air conditioning, there was no sleep. Automatically his hands picked up the sheets of paper she had given. He glanced at them.

In sum, what is her import? I love you. But you got interested in someone else and forgot me. Not just that, you drove me to cheat my husband. She didn't agree. But I forced her. But which girl will submit without force? Did she or did she not surrender herself totally after acceding? Was she not more passionate than I? Thus the idea that I deceived her husband will crumble by itself, the mind felt certain that no justice will accept my guilt. He folded the papers, removed his spectacles, turned and closed his eyes. Still he couldn't sleep. If there was no afternoon siesta, by the evening there would be a dried up feeling. He must sleep. It was half past three and he made a decision that he should tell her point blank that only she was responsible for her madness and she should not involve him in it. The address card she had given was there, close to the pillow and he pressed the digits of the phone.

She arrived in half an hour. A small box in her right hand. He saw immediately that it was a recording machine. She has brought it from America. In the left hand, a bag containing recording cassettes in addition to her purse, etc. He said, 'Looks as if you have come prepared for the lesson.'

'I am ready whenever you want to start,' She said.

He looked in the direction of the bedroom and said, 'Let's go there and talk.' She followed without demur; he sat on the bed, arranged the pillow against the wall and sat leaning on it. She sat a couple of feet away, drawing up a chair. There was no pleasantness on her face. Only a determined seriousness. She had no firmness to meet his gaze. Both of them sat as if listening to the hum of the AC.

'Speak', he said. She didn't speak immediately. After he repeated it, she said, 'You should speak.'

He said, 'Did you give this letter to Vikram directly?'

'I didn't have the courage to give it directly. More than courage, it looked like arrogance. Anyway he was repeatedly asking me to go to Bombay for lessons. He bought this new recording machine only for that purpose. This is an extremely sensitive machine which can record even the slightest variations of tone. He came to the San Francisco International Airport and sent me off. "Don't be in a hurry to restrict yourself only to two weeks. If Guruji is in town and in a mood to teach, stay as long as you like." After moving over to the other side of immigration I went to a phone booth and rang up home, and left a message on the answering machine, "Vikram, please excuse me. I have kept a white envelope on the pillow of our bed. Kindly read it." He would have reached home in fifty minutes. He would have read it immediately.'

He didn't say anything. She didn't either. After a minute she herself spoke. 'It is my habit to call him from London as soon as I get there. But I didn't. It is his habit to call me at Bombay in an hour after my reaching there. He didn't. It is two days since I arrived, isn't it? He hasn't. There is nothing more left for me. I have lost everything. I have severed everything. I am not feeling sorry for what I have lost. But when I think of how much sorrow he is experiencing, I cannot bear it. There is no man as good as him. It is not possible for such a good husband to exist. Why should he suffer this pain? Why should he get such a bad wife as myself? There is no justice in life. If there was, he would have got a good wife.' When she said this, tears burst forth uncontrollably. She tried to control it. But like a lid that had been clamped broke open, fits of crying burst forth. Even without being conscious that weeping was undignified, she kept sobbing profusely. The guru was nonplussed. He also became affected. He stretched forth his hand from where he was sitting, held her shoulder and started caressing the top of her head, asking her to console herself.

After a couple of minutes, she brought herself under control. After a minute or two later, she said, 'I didn't weep for myself. Because this is a situation brought on by myself after thinking about it. I am feeling sad for Vikram. God will not forgive anyone who brings about pain for him. He is such a good man.'

For a moment he felt as if his brain had been immersed in ice-cold water. Couldn't think of anything to say. He just looked at her face. Her eyes filled with tears were looking at him. After some time his voice found expression. 'What you are suggesting is that I am responsible for his pain, that you were spoiled by me, isn't it?'

She looked steadily into his eyes. 'Guruji, you are my guru. If I blame you, my learning will be destroyed. You have not erred in any situation. All that I have done, I have done with full responsibility.

If you did not feel that I was yours, you would not have taught me all the secrets of this discipline. You said that if I offer myself to you completely without reservation, you would feel like teaching me with all enthusiasm. You didn't force me. I gave myself to you only after thinking of the pros and cons. You taught me regularly. After six years I felt like having my own family. I married without telling you and left for America. I knew that if I invited you, you would demand the same thing and that you wouldn't consider me as belonging to someone else. Still, I invited you. You taught me two ragas completely. Now I have come away to learn all the ragas completely. Cheating my husband, forsaking him is completely within my purview. It is not concerned to you. Therefore I have come after telling him what should be told. There is no need for you to get upset. You just ignore my weeping, thinking that it is the natural weakness of a woman. Please teach me right from today.'

'You are talking very cleverly.'

'There is absolutely no cleverness in this.'

'You have come to me because it is difficult to love me while living with your husband. So you have left him and come to me. Now you will completely give yourself to me. That is what you are saying, isn't it?'

She didn't reply. She looked at him intently. Very soon she turned away towards the AC. He insisted, 'Tell me clearly.'

'Guruji, I have to answer you because you have asked me. You shouldn't mistake my plain speaking. If you promise me that you won't, then I will tell you.' Saying so she bent down and touched his feet. He said go ahead. Tell me. Then she spoke slowly. 'I don't see any sense in the expression offering oneself. Nobody should give one's body to anyone else. They to whom it belongs must claim it. Still, many people surrender their body, some give it for money calculating the period of time in terms of the amount. Some do so to get promotion in their career, some for glamour, and some for position—thus people surrender for various reasons. Doesn't a man or a woman have the right to surrender his or her body in order to achieve a goal? But education is superior to money, career, position, glamour and all these. That too, the learning of music is the highest form of education. My whole being is vibrating only for music. What is wrong in surrendering my body for its sake? Staying in the frame of marriage and surrendering to another is wrong. So I have come away leaving Vikram.'

Saying so she looked at his face. Though his eyes were looking in her direction his look was scattered in an unspecified region. 'I will tell you one more thing. I am now thirty. My body may not have the capacity to inspire you. Don't suffer by getting bound on account of some old obligations. My father had given me a large flat registered in my name, many years ago. My elder brother has rented it out for a big sum for a company to run it as a guest house. The rent credited to my bank account will have added up to lakhs of rupees, the cash that I received at my wedding was also credited to the same bank. I will give myself to you as before. But if I don't have the ability to inspire you, I will pay in the form of money. As much as you want. It is my money. I am not taking it from anyone else.'

His gaze was still uncertain. A minute later she spoke, 'I have surrendered to your music. Not that there is no other singer. But your style of singing, emotional interpretation, sophisticated nuances, the ability of art that makes one to spring to the heavens from the earth—this is unique. After learning from you all these years, I must complete the final phase also with you. If I go to learn from anyone else, there will be no co-ordination between the foundation, the mural structure and the pinnacle. The secret of your art will not be obtained either. So, only you must teach me. I must sing till my last breath as a pupil of Pandit Mohanlal.'

He didn't speak even now. She also didn't have anything more to say. She got up, went to the window and drawing aside the curtains stood looking at the sun who was bowing down to the west and checking the waves of the ocean with his red rays. Then turned towards him and said, 'I won't speak anything of this at home. I won't even mention having come away, leaving my husband. I have come since it is not possible to learn music in America. I will only say that I will spend sometime here and sometime there. I have confidence that Vikram will say the same thing. He is a man who acts with great self-control. I will stay in a flat which is sufficient for me and conducive to musical atmosphere.'

4

By the time he brought her from the airport and dropped her in a room on the sixth floor of Moti Sadan in West Bandra, she was extremely tired, ready to collapse, she kissed him and said, 'Sorry, Guruji, I am sleepy.' He returned to his flat. When he went there at three in the afternoon, she had finished her shower and lunch. She understood what was on his mind and took the initiative, caressed him, stimulated his desire and satisfied him demonstrating that she was still the same Bhoopali. Then she slept in his arms. Deep sleep. A difference of nine and a half hours. The taxing sixteen hours' flight. Feeling he should let her sleep away he caressed her but the thought of how to support his arm under her head for six or eight hours, or even for ten hours waiting for her to wake up, bothered him. But he didn't feel like abruptly pulling his arm away and leaving. Yes, she was the one beloved who was his heart's desire, she will be here for three years. He thought that he shouldn't give up the others but also it won't be possible to have the others frequently, as he had turned sixty. In the company of Bhoopali, sixty becomes thirty. Now, he remembered that he had become twenty-five and felt happy with that memory. There is a kind of freedom in this girl. She doesn't impose any moral bondage. It is not just that she is not married. Sheer freedom is the characteristic of that society. Not just freedom. There is also the devotion to the guru. Though she was utterly exhausted with the journey and in spite of the pull of the jetlag, how she went to sleep only after serving her guru with such a deep commitment! He appreciated it. He kissed her lips. It was as though the turmoil he was experiencing for two days got allayed. Accusing the guru. The sense of sin of having deceived her husband and deceiving him still. It seems she left him because of this sense of sin. She says that just as some people surrender their bodies for the sake of money, position and fame, she was ready to give herself for the sake of education. Hereafter I won't teach her a single note. And, I am going to curse her—as legendary Parashuraama cursed Karna—let her forget even what I have already taught, he decided. If music was everything to her, why did she get married stealthily, before she learnt everything? He felt a pain in the left arm. Bhoopali's head was firmly placed on it. Unless he frees himself, the pain will increase. Without a palpable movement he slowly extricated his arm and put a pillow there. She rolled over and turned her back to him. After some time his mind left Madhu. However, the mind was vacant and there was a sense of void. For how long can one stay lying down this way. He got up. He went into the bathroom, had a wash, combed his hair and shut the door. It locked itself from inside.

The next morning, after ringing up the hotel, when he went, Bhoopali had finished her shower and was ready. She said, 'I don't know when you left. When I woke up, morning was breaking. The hangover of sleep had been over. I had a shower and breakfast. Your call came through. Tell me, now, what shall we do?'

He winked. She understood. She smiled consent.

But afterwards he himself felt a void. While engaged in bodily activity no other words are necessary. But when it was all over, there appeared nothing to say to her. She was not from New York. He didn't know anything much about that place. Not about the place where she came from. All that he remembered was Atlantic City. The gambling city where he lost thirteen thousand dollars within five to six hours. The only intimate and truthful thing he could talk to her about was to tell her, 'Bhoopali, after returning from America I was immersed only in your thoughts. I have not touched any other woman.' Realising that to say that he had not touched any other woman would cheapen him, he suppressed that sentence. What else was there to talk to her? Besides on realising that his English was not fluent there appeared a void was it only for this that he was waiting all those months? It was all right with Madhu. There could be inexhaustible talk. Both their languages were the same, the same country, the same town, the same mindset which would understand things the same way. He became aware that it was the same food habits, dress code, the same way of understanding the meaning of every word of the cheez that was sung etc. But she has accused that he had cheated her husband. At least if she had openly accused and quarrelled, he could be pacified. But she has written everything and has even given it to him. Whom did she ask before giving it to him? Did she ask me? Impudence. A moral pride that she was superior to her guru. He told himself that until pride is given up there will be no progress in learning.

'Guruji, when do you start the lessons? I must send an official document from you to America mentioning the date of starting lessons,' Bhoopali asked.

'Today I will show you my flat. It is walking distance. Your class begins at nine tomorrow morning. In twenty days, you can occupy your flat. After that you may practise everyday. If you practise singing in this hotel, the other guests will object.'

That ended the conversation. There seemed to be nothing more to say. He remembered that this was so with the other women he had contact with. After the sex act is over, all the encomiums that were showered like you are the goddess of love, you are a great beauty, you are the queen of my dreams—all such praises lose their meaning. Inventing an excuse that I am expecting someone or that I have to go somewhere, I get them packing off soon. It is very rarely that even after the passion is spent, to lay there dreaming, sharing dreams and keep lying together. That was what used to happen, with Manohari, in the beginning. And with Madhu on the days and nights when Vikram was on tour. Manohari did what she did. For Madhu, she suddenly contracted the fever of chastity—of being utterly faithful to her husband. This turned into a mania and gave a letter to the husband. 'With whose consent did she do that?' He asked himself angrily.

ऽ

It was five days since Bhoopali had come to Bombay. One morning she had her lesson from nine to half past ten and left. At about eleven the doorbell rang, when he went and opened the door, Madhu was standing. A handbag in the left hand. Fruits were visible in the plastic bag she was holding in her right hand. He didn't invite her in. Didn't talk to her. She just came in. Went into the kitchen, placed the bag on the table and came. Meanwhile he was sitting on the sofa. She sat on the floor at his feet, bent down, touched his feet and put her hand on her head like a benediction. He didn't speak. Just sat there ignoring her. After sitting there for a minute she said, 'I am not a new entrant.

Still, today is Thursday. I came because it is a good day to start the lessons. I have brought the cassettes also.'

He didn't talk. She lifted her head and looked at his face. Though his gaze met her face, he at once turned it away. After a minute, she said, 'Guruji, you must forgive whatever mistake I have committed, you must forget even if I have said something wrong, inadvertently. If you are angry, where can I go? You must start the lessons today.'

Even now he didn't speak. He didn't even look at her. After waiting for another minute she held both his feet firmly, pressed her head on them and said, 'I won't let go until you ask me to take up the tambura.' He didn't talk. She didn't let go. She tightened the grip, then she said, 'You must speak.'

Now he spoke. 'Those who have guru-bhakti—true devotion to the guru won't have moral pride. Because of your vow of chastity, your telling the truth to your husband and such rituals, you have belittled the guru. How can I feel like imparting knowledge to you?'

'Let there be no such duality. Isn't it because I want to transcend this duality and solely give myself to my guru that I came away by telling Vikram? Why would I do it if I didn't consider guru as everything?'

'Then why did you say that some people give their body for money and you were giving yourself for knowledge?'

'It was a mistake. Not for education but I give myself to you out of devotion for you. I will give myself to you without any duality. Please come.' She got up and pressed his face to her breast. He didn't talk. He didn't resist either. 'Guruji, everything that is mine is yours. I don't have to be afraid of anyone. I don't have any fear in my heart. Come.' She lifted him up. He stood up. She took him by the shoulder and led him to the bedroom. She switched on the AC, closed the window curtains, embraced and kissed him and whispered, 'Take me. Accept me. You are not just my guru but my master, my companion and my only lover.' He believed her. Anger subsided. He engaged in foreplay. Remembering his loveplay, she started putting out. He reacted. She kissed him, caressed him like a mother. She tried to obliterate all his anger and reserve as a mother. Mentally aroused, he tried to tune up his body. He struggled. She encouraged him with compassion, fellow-feeling, protection and support. Still, the rhythm couldn't be generated. No amount of manipulation would result in perfect tune. She caressed him, 'Keep quiet for a little while. Your anger against me hasn't subsided. It will be all right when that happens. Put your head on my lap and lie down.'

Suddenly he sat up with a jerk. He looked at her with burning eyes. He swung his right arm and slapped her cheek hard. Before she understood what was happening he slapped her again. She felt giddy. She caught hold of him and embraced him with leaning her head against his chest. He didn't notice it. 'You are a great Pativrata. You have to write a long letter to him. You should also carry on a charade of giving yourself to me. Your offering is not genuine. The proof lies in the fact that my body is rejecting you. Just get out. Never set foot here again. Take that recording machine with you that you left here the other day. You can never master music in this birth. Get this. It is the curse of a guru', he blabbered away.

Chapter 12

I

Didn't know where to go when she came down the lift. She knew that there was a taxi-stand close by. Could go home straight. But to do what? Even before the question popped up, the answer that there was nothing but only a void. I had to be honest to my husband. Confession of guilt had been submitted to him. It shouldn't have been made known to the guru. The only thing that bothered me was though I made it clear that I was spoiled and not that he spoiled me, he didn't understand. But without his spoiling me, how could I be spoilt? This hair-splitting logic seemed absurd to her. The husband had been abandoned. Though I offered myself to the guru, he would not accept me. He even slapped me angrily. He pronounced a curse that he would never teach me again and music would never be achieved by me in this birth. When she remembered all this, the feeling of nothingness further deepened. Instead of going to the taxi-stand, she turned left. She reached the sea shore. A large platform about a hundred feet long and fifty feet wide was abetting the sea. A place where children play in the evening. The noise of hawkers selling chikki, lollypop and ice-cream. Now in the scorching mid-day sun, the raised platform was totally empty. She went to its edge. She took hold of the four-feet high iron railings and looked. Twenty feet below, the waves of the sea were assailing the platform wall with a loud noise. There was no high tide. Still, even a big elephant would be dashed to pieces if caught in that turbulent blow. She wondered how she had never noticed that place! While she stood gazing, the tape-recorder she was holding in her hand felt heavy. She put it down at her feet and stood there. When she watched the waves mounting one after another and beating against the parapet wall, she remembered asavari mandra-shadja. A state which confronted the truth. It was the swara-sthaana that exposed the adultery and deceit to a husband who trusted her and who had tied the sacred thread round her neck with a feeling of equal sanctity. She just wanted die.

If she drowned there and swirled with the rolling waves and got smashed against the wall, that would be the end. The conclusion. The conclusion of the raga. The end of life. *Don't set your foot here again. You will never master music in this life.* Just a barrier of four feet. The heat of the midday sun. No one around. The idea occurred that if she jumped, the tall wave would catch her, swirl her around and the next wave would absorb her into itself dissolving life even before dashing against the wall and beat her into an unrecognisable pulp and the next elephantine wave would crush her skull, bones, ribs, knees and elbows into smithereens. Suddenly the resolution to climb the barrier and jump down did appear. Where was there any better tune than death for her who had been given up by the husband and rejected by the guru and there was no more music? Where was there a greater tune? She didn't feel fear. But sorrow came surging up. She started weeping uncontrollably. She folded the edge of the sari and pushed it into her mouth. The fit of weeping pushed it aside and came rushing out. Without even bothering that someone might hear, she wept aloud. Her body became exhausted. She held on to the railings and sat on the floor. The waves of the sea as if losing their turbulence looked like water colour paintings, on account of the colour of the tears in her eyes. She wiped her eyes with the edge of her sari. The roar of the waves filled her ears. Still, she felt that someone was standing behind her. She looked back. An old man. An ordinary, unpressed white dhoti, the kind that is worn at home. A small, stitched shirt. Thick spectacles. A walking stick. Dentures. More than eighty years old. A bald head. He asked, 'Why are you weeping, my child?' She was embarrassed. She felt ashamed that somebody had found out her secret. Couldn't speak. He continued, 'Look, look at that flat on the fourth floor. That is ours. It is my habit to sit out there after lunch on an easy chair, dozing away, looking at the sea. I was slumbering. Suddenly I woke up. Don't know the reason. When I opened my eyes. I could see your figure indistinctly. I wore my glasses and then I could see you distinctly. I saw only your back. Some girl in trouble. I wondered why she was standing there in the hot sun. I got up, took up my walking stick, got down the lift, crossed the street and came. Meanwhile you were sitting on the floor.

Don't feel shy. Come to our place. Or go to your home. Sorrow is like a wave. One wave is not exactly like another. One moment is not like the next.'

She lifted her head and looked at his face. In half a minute she felt ashamed and lowered her eyes. He said, 'Look, my girl. I am not curious to know your personal problem. But sorrow lessens if shared with someone. Some conquer it and come out of it without confessing it to anyone. Such people are really brave. That doesn't mean that those who confess it to others are weak. Do you understand what I am saying? Come on, lift your face and look at me.'

She still kept looking down. Again, he said, 'Lift your face. I want to look at your face.' She then looked at him. He looked steadily at her face. After half a minute, he said, 'I have the power to read faces. You are a strong girl. You will overcome the situation and transcend it. You don't need to confide in anyone. Get up. Take up that box of yours and go home.'

She felt ashamed to keep sitting in front of him. She got up, bent down and prostrated to him, took up the recorder and walked towards the taxi-stand.

5

Though her intellect said that the words of consolation he had uttered were of worldly wisdom, her mind was informing that he might have some special powers. He made me lift my head and just by looking steadily at my face said that he knew physiognomy. He said, you are a strong girl and you can overcome your situation yourself without confiding in anyone. He said that. He probably has that power. Yes, he certainly has. Otherwise how could he arrive at the exact moment I was about to jump into the sea? Her mind favoured the notion that he had special powers. What kindly compassion was there in his eyes! I looked up only once, just for a moment she felt like seeing him again.

She didn't do anything for a week. Didn't go anywhere. Without talking much with anyone at home—her mother, sister-in-law, brothers or their children. She would just keep lying down in her room. In order not to give room to unnecessary speculation she would come out of her room for tea, breakfast and lunch and mingle with others. She told everyone that it was not possible to learn music in America and she would spend more time at Bombay hereafter and that Guruji was not in town. Saying that she had some reading to do she had kept the volumes about music written by Batkhande. Though she wondered a couple of times whether she did an unwise thing in giving her diary of notes to Vikram, her mind had become lighter because she had confessed the truth. Usually when she arrived in Bombay, she would receive a phonecall from him. Then he would ring up everyday. Now, not even once. She had also not expected it after he knew all she had written. Mother had questioned her about this a couple of times already. She herself felt that her mother had not been entirely convinced by her explanation. Mother knows well enough that he could call from wherever he was. Even the sisters-in-law hadn't talked about it. They were behaving as if everything was normal. I must ask for my cheque-book and passbook from my elder brother. Though the money is mine, he was looking after the money matters. I feel shy and embarrassed to ask him. I must search for a flat. If I live in my own flat in Khar, it will be too big for a single person. Let its rent get credited. The decision she had made in America that she should rent an inexpensive flat seemed good. But the guru, the teacher himself had rejected her. It seemed fruitless to go and ask him again. Didn't feel like it. The decision never to see his face again was getting firmer. But from who else to learn? Who would teach with dedication? It was not a question of mere knowledge. Who else has such a genius like him that causes the swaras flow and weave so as to concord with the power of emotion? She decided that if a proper guru was available, why should she stick to Bombay, she could go to any other place, rent a house and learn. After a week, she figured that if she stayed cooped up in her room behind a closed door nothing would happen and that she should talk to some people who are music lovers. But whom to ask? She pondered. Another problem presented itself. Whichever guru she will go to, he would say forget the style you have learnt, it doesn't suit my gharana. They would bind me to their gharana. No matter what a bad man he was, there was no restrictive imposition in Guruji's approach. His method had incorporated the best from all styles. She remembered him again. He is like a bee. He is an independent spirit who collects honey from all flowers and creates his own composite honey. When this comparison suggested itself, her mind forgot his weakness.

The next morning she looked at the newspaper left in the balcony. When she glanced at the Daily Engagement Column, she saw the item that at 6 pm there was a concert by Pandit Mohanlal at the C J Hall. Immediately she was thrilled. Along with it there was contempt. She felt disregard, for when she didn't want to learn from him, why listen to his singing? Harmonium by Rajaram Tipnis and tabla by Omkar Prabhu. The same group. The accompanists when I sang at Sunny Vale, I had invited them to dinner. She remembered they were very nice people. By the time she finished her shower she decided, she must attend the concert. She felt, though she had rejected him why should she reject his music? Came out and looked at the newspaper again. There was a telephone booking number. She rang up. It had been sold out except the two tickets of the upper class at two hundred rupees. She asked, 'I am speaking from Dadar. It is difficult to come there to buy the ticket. Make a note of my name and telephone number. Reserve a seat for me. I will come half an hour early, pay the money and buy the ticket. Is it all right?' They agreed. Half a minute later the phone rang, 'Had you phoned to reserve a seat? Please give your name and address. I am ringing up just to confirm.' The same voice.

She had secured the centre seat in the second row. Close to the dais. He could see her. Even recognise. Somehow she felt embarrassed. She thought if she went up and asked someone in the middle or at the back if they would exchange and occupy the expensive two hundred rupee seat, they would gladly agree. She felt it was right and got up. But she told herself that after all, she had paid good money to listen to the concert and why should she hesitate. She sat down. After a little while she wondered if she should cover the top of her head in the traditional manner. She did so. It is nice in a way—an ancient custom. Five minutes later she told herself whether it was a traditional family custom or for her own will and wish. Why should she disguise herself—and adjusted the edge of her sari to cover her right shoulder, from across the left side, as before. A gentleman came to the row in front of her. About seventy. A thick crop of white hair. A handsome and intelligent face. As she was wondering where she had seen him, she remembered it was Gore Saheb. She felt like going up and talking to him. She thought he may not recognise her and her enthusiasm subsided. He sat on the fourth seat in front to the left. Many people approached him and made polite enquiries. A woman came to the front row. A light green silk sari, a pink bordered choli, kumkum on the forehead, red bangles for the wrists, a delicately built White woman. About twenty-seven or twenty-eight. She wondered if it was the same woman who accompanied him on the tambura and sang along, joined swaras only to Raga Bhoopali at Los Angeles. She had seen her from a distance, from the balcony seat. She couldn't make up her mind. She could be a tourist, or some consulate official or the wife of one. They brought the harmonium, tabla and two tamburas to the dais. Tipnis and Prabhu sat in their places. Girls of about twenty-five entered and held the tamburas. And then, he, Pandit Mohanlalji, entered. The audience gave him an ovation. She was thrilled. She also felt contempt. When the secretary was welcoming, the singer took a look at the front rows. He greeted Gore Saheb. He lifted his hands in recognition of the greeting and making a polite inquiry in the pose of blessing. And then the singer's eyes fell on the sari-clad White girl in recognition. Yes, Madhu felt certain it was the same girl. After that when he was observing the first few rows, yes, he recognised her and his puzzled face was in a state of confusion not even being able to look away, even without realising that the secretary's welcome speech was over. Without betraying any emotion, she just sat there like any other listener as if there was nothing private or personal between them. A minute later, coughing as if to adjust his throat, saying that he would sing Peeloo he entered the shadja. With his usual command and power of swara, an intoxicating soft strength began to permeate. She became aware of his strength and realised that he had captured the audience by beginning with peeloo which was considered a Kshudra-raga by other singers. Remembering the theory of this raga, she also remembered the mixture of the ragas Bhairavi, Bhimpalaasi and Gowri. The mind got caught up in the influence of komala-gandhaara, komala-dhaivata, and komala-nishada and the mind became supple and delicate. Suddenly, she remembered Vikram. She shouldn't have told him, she shouldn't have caused pain to him by informing him. In my concern to lighten my conscience by confessing my deceit, I subjected him to pain. What a devotion he has for music. I destroyed that too. She felt, now he will have no more love and respect left for music. This fellow wouldn't have taught without my giving myself to him. He also, in his innocent devotion, had been reiterating, go to Bombay and learn more. It was impossible for me to be able to live without learning more. She wondered what a magic snare this was. He was immersed in alaap. Rajaram Tipnis was a marvellous harmonium accompanist. What sophisticated nuances he is able to produce in a rather basic instrument with limited swaras like the harmonium! He doesn't simply follow, he moves alongside, there is absolutely no stress of strain on his face. He accompanies with such foreknowledge of the nuances of swaras what the singer may touch, smell and cause shadows to fall and emanate through his gestures. He does it with his inner consciousness. Is what is known as truth also a form of pride? The kind of truth of giving pain to a person like Vikram? This question propped up. She closed her eyes. She felt a slumber. Singing became inaudible. She shouldn't have said, 'I have come because I didn't want to deceive my husband. I am now totally yours. Take me.' The wedding commitment is just one aspect of it. She began to feel that she was a betrayer—having betrayed what is most intimate and what should be offered only in intimacy, surrendering it to this man's knowledge as an exchange. Not just giving myself to him in my own house, in my own conjugal bed, but I should have kicked him and moved away from him nine years ago when he said that he would teach everything only if she gave herself to him totally, without any reservation. What would have happened if I hadn't learnt music? What would have happened if, instead of learning from him, I had learnt it from someone else? These memories entangled themselves into questions. There was no other singer like him. I couldn't find one. By remembering that music is not a knowledge to be gained by only a master but it is a knowledge, the inner secret of which has to be entered and mastered only through the help of a singer who is a genius, her confusion became more complex.

The concert was going on. The mind was grasping the theoretical subtleties of what swaras were being touched, what were being slurred over and on which swara, he is resting, and how many prosodic units and what exactly was the pace of the movement. However, the mind was hitting the tanas and reaching the saam that if he wants, let him call himself and that she wouldn't even turn in that direction, and will not submit her body and mind. The body was sacred and its relationships and intimacies must also be sacred. If that is desecrated what sanctity would be there in learning? This refrain was rising. The intellect which was comprehending the music suddenly felt, 'Yes, I too can create this. There is nothing profound in this that surpasses me.' She just sat there like an examiner studying the calculations of tanas and time and the delineation of the various swaras and their manipulation of patterns, and comprehending the secret of the game of merging the taal with those patterns.

While listening to the second raga, Chaayaa-nata suddenly the light did flash, that after having learnt the technique for so long and developed it, couldn't I grow further without becoming the slave of a guru?

3

She slept well that night. The next morning it wasn't possible for her to locate 'Tipnis, Rajaram' in the telephone directory as there were three full pages under the name 'Tipnis'. There were more than twenty names under 'R' for Rajaram. She remembered that he was at Mahim. She noted down three names under 'R. Tipnis, Mahim' and his was the second try. It was his voice. 'Speaking,' he said. 'Kaka, my name is Madhumita Shah. I had accompanied Pandit Mohanlalji on tambura at the temple auditorium at Sunnyvale in America. You had given accompaniment on the harmonium. My husband Vikram Shah had brought you home. Do you remember?'

'How can I forget? Your co-singing was wonderful. Have you come home? You had mentioned that your home was at Dadar.'

'Thank you Kaka for remembering. I would like to come and meet you. Would you please give me the address and the landmarks?'

She knew Mahim quite well. Even when he was mentioning it she could visualise the street and the buildings. She reached the place in fifteen minutes. As soon as he opened the door, she touched his feet in a namaskar. Tipnis was pleased. He expressed his embarrassment, 'Why such great respect of touching feet for me?' He called his wife who was in the kitchen, introduced her, asked her to get some tea and led her to the music room. Though in Bombay, it was a silent room. The branch of the jackfruit tree which had grown tall enough to reach his window of the third storey just two feet away, was increasing the sense of silence. The floor had been covered by a carpet and a big reclining cushion had been placed against the wall. Five harmoniums in a row. Two tamburas reclined in the corner. By the time the polite enquiries were over, Tipnis's wife brought tea and biscuits and left. Sipping tea, she said, 'I will come straight to the point. I have decided to continue with music. Each time I come to Bombay I stay for four to five months. All the twenty-four hours of the day are dedicated for learning music except the time for food and sleep. You know what stage of learning I have. You must kindly agree to be my guru and teach me. In another three to four years, you must make me an artist who can sing with selfconfidence. I will pay whatever fee you fix in whatever currency you like. I will always sing in the future as the disciple of Guru Rajaram Tipnis.'

Tipnis's face expanded with joy. 'I am happy to hear your words sister. You have the potential to grow into a great artist. I have spent all my life as an accompanist, if it was teaching to play harmonium I would have accepted immediately. But how can I be a guru for singing? Though I have the theoretical knowledge as well as the technical expertise I cannot demonstrate by actually singing.'

'There is no need for you to sing. I will sing. You please explain the theoretical aspect. Utter the notes aloud, vocally. No, not even that is necessary. Demonstrate it by playing it on the harmonium. If you show me the path, if you correct my mistakes, it is enough. If a sitar player can train a player of flute, why can't a harmonium maestro train a singer?'

Tipnis couldn't think of any reason to refuse immediately. He sat silently for a couple of minutes. Then he said, 'Mohanlalji stayed in your house for three weeks and taught you two ragas. He is the one who has raised the edifice of your learning right from the beginning. If you continue with him, learning will be easy. You will become famous soon if you say you are his student.'

She was prepared for this question. 'Kaka, I have come to receive you as my guru. It won't be proper if I hide anything from you. Will you promise me that you will not speak about this with anybody?'

He thought for a moment. He could guess what it was. He knew Pandit Mohanlal for twenty-five years. He cogitated why he should promise and get to know it. He just sat silently. After waiting for a couple of minutes she said, 'I know that wherever he holds a concert, he invites only you to accompany him. If there is a misunderstanding, he might drop you and invite someone else. That's why you kept silent, isn't it?'

He didn't reply. If he turned away, it would be accepting defeat, he thought and was just looking at her face. 'Kaka, I will never tell anyone that I am learning from you till I give an independent concert. I will engage my own flat. You please come and teach me there. Or, I will come to your place. Please, you must listen to what I want to say. Even if he doesn't invite you, you are not in a position where no one else will. You are one of the famous harmonium maestros of India. Besides, I know that other great singers of India not only invite you but insist they want only you. I know that you will not reject when a helpless girl wants to confide her situation with you.'

He felt trapped. He decided to retain his dignity. He said, 'Tell me. I will keep the secret.'

'I was bent upon learning only from Mohanlalji. If I didn't surrender myself to him the way he wanted, he wouldn't teach me properly. After struggling for months, I agreed and gave myself to him. He taught me well. But gradually, I learnt that I was not the only such student. After learning for six years I felt like marrying. I got married. I got a noble husband. There is no opportunity there to learn music. You yourself said that he stayed at my home and taught me two ragas. Even though I begged him that I was a married woman, he mercilessly extracted his fee! I was tormented with the thought, isn't it possible for a woman to reach the top as an artist without surrendering her chastity?... When she said this, she couldn't help weeping which came surging up. Realising that she couldn't stop it, she cried her heart out. Then she wiped her tears and sat with her head bent. 'I know that many women get sympathy by crying. I have never done such a thing. Suddenly crying came surging out. Sorry. I had never mentioned this to anyone. How can I confide in my mother?'

Tipnis was just watching her face. He felt that if he looked away, it would tantamount to ignoring her. Ten minutes passed that way. They were just looking at each other's faces. A supplication in her face that she had no other support. A compassion in his face that if he looked away, she would collapse. Then he said, 'Take that tambura in the corner, the one with the black covering and tune up.' It is a female tambura, from Miraj.

She brought a cloth from the niche, wiped the tambura and asked, 'madhyama or panchama?' 'Anything other than Kalyan and Bihaag. Both of them have been practised for two weeks, isn't that so?'

She began to think. She couldn't decide. Suddenly, she remembered—Peeloo... He drew to himself the harmonium by his side and asked, 'What shruti shall I provide?'

'I will just start. Please show me if there is a mistake.'

He said, 'Sing. Slowly. Right from the alaap.'

She started singing, but she hadn't learnt this raga. It is a composite raga. There is a difference of opinion about the ascending and descending notes and the delineation of swara of this raga among scholars. She felt that she committed a mistake by choosing this because of the influence of having heard it the previous day. Having plunged into it, she couldn't go back and so began to expand it slowly in detail. He followed her. Didn't go forward and direct the path. However, since he was following, she believed that she wasn't making any mistake. She forgot that she was a student aspiring to be accepted and went on embellishing. When she stopped after about half an hour, he smiled. She didn't understand the meaning of that smile. Noticing the expression on her face, he asked, 'Did you come to CJ Hall yesterday?'

'Actually I haven't learnt this—the intricacies of this raga even at the elementary level. I sang from yesterday's memory. Now you please teach me,' she asked boldly.

Explaining the features of the raga he started playing. Now it was her turn to sing it. She sang, understanding the intricate nuances of the raga that cannot be played on the harmonium no matter how good he is. He broke it up into segments and took each one, mouthed it and demonstrated and made her sing. Though his verbal expression wasn't exact, she could understand his concept. She sang it correctly without much difficulty. He would teach, first in the swara, and then in aa-kaara. He made each bit and piece to be sung correctly thrice and after making sure that it had sunk in, then he would go on to the next movement. All along, he would remember and show the different styles, saying, 'This is Amir Khan's style—I had given accompaniment to him, this is Pandit Tiwari's style, this is Maniram's style etc.' He didn't even notice his wife Sonu Tai came to the door and had peeped in. When the lesson was over it was quarter past two. That day the lesson had gone on for three hours—just the extension and expansion of swara.

'Is it enough, practising the alaap this way? Don't think about the cheez. The ups and downs and the bends and sways, and variations of the cheez are at the finger tips for the harmonium player.' There was satisfaction on his face.

'Guruji, when shall we have the gandaa-puja?'

'You started calling me Kaka affectionately and now you are addressing me as Guruji. There is no need for gandaa-puja or any such formality. Press the tambura and the harmonium to your eyes. Please go in. There is an idol of Sarasvati in our puja-room. Prostrate and smear the kumkum. That is enough.'

She did what she was told. Sonu Tai invited her for lunch. The Guru insisted lovingly, 'Shouldn't go on an empty stomach on the first day.' While eating, he said, 'Don't tell anyone that you are learning from me for time being. What special use is there in mentioning it? When I go out of station for programmes there won't be any lessons. When I am in town, I will teach you three or four times a week. The sessions will be for two to three hours. Come tomorrow morning at nine.'

She prostrated to both of them, touching their feet and left. She herself hadn't imagined the Tipnis would accept so soon. Besides, when she remembered that on the first day itself he would teach her in such great detail, she felt her problem was solved and she was flying about in the sky of music.

४

As soon as she went home, her mother who seemed to be waiting for her asked, 'Beti, where did you go in the morning? You didn't come for lunch. Didn't even make a call. Do you know how worried I was!'

'Ma, I had gone in search of a guru. My good fortune. He accepted. On the first day itself he taught me for three hours. He made me have lunch at his home itself. He has asked me to go tomorrow morning at nine,' she said with enthusiasm.

Her mother followed her to her room, closed the door and sat on the chair. This was the time for the siesta of the sisters-in-law. Still when she noticed that her mother had come to her room and closed the door, she understood that she had come to discuss something in secret. She also guessed what it was about. She sat quietly so that her mother herself could start the conversation. In a couple of minutes she started, 'Isn't it two weeks since you came? There hasn't been even a single phone call from your husband. You have searched and found a guru. What's happening between husband and wife? You are hiding something. Daughters shouldn't have secrets from their mothers.'

'There is nothing to hide. There is no opportunity to learn music in that country. I come here and learn for three or four months. And then, I practise it there for three or four months. He has himself agreed and sent me. I have telephoned him twice. He is on a tour. I come here when he goes out on his tours. I go there when he is there. Please don't worry.'

Her mother said, 'I don't know. I don't understand, my dear.' She understood that her mother meant that she didn't believe her words. She fell silent, not to prolong the conversation. Then she went to the bathroom. When she returned her mother had left. It was clear that she was displeased. The musical notations taught by the guru were receding and confusion reigned supreme. I am trying to bring under control the memory of my husband which I should really be worrying about. But her mind was filled with the anxiety of the actual difficulty of answering her mother's questions. The sisters-in-law aren't saying anything openly. They aren't asking anything either. They are silent because of the fear of my mother. She became aware that otherwise, they would look daggers at her. Yes, I must have a small flat for myself. I must find out how much money I have in my account, I mustn't delay. Who can do all this? She cautioned herself that it was not proper to do anything without the knowledge of her brothers. While she sat thinking, it occurred to her. How about conferring everything to the younger of the two brothers? After telling him, it will be all right if I ask him to fix up a flat for me. After dinner, she signalled to her brother Ajay and took him to her room and said, 'I must talk to you privately. Not at home. Tell me when and where. I have music lessons till noon tomorrow.'

He thought for a minute and said, 'Ring me up at the shop at 2 pm. I will tell you where and when to meet.'

5

After occupying a corner table at the Island Restaurant of Hotel Ocean, Ajay placed orders for refreshments and sitting opposite his sister, he said, 'Now tell me.' She began, 'There is no one else in whom I can confide. Not only because they will condemn me but because they will be hurt. That is why I don't want to tell anyone.' It took an hour for her to relate all the important details, beginning with her giving herself to Mohanlal and the latest development. It was the policy of the restaurant that until they were summoned with a signal, the servers would not disturb the privacy of the customers. After she narrated everything, both of them remained silent for a couple of minutes. She asked him, 'Tell me honestly what do you think.'

After exhaling a deep sigh, the brother spoke in a quiet voice, half to himself, as it were. 'I had heard that Mohanlal was that kind of a man. But I was also confident that since my sister is a strong woman, what does it matter what kind of man he was. Just like all parents and brothers believe that no matter what other girls are like, our girl can't ever be like that. Especially after you left after marriage, there was no reason at all for any doubt or suspicion. Brother-in-law himself had sent the cassette of your singing in the temple at Sunnyvale. Listening to it we were all so proud. Because our girl had reached the heights of singing along with that famous maestro.'

He stopped there. After waiting for a minute she asked, 'Isn't there anything else you want to say? Speak plainly and honestly.'

'You see, it is true we are in Bombay. The new, modern world doesn't manifest itself and is experienced as much in any other city as it does in Bombay. Still, I feel that this sort of thing has happened for the first time in our family. I am not saying this in anger against you. I am saying this because ours is a family which has been maintaining its tradition.'

'Nobody in our family had graduated. Only elder brother, you and I did so. Nobody had been given in marriage to someone staying in America. Isn't that so?' He didn't reply. 'I didn't ask this to justify what I have done. Your sister became the victim of an evil deed. But she is also honest enough not to conceal it but to tell the husband and come out. Why aren't you sympathetic that she is also burning with a sense of guilt and contrition?' He looked at her face. Confronting his look, she continued, 'I won't take even a single pie from my husband. Actually, I must make good his loss. But that cannot be measured in terms of money. I have come away taking the decision of dedicating my life to music completely and become a singer of standing in four or five years. The rent from the house that father gave me is the only support I have. Without revealing this to anyone, have a talk with elder brother in a proper manner and make the arrangements. I want a small flat for rent. After four or five years, I can earn by giving concerts and look after myself.'

'I am looking after the affairs of your flat. We are receiving forty thousand rupees as rent every month. Besides, there is a deposit of twenty lakhs in your name at fifteen per cent interest. The auditor has checked it every year and the transaction is clean. Why do you need a separate flat? You have, anyway, your own room in our house.'

'When married girls visit the mother's place for a few days it is all right. But a married girl coming back permanently, let alone the sisters-in-law, how will mother feel? Can I tell them everything I have told you? Can I even tell elder brother? You are five years elder to me. I told you because we grew up together.'

After thinking for a while, he said, 'Yes, that's also true.' After a couple of minutes, as if to change the mood, he said, 'I brought you here so that we can sit here and talk. You do like, don't you, the kachori by the roadside near Tilak Bridge?'

She felt at ease, remembering those days when they would stealthily eat the cheap roadside edibles after playing together and quarrelling.

'I have another thought. This Bombay is filthy-aired, noisy, with debris thrown everywhere. How can music be practised in such an atmosphere? If there is a place for rent available out of town, say, at about ten or twenty miles distance, in quiet surroundings I will engage a cook and stay there, practise and give myself to music. There must be a vehicular convenience to the teacher's place. The worry and bother of maintaining a car and driving it is not good.'

ᥔ

On the days when Tipnis was in town he would teach regularly. Not waiting till she had a flat of her own, she would practise the morning lessons, till the evening in her room. She would also tape the lesson and get the assistance. Since the tambura and the harmonium that were bought before her marriage had been taken to America and left there, she had to buy new ones. Everyone at home agreed to her having a separate flat. The reason given was that staying in Bombay for three to four months at a time and the accompanist—tabla artist coming home for four or five hours was an inconvenience to everyone at home and the noise that had to be borne by the school-going children—and all that. This explanation was accepted by everyone—especially the sisters-in-law who welcomed it.

One day an idea flashed. Guru Tipnis certainly teaches in great detail. But how the details are brought out and presented by the singers can be understood more clearly by listening to the tapes. Not the bits and pieces of the ragas recorded for marketing purposes. But she must listen to the recordings of the concerts. When a particular raga is being learnt, the tapes of expert singers, many singers, must be carefully listened to and studied. And the lessons of Tipnis also must be mastered. And then, she must develop her own style. On consulting Tipnis, he also agreed, yes, each artist must develop his or her own style; they should not be a carbon-copy of their guru. It was his opinion that there was nothing wrong abut integrating several styles. He himself said, 'Do you know Gore Saheb? As far as I know, no one in Bombay has a collection of as many concert tapes as he has. I can introduce you to him. But if I do so, it will be known that we know each other and that you are learning from me. For the present, let it not be known. Try through someone else.'

She remembered that her own elder brother knew him. Ten years ago, after a benefit performance of this same Mohanlal, he had dropped her home in his car. After that she used to see him in all the music concerts. He might have forgotten now. Again, she sought the help of her brother. Two days later he gave her a chit of paper saying, 'I have talked to Mr. Gore. Meet him at his place at seven in the evening. He has given his address and phone number.'

She touched his feet. Though his hair was snow-white and shining, he had a thick crop. The face was as it was ten years ago. 'Please come. It seems you have come to Bombay for three months to practise music. Mohanlalji is your guru, isn't he? Before getting married, you were accompanying him in concerts, weren't you?' He welcomed her.

'He is very busy. I am not learning from him. I want to learn from someone who teaches the theory part also. I want to realise and inculcate it by practising myself what is taught. Besides, if I listen to the tapes of full concerts by great musicians I may learn the intricacies of ragas.'

'Will you please sing a raga? I will tell you after I listen. Please come here. I will give you a tambura.' He took her to his music room. It was about twenty feet long and fifteen feet wide. When the window was shut there was absolute silence. Air conditioner without the hum. Just two cane chairs. All along the floor a Kashmir carpet. He said, 'I don't sing. I don't even know how to sing. But for any visiting musicians, I have kept two female and two male tamburas. Please choose your tambura, tune it and sing any raga you like.'

She understood that it was only if she passed this test would he show the tapes. After tuning the female tambura, sitting on the carpet she queried, 'Kalyan?' Saying, *bahut accha* he sat against the opposite wall, adjusting a pillow. She sang the alaap at great length for three quarters of an hour and stopped, 'Since there is no tabla accompaniment, it can't be continued.'

'You will attain musical expertise. Voice and concept are very good. But still you are a copy of your guru. When will you become independent? A person who can't separate from the guru and achieve one's own identity before thirty, can never be a great musician. How old are you? You look thirty.

'Yes, that is why I want to listen to the styles of various maestros, understand their best aspects and steer my own path. I have come to solicit your help, blessing and guidance.'

He invited her, 'Come here, I will show you.' She got up and went near him. He drew apart the light green curtain from the roof to the floor. She thought it was the wall. Actually, eight-feet high cupboards were there from one and to the other with glass doors. They had six-inch partitions with music tapes arranged. As soon as she saw it, she wondered how many tapes did he have in his collection. It was surprisingly breath-taking. Saying, 'come here', he drew the curtain of the opposite wall. Even there, the same sort of thing, about the same number, full of compartments. 'There are tapes of classical music which can be heard for ten thousand hours. I have secured the tapes of all the great maestros who have given concerts in Bombay for the last forty years. Not just here. I have contacts with Delhi and Calcutta music associations also. I bring tapes from there whenever I go there. Please come and see', he said, drawing the curtain of another wall. There was an index box, the kind you find in big libraries. Drawing each compartment, he said, 'I have prepared an index of the names of artists, male and female. Another index of ragas. The Kalyan which you sang. Look up the cards under. K.A.L.Y.A.N. There is a record of which artist sang it, where and when—all numbered—you will find at least fifty Kalyans. There are also cards showing various versions of it. It also mentions for how many minutes it plays. Saying, 'Come here,' he drew the curtain of the other wall. Half the length of the wall had discs in vogue before the cassettes. 'I have brought the machine which converts these LPs into cassettes. I am searching for a technician who can inscribe the cassettes with the artist, the raga and the accompanist. I still haven't found one.'

'May I pick a raga and record its rendering by four or five great singers? After two or three weeks, another raga the same way—four or five tapes. I am afraid even to ask you.'

'There is the question of copyright in this. These should not fall into the hands of stealers as great injustice will be done to the artists if these are made into cassettes and sold. I don't give it to anyone. But since you are a student and an achiever, I will allow you. Besides, you are Mehta's sister. I will introduce you to my wife. You may come and record even when I am not here. You must leave a chit when you came and what you recorded. My original tape should not leave this room. After you record, they must be replaced exactly in the same spot. Do you know the library discipline?'

'Sir, please trust me. I will never give it to anyone else. Not even a single tape of yours will leave this room. I swear on the tambura. I will come tomorrow and record Peeloo.'

'Peeloo? I have thirty-four of them. You bring a fresh tape. That's enough. You copy only in my high-speed machine. My tape shouldn't be put into a cheap machine.'

'Done. You are my patron.' When she said that, she was full of gratitude.

7

A fortnight had passed. One evening, after dinner, her brother came to her room and spoke in a soft voice. 'There is a good offer. The kind of place which you desired. Our elder brother has said that if you and I like the place, we can buy it. Have you seen Panvel?'

'When I was in high school, they had taken us there on a picnic there. A hilly region.'

'There is a farm there for sale. Four acres. A mango grove that yields income. At the centre an old-fashioned house. It has a borewell, electricity and good plumbing. A very reliable couple stays there and looks after it and maintains two yielding cows. The people selling the farm are our clients. They also have business in Bombay. Their business has flourished because of our help and co-operation. Tomorrow morning I will take you there. The owner of the property will accompany. If you agree we will buy it.'

'How much will it cost?' She asked anxiously.

'Don't think about it now. We will talk later. Come with me tomorrow morning.'

At nine in the morning, the owner of the farm, Satish Chandra came home. The elder brother seated him in the drawing room and talked to him. Then Satish Chandra took both of them in his car. The junior brother sat in the front and she sat at the back. Satish Chandra was explaining, 'By road, it is an hour and a half from Dadar. There are also State Transport Buses. One every fifteen minutes, the farm is three kilometres from the Panvel Bus Stand. One can walk if one wants to. Otherwise, autorickshaws are available. There are cycle-rickshaws. If you go to Kurla from Dadar, there is the harbour-line train. Once every thirty minutes. There is an auto service from the station also. Cycle-rickshaws are available too. With all these conveniences, though it is so close, you are totally away from the atmosphere of Bombay. Just like going to Mahabaleshwar. But it is not a tourist place. As you are going to see for yourself, though it is so close, it is not polluted by Bombay.'

She entered into a dream world just by listening to his description. As they were proceeding, Satish Chandra was talking about the places they were passing through—this is Vashi, this is Sanpad, Juyinagar, Belapur and now we are reaching Panvel. There, to the left is the State Transport Bus Stand. Here we turn left. The place was full of small gardens, cultivated green fields. After one and a half kilometres, turning right into a small road there was a small mound full of verdant trees. Just at the foot of it, to the right there was the gate with the name 'Aambagh' written in Devanagari letters. He stopped the car, got down, opened the gate and drove in. A place she couldn't even imagine in her dreams. A farm and a great number of mango trees. About thirty-feet tall teakwood trees stood around the fence at an interval of fifteen to twenty feet from each other. At the centrem there was a fairly large house of the Konkan style with a mortar floor. The loft also had a gravel floor. About a fifteen foot high wooden ceiling and on top of it a Mangalore-tiled roof, preventing the heat of the sun in summer. A large lounge downstairs with two rooms, kitchen, bath, toilet and a sun-shade. Upstairs, a lounge, two rooms, toilet and sun-shade to sit out. Running water for all bathrooms and regular electricity supply. Satish Chandra explained, 'We have never found the necessity for air-conditioning here, in the hottest summer. Even on summer nights, we have slept here switching off the fans.'

Madhu thought of the upstairs lounge as her place for practising music. While coming on to the sun-shade sit-out area, she thought it was a great natural beauty spot, greater than that of Los Gatos. Not just the green-covered mound to the right. But right in front, about a kilometre away, a line of rolling hills, clear blue sky. Silent atmosphere. Pure air. Satish Chandra continued, 'One can stay alone here. No thefts and robberies. Besides there is the servant. He and his wife belong to the golden era of Satya-yuga. Come, you can see for yourself.' He led them to the back of the place. In a house which had been built specially for the servants there was a man, about fifty and his wife, about forty-five. The moment she saw them, she felt they were trustworthy. Right in their presence, Satish Chandra said, 'Vaghe is this man's name. He has been maintaining two cows. They graze in the farmland. The cost of their maintenance and the income from them is totally his. He looks after the cultivation and maintenance of the entire place. Cultivation means only the mango grove. He has to dig at the base and manure the trees once a year. He has to water the plants from the pump every fortnight, i.e., except during the four-month rainy season. All this is his responsibility. He gets a pay of one and a half thousand rupees per month. The household chores, she will attend to. She does all her work efficiently. Her name is Malakshmi, you can fix up her salary. At the flowering season of the mango, the contractors from Bombay will come and buy the entire yield in advance. I will teach you that business. Until you get the experience, I will come for the next four or five years and look after it. All the trees are of the Alphonso variety of export quality.'

Saying that they would go round the place, the brother took his sister along, inside the garden after going round the interior, he said,

'Your face itself is indicating your approval. Let us buy it. For others, it costs thirty lakhs. Satish Chandra will sell it to us for twenty-five lakhs. He has benefited from our business. He is still benefiting and will, in the future too. If we bargain, it may even be reduced to twenty lakhs. Or, it may be a lakh more. Don't discuss money with anyone. When once the daughter of the house leaves after marriage, the sister-in-law will object even parting with a ladle or a spoon. After your marriage, nothing has been given to the son-in-law like furniture, utensils, fridge, car or anything of that sort. What can we give for a person who has gone to America? Since childhood, you have never been interested in gold and silver. Besides, in the future my elder brother and I want to split up the business into two. All this is strictly between the two of us. An arrangement only for tax-purposes. Not something which should be mentioned to the sisters-in-law. Our present business was started by father. According to law, you also have a share. But you never came to the shop. Never worked there. Still, it is the wish of our elder brother that we should obtain a letter of release from you saying that you have received your share. We will pay whatever the expenses incurred in the buying of the farm. The sale will be in your name. At home, you say that you have brought this money from America. What do you say?'

She felt grateful. Didn't think of anything to say. Her eyes were filled with tears. She wiped them with the edge of her sari and said, 'I hadn't expected this. I will give a declaration as you have said. Please don't feel you are giving me partition. I will accept if you give with the feeling that you are giving this as a gift—a blessing from the mother's place.'

Chapter 13

I

One morning at seven, the door bell rang. He was upset, wondering who it was troubling him at this unearthly hour. Recently when he was practising he couldn't concentrate. The voice would set itself because of long-standing habit. The ragas and the nuances of the swaras would appear because of memory. But the subtle and pinpointed target or the thrill of quest that is achieved in the advancement at the end of each movement, which could be had by deep concentration was not taking place. Though he had thought about it for many days, no explanation had been found. One day, suddenly, a memory flashed. This defect was perceived for the first time when he sang at the C J Hall. He could not fathom the reason. Another day, like a corollary to it, a thought occurred. Kalyani, no, Madhu was sitting in the second row in front of the stage and was staring at me. It wasn't clear whether it was anger or shame or relapse of desire—whatever it be, some unexpected emotion was affecting the mind and had ruined the absorption of the flow of music. Yes, it was since that day. I had gone to Jaipur, Bangalore and Kolhapur. But nowhere could I get the concentration. The audience applauded, all right. But on sitting down for practice at home in the morning, the same problem. Had she performed black magic on me? You can't say anything about these business people. I must find a good astrologer. But how to find a genuine astrologer who can predict the future? He saw that all of them were expert publicity-mongers. After a few days he consoled himself that she was not that kind of a girl; she would be aware that if the guru is harmed, all that she had learnt would become infructive. But still, why is this happening? It was a mistake hitting her and throwing her out. She is the only one who is truly inspired. Which other pupil do I have, who can understand the delicate intricacies of music as she does? Bhoopali doesn't have the innate knowledge of Indian music. He came to the conclusion that the reason for this obstacle was his lack of inspiration. Though an instant solution appeared that if he called Madhu and consoled her, she might be pleased, yet, an inner voice told him that she would never come back. Will she ever inspire him again, offering herself to him, she whose head was full of betraying and cheating her husband, prostitution and the vision of truth that is available through mandra-shadja? These reasons appeared later. He had engaged in practice after a week, telling himself that concentration would certainly be achieved if he strengthened his willpower and persisted. After all, music means yoga and yoga is submitting the mind to willpower and mastering it: what willpower is there, that is not possible for this Mohanlal to achieve? It was four days since he had begun. He had been at it for an hour this morning. Still, he hadn't achieved concentration. Meanwhile this doorbell. He hadn't bolted the door. He shouted 'come in'. The fingers were playing on the strings of the tambura. Even after a minute, the door hadn't been pushed open. Again, the bell. Tut, tut! I must change this harsh-sounding thing. The sound inside cannot be heard outside. The outside noise cannot penetrate inside. Thinking how nice it would be if he had a machine, by his side by pressing which the door would open automatically as they have in America and France, he put aside the tambura on the carpet, went and opened the door. There a girl was standing, no, a woman about twenty-five or thirty. She was wearing a salwar kameez, long bob-cut. A handbag, the sort that is carried by office-going women. A feeling that I have seen her somewhere! No, not really. He demanded unpleasantly, 'What do you want?' She bent down and touched his feet. Since all people touch his feet this way, he didn't think it was any special kind of greeting.

'Can you recognise me?' She asked.

He looked hard at her face. As if he had seen it somewhere. How many places do I go to, thousands of people come to every concert, at least hundreds come to greet me and touch my feet. He said, 'No, I don't remember. It is better if you identify yourself.'

'May I come in?' she said.

He understood that she asked because he was standing at the door. 'I was practising music. It may take an hour or more.'

'If you have no objection I will come in and listen to. Otherwise, I will be standing here, outside. I also have to reach my office at nine.'

'What do you want to talk about? Do you want to learn music? Come in', he said. This girl looked attractive. A trim physique that had not given birth to children. The mind became lewd. But can this girl inspire me the way Madhu could? He was curious. She came in and sat in front of the reclining tambura. 'What have you learnt so far? I don't teach beginners. There are other teachers in my school. I teach seniors, and only after examining them. I don't have time even to teach the present students', saying so, he sat at the place he was practising. There was a distance of only four feet between them. In the middle was the tambura. Since she had come from outside, her face and neck were moist. She was looking fixedly at him. He couldn't understand that look. If she has to come so boldly, sit so close and stare like this, she must have played enough. How can such a girl provide inspiration? He decided not to have anything to do with such a courageous girl and said, 'Tell me. I must continue with my practice. If a stranger is sitting in front, it is not possible. You have come without calling earlier and fixing up an appointment, at seven in the morning. Tell me quickly.'

'Didn't you recognise me?' She asked again.

'How many times do you ask the same question?' He got angry. He raised his voice. A million people come and introduce themselves. How can I remember?'

Her staring eyes became wet like ghee that melts with heat. 'My name is Bakula. Bakula Lal.' When she said this, her voice was infirm.

His eyes lost their direction. Without his knowledge his sight lowered like a weak voice missing the shruti and falling off while singing. It was as if consciousness had suddenly taken a downward plunge and descended to its half level. In spite of the effort he couldn't raise his eyes. The pressure of the silent droning inside the ears. Though she asked again and again, 'Can't you recognise me?' memory failed and imagination ran riot...shame occupied his inner being. As soon as she came, only if she had identified herself, there would be no room for wild speculation. She has come with the intention of testing him. This thought began to console him. He also thought he knew why she had come now. How many days is it since her mother refused one lakh? This girl might have come to claim it. What was intended for her must be given to her. There was no cash at home. It will be fine if I give a cheque. Or, I may go to the bank, get the cash…while he was thinking, she spoke.

'Is it difficult to recognise me? It seems you saw me till I was six, when you used to come once a month to give some money to mother. You would, it seems call me who was playing downstairs and give me chocolates. It seems when I was little, if I was crying, I would stop and become silent if you started singing, playing on the tambura. That is what mother used to say when I was a little girl. Of late, she never speaks about it. When I started going to school, when I asked about my father, she might have invented this lie. It was she who said that you were my father. Even now, she doesn't deny it. She just doesn't speak about you, that's all. The reason for my coming here is to ask you and ascertain a certain truth. I will tell you the background. According to the date of birth recorded in my school certificate, I am now thirty. Since going to college, I have loved music, to listen to and to learn. But mother was afraid of it. It was her feeling that people get spoilt by getting involved in it. After I finished college, got a job and started earning, I started learning music. Stubbornly, I even started going to concerts. I had a colleague. His name was Avinash. He didn't have training in classical music. But he would sing semi-classical music with feeling. I took him to classical music concerts and created a taste for it. One day, he went to your concert and became your admirer. When we met in the office next day, he was not just praising your music but adoring it. My eyes were full of tears. I told him that I was your daughter. He also agreed saying that there was facial resemblance. Maybe because of his love for your music, he developed love for me and it reached the level of marriage. It came to the stage of his parents coming to our house and fixing up an engagement. I used to tell him a lie that my father is staying with us and looking after us with love. I was ashamed and afraid to tell him that we had no contact with you. His parents said that the father should arrange for the engagement. What's wrong with that? I called Tipnis Kaka and asked him to tell you. I was afraid of meeting you directly. Doesn't one feel afraid to meet a father whose face one doesn't remember and one who has abandoned us completely, though living in the same city? But you just sent one lakh. You said you wouldn't be present at the engagement ceremony. In whom should I confide? Who is dearer than Avinash, the man who was prepared to marry me? Then I told him everything. "It's true that he is my father. But we have no contact with him. He married again and left us. I am the one who will be marrying you. Please believe me. I will be a good wife. Don't insist on his coming to the engagement and giving away the bride in marriage. "I begged him. He found out the house of your second wife at Kurla. He got hold of the address from your latest cassettes which have been released as Mohan Melodies, interviewed your second wife, Champa Mohan by pretending to be a journalist from Delhi. He had asked her, "It is said, you are the second wife of your husband, and his first wife, a daughter and a son are living in Borivali. What do you say?" She had answered, "It is possible that before marriage he might have paid some money to some woman to satisfy his sexual need. I have heard that charwomen, servants and cooks earn money this way clandestinely. Even some respectable gentlemen keep such women. Sometimes, it is possible that such women get pregnant, give birth to children and mention the name of some famous person." This is what she said. So Avinash suspected the legitimacy of my birth. Anyway, the parents were not fully in consent. He ditched me. "Why did you say that someone whom you don't remember seeing was your father?" When I said that I had love for my father though he deserted us, he simply said, "Every word that Champa Bai said rings true. If the talk continues, indecent questions have to be asked. We are colleagues. We shouldn't quarrel. Let's forget the question of marriage." He might have felt that seeing each other everyday would be embarrassing. A new Sales Division of our company had been started in Bangalore. He told the Managing Director and got a transfer and left.'

Not even noticing whether he was listening or not, whether he was showing any reaction, she finished her narrative. And then she lifted her head and looked at him. He also had not faced her. He was looking at the strings of the tambura. A minute later she spoke, 'Now

I am going to ask you some questions. Please give me an honest answer without any reservation. I am educated and have a job. My brother is also employed. Our mother brought us up by working as a cook in a lawyer's house. She is still working. She says no matter how old she gets, she won't beg for food from anybody. She says she won't ask even her children. You must speak the truth without any fear of shouldering the responsibility. Has my mother begotten us to someone else and afterwards mentioned your name? Or, did you get my mother pregnant by paying her money to satisfy your sexual appetite? My mother swears on god that you married her in the Bhavani temple. The priest who married you is not alive now. Therefore a witness is not available. It seems there was someone in our locality and they sent for mother who was brought here and got you married. This is also mother's statement. But twenty years ago they sold their house and left. Since it has not been possible to verify the relationship between you and us in any other way, I have come directly to you to ask you. Even if you speak the truth there is no responsibility attached to you. You sent one lakh with Tipnis. Why did you send it? Even if you offer it to me again, I won't touch it. All I want is the truth about my birth.'

Even when she stopped speaking he was still looking at the strings of the tambura. After waiting for a minute she said, 'I am finished with my question. Answer me.'

Suddenly he summoned up courage and blurted out what came to him, 'I don't want to talk about that old story.'

'I have also not come to listen to a story. The answer I want from you is just for this question, "Did you marry my mother and sire us? Or did my mother receive money from you and in copulating with her, were we born accidentally? Or is our mother mentioning your name just like that, without any relationship? If you answer in the affirmative for any one of these three questions, it won't be a story. If you say that you have never seen Borivali, even that will answer my question.' Saying so she started looking steadily at his face. Now it became difficult for him to escape from her quizzical gaze. Looking away would be tantamount to accepting defeat, he also looked keenly at her. He felt that her forehead, nose and eyes resembled his own.

For a moment he wondered if they resembled her mother's. But he couldn't recollect the features of her mother. He started searching his memory. But he didn't reveal in his demeanour the thoughts that assailed him. After the battle of looks that went on for some time, she said, 'It may be difficult for you to remember the details to answer me immediately. Take your time and tell me.' She took out a card from her handbag, put it in front of him and said, 'This has my office address and phone number. Also the home address.' She picked up her handbag and left.

After she left, his fingers moved automatically on the strings of the tambura. It was that time of the morning when maestros practise the command over their voice. His mind had been perturbed that a lot of people didn't have the sense not to disturb at this time. His saying that he didn't want to talk about ancient history hadn't come out because of anger. It is an actuality. He justified himself by telling that a man should look forward and not at the past. After all, what would be gained from remembering the past? Recollecting her retort, 'I have also not come to listen to your past escapades but just to know whether you married my mother properly and engendered us, or whether you just paid money to my mother and...', he came to the conclusion that she had come only to condemn him. Insolent one. As a result of this anger the buzzing of the tambura came to a halt. Her mother who had the right to question this had not come. This chit of a girl, who was six year old then, comes here... He was filled with anger. The strings of the tambura were reverberating. No one has the right or authority on me. I am an artist. The right belongs only to tambura only to shruti, only to the purity of swara. At no time or not even one day has the tambura asked me or accused me that you have made a mistake or have uttered a discordant note. Defending himself like this, he struggled to involve his mind on shruti, and found it. Practice, the practice of fifty years. It was the strength of a sage, that could absorb in meditation, in any kind of disturbance, and this comparison gave him a little solace. Which singer of sixty years age gives himself to music like me, the moment he gets up every morning?

Which young man of thirty can hold the breath and perform in all the three saptakas and exults making aavartanas upon aavartanas without deviating in even a pinpoint of the swara, while extending the tana? He told himself that even after forty more years this Mohanlal no, this Mohansen is going to exult as the crowned monarch of the swara. He started with shadja. Even before he consciously decided on the raga, he became aware that it had taken the form of komala-rishabha asavari. Recollecting its ascending and descending and subtle movements he enjoyed himself. He paused at leisure at each step of the mandra, concentrated his mind without any distraction and invoking the emotion he started to descend. While descending from *ma ga* to komala-rishabha he suddenly became perturbed. He remembered that, when Madhu had reached the mandra-shadja of this raga, the rights and wrongs of her had been visualised by her. It is true that mandra-shadja is the locus of meditation. The sangeeta-shaastra also says the same thing. It is the point of origin of the raga. If that is lucidly attained, from that vantage point any saptaka of any raga or swara appears clearly. Instead of that if mandra-shadja is mistaken for the witness stand of life's rights and wrongs, the head will reel and music will dry up. That is what happened to her. She lost the way of music. She is affected by the madness of becoming a saint. Let her go to the Himalayas and become a disciple of the yogis. There is no relation between her and me. The thoughts arose that she had fallen a prey to ethical arrogance as a result of abandoning music. His concentration of the swara was perturbed. But he remembered his sadhana of fifty years. The throat easily reached the shadja from the rishabha, the mandra-shadja of asavari. It has reached that point effortlessly and rested on it. From that eminence, it is looking at all the swaras of all the three saptakas clearly. There is no duality of any kind. Art must be looked at as art. He felt that if it is perceived as an instigation to the dualities within oneself, it results in the kind of madness that she has contracted. Now he converted that shadja into a spring of art experience and spent a lot of time enjoying it. Then even after giving rest to his breath, he immersed himself in the play of swaras focussed and played with them. He was satisfied. After reaching the shadja of madhya-saptaka by gradual ascension, he suddenly got angry. Why did she have to examine me by asking, 'Can you recognise me? Couldn't you recognise me?' Why didn't she straight away say, 'My name is Bakula, Bakula Lal.' If she had told, when he thought about it, he felt strangely embarrassed. Had I known she was my daughter, if she had said so straight away, my mind wouldn't have wandered the way it did. Did she lead me up the garden path, teasing me by asking can you recognise me, can't you recognise me? The sharp girls of these days, she came only to criticise me. She must have known that I play around with girls of her age. Had she come with the plan to examine what kind of man I was by watching, by seeing what feeling my face would indicate if she came and sat in front of me without revealing her identity? The voice which was singing stopped. The fingers were moving on the strings of the tambura. He got angry, 'Who is she to interrogate me? Her words which had been carefully prepared to prosecute me like a lawyer! Her questions! Did you sire us rightly by marrying our mother by tying the mangalasutra round her neck? Or, were we born accidentally when you paid money to my mother and copulated with her to satisfy your physical need? Or is my mother simply mentioning your name without any relationship? Even if you say that you have never seen Borivali, I will get my answer. These three questions and the fourth suggestion started strumming like the four strings of the tambura and the mind got entangled and went round and round. Without his knowledge the fingers had stopped playing on the strings. For quite some time the mind was circling the three questions and a suggestion.

A knock on the door was heard. The inner voice said it was Bhoopali. She doesn't ring the door bell. She says it is a sound detrimental to that of music. Even while tapping on the door she moves her fingers like the rhythmical sound on the tabla. She can't hear his saying 'come in' but then she opens the door slowly, silently it opens.

Saying, 'Are you still engaged in sadhana?' she came and sat in front. He didn't speak. She herself took up the female tambura and tuned it. 'Keep practising. I will go, have a shower and breakfast.' He got up and went in. While taking the bath, though her singing was audible, he wasn't aware of it. When he asked, 'Will you have some cornflakes?' She replied, 'No, I have had my breakfast. If I eat more, I won't be able to sing.' He was not in a mood to teach. But he came and sat in front of her because unless he forcibly engaged himself in teaching though reluctantly, there was no way in which he could free himself from the nagging questions of Bakula. Besides, she is an American. He was aware that there was no excuse for not teaching during that time. After practising for two hours, she asked, 'Guruji, you are absentminded for some reason.'

He evaded the question, 'The mind is like that. It won't always be alert.'

'Come close, let us make it alert together.' She put down the tambura came close, embraced and kissed him. It was a week since he had taken her to bed. She was also in need of it. She looked at him gladly and said, 'Let's go to the bedroom.' After realising that this was a welcome opportunity which had presented itself to lighten his mind, he got up. She bolted the door and came. In bed, his mind again became preoccupied. Bhoopali is of the same age as Bakula; may be a year younger, his mind calculated. Realising his mental state, she took the lead in everything, actively engaged herself in love play and encouraged and provoked him. In spite of it, his mind was still preoccupied. She, being aware that such a state was not unnatural, said intimately, 'Guruji, something is bothering you. If you can tell me, please do.' He thought of mentioning Bakula's visit in the morning and confiding. But she is a student. He became aware that he might become light in her esteem. He certainly couldn't tell her the lustful thoughts that arose in him when he saw Bakula. He couldn't tell anyone. He also saw the possibility of this American girl not seeing anything wrong in entertaining erotic feelings towards a daughter, not knowing her as such, having grown up in a free society where anyone past sixteen can have an affair with any one, irrespective of age difference by mutual consent. However, she might get angry getting to know about an intended alternative affair with another girl her age when he was having an affair with her. He was cautious that no matter what country or society, there is a possessive instinct in such relationships. To lie naked in bed with her was a torture. He said, 'Sorry, I am not all right today.' She accepted it saying, 'OK'. After both came out of the room she said, 'Bye, take care', went out and shut the door. He went back to the bedroom, drew open the curtain and stood looking at the brown sea. Even after a long time the anger against Bakula didn't subside.

He could not sleep well that night. Anger. In addition to that, a feeling of having lost everything and a sense of void and emptiness of having nothing left. A feeling of the whole sea turning incarnadine and the red waves mounting with force. Hitting. He kept rolling over in bed, and sleep evaded him.

Two days passed like this. On the third day he began to remember her words clearly. It seemed she was also very fond of classical music, and a votary of my music. It seems that boy, what's his name...Avinash knew that because of her love of my music, he believed that she was my daughter. He got close to her. It was a matter of pride. Had I gone to the engagement and had given her away in marriage, the wedding would have taken place. Why didn't I go? Was I ashamed to show my face? Or was I afraid of facing Ramkumari? She had refused the one lakh I had sent. Perhaps she might not have rejected it had I personally given it. He began to feel guilty. Suddenly he felt that in this whole affair, it was Ramkumari who had suffered the greatest injustice. After departing from Manohari and returning from Delhi, there was no question of rejoining Champa. But why didn't I go to Ramkumari? Was it the fear that Champa who had the backing of legal registration of marriage might create trouble? But if I had made up my mind, there was a way of keeping Ramkumari and the children with me in spite of the fear of Champa. I could have even lived separately, looked after the family and even visited them now and then. It was possible to make her agree, telling her that she could stay in the house and he would live in the flat in order to teach the students. But the mind never moved in that direction. Manohari who not only was very inspiring but gave a maddening sexual bliss abandoned me. She trampled on my music. Leaving her itself was a new birth. He came to a decision that he shouldn't get caught in any woman's stranglehold. But at the same time it was his true experience that there is no inspiration without a woman. But why should he get arrested in the grip of any single woman? Getting caught in the stranglehold of a woman is like the drying up of the spring of inspiration and living in a desert. Marriage is such a permanent stranglehold which makes life a desert. It became clear that it won't do to get caught in it even to an infinitesimal extent. Even with her old husband there, with what mad ecstasy did Manohari make love to me! What great intoxication did she create, a fountainhead of erotic ecstasy! But gradually she lost the intensity and got enamoured of Karthik. Or to put it in another way, it was because she got hold of Karthik that her feeling for me diminished. Then I got angry with her. But it became my path, my way. How many ragas does a musician sing! Just as a raga, hiding somewhere, presents itself when it is invoked suddenly, with all its myriad forms of beauty and its bends and sways, so does a girl provide her own individualistic, unique inspiration. While singing that particular raga there shouldn't be the awareness of any other raga. And then, when some other raga is being sung, the memory of this raga shouldn't be there. It became clear that no raga should have a permanent hold on the singer and he should enjoy total freedom. By that time, four years had passed. Ramkumari was working as a cook in Gore Saheb's house and was maintaining the family. She had established herself in her own home. When he remembered that he had stayed away with that view, he also remembered that she was a woman who could never identify what raga it was even if the same raga had been sung in her presence for two years continuously. Of course, she was a good cook. Had I gone back to her, what inspiration would I have got? That too, after enjoying the connubial bliss with an artist and such an ecstatic intoxicating experience with Manohari? Where was the attraction to reunite with Ramkumari when girls with love of music and knowledge of music were available galore who would give themselves to me without reservation just to be able to learn music from me? The attraction for Champa who understood music was dead with the realisation that she not only had the mean mentality of keeping me and my earnings completely under her control but the capacity to inspire me musically was dead—no, not just dead but it was never there. Until then I had never met, touched and enjoyed a city girl. I had never met any woman with knowledge of music until then. Both Chunni and Ramkumari were alien to music, uneducated villagers. It was also clear that though Champa knew music she was totally business like and much interested only in the commercialisation aspect. With the decision that I didn't want either of them and I wanted independence, I remained aloof. But she had the right of governmental registration. He remembered that he was throwing a fixed amount of money to her monthly. He felt something was piercing the eye. He opened his eyes and looked. Sunshine was emanating from the window. He sat up with alacrity.

3

In a week's time his mind started mellowing. I will myself arrange the engagement. I will give away the bride. I am an artist. A musician. My lifestyle is different. They are my children. Their mother is a virtuous woman. Before I married the woman from Kurla, I was married to this woman. I will convince them. He felt like telling his daughter to make a call to that boy and get him over. Give me the address of his parents. That boy had gone to Kurla and asked that wicked woman. He believed her and left this girl. Why didn't he come straight to me and ask? He thought, what sort of husband will a man make if he listens to one-sided account and doesn't have the patience to check a lopsided story. He wanted to call Bakula's office and tell her this. When he searched for the card she had given his mind became hesitant. She spoke like a cross-examining lawyer. He doubted that if he had softened and made a conciliatory offer now she might react sharply. He was afraid, and thought, she may say even if you come now he won't agree, what is the use of your coming now when the marriage proposal has broken down? Though he found the card, he simply put it away. No need to talk to anyone. No contact necessary. He tried to forget the entire relationship by telling himself, 'I am not responsible for the lives of all the people in the world.' He experienced a bit of relief.

But boredom made its appearance. A feeling of uselessness. An experience of arid feeling while holding the tambura. A perception of dry sterility like the sight of the midday hot sand as when a flight flies over desert landscape. Interest was lost even in food. Didn't feel like asking any student to stay on after the lesson was over. Even Bhoopali, the source of inspiration, as if understanding his inner arid weather was leaving mechanically without giving any encouraging signs of intimacy. Though there was a feeling that it was good riddance in a corner of the mind, the feeling that his entire mind had become a desert made matters worse. Meanwhile, there was a concert in Varanasi. The secretary had intimated earlier that there was no need for him to bring the accompanists as there were efficient accompanists who were able to provide him the company. When he went there he found that it was Ramratan Yadav on the harmonium and tabla by Kishan Maharaj himself, a pair whom any accomplished musician had to respect and, anyone if he is not an expert to be afraid of. A hand that can mould a frame to any rhythmic movement, and if an opportunity was given, could challenge by striking new rhythms and beats, and create the mood of raga in the tabla and create inspiration. He was afraid. He doubted if he could stimulate their art in his lacklustre state and get himself inspired and sing. When he started the alaap he experienced that his fear was very real. The audience of Varanasi were highly accomplished. They can penetrate and analyse any sophisticated hidden chinks of aesthetic nuances. Most of them had either by singing or playing instruments gained experience of theoretical knowledge of music. They had insightful knowledge to recognise the feature and intricacies of a raga without touching its pulse. He knew that his delineation of the alaap was according to prescribed rules. But there was no swelling up of aesthetic emotions though there were no discordant notes or wrong moves. He was aware that he was struggling alone. The audience was showing their appreciation out of politeness and the ethics of assembly, in order not to discourage the artist. An old man in the front row was vocally expressing his appreciation. But Mohanlal became aware that he was not the kind of a rider who moves on these kinds of compensatory favours and he must summon his original strength and sing as an artist. Suddenly a plan flashed forth. He brought his face close to the microphone and said, 'You must kindly excuse my mistake in starting the alaap when Kishan Maharaj himself is present here. So I now begin again the alaap of the same raga in vilambit ek-taal' and looked at him. There was a mischievous smile on the face of the Maharaj. He, who was sitting in a reclining half padmaasana sat up in his usual vajraasana. He started the alaap and showed him the saam. Timing went into Kishan Maharaj's hands. Without any effort, he took it into his control. Mohanlal got the accompaniment he desired. He got the inspiration. Even in this wholehearted co-operation a spirit of sportive competition was created. The dryness disappeared and emotion flowed forth. The same raga. The same ascending and descending movements, the same vadi and samvadi. A lively, bright atmosphere shone forth just like the sunlight is reflected from the leaves on the day after rains. He understood that what was now being expressed as admiration from the audience was not polite condescension but an appreciation overflowing the spontaneous powerful emotion, which had been demanded and accorded by his authority. The concert became a great success, especially when it came to madhya and drita-laya the thrilling sport that was carried on with the tabla, brought forth and flooded many supportive sentiments of the emotion of raga hitherto unknown to himself. He concluded with the feeling that he had conquered the town.

The whole of that night, even in sleep, the mind was in a happy mood. However, the next afternoon, on the return flight, the mood of emptiness set in again. Like the monotonous dry drone of the flight filling the ears. After requesting the airhostess for earplugs and plugging the ears, it lessened. While looking down the window the wandering mind created an exclamation whether the emotional satisfaction provided by art wasn't only temporary. He couldn't understand this exclamation. In the definitive dam of rhythm that had been built up by Kishan Maharaj and the appreciation on the faces of the elite audience, my mind dug the dry land and brought forth abundant spring water. After the concert ended and the euphoria was over, it felt as if it was the arid weather which had been boiled and evaporated of its water content completely and was expelled as vapour. He felt some new meaning did flash. But what it was, was not clear. He didn't have the habit of thinking clearly either.

When he changed the flight at Delhi, the seat next to him was vacant. Five minutes after the plane took off and reached steadiness and the indication flashed, 'Now you can unfasten your seat belts.' A girl approached and said, 'Hello, I never miss your concerts in Bombay. I just love your music.' He looked at her face. A thick crop of hair, bobbed, descending upto her shoulders. Wore trousers and a half-shirt tucked in, revealing the shape of her breasts. Sharp eyes. About twenty-five. Taller by a couple of inches to the air-hostess who just passed by. He said, 'I am glad.' She enquired intimately, 'Is this seat vacant? May I sit here?' He felt happy. His boredom receded. He said, 'Yes, please do.' After she sat down, he asked, 'Do you learn music?' She replied, 'I used to. After joining the medical college, I don't find time. Now I am doing my MD from Delhi's All India Institute of Medical Studies. I never dreamt that I would have the opportunity to sit next to you and talk to you. I am thrilled. Are you coming from Delhi?' He got interested in her. She was really a fan. Not one who would want to learn music. But still...He looked at her face. She was gazing at him with adoration spilling from her eyes. A part of his mind was calculating whether while getting off at Bombay he could give her his visiting card and tell her to come when she had free time. She is doing MD at a premier institution of Delhi. She is a native of Bombay, perhaps, she must be from a well-to-do family. Otherwise, how could she travel by plane while visiting home instead of travelling by train in the Second Class? Such people meet and talk to people pleasantly. They take autographs. While leaving they say, 'It was very nice meeting you, thank you so much.' Another part of his mind cautioned, I shouldn't volunteer to give a card myself, show interest and make a fool of myself. She was saying, 'Nowhere else does one find the kind of joy as in your music. Such music does not come forth except by divine inspiration. I have a friend. She also thinks the same.' His inborn talent of accepting with a smile at least for courtesy of women spoke words of praise to and encourage them to continue became alerted. The girl was in a mood to speak further. He looked steadily at her face. He was not very enthusiastic even with the girls he had at present. It was a month since he had touched Bhoopali. Then a lack of enthusiasm set in telling himself what was the point in engaging himself in polite conversation with this girl for the next hour and a half. As if a yawn broke out, he shielded his face and opened his mouth wide. After that he said, 'Sorry, it was a night concert. Didn't have any sleep' and closed his eyes. After a minute, he heard the sound of her getting up and leaving. With his eyes closed still, he thought Bakula is, after all, a girl of these modern times. She has all the grit and anger. Like the girl who left as soon as he closed his eyes. What should I do? Meet Bakula's mother, ask her what he should do to allay the suspicion of that boy—Avinash and establish a rapport. He felt it was a momentous decision. Meeting after twenty-four years. He was afraid she might ask him why he had deserted them. By the time the airhostess came pushing the refreshment cart, he had come to see a way out-telling Ramkumari, 'Fate had willed so. Do you think I am happy? I left her also, she who came between us like the planet Rahu. A great astrologer of Kashi, by reading my palm, had said that I had no marital concord. What is written on your forehead is only service to music. There is no use now in delving into all that. Now tell me what I should do to get our daughter married. You also give up the job of a cook. I will say that I will deposit a fixed deposit amount in your name from which you will get a regular income. If she is still grumpy, console her by clever appropriate talk. He thought of this way out. He felt consoled with the decision that he could deposit an amount of four or five lakhs in her name also. He felt sympathy for her that at a time when the desire had become uncontrollable and he was about to resort to the prostitute's den, she had got married to him and had borne him two children. He calculated that after all, five lakhs, wasn't a big deal.

By the time he got off from the taxi and reached the flat, he started feeling afraid. Giving money was right. It was also just. But to meet her face to face, one who had returned one lakh with pride. While going up in the lift, he thought how about sending it with Tipnis? If she says that she doesn't want five lakhs, it isn't my fault. It is not my fault even if she says I have no part to play in the daughter's marriage. He felt relieved that after that, he could live in peace.

४

After wavering about this way and that, he came to the conclusion that it would be best to go personally and solve the problem. He decided to go unexpectedly in order not to give time and opportunity to concoct some excuse. He remembered that Tipnis had mentioned that she would return from Gore Saheb's house around half past four or five. When he thought that he remembered the way from Borivali to the extension, though it was twenty-four years, he realised that it wouldn't be the previous Borivali but would have become a part of the congested Bombay. He pocketed the card that Bakula had given and descended. He remembered that for the past twenty years he hadn't boarded the local train. Thinking that even if he took the train, he would have to walk to the place, he got into a taxi.

Though the door and the walls had been painted, he could recognise the house. The door was half-open. He could see that inside there was a partition that led to a room. No one was in sight. He rang the bell next to the door. Yes, though he had not seen her for twenty-four years, it was the same woman who came out of the kitchen with a rough-skinned face which had never seen any makeup and had weathered in the cold, sun, frost and heat. Kumkum on the forehead. A simple white sari with grey spots. A braid with white hair parted at the centre of the top of the head. A mangalasutra with black beads round the neck. Two red glass bangles on both the wrists. Though the sari hadn't been worn in the typical Maharashtrian style, it was clear that she looked like a middle-class Maharashtrian.

'It is I,' he introduced himself. She was confused for a minute. She lowered her eyes. Again he repeated, 'Don't you recognise me? It's me.'

Meanwhile she recovered. 'The children are not at home. You can meet them if you come after eight.'

'Can't you recognise me. It's "I"', saying so he entered and sat on the sofa.

When she said, 'I don't recognise anyone', he understood that she had recognised him and was speaking in anger.

'Bakula had come. It seems that boy got angry that I hadn't come to the engagement function and said he didn't want to marry her. I won't always be in town. If I am in town for a day, I will be on tour for the next fortnight. So I didn't come. If you inform me earlier about the date of the engagement, I will come and perform kanyadaan on the fixed date.' There appeared confusion on her face. He volunteered, 'If there is no space here, the meeting can be arranged in my flat. The marriage can be celebrated in a big marriage hall. I will pay.'

There was greater confusion writ on her face. As if coming to a decision she said, 'Has Tipnis told me a lie? I have his number. Shall I call him and confront you face to face?'

He was thunderstruck. He reeled for a minute uncomprehendingly wondering how a woman who used to emanate only helplessness, obedience and pity had become so sharp. He didn't know what to say. After a couple of minutes, he felt that he must say something or it would be accepting defeat. He blurted out what came to his mind at that moment. 'Let bygone things be bygone. Don't think I am happy. Bad luck dogs men also like as it does women. She caught hold of me like a cluster of evil, unfavourable stars. It is true that I was under her control for four or five years. After that I kicked her out. I haven't entered the door of her house. I haven't seen her face. Do you know that? Eating in hotels when I am on tour and in a mess, feeding on cold rotis, that's how I am living.'

When he completed the last sentence he found comfort that not only had he confessed his difficulties but had made it clear that he had abandoned his second wife, her rival. He thought he had touched her heart. He observed her face with the hope that he had softened her. She replied in half a minute. 'People with money can make any kind of arrangement for food that they like. Why should I be interested in such stories!'

He felt he had been slapped. However, he decided not to get defeated. He had the experience of having had lovers' quarrels with many women. Women who were not students but many who had a relationship because of the love of art. Many a woman would come and quarrel that he was neglecting them and he was not responding even to a hundredth of their love for him. One of them had gone to the extent of challenging him that she would abandon her husband and children and he had to marry her to accept that his love for her was a sham. With the memory of how he had overcome all such difficult and tricky encounters he developed self-confidence. He got up, went to her, and whispered holding her shoulders, 'Rami, please believe me. It may have happened like this now. I will marry only you in the next birth. I will pray to Amba-Bhavani that only you should be born as my wife. I will give you five thousand rupees every month. Give up cooking in someone else's house from today itself,' saying so he let go of her shoulders, caught hold of her face and kissed her lips hard. As if disgusted, she broke herself loose, and walked away. From the force with which she broke away he felt that she was stronger than himself. He started looking at her who had moved quite far away.

She was spitting fire with her eyes. In a minute there were tears. But they didn't extinguish the fire. Though she looked like about to weep, her face hardened. She seemed possessed. The lips began to utter words, 'Will you marry me in the next birth? Look here. I am wearing this mangalasutra around my neck which you tied in the temple of Amba-Bhavani because it shouldn't be removed. Even if you fall at my feet and beg me, I will never be your wife in the next birth. I have already prayed to Amba-Bhavani. If I am to be born as a woman, make me Gore Saheb's wife. Otherwise I don't want to be born a woman.'

He was flabbergasted. He remembered the many women who had said that they had vowed to become his wife in the next birth and he had reciprocated the same way. Has she played such a game with Gore Saheb? He suspected immediately. He asked at once, 'Tell me the truth. For how long have you had a relationship with Gore Saheb? I also know a bit of truth.'

'What is the truth that you know?' She became aware that she shouldn't have spoken her mind so excitedly about Gore Saheb. To prevent any damage done, she retorted, 'Where is there a man like him? When I entered his house as a cook, I was thirty. If a despondent young woman had sought your protection, would you have left her alone? An evil thought has never entered his noble mind, even once, not even on one day. Which woman will not pray to Amba-Bhavani to give such a godlike man as a husband in the next birth—a man who paid a handsome salary to a destitute woman, helped in the education of her children and even got them jobs? I haven't touched him, except his feet. How can a vile fellow like you understand it? You said you also know a bit of truth. What the hell is it? Bark it out.'

He was silenced. She started staring at him. Unable to meet her gaze, he lowered his eyes. He was aware even after lowering his eyes in every limb that she was spitting fire and brimstone. It was difficult to keep standing. He felt like collapsing on to the sofa. But what to do after sitting down? He foresaw that it would be difficult to get up later. Without uttering a single word he turned back and went out of the door. He descended the steps and moved to the street with long strides.

He felt he had never suffered such a defeat in his life. Really, never. He took his time to remember. He felt that not even when Manohari kicked him out of the greenroom, it was not so humiliating a defeat. He calculated that it had happened seventeen years ago. Manohari, the wench came herself and fell at my feet. He remembered with satisfaction that he had put her in her place even after that. But this woman, it seems, has already prayed for this tax advocate to be her husband in the next birth. It seems she has not touched him anywhere else except his feet. His whole body was set on fire. He felt that he should take revenge on this scoundrel. He may have money. Big merchants and industrialists may be his clients. But the question shot up like a serpent's hood, what right did he have to capture the heart of another man's wife, that too the wife of an incomparably great artist? The question whether he and she had no relationship began to bother him. If there was, why would she remain like a lower middle-class woman? A face that had never seen make-up. Hair which had not even been dyed black. Not a piece of gold around her neck and or her wrists. The hope of the next birth must be just her dream. If she had even an iota of interest in art, she would have told herself that an artist-husband was not completely hers in this birth and would have prayed for its fulfilment in the next birth. The mind was seeking consolation thinking how an uncultured woman like this could have him as her husband in the next birth. Suddenly another thought flashed; that man Gore was not only a tax consultant for big businessmen and industrialists but a patron of all the music associations of Bombay, not just that but he was their very backbone. He has every singer and instrumentalist in his grip. His knowledge of music is also perfect. He became cautious that it would be difficult for any musician to survive if he antagonised him. Why should I get into trouble? It is not possible that this well-to-do music connoisseur and who is so good-looking himself to have even glanced at an ignoramus like her. Though the explanation that she was only dreaming about being the mistress of the big house where she was only a cook now, brought him some peace, the pain of his defeat did not lessen. He could not forget her effrontery of denouncing him who was welcomed with a standing ovation at music concerts.

About a week had passed. One afternoon he called Bakula's office. 'I have to discuss a couple of things with you. Meanwhile I have to answer your questions. Can you come by this evening on your way home?' She didn't know how to answer, when he said, 'Even if your anger hasn't subsided, do come. After all with who else should a daughter be angry except with her father?' She softened and said she would come by half past five.

When she came, she was feeling embarrassed. He enquired after her work and salary. He asked with whom she was learning music and what level she had reached. He came to know what her brother was doing by round-about queries. Then he said, 'I teach music to all kinds of people. I don't take any fee. That I should not is my guru's principle. Would I say I won't teach my daughter? But I cannot teach beginners from the fundamentals. Learn from your teacher whatever you can with dedication. After that, I will teach you at an advanced level.' Her eyes sparkled with joy. 'Till then, I will pay the fee. You are my daughter. You tell him that I said so. He will teach you with interest.' Now her eyes shone. 'You tell that boy, Avinash, you tell his parents also. I will take part in the engagement function and I will give you away in marriage. I will celebrate it in a good marriage-hall. My programmes will be fixed up months in advance. Only the date must be fixed well in advance. Now, does Kishan say that he has no capital to start a business? Tell him that I will give him three to four lakhs. It is important that in his business he should not lose money, but develop it responsibly. Tell him to come and meet me.'

Bakula's eyes were filled with tears of joy. 'I had come to Borivali a week ago to speak about this. Your mother must have told you.'

'No, not at all.' Her face showed surprise. 'I went there only to discuss your marriage. I told her that I would shoulder the expense of engagement and wedding. I asked her to send for the groom's people. She showed anger that I had not come all these days. When I tried to explain my difficulties, she wouldn't listen. She told me straight-away that she would marry Gore Saheb in her next birth and that he would marry her. What's all this talk? Would he help to this extent if she was only cooking for him? I didn't say a word. I have seen all kinds of women in my life as an artist. But I never thought that your mother was this kind of woman. My marrying a second time was a mistake. But I haven't seen her face for twenty years. I haven't set foot on her doorstep. I swear by god. She has told a lie to Avinash. I will deal with it accordingly. But what is the meaning of this woman saying that this rich lawyer, Gore is going to be her lawfully wedded husband in her next life? Is this the kind of talk that can come from a respectable woman?'

ङ

Though Bakula and Kishan were grateful for their mother that she had looked after them and brought them up to the present state, they did not have attachment and love for her. With the idea that without the fear of the presence of a man, the father, she had to play father as well as mother, she had brought them up very strictly lest they should go astray. They should study all the time. They should come home early in the evening. She would get angry very soon. If the children were mischievous, as children tend to be, she would thrash them. Afterwards, she would weep upbraiding them that they didn't know with what great difficulty she was bringing them up and still they would trouble her. Her weeping would generate in them the feeling of guilt and augment the intensity of punishment. Both the children had developed a feeling that the man they had to fear in their life was Gore Saheb. Their mother would take them with her to him to tell them what subjects they should take in high school and what optional they should choose in college. As soon as they saw him they should touch his feet with reverence. After that they should keep standing. They should bow down to Suniti Tai also. Their forehead should not be placed on Tai's feet, but should touch the ground at a marginal distance. All this their mother had taught them. Though the boss talked to them politely without any anger, there was no other emotion except fear regarding him. They had met him only five or six times. The last time they met him was when their mother took them to get a job for them. He was the one who had said that after graduation, typewriting had to be learnt and then the computers. A suggestion by him was considered an order by the mother. Bakula had nursed the feeling that she had to join B.Com against her wishes. Gore Saheb had said that after she got a job, she could learn music also but in her present state, going in for music right away was not right. She had suspected that mother had told him to say so. The anger against her mother would sometimes turn on Gore Saheb also. One of the reasons was that from time to time mother would say that she would tell on her to Gore Saheb. She had an intensely bitter feeling that both of them had joined together in preventing her from learning music from young age itself. She would also feel grateful that without his guidance and help, she wouldn't have found a job. In addition to the fact that her mother would obey Gore Saheb she had an unpleasant feeling that he was controlling her through her mother. She had learnt from her college friends and from her guru that he was helping all the music organisations of the city. But there was also the dissatisfaction that he had come in the way of her learning music. More than in the case of her father, the controlling power of Gore Saheb was more resentful in her mind. The single dissatisfaction that her father was a deserter became only tangential, lost its intensity and his existence had been relegated to some distant corner of her mind. Even that, because she was interested in music. Kishan didn't have even that much of feeling. He didn't know anything more than that one Mohanlal, who would earn one lakh per concert was his father, that he got involved with a student of his and abandoned his mother. That he hadn't seen him at all since his birth and that now he was philandering with his students and women mad after music, gives concerts all over the country and lives in West Bandra. He had no desire to know anything more either. He was also a bit afraid of Gore Saheb. He had told him that if he didn't complete his graduation, he would be ruined. If he cleared the exams, he himself would get him a job with some auditor. He could do his CA. He had said as an alternative, he could get him a job in some company as he had, for his elder sister. Another day his mother had taken him to Gore Saheb's house and got him scolded. He entertained both fear and dissatisfaction regarding Gore Saheb. He was filled with the idea that because she could not abuse the son herself, she had got him to do it for her.

Now, all of sudden, the relationship changed in the minds of both. Bakula's mind was completely changed and her father's image altered when he offered to arrange the engagement, pay for a wedding hall and give her away in marriage. How was it possible for him to live with this woman who simply didn't have any music in her and who spits fire at the very mention of music? That is why he married someone else. Now he has left her also and is living alone with no one to look after him. It is possible he has relationships with other women. The justifications did appear in her mind that artists do have such relationships. People without any taste for art might make much of it and indulge in loose talk. How can art grow without inspiration? She threw back that one lakh he had sent for the wedding. Now when he has come of his own accord searching for the house, she sent him away saying that she wants Gore Saheb to be her husband in the next birth. Which respectable woman will talk like that? She was very angry with her. She couldn't contain her emotions for many days. One evening, on coming home she asked, 'Why have you hidden all these days the fact that father came and said that he would bear all the expenses of engagement as well as marriage?'

The mother became nonplussed. She couldn't think of an answer. She mounted a counter attack, 'Had you gone to visit him?'

'How can you speak in the singular of a man who is great enough for the whole country to come and touch his feet. It seems you said that you wanted Gore Saheb to be your husband in the next birth. Tell me, what is he to you in this birth? If he was nothing to you in this birth, why would you talk about the next birth? It is possible that it is because you are that kind of woman that father left you, who knows?' Having said this, she realised that she had gone too far and shut her mouth immediately.

Meanwhile the mother had been struck dumb. Couldn't think of even a word in reply. No thought passed through her head. It seemed the floor gave way under her feet. She remembered how, many years ago when she was standing at this very spot she felt the whole building shaking during an earthquake. It was the same experience all over again. But this was not an earthquake. Afraid that if she kept standing she would fall, she supported herself against the wall and sat down. The daughter who withdrew her lips into her teeth, shut her mouth, didn't stay there but went into her room and shut the door. After a couple of minutes the mother found her balance. She felt sure she wouldn't fall. She walked out even without bothering to wear her slippers. She came down the steps and walked down the street. Wading through the evening rush and traffic in the narrow streets, she came to the temple of Amba-Bhavani. There was a rush of people even there. She made her way to the sanctum sanctorum, stood in front of the marble image of the Mother Goddess who was seated on the tiger with a sword in hand and filled her eyes with that image and closed her eyes. If I have sinned and have entertained sinful thoughts, mother, cut off my neck with your sharp sword. Otherwise, cut off the tongue of those who talk of sin. You, you mother of all humanity, you tell me how is it a sin to pray to you to give me a good husband at least in the next birth. She confined these words within the firmly closed eyelids and stood her ground. For some time those sentences imprinted themselves like word pictures on the inner screen of her eyes. But then, I have stood before you and have prayed to you that Gore Saheb should be my husband in the next birth. If it was a sin, you yourself should have told me so. You didn't tell me. If it is, tell me right now. These words took shape. The closed eyes had remained closed. She never got an inner message that it was a sin. After some time she opened her eyes. The priest applied the kumkum paste vertically on her forehead. She put her right palm above her left and requested the priest to let her have some of it to take home. He collected a bit of it, mixed it into a pulp and put it on her right hand. She touched it, to her eyes, circumambulated thrice where she was standing and came out of the temple. While retracing homeward, her steps were steady. There was firmness in her gait.

The emotional excitement had given acceleration to her walk. She reached home quickly. When she climbed the steps and reached the door, it was shut. She rang the doorbell. 'Who's there?' It was Kishan's voice. After she announced herself he opened the door. After she went in, he closed and bolted the door. He hadn't yet removed his shoes. He was wearing jeans with his striped half-sleeve shirt tucked in. The lid of his handbag was open. There were hundred-rupee bundles. She understood immediately that each bundle contained ten thousand rupees. He was counting the currency notes. Though she understood that it was company money to be handed over to the boss, she didn't pay attention to it. The door of the room was half open. Bakula was sitting on the cot strumming her tambura. The mother, on entering, transferred the kumkum from her right palm to the left, collected half of it on her pointing finger and applied it to the forehead of the daughter vertically and said, 'I had gone to the temple. I begged that if my request was sinful, to cut off my neck with her sword. The goddess has told me that I have not committed any sin. Your tongue will be shrunk. Yes, I had prayed to her. Not today but have been doing so for sixteen years. Praying that at least in the next birth, to give me a husband like Gore Saheb. I had told your father about it when he had come eight days ago. He has slandered about me. You come and ask me about sin. Your tongue will be silenced. What I have applied to your forehead is not the boon of the devi but her curse. For having brought up a chit of a girl to a level where you call me names, do you?'

Her voice had been raised. Though the door was closed, there was no guarantee that it hadn't been heard across the walls as the house was a portion of a condominium. The daughter looked up at her mother's face. The kumkum that had been passed vertically had given her face a fierce look. She has pasted it to her face also and had pronounced a curse on her. Though she remembered that she didn't believe in gods and goddesses and curses and blessings, yet, she was afraid. Meanwhile, Kishan who had come to the door of the room, asked, 'Mother, what has happened?' The mother who heard the pacifying tone in his voice believed that he was on her side and narrated everything, the pain that she suffered and her going to the temple immediately. Kishan took his sister to task, 'Because you are learning music you think that musician-father is a god? After engendering us, what has he done? It was our mother who brought us up. You extract whatever you can from father. Who the hell is he favouring by shelling out money? But beware of hurting mother's mind. This evening I had also gone there. He gave me two lakhs for my business. I have brought it. He asked me also, what does it mean that your mother has prayed that Gore Saheb should be her husband in the next birth? Just because of that I wouldn't come home and ask mother about it. Merely because you have passed your B.Com and have learnt computers, do you think you have become a genius?'

She felt comforted that at least the son was on her side. But after a minute, she began to understand the implication. Without her own knowledge, her voice had become a screech. 'Did you go and cringe before him because he pays money? Do you have any shame? Is it for this, that I conceived, gave birth and brought you up? Just go immediately and return the money.'

Kishan didn't show any anger. 'Mother, it is natural that you got angry at what this girl said. But why should the money be given back? Don't I know that he did nothing and that it was you who did everything? Do you know how much he has given to the children of the second wife? That son plays cricket in the Brabourne Stadium. You don't know what a luxury it is to play cricket there? He has a BE degree and is going to England for higher studies. He pays lakhs for those children. Why should I give him back the measly sum of two lakhs which he has paid lump sum? What justice is there in rich people getting richer, and poor people remaining poor? And then such luxury for the children of that concubine. Why can't the children of the lawfully wedded wife touch even an iota of his money?'

She couldn't think of an answer. She was pleased in a way that her son had not only identified himself as the son of the lawfully wedded wife but had called the other woman a prostitute. She saw that such a word hadn't been used by the daughter. The son saw the kumkum on the right palm of the mother. Paste devi's prasadam on my forehead also. He bent down and brought his face close to her. She applied the prasadam to his forehead. She couldn't understand immediately that if her son invested the money in business to bring profits, it was as good as her blessing him with that money from his father. She couldn't sleep that night. She could never give him two lakhs. So the children would never listen to her if she said not to take the money. She began to ask herself whether it was right to ask them not to enjoy the money when the children of the other woman were doing so with such aplomb. The other voice said that these children extending their hand to receive money from him would be below their dignity. No matter how long she rolled about and struggled there was no solution. Isn't it possible for my son not to accept filthy lucre from him? Can't she get married at all if that fellow doesn't give her away in marriage? If she says right away that he is my father. He is a philanderer. My mother worked in some one else's house and brought me up. I am in such and such a job. I get so much of salary. Suppose she said this, what happens? Won't anybody marry her at all? When these questions cropped up she got angry with her children. She felt that they, whom she had nourished all these years had forsaken her. She felt like crying. If she cried, he who was sleeping would awake. She who was sleeping in the room might also hear it. She would lose face. After she regained her self-respect she felt why she should belittle herself before them, and then it was easy to control her crying fit.

However, in a couple of days she felt that he was determined to take revenge by alienating her children from her. She had no one to confess to. She went a little early, waited for his wife to go to take her bath, approached Gore Saheb and told him that she had something to discuss with him. He asked her to come to the office the next evening.

When he heard everything she told him, he was surprised. He was helping her at home without the knowledge of his wife. He would listen to her problems and comfort her. It was true that when his wife was away he was interested in her. But she rejecting bodily relationship, because Goddess Amba-Bhavani in whom she believed appeared in her dream and told her it was wrong and he had honoured it. He remembered all that. But he was surprised that she had prayed to the same goddess to make him her husband in the next birth. He didn't believe in previous and future births. She did. Though he was meeting her in the office at least once a month when no one else was there and enquiring about her welfare, never had he spoken a word of intimacy or endearment. That feeling hasn't remained with him at all. It got extinguished within two months of its occurrence. What was left was only compassion. Even tenderness. But her resolution is strong to get her desire fulfilled in the next birth without committing a sin in this life. For its fulfilment she has requested the permission and blessing from the goddess she believes in. He experienced endearment in addition to surprise. But he didn't show it. He asked, 'No matter what you have in your mind. No matter what you have prayed for. But if you blurt it out openly to your husband, won't he be angry? Why did you tell him that?'

She answered at once, 'His coming close to me suddenly, taking hold of my shoulders, saying that he will marry me in the next birth, I will pray to Amba-Bhavani to make you my wife in the next birth, saying that he would give me five thousand rupees every month and asking me to discontinue working in someone's house...Can he say these things? Would Amba-Bhavani listen to the one who has been praying for the last fifteen years or to his manoeuvring scheme now? How is it possible not to get angry? I blurted out what I did without hesitation.'

'Won't he think that there is a relationship between you and me? Won't he use this by telling others that his wife is carrying on like this just to hide her mistake? What will happen to my reputation by this?'

She became extremely serious. Her face registered the feeling that she had committed a great blunder. She was in tears. 'I didn't think any of this.' Saying so she approached, bent down and touched his feet.

'Leave it alone. Remember that those who don't hesitate to do anything won't hesitate to say anything.'

She confided in him her sorrow about her children whom she had brought up with such loving care and affection were slavishly licking his feet for his money. 'With grown up children you can confess your feelings. Is it possible to bind them? Don't worry too much about it.' He consoled her.

೬

It was half past seven by the time she went home. Bakula had come home and was practising music. On coming to the door and opening it, she asked, 'Why are you so late?' The mother felt a setback. Does she know where she had gone? Still, without showing it she just went inside, washed her feet and went into the kitchen. The daughter who had come home earlier hadn't cooked anything. She had just prepared tea and hadn't even washed the cup. She had to wash all the dishes, cut the vegetables, do everything herself. She was angry. She had to earn a living and do the household work too. She felt like asking the daughter what did she think of her mother. She pushed the door open and stood there. The daughter was sitting on the bed strumming the tambura. On the wall behind her was a large photograph with glass and frame. She couldn't make out at once whose picture it was. She looked steadily at it. It was his. Bakula's father's. The pose of singing open mouthed in concert. When did she bring it? She hadn't seen it in the morning when she swept the room. She must have just brought it and hung there. What she wanted to ask remained unasked. She stared at the one sitting there with the tambura and at the fellow in the photograph and went back. When she went into the kitchen, the question recurred why she should serve them. Still she started slicing brinjal and potatoes. When she was cooking, the daughter barged into the kitchen and said, 'Why did you spit fire the moment you saw that photograph? Looking at your angry demeanour, the mood for music dies. I know that you don't like him. But thousands of students who aren't his direct disciples have his photograph and practice music sitting in front of it, all over the country. Why can't I, his own daughter, have it? If you don't like it, don't come to the room.'

The mother didn't speak. As if she hadn't heard it, she automatically poured the vegetables and some water into the pan. Now she couldn't keep silent any more. She blurted out, 'Those who screech and scream let them have his photograph or even a statue of him. I won't allow the photograph of a fellow in my home, who married by tying the sacred knot, and begot two children and left unceremoniously. This is my house. After you get married and go, have a hundred photographs of his to fill all the walls. I won't ask you.'

The daughter spoke with the self confidence that the truth was on her side. 'I won't get angry because you do.' In whose name is the rental of this house? Is it in you name or his? Are you or are you not staying in his house?'

'Is this his house?' She was quite upset by this new question.

'Is it yours? Is the rental in your name?'

She had never thought about this. It was true that the rental was not in her name. She remembered that she had paid the rental every month all these years.

'The house is in father's name. Remember that. It doesn't work if you say you won't admit him. If he likes, he can throw you out.'

She felt the floor giving in beneath her feet. She caught hold of the cooking counter and got her balance. In a minute, though the floor became steady her mouth was tied up. The daughter said, 'If I like I can hang his photograph in the living room. I didn't do so because I didn't want to embarrass you. I won't tolerate if you speak disrespectfully about him.'

The mother didn't reply. She cooked, her mouth shut. After the cooking was over, she put chapatti and curry in a plate, put a bowl of dal and a bowl of curds and said, 'Dinner is served. Those who want may come and take.' The daughter who was just sitting without playing on the tambura came and took it away. Mother had decided not to eat. But the daughter did not understand it. She approached the daughter who was eating, sitting on the sofa and asked, 'You said that if he wants, he can throw me out. Is it what you are saying or did he say that?'

The daughter didn't reply. The mother repeated the question as if to say that she wouldn't leave her alone until she answered. The daughter's face turned from boredom to disgust. 'Why all that now?'

'This is not an investigation. Just tell me whose words are these? There is the witness of Goddess Amba-Bhavani. The tongue of the liars will be shrunk. Beware.'

The daughter was afraid even though she didn't fully believe in Amba-Bhavani. Still she couldn't summon up courage to utter a blatant lie in the context of the threat. Without replying she put a fresh morsel of food in her mouth and went on churning. After waiting for a minute when the mother said, 'Will you speak the truth now or shall I right away rush to the temple and take a pledge?' The daughter was searching for a way of escape. What came to her mind was. 'He didn't actually say that he would throw you out. This is my house. In those days when I didn't have much income, who was it that leased this house? Even now the rental is in my name. If I say that this is not my house, the owner will throw you out. That is what he said and what I said.' The mother fell silent on that. She went into the kitchen, prepared enough chapattis for Kishan, put it on a plate, covered it with another and came out. Meanwhile the daughter had retired to her room. The mother, as usual, spread a mat on the floor, put a pillow and resting her head on it lay down under the fan. She slept after a long time.

She got up early in the morning, cooked for both the children prepared their lunch packets. She herself didn't eat. They never had the concern to know whether she had taken food or not. With the resolution that she wouldn't die if she didn't eat anything till the afternoon when she would have lunch in the afternoon at the boss' house, she washed the dishes and started mopping the floor. The fire of anger was burning in her that he had spoken about throwing her out of the house. Since that day she left eating, except what she had earned and cooked in that house. She ate only once a day in the afternoon. The children didn't know this. She didn't feel like telling them either. Both the children were taking his side, he who had deserted them and now whom she had deserted. For her, her father's name and music were sacred. This fellow wants his father's money. Thinking how could she confide her self-respect, the plights she had undergone with such people she kept quiet with a sense of loss.

A week had elapsed. One morning when she went, Suniti Tai was not at home. The Saheb said, she has gone to the Ganesh Mandir. She will come now. Afterward, he himself said, 'For the last one week, you have been very dull. Since the day you spoke to me last, if I remember correctly. What's the matter?' She began to cry. 'Come to the office tomorrow evening. Let's talk.' He went into his room. She entered the kitchen. Suniti Tai returned in five minutes.

The next evening when she narrated the exchange with her daughter and how she hadn't eaten at home since then, he observed her. Within a week she had grown thin. The cheeks were shrunken. There were hollows beneath her eyes. 'You are the one who is paying the rent. In Bombay the house belongs to one who pays the rent. It is the food you have earned. Why are you starving?'

'The house belongs to him. It is registered in his name isn't it?'

'In whose name have you paid the rent all these years?

'Only in the name of Mohanlal. If I tried to pay in some other name, the owner would have made us quit using that as an excuse.'

'That isn't possible. According to the law rented person includes his wife and children.' He fell silent. She herself reminded, 'According to law, I am not his wife at all!'

Without talking, he started ruminating. With the feeling that she shouldn't interrupt when he was thinking, she sat silently. After ten minutes he spoke, 'Till now, even I, hadn't realised it. Now the time has come. He is also transgressing the limit. Listen to me. I will fix up an intelligent advocate. You sue him.' He will bring the charge that he hasn't married you at all. Then you must ask the court to conduct a blood test on him and these two children. It will be established in the blood test that these are his children. Then he has to say that they were born out of wedlock and you are a prostitute. We can bring in witnesses to show that it is a lie. Besides, circumstantial evidence will establish that his has been a marriage. Our advocate will see to all this. This means that his second marriage is illegal. He will go to jail for having married a second time. If all this appears in the newspapers he will be terrified and come and fall at your feet. He will ask for settlement. We may settle by bringing the court order that he should pay a compensation of ten thousand rupees every month. Or, we may get ten to fifteen lakh in a lump sum and leave it. If you put fifteen lakh in the bank, you will get an interest of fifteen thousand. You just agree. I will fix up a lawyer in a week. You don't have to pay him a single pie. After the case is won and the bumper money is obtained, I will tell you how much you should pay him.'

Her face beamed forth. She forgot even to close her mouth which fell open to exclaim if this was possible.

'Remember I am a lawyer. But my cases belong to a different category. I will appoint a lawyer who is famous for dealing with cases pertaining to marriage, divorce and compensations and settlements. That man will see to it that no matter what lawyer he engages, he will have no chance. Don't have the slightest doubt about this. Just go back and have your food properly from today. It is what you earn.'

'Yes, I will,' she promised.

'Come to the house a bit early tomorrow morning. You narrate to me before Suniti what you told me. I will tell the same thing to you. Because when once the case starts there will be things you want to tell me and I want to tell you. Every time you don't have to abide for a time and come here. In this matter Suniti also has great sympathy for you and anger against him. For the present don't talk about any of this in the presence of the children. In case he argues that these are not his children or that he is the father but he has not married you, these very children will turn against him. Understand that too. For the present, don't say a word.'

7

On the third day after this talk, he went to Delhi, there was a big income tax case for which he had to stay there for four days. After coming back to the hotel room and a light refreshment, he had to go to another advocates' office and collect some information. But by the time he returned to the hotel it would be midnight. Still, in the midst of all this and in the mornings and till he went to the court after breakfast her or Mohanlal's state would occupy his mind. A great singer. It was quite unpredictable where he creates a new path, where he takes an astonishing turn, where he suddenly attacks and in which curve he dashes forth. The themes, patterns of weaving, the depths and variations which do not occur to any other maestro flash forth to him in a hundred, nay, in thousands of ways. He is sixty-one. No matter to what gharana, tradition he belongs, there is no singer of the younger generation of Hindustani classical music who doesn't imitate him or who has not been influenced by him. Being such a genius, shouldn't he have at least elementary moral sense? Are all artists like this? Or, only performing artists like this? Even if you say that private lives of artists shouldn't be bothered about, is there no limit to their misbehaviour? Even after all this, he was not disgusted with Mohanlal's music. The attraction hadn't decreased. Remembering it, he was surprised. Isn't it one year since he came to me with the complaint that his second wife was making tapes from his concerts and selling them commercially? Since I sent him with the message that he should make up his mind about what kind of relationship he wants to have between himself, his wife and children and then I would fix up an advocate for him. He didn't come back after that. He does not have the capacity to bring the problems of life together under a framework. Are all artists like this? These thoughts were revolving in his head. Yes, he must be taught a lesson. When he was a nobody, he married a poor girl and having begotten two children abandoned her and didn't give her anything even when he was earning thirty to forty lakhs a year. Besides, what a mad womaniser! How can any respectable girl, learn music from him? Gore got angry. He thought Mohanlal must be punished. But such people, when they go to court, they don't fight it out. His professional experience told him that they manipulate, bargain and get away scot-free. A two bed-room flat must be bought for her. On top of it ten lakh rupees, this must be the inflexible demand. No concession. He decided to tell Ramkumari strictly. Though he wanted to ring up advocate Gupte from Delhi itself he couldn't find the time. Besides it was not an urgent case to call up from Delhi itself. He kept quiet.

On the fifth day even on reaching Bombay by flight, he couldn't stay long at home. He had just time to deposit the suitcase and go to the office with the box of case files. He was not in the habit of enquiring about the welfare of Ramkumari and soon as he saw her. It was Suniti Tai's habit to make such enquiries. Besides there were urgent things to attend to in the office.

The next afternoon at half past three Ramkumari called him at his office. 'Have you fixed up a lawyer? I am calling to tell you not to do so.'

'Why, what's the matter?'

'I will come to the office and speak to you. Not in the presence of Tai.'

'Did she say anything reproaching?'

'No, certainly not, she asked me to go to court against him. Just make him cough up the money. Still, there is something which I want to speak about alone with you.'

'Come tomorrow at six.'

Six meant six. She doesn't have a wrist watch. But he knew that she would come early, enquire about the time from someone who had a watch and come exactly on time. If it was a minute or two this way or that, it would be the difference on account of the time in the watch of the person she enquired. Now she came and sat as usual on the chair opposite. There was not the usual ease on her face. There was seriousness. Knowing that she wouldn't say anything unless he himself started the conversation, he asked, 'What are the things which you wanted to ask during the case hearing? What are all the things which Suniti wanted you to ask?'

'Tai told me to ask for as big a flat as he has given to the other wife and for the same amount of money he has paid her all these years. But I have decided not to ask anything and not to go to court. No case.'

'Why did you change your mind all of a sudden?'

'All these years I have eaten from what I have honestly earned. I have brought up the children. All this wouldn't have happened by my earning. You looked after us. You gave money from time to time and made a deposit out of it. Now the children are independent. They have stretched their hand to his dung. He is their father. They don't listen to me when I say "Don't". Besides, who am I to tell them not to do so? But why should I eat the food at his expense? My lunch I have at your place. After I told Tai everything the other day, she keeps some breakfast and gives it to me as soon as I come to your place. She has told me to work only after eating. All that I need at night are a couple of rotis. They are building a new complex of flats at Dahisar. It seems for one lakh and half, there is accommodation of a room, toilet, bath and kitchen. It is far away from Borivali, less number of local trains also. It doesn't matter. I will buy it with the deposit I have in the bank. I will leave the house that is in his name. Let him take possession of it, or let Kishan and Bakula stay there. It is none of my business. It is dignified for me to live away from them.'

'If you withdraw the amount from the bank and invest it on a dwelling, you will die without food in old age?'

'How will I get old so soon? Isn't it economical if I live alone? I can save. And another thing came to my mind. If I reach a stage when

I have to die without food, I myself will go on a fast in god's name and if I give up food and water, life will cease to be itself. There is no question of dying from hunger.' She laughed.

'Where did you get this idea'?

'I stood in front of Goddess Amba-Bhavani and begged. It flashed.'

He didn't ask anything else. He began to ruminate on her words. It looked like escapism, giving up her legal right.

'Are you afraid to go and stand in a court of law? Did you come to this decision because of the fear that his lawyer might ask all kinds of embarrassing questions?' He asked.

'What fear do I have? I can answer any question asked by any lawyer in whatever court. Why should there by any fear for one who has suffered for so many years?' When she said this, courage and self-confidence shone in her eyes.

He didn't speak. He was struggling to understand the nature of her inner strength. After a couple of minutes he asked. 'Aren't you bothered about who would look after your children if you left? Didn't your mother's heart bleed? Have you thought about it?'

'I have hardened my heart. They have not remained just my children. I have made up my mind that they are not my children any more if they want to exploit me as well as receive benefits from him.

'Don't touch your deposit in the bank. I will buy you the flat.'

She didn't speak. Her eyes were filled with tears in a minute. He sat looking at her face. She herself found the words and said. 'Even the money in the bank is yours. The money you gave from time to time. Now...' She began to cry profusely.

He who was listening quietly, said after a couple of minutes, 'Tell me without hiding anything? Yes, tell me without hiding anything.'

'You went to Delhi. I had to cook only for Tai. There was not much work. I left early and instead of going home at Borivali, I went straight to Amba-Bhavani Temple. While I sat with closed eyes, leaning against a pillar I thought that you were looking after me for fifteen years, me who wanted to become your wife in the next birth. You have enabled me to have a deposit in the bank. Now, why should I stretch my hand for his compensation? Where is the relationship between me and him, I thought. Then it occurred to me not to go to court and register a case against him. When you were not in town, Tai enquired after my problems with loving care. She said that I should eat something first and then start the work. She has never treated me badly. But after I sat in front of her that day and told her all my problems she has been bestowing greater affection on me. The saris that I have been wearing all these years were given to me by her after she had worn them. I had given the same ones to Bakula. After she got a job, she spoke proudly why she should wear something already worn by someone else. Let that go. On the day previous to the day you returned from Delhi, I was sitting alone, leaning against a pillar meditating at the temple. Suddenly, an idea occurred. If I become your wife in the next birth, who would be Tai's husband? Isn't it justice that for a faithful wife who looks after her husband with loving care, that she should get the same husband in the next birth also? I am a woman who cooks for receiving a salary. She is the one who wears the mangalasutra, the mangalasutra tied by you. How can I wrest from her the right in the next birth? Is it justice if I seize it? I thought, what a sinner I am! All that night I was only thinking of that.' She stopped and closed her eyes, adjusting mentally what she should say next. He was just looking at her face. A minute later she opened her eyes and spoke. 'When I had the feeling that I would be your wife in the next birth, I used to take whatever you gave. Now when I know that there is no such thing, how can I take the flat?'

He became silent trying to understand her turmoil. Their eyes were viewing each other. After a little while, she lowered her gaze and started looking at the edge of the table. After a couple of minutes he said. 'I have no belief either in rebirth or in the belief that a man will be reborn as a man and a woman as woman. If one wants to help someone, there is no rule that they should be man and wife now or later. Don't you help someone who is not related to you? You have decided not to be obliged to Mohanlal for your food. It is praiseworthy. The same way I have helped you till now without even imagining that you would be my wife, the same way I will buy you this flat. You be independent. Don't tell anyone. Don't think about how you can repay this help. I have not given you with the idea that you should pay back. Now let's go. I have some other work,' saying so he looked at his wrist watch.

Chapter 14

I

Mohanlal became worried when not only in other things but in his voice also he found an aridness. There was no question of striking a discordant note. But there was no emotion in the resultant voice. The power of his music lies only in the full, rich, overflowing emotion. His strength was in expressing the emotions of pity, valour, delicacy, tenderness, sorrow, exultation, surrender, and such feelings which transcend calculation or imitation, which would be lighter than the air or deeper than the ocean and any sophisticated nuance between the two. He would become upset at remembering the days when he would proudly declare that if there was essence in the personality of the singer, the emotional upsurge would well forth from his throat. When the emotional power dries up, what value does life have? This was his anxiety. There was no enthusiasm in practising swara in the mornings or even in teaching. The other springs of happiness of life were closed. After ruminating for a long time why this was so, one midnight the reason flashed forth. He had pawned the tambura that his guru had bestowed on him with his blessing. He must get it back and worship it. If he practises with that tambura then aesthetic emotion will again flow in his singing. He thought that was the reason. The man with whom he had pawned his instrument had demanded a redemption fee of one lakh, Mohanlal's rate for a concert. He decided to throw it at him and bring it back. So many years ago when his fee was very small, then alone he should have redeemed it. He thought he had been an idiot to get involved with that rascal. After some time he managed to sleep.

By the time he got up and finished his shower and breakfast, the charwoman came and finished the morning chores. He opened the safe-deposit locker in his almirah, took out bundles of currency notes of one lakh, put them in his handbag and took a taxi. He remembered it was fifteen years since he had seen the face of Junnarkar. Now he was eighty-five. His son would come to the conferences where he would meet him. He is of my age. He doesn't talk to me. I also don't talk to him. He remembered that he would slander him with others saying, 'There was a time when Mohanlal would beg my father to get him a programme since he didn't have money to buy his next meal. Now look at him. He doesn't even invite me to accompany him on the harmonium. How long will the vanity of such people last?' Even now he continues to cast aspersions on him. He might also be at home. He felt unhappy that if he went to his place, the ego of junior Junnarkar may hit the roof. He felt like asking the taxi driver to go back. However, he took courage that when the spring, the source of his inspiration was lying imprisoned in that fellow's house, it won't do to dilly dally instead of freeing his instrument. Besides, seeing the bundle of bank notes of one lakh, he would not be able to refuse.

The son Anand was not at home. The father, Vittal Junnarkar was reclining on the divan supported by a pillow. It was possible that the lady who opened the door was Anand's wife. She asked, 'Whom should I announce? The old man heard the name Mohanlal. Still he was sitting silently wanting that the visitor should speak first. He himself approached him and said, 'Salutations Panditji. I am Mohanlal.'

After he said it a bit loudly, Junnarkar said, 'Who is Mohanlal? Which Mohanlal? There are a lot of people with that name in Bombay. If you open the telephone directory, ten pages full.' Mohanlal understood that the old man was deliberately being contemptuous. At that moment he didn't remember, that was his very nature.

'The Mohanlal who had pawned his tambura with you. I have come to reclaim it with the money—my fee for a single concert.'

After he said it, he called out to his daughter-in-law. 'Then, you must say Pandit Mohanlalji. Please bring a chair to the Emperor of Music who has graced us. Please prepare some tea.'

Mohanlal noticed sarcasm in the word 'Emperor,' After enquiring after his health and drinking the tea, he said, 'I have brought one lakh. Please count. Give me back my tambura.'

'You have reached a level of getting one lakh for a concert. I am very happy. Why don't you take my son for accompanying you in your concerts? Why are you saddled with that fellow Tipnis?'

'There is no question of being saddled. It is not that I don't want to take your son. But there should be an artistic rapport, shouldn't there? All right, I will take your son also.'

'Don't say your son also. Say, only your son. I was the one who pushed you, didnt I?'

This angered him. How was it that he made me famous? 'Vittal Rao, nobody can launch anybody and make him famous. It is also not possible to trample on anybody who has innate talent. Take this one lakh you asked for and return my tambura.'

Junnarkar said contemptuously as if he was being swept out like a piece of dirt, 'Oh, that's your tone is it? What tambura are you talking about? If it has to cost one lakh, its rotund must have been made with gold. We don't have any such tambura in our house!'

'That tambura which I pawned with you for twenty-five rupees and then when I came to retrieve it you demanded the fee of a single concert of mine. When you demanded it, my fee was twenty thousand. I had said I wouldn't pay. Now will you just take this one lakh and give it to me or not?'

'Am I so stupid to reject Mahalakshmi in the form of one lakh? I don't have your tambura. It is as old as thirty-two years ago, isn't it? So many tambura's get broken. Some people take them and don't return them. Something like this has happened and it is lost. What can I do?' The old man spoke quite calmly without showing anger.

Mohanlal, realising that it was the style of this rascal, got up and started climbing the stairs at the right hand corner. Ignoring the old man's shouting, 'Who had given him the right to climb to the loft,' he found that there were five tamburas, all tied with covers. By an instinct he untied the fourth one and on removing the cover found that it was his indeed. On either side of the head of the instrument there was the insignia of Chittarpur, design of a peacock, all inlaid in ivory. Though it had been covered, it was full of dust. He took it in his hands and pressed it to his eyes. He felt the image of Raja Saheb emanated from his eyes and became visible; he saw in his mind's eye the idol of Lord Shiva of the temple and in the immense precipice the River Narmada become visible, flowing deep down in mandra-shadja. He could even find the correct swara. He felt that he had obtained each hue and mood of the swara. By the time he started back holding the tambura, he found that the old man's daughter-in-law, Anand's wife was standing at the steps, blocking the way. He said softly, 'Sister, please allow me to pass, I must show this to the maestro.' She descended. He also descended and said, 'Old man, you told me a lie that my tambura is lost. If you had given it to me voluntarily, you would have got one lakh. Now, see this.' He put his hand in the pocket of his jubba and said, 'I will give you just the amount of twenty-five rupees which you had given me.' Saying so he just threw the currency notes in front of the old man and walked out. Though he shouted to his daughter-in-law, 'Stop him, and catch him' she was just standing still, confused. Reaching the street Mohanlal disappeared in the crowd. He found a taxi a little distance away.

After reaching the flat, he dusted the tambura and then wiped it thrice with a wet cloth that had been rinsed clean, and then it could be touched by hand. The knobs had become so tight that they couldn't be turned even to a pin's size. He was afraid that if he turned them forcibly they might break or develop cracks. The strings had all rusted. It was because of the salty humid weather of Bombay. He remembered that it had been kept in the same place for thirty-two years. He decided to take it to the Sarasvati Musical Instruments Shop at Dadar, get the knobs corrected, get new strings tied and get the bridge examined. Didn't feel like going immediately. He was still in a mood to tune it, practise the swara and then sing a Badaa Khayal. He laid it down, took out the kumkum from the container, applied it in three different places on the tambura, the same kumkum he would apply to his forehead every morning after bath. He took a pinch and applied it vertically from the middle of the eyebrows to the centre of the top of the forehead. He applied it to the tambura of his daily practice, tuned it and started strumming. In front was visible to the half-closed eyes the tambura that had been presented to him with the blessing of his guru. He felt, even with closed eyes it was only the tambura that he was strumming with a full, overflowing heart. The swara was achieved. Not just in the throat but in the entire gamut of emotions. Now it is getting to be morning. There is the hint of twilight, dispelling the darkness, gently emanating from behind the edge of the east towards the sky. Quite unselfconsciously, the mood of Bhairav is taking shape. The lack of emotional involvement which was bothering and teasing him in recent months has disappeared. His voice means, it was a fertile cool land, and as soon as you put forth a crowbar, water would ooze out. For the last few months, his throat had become a sterile waste land. Now the original strength had returned. It was the grace of the tambura. This was the benediction and blessing of the guru. No matter if that tambura is not repaired. He felt that it was enough to apply kumkum to it, touch it with his eyes and then emotion would surge up. Descending into *sa ni dha, da* again and again and experiencing the mood of the raga, he was totally immersed. He was absorbed in the blessedness that he had been re-incarnated and that the life that had been lost was restored.

At that time the doorbell rang. He was angry. He remained immersed telling himself he wouldn't open the door. Not for anybody. Let them go back thinking I am not in. If it is someone known, they will push the door open gently and they should just listen to music. No, I won't speak a word. I won't even open my eyes, he decided and stayed on the music. The bell rang again. He felt he should remove and throw away the bloody thing. Still he continued, not opening his eyelids and not ceasing the swaras, sat determined not to give any let-up in his recital. Meanwhile the door had been pushed. It opened. He felt that no disciple of his or anybody from the music circles would push the door open so rudely. He opened his eyes and looked in that direction. The person who had entered was a policeman—not just a cop but an officer. From his uniform he looked like an Inspector. As soon as he saw that he had been noticed, he saluted. Then he turned back and stood aside. The man who came in was Vittal Junnarkar. Behind him was his son Anand Junnarkar. Behind both of them was a constable. He understood the situation immediately. The old man turned to the Inspector and pointed out, 'That one. The one which has been laid horizontally in front of you.'

The inspector asked, 'Panditji, this person has given a complaint that two hours ago you trespassed into his house and took away this tambura. Is it true that you did it?'

He was angry that when he was immersed in inspired emotion and the swaras were moving, this old man had brought the police. But he summoned all the patience at his command and narrated the whole story from the beginning when he had pawned it for twenty-five rupees till he had gone in the morning with one lakh and said, 'Yes. I brought my property by climbing his loft. Look at this. Can you understand the condition of the tambura? I have just cleaned the rusted strings, the tight knobs and wiped the instrument clean, performed the puja and kept it here. Right now, in your presence I will throw one lakh. Get me a receipt from him.'

The Inspector sat on the sofa and asked the old man Junnarkar, 'Is all this true?'

'The instrument became mine thirty-two years ago. Is he the only one who has seen money? When I say I won't return it, I won't. That's all.'

'You bastard, I am going to hit you,' Mohanlal said. He got up suddenly and took out a shoe from behind the door.

Junnarkar appealed to the Inspector, 'You are a police officer. You must record what he said in your presence and what he intends to do.'

The inspector said, 'You must have patience,' and then told Junnarkar, 'he is a musician. So are you. This tambura has rusted and has reached the stage of being thrown into fire. Because it is given to him by his teacher he is prepared to give one lakh. Instead of coming to an agreement between yourselves, you shouldn't bring the dispute to us. Though you are aged, because of some old hatred you are stubborn.'

'Hatred is his. Why do I want hatred or war?'

Though the inspector argued for about an hour, Vittal Junnarkar didn't relent. Didn't give up his smooth talk. He was also sitting next to the inspector on the sofa and was arguing. Mohanlal shouted, 'You old fellow, I was singing Raga Bhairav with great concentration, full of emotion after I brought this. If you were born to your father, you would have sat down and listened. If you were a true harmonium player, you would have picked up my harmonium and would have given me accompaniment. You say you don't want one lakh but want hatred.' He rushed forward and started beating up the old man.

The inspector stopped him only after a few blows either because he wanted the old man to be hit or because of the respect he had for the great musician. The son Anand Junnarkar came up and lifted his hand to thrash Mohanlal. The constable held him back. The inspector said, 'You have given a complaint that he came home and has carried away the tambura. It has not been stolen. He is saying that he has retrieved what he had pawned. As you wouldn't give it back, he is saying that he had brought one lakh to give you and is prepared to give you even now. You have also agreed that it had been pawned. Both of you come to the police station. Our clerk will record both your statements. Both of you sign it. Let the court decide whether it is a civil or a criminal case. I will now take the tambura, keep it in the station and give it to the custody of the court.'

Mohanlal shouted, 'Leave the tambura here. Go to any court you like. I am not afraid of this bastard. I know a thousand lawyers.'

The old man Junnarkar was stubborn. 'The case will not be complete by just this. This scoundrel calling me a bastard, taking up his shoe in his hand, beating me up before you, all this has to be recorded. Otherwise I won't leave it alone.'

The inspector looked at his face, there were no marks on the face to be reported to a doctor. He said, 'Look, I won't be a witness to all your quarrels. The main case is about the tambura. I will record that.' He ordered the constable to take up the tambura and told Mohanlal to come to the police station.

5

By the time he came back to the flat and had his lunch, there was a feeling of having been defeated. If I had gone to Dadar and had immediately given the tambura for repairs when the police came, I could have taken the stand that I had never gone to his house and I didn't know anything about the matter. This was an after thought. He felt sorry that he couldn't even guess that the old man would bring the police. Immediately a sense of defeat overtook him. He couldn't even go to bed. He felt that he should meet someone, that he needed someone and being alone would be very repressive sadness. When he was thinking about inviting someone he started thinking about which student could be asked to come. He become aware that each one would be busy with her own work and it would be difficult if he didn't decide about it a day earlier. He felt that it would be a change if he himself went to Bhoopali's flat instead of asking her to come. He called her, 'Hi, how about my coming to your flat and staying till evening?'

'Guruji, great! Shouldn't be upset by the chaos in my room. Please come right now,' she said.

It was quite a few days since he had slept with her. He felt it was a good change. The stress disappeared. He felt that she had that kind of power. After he had a short nap in her arms he told her about the events of the morning. She said, 'The old man must be a cantankerous scoundrel. I have heard the harmonium playing of the junior Junnarkar. His playing is not peaceful. His rendering doesn't suit your temperament at all.' He felt comforted. She continued, 'Guruji, stay the night here. It is months since we slept together during night. No matter how intense it is during the day, the peace and enjoyment of sleeping together at night cannot be obtained.'

On getting up in the morning and washing face, when he came to his flat in a taxi, he noticed that there was a newspaper stuck in the chink of the door. On opening it, there was a big title in the first page itself: 'Quarrel between two musicians. Prized tambura in police custody.' It also carried his large size photo. Surprised, he read on. They have printed everything, his invading the house of Junnarkar, going up the loft and bringing the tambura, Junnarkar giving a complaint to the police, everything had been given in detail. His statement also had been printed. When he was wondering how the newspaper men had got hold of all this information Wadekar came. He had come fifteen minutes earlier than usual. On seeing the newspaper in his hand, he said, 'There was this news in the morning papers. What's all this?'

'You also know about his keeping my tambura and irking me? The paper men have not written lies. But I was wondering how did all the papers get this information.'

'The police themselves give the information about their cases to the newspaper. Since you are famous, they have printed it on the first page itself.' When Wadekar was saying this, the phone clattered.

'This is Paranjape. I was ringing you all evening and till eleven at night. You weren't there.'

'Someone from my native place had come. I went to visit them.'

'You have seen today's newspaper, haven't you? The paper office received the information by four in the afternoon. I tried to meet you so that I could interview you and print it alongside. It doesn't matter. Even if there is a day's delay, it has its own advantage. Now please answer my questions. I will expose that fellow, Junnarkar.' Paranjape started asking questions. The interview on the telephone itself took half an hour with all the facts and explanations. After that, he asked, 'Which lawyer have you engaged?' 'Lawyer? Why should I engage a lawyer?' Mohanlal asked with surprise.

'Mohanji, what are you saying? There is a complaint against you of trespassing and taking away an object. No matter for what reason. You have accepted it. The property was in your house and the police confiscated it in your own presence. This old man has determined to bring a bad name to you. You employ a competent lawyer right away and follow his advice. I would suggest you meet Gore Saheb. He will fix up a good and able lawyer. Isn't it better than entering some unknown lawyer's office by looking at his name plate?'

He felt it was right. He was also concerned that he had not yet engaged a lawyer. When he was thinking that it was the right thing to see Gore Saheb, the phone rang. Hundreds of people who had read the morning newspapers began to call. Though all the details were in the newspaper, they started asking the same questions. There were calls from newspapers also. He felt tired after talking to them. While having his lunch, he disconnected the phone. Eating silently he began to perceive difficulties in seeing Gore Saheb. He remembered the words of Ramkumari that she wanted Gore to be her husband in the next birth. His mind concluded that there must be definitely some relationship between them. Because Bakula told her that the tenancy of Borivali house was in his name, it seems she has left it and has got a shack in Dahisar. It seems she is also angry that after she had brought up the children with such care all these years, they had fallen for the money of the father. Is it possible she hasn't mentioned this to Gore Saheb? If I go to him now, he might get the case spoilt, get me punished and take revenge. He was afraid. Paranjape doesn't know these details. He felt that he should engage a lawyer himself. Actually, many lawyers came to his concerts. There are even those who come directly from the court. After putting the dishes in the sink, he reinserted the telephone plug. It started bellowing right away. When he put the receiver to his ear, it was Tipnis, 'I have tried a score of times since morning but your phone was constantly busy. I had even called the telephone exchange to find out if the phone was out of order.'

'A hundred people have called since morning for the same reason you are calling me now.'

'I never thought that the old man would go so far, to such length.'

'He said that he would give me the tambura if I take only his son to accompany me and no one else. I got angry at that and did this.'

'A lawyer must be employed.'

'I wanted to see Gore Saheb. But he is angry with me an account of Ramkumari. I am afraid he might take revenge.' But he had not told Tipnis about the words Ramkumari had uttered about the next birth, though he wanted to, he felt ashamed and suppressed it.

'A year ago when Champa Bai was selling your cassettes, you had seen Gore Saheb hadn't you? Even then Ramkumari was a cook in his house. In spite of it he never spoke a word about it, did he? Remember one thing. His love of music is so great that he will swallow any defects of musicians. Don't you know this?

No matter how true Tipnis's words rang, he couldn't summon enough belief in Gore. When he was rolling about sleeplessly for a long time, the name of one Desai came to his mind. His house was in Girgaon. He had arranged his concert as a part of the celebration of his father's eightieth year. It seems he is a prominent advocate. He got up immediately and opened the box where he would put all the visiting cards. He went and started rummaging, one by one. After half an hour, he found it, Chamanlal Hirabhai Desai. High Court Advocate. Yes, this was the man. He felt comforted. He lay down and slept. In the morning, he fixed an appointment with Desai.

There was a front-page write-up by Paranjape in the morning's paper. He had written in great detail covering the details discussed over the phone, and the similar questions he had asked of Vittal Junnarkar. He had started by saying, 'Though it is natural for envy to exist between two people in the same profession…' he had gone on to mention how an important musician had pawned a tambura which he had considered sacred, now in a ruinous condition and how much money was demanded at what stage, how even one lakh was rejected, how he had put a condition that hereafter only his son should be taken for harmonium accompaniment—all these details had been mentioned. He had also set down the questions he had asked Junnarkar and how he had given evasive, non-committal answers. He had taken a picture of the tambura with rusted strings and had printed that too.

Mohanlal felt happy. He called Paranjape and expressed his gratitude. When he went to meet the lawyer Desai with both the newspapers, after looking at them, he said, 'There is nothing in this case. In the cross examination itself, the old man will flounder. Besides, it is not a case of stealing valuable ornaments or money. If it is put up for sale, the tambura will not fetch anything. But it looks as though the old man will stick to the case only to harass you. We will look after that. You shouldn't speak about this to anyone. He has also agreed that he has kept the tambura as pawn and for twenty-five rupees. Has he got a licence from the government to do the pawning business? He will stumble with just that point. But he might cantankerously manage to go to the high court. It might take six to seven years for you to get your tambura. That is the way our legal system works. You must be prepared.'

His mind was not prepared to accept this inevitability. His conviction that without that tambura his music would not acquire its original force of emotion was firm. He begged, 'Isn't it possible to get it to me soon?'

'If your opponent also spends money and drags on the case, it won't be possible. I am telling you from my own experience. Those who are intent on revenge are prepared to spend money. Or, it is possible that the lawyer is a friend or a relative of his. By the by, isn't Gore Saheb your well wisher?'

He was peeved that even this man had mentioned Gore's name. He didn't reply. Desai himself confined, 'I mentioned it because he is very concerned with the welfare of musicians. Actually, it was he who suggested that I should arrange a music concert on the occasion of my father's birthday. It was he who recommended your name. I don't know much about music. Neither does my father. Gore Saheb says everywhere that well-to-do people should arrange cultural events like dance and music on occasions of celebration and thus encourage art. He hands over his criminal cases only to me. Even if you had gone to him, he would have sent you to me. You came directly to me. I am happy.'

As if to escape from his dilemma, he was nodding ascent.

Three days after this, Desai called him in the morning. With the anxiety that something regarding the case had transpired he said, 'What has happened Sir?'

'Yesterday I had run into Gore Saheb in the High Court campus. I told him about you visiting me and about the case. It seems he too had read the newspapers. He said Pandit Mohanlal is a great singer. I am content that he has brought the case to you. He told me that I shouldn't accept the fee of even a single rupee from you, I accepted and said "yes". I will instruct my office today to that effect. My junior by name Pancholi will handle your case. I will also tell him. You please speak to him about anything concerning this case.'

Mohanlal was dumbstruck. He couldn't even think of thanking him. When he himself was asking, 'Hello, are you listening?' He was stammering like a student who had forgotten his musical notes.

For a fortnight this was the news in all papers—big and small. Several letters by the readers. Many people had condemned Junnarkar in hard words. They had raised the question of how such a philistine could be a musical accompanist. Since the English editions of the newspaper were being printed in Ahmedabad, Delhi, Bhopal, Lucknow, Jaipur, Hyderabad—places where Hindustani music lovers are in great number, the news spread everywhere. It became the feeding source for small newspapers; the readers wrote letters by spicing it up. Mohanlal was elated, finding that the entire world of music connoisseurs was on his side.

A week later, another happy news was published. Mohanlal had been chosen for that year's Tansen Award. Throughout the country people were saying that on account of his name and fame which drew millions of educated people to music who couldn't understand the technical aspect of classical music, who instilled music culture in scientists and technicians and attracted them to art, such a person should get the award. A flow of congratulations, letters phone calls and invitations of felicitations. His sense of inner emptiness receded. Enthusiasm began to flow forth when he took up the tambura. The scoundrels had delayed it all these years. Every year they have superseded me. He thought of hitting back at them by rejecting it. He thought in his pride that since he was bigger than this award, why should he demean himself by accepting it. But he kept quiet with the thought that if he did so, he would be antagonising the award, his predecessors who had received the award, millions of listeners who honour the awardees and the establishment that decides the award.

Paranjape rang up and said, 'Do you know that the old man Junnarkar is responsible for your getting the award this year?'

'How is that?'

'On account of the tambura episode your name had appeared in all the Indian newspapers. Its effect will certainly be there on the selection committee. I am saying this with my experience in the media. No matter how mature is the artist, unless he is in the news, he will not attract the attention of the selection committee.'

Mohanlal said, 'If you write this, the old man may say in his appeal that half the award money should go to him!' Both of them had a hearty laugh.

'Another bit of news. On account of your having received the award, all the music organisations of Bombay have decided together to give you a public felicitation. They want to give it a big publicity and arrange the function in the Wankhede Stadium so that a million people can come. After the felicitation you should sing for four to five hours. They are thinking of making Gore Saheb the President of the felicitation committee. I am telling you right now. You agree to sing. You tell them that you won't accept any money. That only the accompanists should be paid their fee. With this your prestige will increase.'

He felt happy. 'Yours is the last word,' he said.

The music lovers of Bombay said that never before had happened such an enormous classical music concert in Bombay. The entrance was free. There was immense publicity in all the newspapers as it was something arranged by all the music associations. The felicitation programme was from eight in the evening till quarter past nine. The concert was from half past nine to half past four in the morning. An interval of half an hour. Mohanlal himself felt that it had been quite some years since he had sung with such great enthusiasm. What Raghuvanshi, the secretary of the Mulund Music Academy said in his welcome speech, that more than a million people had gathered was true. What more was needed to boost his enthusiasm than the fact that so many people had come to felicitate him and listen to his music? A garland of fresh red roses as high as himself had been laid in front of him in the form of a bow. Though he sang continuously for six hours, he wasn't tired. His voice did not shrink. There was another reason for his euphoria. At the conclusion of the concert, Ram Tekekar, the President of the Bombay Fort Music Association, offering the vote of thanks said, 'Thirty-two years ago, such a great musician had pawned his tambura when he was in financial difficulties. The son of a harmonium player who makes his living as a harmonium accompanist has lodged a police complaint in spite of the offer of one lakh rupees to redeem it. If that man doesn't voluntarily withdraw the case and return the tambura to Mohanlalji by taking twenty-five rupees within two weeks, no music association in Bombay will invite him to any programme. We have, through this declaration, sent out a message that no vocalist of India should invite him to accompany. He should not be invited by any music association.' The audience clapped and cheered when this was announced. This applause was enough for the great encouragement of that night's performance.

All the newspapers carried a front page report and large photographs of the felicitation and the ocean of people, the audience next day. On the second day, Paranjape called and said, 'The warning that was given to Junnarkar was by the instruction of Gore Saheb. Both the father and son are frightened. It seems they have already asked their lawyer to prepare the application for the withdrawal of the case.'

Mohanlal felt grateful to Gore Saheb. He remembered that Gore Saheb was helping him continually. Paranjape said, 'It's good if you meet Gore Saheb and thank him. He has arranged for the biggest felicitation given to any musician so far in Bombay. If he was not at the back of it, it wouldn't have been possible for so many music associations to come together.'

'I will see him', he said.

He felt embarrassed to go and meet him. Gore Saheb knows that Ramkumari has moved to a different house. It is not possible for Gore Saheb to have any respect for Mohanlal's personal life. Yet, he has ignored all that and has done this without uttering a single word. Mohanlal was afraid to meet him face to face. Still he felt he should go and meet him without fail. He could not sleep properly because of the anxiety of facing him. He felt it would be good if he went and met him first thing in the morning and get over with it. He decided to call him that day itself and fix up an appointment. He had the office number. The number of the residence could also be found in the directory. But he was afraid that Ramkumari might also be at home. He could contact him when he called at ten. He said, 'Sir, this is Mohanlal. I would like to meet you and obtain your blessings. I called to find out when you would be free.'

'Oh, I wanted to call up myself. I was very busy for the last three days. Is half past four this afternoon convenient for you?'

'I have no other plans. I will definitely come.'

He went to fruit stall cum florist, bought expensive fruits, got them neatly packed in a bamboo basket with a rose-coloured gift packet. He also bought a large bouquet, carried them to the chamber of Gore Saheb, delivered the bouquet into his hands, made him touch the basket of fruits and placed it on the table and bent down and touched his feet. Gore embraced him. Mohanlal himself started the conversation by saying that it was because of his grace that all this had happened. 'Nobody's grace can do anything if there is no innate artistic merit. Please sit down.'

After chatting about the music in general, he asked, 'Sir, how was the concert the other night?'

'Didn't the audience listen with rapt attention?'

'Yes, the audience listened but what did you think of it?' He didn't reply at once. With the desire to find out whether he could get an answer to his inner feeling of emptiness, Mohanlal pressed for an answer.

He merely said, 'I am already seventy-one.' Didn't give a direct answer.

'You are a mature listener. Please don't hide anything. Tell me.'

'It was all right. It is not possible for any technical fault to be in your singing. But it was mechanical. As if the feeling was dried up. The same movements, the same beats. It was as though you were singing with the strength of old practice. There was nothing new. There was no innovation. There was no experience of any novelty. There was no unexpected turning.' He was just watching his face as if he was in agreement with him. A minute later, he said, 'Anyway, I don't know much about the shastra or theory part of it. I am just an ordinary listener.'

'You are an initiated listener, only the opinion of people like you is important. The scholars will have lesser understanding of the emotional aspect,' he said.

'Have you thought about why this has been happening to you? I had this feeling when I listened to the cassette of your Chicago concert. I think I even told you about it. Certain questions arise in my mind. Should every artist refine and revise his own method of singing from time to time? Or, should he understand anew the nuances of the raga? Or, is it that our musicians don't have the habit of reading serious literature and philosophical works to nourish their mind apart from just singing? Or cogitation about why do I sing and what meaning I am putting forth through a particular raga. Is it that they don't have a clear notion of it? Because emotion is also a sort of meaning, commentary and criticism. If the flash of meaning stops, do only habit and practised sounds come out? Such varied questions do arise in my mind. I was thinking of sitting down with you and discussing these things. I am very happy you yourself turned up.'

He couldn't think of an answer to any of these questions. Though he was looking at Gore Saheb's face, his eyes were betraying emptiness. After a couple of minutes he changed the subject. He talked about the changes that were taking place in the music concerts, the singers of the new generation etc. Tea was ordered. After speaking to him for about forty-five minutes, Mohanlal got up, prostrated and left.

He began to think that his own feeling that the emotion in his voice had dried up and the judgement of Gore Saheb that his music had become mechanical meant the same thing. He also began to understand that at the Chicago concert itself, the mechanical nature had set in and he hadn't noticed it. He couldn't think of why. He began to ask himself whether it was because he had no intellectual hobby, as Gore Saheb had suggested or because he simply didn't have the ability to understand the meaning of emotional involvement.

४

It is the custom of the three day festival of music, held in Gwalior, where Tansen's grave is situated, to begin the overnight programme of the first day, by conferring the award. The award winning musician must sing that night. If his concert is immediately followed by receiving the award, many listeners may leave. It is a trick of the organisers to arrange the programme of the famous and crowd pulling singers at the end. Many artists have the feeling that to be placed last is a sign of bestowing honour on them and showing their greatness and importance. It had been decided that Mohanlal should sing by dawn at the very end after five singers. The last singer could sleep and take rest in the hotel and arrive a little before the start of his concert. The organisers would arrange for the hotel people to wake up the singer on time and provide him with a wash, tea and bring him to the concert. Half an hour before starting off to receive the award, a woman who looked like a singer came to Mohanlal's room. Thick hair, dyed black and parted in the middle. Silk sari. A choli with a wide border, gold bangles, a necklace, and diamond ear rings. She touched the ground near his feet with her fingers and touched the top of her forehead, where sindoor was applied. She had no place to sit. She said, 'Guruji, I have a request. Mine is the second item this evening. I have one hour's duration. You must kindly listen to me and then go for rest. I came only to make this request. I will consider myself blessed if you listen as I am not a famous artist.'

Mohanlal greeted her and got up to provide some place for her. One of the visitors got up and gave up his place. But she didn't sit.

'My name is Jawahar Bai. I am from Jodhpur. If you promise to listen to me I will leave.'

He said, 'Certainly I will.' She left.

He was looking at her attentively when she was singing. A vague remembrance of having seen her somewhere. He couldn't place her. Not a very talented signer. But she was singing what she knew with feeling. The diamond ear rings, the gold ornaments and the silk, embroidered sari were giving the impression that she was from a rich family. He thought he might have met her when he had gone to Jodhpur. Or she, might have invited him to dinner. Her age couldn't be guessed. He became aware that the faces of some women have the magic of concealing the age. In such music festivals the singers won't have the choice to select the raga they are going to sing before and, they must sing some raga relevant for the time. They must select from what has been left over from the first singer. Still it was not bad. Bihaag. While singing she was glancing at him from time to time as if to seek his approval and as if to say she did not have power to express more nuances and expansion than this. It seemed she was implying that if she was committing any mistake, to forgive it. He nodded a couple of time as if to say 'excellent'. Another time when she reached the saam, he intoned fairly loudly '*Kya baat hai*,' and showed the gesture of saam with his right hand. She registered gratitude and fulfilment on her face. She bent down her head, neck and chest in a gesture of prostrating to him.

Mohanlal came out of the enclosure as soon as her singing was over. The volunteer who had been assigned exclusively to him approached him. He took him to the car as soon as he mentioned the hotel. Mohanlal couldn't sleep. There were only three more singers. It was midnight already. It was not just the anxiety that he would be woken up at half past three. His mind had been elated by the award that had been given to him. So many associations and organisation had bestowed honours on him. But somehow there was something special about his experience this time. The name of Tansen was one reason. He had been honoured on the platform erected right in front of Tansen's tomb. In the citation they have written that he was the present day Tansen in the opinion of the connoisseurs. How many ragas are still prevalent today in Tansen's name! Miyaan ki Malhar, Miyaan ki Todi, Darbari, Miyaan ki Saranga, Deepak, Basant, Megh-malhar. What raga have I created by which I will be remembered after my death? What new forms have I given to the old ragas as he has done? These questions made him sad. What raga shall I sing here today? I have not created any raga which can be called Mohan-Bhairav, Mohan-Lalit or Mohan-Todi? I have not created any raga which can be called after my name. The idea itself didn't occur to me. He felt, 'When Mohanlal dies, nothing will be left. No disciple has been trained who will mention my name. The guru must be spiritually meritorious to find a disciple who will keep alive the name of the guru.' The awareness that he didn't have such a good fortune deepened his sense of sadness and he kept rolling about.

Though it was half past four in the morning, the audience hadn't moved a bit. Those who felt sleepy had taken a nap just where they were sitting and had got rid of their somnolence. The secretary mentioned in his welcome speech that so many people had come and were waiting just to listen to the singing of panditji. Though it was the Indian style of sitting on the floor, due to lack of space, the people were sitting back to back with folded legs. When he saw this ocean of listeners, he got enthused. Self-confidence dawned. The singer from Jodhpur was sitting in the reserved enclosure for artists and special invitees. By her side was her husband who was sitting leaning against a fat pillow, stretching his legs a bit. The royal head gear of a king and a black Jodhpuri coat. White sherwani. His hair as well as sumptuous moustache had been dyed black. Age, nearing seventy, two rings—must be diamond—for the fingers of the left hand and one for the right hand. A wrist watch with a gold chain. Is she from the royal family? Her colour and physiognomy indicated she wasn't. When the secretary, at the end, of the welcome speech, mentioned that since it was the Tansen Music Festival, Pandit Mohanlalji, the winner of the Tansen Award would sing Miyaan ki Todi, the entire audience clapped lustily as if this was what they wanted and expected. He got enthused. In how many places and how many times had he not sung this raga? He entered the shadja with the self confidence of the one who knew all the spots of aesthetic essence, sophisticated intricacies, the variations of emotions, its twists and turns and its movements of rasa. The audience was totally silent. He got completely absorbed as if even Tansen was listening from the other world. Like a captain of a ship who has moved about the ocean thousands of times, and has the perfect knowledge of the route, Mohanlal plumbed the height, width and depth of the raga. Tipnis was playing harmonium and was moving with him with all the knowledge and was following with able sophistication and giving support. Prabhu, the tabla player, in addition to following the rhythm of the ebb and flow of the sea was also showing the time beat. Mohanlal experienced within himself the inner knowledge, that the feelings of wonder and marvel have captured the mind of the audience, and he felt the exhilaration of a magician, when he knows that he has completely mesmerised them who were experiencing the wonder of it all. He sailed forward, cutting across the waves of emotion with a sense of fulfilment thinking what else was needed more than that. He himself felt that when he reached madhya-laya, the heartbeats of the audience had surrendered their own natural rhythmic heartbeat and were beating to the rhythm that he had created. No matter how much he elaborated and how many patterns of rhythms he changed, they were unaware of the passing of external time. When he touched the final crescendo of shadja, the audience was so dumbfounded they didn't even remember to clap and applaud.

Meanwhile, it was sunrise. After the audience had listened to such an elaborate expansion of Todi, they even didn't have the desire to request for another raga. When the secretary stood up to express a vote a thanks and said, 'Mia Tansen's body may be inside the tomb. But his living consciousness has proclaimed that Pandit Mohanlal is the emperor of music, after listening to this Todi.' The entire audience went on applauding for a long time in approval.

When he came back to his hotel room, had his breakfast and lay down, he chastised himself as stupid for thinking that his inspiration had dried up when, actually, there would be high-tide and low-tide in the ocean and such was his case. In a little while he got deep sleep. Though there were some ups and downs in his sleep, he wasn't awake until half past three. It was a polite understanding that the award-winners should stay for all the three days. It had been decided that Tipnis and Prabhu would leave in the morning. After rolling about for another half an hour, getting up, shaving and taking shower, the euphoria came to an end and the feeling of a lack-lustre downward trend began. Where was anything new in what I sang in the morning? The same old movements, the same variations and the same tanas? He felt what was it except mechanical repetition? But so many were utterly captured. How they clapped away in ecstasy after secretary's speech. But the speeches of welcome and thanksgiving are always concluded in exaggerated language. It has no value. It is true the people have liked Todi. Many of them have listened to my singing for the first time. The rest of them may have listened to my rendering of other ragas. Even if they had, it might have been several years ago. It was new to them. What's new in it for me? Such negative questions began to appear. But then, which singer can really sing new and newer things? Everybody sings the same ragas, in the tradition of their own schools. Why should I think that only my own was mechanical? Consoling himself thus, he put on his clothes. It was past lunch time. Telling himself that he would have dinner by seven and go to the festival, he rang up room service and ordered some snacks. Right behind the waiter came the singer from Jodhpur. She touched his feet and said, 'Guruji, there are some twenty-thirty people waiting to see you. You have hung the "Do not disturb" sign on your door. I was also waiting. I just barged in with this boy. I must have a private conversation with you. There is a personal matter to discuss. You have forgotten me. My husband will leave for the venue at half past six. The others also who are staying in this hotel leave at the same time. Please go late by at least one hour. I will stay and talk to you. If you think that people will come here, come to my room. We are also staying in this same hotel.'

His curiosity got inflated by her saying, 'You have forgotten me.' 'Please identify yourself,' he said. 'At seven when you come. Now people are waiting. Please finish your snacks soon,' she said and went out.

ऽ

He had an early dinner and returned. She came and took him to her room. He found that this was a suite—with a drawing room to receive the guests, a boudoir, a master bedroom and a bath with a large tub—the sort that is given to very very important people. She closed the door of the room, sat him on a chair and she sat on the bed opposite and asked, 'Don't you still recognise me?' He remembered the same question asked by his daughter Bakula and his distasteful situation when she didn't say directly who she was and he thought she was just another desirable girl. She persisted, 'In the course of my singing Bihaag I introduced the gait of Maarubihaag to induce you to recognise me. Purposely I experimented with Komala-nishada. Didn't you know even then?' He was chagrinned that she was teasing him without talking directly.

'No, please tell me directly.'

'Thirty-four years ago you had come to my room in Bombay. An old harmonium. You corrected my faulty Maarubihaag. After that you sang for an hour and demonstrated.'

Now suddenly he remembered. The picture of an old memory bothering him of having seen her somewhere was placed correctly on the page of memory and the links tagged themselves on to form a whole picture. He looked at her face steadily. Then she was thin and anaemic. She had artificial ornaments on her body. A cheap and gaudy sari. Now she was wearing a gorgeous, embroidered pure silk sari, diamond earrings, gold bangles upto her elbows, a thick necklace covering her entire neck. Remembering the time when he was finding it difficult to get a programme though he offered to sing for twenty-five rupees and recollecting his state of going to whore houses to satisfy his lust, his body began to shiver. Now she was certain that he remembered. Noticing his face was getting contorted, she said at once, 'It was a situation of my life which couldn't be shared with anyone. I guess the same is true in your life too. Now that we have met, we can reminisce together. You know, that day I listened to your Maarubihaag for one hour. You left. I yearned for you, not for making love. Not the way Radha longed for Krishna. But to learn music from you. But where to search for you? Perhaps if I had sent Bhaaijan after you, he would have found out! But what means of livelihood was there in Bombay for someone like me? One must earn by giving concerts that means, by selling music. I didn't have the level of musical education to do that in that big city. Or, one must earn by selling one's body. After all, it is a commercial centre. At what a big scale the flesh trade is carried on there quite shamelessly! I determined to leave that city. Again, I went back to my native city, Udaipur. It is much better. At least ten or twenty connoisseurs would come in the evening. They would chew paan. They would ask me to sing their favourite song. After each song, when I saluted them, each one would give at least a rupee. Some would ask me to give them paan with my own hand putting it in their mouth. That would be five rupees. All in all, by eleven in the evening, I would get a hundred to a hundred and fifty rupees. After paying the tabla and harmonium accompanists, I would be left with a fifty or seventy-five rupees. It was left to my will and wish to take a customer to bed or not. It was entirely my option. To tell the truth, after I served you that night I never went to bed with anyone. I am a singer, I decided not to serve anyone who couldn't sing better than me and who could be my guru. I remained that way.'

'Your present husband?'

'Why do you use the respectful plural "aapka"? Say "tumhara". Didn't you understand I called you Guruji? It is not good for the disciple to be addressed in the plural. One day, this person came. He remained even after the other connoisseurs left. Or, the others left early noticing his royal look and dignified face. This person said, "I want to remain the night or you come to my place." I said, "I don't do that kind of business. If you want you can stay the night, I will sing the whole night." He said, "All right. I don't like Thumri, abhinaya and erotic songs that these people want. Will you sing pure classical music? The raga I want?" I felt happy that he had knowledge of music. I was also afraid. I said, "I am not an expert. I will sing to the extent I know." He looked at his pocket watch. It was ten. He said, "Will you sing Megh-malhar? I feel like listening to it." I sang as elaborately as I could. I further extended it with repeated variations. It was obvious from the expression on his face that he was happy. I understood that he could recognise and enjoy the raga, its variations but doesn't have the knowledge of swara or shastra. Where could one find even such a connoisseur! After that he asked me to sing all the forms of Malhar. I sang to the extent of my acquaintance of the raga. Where did I have the knowledge to sing each variation in depth and detail? Meanwhile he felt sleepy. He asked, "Do you have whisky with you?" I said, "No". He left, saying, "OK I will come tomorrow." He didn't pay even a rupee. Nothing for the accompanists, either. After he left, the accompanists laughed, calling him a stage-king! I couldn't tolerate their speaking lightly about him. Wouldn't they feel bad about making them work for two hours and leave without paying anything? As for me, I was feeling happy that a person who could appreciate music had come. It was morning. He turned up again around midday. Which singer's house will be ready at that time? Even if the floor has been swept, the carpet will not have been spread. The singer will not have decked herself with make up. The preparation starts in the evening. It is a strict rule that without make up, the face shouldn't be shown to anyone. But I had opened the door myself and had shown myself. He had come in even before I had invited him in. He ordered the coachman to leave. A small handbag in his hand. He put it before me and said, "I know that at this time you won't be ready. What do I care about your make up! I have brought lunch in this bag. You shouldn't be engaged in cooking. I have come to listen to a midday raga. Which raga will you sing? My liking is both Brindaavani-saranga and Bheempalasi. After them you can sing what you like." His request was an order. I didn't have the strength to say no. Where did I have the knowledge to sing the ragas one after another thus, I said that it was not possible to get the accompanists just like that

"Don't want any accompaniment, you sing by yourself. Don't you have a tambura?" I was excited that there was someone who asked for a tambura. I took out the dust covered instrument leaning in the corner, tuned it, placed a soft big pillow for him to lean on and sat before him. Though I had taken bath, I was wearing an old sari. No make up for the face. No ornaments. Still I sang. He was immediately coming out with an appropriate response. I sang with aplomb. After the two ragas, he asked, "Your choice?" I queried, "Multaan?" "Yes, do sing," he said. By the time I finished, he put his hand in the breast pocket of his Jodhpur coat, took out a watch with a gold chain, took a look and said, "I have some other work. I am very pleased. Here, take this." He took out a wad of hundred rupee currency notes, counted ten and held it before me. I got up, approached him, saluted him in the traditional manner and extended both my hands. After he placed it in my hand, he drew out two more notes and said, "Give this to the artists who gave you the accompaniment." I touched the money to my eyes and walked backwards a few steps as is the custom in the presence of royalty. He stated to go out.

"His Highness doesn't seem to be from Udaipur. I was not favoured with information of where he is from."

"Jodhpur. Business brings me to Udaipur. I will come again." He asked, "Can you fetch me a carriage?"

Mohanlal remembered his guru, Raja Saheb. She continued, 'Since that day his memory started to bother me. Not anything else. If someone like him became my patron, I could give up my profession of *ganewali* and could learn music seriously. I prayed to god daily. He came after three months one afternoon. He got the horse-carriage up to the door and knocked. He came in said, "I didn't ask your name. You also didn't mention."

"Jawahar Bai."

"Listen. The property dispute in this town has been settled. There is no possibility of my coming this way. Now, there is no kingship. Not even the wealth of a king. I am not even the direct descendent to the kingdom. Still I belong to the royal family. If you come to Jodhpur, I will make you a paaswaan. Do you know about the practices of royalty? Do you know what paaswaan means?"

"My mother was paaswaan in Udaipur. After the kingship was gone, I descended to this position."

"Don't worry. I will buy a house in your name. Two shopping complexes that fetch rent. Ornaments galore. And also, I will look after your expenses as long as I live. The paaswaan should remain as faithful as the wife herself. Should always be learning and practising music. I will make arrangements for you to learn from any maestro in

Jodhpur. After you reach proficiency, there are no restrictions on your going out to give concerts. You must always act with the honour and dignity in keeping with the position of paaswaan. Will you come?"

'I couldn't believe my own ears. I was hoping for just such an opportunity. It was beyond my imagination that he would come and invite me. I just stood dumb founded. "What do you say? If you want, you can think about it until tomorrow."

Immediately a question sprang up in my mind. "Won't Her Royal Highness hate me? Won't it create disruption in the royal household?"

"The queen is born into the proper Rajput household. One who knows the habits and ways of the royal Rajput men. Her Highness will never descend below the level of her dignity."

'There aren't many great singers in Jodhpur. Are there?' Mohanlal asked.

'There are theoretical, knowledgeable experts. This is an art that should be learnt from an artist. For four years, I would travel to Jaipur by train twice a month and would have my lessons. To develop music, a singer stays in a place where there are musicians and where concerts take place frequently. Thus I didn't develop much.'

'Still, you sang well,' he uttered words of enthusiasm.

'I had seen you in Bombay, hadn't I? I couldn't forget your face. Afterwards, whenever I saw your photo in the newspapers I felt that this is him. It had also appeared recently in the newspapers that a harmonium accompanist was harming you without returning you the tambura which you had pawned and that you encroached and brought back. My Lord, the Raja Saheb himself saw it and showed it. Even when I looked at that photo I thought it was you.'

He was about to burst out that it was with that money that he had visited her, but suppressed it. She enquired, 'I am talking myself all the time. I have told you my story. You haven't said anything. Tell me, 'How many children do you have?'

'Children!' He became introspective. After waiting for a couple of minutes, she said, 'No matter. I also don't have any children. Our disciples who mention our name are our children. Do you know what I had imagined? You are the star of this celebration. All your disciples would have come. The important among them would be sitting on either side of you, playing the tambura. From time to time they would be lending support. When you allow them, they would even sing a little. The number of Pandit Mohanlalji's tradition of disciples is growing, people should find satisfaction that his style of singing is continuing. Some people who were sitting behind me were talking about it. Such a great maestro, why hasn't he brought even a single student to such a prestigious occasion? Hasn't he trained any disciple at all! For artists who are always on the move, don't have time and inclination to train up students. Didn't any of your children have the music culture? Weren't they musically inclined?'

He couldn't think of an answer to get out of this predicament. He looked at her with lacklustre eyes. She said, 'Jodhpur and Bombay are so far apart. Otherwise, I entertained the hope of sometime coming to Bombay once a month and learning from you. But you are such a busy artist. I kept quiet because it wasn't possible. Besides, I was past the age when I could travel so far and learn. Even to learn, one must have strength in the body.'

Perhaps she would have gone on and on this way. He couldn't find anything to say. He began to get depressed. He didn't have the energy to sustain what she was saying. He began to feel that she had come to hurt him. He got so angry he wanted to call her a whore. He refrained and looked at his watch. He said, 'Very good, I felt very happy meeting you. The programme is going on. If I am not there, people will think I am arrogant.' She touched his feet in obeisance.

६

He was sitting right in the front row, learning against the comfortable pillow meant only for him. All the singers would begin only after paying him respects by folding their hands in a namaskar. The person who came to the platform now was Kalindi Prasad Tiwari from Darbhanga, about sixty. His own age. Drupad singer. Behind him two tambura playing disciples. The boy was thirty. The girl was twenty-five. Two young people—a young man and a young woman. They took their place in a dignified manner, as Drupad singers do. The secretary who in his welcome speech after describing the musical achievement of Tiwari, introduced the fellow artists. 'The person sitting on his right with the tambura is his son and disciple, Kalindi Prasad Tiwari. The lady sitting to his left is his disciple Janhavi Sinha. Both of them will assist their guru in his singing. Besides these, the three, sitting at the back are also his students.' Like all Khayal singers, Mohanlal also had great love and respect for Drupad. That is what Tansen sang. Not just because it is believed that Tansen's guru, Swami Haridas taught him that, but Mohanlal was fond of it because he loved the quality of Drupad which would dwell on the swaras with dignity, and the purity of mind that of a sage. Tiwari also began with the same impeccable austerity the swara-alaap of Bageshree. He was giving a chance to his son, from time to time. Even the son had perfect purity of swara. The meends like boats touching the waves and swimming and attaining the destination. Excellent training. Mohanlal felt, the son would do credit to his father's fame. Then the second opportunity to the girl—disciple. She wasn't bad either. The dignity of the River Janhavi. He felt that she had been given a disciplined training. He sensed someone speaking softly at the back, 'Though a female voice, how mature the achievement of drupad!' Mohanlal looked back. The people at his back were Jawahar Bai and her Lord and Master. Jawahar whispered, 'Please speak softly.' The son had reached the level of giving independent concerts. Mohanlal felt even the lady disciple was all right. He remembered all the three questions of Jawahar Bai. How many children do you have? Did none of them have music culture? Didn't they have a desire to learn music? Why didn't you train a disciple who would perpetuate your name? Statistically, he engendered five children. None of them had remained with him. For the first time, the reality that he hadn't tried to keep them with him dawned on him. He remembered that of the five, the first one couldn't even be mentioned as his and felt sad. He had never bothered about that child of the coolies of Chittarpur territory who appeared vaguely in his memory and disappeared. Now it began to trouble him. Supposing I meet him now and tell him 'I am your father,' will he listen to me? When the question arose, 'Do I have the courage to say so?' he was further perturbed, and there was an inner turmoil. The alaap of Bageshree was proceeding at a dignified pace. But his mind was occupied by Chunni who wanted to have a son and his lusty copulation. Though her object was to have a son, it was not without her sexual desire. She got both the things she wanted. My mad urge found a tolerable pace of calmness. Again the mind engaged in the practice of music. Why should the memory of that child trouble me now? If every incident of life falls like a rock of moral magnitude, how can the outlet for the riverbed of life open up? The explanation occurred that it is only in smooth-flowing rivers without rocks that boating and pleasant ramble are possible. The other four children anyway are legally mine. If everything was all right and they had grown up with me, one or two of them, a boy or a girl perhaps might have become a singer. Even now, Bakula is fond of and devoted to music. The thought that if he had taught her since she was a child, was diverted by the anger thinking what kind of mother she was who had moved away from both son and daughter because they had come to him. In what way is she better than me? I am better than her. I have given two lakhs to Kishan. I will give him two more if he asks. I am ready to spend money and see that the bride is given away properly. What sort of a mother is she who deserted her daughter at the stage of her wedding? The thought brought him some comfort. The sentence of judgement that she was a mean and stubborn woman pronounced itself. The alaap reached its crescendo in Tiwari's singing and his face became contorted. He turned to his left and said, 'Beti, bring the Tambura close to my ear.' It is always like this when the tambura accompanists, in about half an hour, lean the instrument against the shoulder, as if the sound of throbbing is to fill their own ear and not the singer's. I also get angry like this. But I have never addressed the person as Beti, had never felt like it. In big cities, it was usually some local professional or some glamour girl of the town who would rush in to accompany the singer. He remembered he had never addressed any of them as daughter or sister. I have never rejected any boy who came to learn music. But have never taken the interest I have in girls. It is perhaps because of the memory that even among girls he had rejected teaching girls who didn't submit themselves, that he had no student who would perpetrate his name as a guru. How many even among girls, stuck to music? Marriage, children and family, when he thought how many of them would perpetuate his name, he remembered Madhu. She was ready to marry me if I was prepared to divorce Champa. Not even that. Had I even promised that I wouldn't touch any other woman and had garlanded her in a temple saying, 'I am for you and you are for me,' even then, by now, she would have become a singer of national level who would be known as Mohanlal's disciple. She madly went off, marrying. A mad one, she then suffered the guilt of infidelity towards her husband...Now for the first time the question arose whether it could be called madness. It could be her self-criticism that appeared. I must have accepted it as not my criticism and should have started the lessons. She would have reached a considerably high level in this one year. Within two or three years she would be able to mention the name of her guru in the entire country. He realised that she had a moral pride and his decision to destroy it was responsible for the breakdown. For the first time suddenly in his life he realised how simple it was if one could think of the disciple as daughter, how simple the relationship would be. Tiwari was sitting like a statue and was building the raga as an edifice. He announced in the middle, 'This is the pure style of Tansen. Tansen was singing in Drupad,' and continued. Did he make this comment on observing me? Mohanlal suspected Tiwari might be deriding him by implying that he himself was the next in line for Tansen and not me? He got suspicious. But he should not show any reaction. It was not decorum of the assembly. Or, was he suggesting, 'Why did you give the award for this Mohanlal, overlooking me?' He felt jealous. But Tiwari was singing in all seriousness. He felt a bit comforted noticing when Tiwari said this, he wasn't looking at him. Drupad singers were always saying this. The explanation also occurred that he said it in anger that the audience won't come if it is only a Drupad concert. There is no levity in this. There is no attraction of swings. Everything is sublime, like the Vedic chanting. It is fit to be sung in rituals and sacrifices. It doesn't have the quality of making the mind dance about in merriment. The gurus who teach this, what else can they call their disciples, except 'beti'? In true art all the rasas must be there. The sentiment of eroticism must be present even to a little extent in all the rasas. He comforted himself by telling himself, 'What do the Drupad singers know about erotic sentiment?'

In the wee hours of the morning he left out the last singer, went back to the hotel and went to bed. He couldn't get to sleep for a long time. All the Hindustani singers claim that they belong to Tansen's tradition in one way or another. Whoever is going to mention my name? I am neither an establisher of a gharana nor have I trained even three or four disciples who can perpetuate my name. This emptiness began to tease him. Has any rumour spread that Mohanlal doesn't accept male students, even without my own knowledge? He suspected may be that was the reason why talented boys were not coming to him. After some time he wondered if the parents are not sending their sons to him thinking that Mohanlal was a man without character and their sons would ruin themselves in his company. However, girls are coming. If there was any such objection, the parents of the girls should prevent them. He found some solace. After some more time the question arose—should an artist be a saint? Otherwise won't art favour him? Meanwhile he fell asleep.

When the concert was going on, he went to Tansen's grave and sat there. Though the music was audible, since the loud speakers were turned away in the other direction, the sound was not piercing the ears, he remembered that he had never come like this to Tansen's grave and sat there. How did Tansen get such mastery over music? Is it purely congenital? Is it continuous devotion and practice? If it is practice, haven't I practised? Am I not still practising? He plunged himself in thought. He couldn't find an answer, no matter how much he thought. By midnight, the secretary of the event came and said, 'Panditji, you are sitting here. We were searching for you. Now the Dagar family is going to sing. Everyone has decided that it is proper that you should garland them. Would you please come?' He went. After garlanding, he sat leaning against his pillow. He remembered that this family boasted that they were the perpetuators of the pure form of Tansen's tradition. 'May be so,' he thought and started listening. In a little while, he remembered the prevalent story regarding Tansen's rendering of Deepak and Megh ragas. Tansen implored Emperor Akbar not to force him to sing Raga Deepak fully as he would catch fire and die if he did. Still Akbar was stubborn. Knowing that he was in grave danger, Tansen taught its counterpart opposite Raga Megh to his daughters Sarasvati and Gurubhaagini Roopavati. He arranged for them to start singing the alaap for Megh at home as soon as he begins Raga Deepak and then he came to the palace grounds and sat on the dias. In order to witness this extraordinary rendering of the rare raga and its effect, people in thousands gathered—citizens, officers, royal family relatives etc. A little while after the alaap of Deepak began, the entire area in which it could be heard, a hot summer's heat started. The people and Emperor Akbar were wiping their perspiration. By the time the raga touched the second stage, the eyes of Tansen became blood red. On reaching the third stage, Tansen's body got lit by fire. By the time the fourth, final stage was being completed, the entire area was enveloped with the flames of fire and spread and it spread. Everyone—the citizens, Emperor Akbar, the officials, the generals and the royal relatives—everyone started screaming and running helter skelter. Tansen came home, running, with a burning body. By that time Sarasvati and Roopavati concluded the worshipping part and had started the alaap of Megh. The moment she saw Tansen entering, flaming, Roopavati started singing with all intensity. That very moment the sky became overcast. The entire city was plunged in darkness. Whirlwind started blowing. There was thunder and lightning filling the firmament with frightful fits. Sarasvati picked up the second stage of the raga. The clouds in the sky became deep black. It started raining in torrents and the whole city was drenched and there was water everywhere. Tansen's burning body became cool. After that he had to stay in bed for a month for the wounds to be healed. Therefore Tansen never used to sing the Raga Deepak in detail. He would just introduce the raga and stop. He remembered that a variation of the story was prevalent all over Hindustan. He had heard the story on the banks of the Ganga, narrated by the sadhus at Har-ki-pauri, even before he joined the Omkar Ashram at Hardwar. Every music guru and musician narrates this in some form or the other. What is its meaning? When he had asked this question with Raja Saheb the latter had said that music was fundamentally an act of yoga, and that through the yogic act, it was possible to influence the five elements. He said that it is mentioned in the shaastra that if music is attained at the highest yogic level, it was possible to influence the corresponding elements with the singing of appropriate ragas. It is said Tansen brought on the darkness of midnight by singing the midnight ragas at midday. He brought on the sunshine of midday at midnight by singing midday ragas. Though he remembered that he had understood all this as mere symbolic, allegorical, figurative representations of describing the power of music, his mind became absorbed in the yogic level of music. He began to feel that music was but another face of yoga, indeed a mantra.

By the sunrise, when the festival came to a close with the Todi by Dagar family and everyone left, Mohanlal went again to the tomb of Tansen, placed his forehead on it and prayed that his music also may acquire the yogic powers that Tansen had. All of a sudden something flashed forth. Tansen got the power of his music from his music guru Swami Haridas. He was not just a musician but a great yogi. But I learnt from a temporal king, Raja Saheb. Though he was also talking about yoga, he was not a total yogi—a spiritual seeker. Mohanlal remembered that though he was singing only in the Mahadev temple, it was because he had been bound by his word of honour to his ustad Asad Ali Khan. Suddenly he felt like visiting Brindavan, having come so near. There are any number of trains from Gwalior to Mathura, from where Brindavan is only a matter of six or seven miles. The moment he felt about it, he decided. As soon as he got to the hotel and had finished his shower and breakfast, he asked the secretary to send him to Brindavan. He got the eleven o'clock train.

7

A field surrounded by well grown thick holy basil plants. River Yamuna to the right. A statue of Swami Haridas in the temple. No rush of pilgrims in this temple. Famous as the 'Guru of Tansen' in the outer world, but here, in this temple the focus was not on the famous disciple. Though in this city also, as in all pilgrim centres, there was noise of visitors, menace of priests and invasion of merchants, selling local souvenirs proclaiming the greatness of the place and the ubiquitous flies flying about noisily, Mohanlal found a sort of peace in this temple. Sitting in the temple for an hour, he went to the nearby hotel where he was staying and slept. Got up in the morning and walked about on the banks of the Yamuna near the tree where Lord Krishna was supposed to have tied up the saris of the gopis. The next morning he woke up very early. Looking at his watch, he found it was half past three. He felt like going to the Haridas temple at that time. Had a wash and walked in the darkness. On approaching the temple he heard the sound of music—someone practising the swara-sadhana. He wondered if Swami Haridas's soul was engaged in achievement of naada. Walking softly to avoid the noise of the footwear he approached the temple and sat on the platform. Yes, someone was actually singing. There was a certain method in that practice. The *sa* and *aa* syllables are not pronounced. The sound of Om is intoned in an elongated manner. Each pronouncement of Om takes its birth in the region of the navel and reaches the top of the head resounding for a long time. Starting with the shadja at each one of the twelve steps, one prolonged Omkara emanates. After reaching the mandra-shadja, in the same order of descending, there is an ascent of the twelve swaras in Om sound and the shadja of madhyama-saptaka is reached. From there he ascends the twelve steps of madhyama-saptaka. And then the twelve steps of tara-saptaka. Like this to complete one round of ascent and descent it takes seventy-two Omkaras. No deviation, no infirmity even to the extent of hair's breadth in any swara of any saptaka. No transgression of the place or contracting of the place of the swara. Such precision. Not the slightest defect in the essence or strength of breath. Mohanlal calculated that even if it was one minute to one unit of the completion of the Omkara it takes seventy-two minutes to complete a 'round'. He couldn't imagine for how long he had been singing and how many rounds he had completed. He concluded at daybreak. After that, total silence. This is the pure form of attaining the perfection of swara. In this method, no particular raga is perceivable. He understood that it contained the foundation of all ragas. He felt he had plumbed the depths of music. He remembered his practising in Raja Saheb's forest temple. He understood that this was a profounder method.

In a short while the sun rose and the golden rays sprouted everywhere. It sounded like the person that was practicing inside was coming out. He turned that way. He was a sadhu—an ascetic. Black long hair tied up in a tuft. About forty. Sparsely clad in a small dhoti tucked up tightly around the waist. The remnants of the mark of the kumkum fallen away. No other apparel. Mohanlal got up with alacrity and touched the sadhu's feet in a namaskar. The sadhu's eyes which had concentrated their gaze at the tip of the nose looked at him. He did not know what to say. The sadhu just went away. He couldn't think of following him. That entire day his mind was occupied by the sadhu's practice of the Omkara. It was firmly rooted in his mind that the sadhu's power of rendering was deeper, more profound and sublime to summon the infinite than that of his own practice—past and present. Though he was lying in bed he couldn't sleep. He dined early and slept. But by midnight his ears were filled with the sound of omkara and he got up. Switched on and looked at the watch. It was midnight. Washed his face, locked his room and walked up in the direction of the Haridas temple. There was only moonlight illuminating the area. It was as though the original Brindavan had emerged, re-born again, and the Brindavan, polluted from the contemporary commercial trade had disappeared. It was as if Yamuna, Lord Krishna, Radha, the gopis, the sacred dance, the sands—all the tintinnabulation of the best was alive and right there, for the eyes and ears again. Walking up slowly towards the temple amid the basil plants, all that did vanish and the pure and unpolluted sound of Omkara became audible. When he thought that the sadhu must have been practising all night, he walked up silently and sat in the same place as the last night, leaning against the same pillar. He was uttering the same Omkara in the same sublime tone, in the same order. Since it was very clear what swara of what saptaka and round he was transforming into the Omkara, there was no need for any arithmetical calculation of the cycle. Though he felt like singing along softly in accompaniment, he felt that it would disturb the concentration of the sadhu who was in an extremely subtle state and he might get angry. With this awareness he participated silently.

As yesterday he completed his sadhana by dawn. For a little while silence reigned inside. Then he came out at the time when the rays of the sun spread on the horizon. As yesterday he got up and touched the sadhu's feet. Standing for a moment the sadhu diverted his concentrated look from the end of his nose towards him and asked, 'Are you a musician?'

'Yes, my name is Mohanlal.' He said but withheld adding, 'this years Tansen Award winner.' He understood that he didn't add this because his inner logic told him that it was enough if he just mentioned his name because who was there interested in music who hadn't heard his name? He had an after thought that his question didn't require his name to be mentioned. He saw the man didn't seem to have heard anything special about the name Mohanlal.

'Yesterday in the early morning and tonight at midnight you came. I chose this temple in order to do my sadhana as it is an uninhabited place.'

'Kindly pardon me if I caused any disturbance.'

'All right. But don't come from now on.'

'I won't come transgressing your order. I came with the desire to learn the hidden power of music after listening to you. I will ever thankful to you if you would take me as your student.'

'What I am doing is not sadhana in music. It is yoga-sadhana. This is just one aspect of yoga that's all.

'That is what I am asking for. To learn the unknown power of music. If you would teach me that, my music will gain new strength. Isn't it through the yoga-shakti that flowed through music which was taught by his guru Haridas that Tansen was able to light up the lamps by singing the Raga Deepak and brought rain by singing Raga Megh? If such power is achieved by me through your grace I will also be blessed.' He again prostrated.

'Oh, I have also heard these concocted stories by the musicians about Tansen's mantrasiddhis which are believed by music lovers. These are also some of the stories concocted to spread the personal glory of Emperor Akbar. It is not possible, is it, to have the stories of Tansen signing the Deepak and Megh without mentioning Emperor Akbar?'

'Yes, yes, Akbar was a great lover of music. He was paying a better salary to Tansen than he did to his minister.'

'Do you know the truth? When Swami Haridas sang the Lankaadahana-saranga right here, in Brindavan, the forest which existed then caught fire. Then he sang Megh and quenched it. He was not just a musician. He was a great yogi. What is the first quality of a yogi? Though Emperor Akbar sent word to him in various ways, Swami Haridas never left his ashram, right in this place and never went to accept the patronage of a king. In order to enable the emperor to listen to the music of his guru, Tansen made him come incognito, sat him up outside the precincts of the ashram, went in alone and begged his guru to sing a particular raga. The emperor heard it sitting outside and returned. Did Tansen have this character? Did he not seek the patronage of the ruler? Did he not compose several songs singing the praises of the emperor? Did he not make his own children compose songs of praise flattering the emperor, corrected them and got fat salaries paid to them at the king's court? In the ragas that he composed was there no ulterior motive to pander the emperor's taste? Did he not abandon his own religion and convert to another in order to have the woman he desired? Did he not get special benefits and privileges in the court and among the courtiers? He was a singer and artist. A big genius. But the power that is possible only to the yogis is attributed to him by musicians like you. No matter how much he fell for the luxury and temptations of court life, no matter how worldly he became and though he abandoned his own religion, the great sage Haridas from the same religion and a very great saint at that, did not abandon him, reject him and curse him. That is another great quality of the power of yoga.'

Mohanlal was listening to it standing respectfully at a distance. He looked at him quizzically as if asking him if he had anything more to ask. Mohanlal couldn't think of anything. His look again turned inward. He walked out of the temple and went in the direction of the river. Mohanlal just stood there looking at the rhythmic movement of the yogi's steps.

On returning to the hotel and stretching himself on the bed after shower and breakfast, a mixed feeling of both comfort and a sort of unpleasantness appeared together. Tansen was also a singer like me. Much better. A genius. Mohanlal felt comforted that Tansen also had the attraction for money and fame as I have. No miracles can be wrought in music unless one is a yogi. He felt dissatisfied that he could never attain it. Perhaps Tansen never suffered from the feeling of void that I have suffered because he was satisfied with his wife, children and disciples. In a short while he fell asleep. Before waking up, the sound of the Omkara of the sage was audible in the dream state. Then he woke up. Even after waking up, its attraction continued to posses him. Tonight also he is going to engage himself in the sadhana at the temple. There was an irrepressible desire to go and listen. But he had clearly stated that he had chosen a lonely place for his practice and had asked him not to go there. If I go there stealthily and run away the moment he stops singing, yes, he will know. He was afraid that he might be punished for his transgression. Suppose I beg him, Maharaj, I have decided to be your pupil, kindly give me yoga-diksha? There seemed to be a way out. But he will ask me, 'Will you give up all your worldly ways? Will you refuse to sing at court as Swami Haridas did?' Then what? This question occurred. He started searching within himself. He remembered the words he had heard that all other types of happiness are incomparable to the inward bliss the yogis enjoy. He was immersed in the magical contemplation of these words for a long time. Then he felt hungry. While eating at the dining hall he felt he should have brought Bhoopali along with him to the award receiving ceremony. Once the sumptuous meal was over, he felt the need for a woman. He felt yoga-sadhana was not for him. By the time he returned to his room, the desire for woman had also receded. Again the feeling of depression and void. Now all eyes were on him after the Junnarkar episode and the award. If he had brought any female pupil and especially the white-skinned Bhoopali, it would have attracted the attention of the media. If some mischievous journalist had started a scandalous propaganda, the other newspapers would pick up the cue. He felt comforted that it was a good thing, coming alone.

He couldn't sleep that night. The desire to listen to the Omkara persisted. But he couldn't go to the temple. After rolling about for a couple of hours, he locked up the room and walked to the banks of the river. After walking on the sand for half a mile he sat a little distance away from the water on the dry sand. He imagined the shruti in his mind and started practising the swara. As that sadhu was doing, he descended twelve swaras in mandra-saptaka and ascended twelve swaras. Then in madhyama-saptaka. Then he achieved this in tara-saptaka. He felt that he could also do this. But what is it that is gained by this? No matter what swara he conceived in which saptaka, he felt he had the power to control his voice and produce it like an arrow released by Arjuna. Raja Saheb had made me achieve it in just six months. And I have been singing on that foundation all these years. Can that sage produce all the variations of swara that I can? Has he had the sadhana that I have achieved? These questions arose. But when he got the explanation that what that sage was achieving was not sadhana in music but in yoga, he became aware of the wonderful, special power of the Omkara . A mood of helplessness took over, torn between the desire to go over to the temple and the disappointment in the sadhu having forbidden it.

After a couple of days the question arose as to what he was to do and what he was doing, sitting here in Brindavan. Just six miles away in Mathura he could get a direct train to Bombay. Or just two hours away if he went to Delhi he could fly from there. But the uselessness of what he could do at Bombay confronted him. Meanwhile, he would have received letters, telegrams, telephone calls inviting him to give concerts. Now everybody knows that my fee is one lakh rupee. Nobody would bargain. In the wake of the winning of the Tansen Award, the enthusiasm of music lovers and music associations would have increased. This enthusiasm will abate after a month. He remembered that at this juncture he had come and entrenched himself in an unknown destination without an address. The decision to just pick up his suitcase and get to the Mathura railway station occurred. But he was just lying down not having the will power to get up from his bed and packing his bag. Yes, he must go. But it was not clear where to. No town was attracting him. He had nothing to do anywhere.

After a couple of days, suddenly he felt like going to Chittarpur and just sit silently in the temple which had been built by Raja Saheb in the middle of the forest, facing the River Narmada. Then sing for a couple of hours to himself. In half an hour, he got up and packed his bag. Even without making any enquiries about the train timing, he took an autorickshaw and went to the railway station.

ड

The next morning, getting off at Ujjain and going in a taxi to Chittarpur, he came to Shakapur en route. Immediately, he remembered Bhupatram. Most probably, he wouldn't be alive. Thirty-four years had elapsed. If he was alive, he would be past a hundred. Just wanting to take a chance, he asked the taxi driver to go into town. He could recognise the street and the house. He enquired. The tabla maestro had passed away twenty-five years ago! His sons had sold the house and left. One of them was in Calcutta. The other in Dhanbad. There was no one in Shakapur now. Mohanlal felt sad. He directed the taxi to Chittarpur. He noticed that the road had been asphalted. It was not the same dirty, dusty street with potholes that he used years ago. He asked the driver, 'How many years since this road was asphalted?'

'About fifteen to twenty years. This is the best road in the entire Malwa region.'

'How is that?'

'Many foreigners come here. Tourists from England, America, Germany and Europe come to the Chittarpur Resort. It is full, nine months in the year except for the three summer months.'

'Who runs the resort?'

'Don't you know? It is Raja Saheb. Raja Ajit Singh is a very intelligent man. Because he has made this into a resort, we get some business. Otherwise who would ask for a taxi in Ujjain?

Mohanlal got excited to see what it was like. Whatever could have happened to the place, which he had left thirty-four years ago? He felt like asking the driver himself. But since it was a good road, the taxi was moving fast and most of the distance had already been covered. A good, modern bridge had been built which could withstand any flood water to cross the River Chitra. Prince Ajit Singh hadn't got this road built and the bridge erected by spending his money. He thought the prince had used his influence with the government and by bribing the officials. When he was remembering the palace of Raja Saheb, his guru, the forest path and the temple in the wood, the taxi driver stopped the vehicle at the entrance of the palace. Immediately, a liveried attendant, the sort that is at the door of luxury hotels, came forward and saluted him.

Mohanlal asked the driver in confusion, 'Why did you bring me here?'

'You didn't mention any specific place. Now, please direct me.'

Mohanlal's confusion got worse. He had to stay somewhere before going to the Mahadev temple. Who does he know in this town? What other alternative arrangement is there? He couldn't think of anything. The driver switched off the engine and sat quietly. After thinking for a minute he asked the doorman, 'I have come to worship at the Mahadev temple in the forest on the bank of the river. Can you tell me where the priest lives? Or, can you get him over?'

'Outsiders cannot enter the temple. Only those who are lodgers at the resort can enter the forest. After entering the forest, one can visit the temple.'

'Doesn't anyone from the town go to the temple? For worship at the time of Shivaraatri, for instance?

'Sir, this is a private temple of the king, the Raja Saheb. Others cannot enter it.'

Mohanlal felt helpless. He got off the taxi, ascended the steps of the palace which had the big name board 'Oriental Royal Resort' and went to the reception. He was not unfamiliar with five star hotels. He would also put the condition that he should be lodged in a hotel not beneath a four star hotel to the organisers whenever he was invited to a concert. He went to the reception desk and said, 'I want a room.'

'Sir, there is no arrangement for renting rooms here. There are cottages for single occupancy, there are small cottages in the forest.'

'What is the rent for a day?'

'Two hundred dollars, plus tax. On the board in front, the exchange rate for pound sterling, dollar, Deutsch mark, the frank etc had been mentioned in rupees. Which meant that he had to pay seven thousand rupees for the lodging per day. Never had he stayed in such an expensive place in his life when he had to pay for himself. But there was no alternative to pray to his deity, Mahadev, who had been the source for his musical practice and achievement. After paying off the taxi, he registered. He was transported to the cottage allotted to him in a cycle rikshaw along with his suitcase. All over the forest, hundreds of cottages had been constructed. There was vegetation around each cottage. The entire area had been designed in a way that while riding on the cycle rikshaw, not even a single cottage was directly visible. The cottage that had been allotted to him was of the same size where he had lived for six years. However, the interior decoration was such as is found in five star hotels. It had a bed, a sofa, a bath and toilet. In every cottage there was a light weight bicycle as is found in foreign countries. It had no bell. The table had a map of the entire forest showing the cycle route as well as the trekking footpaths. For dinner one could cycle up to the dinning hall situated behind the reception. Or one could order with individually priced dishes by looking at the menu which would be brought to the cottage.

He sauntered out after shower. Though a cycle was available he had been out of practice for thirty-five years. He remembered that one should walk in order to get a real feel of the forest. Though the forest was visible before the eyes, inside, it was filled with luxurious cottages. He knew that the population would not be noticed because the Western people are not given to shouting and making a lot of noise. Some peacocks could be seen here and there. Well planned networks of streets, wide enough for two rickshaws to pass each other from opposite sides. Little footpaths, stone paved and braid-like, intertwining each other. Three feet high, arrow shaped direction—showing name plates stuck on metal frames. He felt this was not a forest. Interspersed with hand holding White couples. Single men and women too. Here and there a couple, leaning against a tree, absorbed in prolonged kissing. Not even a single Indian. He was greeted by a 'Hi' or 'Hello' with a smile. He was not in a mood to engage them in conversation. It was not in their culture to do so either. By instinct, he moved in the direction of the river, from there he proceeded to the temple. The door was open. Outside the door, the legend about the worship of the lingam had been inscribed in English on a board: The ancient Indians were following the practice of free love, they considered the vagina and the phallus as goddess and gods and were worshipping them. They considered the union of these two equal to the highest from of spiritual experience. They established the Iswaralingam, as an artistic, symbolic representation of such a union. Indians still worship this idol. He peeped in though the door. Four pairs of couples were intently observing the idol. In the eyes of those couples, holding hands or embracing, the desire to copulate was evident. He looked around. Not even a single almirah —he remembered there used to be three of them there. The three cupboards contained three tamburas in one, harmoniums and the folded spreads and pillows in the second and the third with the glass door was packed with books on music. He remembered the words of Raja Saheb that the lingam means the spherical world around which naada, the musical sound would return with circumambulance. It is the image in which one is absorbed in meditating on naada by inward concentration. He felt that concept had disappeared here. This was no longer a shrine. It was just a stone building. He felt that even if he sat there a whole night, not a single ripple of music would come out. He came out and sat on the platform pediment of the temple gazing on the River Narmada. The feeling that he was completely alone filled him. In these thirty-four years, even Narmada had thinned out like an emaciated mother who had nothing to feed on but had fed away everything to her children. At the right hand side confluence, at the basin of the Chitra there was not even the amount of water found in a gutter.

When he was sitting there for half an hour a White man approached him. About thirty-five, he was wearing a shirt of faded ivory and black trousers. He came up and said, 'Please excuse me, I am disturbing your privacy. Aren't you the singer, Mohanlalji?'

Mohanlal's feeling of loneliness was alleviated a bit with the idea that there was at least one person who could recognise him even in this atmosphere. He looked up. The man himself said, 'My name is Winston. I am from Houston, Texas. I had come to the Gwalior Music Festival. Your music overflowed with inspiration.'

After the customary pleasantries Mohanlal asked, 'Since when have you been here?'

'Three days. Tomorrow I am going to Rajasthan.'

'Why did you come here?'

'Looks as if the owner of this resort, the Maharaja is an expert salesman. All the travel agents in America and Europe have given tremendous publicity to this resort. Everything is booked right from there', he smiled.

'What are the attractions here?'

'There are badminton, tennis and basketball courts. There is a huge swimming pool. Tiger and deer hunting. The dinner feast with the Maharaja. These last two are special attractions. If at least ten people get together, buy a ticket at two hundred dollars each, they will get the opportunity of dining with Maharaja Ajit Singh. The cutlery of previous kings—the great dining table, the traditional chairs, silver plates and containers, spoons and forks. The Maharaja will appear in full regalia, traditionally. The etiquette that is to be followed would have been already instructed to the aspiring dinner guests. The Maharaja will receive the honours with great dignity and formality, with a smile on his face. He carries on a pleasant conversation during the dinner. Those that have paid two hundred dollars get a feeling of fulfillment that they have experienced the royal culture of ancient India. But the ordinary tourists don't understand that the culinary specialties are mostly of the Moghul times and not of ancient India. The resort makes a profit of more than fifty thousand rupees every evening, even if there are only ten guests dining. On many days, twenty to twenty-five guests are there for this dinner.'

Mohanlal remembered the prince, four years younger to him who was studying in Oxford way back. Why not meet him once, he thought. May be he has even a fixed rate of many hundred dollars for a meeting, he suspected. Meanwhile Winston looked at his wrist watch and said, 'Now there is a tiger–antelope hunt. If you are interested, come, let's go.'

Mohanlal followed. Winston studying the map in his hand, trekking across the five feet wide roads and the intersecting stone paved footpaths in a zig-zag manner, warding off the peacocks on the way by clapping his hands, led him to the centre of the forest. A hundred people had gathered there as if to see an extraordinary event. Seventy to eighty Westerners, about twenty Indians. Even the Indian women were wearing jeans and T-shirts like the Western women going out for a forest adventure. Rough sporting trekking footwear worn by people who move in the forest. In front was an enclosure with a twenty feet high finger-size wide wire mesh and on the other side an open space of an acre and a half without any plants and trees. Here and there were two feet wide bushes, guessing that some extraordinary event was going to take place there, Mohanlal looked at Winston's face. He said, 'The sight of a tiger hunting down a deer—a real tiger and a real deer. This gives the forest a natural awe-inspiring ferocity, doesn't it?' The gathered people were absolutely silent, as if they didn't want the tiger and the deer to know about their existence. Many of them hid themselves behind trees. Some climbed the trees and perched themselves amidst supporting branches. Everyone had a camera. Since there was sunlight in the area of the hunt, there was no need to use the flash for the cameras. When everyone was looking, a deer entered the enclosure. In a short while the roar of a tiger was heard nearby. The deer got frightened and started running. But no matter in which direction it ran, the fence was there obstructing it. It ran backward, forward, to the sides and hid itself in the bushes at the centre. Then a huge tiger entered the enclosure with a slow, unperturbed pace. Spotting the deer, it ran towards it. Confronted by the fence, the deer suddenly changed its direction and ran backwards. The tiger turned slowly and followed. Tired after running about frantically the deer stood still, panting and looked around. The tiger that came from behind roared once. The frightened deer, though exhausted, ran fast, dashed against the fence and changed direction. The tiger, knowing that it was its prey, and meant for it, was palling around in a leisurely manner without a need for any hurry. Each camera was clicking away madly, twenty, thirty times, in about half an hour, the deer, running about, twisting and turning, realising that any attempt to escape was in vain, as if accepting its inevitable fate stood there panting expecting death. Then the tiger, in one jump, held the deer firmly in its front claws and bit into the neck of the deer.

When the deer was becoming still after writhing frantically in vain, the blood that filled the mouth of the tiger began to drip. Then the tiger held its prey in its mouth and went to the right side. Winston, gesturing to Mohanlal to follow him walked away briskly. To make it convenient for the tiger to enter with its prey was an iron gate which led to another enclosure which the tiger entered. Then the door closed automatically.

Winston explained, 'Now do you understand the manner of the hunt? As in a zoo, the tiger has been imprisoned in a cage. Once in two days, a full-grown deer is its food. It has been trained not to jump on the deer at once and devour it. It knows it is a prey reserved for it. But it is a new experience for the deer. In a twenty acre farm a mile away from the forest, they have reared and maintained a deer park. We can go and see them too. If you observe the swiftness of their run, the graceful beauty of their jump, the way they turn their ears and listen intently in the direction of sound, you will fall in love with them. They select a deer, bring it and arrange for the hunt. The tiger knows that after drawing the deer's carcass away, it has to make it last until the day after tomorrow. After the tiger has been let into the hunting zone, a servant closes the door, cleans up the cage of the debris of old bones and the refuse of the tiger, and cleans up the cage.'

Mohanlal felt that the entire sport was cruel. He remembered the graceful movements of the frolicking deer, moods of the Raga Saranga which reflect it. Meanwhile a servant came out from the tiger enclosure. In his hand, a key chain with a number of heavy keys attached. Around forty years. His uniform was that of the employees of this Oriental Royal Resort, on both sides an inch wide, yellow striped, parrot–green pants, a light yellow shirt with two pockets, a big collar, shoulder–belts and a wide, shining belt. Boots for the feet. Sumptuous moustache. Clean-shaven face. Winston pointed him out and explained, 'The man who looks after the tiger. He is the one who releases the tiger for the hunt. He is in charge of the deer park also.' Mohanlal felt he had seen him somewhere. He walked forward. In a few seconds, another employee called out to him, 'Giri, hey, Giri.' Giri, the man-in-charge of the tiger and the deer stopped. Mohanlal again looked at his face steadily. His mind started to remind him that he had seen him, seen his face, without the moustache. Winston bade him goodbye, saying, 'I am hungry. I must eat and take a nap. Goodbye.' Mohanlal also felt hungry. He remembered he hadn't walked about so much in recent times. He guessed the direction of his cottage and started walking.

He ordered for the dinner to be arranged in the cottage. When he changed and stood in front of the sink to have a wash, the memory of where he had met the man in charge of the tiger and the deer began to take shape. When he remembered that he had been addressed as 'Giri' by his colleague, Mohanlal shuddered. He began to wonder 'could it be true' and since he was of the parents, both in the employ of the palace, it was possible he was also in the service of the palace. This conclusion began to take shape. He was not only surprised but sad that in his desire to sit and practise in the Mahadev Mandir, he never remembered Chunni and the child he had fathered. But the time he returned from the wash, the question arose whether he would have avoided coming here if he had remembered. Even now, it was uncertain whether he was his child. He began to console himself thinking whether it was not just his fancy that he had joined the word 'Dhara' with Giri. Suppose it was he, what could he do now? Could he tell the old story that Giri was engendered by him? That tiger trainer might just fell him with one blow of his paw. He told himself, who would keep quiet, listening to such a thing. Until the dinner arrived, he tried to quieten his mind by thinking. He had this irrepressible urge, and she wanted to have a child. So he had impregnated her. There was no point in worrying. The servant who brought the meal on a cycle said, 'Sir, please see that it is warm. If you want it hotter, I can heat it up in the microwave right here in the cottage.' When he said it was hot enough for him, the servant began to lay the table and serve him.

While dining, he asked him, 'Are you from this place?'

'Yes, sir.'

'What's your name?'

'Banwaarilal.'

'The man in charge of tiger and deer, Giri, where is he from?

'Just four miles from here. A town called Gowriganj.'

'What is the name of his mother and father?'

'Mother's name is Chunni. Father is Bansi. The father died about five years ago. He was suffering from a breathing problem for many years.'

His speech stopped and he couldn't continue. He started eating with his head bent down. He could hardly enjoy the taste of anything. He heard indistinctly what the servant asked, 'Why, sir, do you know them?' After he finished his meal, the servant cleaned up the table and before leaving, collecting the cups and saucers, he said, 'Sir, the ingredients for making tea, and biscuits are in this cupboard. The milk and a number of other drinks are in the fridge,' and he left.

When he went to the sink, the image in the mirror said, 'This is my first son, the one who looks after the deer and pushes them into the tiger's mouth.' He felt like telling him to quit this job. It followed up with words, 'I will pay you two lakhs. Take up some other job.' Didn't I pay two lakhs to Kishan? What did he do with it? He remembered that he never asked him how his business was progressing. The reasons were, where was the time to enquire, with all his programmes, travels and while he was in town, his own practice and teaching work. He yawned. Night journey. No proper sleep. The ticket collector who took a bribe of a hundred rupees had given him only a berth in a non-air-conditioned, three tier compartment, the bastard. A series of yawns, couldn't sleep. He had paid money to Kishan not out of love for his son but to draw him to his own side. He remembered how she had said that she wouldn't be his wife in her next birth and would be Gore's wife. He wanted to teach that slut a lesson. He became critical of her and thought, what sort of a mother was she who left both her children and went to live in a place of her own? I didn't tie the mangalasutra to Chunni. She had a husband who had done it. The name of 'father' is his. He derived some satisfaction and justification. But why was the memory of the face of Giri troubling him? The question arose again and again without finding an answer.

After rolling about for five minutes, he suddenly sat up. He called the reception and asked for a cycle rikshaw to be sent to him. By the time it arrived, he prepared some tea, dressed up and got ready.

He sat in the rickshaw and said, 'I want to go to Gowriganj.'

'Whom do you want to see there, Sir?' Asked the rickshaw driver.

'I want to see the town.'

'It is a small village. Too small, in fact. What is there to see, Sir?'

'You just take me there. I want to see a village in these parts. Leave me there and return. I will come back on my own.'

ऽ

When he reached there, he understood that Gowriganj was a very small village with just fifteen or twenty houses. After paying and sending away the rikshaw fellow, he asked a woman who was sitting on the platform in front of her house which was Chunni's house. She asked, 'Which Chunni?' After he explained Giri's mother, Bansi's wife, she said, 'Their house is not in the village. They have built a house on their own land. I will show you.' She came to the street and pointing her finger in a certain direction, continued, 'That is the only house in this direction. Tiled, tall house. You will see it as you go along.'

He walked along the tiny border path of someone else's land. He felt there must be a separate cart track which he didn't know of. After walking for a furlong and ascending and descending a mound, a further furlong away a house was visible. He walked briskly. When he was still a little distance away, two dogs started barking. Then they rushed forward to attack him. After trying to ward them off with loud noises and shouting aloud, 'Anybody home?' A woman of about thirty-five came out of the house and quietened the barking dogs. After they were reprimanded, the dogs were reduced to mere growling, she asked, 'Who are you? Whom do you want to see?'

'I wanted to see Chunni Chowdhurani.'

'Please come. These dogs don't bite after the people of the house quieten them,' she invited. She was good looking. He seemed to have seen her somewhere. The body build and colour of a woman who was working in the fields. The house was not very poor looking. On the concrete floor of the veranda there were a wooden bench and two cane chairs. She gave a shout, 'Mother, there's someone here to see you.'

The old woman who came out was nearing seventy. A mouth, that looked like a small open door with two teeth missing from the top row and one from the lower row. Sparse white hair. A shrunken body. She came up and looked. She said, 'I can't recognise you. I have cataract in my eyes. It seems they will remove it after they are fully developed. Till then everything is hazy.'

'My name is Mohanlal, I was learning singing in the Mahadev Mandir at the time of the great Raja Saheb.'

Memory flashed on her face. There was confusion, embarrassment and fear. The young woman was standing right behind her mother. In a couple minutes, the perturbed lines on the face of the old woman came under control. She said, 'At the time of the previous Raja Saheb, great musicians used to visit the place. Now, times have changed. I am not able to recognise you. It is thirty-five years, isn't it, since he passed away? Come, please sit. Sit down on the chair. She said, 'Beti, the gentleman has come in the hot sun. Prepare some tea.' The daughter went in.

He understood that she had created a situation where they could be together alone and asked in a soft voice, 'Do you remember?' She didn't talk. He continued, 'I came in search of you to see you.'

Still, she didn't speak, but he observed that her eyes were moistened. A minute later she engaged in customary polite conversation, 'Where are you now? Can you make a living by singing? When the grand old Raja Saheb was there he would give plateful of coins to singers. Now it has all become a hotel. Are you married? How many children?' Chunni was a smart woman. Even when she was meeting him she would give him courage too in addition to direction. He understood that even now she is engaging in customary polite conversation, in order that the daughter who was inside should not know anything. His mind began to suspect. Was it her daughter who had gone in? Bansi, anyway, was impotent. Did Chunni have an affair with someone else and gave birth to this woman? Or, did she address her daughter-in-law as daughter? The young woman brought tea. After he drank it, Chunni turned to her and told her, 'Beti, this is a great gentleman. Hold his feet firmly and prostrate to him.' Treating it like an order, she pressed her forehead to his two feet, held the upper portion of his feet and prostrated for a full minute. Then she said, 'Look after the house. I will accompany him and drop him near the main street and come.' Saying so, she took hold of the walking stick which was leaning against the door corner. After taking a good look at the young woman who had so fervently pressed her head on his feet and had filled in him a deep feeling, he took a good look at her again to his heart's content and he started off.

Chunni didn't need the support of a stick to walk about. She was using it to find the ups and downs on the road because of the cataract. After walking for a furlong, she said, 'You see the mound to the right? If you go up and climb down, there is a huge banyan tree. We can sit under it and talk. No one comes there and it isn't visible to anyone. Let's go.' Thinking that was the kind of place he wanted and it was a good opportunity, he led her on as if to show the place. Under that ancient banyan tree with almost fifty aerial-roots descending from it, he sat on a stone. Sitting at his feet on the ground she asked, 'You remembered suddenly and came. Tell me why?'

'I am also sixty-two. I wanted to see you and my son once before I die.'

Her eyes moistened. 'Why do you say only son? You can see the daughter too. I found out that I was pregnant again after you left. The daughter who prepared tea for you and who prostrated touching your feet. That girl, I named her Poonam.'

'What are the two children doing?'

'You know your son Giridharlal. You remember I used to bring you food, carrying him in my arms. You used to hold him. He had relieved himself on your jubba three times.' He remembered the rest. Though he was a six month baby, while he was laid down on the ground, he would happily chirp away throwing about his hands and feet. But when his mother was embraced in his presence, he would start crying aloud as if someone else was seizing his property—as if his mother would not be his, anymore. Afterwards Chunni would leave the baby in her friend's home and come alone.

'What is he doing?'

'He works in the palace. A salary of one thousand and five hundred rupees. He tackles the tiger boldly. He looks after the deer. All the manure from them is ours. He is married. He has two sons—thirteen and eleven years old. His wife is a good woman. She has gone to her parents with her children. Poonam has two girls and a boy. She has been given in marriage to Duni, in the neighbouring town. He owns four acres of land. Her husband is also in the employ of the palace. He gets a pay of one thousand and two hundred rupees.'

He was struggling to come out of the new situation of having five grand children in this town. In order to come out of it he asked, 'Can you remember me?'

She didn't reply. Her face registered discontent. 'Answer me', he asked.

'Can you remember me? You tell me.'

'Have I come in search without remembering?

'You came today, after thirty-five years. Why didn't you come all these years? How could I know where you went and in which city you were living? Even if I knew, how could a simple woman like me come to meet you? You knew where I was and what I was doing. Then why didn't you come?'

'I wanted to come. I was afraid of what people might say and what Bansi would think. For how long did you think about me after I left? How frequently do you remember me in recent days? Tell me.'

'Why do you ask me in how many days? Whenever I see the faces of the children, the memory of one who gave them to me comes naturally. In the wake of your leaving, I used to get very angry. Then this house hadn't been built. Didn't I tell you not to go anywhere? We will build a house in our land. Stay there with us and practise your music. Though I begged you in so many ways. Afterwards, I understood. Musicians want royal patronage. They go in search of it. What do they get if they sit in a hut in the middle of a farm? Still my heart was throbbing, hoping that you would come to see me and the children. Why were you afraid to come? Didn't you know that my husband, Bansi looked upon you with great respect?'

Mohanlal couldn't think of anything to say, he just sat there, silently. After a little while, Chunni said, 'It looks as if it is getting dark. Get me to the path of my house and leave. Where are you staying?'

'In the Oriental Royal Resort.'

'Oh, my! It seems they charge eight thousand per day. You have become that rich have you? I spoke all kinds of things. How could a person like you stay in my hut?'

He felt he shouldn't have said that. He didn't understand that the difference in money matters would create such a big chasm. Immediately he replied, 'After coming here I didn't know where to stay. The rickshaw fellow took me there. Had I known where you stayed, I would have come to your house right away.'

Now she was satisfied. After a couple of minutes she said, 'I could have told the children that the maestro was learning music from the great master. Your father used to carry the food for him. He has come with that acquaintance to see your father.' Two minutes later, she herself spoke, 'I can't see properly. Don't people see that Giri's face resembles yours? Would Giri suspect it either, would he? You went away. Your facial contours became musty in my memory. But when Giri attained manhood, the memory was revived and I began to feel that he was yourself. You know, don't you, that my husband was such a stupid man that he could not understand any of this?'

He thought within himself that women are more afraid of their sons than their husband. Perhaps men are also like that. He remembered that he had never grown up with children. 'Shall we go?' Chunni stood up. It was sunset and dusky. He didn't think of telling her anything nor asking. He took the lead and showed her the way. After surrounding the mound and leaving her at the road to her home, he said he would leave. He couldn't think of any emotional or sentimental talk. Saying, 'Now I know my path. I can reach home even with my eyes closed,' she turned left and starting walking away. Turning right he reached the road leading to Chittarpur. He thought that there was no means of transport there and he had to walk the distance. Though it did occur to him that if there was a phone within reach he could have called the resort and get a vehicle sent, he preferred walking alone. His body was tired but still he started walking. He remembered that he was giving more than enough money to Champa's children, right from the beginning, didn't give any money to Ramkumari's children when they were growing up but compared to this he had given absolutely nothing, not even a rattle to the children of Chunni. He didn't tie the holy knot to her neck. She didn't desire it either. There was not even the name of father. Knowing all this, Chunni gave birth to two children. Without even an idea of the consequences of begetting children etc., I had satisfied my inner urge, the madness of lust. This being the case, how can there be a father-children relationship? Though there appeared this consolation, the fact that they were born to me, his face resembled mine, and even without knowing she was my daughter, when she had placed her head on my feet and held the back portion of the feet firmly with her hands he had experienced a special relationship—these facts pulled him down. Chunni said Giri had two sons and Poonam had two daughters and a son. He got curious about how they looked. Not just a curiosity but an intense desire—a desire to see Giri's wife and Poonam's husband.

Meanwhile it became quite dark. He could see the road. Wondered how far the resort was. He was feeling tired. Night journey by train. Wandering about in the morning in the forest. Remembered he hadn't slept during the day. He was dragging his feet along. Meanwhile a cycle came up from the front. The light of the battery dynamo pierced his eye. The rider went past whistling. But after proceeding for fifty feet, he came back and talked to him. 'Sir, you are walking alone. Where do you want to go?'

'Oriental Royal Resort.'

'Can you sit on the carrier, at the back? I will take you there.'

He felt he had his life back. After he got settled, the cyclist peddled off, continuing to whistle with joy. A whistle full of feeling—joy of life. Not classical music. He knew that the folk tunes of Malwa region were full of emotion and filled with exuberance. The cyclist was putting forth such an intense feeling with an exaggerated enthusiasm in his whistling. It was as if he was using two major tunes as pallavi and a different movement in another tempo as anupallavi. He felt that his whistling was even more emotional than the flute rendering by the famous flautist Pannalal Ghosh. Throughout the ride he was repeating it without being aware that he was repeating. Mohanlal also felt that no matter how often he heard it, the source of its inspiration was inexhaustible. That too, in the darkness he thought that the expansion of its rasa was endless.

At last the lights of Chittarpur appeared. The cyclist went straight to the steps of the palace door, put his left foot down to stop the cycle and said, 'Get down.' Mohanlal put his hand in his pocket, took out a hundred rupee currency note and held it out for him. He took it and said, 'Sir, in this hotel a tip means one hundred rupees. I have cycled four miles. That too in the dark. Please give me at least one thousand rupees.'

Mohanlal felt it was nothing short of robbery. Even in Bombay it is six rupees per mile by taxi. If it was to a distant place it is three rupees. Yet he thought it was a mistake not settling earlier how much he had to pay. But still he felt giving a thousand was surrendering to injustice. Meanwhile it came to his notice that the cycle rider was wearing the uniform of the resort. He said, 'My dear fellow, there should be some logic for your demand. Actually, I had walked a mile already. How can it be a thousand rupees for a three mile cycle ride? Come to the reception. Let them decide the right amount. I will give that.'

'This is not related to the duty at the hotel. I had finished my duty and was going home. If you want to give at all, give me five hundred. Otherwise, I myself will leave it to you as tip,' he was blustering, with impunity. Not wanting to continue the quarrel he again took out four more currency notes and held it in front of him. When he was counting them, suddenly, on an impulse, he came forward a little and looked at his face—Giri! Afraid that if he stood in front of him in the light, he might look at his face properly, Mohanlal started ascending the steps of the reception building.

ೲ

Going to bed immediately after dinner, Mohanlal fell asleep. Throughout the night, the emotional impact of the whistle could be heard in the dream. When he awoke at four in the early morning, the question to which raga this may be placed began to trouble him. Though he was angry that a thousand rupees had been demanded for a cycle ride of three miles, he consoled himself that everything here was in terms of dollars and a thousand rupees meant only thirty dollars. He wondered if he knew I was his biological father, he would have touched my feet! Not only he, but his wife and children, Poonam's husband and children, everyone. But supposing they knew now! He was embarrassed even with the thought. He was afraid. He felt like giving them something, he must pay back his debt—his obligation. He got up and counted the bundles of currency notes. Even after paying the hotel bill and the ticket money for the train to Bombay, he would be left with seventy-five thousand rupees. How about paying fifteen thousand for each grand child? Or, how would it be if he went to Chunni's house and gave her the entire amount and say this is for you and ask her to take the money and distribute it among her children and grand children as she liked? No one will suspect if I say that I was learning music here and I am giving this money in gratitude for Bansi bringing me food and cleaning my lodge for six years. He got up, had a wash, prepared tea and after drinking it with the biscuits, came out. It was getting to be dawn. Though there were misleading paths, he guessed the direction and reached the temple. The door was closed. Not locked. He pushed it open and went in. In the dim light the lingam was appearing as the form of the shadja taken shape clearly. He started intoning the sound Om which in a short while assumed the form of AUM. Even before rested as the shadja of madhya-saptaka, the meend of *saa re ma pa* had formed and the Omkara had taken the definite shape of Asavari. He steadied the same movement and repeated the Omkara seven times. Then he started descending into mandra by designing each of the small knots of the swaras into the form of Omkara. The raga which he had practised for a whole month in this same temple and had sung to himself at least a thousand times, began to appear in a new dimension now. The plethora of emotions; sorrow, contrition, profound sadness, distressing beseeching of forgiveness all these began to reach the proximity to divinity and appeared in the ripeness of spirituality. By the time he descended into the cave of mandra and came up, new variations and alterations of points of swaras were visualised, hitherto unknown to him. Each one seemed the composite Omkara of different levels of, and different combinations of musical meanings. He wasn't aware that he was singing without the support of tambura. Meanwhile two people, talking to each other entered the temple. He opened his eyes and noticed the outside light penetrating into the interior of the temple. He felt singing here wasn't possible any more. He got up immediately and went out. But the mood of the Omkara hadn't been snapped. The basin of Narmada which could expand its heart with the vast expanse and great depth was sighted before him and gave a new dimension of the Omkara. It was a good thing he had come out of the temple. After coming out of the cave of mandra, the imagination took form that the entire expanse of the earth in the madhya-saptaka and the galaxies of the sky in the tara-saptaka could be included. He started singing right there. Whether he sang sitting or standing, the foreign tourists might think that it was another attraction of the tour and might come and surround him. With this awareness he started descending through uneven and edgy path of boulders into the river basin. However, the throat was sounding the Omkara in the form of the clusters and combinations of the swaras of madhya-saptaka. By the time he reached down in the meandering path, he had searched and explored the places of the Omkara in the madhya-saptaka. The moment he saw the water, he removed his outer garments, got into the water, descended till the waters were up to his neck and started singing from the beginning. By the time he completed the cycle of tara-saptaka and reached madhyama-shadja, the sun had come up.

On coming out of the water, stretching his limbs and putting his clothes on he started ascending, then he became aware that if he didn't vacate his cottage before mid-day he would have to pay an additional seven thousand rupees. He looked at his watch. It was half past ten. He decided to vacate before noon, deposit the suitcase at the reception and go to Chunni's house. When he moved towards his cottage, he felt he had lost his way. He hadn't brought the map. He finally reached the cottage at 11 am. When he was counting the currency bundles to make up seventy-five thousand rupees, and putting them into a separate bag to give to Chunni, a thought occurred to him. If the money is paid could the feeling of obligation be got rid of? Recently I gave two lakhs to Kishan. I have promised to give money for Bakula's wedding. To Swarmohan and Srutimohini I have paid all along. Did that complete the father's moral obligation and relationship? Now if I give money to Chunni saying that it is for expressing the gratitude for her husband bringing food to me and hide the fact from her son, daughter-in-law, daughter and son-in-law, how could Chunni understand it? Suppose she understands it as a pay-off for her sexual favours enjoyed by him! Chunni did not come for the money. She wanted babies. In full knowledge of everything, only to have me, she changed her husband's duty of bringing food to me to herself and came instead. Without being conscious of it myself, I must have looked at her with lustful eyes. She must have observed that and my youth and must have selected me. If I go to give her money, it would be insulting her. He thought it would demean the friendly relationship and decided not to give the money.

After going to the reception and paying the bill, he asked, 'Is it possible to meet the owner of the resort?'

The receptionist corrected him, 'You mean His Highness?' After he said yes, she explained, 'It is very difficult to have an interview with him. If you give your introduction in writing, your address, the reason for meeting him—all these details—we will forward it to His Private Secretary. He will let us know whether it is possible at all, and if so on what day and time.'

'I can't wait for days that way. I am leaving now. If it was possible I wanted to talk to him for half an hour. His father had helped me a great deal.'

'Please wait. I will talk to his Private Secretary.' She communicated his message. 'It seems there is a possibility of dining with him tonight. You can meet him there.' It means that I have to stay here one more night. The rent of seven thousand. Two hundred dollars plus tax for the dinner. Which means another eight thousand. I just wanted to meet him casually.

She beamed a professional smile. Though he felt like telling her what a famous maestro he was, he didn't say anything thinking that it would be dishonouring music. He got into the van which was proceeding to Ujjain.

In the train and even after reaching Bombay he was completely in the grip of the Omkara . He closed the door and window, put the tambura next to his ears and started strumming. His experience of decades that the tambura emanates only Omkara now began to be heard clearly. He started singing only that. The feeling of losing shelter, wretchedness, sorrowful feeling of beseeching to be taken again into the fold, strange, feelings bereft of relation, slow sighing moves that yearn for relations. Then ascending the shrutis step by step, and finally reaching its culmination in the roaring sound of 'mm' utilising the theory of sound—raga-shastra—and his technical accomplishment, he gave the form of alaap to asavari for a period of forty-five minutes. There was no accompaniment of harmonium and tabla. Sometime right in the middle to the same Omkara creation of a complex rondo structure of shruti. Only the twin tamburas. The music got converted into a meditation and attained a form of inwardness. He felt a sense of achievement of having created something new. He began to believe that he was being elevated from an entertaining art to the level of spiritual enlightenment. He began to visualise the ideal of transforming every raga as a medium of expression of spirituality. If it was not possible in the noisy and crowded atmosphere of Bombay, he thought of getting away to some mountain peak. He must meet the kind of sadhu he met at Swami Haridas Mandir at Brindavan and must obtain a new feeling. He contemplated going away to the Himalayas, the shores of the Ganga or at least to the nearby Brahamagiri, the place of origin of River Godavari. Tansen transformed the Raga Darbari-Kanada to reflect the dignity of the Durbar of Emperor Akbar's Court. Just like that, by structuring some swaras and some movements as the expression of basic sorrow that is created by Maya, why can't I invent a raga as Maya-Kanada and publicise it? Or why can't I call it Mohana-Maya-Kanada?

At the annual music night programme of the Gandharva Mahavidyalay at Bombay he sang komala-rishabha asavari omkara for the first time. After explaining to the audience that he envisioned this new form after he knelt at the samadhi of Tansen and after he was blessed by the sadhu at Swami Haridas Mandir, who had perfected Omkara sadhana, he began to sing. He always had the long hair of a musician. That day, he had a large kumkum mark on his forehead. He was wearing a saffron jubba. A posture of closing his eyes and getting absorbed in the shruti. The listeners got immersed in bhakti-bhava. His singing became the crowing item of that evening's six concerts. When he concluded, no one applauded. They didn't open their eyes. The sound had lost its mobility and had become still. The two tamburas that were strumming in the back were also intensifying and mystifying the silence.

Two days later, that was the news in all the Bombay newspapers. Praise, Paranjape spoke to him on the phone for half an hour. The next day he wrote under a big caption: 'New heights in Indian music. The Omkara that was vocally attuned by the winner of the Tansen Award Mohanlal elevated our music from the level of art to spiritual heights at the annual music night of the Gandharva Mahavidyalay ....' Making use of the details of information, obtained by Mohanlal himself, he wrote a detailed write-up with many magnificent adjectives and embellishing his writing using all his flourishes of style. He had concluded by saying, 'When our famous musicians are gaining cheap popularity with the support of technical help like loud speakers, lighting tricks and crowd management popular devices, a saadhaka, a spiritual master like Mohanlalji preparing to reach the very acme of tradition has opened up new horizons in the artistic world of our India...' Right in the centre of it a large new type picture of a face with a smear of a large kumkum mark.

Though not as extensively as this, the other newspapers had also reviewed this musical achievement, giving it considerable importance. The newspapers had praised and complimented that throughout the raga, at all the levels, the Omkara alone was made to exult in his rendering of Asavari and this provided an aura of spirituality, which made the journalists appreciate it. The audience were also spellbound with the mood of devotion. After this, it became a convention for organisers of music concerts and even the audiences to request him to sing the Omkara.

Chapter 15

I

Manohari was filled with the bitterness that she has always been cheated by men. During the three or four years when Guruji had very little stamina in him, though sexual instinct had not been awakened in me, I served him and gave him comfort. After that I danced my prime life away for Mr. Mittal, a man of mature age, thinking that was the only tempo of dance and had derived contentment. Until the friendship with Mohan, there was no occasion to experience the enjoyment of equal pace. Those were the peak years of happiness. He who was a companion in the equal pace has rejected me, calling me an old woman and thinking about a woman of twenty-nine yers in my presence. I should have strangled that musician bastard who was never my equal in physical strength. Besides he had lost control by drinking, so in order to save his face, did he deride me as an old woman? She doubted. She felt at ease. She developed a generosity to forgive him. I myself lost patience. If I had traveled with him to Delhi and played the host, perhaps he would have got physical strength and successfully made love to me! Didn't the packed hall full of spectators of Paris congratulate me on the charm and delicacy of my dance and the ascending dance movements of Raga Bhoopali? How orderly she had gesticulated the peace of the morning, the enthusiasm of welcoming a new day and the feelings and emotions so soft and delicate! When the critic Daniel said this, in what congenial rhythm the audience applauded in agreement and approval!

Anna Batsky said, 'Give away your two eyes to me which by transformation of the view will show a new world and new life and I will change my whole life.' Was Mohan envious of this and therefore derided me like this? But he too got an equal amount of praise, no, even more. Was it a small appreciation saying, they did not have the concept that a whole ocean of emotions could be created with just one voice? It was I who created this opportunity for him. He himself complimented me by saying that I had transformed myself into an innocent girl who lights up the line of lamps in front of the house in the evening!!

No matter from what angle she thought about it, let alone forgiving his rejection of her, she couldn't move forward at all. It is true that he may not remember the words I spoke. But he is not so innocent as not to notice my wooing him and cajoling him for more than two weeks. He is an experienced lover. He behaved as if he didn't know a thing. Did he want to avoid quarreling with an old woman? Or did he put on an act of being drunk in order to hide his cruelty?

The dream of receiving new inspiration for dance from his singing was destroyed. How is it possible to admire the music of a man who destroyed the very source of friendship by disgracing me? She thought, how is it possible to get inspiration without admiration? He was not the only bloody big singer. Dance doesn't have to live only by music. She comforted herself that her beauty need not have to be defined by the taste of a tag-rag musician. She even forgot that incident.

Two months had elapsed. She felt like choreographing again; a composition similar to what she had created with the co-operation of Kartik. Though she asked herself why the composition she had abandoned fourteen years ago after suffering humiliation was still smothering her, she couldn't find an answer. It is my own composition. Not that of any one's. I don't need the music of anyone. I don't need the support of any cowardly dancer. I will prepare and train someone. Instead of Kartik, I will train Devaraj. She decided that it would be an advanced training for him. The rest are the usual roles. Our own girls are sufficient. I am Radha. Devaraj is Krishna. 'Devaraj, I will give you the role way beyond your capacity. Special training for four hours every day. There will also be the lessons for your Praveen Examination. Do you agree?

'Yes didi,' his face beamed.

'If this composition is carried and the programmes are arranged all over India would you be able to get leave of absence? This is a problem with employed people.'

'I won't utilise my leave for anything else, didi. If I don't have sufficient leave at my disposal, I will apply for sick leave. I will apply for special leave. My boss is an art lover. He won't come in the way!'

Devaraj had studied in Banaras. He was learning dance even when he was studying. Two and a half years ago he landed a junior officer's job and came to Delhi. After a month he enrolled with her school to continue dance practice. Twenty-four years old. Though he is keen on learning, he doesn't have any convenience to practise in his rented room and so there wasn't satisfactory progress. Besides, he was shy by nature. She started special training for him in the evenings, she would teach him alone till half past eight or nine. After a couple of weeks, she asked, 'Do you feel bored to dance for this long?'

'Didi, no one had taught me so intensely. In these two weeks I have learnt the secret of dance. You must kindly teach me completely. I want to give up my job and become only a dancer.'

'Do you desire to become totally a dancer, like me?'

'Yes, didi, if you would teach me.' He bent down and pressed his forehead on her feet, pressing them firmly.

'Understand one thing. It is not possible for anybody to grow as an artist without the grace of a guru.'

'I know that, didi. That is why I have surrendered to you.' He pressed his forehead again on her feet.

'I will never abandon a student who completely surrenders to me. Will you continue to have the same devotion till the end?'

'I swear.'

'Get up,' saying so, she put her right hand on top of his head and embracing him with her left hand, assured him, 'I will make you a well known dancer. This Manohari doesn't go back on her word.' She tightened her embrace and looking on him with a graceful eye, asked him to observe a trivet which she danced.

kdaa n dhaa dhaa dhaa dhaa ti ta ka ta ga di gi n dhaa
dha ki tta k dhu m ki tta k dhu mki t
dha ki ta ta k dhu m ki ta ta k dhi ta ta ga na dha
kdaa n dhaa dhaa dhaa

'Now observe the difference.'

ga di ga n na gdhe t ga di n kdaa n ki dna g.......

'Now you do this.'

He tried. The strike of the feet didn't correspond with the bols. 'Look, if they don't coincide, the sound of the jingle bells don't correspond. If you miss the beat it will be Betaal. Tell me what Betaal is. It is the goblin spirit of the story of *Bhatti Vikramaarka*. If you miss the taal, the Betaal with come and catch hold of you.'

Another week passed. The practice would go on till ten in the night. 'You go to your room alone at this time. What do you have for dinner? Isn't your room in Patel Nagar?

'Yes, didi.'

'Vacate your room tomorrow itself and shift to a room upstairs. You will avoid the fear of going alone so late in the night. Also, you can get up early in the morning and practise for an hour.'

'The same rent, I can...' He began.

'Will you ever bring in the question of rent for the education you are getting? If you do, look here.' She playfully slapped his left cheek. 'I got an inner prompting that I should keep a student like you with me and teach you.' She caressed the cheek with the fingers of her right hand, blew a warm breath with her mouth and comforted him.

His face blossomed when he said, 'If it is this kind of a blow, I would like to be slapped every day.'

Just as she asked him to do, he shifted the very next day. 'When I come in the morning, I will get you your breakfast. You will have your lunch in your office canteen. In the evening I will bring dinner.'

'All that is unnecessary didi.' He felt embarrassed.

'If you don't just listen and agree, you will get a slap.' He smiled. 'Why did you smile? Is it because you will get a caress after that?' His face reddened.

Two days later, after the school was empty, before starting the lesson, she said, 'All these days, the footwork has been practised. Along with it must follow the abhinaya part. Come here. Hold both my hands. Look steadily into my eyes.'

He did so. 'Look here, you are not mingling your eyes in mine. Eyes are the essence of abhinaya. As life unites with life and achieves oneness, so should looks melt into looks and become one. Come. Come close. Hold my face in your hands, like this.' She held his face and steadily gazed into his eyes. His eyes were shifty, trying to slip away, unable to receive that look. 'Look, you are Krishna. I am Radha. Imagine so, imagine so, completely. Otherwise acting is not possible. I am not Manohari. You are not a student. Get another thing straight. Krishna is sixteen years old. Radha is senior, a mature person. It is because she is a veteran in experience, that there is a mellowed love in her. She has the deep love which is capable of immersing him in it. That is the reason why the love of Radha and Krishna is exceptionally capable of inspiring poets and artists. You are Krishna. My Krishna. Think of me as your Radha. Now merge your looks in mine.'

His eyes were revealing confusion. Unable to meet her gaze, his eyes were evading. 'You grasp the footwork so easily. Why this confusion in acting? Tell me why?'

'It's nothing, didi, I will learn.'

'If you say, didi, look what happens.' She slapped him hard. Then she kissed him ardently, pressing her warm lips to the spot and said, 'Call me Radha. Didn't I ask you to forget the guru-shishya relationship? I am your Radha. You are my Krishna. Get into that mood completely. Become Krishna. You see, though Radha is mature, Krishna must invade her. He must master her. Is it possible for Radha to teach him everything? Now turn your eyes into mine. Do you know the meaning of the line *Gopi pina payodhara mardana chanchala karayugashaali*?'

'Yes, I know.'

'Say, yes, Radha, I do know.'

'Yes, I do know, Radha',

'Then do as you find in the poem. It says kara-yuga, a pair of hands. Here, give me both your hands this way.'

He followed. He became Krishna completely. He kissed her ear and whispered, 'Radha'.

2

After the general classes got over by half past seven and after the front door was shut when they went to bed in his room, she wouldn't feel like going home. He wouldn't let her, either. On the fourth day she said, 'Why should we sleep separately, you here and me there? Come with me. Guruji would be sleeping by now...Though he is awake, he can't see you coming up the stairs nor can he hear you. Though just in case he is sitting on the sofa, I will call you after I put him to bed. You come in and go straight up the stairs. Why should we miss the comfort and peace of sleeping together?' He was afraid. She got him up and led him saying, 'Why are you doubtful when I am telling you why any consternation? Guruji had never climbed the stairs. Now, of course he is ninety-eight. It is impossible. He can't even hear if spoken softly.' Still, he is in this house. Otherwise, there was no need to bring Devaraja by stealth and send him away secretly in the morning. If the lovers sleep together how peaceful it would be. How comfortably one can sleep! When there is a slight wakefulness during the night, the feel of the embracing arm of the beloved is experienced, how easily sleep envelops one! When he is facing the other side, even if I embrace him with my arm, there is the same feeling of security, well being and continuing sleep. Now I have gained it in my life. I didn't even have an idea that he was capable of such deep love. Devaraja, I will call you Raja. You are not the king to the gods, but for me. I will address you so publicly. Whom should I fear!

'Are you asleep?' She would whisper.

'No.'

'What are you thinking?'

'It is my good fortune that I found you as my teacher. I, who didn't at all have any experience of love, how could I act the role of Krishna? Now, I think there is no need for you to instruct me and correct me again and again.'

'My Raja,' she embraced and kissed him. 'Do you say that this is only a part of dance training?'

'Did I say that?'

'Love is always immortal, eternal. It never diminishes. Tell me that, holding my hand.'

He held her hand in the dim light, squeezed it and took an oath, 'This love will never diminish, my queen. I swear by me, my life and my love.' Her eyes watered. Her breath warmed up. He got further melted by the warm teardrop on his face.

'Shall we get married, my love?' he asked.

'Would you?'

'Would I ask you if I didn't mean it?'

'At your place? Won't there be a commotion if you say you will marry someone older than you?'

'Who will say you are older when they see you? Even if it appears so, it is only by two or three years. If I just send them the money regularly, they will accept you as their younger daughter-in-law. Even if they don't, they will stay by themselves in the village. We will stay by ourselves in Delhi, if just a grand child is born they will come running.'

She felt a shiver go through her at the mention of a child. She felt that he didn't know that she was approaching fifty-seven. He thinks that I am a mature person, a little older than him and a woman who can still bear children. Shall I tell him my real age? She thought. But she was afraid that he might move away.

'Do you desire a child?'

'Don't you?' She felt suffocated by his question. There was an upsurge of sorrow. She started crying in fits. He pressed her to his chest and caressed her head. 'Why did you weep?'

'You asked if I didn't want a child.'

'There isn't even a single line on your stomach, not a fold either you don't have even an unnecessary gram of flesh on your body. So I thought you have never been pregnant.'

'You don't know. Keep quiet.' She closed his lips with hers. She felt impelled to tell him about her pregnancy and her getting an abortion and surgery to prevent any further pregnancies. She didn't feel that his love could bear all that. He is still with the ashta-padi. He has read it again, the erotic extravaganza, noted down the details of the beauty of Radha's body and is giving expression to them relating it to my body in detail. He quotes the details of the entire love making—he repeated, hot kisses, the full and heavy breasts, the shyness, the intimate whispers, the gentle parting of the cloth covering the intimate private parts etc. My breasts are not of that size and heaviness.

Chaaru chuchumba nitambavati, nakhalikhita Ghanastana bhaaram
Prathama samaagama lajjitayaa patuchaatu shatairanukulam
Mridumadhurasmita bhaashitayaa shithileekrita jaghanadukulam

Kisalayashayana niveshitaya chiramurasi mamaiva shayaanam
Kritaparirambhana chumbanayaa parirabhya kritaadharapaanam

He is worshipping me as Radha. Would he accept me as Manohari? She decided not to mention the details about Manohari. She merely said, 'Raja, Radha is someone else's wife. But an immortal lover of Krishna. They didn't marry. If they had, the intensity of their love would not have survived.' She remembered her husband. He is ninety-eight. Still alive. He won't object to my marrying Raja. He won't attempt to establish his right. If I say, 'I will continue to look after your material needs like food and clothes. After all, your role of a husband ceased thirty years ago,' he has no choice but to accept. If it becomes necessary, the formality of divorce can be completed, she thought. But is it proper for her to shift her place from Radha to that of Rukmini? She thought for a number of days. It was difficult for her to come to any conclusion. The memory that his mind had made a provision for a child too, made her further helpless. She embraced and made love to him ardently and whispered, 'My Krishna, marriage is but a mean thing compared to the immortality of love. Have you understood?' He said, 'Yes.'

The choreography was successful. The production was exhibited in several cities. There were eight performances in Delhi alone. The spectators had forgotten the same programme, given with Kartikaram fifteen years ago. There was one critic, however, who had written thus: One remembers that Manohari had performed the same item a decade and a half ago with one Kartikaram of Jaipur Gharana. Since Devaraj is younger than Kartikaram, he is more suitable for the role of Krishna, naturally. But he still has to achieve the sense of rhythm which Kartikaram could bring out spontaneously. On seeing it a second time, one feels that he is mechanically repeating like a parrot what he has been taught. However, the mature Manohari, in keeping with the maturity associated with the mature Radha is still shining forth in a mature fashion both in dance and acting aspects.

Devaraja read that newspaper in his office, brought and showed it. Manohari noticed the clever subversion of repeating the word mature three times in just one sentence. Rascal, she thought. She had noticed that after she had become influential in the government sponsored programmes, she wouldn't be mischievously criticised. Now she was a dignitary in the dance circles. She thought that no one had the courage to think and express it that way. Who is this critic? No name had been mentioned. Was it deliberate? It wouldn't be difficult to find out, she thought. But Devaraj said, 'I was displeased when I read this in the morning. That mine was just a parrot like repetition. By evening, it abated. He has identified something which no one else has. It is finished with the role of this composition. Teach me regularly. Teach me each and every movement of the taal in great detail, every step of the way. I don't know how I can go from one rhythmic movement of the taal to another effortlessly, play with it to your heart's content and return. Teach me for three hours in the evening. I will practise by myself in the morning.'

She thought what he felt was true. She said, 'Let's start from tomorrow.'

But as soon as he got into bed after dancing for three hours he would immediately go to sleep and start snoring. She thought of the consequence of not enjoying the happiness of touch, foreplay and pillow talk. Just like she was going to sleep immediately when Guruji would make her practise the whole day after her marriage. She felt perturbed on remembering that she endured whatever the old man did in her sleep of fatigue. Now I might...after this fellow slips to slumber. The old man is forty years older than me. I am thirty-three years older than this fellow. The discomfort increased. Raja is not given to talking much. He is an introvert. Is he also enduring like me? Or, in the vicarious role of playing Radha and Krishna, these differences are not occurring at all? This fellow is inexperienced. I am the one who opened the door of experience. He is not aware of comparison. She suspected, that was the reason why he had a single-minded devotion. What immediate difference is there for comparison? I am a bit older, that's all. Whoever can say that I am older by more than thirty years? There isn't a single crease on the neck. Breasts are not sagging. The facial muscles haven't loosened. He has himself admired the trimness of my stomach. Which dancer has done the yoga exercises that I have and am still doing? She consoled herself that what was visible under the eyes was maturity, not old age. That night when he called her by endearing names like Rati and Madanika, what small doubts she entertained, vanished. She awoke early in the morning. His breath of deep sleep was caressing her neck. Yes, she must start the advanced lessons regularly from this evening. Three hours a day. At intervals, Jaswal, the accompanist on the tabla must be summoned. If it is for three hours, he will demand at least two hundred rupees per day. While pondering that taal will not be perfected without the tabla, a caution lifted up its head. It will take at least three years for the completion of the training and she will be sixty years of age. The dirty journalists won't forget and will write articles. The fans will arrange a felicitation. After receiving the full training and after it is advertised that she is sixty will he remain attached to her with the same intensity? Her entire body shivered. In all the pores of her skin, particles of sweat sprung up. His breath was fanning her neck still. After he woke up in the morning and she went down the steps silently and signaled that Guruji was not in sight, and after he descended silently and pushed the scooter noiselessly for some thirty and forty feet and then started it and sped away, even then her perspiration persisted. Even after she doled out biscuits and tea to Guruji it didn't stop completely. The cook arrived the time she finished her shower. She thought of a plan. When she sat in the car and started it, how about marrying him and keeping him firmly in a matrimonial stranglehold? He had himself proposed it. Remembering that she herself had proposed to just live like Radha and Krishna, he will agree readily, quite happily. If caught in the shackles of law, it isn't possible to escape. Another tie up appeared, he was a government servant. Her enthusiasm dampened when she realised that it was on record that she was Guruji's wife and this impediment showed that the marriage was not possible. He is ninety-eight. He is still sitting around like the legendary Jataayu without a care in the world. She was irked that such people don't die early. After coming to the dance school, going up the stairs to Raja's room where he was ready to go to work after a shower, gave him the packet of breakfast and exchanged kisses and said, 'this is till the evening'. While she was giving the lessons to senior students, she saw a way out. How about meeting the advocate Ramoo Walia who would plan an escape by making the Guruji sign a pre-dated document or through some other legal trick he would make my wedding with Raja legal. This confidence appeared. Wasn't it nineteen years ago that he made Mohan's wife write out in her own handwriting that all her property and bank deposits were made with the money of her husband! Remembering this, her confidence in the ability of the advocate Ramoo Walia was total. With the decision that marriage was the solution she started correcting the girls—the hand and the neck movement and the footwork of each student. The memory of Mohan engendered by the memory of Ramoo Walia began to bother her. That bastard called me an old woman. He thought about a twenty-nine year old girl of French origin in my presence. If he had accepted me, I would have advanced his career. I would have introduced him to a dozen ambassadors. I would have recommended him to the titles Padmabhushana and Padmavibhushana. What a fool, he ruined his chances. He mentioned Bhoopali of twenty-nine years, didn't he? She comforted herself, by thinking, 'I am going to marry Devaraj of twenty-five, get the wedding pictures published in the newspapers and I will send that rascal the cuttings by mail.'

She started the lessons to Raja in the evening. Explaining each calculations of every taal in detail about the additions, subtractions, multiplications and divisions and which laya may be obtained by what sort of division and calculations, she demonstrated herself and made him dance accordingly. No matter how much she danced, she didn't feel tired, she didn't gasp for breath. He wasn't sufficiently trained. After dancing for two hours, he was tired. She thought she should make him practise yoga and pranayama. She told him let's have an hour's practice in the morning and for two hours in the evening. In addition, you practise yoga. After the session, he stood still. She commanded, 'I am the guru here. Touch my feet here in keeping with tradition. After that I am your lover.' She smiled with love.

It happened just as she had expected. He quickly slept off. Dancing till the limbs ached. After that the hot shower, which they took together. Then dinner. Her efforts to keep him awake at least for an hour were in vain. She must shake him by the shoulders and whisper, she couldn't speak aloud. Though the door of the room was shut, there was that anxiety, if accidentally the eagle ears of the old man who was sleeping downstairs heard it in the silence of the night! He slept off breathing down her neck. Though she had danced as much as he had, she wasn't sleepy. Yes, I can keep awake for any length of time. I can dance for two more hours. Who is the one that is young? She comforted herself in pride and self confidence. After half an hour an impediment appeared. Marrying means surrendering herself to him. The respect and reverence for a guru will transform itself into authority. After accepting him as a husband she must act with obedience in public as well as in the presence of the students. He will exercise authority. The freedom she had enjoyed for years on, will disappear. The mind was caught up in turmoil.

The next evening after coaching him for two hours when they were having a warm shower she asked, 'In the area where you come from, do the husbands beat their wives?'

'Why?'

'I have heard that it is an old habit in your part of the country.' His face broke into a smile as if he had remembered something. She asked, 'Why did you laugh?'

'I have an aunt. My mother's elder sister. An extremely good lady, totally innocent. Once it seems she complained to her mother that her husband didn't love her. When she was asked why, she replied that he had never beaten her, not even once.'

'What you are saying is that you will beat your wife.'

'When did I say that?' he asked in misapprehension.

'There was a smile of joy on your face when you spoke about your aunt.'

'It was a remark that gave rise to laughter.'

She left it at that. But the mind was sorrowful within her. It was decided that if she married him, he would certainly beat her one day or the other. He also didn't say anything after that. The day after that while taking the shower she asked, 'Is there a dowry system in your region?'

'Why?'

'I just asked.'

'Recently it has developed a great deal.'

'How much will you get if you marry?'

'The question arises only if I do. I have my Radha.'

'Krishna married eight times after he left Radha. Answer my question.'

'It seems there is a landlord. He has proposed his daughter and he is repeating that if I marry her he will get a house built for me in Delhi. They had written to me.'

'Why do you miss the opportunity? Reply immediately giving your consent.'

'What are you saying?' He slapped her soap smeared back. It was not a playful slap. There was the force of anger. She liked it. She gazed at him with love filled eyes. She embraced and kissed him.

That night he didn't go to sleep at once. He was talking for a while. He had understood that she would be happy if he praised her beauty of form and shape which never got tired no matter how much she danced. He made love to her calling her with a new description 'sweet seventeen'. After he slept, her mind engaged itself in thinking. Both the school and the house are registered in my name. After the wedding what part of this will come under his right legally? She must consult a lawyer. What would she do if, after the marriage he starts trouble by saying that he would not live in his wife's house and ask her to change the ownership of the house to his name? He might say that if he had married the daughter of the landlord from his place, he would get a house built in his own name. If she said that she wouldn't, he might even beat her. How would he take it if he came to know that she couldn't bear a child and that she was also past that age! Wouldn't he create a rumpus if he knows the exact difference in age? She felt that if she married, problems would arise and multiply.

The two hour training had been going on for a month. Besides, he was practising by himself for an hour and a half to two hours, in the mornings. He would tape many parts of the previous evening and would benefit by them. One evening she told him, 'I am teaching you at such a rapid pace. But it must become a part of you—your torso and feet. If the bottom brick is not laid firmly the brick that is put on top of it will be wobbly and tomorrow the whole structure will collapse. An hour's lesson is enough. Thrice a week. After you attain proficiency in the morning's practice, then the next lesson. That is the right method.'

He agreed. She expected that he wouldn't agree and would argue. After going home in the evening, the opportunity to enjoy intimacy before falling asleep was found. But of late, even in bed he would talk only about the lessons. He asks critical questions regarding the result of changing the bols. She would make love to him by telling him, 'My Raja, when you are in bed you must talk of love and engage in it. Without the anklets tied to the feet and without standing on the wide dance floor, discussing dance is useless.' He wouldn't reply. He doesn't transgress the limits of a student. Her mind questions itself in asking whether it is not a mistake to slow down the pace of teaching a pupil like this. Everyone will be obedient as long as they are learning. The suspicion hardened that he will slip away the moment his education is complete. No rent for the room. Morning breakfast and dinner in the evening is free. No fee for the lessons. The mind plans, let him learn for eight to ten years. By then he will be thirty-five. Then where can he go? Who will offer their daughter to him? If he remains faithful till the end, I will give him both my buildings. She justifies in complimenting herself that she won't do injustice to him and embraces him firmly. She would understand that he would accept but his mind was engaged in the rhythm and time in dance. She would whisper, 'If you are thinking about it incessantly, learning will not be easy. You must give interval to it from time to time,' and she would draw him closer.

३

She received a letter from the government. The United Nations had arranged a lengthy workshop at Tokyo to study the various Asian Traditions of dance comparatively. It had been decided to send her as the representative from India. The United Nations would bear the expenses of the trip to Tokyo and hospitality of three months there. Further details would be communicated by the cultural office situated in Paris.

She became ecstatic that she would be honoured not only at the all India level but also in the United Nations. She had already become famous internationally. Gradually she would be considered an international celebrity. She guessed the concerned Indian government officials who were in the selection committee. She expressed her thanks by phone. She went to the Secretariat fully dressed as a dancer, minus the ankle-bells, obtained an interview with them, praised their artistic taste and thanked them. She put on an act of anger and asked, 'Why aren't you teaching dance to your daughter? Shouldn't I have the opportunity of teaching her?' She displayed her coquetry. When the officer in charge replied, 'Where do I have a daughter of a young age who can be taught dancing? She is already married and has two children.' When the old man who was trying to look middle aged by dyeing his hair black, she pretended to be surprised and made him happy, 'Is it? You don't look like that.'

When she realised that in all these years she had never left her school and her home for three months at a stretch she was worried. Naturally she had to put Omprakash in charge. But he is lazy. If I am not around to keep him in check, he would absent himself, giving some excuse or the other. When there was no one to question him for three months, he might abscond for weeks. Even if he turned up, he might not engage the classes for the full time. Everyone knows that Devaraja who was also a student was living in the same building. Omprakash also knows it. After all Devaraja was working as an officer in the government. She decided to tell everyone that he would be the supervisor. The same would hold good for the home also. He should sleep there. He would be introduced to Guruji as a student. He should go home early in the evening and dine there. He should stay there in the morning till the domestic help would arrive. This was the arrangement she made. She explained everything to Devaraja. 'Be careful about one thing. Both boys and girls learn together at the school. What they learn is dance. The erotic element will be the primary emotion. If the students go beyond the limits, the parents will attach a bad reputation to the school. Be careful. Be strict about attendance. Everyone knows that you play the role of Krishna in all our programmes, that you stay here and that you are an officer. Everyone will be afraid of your authority.'

He accepted the responsibility. Before leaving there are a hundred things to take care of. The passport must be renewed, the visa must be obtained and the government officers have to be visited. Also, the letters received from Japan must be replied to immediately. With all these things, the students at the advanced level couldn't be given enough coaching. Not just this, even Devaraja could not be taught regularly. There was this vague anxiety. The worry that he might betray her. How wonderful it would be if she could take him along, she thought. If she could bear his expenses? She felt that it would have been easy to get a visa etc if she was married to him. Three months. But he might not get three month's leave of absence. The night before leaving she made love to him, hugged, kissed and said, 'My Raja, you know, don't you that my life is within you?'

He replied, 'Both our lives are within each other.'

'If you ask me not to go, even now I will cancel the trip. You are more important to me than a foreign trip.'

'It is a once-in-a-lifetime opportunity. If you cancel it in the last minute without giving them time to choose someone else, the United Nations will never again select you.'

'My Raja, you have understood all this. After I return I will teach you for three hours a day,' she burst out. Immediately, she corrected herself. 'By then you get perfected by everything you have been taught. Without perfecting what has been learnt, what is to be taught will not be effective.'

He assured her, 'Yes, I know. Don't worry.'

She didn't take anyone else but him to the airport. She sat in the back seat of the taxi holding his hand. After putting her luggage in the trolley and crossing the gate of 'Passengers Only' enclosure, while bidding good bye holding his hand, she was in tears.

Her visit was packed with events, watching the dances of various Asian countries and understanding them, demonstrating the highlights of Indian dance, performing in various places and participating in the arranged programmes by dancing to the sound of the recorded tapes of music, refreshing the knowledge and practice of dance twice a week to the wives of the officials of the Indian Embassy who had learnt dance but who were out of touch.

Like this her time was totally taken up in a busy schedule. Still, she would remember Devaraja. The desire of bringing him along by marrying him would bother her. She would ring him up when possible. But the difference in the time between the two countries and the opportunity for him to pick up the phone when he was alone was an impediment. At home there would be Guruji. At school the phone was in the office. In his place of work, he didn't have a separate room to himself; no independent phone either. It was disappointing. She had never written anything emotionally. But she felt that the prose she was using was getting to be more poetic than the poetry of the poet Jayadeva. She wrote a two-page letter and mailed it. The next day also, after coming to the hotel she wrote another letter. Upon returning to the hotel, she was all alone. Though the dance representatives of various countries were lodged in the same hotel, she, as a woman going to their rooms or calling them out was not proper conduct. Though there were three female dancers, they were not friendly, perhaps because they were envious of her. Her mind would find consolation only in writing letters to her Raja.

4

Her Tokyo visit was extremely fruitful. The secretary of the cultural department of the government of Japan invited her along with a delegation of ten artists to come and give eight programmes without fail—three in Tokyo, two in Kyoto one each in Nagoya, Osaka and Hiroshima. He also suggested that in addition to her prepared items, at least one composition could be presented about Lord Buddha. The representatives of Thailand, Malaysia, Korea and Indonesia also praised her knowledge and expertise in dance and said they would try to get her invited to their countries. The Japanese dancer Teeko who had already learnt Indian dance for two years requested her to accept her as a student for three years to learn Kathak at her school and she would come to Delhi. She returned with the happiness that she had truly earned international recognition. She purchased for Raja not only a shirt and trousers but a suit as well.

He had come to the airport in the morning. He shook hands saying 'Welcome'. He didn't embrace and kiss her. She comforted herself thinking, 'This is Delhi, India not Paris. She sat in the taxi holding his hand. There was no privacy to get more intimate. The long line of other taxis and cars were shedding their lights around. After dropping her at home he said, 'Guruji hasn't yet woken up. You sleep for a couple of hours. I must also get some sleep.' He started off for the school. She signalled to him to come up and sleep together. He signalled back declining the offer. Morning was breaking. She understood that he implied that it was an odd hour. Though she felt that he could come up and engage in a silent embrace and a kiss, she did not put it into words. He just left. She heard the scooter starting off. She felt he had changed. Had the heat of passion cooled down? She wondered if the English saying 'Out of sight, out of mind' had come true. No, he hasn't slept. He had come to the airport at midnight itself and had been waiting. Also, the flight was late. He hasn't the ability to forego sleep. Let him sleep. The entire evening is ours. From today the entire night too. She imagined getting twin rooms in the hotel at Japan and sleeping together. If it was just the two of them, they could have stayed in the same room. But going in a troupe it would cause a scandal. She had exercised caution. She realised that it would be the same in the other Asian countries also. The solution appeared that no tongues would wag if they got married. Took a shower, ate some bread, swallowed a pill and lay down. She got some sleep.

It was a bit late when Devaraja came back from the office in the evening. By that time she had met the students and had enquired after their welfare. She had told them about the Tokyo workshop. Omprakash was quite happy. On informing the students about the possibility of going to Japan again, the senior students asked her to take them too. She told them proudly and encouragingly, god willing, she would since their school was the very first in ranking in the whole of India. By the time she closed the front door of the school and went up, Devaraja had come, had a wash and had changed. He begged her pardon. 'The Joint Secretary had called a meeting and so there was a delay.' But he didn't approach and sit next to her. Didn't hold her hand, didn't embrace either. Noticing the change in him she sat on the sofa. Sitting on the bed, he informed, 'There was no problem at school. The students of Praveen level didn't come as you weren't here. However, three of them used to come and practise. Omprakashji wasn't absent too often.'

'Don't you have anything else to say?' She asked pointedly.

'Since the senior students themselves weren't coming, there was no problem of discipline.'

'And?'

'What else? You must tell about the international news?'

She looked at him steadily, silently. He seemed to have gathered courage and met her gaze. After a couple of minutes, she asked 'Why did you use the respectful plural in addressing me?'

'You shouldn't address the guru in the familiar singular. I was forgetting.' He got up, approached her, touched both her feet and she stroked his head. 'I am waiting for the three hour coaching from tomorrow.'

She was still more angry. It was certain he was hiding something. She said, 'Just say what you want to, directly,' arresting his look. He looked vanquished. For a minute he lowered his look to the floor. Then, as if he had decided, he looked up and meeting her gaze, he said, 'You know Alka, the girl who is learning at the advanced Praveen level, I am going to marry her. Her parents also have agreed.'

She felt suffocated. A girl of twenty-one. She has just completed her B.Sc. degree. She is interested in learning. Not very bright. Slim and five foot three. Even when the picture appeared before her eyes, she felt giddy and leaned her head against the back of the sofa. One minute. Another minute. Her thinking became clear. She decided not to show what had happened to her. After another minute she lifted her head and sitting up straight, asked him point blank quite firmly, 'Were you waiting for my absence to cheat?' He didn't reply. 'This is an event that developed in my school. How did this happen?' She demanded as if she was conducting an inquiry.

'You know she used to come to our programmes. She used to perform the role of the companion of Radha. I had seen her. One day she came to discuss a lesson. We talked. I was attracted. In a week we became close. I myself asked her if she would marry me. She didn't show any further intimacy. 'What if didi gets to know about this?' She was afraid that there was a school regulation that boy and girl students should not get familiar and get married. It is against school discipline. I myself consoled her that there was no need to be afraid.'

'Did you take her to bed? In this room, on this very bed?'

'No, I didn't have a bodily contact. Didn't touch her intimately. I am telling the truth. I invited her. She didn't agree. She said strictly that it shouldn't take place before the marriage.'

'What is the attraction you found in her?'

'Her innocent beauty. Her pure innocence.'

'You say that you haven't made love to her. That you haven't touched her, how did you discover her innocent beauty?'

'Though a blossoming bud is at a distance, doesn't it send forth fragrance? Do you have to examine its beauty only by squeezing it?'

She didn't talk. Her lips quivered as if she was trying to speak. Her eyes filled with vapoury tears. She suddenly got up and stood before him. He looked up, sitting just where he was. Before he became aware of it, she lifted her right hand and slapped his cheek hard. Before he understood what was happening, she slapped him again. He hardened his face by biting his gums in order to bear the pain. She lifted her left hand slapped his right cheek. After hitting him hard with seven or eight blows she stood still. He had bent his head. She understood it was with shame. She screamed, 'She is a blossoming bud. After enjoying me all these days, are you calling me an old woman and insulting me?'

'I didn't mention anything about you. I won't either,' he said, recovering. His cheeks were swelling.

'You didn't say it. You suggested it. Let me see how you are going to marry her. I will myself tell her and her parents about our relationship. I will tell them that you had even talked about marrying me. Did you or didn't you propose to me. Just blurt out.'

'You are a guru who taught me. Therefore, no matter how much you beat me up, I didn't lift my hand to you. I am twenty-six and if I hit you back, you won't be able to endure it. Did you think that I didn't know you delayed the process of teaching me because you wanted me to hold on to you? If the relationship you dragged me into is known to my Alka, she will be pained. I won't tolerate it even if she is hurt a little. If you try to take her away from me, beware, the letters that you wrote to me are the evidence. I will bundle them up, give to the newspapers and tell them everything about how you seduced me and how you are managing to keep me under control.'

'You want to tell them. Do!' She lifted her hand again but changed her mind and opening the doors of the cupboard, started rummaging, throwing out the papers and clothes and started searching. Removed and overturned the lower compartment box.

'What will you find there if you search? I knew you would do it. The letters are not there. They are not even in my office. They are safe in a secret place. I don't want to make public the private letters. I will return them to you if I get a guarantee that you won't harm my marriage with Alka and that it will not happen in future also.' He began to gather his clothes which she had thrown helter skelter, fold them and pack his suitcase. He went into the bathroom brought out the soap, tooth paste and brush and put them in the box. She understood that he would leave immediately. She was stunned. The limbs went limp. She sat on the sofa and stretched her legs. He threw the two bundles of keys next to her that were in his hands, took up the suitcase and the bag, and just walked out.

Chapter 16

I

One day Paranjape called. After the usual polite enquiries, he made a proposal, 'Several people are asking me to make the cassettes of Omkara. I have decided to do whatever is possible for the cause of music. There is one, Shashikanth Pokale, son of my friend. He has started a new cassette business. It would be an encouragement to him. If you could kindly come to the studio and sing, we will look after the rest.'

'What are the terms and conditions?'

'I said he is my friend's son. An extremely honest fellow. If it sells well, he will pay royalty. In the beginning I will arrange for an advance payment of twenty-five thousand rupees. It is nothing for your status. You must consider it as just a token of gratitude.'

Mohanlal didn't know much about the cassette business. He had not made up his mind to prevent legally the deal that Champa had made. He had also a feeling that the cassette companies doled out a raw deal. So it was difficult to reply immediately. Besides, to a musician of his fame and standing, who attracted the people everywhere, the honorarium of twenty-five thousand seamed trite. Still, without saying 'No' at once, he said, 'You know I haven't made even a single cassette. Give me some time to think it out.' 'Let it take its time, there's no hurry,' Paranjape also didn't push it.

That evening Mohanlal had been invited for dinner at Jhunjhunwala's place. Tipnis was also there. Jhunjhunwala had said that he would invite four of his friends. It had been arranged that Tipnis should come to Mohanlal's flat and the car would be sent there to pick them up. Since Tipnis was not busy, he called up and came an hour earlier. When he came, Mohanlal told him about Paranjape's proposal. He noticed that the moment Tipnis heard it, there was a mischievous smile on his face which he suppressed. He asked, 'Why did you smother your smile?'

'My grandson had come home. I remembered his mischief.'

'Not that you should not remember your grandson's mischief the moment I mentioned Paranjape's proposal. But your face shows that it is a lie. Tell me the truth.' Mohanlal looked steadily at his face.

Tipnis didn't have the acting skill to produce a natural expression, instantly on his face. After Mohanlal insisted, he extended his hand and said, 'Swear that you will not mention to anyone at any time that I told you.' After Mohanlal vowed, Tipnis withdrew his hand and said, 'Come to think of it, it has not really remained a secret. But these small things don't reach your ears because of your high status. The name that he mentioned, Shashikant Pokale is not at all his friend's son. He is a boy who has been hired by him. He is running a cassette company called Vittal Cassette Company. Vittala is the name of his family deity. Since he is in the newspaper business he knows artists and holds out the temptation that he will give them publicity. The twenty-five thousand that he offered you is a very big amount. He had paid just a thousand or two to other artists and has washed his hands. There is no account of the sales. If you give away your cassette of Omkara to him, he will make a profit of fifteen to twenty lakhs. It is even possible that he has already recorded your singing in various concerts. Do you remember that two and half years ago I and Prabhu had asked you about the cassette that Champa Bai had made under the name of Mohan Melodies and marketed it? Someone told me that it was Paranjape who gave her the idea and supplied the cassettes. Isn't Champa Bai the daughter of Pratap Rao Naik who promoted his career in his profession? He has a secret sympathy for her.'

Mohanlal contemplated, 'What a bastard! Did he write so extensively about it only with the nefarious intention of making it into a cassette and selling it?' He suspected. Yes, there's such power in its composition. He wrote about it. He didn't invent the innate power it possesses.

The next morning there was a phone call from the Globe Musical Voice company. 'Our executive director would like to come and meet you. If you would come to our office yourself, it would be our pleasure. We will send the car. We would like to make a cassette of yours. We want to discuss it.' He agreed to go himself. When he went to their office situated in the Fort area, he saw that it was a very big company with an international standing. Their deal was straightforward. 'We have thought about making a cassette of your recent Omkara rendering. It can be marketed in India as a variation on Raga Asavari. But it will be marketed in the West as a form of meditation which is spreading there as representing Indian spirituality. People like those in the Hare Krishna movement will welcome it with open arms. Besides, there is a possibility to use it as a therapeutic background, as a means of giving peace and tranquillity in the alleviation of mental diseases. We will sell it in various places under different titles. That will be taken care of by our marketing department. We will pay you fifteen lakh as an advance honorarium. This is just an advance. After the sales, we will give you an account of the details of what cassettes were sold where and how many and we will pay you royalty on a percentage basis. If you agree, we will pay you one lakh right away and fifteen lakhs as soon as the recording is over. You must come and record in the studio we choose within two weeks at your convenience. After that there is a possibility of recording some other ragas.'

He hadn't seen fifteen lakhs in one place in his whole life—it was money collected from fifteen concerts. At many of the concerts, on account of some pressures ten, twenty and even thirty thousand would be exempted. Mohanlal became aware that there would not be any travel or concerts for a few months. He signed the contract and returned in the company car. The very idea that there would be fifteen lakh in his bank account gave him pleasure. The next day he received a phone call from Paranjape. He began thinking about what to say after the preliminary polite inquiry was over and after coming to brass-tacks. The signing of the contract is already over. In a couple of days everyone will come to know about it. He will also come to know it. When he decided it would be better to tell him right away, he said, 'I have already recorded your Omkara in four different places. Can I use one of them or would you prefer to sing in a studio?'

'The day before yesterday the people from the Globe Musical Voice had come with four of my friends. They didn't give me a chance to speak at all. The friends got together made me sign right away. Sorry. I will help your friend's son in some other way. Promise,' he said.

Paranjape fell silent for a minute. Thinking that the phone connection was cut, Mohanlal said, 'Hello, Hello!' He spoke, 'You said that there were four friends. Who are they?'

'Oh, those people. You don't know them. From Calcutta—from among those who came to my concert there.'

'There is no one in the music world I don't know. It isn't possible. Give me their names,' Paranjape said.

Mohanlal was angry that he was being cross-examined. Still, not showing it he said, 'One Banerjee, one Dasgupta, a Sengupta and one Roy. They learn from me when I go there.'

'What are the terms and conditions?'

'An advance of fifteen lakhs. International distribution level.'

Again he was silent. Wanting him to react, Mohanlal didn't say 'Hello Hello'. Two minutes later, Paranjape himself said 'Hello,' and hearing the response, continued, 'Your singing. You have the freedom and authority to give it to whomsoever you please. But you too gave greater importance to money than friendship. It makes me sad. All right, that's the way the world moves, isn't it?'

When he asked, 'Where is the question of friendship in this?' he remembered what Tipnis had said that this fellow had a say in Champa Bai's selling the cassettes. 'If you had remembered at what critical times I have helped you, you wouldn't have asked this question. Though you treated my patron's daughter badly, I supported you. When you got kicked out by the Delhi dancer and came to Bombay as an orphan, I kept you at Koregaon. I gave publicity and established you again in Bombay. I have helped you all along. It was I who gave you supporting publicity in your quarrel with Junnarkar and made him return the tambura. I was the one who arranged for an unprecedented and never to be seen felicitation. Now, you were lured by fifteen lakh advance, you betrayed friendship.'

'If you had truthfully said that Vittal Cassette company was yours, I would have given you the contract. You told a lie that it was for the son of a friend. Answer me first.' He himself continued, 'It is true you helped me. But don't I have any merit myself?' he said. Paranjape put down the phone.

2

Whenever Mohanlal remembered that Paranjape had supported him he felt bad about the conversation. Not just for him either. The newspaper he was working for was giving him a lot of space to write about music, dance, drama and film. Not just in Bombay but it would carry a report from many a city in India of the good cultural programmes along with impressive photographs. Since he was an aficionado and had fundamental knowledge of the arts, that newspaper had retained Paranjape as the sub-editor of that section for the past twenty-five to thirty years. As his seniority was established he would write for the other sections also and would supervise them too. Regarding the performing arts, not only the chief editor but the entire editorial staff considered him an expert. Thus it was easy for him to either promote or create an opinion in favour of any artist. Since he was looking after the critical opinion of those areas for many years, he was influential in circles organising music and dance. Even the film people greeted him respectfully. However, his influence was greater in the music and dance world than in the film world and its many affiliated aspects involving millions of rupees. Though on account of his age he had retired, the same newspaper where he was working had re-employed him to do the same job as a consultant.

After he had the bitter exchange with Mohanlal, there appeared one article in the Sunday edition. It had been written by Dr. Vajrakishore Jani, professor of music section in the university. There was a big photograph along with a write up on his research and a list of his published books. He had begun with some general observations on music but with the specific purpose of hitting at Mohanlal. 'It is a well known fact that recently some ambitious, self-appointed experts in the musical field are giving wide publicity to themselves as if they are the only ones who have drunk deep from the spring of Indian spiritual music. Mohanlalji, who has manoeuvred to get this year's Tansen Award (I am not forgetting that he is a close friend of mine) is publicising that he has attained greater heights of yogic musical mastery than Tansen and that he has been inspired by Swami Haridas, the guru of Tansen and it is common knowledge that he is taking the music lovers on a ride and mesmerising them by singing the Omkara. It is only substituting Omkara for Aakara in the alaap of the Raga Komala-rishabha Asavari. Even there he has polluted the raga by mixing up Asavari with Jeevanpuri here and there, either knowingly or unknowingly. Mohanlal who is now basking in the euphoria of popular fame, let him, if he has the courage, sing the same alaap publicly sitting in front of me and in the presence of music critics. I will point out right there where he is committing the mistakes. Pleasing the uninitiated masses who are without the theoretical knowledge of music is one thing, but convincing the experts with subtle aesthetic perception and theoretical knowledge is quite another. The musician who wants to raise it to spiritual heights must first of all have a good character. No one, who knows the personal life of Pandit Mohanlal can be cheated by his pretensions to spirituality...' About half a page had been written.

The moment he read this, Mohanlal understood that this was Paranjape's manoeuvre. He did not know Jani from the university very well. He only knew that having been unsuccessful in the field of music; he had obtained a Ph.D and was living on the salary of the university. The journalist had used him. He understood that he had tried to become famous in a vain attempt to throw a challenge on Mohanlal. He didn't care for it. But when he went to bed after dining he began to feel sad. He was worried that not only had he lost Paranjape but that the man whom he had thought as a well-wisher, had descended to such a low level. He remembered the words of Tipnis that Paranjape had a soft corner for Champa Bai. Paranjape's words also came to his mind that he had supported Mohanlal in spite of the fact that he had hurt Champa Bai. He couldn't sleep well that night. Three letters from the reader's response column had been published in Tuesday's paper: 'After reading the Sunday special article by Sangeethaarcharya Dr. Jani, it is a matter for joy that at last a music expert has written boldly the truth. I have been listening to Pandit Mohanlal singing for the past twenty years. There is nothing new. The same old stunts, the same old gimmicks engaging in the circus of repeating and extracting the applause from the audience. Since his luck is good he is doing business as the most expensive singer. Another letter: Mohanlal is now sixty-two. Still, why is it he has not trained even a single disciple? Even among those female disciples he has accepted, why is it that no one has made a name? Third: In this context, the newspapers must publish impartial and fearless critiques about every musician. After that almost every day one or two severely critical letters started getting published. No just that, in the other newspapers of Bombay also small items against him started appearing. The Marathi, Hindi, Gujarati, Sindhi and Kannada made a bit of news with this. If letters supporting him appeared in some papers, none such appeared in Paranjape's. One letter went to the extreme limit of writing: The Bombay music associations must teach a lesson to singers like Mohanlal by boycotting them—the kind that say they won't sing for less than a lakh for a concert. All the associations must decide never to pay beyond a certain fixed amount. The musicians like Mohanlal must remember the days when they had to pawn their tambura for twenty-five rupees.

It was not as if Mohanlal didn't have well-wishers. After the publication of the Sunday article, several people had called him and expressed their unhappiness. After that, many people came and met him and talked to him. Those people who were insiders to the music world had understood that this was the handiwork of Paranjape. Some of them asked what had happened between them. He told them what had transpired. Some of them wrote readers letters supporting him. But none of them got published in Paranjape's paper. But the sordid affair didn't stop there. In two weeks, the newspapers who cared for decency and respectability put an end to this whole affair. Then the 'yellow rags' took it up. They fished out old photographs of his concerts with women tambura players on either side of him, printed them on the front page with captions like: 'Won't men do? Are only women required?' They made an uproar about his going to Delhi with Manohari Das twenty-one years ago. They printed the photographs of the White girl Bhoopali and gave titles like, 'Can't an Indian find inspiration in Indian girls?' They would end by promising salacious details in the next issue, after a good deal of mud slinging. No educated and cultured persons would read such newspapers. But someone was sending them to him by mail.

Mohanlal would get angry. He would feel like beating up these newspaper fellows. He felt like suing them in the court of law. He consulted some well wishers. Their advice was 'Don't'. The lawyer representing them will ask hundreds of dirty questions. The newspapers will use the same details as the food for their next issues. They write such things about film actors and actresses everyday. None of them goes to court. They just ignore it. You also just keep quiet. He didn't think of any way out. It was unusual for him these days to invite female students to his flat. Now he was afraid to do so. These suspicions assailed him. Suppose these newspapers somehow photographed him when they were with him in his flat; if they have bugged my flat and hidden surveillance cameras! Or the residents in the opposite flat are spying secret agents for papers! He was afraid even to close and bolt the door when Bhoopali came to him for lessons. But if he didn't close the door, the outside noises would disturb and spoil the niceties of the singing. Yes, he must himself go to her flat when necessary. Not here, he decided. But he would worry. How could he be sure that her flat wasn't bugged and there were no spies?

Though a month passed, there was no news from Globe Musical Voice Company. There was no phone call either. In all this hullabaloo he had just forgotten it. One day he remembered. He himself called, 'You said that you would record within two weeks and give me the cheque. What happened?'

'Sir, this project was not approved by our MD. It looks as though it has been dropped. He has said that your singing of other ragas may be considered later.'

'But you made me sign the contract.'

'That we do. Until the MD approves it and it is signed by the Manager, the contract will not be final. I myself wanted to telephone you and let you know. But I had gone to my native place as my mother was ill. How is your health, Sir? Which new raga have you composed?' He started making polite enquiries. I did not even get their signature or bring a copy! There is no way in which I can take action against the bastards. I trusted them. Mohanlal felt sad. After his anger subsided, he understood that it was a big company and wouldn't go back on their word and they had been scared by the rumpus created by Paranjape.

What should he do to this fellow, Paranjape? He should pay some ten or twenty thousand rupees to some hooligan and get his limbs broken, when he was going from the office to the railway station but he shouldn't get killed. How to find such a man and how to negotiate with him? This thought became obsessive. If he is beaten up at this juncture won't it arouse a suspicion that I got it done? He thought cautiously, what if I get it done after a couple of months! There was no need for hiring somebody. It is more manly to go myself and slap him. Though this thought occurred, the caution that it might result in a police case and further rumpus.

On the fifth day he received a call from Hubli that they would arrange a programme in Belgaum and Hubli in such a way that both the engagements could be fulfilled with just one trip, requesting him to give them a date. Then he remembered. A similar request had come from Goa, asking him for a date. He himself called them. They agreed immediately. When he was planning three dates he received a call from Hyderabad. He adjusted all the four engagements. Four concerts in one week. Four lakh rupees. Fly to Goa for an evening concert. Next morning to Belgaum by car, the morning after that to Hubli, from there to Hyderabad by train, return to Bombay by plane. The special request from every place that he should sing the Omkara. In all the places it achieved tremendous success. Everyone was transported. They closed their eyes and were immersed in meditation. Not being able to suppress his curiosity, he himself asked the Hubli secretary, 'What did you feel about the Omkara ?'

'It mesmerised everyone. They felt a religious devotion towards you, the way they never have, about the pontiff of any mutt.'

'Some newspapers in Bombay had created a rumpus about this. Do you know?'

'The Bombay newspapers come to this place also. Everybody knows. Our Hubli papers also had published some salacious details. The paper is read for entertainment. No music lover changes his mind on account of newspapers stories.'

'Then do the people here still think that I am a saint?'

'No, they cannot be misled. The people here go crazy about artists. They prostrate to them. They worship them by carrying them on their heads. But none of them keep them as a guest in their homes. They arrange for the hospitality in a hotel and send them off.'

Even before Mohanlal completely understood this, five or six local musicians came to meet him with garlands.

Another incident took place in Hyderabad. It was a morning concert. As peroration, he sang the Omkara instead of Bhairavi. The listeners attained the heights of samadhi. He was scheduled to leave for Bombay the next day. But he received an invitation for a chamber concert in a private house. Tipnis and Prabhu who had accompanied him also stayed back. Saying that he wouldn't meet anybody till the next evening and he wanted to rest, he went to bed in the five-star Hotel Golkonda. The organisers at Hyderabad also knew about the smear-campaign of Paranjape. The audience also knew it. He sang the same Omkara here as well. The listeners were totally immersed in the devotional fervour. He began to feel forgiving and generous and thought what would he gain by getting that bastard beaten up? When he was lying down, he remembered the origin and genesis of this Omkara. The sage at Haridas temple was using this as meditation. I converted this only under yogic inspiration into the alaap of Asavari. And then I shaped the ascending and descending movement of aa-kaara, u-kaara and ma-kaara and I adjusted it to the shruti of tambura and moulded it into pure art in the inspiring spiritual ambiance of the Mahadev mandir and River Narmada basin. If I had not done it, it wouldn't have touched the minds of people. It wouldn't have plundered their hearts. If the achievement of the yogi of Haridas Temple had been sung exactly as he sang it at any concert, people would be bored in ten minutes and they would walk out. After it had become art, then, creation, exhibition, money and business. The clever plan of Paranjape, and the talk of the fifteen lakh advance offer of the globe musical voice company... How much profit they must have contemplated if they had talked of an advance of fifteen lakhs? I shouldn't have told Paranjape about the offer of the Globe Company. He started the smear campaign only to destroy it. The offer of fifteen lakhs didn't materialise. So what? People will certainly admire it. The admiration will continue till it is heard in two or three concerts. Why should I get that bastard beaten up? Why should I beat him up? Why invite unnecessary problems?

He slept well that night. By the time he shaved and had his shower, the phone rang. The receptionist asked, 'Sir, there is one Prabha Rao here who wants to see you. Would you speak to her?' After he said 'yes', a lady started speaking to him. Her voice was shaky, 'Panditji, I am a singer. Not well known. I listened to your concert yesterday. I want to see you. If you would please...' He said, 'Yes, come.'

Mrs. Prabha Rao was a lady of about thirty-five. A silk sari, diamond ear rings, nose ring, diamond studded bangles, wrist watch, and smooth skinned and looked like she belonged to a well to do family. She came in as if she was quite familiar with five star hotels. But in addition to well-being, her face indicated anxiety and trepidation. She sat on the sofa, pointed by him. He sat on the opposite sofa and talked to her. She mumbled with hesitation, 'Singer means in no way to be compared with you. I have learnt a little. I adore your music. After listening to your Omkara yesterday, I have been your devotee. The kind of devotion...how can I put it...'

He who had treaded that path with many years' experience, understood. It was six days ago he had left Bombay. Three days earlier, he had made love to Bhoopali in her flat, even that in the fear that a yellow journalist might be hiding somewhere. Thinking that he shouldn't touch her he asked, 'Devotion means, of what kind?' She bent her head. Didn't reply. After he repeated the question she said, 'Don't you understand that it is difficult for me to answer?'

'Don't feel embarrassed. You are an artist. I am an artist. Please speak freely. He got up, sat next to her and asked. Even then she didn't speak. 'If you don't speak, how can I make up my mind?' he asked.

'The devotion of Radha, the devotion of Meera,' she looked up at him and suggested with her eyes. He went up, hung the 'Do not disturb' card to the door, bolted the door and came back.

After sending her away at mid-day, he went to the dining hall and sat down. He began to remember her words. When he mentioned that she would have been impressed for the AahirBhairav if not for the Omkara, she explained, 'I had been captivated by your music fifteen years ago. But what made me mad for you, overcoming all fear of any suspicion by anyone and made me come to you boldly was the

Omkara. It was that absorption, that identification of oneness was that which impelled me to offer myself. It was that Omkara which made me consider me a jeevatma and consider you the paramatma which attracted me to become one with you. Would you kindly send me a cassette of that? I will listen to it daily and think of you.' He had agreed to send it, he remembered. He also remembered that after Madhumita left, he had never taken out the recording machine from the cupboard. He became sorrowful.

In the evening he had been invited for the private concert. Private music performance gives inspiration if a limited number of music lovers sit in close proximity. It was not as if he didn't know that the new-rich invited other Nouveau riche like themselves for a formality to show off their wealth. Raja Reddy, the industrialist had arranged this in his palatial residence. About thirty guests. It was evident by the introduction that though all of them were not adept in the theoretical knowledge of music, they were initiates. When he saw the Ramana Rao couple who were introduced at the end, his mind sent up waves of excitement. It seems Ramana Rao runs a business of manufacturing automobile spare parts and has his establishments at Vijayawada, Guntur, Machalipatnam and Nellore, in addition to at Hyderabad. It was a business, developed by his father. His wife, Prabha Rao was introduced as a singer herself. One of the people who sat behind me with the tambura was Prabha. She was wearing the same sari she had used in the morning. The same diamond ensemble too. She was wearing a French perfume now which she hadn't, in the morning. He noticed that they were recording what he was singing now. He mentioned at the beginning itself that these recorded cassettes were only for the private use of Raja Reddy and shouldn't be given to anyone else. Prabha Rao who was behaving as if she had just been introduced to him said, 'The recording machine is ours, I assure you that it will never be misused.'

The audience insisted on his singing the Omkara after one bada-Khayal and two chota-Khayals. Some seven or eight of them stood up and made a request that they had come only to listen to that after hearing it the previous day. For that there was no need for the accompaniment of harmonium and tabla. He tuned the tambura afresh and made the two women players come closer and closed his eyes. Prabha Rao sat closer than was necessary. He was filled with the memories of that morning. Even after five minutes he couldn't concentrate. He was dissatisfied. He felt defeated. After struggling for some time he persuaded himself that he was an artist, a singer. This was a work of art. Creating this is my only business. Yes, he must capture the minds of these thirty people and enrapture and inspire in them the same feeling of yearning and dedication that made her go mad the previous day. Well, the required mood ought to come if he sang with perfect harmony giving the right stress, pausing, touching the particular sophisticated nuances of the swaras. I am not a yogi, nor a saint, not even a pious individual. I am just a singer, a pure singer, and nothing else. He put all these ideas and emotions together, supported himself firmly with these thoughts and started singing. In a couple of minutes, the right emotion was achieved. In another two minutes he got totally immersed. All the listeners had half closed their eyes in a mood of surrender. He took the singing completely into his control. He resurrected all the latent power of the asavari, searching and bringing them out which he had not found till now, and began to express them in the pattern of the Omkara. He was himself aware that he was singing better and more effectively than he had in his practice and in any other earlier concert. Though he felt that he was repeating, he experimented with them, made variations in tempo and movement and built a tower of Omkara of new and newer dimensions.

It was one in the morning when he finished. For a couple of minutes the entire gathering was in deep silence. Then the head of the house, Raja Reddy came up, touched his feet and prostrated. The others also came up one by one and prostrated. Prabha's husband, Ramana Rao held both his feet and said, 'The experience was that of visiting the temple of our family deity' and commanded his wife, 'Get up and prostrate to him.'

In the morning, before he started off for the airport, Prabha and Ramana Rao came. Rao took out three cassettes from his pocket and said, 'The person who gave the idea to record the entire concert of yesterday was my wife. Your last song, Omkara is such that it must be preserved for ever. Yesterday's rendering was even better than that of the day before, more alive and vibrant. We brought it so that you can have a copy.'

उ

After sounding his triumphant trumpet in four cities and with four lakh and thirty thousand rupees, his mind started neglecting the criticism in the newspapers and the dirty stories of the yellow rags. He even lost the fear of hidden spies and hidden cameras. After all what can they write? It is just saying that such and such a woman went in at such time and the door was closed. He began to feel that why should he bother about them? The newspapers also lost interest in him. He was getting invitations from various places through letters and phone calls. But his enthusiasm, and even the feeling that through Omkara and yoga he had ascended the first step of philosophy was vanishing. There was a feeling of emptiness and void. What was there in life except giving concerts and making money. There was no connection with Giridhar and Poonam. Nothing with Chunni, in the same way with Ramkumari and her children. Not with Champa and her children either. All those with whom he had contact would stay only as long as it was necessary. That was the arrangement I had made. Some got married and went away. It was not proper to call those who were married. There was no steady relationship with anyone. These days, the idea that art was inspired by women had also ceased. Then what was it that provided inspiration? These days there was no inspiration at all. He felt he was singing mechanically.

On a morning around eleven, the phone rang. A woman's voice. 'Do you recognise me?' He said no, 'Have you forgotten so quickly?'

'Perhaps it is the first time you are ringing me up. If I see you I might recognise you.'

'Then shall I come right away?'

'Please give me your name.'

'Prabha. Hyderabad.' He got enthused. He begged pardon for not recognising the voice.

'It is one month since you left. Have you thought even once about my condition? I am calling from a booth outside. I will be brief. I have thought about something. Once a month I will come to Bombay to get lessons from you. My husband may agree if I tell him that I will take the first flight in the morning and return in the evening. I will convince him somehow. It is enough if you just inform me the day on which you will be in Bombay. You have your own flat. You said there was no one else. You must teach me for two hours and also enjoy my company. You understand? I can't talk on the phone...I am becoming mad for you. You must accept. Please. If you say yes, I will discuss it with my husband.'

His depression lessened a bit. He felt the enthusiasm one would get when a comparatively young rich woman says she is mad after him. But it subsided at once. After a few days this will also become a tame affair, why get entangled? He was uninterested.

'Coming to Bombay from Hyderabad is not workable to get lessons. I myself won't know when I will be in town.'

'Even if you tell me a day earlier, I will come.'

'No, Madam.'

'You are in Bandra West, aren't you? I have a relation in Matunga, saying that I will be there, I will come for just three days. Both of them go out for work. I will come to your flat during the day. I must see you at least a couple of times, please.'

'Let us see!'

'You must ring me up. From ten in the morning till one in the afternoon and four in the evening till eight, I will be alone at home. Would you please call? Please, there are some four or five people here waiting to use the phone.' She put it down.

He decided not to get caught in this. He saw a sort of self-confidence and self-determination in him as he had rejected a voluntary offer like this for the fist time in his life. But the next day he felt that what he thought as self confidence was only a form of vanity and egoism. His memory coursed variously—Prabha, the French perfume, then to Paris and on to his curbing the pride of Manohari. He was curious about what she was doing now.

One day the manager of the diamond merchant company Jhaveri and Co., rang him up and came. Rawal, who was about sixty was known to him. Not only would he attend all the music concerts wherever they took place, he would be in the first or the second row. If the concert was very good, he would come to the stage and convey his congratulations. The reason for his visit was that the company where he was working was celebrating its golden jubilee. As a part of the celebration, there was a music concert also. It is their wish that only Pandit Mohanlal should be invited for the concert that was to be arranged in the Birla Matrusree Auditorium. Though the concert was free, those who are uninitiated won't be allowed. Those who want a free invitation must come to our shop and request the invitation. Before giving it, one or two fact finding questions about things like how many concerts they have attended will be asked. The invitation will be issued only if the answers are satisfactory. I can assure you right away that it won't be a case of throwing pearls before swine. Then he added, 'We know that your fee is one lakh everywhere. We will pay two lakhs as it is a special occasion. Also before the concert, we will put a diamond ring on your finger. You must sing wearing that. In future also you must always wear it.'

'You will photograph the hand that is wearing the diamond ring. Then you will publicise it in the newspapers, won't you?'

'You are really very astute in business matters. If you get into the business world, you will buy our company itself,' Rawal laughed. He further mentioned that the tabla and harmonium accompanists would also be paid double and they would also be presented with diamond rings and asked whom they should invite. He added, 'You always take Tipnis and Prabhu everywhere. Still we shouldn't decide without consulting you, isn't it right?'

Then, as if remembering something, he said, 'You know, once in a way, I come across Tipnis Master. My boss has a farmhouse in Panvel. It is his custom to go there for a whole day for a saunter when there is a holiday for the shop. I also accompany him. You know what happened? About six months ago, my wife's health suffered a set back. The doctor said that I should send her away to some place from the polluted weather of Bombay. Where to send her? My boss said that both my wife and I could go to Panvel and stay in his farmhouse and that I could commute by bus or train. Then I used to see Tipnis Master now and then. He goes there to teach a lady. One day, I also went and sat listening to the lesson. Music is better understood by listening to the lesson being taught than by listening to a concert.'

'What is the name of that lady?' Mohanlal asked with curiosity.

'Name? I forgot. She stays alone in her own farmhouse, practises music all day. A name something like Madhavi. There is even a raga with that name, you know—Madhukauns—you sing it very well. Yes, her name is Madhuben.'

Mohanlal didn't show much interest in this. When Rawal stood up to leave, Mohanlal asked him, 'You are going to publicise in the papers that you have paid me two lakhs, right?'

He asked, 'We will do it if you ask us to do so. Why?' Mohanlal just smiled. Rawal said, 'Yes, understood.'

'What did you understand?'

'If two lakhs are paid by someone once, that itself becomes your standard, won't it? Can't we, who are in business understand?'

He accompanied him to the lift.

He inferred that Madhuben was none other than Madhumita. He was angry with Tipnis that he was secretly teaching her without telling him and thought Tipnis didn't have commitment. I don't invite anyone else but him. Still ... his anger surged forth and he wanted to take him to task immediately. Still remembering that he had been honest and loyal in a number of ways for twenty-five years he controlled himself. Has she bought a house in Panvel? Is it someone else with that name, or is it his some distant relation on his wife's side? Or, meanwhile has he purchased a farm house himself at Panvel and has kept one of his students as concubine? Mohanlal became suspicious and thought that Tipnis was secretive about everything and didn't let out any information. If it is so, I don't have the right to ask him why he didn't tell him. He has never poked his nose in any of my affairs. Even if he knows something he has remained as if he knows nothing. There are fans for the main singers and assistants. Who ever talks to harmonium accompanists? He felt that it would be best for him to remain silent.

By the time he had his lunch and a nap, there was a call from Tipnis himself. 'It seems they are going to present you a diamond ring.'

'For you and for Prabhu also. Didn't they tell you that?

'When the main deity is offered panchaamrita sumptuously, even the priests should have to be served a ladle each.'

Remembering that this was the style of Tipnis' talk, he felt happy. 'What are you doing? Come and let us have a talking session.'

Tipnis brought fresh home-made poha to munch. Mohanlal prepared some tea. After sitting opposite him at the table, looking steadily at him, Mohanlal asked Tipnis, 'I heard you are teaching someone at Panvel, and she practises all day. Who is she?'

Tipnis knew that he was being steadily examined, when questioned gazed at, examining him. His face lost a shade. However, as if he had committed no mistake he replied quite naturally, 'Your own student. The one who sang with you in America. Madhumita Shah. She has bought a house at Panvel and she is practising there. She came here to learn properly. It seems she asked you to continue teaching and you said that you won't be in town continuously, so regular tuition was not possible. She came to me. When I told her that my instrument was the harmonium and I could not teach vocal music, she wouldn't take "no" for an answer. She said she would practise herself and it was enough if I corrected where she erred and if I showed it on the harmonium. I wouldn't have agreed even to do this but my wife persuaded me that when you were in town, at least for a couple of days in a week, we could stay there and breathe fresh air, so that her health would improve. Of late, my wife has developed asthma. The doctor says it is because of the weather of Bombay. When I am free I go there, stay for a couple of days and teach what I can.'

It was nothing new to him that this Rajaram would eliminate what might be irksome and speak only what is pleasing. He suspected, would she not have told this man about betraying her husband because of her guru, her confessing everything in a letter to her husband, unable to bear a guilty conscience, her coming away to Bombay, meeting her guru, and telling him that she had freed herself from her husband and offering herself to him to be used as he liked—all this, is it possible she has not told this fellow? Now he felt that it was the harmonium accompanist who was examining his face. Mohanlal decided not to give away anything by himself. Aware that if he remained silent tamely, it would be tantamount to accepting guilt, he said, 'Yes, it was enough if the salary of Wadekar Master is realised. I am not accepting at my level. How is her sadhana?'

'When the foundation has been laid by you, what is there to be said? She is practising with great commitment. She is in the same mood all twenty-four hours, she develops the raga herself. I demonstrate on the instrument how it can be further developed. In the process, if the shades of the jnaati-ragas are touched, I will let her know them. That's all. It is impossible to learn from me and get trained as taught by you. She must have come to me only because I am your accompanist and can explain and distinguish, approximately your movements.'

Though he understood that even here he was saying what would please him, he found a little comfort in thinking that he would not ruin his peace of mind. He found an inner assurance that she, being a lady of a respectable household, might not have told him about their personal relationship, leaving her husband and the reason for her doing so. If he stared at his face unflinchingly he might be able to plumb the depths of truth and falsehood, he was afraid that if he did so, Tipnis also might look right back into his eyes and examine him. After a couple of minutes he felt that the proper thing to do was to change the subject in order get out of the predicament. Since he couldn't think of any other subject immediately, he struggled and came out with this. 'You also know that the Jhaveri Company will pay me two lakhs. It seems they are also going to publicise it in the newspapers. Hereafter, I am going to increase my fee to two lakhs. You know Paranjape got an item written by someone in his paper that all the music associations of Bombay should reduce my fee to fifty thousand. This is my retort. What do you say?'

'Why should you bother if a nobody wrote something or got something written in some newspaper? No matter how much you demand, your admirers must pay that amount. But if the fee is increased, it may be difficult for music associations to cope with it, isn't it? Only diamond companies and others of that financial standing would be able to arrange your concerts. But it does take away the opportunity of real music lovers to enjoy your music, wouldn't it?'

'Look here. If my fee increases, so does yours, correspondingly. It is profitable to you also, isn't it?'

'If it comes automatically, who would say no? Still we should be within reach of those who invite us. That's the reason I mentioned it.'

Even here he felt defeated in the exchange. He wondered whether he had trounced him with polite words. He got up with the pretext of removing the tea cups from the table.

Chapter 17

I

Earlier, there was the feeling that anger, rejection, contempt, hatred—no matter what a mean emotion it is—when it is elevated to the level of alaap in music, it gets ennobled; even a mean material is elevated into sublimity. But now it is being felt, not just in alaap but whatever may be the form of singing when it gets merged in the shruti, there is absolutely no place for low, mean and dirty feelings. Now I am feeling that when these emotions remain, they do not change to music. There is no individual in my life who should be hated and rejected. Even the rare instances of small-mindedness of the sisters-in-law or the envious intrigues of a fellow student while studying in college had never given rise to hard feelings of hatred and contempt—certainly none that could have lasted lifelong. While I was taking leave after my marriage both the sisters-in-law had given me a tearful embrace. During the class socials of the final year when we were taking leave with no possibility of meeting again, even those who were not close friends had gotten close. Mohanlal who had forced himself on me, ruined my character and afterwards destroyed the chastity of my marriage. And when I came and surrendered to him, leaving my husband, after confessing the truth, his throwing me out, accusing me of having a moral egotism which was greater than the dedication to the guru and his slapping and cursing me...

In this house, in the middle of the garden, which is like a penance grove, as if, purposely built for practising music, when I sat holding the tambura, the mind would be filled with hatred. Such an intense hatred that would stir me to curse: Let him lose his limbs and become lame. If there is justice, a sinner should be punished. Yes, he must be immersed in boiling oil as described in our description of hell, yes, he must be pierced by the beaks of crows, hard and sharp like iron nails, or at least the kind of punishment that is sanctioned in our legal system. Imprisonment for seven years. Not just seven years, but as many seven years as the number of girls and women he has ruined who had come to him begging for knowledge. If such anger fills the mind, how can the mood of the raga arise? How could I have had the wisdom then, that even in the raudra-rasa when it has achieved maturity, the raw anger and hatred shouldn't exist, shouldn't ever remain. The main purpose of engaging in sadhana was to excel him, must learn even if he didn't teach. It was with this resolution that I was practising. On account of this, though I had totally given myself to severe, intense sadhana for a whole year, I couldn't extricate myself from my past and his existence in the background. No matter what alaap I began and what tonal variation I made, it was his model and his pattern and the resolution to transcend his method and style. One day Rajaram Kaka said, 'I have thought a great deal about your style of singing. You are practising only in the style of Mohanlal. Though your learning has been completely under his tutelage, unless you find out your own individual method and manner, you won't be an independent artist in your own right. Right now you are not learning from him. I, am not a vocal singer myself. Therefore, you must grow in your own way. You must come out of the influence of the teachers. Do you understand?'

What Rajaram Kaka said was in the context of music. I did try to get out of Mohanlal's clutches right from the next day to free myself from his influence. Within six months my own method started taking shape. Kaka also admired it and said, 'Yes, now you are becoming independent.'

Either because I got free from his style of singing or because I freed myself from anger and hatred generated from his memory and got the strength to concentrate I achieved absorption in singing. I enjoyed my singing. I am experiencing that, when freed from dark lowly emotion like anger, how lucidly and spontaneously the form of raga would reveal itself.

It is more difficult to extricate oneself from sin than from anger. There is no redemption from sin without suffering internally and getting purified by repentance. But repentance is not an obstacle, it is complementary to music. Asavari is quite well known for it. In Marva, in various versions of Todi, in Bairagi-Bhairav through *ma-re* and with *ma pa dha s ni s pa, ni sa re dha sss ni s pa*—when merging in Darbari—in all these cases contrition itself seems to have been personified. It plunges one in self-searching.

For the past three months, contrition and self-analysis have been the motivating factors for the ragas I am practising. They have been helpful in reaching greater depths. Contrition is a moral achievement—the first step in spiritual realisation. Therefore it is an ennobling act. It doesn't impede artistic concentration.

I am now beginning to understand my mistake. One cannot mix repentance with any sublime raga. No I am mixing it. As a result I am ruining the individuality of ragas and am lowering it to the level of a supplication. Is there no difference between Bairagi and Bhairav and Bairagi-Bhairav and Aahir-Bhairav? There is detachment in Bairagi. There is non-attachment and selflessness. There is profound sorrow of intense loneliness. But if the colour of repentance is added to it, their uniqueness will be lost, like the same gravy that is mixed with all vegetables in restaurants reduces them to the same taste and smell. Here also, I am mixing my own feelings to the emotions of the raga.

The awareness that I shouldn't mix my own sentiments with the mood of the raga has transported me to another higher step in my learning. Each raga has a sthayi-bhava, a basic constant emotion. The river of constancy gets joined by several transitory emotions of the pits, streams, rivulets; gets it fullness and flows on. The secret of achievement is discovering the sthayi-bhava for each raga and finding the complementary transitory emotions and pulsate the places of vadi and samvadi with particular pattern of swara special to that particular raga and articulate them. Neglecting this and merely weaving melody with sweet decorative swaras doesn't result in the creation of the raga.

In order to understand the method of unifying or harmonising the sthayi and sanchari emotions of each raga, the process must be of a visionary enlightenment, just as in the comprehension of a poetic masterpiece. Deep contemplation of life must take place. It is necessary to identity through detailed analysis each and every occurrence of daily life and relate it to the possible connection with each other and all other objects. Then music becomes poetry. It transcends poetry. Sages like Swami Haridas might have envisioned the ragas at this level of realisation. That is why such musicians might have been called yogis.

It is true that the purity of music doesn't remain if it is touched by the raw emotions of everyday life. But by immersing oneself in practising music for eight to ten hours of day, the raw emotions will not be obliterated. The question why did this madness of music catch hold of me and still has a stranglehold on me often bothers me. Even while studying at school and college the attraction towards music was so great that I asked myself what was the use of formal education? What meaning does it have? After that I sacrificed my virginity for it. In the interim, I went to America with the intention of leading a family life. For the sake of music, I even sacrificed an enviably happy married life and ruined its sanctity. What will I gain by sacrificing such conjugal happiness by staying in this uninhabited ashram—like a forest abode? Is this not madness? Such questions too arise now and then.

I may sacrifice anything and may do anything in order to satisfy my madness. But what justification can music give for having deceived Vikram. I did not tell him about having lost my virginity before marriage. He didn't ask. No man in America expects his wife to have been a virgin before marriage. Didn't Vikram ask because he was settled there and knew it. But he was born and brought up in India. Perhaps he didn't ask because etiquette demands that such a question shouldn't be asked. Or was he silent because of the innate understanding that an Indian bride would be a virgin? If sanctity and purity and the belief in them had been maintained at least after marriage, the pre-marital affair would have been forgotten in course of time. Though it was true that Mohanlal had forced me, I would not have agreed, if I was not mad after music. I wouldn't have invited him to stay in my home. Shouldn't butter have the sense that if fire is allowed to come near, it would melt?

For a week I was very angry with Vikram. He hasn't tried to contact me. He hasn't called even my brother. Had he called my brother's place, he would have got this number. Why didn't he call me and scold me? After all, he is not a saint who has conquered anger, and when angry, angry on his wife, would not talk sharply with her. I would have felt a little relieved had he called and scolded me as an unworthy rascal and an untrustworthy woman. If he hasn't called at all for a year and a half even after I left the leaves from my diary on his pillow, it means that his anger hasn't subsided. Or, he is still feeling hurt. Anger and pain are both transitory forms of the same emotion. Won't there be tears in anger and a curse in the tears?

Since the day before yesterday, a new question has taken shape why has he not sent a divorce letter even after a year and a half? He might feel contempt to write it himself on the computer. But nobody writes a divorce letter personally. It is given to an attorney. I had written clearly that he should marry someone else and had pleaded that he shouldn't ruin his life. Still he hasn't done it. He may not like a divorce. Would he ever accept me If I went to him as a supplicant and say that the past is irredeemable, I would be utterly faithful hereafter and implore him to take me back? Would he accept me? Was it his expectation that since I was the erring person, I should go to him, call him or write a letter? She was thrilled. The feeling, 'Vikram, I won't just volunteer to call you. I will beg you placing my head on your feet. Even now, would you take me back?' This feeling was only for half an hour. Then it was only a day dream. How can he accept me? Not only that. Even if he accepts, it is not possible even for me to live with him as a wife without a trace of black shadow always hovering around? The milk that is spoilt and congealed cannot become milk again. Engaging oneself in such speculation would result only in further agony. Abandoning family, I have come to music. Why remember the past? Since yesterday another doubt has brought me fear. Doesn't he know the damage caused if divorce is not obtained after separation? According to Californian law, half his property will come to me, legally. It is nearly two years since I gave it in writing that I wanted nothing and that I must compensate for having ruined his life. As time passes, the authenticity of the letter in the diary might abate. It might even cease to be valid. Even being aware of this danger, if he was to keep quiet, has he deteriorated to the level of negligence about life's responsibility? Has he started drinking with disgust and contempt? When a man, after working hard from morning to evening comes to an empty house, to a broken home, broken by an unfaithful wife, he is easily lured by liquor. What has happened to him by now? I have selfishly indulged myself in the world of music—in researching into swara, raga and taal. Is it not my duty to look after his welfare? It is not difficult to find out at least how he is. But I don't have the courage to do so. I can call up someone in the area of San Jose. But the news will spread around. The suppressed news will get renewed publicity. It is just possible that my brothers may know something. Even if they do, they won't volunteer. How can I ask them directly?

ऽ

Since the last two days my mind has been in turmoil. It has been difficult to engage myself in practising the swara. The turmoil can be overcome if what is gnawing inside is thrown out. But how to throw it out? The day before yesterday around nine in the morning, I was practising. Malakshmi came up the loft and said, 'An old couple is here. They said they wanted to see Madhumita Shah. When I asked them for their names, they said just to call you.' Nobody comes here to see me. Once in a way Ajai Bhai comes. Not in the mornings. Very rarely the sisters-in-law come with their children for a picnic. No one comes without calling. No one except Rajaram Kaka and the tabla accompanist, Kalimulla. Reclining the tambura on the carpet and coming down, I found that the people sitting on the cane chairs were my in-laws. I was dumbstruck with this unexpected visit. Both of them saw me. I just stood transfixed on the last step. They have come suddenly. Without calling earlier. How did they know I was here? Not even such questions found expression. Without thinking, I just proceeded forward and prompted only by tradition, I approached them, touched their feet and smeared the dust on my head. I didn't have any words. Since I prostrated to them, their faces registered pleasure. Meanwhile I understood what they had come to talk about. Whatever the conversation I became aware that it shouldn't be in the presence of the servants. I invited them to come upstairs. Both of them started ascending the stairs. I got some tea prepared by

Malakshmi and went up with some biscuits and fruits. They were sitting on two cane chairs. I could see the taxi parked near the gate. I placed the tea and fruits on the tee poi and said, 'Please have it. When did you come to Bombay? I sat on the carpet near the tambura. Mother-in-law was silent. Father-in-law extended his hand towards the tea cup. I remembered then that he would drink tea once every hour or two. They had both come to Los Gatos when I was there. They would ask, 'My dear child, Madhu, get me a cup of tea.' I was wondering how I should talk to them now. I would then address him as Pitaji and would call her Maa. Affection and love had grown between me and them. But now, when I had come away leaving their son, what is wrong in continuing to address the elderly couple respectfully. Isn't it our tradition? Getting up and approaching her, I said, 'Maa, please have some tea. The apples are good. Taste them,' and poured the tea to her cup.

Mother-in-law spoke, 'Only if you answer my question correctly will I drink tea served by you.'

'Why do you connect the two things? Has she shown that she isn't going to answer your question truthfully? You haven't even asked the question. She hasn't spoken. One should never start a conversation with a condition. Drink your tea first,' father-in-law spoke. 'Madhu beti, do you grow the vegetables that you need yourself? Tell me.'

'Waghe grows various vegetables. I don't go there. No chemical manure is used,' I said.

'That's why I asked you. What curry are you getting prepared for lunch? It's been very long since I have eaten vegetables that are grown without using chemicals! Even rice and dal are suffused with chemicals. I would love to get our food grown this pure way without using chemicals. Eat and live.' He put the biscuit in his mouth. I went down and told Malakshmi to prepare two kinds of curry, salad, dal, phulka, rice and curds. By then mother-in-law was drinking tea. The turmoil within me when I saw them had abated a bit. I again sat near the tambura.

'You aren't having any tea, yourself?' father-in-law asked.

'I had it in the morning. Don't feel like it again.'

'Look here, my child. I don't know how to begin this matter. We never knew about you having come to Bombay or your staying here in the farmhouse, practising music. Both of you would ring us up from Los Gatos every Sunday. One after the other and sometimes both of you together, holding one receiver each. You would tell us about the news there. You would ask about the news from India. You would enquire about our health. Two years ago there was no phone call from you on a Sunday. We thought you were busy. There was no call the next Sunday either and not even the following Sunday. I was anxious and called myself. No one received the call. I left a recorded message. After a couple of days I called again when it would be around ten in the morning. Maria answered. Neither of us understood anything much because of her accent and my accent. All I could make out was that Mr. Shah was not in station. When I asked about Madhumita Shah she said she was not either. Was it possible you had come to Bombay? I wondered whether I should call your mother's place. It was difficult to believe that you were visiting India without informing us and we had to make enquiries from your mother's. You are not that kind. Then one day after waiting, I could contact Vikram when it was nine in the evening there and asked why he hadn't called. He said he was continuously on tour and said, 'Sorry Daddy. Hereafter I will call from wherever I am.' When I asked, 'Where is Madhu? He said, 'She is going for advanced music lessons to San Raphael in the evenings—to Ali Akbar. She has to drive for two hours going and two hours coming back. She is all right. She misses you a great deal! Afterwards he would call without fail. None from you. A year passed that way. We kept quiet without suspicion. But one day I suspected that he was hiding something. We asked quite directly, 'Son, isn't it possible for her to call us some morning or afternoon if she goes in the evenings for music lesson? Even if we call when it is morning or afternoon for you there, she is not available. Tell us the truth. Where is she?' He didn't reply. He was silent. We didn't leave him at that. Finally he said, 'Daddy, you are an educated man familiar with a modern life. Please understand I don't want to say much. Since she felt that it wasn't possible to pursue music in America, she went away to India a year ago. I respect her decision. I have also given my consent. We are not in touch. Don't contact her please. I am all right. Don't worry about me. Please tell mother to receive this news calmly.' We, especially I, received an unbearable shock. We had thought that he who had such interest in and devotion for music had found a suitable wife and was very happy. He is the kind of man who would do anything to promote your musical progress. There was no need to come away to India severing the connection. We understood that he was not telling the truth. We felt that we should visit him in this condition and give him moral support. I called and asked him when it would be convenient for him. He asked us not to come then as he would be travelling. He spent four months that way. He said that he would be coming to Hyderabad and would spend two weeks with us. He had come three months ago and stayed for three weeks. He behaved in such a way that there was nothing to worry about him. When we asked about you there was no answer. He would simply say let's not talk about that. Knowing that it would be painful to him we also kept quiet. When I called him a month ago I told him firmly. 'Look here. If you think it is not at all possible for you and her to adjust to each other, you finish the legal formality. We will look for another girl or you yourself find some girl of Indian origin in America. It is not good for you to stay alone.' He said, 'Daddy, why do you insist like this? Isn't it possible for a man to be happy if he is single? If I go astray, then you question me. Please don't discuss either about her or marriage.' He is not happy. He pretends to be. We decided, why not trace you and talk to you. We didn't feel like ringing up your home and ask them. If the daughter of the house comes back, it is the elders of the family that should contact us. But they didn't do so. Why hide things from you? We engaged a detective agency, found out that you were living here, practising music and found out who the guru was who came here, now and then, to teach you. Now tell us directly. We won't ask you to go and lead a family life with him. But tell us at least why the relationship between you is broken. He is our only son.'

When he was saying all this my mind was surfeit with emotion. Vikram doesn't even want to think about marrying again. He has not told even his parents the reason for my coming away, leaving him. It is simply not possible for him to have told anyone else. Has this control arisen out of pain? Yes—besides, basically he is a man of noble nature. I felt tears welling up in my eyes. Thinking that I shouldn't weep in front of them I immediately went downstairs. Malakshmi was cooking. I went out from the back door and stood looking at the banana plant which had just developed shoots. I felt I had to cry. I wept nonstop. After half an hour I felt I shouldn't keep standing here, leaving them upstairs by themselves. I washed my face, went up the stairs and sat down as before and said, 'Pitaji, I came to understand that my marrying itself was a mistake. I cannot look after my husband properly, I was immersed in music all day. This doesn't mean that he was very demanding. There is no better husband than him in the whole world. Still, I am not interested in family life. Please get him remarried. Kindly excuse me for having married him and made him a divorcee thus preventing his marriage with a really good wife. Please don't ask me anything else?'

'Even if you are immersed in music all the twenty-four hours, he who worships music must be happy. Why should the marriage be severed?' He asked.

I have never been able to tell a lie, right from the beginning. That too after practicing shruti, it is impossible. There was no way but to accept his question. But the inner truth cannot be told. If it is not told, doesn't it tantamount to lying? Why not make a clean breast of it? This pressure appeared. Why should I hide the truth from him? I, who has suffered and is suffering from the sense of sin and contrition? Why not bring a copy of the diary from my box and place it before him and ask him to read it and understand for himself. Why this? Not only did I marry Vikram according to traditional sacred rites but I became the daughter-in-law of his parents. I felt, why not tell them what I told my husband? But there was an impediment. When the son himself hasn't told them, why should I, the daughter-in-law? The actual fact was, I was ashamed to confess to them. An excruciatingly intense shame.

'Pitaji, I cannot answer your question, please excuse me,' I said.

Now my mother-in-law cut in. 'There is something to be ashamed of and both of you have joined to hide it.' There was not just anger in her voice but fury. I saw that it was natural. I was not displeased with her. I felt it was only natural for anyone to be furious in that predicament.

After the meal, father-in-law said, 'The curries were very tasty . We can't get such fresh vegetables in any market. Would you show me the vegetable plants?' He came out alone with me. After looking at the plants he said, 'What I feel is this—from one of you some mistake has been perpetrated. One doesn't feel like betraying the other. Which means that there is mutual love. Without giving room for unnecessary reservations and embarrassments, it is wise to have an honest talk and solve this thing. You have his phone number, of course. I will give him your number.' I didn't reply. I understood then that he had brought me out here only so that he could talk separately without mother-in-law's presence.

When they left, again I touched their feet and prostrated. They didn't say anything more. I certainly had nothing to say. My ears are filled with his benedictory words that we should solve this impasse through mutual heart-to-heart talk without reservations of any kind. If it is the common sort of misunderstanding between husband and wife, it can be solved with a free and honest talk. But this was deep rooted. It has happened deep down at a depth of more than ten saptakas below the mandra-shadja.

३

Haven't written anything for a year. There was nothing to write about. What is the use of writing again and again the same moral grinding that is experienced daily? Many new ideas, new dimensions and deep insights have opened up about music. Those should be realised and given a concrete form in actual experiment. Ideas that should be discussed with Rajaram Kaka and clarified. Or to be tested by reading in music manuals. There was a pressure to write only those that cannot be told to anyone.

Last week I had gone to Gore Saheb's house to listen to the tapes of Raga Kalingada. It was one of those rare occasions when he was home. He made polite enquiries about how my music practice was progressing. 'Isn't it three years since you started? Why can't an opportunity be given to me to listen to?' I said, 'I haven't reached that stage.'

'You are not the one to say whether you have reached that stage or not. We should say that, after listening.'

I thought it was just polite formal conversation. But he had asked quite seriously. If I had still demurred it, it would be showing discourtesy to his wish. I said, 'Please come to the farmhouse for a holiday. Since it is my own ambience I may find the courage to sing.'

'A very good idea.' Looking at his diary he said, 'Is next Sunday all right? I will come there by nine in the morning, along with Suniti Tai. We would have finished our breakfast here, as soon as we get there, a cup of tea and biscuits. Two ragas, one morning raga and another of the forenoon. Lunch. Half an hour's siesta. Then a raga of the afternoon and one evening raga. I will let you know which ragas after coming there, depending on the atmosphere, ambiance and mood. I won't tell you now,' he smiled. I understood at once. It was his innuendo that if there is advance information the student might make special relevant preparation and the examination will not be complete. I also smiled. He asked, 'Why are you smiling?'

'If you ask for rare ragas, I won't be prepared. I am telling you right away', I said.

'These are times when university students go on strike that the questions are outside the syllabus. It's OK,' he smiled again.

After inviting Suniti Tai to come on Sunday without fail with her husband, I returned. I called Rajaram Kaka, and informed him about the programme and said, 'You must kindly come that day and accompany me. Accompaniment means leading further on into an unknown dimension. I am feeling afraid.'

'There is no need to be afraid. I will inform Kalimulla also,' he said. It was decided that Rajaram himself should go to Gore Saheb's place and bring him along, showing him the way.

Gore Saheb liked the atmosphere very much. He came back after taking a look at the garden. Though there were cane chairs, he came up the stairs and sat on the carpet. 'Open the window and stop the fan. Otherwise the tune of the tambura will go down.' Suniti Tai sat on the chair. She didn't have either the habit or the love of music to sit on the floor and listen. He asked for the ragas—Todi and Bilaval. I sang from the shadja itself imagining every little movement. There was no need for Kaka to forestall and show the way. Since the singing itself was in slow motion there was the opportunity to think. With eyes closed, it was possible to perceive the horizon and beyond it with all possible meandering movements, rise and fall. I myself didn't know that I could sing Todi this way for an hour and half. After that Kaka asked me if I needed a cup of tea. Declining it, I started Bilaval. I forgot that I was the host and as such should ask Gore Saheb and Suniti Tai whether they would like some tea. I sang Bilaval also slowly for an hour and a quarter. I was watching the eyes of Gore Saheb who was sitting opposite. I felt that ten thousand spectators were watching me. I am singing in front of Gore Saheb, he is listening with absorption. I can see aesthetic enjoyment in his eyes and his forefinger is moving at the right places. When I would give the saam unexpectedly, he would smile and his right hand was quickly showing the saam as required. I experienced the joy and self confidence, that I was singing in a concert with an audience in front of me uniting the aesthetic consciousness of all of them into one consciousness. As in the case of concert with full audience, without any direct contact with any individual, my singing continued unhindered though my eyes were in contact with those of Gore Saheb.

When I concluded, he nodded his head for a couple of minutes. Didn't say anything. Didn't talk during lunch either. I was making polite conversation and was playing the host to Suniti Tai. After a bit of rest when I again sat with the tambura, Gore Saheb said, 'Now I don't make any special request. I will leave it to you.'

I said, 'I won't be able to make up my mind if you leave it to me. It would be easy for me if you make a specific suggestion.' Nodding his head he said, 'Brindaavani'. I sang for fifty minutes. Then he requested Raga Bhimpalaasi. That took fifty-five minutes. After finishing it, I looked at his face. He asked me if my throat was straining.

'How can it be strained? She practises for eight to ten hours a day. There is a quota still remaining for today,' Guru Rajaram Kaka replied on behalf of his student.

I went downstairs, asked Waghe to bring up some poha, apples and tea. Came back quickly and sat in front of the tambura. The music expert Gore Saheb said, 'All the four ragas sung today should have been taped. I did not think about it. I have a mind to ask for an evening raga after tea. But one shouldn't eat too much on the same day,' he said. Then there was some talk about music.

It was sunset when they started back. At half past nine, Rajaram called, 'Gore Saheb has liked your singing very much. "There is something original. No one else's influence is seen. I didn't imagine that she had advanced so much. She had taped so much from my collection and taken it. I was suspecting that she might have made a mix-up amalgamation of a dozen styles. Allow her to give a concert. I wanted to tell her that right there, myself. But it is proper that I should tell you and leave it to your discretion. So I am telling you now. We will create an opportunity at some music festival. Or, we can tell some associations in Bombay itself and make a beginning. I have not heard anywhere these days any male or female singer of her present generation who can sing at that level." I was very pleased with his appreciation. She is still in a mood to practise by herself for another year or two, I said. He said, "Yes, it is a good thing. However, singing in the presence of connoisseurs of music is itself a sort of sadhana. Both the enjoyment and criticism of the audience, in a sort of silent, magical, mantric, communication support a singer's realisation of raga. One must sing in public as well as practise in private, analytically. Then music will strengthen and mature. Now she is thirty-three or thirty-four isn't she? There should be no more delay to appear in public. Tell her," he said. I also feel it is correct. I won't be in town for another week. So I am calling now.'

Listening to this not only was I just happy but also felt a sense of gratitude. But I said what I thought immediately, 'Kaka, god has saved me from the necessity of making a living by giving concerts. Why should I be in a hurry? I feel sometimes that I shouldn't give any public concerts at all but just stay in this ashram, a penance grove and sing to myself.'

'Take money or don't as you like. But it is the obligation of a learned person to provide a feast for millions of music lovers. We shall do it, all in good time.'

4

I haven't written my diary for a fortnight. There is no other thought in my mind except whether to give a concert right now or not. It is time and having sung in the presence of an expert has given a further impetus. I have understood the creative criticism from his facial expression and look in his eyes though he did not put it into so many words. But my mind is filled with sorrow since yesterday. I know that there is nothing new in this. Still, I am not able to catharsise the sorrow. Yesterday morning I went to the house of Gore Saheb. I wanted to copy the cassettes of Raga Gowri. Suniti Ma received me with great affection. I have been going to their house for the last three years once every twenty, twenty-five days. She opens the music room for me and I can stay as long as I like. I can record as many cassettes as I want. She never interferes. She invites me in at the time of lunch or breakfast. But I have never dined there. I have just had tea and snacks. She is a very dry person. I have no evidence to call her a bad woman. She is good looking, in physical appearance and is of a classical type, with a well-bred family background. The form like a statuette carved out of white marble. Silk apparel in keeping with wealth. Jewellery rich but not gaudy. Not the kind of stupid woman to cover herself with excessive ornaments. A graduate. Civilised talk of an educated city-bred type. But an emotionless, static nature. However, the husband, though a prosperous lawyer, that too an income-tax attorney was an emotional type. Otherwise, would he love music more than life itself? Would he rush forward, otherwise to promote music without hesitation? This lady is simply not interested in music. I haven't seen her accompanying her husband to any concert. She is a white marble statue. Today she spoke with some extra feeling. She herself said, 'Actually, I get bored of classical music. I can listen to some bhajans and dance-music. How can one listen to someone intoning A-A-A without any meaning? Actually I was not interested in coming to your farmhouse the other day. My husband said, 'Stay for sometime. If you don't feel like listening you go to the garden and take a walk. It is good for the constitution.' I came because I thought I had nothing to do, sitting here. Though what you sang was also A-A-A, I liked it. I thought it had some meaning. There was a kind of feeling, like in a conversation. I listened to it fully.' I felt she had paid me a great compliment. I selected the cassettes I wanted and pressed the button to copy them fast. She was sitting there, just watching. She would never come to the music room and sit there watching me, what cassettes I was copying. Sometimes I would sit there, playing the cassettes and listening to them before deciding whether to copy or not. If I remained there for a long time, she would send something to munch and some tea with the cook. But she wouldn't come inside. Noticing that she remained there, I understood that it was due to her new found interest in music. She asked, 'Do you listen to all this, understand the uniqueness of each and incorporate if into you music?' I said, 'Yes.' She insisted that I have lunch. The cook served. I thought that this lady was lucky because this cook was better than my Malakshmi. After the lunch she took me to the music room again, closed the door and asked me to take a seat. She drew a chair opposite mine, sat down and asked, 'You saw the woman who served us. What do you think of her?'

'She cooks very well. Very good behaviour. She has brought me tea so many times.'

'Do you know who she is?'

'No.'

'You know, there is a famous singer called Mohanlal. His first wife. There is a daughter who is thirty-three years old and son who is twenty-seven. When the daughter was five, he married a student of his and left this woman. Then he left the second wife also and ran away to Delhi with a dancer by the name of Manohari Das.' She mentioned about Mohanlal's married life. It was clear that all these details mentioned by her were learnt from his first wife who was working as a cook in their house. So many new things and details. There were a lot of details about his immoral acts in the newspapers recently. You don't seem to have read them. Do you get newspapers to your farmhouse?'

'I don't subscribe to them.'

'My husband also knows what a philanderer he is. He knew about it even before they were made public through publication in the newspapers. Still, when he got the award, my husband was the main person who arranged for his felicitation. I asked him why he was felicitating him knowing what sort of person he was. He said if you establish a relationship between art and the artist's private life, art itself will not survive. I argued whether it was not life itself which inspired art and art is born out of life. He couldn't convince me. I kept quiet thinking that those who are mad for art also have the madness of helping artists at any cost.'

Though I wanted to ask about the details of what those immoral acts were, that were published in the newspapers, I didn't speak. I felt immediately that showing any interest in this matter was unwise. I was also anxious whether my name was also there. But I reasoned it wouldn't be or she wouldn't discuss it with me. This was an event of a long time ago. This lady is mentioning it because of the confidence she found after she came to my place two weeks ago and heard my singing. It also occurred that this was the first time I was meeting her after that.

The woman who was serving as the cook in Gore Saheb's house all these days, without any emotional contact with me, now acquired the position of a sister who had been ruined by the same man who had ruined me. Her memory began to tease me, thinking of her white-haired darkish face which had become hardened as a result of suffering blow after blow of penury, sorrow and hardship. The memory that at one point I had desired to marry him if he gave up his relationship with other women, fills me with shame—the kind of shame that I should give up going to Gore Saheb's house altogether.

After three weeks, I had again gone there. Suniti Tai again gave me lunch. I observed Ramkumari closely. Even today Suniti Tai sat in the music room and told me some more about his conduct with Ramkumari. How could I tell her not to discuss him with me as it would disturb me? Suniti Tai has great sympathy for Ramkumari. I think she won't discuss this with anyone else. She might be telling me because I also belong to the world of music. Gore Saheb might know more than her about the music world. Yes, he certainly does. Does he know about me also? It seems it was Rajaram Kaka who recommended Ramkumari to Gore Saheb to give her some job. Suniti Tai told me that today. Rajaram himself hasn't told me about Ramkumari working in Gore Saheb's house. Has he told Gore Saheb about me? Perhaps not. He being an advocate, hasn't the curiosity arisen in him, why this girl had left such a good husband and is living in this farmhouse? Even if he knew, he didn't belong to the class of people who would reveal it.

ॾ

Last week it was my elder brother's birthday. I had gone home. A bit of exciting news. Sister-in-law Revati is pregnant. This is the third child. These days no one has more than two children. That too, in an educated family. The feeling that to have a third child in an educated family is considered a blemish that has developed lately. Sister-in-law took me to her room and confided, 'It happened accidentally. Your brother said that we should go to a doctor and get it aborted. I didn't agree. Let those who want to laugh, do so. I said when god has blessed us why shouldn't we be happy?' Her face was beaming. Of my two sisters-in-law this one was closer to me. She was of my age. I came back to my farmhouse in the evening itself.

After two days, the happiness on Revati's face began to haunt me. The thirty-four year old sister-in-law's third pregnancy began to compare itself with my barrenness. I had scarified this joy for the sake of music. After getting married and going to Los Gatos, I had told Vikram, 'A child. Looking after it, would be an impediment. I feel like having no children. If you want it I don't oppose it.' He agreed even for that. After leaving him and coming over here, even the idea of being a mother has been beyond imagination. It is not possible either.

Now suddenly the desire to become a mother has arisen. The mango trees in the garden have flowered. Truly, this is spring. This is the time to practise Raga Basant. I am finding new meaning in it. I had understood that Basant meant the season of flowering of love, separation, the desire for re-union and the season when bees fly about from flower to flower, fertilising them. I had understood Basant raga only to mean this. But now it has become a season of intense desire for motherhood. What meaning is there for separation and union if it doesn't lead to motherhood? A new meaning regarding the love of man and woman. I now feel that without the basic tune that mutually assists to become a mother, a father, what meaning is there in affection and love? The latent intense pain of having been permanently deprived of love and affection is burning me up from within. I should never sing a raga like Basant. If I sing it, my inner emptiness will emerge out and make me cry. The Raga Madhyamadi-saranga also inflames the pangs of separation. I thought that those who are not initiated were saying madhumaasa-saranga wrongly. Now I am beginning to understand that even that mistake speaks the truth. In the very word madhumaasa there is the agony of separation bursting forth. Hereafter, I shouldn't sing even that.

Since the day before yesterday a thought, not a daydream, a mad dream is coming afloat. If I consider myself as a Devadasi, I may become a mother without the bondage of a husband or family. I have a dream, a dream of a child, even while it is in the womb, my continuous practice of swara-sadhana would imbibe in its nerves and veins the musical excellence and born with the natural inclination for music, and with my training from the childhood itself, she or he by the age of only twenty, should become a singer capable of conquering the music lovers of entire India.

For the last three days only the dream of becoming a Devadasi is haunting me. This morning a question arose and exposed the absurdity of my dream. Even If I become a Devadasi who should be the man who impregnates me with his seed? Another musician. Though all musicians are not like Mohanlal, on what basis should I select him and sleep with him? Love? There is no likelihood of my finding such love with anyone. For one who deceived and left Vikram, for one who is unable to extricate from the piercing sin, how is it possible to love another? Even if I love, if he is a married man, won't I be perpetrating injustice to his wife and children? If he is unmarried, how is it justly possible to disengage himself by breaking the relationship and marry another woman? If I say that he should marry me, won't the whole conceptual dream of Devadasi become falsified? If all these aspects are carefully analysed, it brings sorrow. It even brings forth laughter.

Since yesterday, the mind has reached a decision. If I have to become a mother, only Vikram has the moral right to make me one. Another noble aspect of his character is becoming clear now. He is the only son of his parents. A growing company. He is a generous man who even gave up the right to expect from his wife to provide an heir to the whole family's endeavour. It is a sin even to contemplate about my motherhood without him. But I have lost him. Therefore it is wise to reject the desire of motherhood and just engage myself in the practice of music.

Chapter 18

I

Lauren Smith clearly knew the difference between the Indian classical music which she had learnt at Varanasi the last time for two years and what she was learning now in Bombay. She was still young when she was in Varanasi. Twenty-four years. The age when dreams would sprout with new vigour. Every new raga was putting forth new emotions and dreams. Besides, it was the city of Varanasi. Since the time of the legendary King Harishchandra and even before that and even now in continues to vibrate with the mythological imagination of ancient traditional lore. Whether sitting on the banks of the River Ganga or sailing in a boat feasting the eyes with the rows of tiered steps of the ghats, or standing in front of innumerable temples nestling in the narrow streets, in the atmosphere of the mythological world that emanated in the eyes of the people with their foreheads smeared with kumkum and the garlands of marigold flowers hanging from their necks, intoning the praises of the gods while greeting with Jai Vishvanathji, Jai Annapurnaji, Jai Kotwalji, Jai Ramachandraji, Jai Jai Tulsidasji. In each raga, the power of the presiding diety was experienced. That guru was different. Even in the name Acharya Shrutisagar Pandey there was a tremendous imaginative potential. Ocean of shruti does not mean a sheet of water which can be crossed in a few hours by an airplane or in a few weeks by ship. Immense, endless, immeasurable, boundless, the repository of all divine gems in its womb, the depth and expanse of the element of water. A natural phenomenon. The name echoes the ocean like power of shruti. His devotion was such that after getting up in the wee hours of the morning and chanting Om unceasingly he would get neck deep in the waters of Gangaji and perform swarasadhana, then return to his ancestral home, worship Lord Krishna in the puja room, built privately, smear kumkum, come out and then only he would hold the tambura. Not even on a single day had he looked at his pupil with a look of carnal desire. There was absolutely no room for any intimate feeling. He would illustrate each raga with reference to a Sanskrit shloka, and generate the concept of the appropriate god or goddess of that raga and would say, singing that raga means involving and actualising the presence of that deity. She could not understand any of those concepts. But her mind would experience a sense of mystery. The secrets and the mysteries of the eastern hemisphere, the origin of the source of Indian life would rise in her mind. Now she had understood the difference; he was not explaining music with the comprehensive analytical or critical concept of art, but would explain as a method of spiritual sadhana of Puranas. Amidst the heat, noise and the bad weather of Bombay, and the multi-storied apartments, that are built, as if a crowd of ugliness is made to stand, to avoid the disgusting sight of underwears, petticoats, saris that are hung in the balconies to be dried and the people who lie down there on the mats, half clad and sweating. Sitting in her flat on the sixth floor she had to tune the tambura and close the eyes. If the window was not firmly shut, the noise of the television of the neighbouring flat would assail the ears. This is a country where nobody can tell anyone else that they are inconveniencing us. She was thinking that the only way of getting privacy here was by shutting out everything and switching on the air conditioning. This disappointment was troubling her. How was she supposed to invoke the spirit of Indian music in such circumstances? The answer to that had been shown by her guru, Mohanlal. Music is an art. The secret of the art of music is creating it in a place where an emotion could not be born—could not at all be born. Understanding the main pulses of raga and strumming it was the method. He taught the secret of shutting out Bombay and being enveloped by the raga just by the tuning the tambura and adjusting the voice to the shruti.

She didn't see anything unnatural in her relationship with him. She was the one with the most outstanding personality and beauty in the New York workshop. He got enamoured. He showed it. Making it known was his right. Accepting or rejecting it was her prerogative. We got together without infringing on anybody's right. He did not exploit my need for money. By all means, an artist, a brilliant artist, the birth of feeling, the expression of desire, their union took place rapidly. It is not that it should not happen so fast in non-artists. The fact of his involvement with other women did not surprise or upset me. He is away from his wife and he is an artist too. After she came to India he is making suitable arrangements and desiring my company. Doesn't she know that asking her to come to his flat was to see that she didn't suspect his other relationships? To expect him not to share intimacy with anyone else, this was not a boyfriend-girlfriend relationship. Though she knew all this, she would get angry with him. An age which showed a sagging face. Why should he distribute it in a dozen places? Though everyone knows that while making love the woman is praised that she is the greatest beauty in the world, who doesn't know that the compliment is momentary? However, who doesn't like to extend its range? She had also mentioned it. She had even shown it by getting angry. But she had not taken it to the level of creating a scene and breaking up the relationship. His life is his own. There was no rule that she shouldn't have contact with friends of her own. He also didn't mention it. In the music concerts when he himself came, talked with her, desired her company, she had given permission to Kapur to visit her at her flat. He had come several times. Nothing more than physical pleasure had emanated from it. He was married and was extremely careful about maintaining secrecy. There was nothing else except the body to be shared. She had herself cut off the relationship. After six months, Vijayanand Bhat approached her. Good looking. Her own age. He was a graduate, a Bachelor of Arts. He spoke good English. He was a singer, struggling to live by music in Bombay. He explained to her the ways of various ragas. When they were bodily united, there were also other interests to be shared. But his parents were trying to get him married to a girl from their own caste, a girl who was well employed in Bombay itself. He who was not well settled in the profession of music felt it was a wise thing. He was behaving with fear lest his moving about with a foreign girl might come in the way of finding such an opportunity. The thought of telling her that she was also learning Indian music and that they could work and earn their livelihood together never came to his mind. She felt that this was a demeaning friendship. She herself kept away. Indians also have natural desire but they are afraid as theirs' is not a free society. Though she explained to herself that for her who had grown up in the free society of America this was tiresome, now and then she would chafe within herself. But she engaged herself in learning music with dedication in order not to deviate from the purpose with which she had come to India. Whatever the other irritating aspects, there was always discipline in the lessons of the Guruji. He never missed a class, three times a week when he was in town. When he said that he would come at half past eight, he always did, though he was late by a few minutes. When once the lesson began, it might go on for a couple of hours and even for half an hour more until he corrected everything and made the lesson sink down in the mind. Since everything would be recorded, there was no problem in practising it later. Whether there was the desire to invite her to bed or not, the lesson would never be suspended. This one quality was enough to admire him.

She had also read the scandalous remarks published about him in yellow journals and newspapers. He had never talked about it to her at any time. She had also not mentioned it. She had wondered that such journalism was found in India also as in America. He had not taken her along to accompany him on the tambura in India as he had done in America. He never showed his intimacy with her outside. She thought that it was perhaps necessary given the conditions of this country.

She had learnt music for three years, and had got her student scholarship extended by one more year. There was a chance of it being extended if a recommendation from the guru was obtained. But she herself had lost her enthusiasm. She could practise further in expanding the alaap and refining the tanas. But what could be gained by it? What would she lose if she discontinued? The comparison had taken hold of her mind. Indian music had become an art for her now. It had not remained a call of a mysterious experience as it was in Varanasi earlier. On thinking about it, no answer was coming forth. Would I go back to the American way of industrial life like the hippies who wander about in search of a new world and after they are disillusioned go back and settle down? Would the alaap which would make time suspended become the steady quality of my consciousness? These questions began to trouble her. Besides, there was a clear change taking place in her guru himself. He looked depressed. The look is downcast. There is no enthusiasm on the face. He teaches as if it is a duty. There are no flashes in it. Gets angry suddenly. Afterwards withdraws himself as if he has made a mistake. She has also tried to soothe him, draw him into pleasure many a time. But he has thrown cold water on her friendship saying, 'What has happened to me? I am all right. You do your practice.'

ƹ

She decided to put an end to her learning and return to America. 'Then learn Bhairavi,' said her Guru. He had not taught her that raga. She had learnt upto that level in Varanasi. She had heard it in every concert. She had collected a few tapes. When she was in the mood she would sing that movement to herself. It was a delicate raga which could be bent and coiled like a creeper that has spread out everywhere. Wanted to learn it right from the beginning. She had even asked him to teach her. He had postponed it saying, 'Not now. It is not so easy to learn Bhairavi.' Now he started teaching it. After pronouncing the unique characteristics and playing it on the harmonium he explained, 'Nobody sings it in the Khayal style expanding it to its full extent. If attempted, the extremely delicate nuances and the emotion of dedication will disappear in a vapour. Only through love, separation, devotion and bhajans the new and newer pulses of this raga could be searched and made to throb. In order to do that one must know the meaning of bhajans. One must know the Vedanta or the metaphysical implications of it.'

Though he taught her for a month and though she practised diligently, he was not satisfied. He would say, 'You are not understanding the secret of the raga.' He would say it again and again. He got angry, 'You leave this raga alone. You cannot understand the Indian bhakti. You people cannot understand the relationship between devotion and love. Why did you come to learn Indian music, wasting your time as well as mine? Go back to America. You say you stayed in Kashi, what the hell for, I don't understand.'

'Are there any mistakes in my intonation in the rendering of the swaras?' she asked.

'If only the places of the swaras are all right, the raga does not get the complete emotional level. You must have that emotional culture within you. You don't have it. Madhu grasped all the sophisticated nuances of Bhairavi in one stroke. You are a White girl. You won't understand even if you take seven births,' he shouted.

'Who is Madhu?'

'An Indian student. Who are you to ask that?' He screamed again as if she had committed an unpardonable mistake.

She felt she had been insulted. 'Correct me if there is a mistake in my singing. But don't compare me with some other girl. Don't talk about my country, my colour and my culture. I have been quite fed up for the last one month. I can do without this raga,' she said.

'Can you do without Bhairavi? What do you know unless you understand the connection between love and devotion? Have you reached the level to oppose your guru? You can never comprehend Bhairavi.' He raised his hand and slapped her hard. Immediately she put down the tambura, lifted her right hand and slapped his left cheek. He was astounded. 'Do you hit back your guru? May you forget everything I have taught. This is my curse. Yes, this is my curse.' Saying so, he slapped both her cheeks hard seven-eight times. Then he left abruptly.

A couple of minutes later her mind came under control. Meanwhile he had descended in the lift. Now if she ran behind him in the street caught hold of him and beat him up, it would create a scene. People would gather around. Discretion prevailed. She stopped the weeping which was welling from within. She made up her mind to punish him. She thought of a means to do so in a minute. She got up, took up her little bag with her wallet, put on her footwear and got down the lift. She took an autorickshaw to the railway station to board the train at Churchgate. The stink of heat, dirt, and the sweat of the crowd. Her anger against the whole of Bombay was swelling. She went to the office of the *Asian Tribune* and said, 'I want to see Mr. Paranjape.'

She knew Paranjape. He had published a small interview with her when she had come to Bombay. Then he was a fan of Mohanlal.

She knew that lately he had turned against him and had exposed his escapades. In a minute the receptionist took her to the second floor. Said, 'Room number twenty-six.' Paranjape got up from his chair extended his hand, shook her hand, showed her the chair opposite and said, 'Welcome. What is the matter? You seem to be in pain. What is that mark on your cheek?' His face was showing concern and sympathy. Her feeling grew intense. She felt like crying. He remonstrated, 'Lauren, why are you upset? Tell me.'

She wiped her eyes and said, 'I have come only to tell you. You can record my statement.' He took out the tape recorder from the draw of his table, put it in front of her and pressed the button. 'He beat me up. Look here. Both my cheeks have swollen up. They are showing his finger marks. He is cruel. Merely because he teaches, how does he have the right to beat up his students? If I was in America I would have immediately called the police. But I don't have confidence in the promptness of justice done in this country. I came to you, so that the people may know.'

'Why did he beat you?'

'Because I did not understand the nuances of Raga Bhairavi.'

'Was this the first time he beat you?'

'Yes.'

'How did he get the lenience to do so?'

'Lenience? Is he not my guru?'

'By merely being a guru, there won't be that much of freedom. That lenience is possible only if there is a greater intimacy. Everybody knows that there is intimacy between him and you. Where and how did it start? Tell me.'

'In New York where he had come to conduct the workshop. A week after we met.'

'Did he make the overtures immediately? Did he make love?'

'Of course we did it.' Immediately, as if she had woken up, she said, 'Mr. Paranjape, you are asking for the full details of our relationship. How much money will you pay if I tell you the full story? If a scandal story is given about a singer famous all over America, they will pay at least half a million dollars. How much will you pay?'

'We don't have either the practice or the opportunity to sell such a story. Publishing it is itself the price we pay in our country.'

'Which means that by exploiting our private affairs, you increase the circulation of your paper.'

'Did I invite you to come and tell me? You yourself came in search of me to give a statement. Proving the background by probing questions is the accepted method of a journalist. If you don't answer my questions it will be difficult for us to publish your statement.'

'Would it be difficult? Then you wouldn't publish it?' Lauren sat still as if lost. He was looking at her steadily as though to capture her. She felt she had voluntarily walked into a trap. After a minute's turmoil saying, 'Would it be difficult? You won't publish it? That is exactly what I want also. I came here in a fit of anger and talked all kinds of things. Sorry,' and left suddenly.

She went to Churchgate, caught the train and went back to her flat. Her anger against her guru hadn't subsided fully. But she felt she shouldn't have gone to the newspaper office. She fretted thinking that instead of just recording what she had to say, what right did he have to dig into all kinds of things? Even without cooking her lunch, she just switched on the fan and lay down. By evening she felt hungry. She got up, cooked and after she dined she began to think. May be what Guruji said was right. Perhaps I can never understand the relationship between love and devotion as the people of this country do! It was impossible to think of god as a lover. I grew up in a culture which said anybody who said it is possible, would be guilty of sacrilege. It is the code of conduct here that even when the guru raises his hand on his pupil, he or she should sit quietly with the head bent down. These people believe that the hand of a disciple who hits back a guru will be shrunk and lose its function. They raise the guru to the level of god; they even say that 'Guru is God'. Not only in music circles but in spiritual attainment and other disciplines also. That must be the reason why they have protected and built up on the same old, original values a superstructure without giving in to new approaches. Every time the characteristics of a raga is described, they start their lesson after how it is defined in the Sanskrit texts. They illustrate with special care how they have not transgressed the tradition. They say that their music, dramaturgy, philosophy and yogashaastra are all different facets of the same vision. Perhaps an outsider like me can never fully understand it! She thought. The mind again remembered her guru in Varanasi. For him I would be an outsider. But this man is a complete artist, living a free life like the American artists. While giving details about the greatness of the music of this country, the references to Veda and yoga were made, he would understand and sing music only at the level of art. He lived his own independent life as American artists do. Why can't I master the feelings and emotions which he can? Why not? She struggled. She didn't even switch on the light. The churning went on even in the darkness.

Couldn't fall asleep. She felt it was late when she woke up in the morning. After twisting and rolling about until she was fully awake, when she opened her eyes and realised that she hadn't taken off her wrist watch last night and looked at it, it was showing 9 am. Opening the door, she picked up the milk packet and the newspaper. Suddenly she felt anxious and turned the pages over. What a rascal! He had published it. After I left, making me feel that he was not going to publish it, he had published it by giving a sensational title: 'Singer Mohanlal, who, after sexually attracting an American girl, exploited and brought her to India is physically torturing her.' She read it quickly: 'Putting on the pretence of propagating the spiritually-oriented Indian music in Western countries and going to America four years ago, Pandit Mohanlal took upon himself the responsibility of conducting a six-week workshop, dragged to his bed a White girl who came to learn music, got her a student scholarship to come to India, arranged a private apartment, exploited her physically. And when it was almost time for her to leave, without learning anything, saying that she doesn't have the cultural background to learn Indian music, putting the blame entirely on her has beaten her up until her cheeks had swollen up and this had made her come to our office to share her sorrow not wanting to go to the police, for not having any confidence in them. This reveals yet another instance of Mohanlal's mean mentality and low moral calibre of his life as an artist...' Starting thus, Paranjape has strung up a whole fabric of lies. No, no, no, this is not what I said. This was not my meaning. Or, what did I say in my anger! No, I remember. I did not say these things, not this way. Should have brought back his tape. Shouldn't have believed his word that he was not going to publish it—dirty fellow, dirty Indian, she thought.

All at once, her body experienced fatigue. She sat on the chair. Then she opened her eyes and read the whole story. My stuff appears only tangentially here and there. She felt that Paranjape had filled in his own story and sub-stories which I couldn't have mentioned and not even suggested. Immediately she looked up his number in the directory and called and asked him, 'Mr. Paranjape, I came out after you said that you wouldn't print the story. I believed you, thinking you are a gentleman. You have prepared your report after weaving in a twisted account of what I have not said; not even suggested.'

'Madam, if you wanted only to appear in print what you wanted, you should have written a letter to the editor. To investigate the news as well as its entire background and commenting on it is also the duty of the reporter. He collects information from various sources. Please understand that he knows more than what you do.'

'But those are not my words.'

'The words may not be yours, but the subject matter is related to your words.'

'Nonsense,' she said, not knowing what to say.

'If you want, you can send the corrections through a letter to the editor. We will publish it.'

'You won't, will you, add a note by the reporter and twist the subject-matter of the letter?'

'You don't have the authority to confiscate the right of the reporter to justify his own stand.'

She couldn't think of anything except shouting 'nonsense' for the second time. He put down the phone on the other side.

After five minutes she called Mohanlal, 'Guruji, it's I, Bhoopali speaking. Please excuse me. After you hit me and left, I was angry. In my anger I went to Paranjape's office and told him about your hitting me. He asked me where and when our relationship started and such things. By the time I told him it was in New York, I got my senses. He himself said that he wouldn't publish what I told him. I returned with that belief. He has betrayed me. I will stand by you whatever action you want to take against him. I don't know what to do in this country. I am leaving in two months time.'

'You bitch, after doing what you have done, you say that you will stand by me? If you come to my flat, I am going to hit you with shoes.' The phone screeched at the loudness of his scream.

Chapter 19

I

Husband Sohanguru had completed hundred years. Could a celebration be made to mark it? This thought came to her mind. It is quite an unusual event to live up to be a hundred. Besides, in his time he had been famous in the whole of India. If she wanted, it wouldn't be difficult to arrange a grand celebration. She thought that it was the kind of combination when a minister from the Central Government itself could be invited, arrange for a two and a half hour programme of attractive dances, sell tickets and make enough money to save some even after meeting all the expenses. But Guruji wouldn't remember anything. If the nurse employed to look after him washed his face, attended to his toilet, gave him a bath, and gave him a cup of tea, he would drink. If available he would eat soft halwa. You would have to speak loudly. If you ask something, he would answer something else. He doesn't complete sentences. He leans in his own chair, goes into a slumber and snores softly. It is difficult to get such a person on to the stage also. If he could speak for ten minutes after the show and at least demonstrate dance for five minutes, the programme would be colourful. Otherwise it is no use. Besides if she presents him to the public and remind that she was his wife, people might think that she was older than she actually was. Why should she advertise the fact that he was forty years elder to her? Caution prevailed. Why do something for him when he wouldn't know anything happening? She kept quiet.

At a hundred and one, he completely lost his memory. Though he could hear, he couldn't understand what was said. Bathing, feeding, lying down, these when administered to him, he accepted. Sometimes the thought came to her that why shouldn't he least die soon. She enquired whether there was any institution which would look after people like him. She couldn't find any. One day he started mumbling something. When the nurse came and said, 'He is saying something. I can't understand. Please come and listen.' She went and sat close to him. When an effort was made to follow his lip movement and join together unclear utterances, it was possible to piece up a sentence. 'She should have been married off and put in the care of a suitable husband.' She wondered who he was referring to. When her mouth was brought close to his ear and shouted aloud several times, 'To whom?' he couldn't comprehend. But once in a way, the mumbling to this effect didn't stop. He had repeated it six times since morning. 'Since this morning he said it eight times,' the nurse would report. One day when Manohari herself was sitting next to the bed, the same mumble. She felt that the word 'her' referred to herself. She decided, yes, it was so. She was surprised. That night when she was lying in bed in her room, she felt happy that he himself wanted to get her married to some suitable man. Was this thought dormant in his mind? For how many days? Or was it for years? Was it possible that it was there for as long as he had become weak and unable to be a husband to her? Nothing was clear. But it was pleasing to the mind. For a long time she couldn't sleep and was rolling about. What if he had searched for a suitable husband and put her in his care? If he had done it thirty-five years ago! The pleasant reverie took shape. Another pleasant idea took shape. It should have happened before she got operated for not bearing any children. The mind became numb. A vacant state of mind when not even the silence of the night was experienced. Suddenly she felt like crying. She sobbed profusely. After a long time she got sleep.

She had not yet woken up in the morning. The nurse had come upstairs and was calling from the door. 'Madam, Guruji has passed away. I had seen him once at midnight. When I woke up in the morning I couldn't hear him breathing. I went close and examined. He has died some time ago.' Manohari sat up suddenly saying, 'Is that so?' She cried. A minute later her mind became light.

She got the funeral rites and obsequies performed according to scriptural injunctions, got a photograph of his enlarged and hung it on the wall next to his cot. She sent away the nurse paying her not only her salary but a tip as well.

Ƨ

There was her programme with her troupe in Bombay. A journalist by the name of Paranjape had telephoned. 'You must kindly give me two hours in Bombay, I must interview you for our newspaper.' The next morning after the programme between nine and eleven. She said that it could be at the hotel where she had been lodged.

She remembered having heard the name. She enquired from Chawla, close to her among Delhi journalists, about him. A journalist very influential in the art world of Bombay. Looked after the Art and Literature sections for the *Asian Tribune* for many years. A newspaper published in five places. He was very close to Deshmukh, the minister for Art, Culture and Youth services. He stays with Deshmukh himself when he comes to Delhi. After giving this information Chawla added, 'Recently he has developed dislike for Mohanlal. I believe the quarrel started with Mohanlal not giving his music for the cassette company that Paranjape runs in his wife's name. There is a latest article attacking Mohanlal. He also has letters by readers relating to it. I will send them to you.'

After reading it she could imagine what kind of a fellow Paranjape was. He had written a letter to the editor: 'On account of a fascination for a girl, he promised the American government that he would teach her, sent from time to time progress reports that her progress was good, got her a scholarship, used her for his physical pleasure and was now punishing her physically saying that her progress was not satisfactory and the letter said that the American Consulate must take note of this and take suitable action on him. A visa should not be granted to him so that any further visits by him to America must be prevented.' There were letters by Paranjape or maybe he had written them under a fictitious name. She understood this immediately. She thought that she should never have agreed to be interviewed by him. But now she had already agreed. Her mind warned her that he would ask searching questions about her relationship with Mohanlal twenty years ago. She decided that she, who had made a name for herself in government circles, and in the embassies of several foreign consulates should not fall a prey to his evil design. Besides, no matter how much he had shamed me in private, as a public figure Mohanlal was an artist, a great artist and saying that she was cheated by him would make her cheap. This awareness took shape.

She came to a decision in two days. She challenged herself into thinking whether he would use her or she would use him.

Paranjape met her at the greenroom even before the programme, exchanged pleasantries and confirmed his meeting her the next morning. She informed the hotel management that she would need a small interview chamber for two hours and arranged for tea and snacks. In the middle was the table, chairs facing each other on which they sat. She started the conversation herself, 'Mr. Paranjape, it seems you have such great experience about the art world of Bombay that you can write a whole history of it.'

He started with a mischievous smile establishing familiarity, 'Madam, what is your age?'

'A dancer doesn't have an age of her own. When I am Shakuntala I am sixteen. When I am Radha, I am twenty-five. When I am Meera, I am between thirty and forty.'

'When you are Manohari Das?'

'Manohari Das is a purely private individual. What do your readers have to do with that? By the by, what's your age? Sixty? When are you retiring?' She smiled. Her eyes with make-up were smiling mischievously.

'In the past, when you and Pandit Mohanlal were together for four years—a question regarding that. Not personal. How was the artistic explosion when brilliance of song and dance united?' He asked with a sugary intimate smile.

'Together? Those were stories made up by newspapermen. Dance gets embellished if it is accompanied by good music and music also gets a boost when accompanied by good dancing.'

'Still, with your quarrel...'

'There was neither a quarrel nor a battle. He is basically a pure classical singer. How long is it possible to simply accompany a dance? Don't you know how difficult it is to find permanent singers?'

'Haven't you heard Mohanlal's concerts lately?'

'If the programmes are there with a difference of a day or two, this way or that, it is possible to listen. It has not been possible. He is a brilliant singer. I would like to listen to him.'

He told himself that she was a very clever bitch. When he was rattling to himself as to how he could drag her into conversation from his angle, she asked, 'Paranjapeji, I will talk about something personal. Would you please stop the recording?'

'Sure,' he said and pressed the button. She continued, 'You asked about my age. Actually I practise yoga everyday. So it is difficult for you to guess the right age. That is exactly the source of our Indian dance. I know that you will be coming to Delhi. I also know that when you come, you stay at the home of the minister for Art and Culture. You please visit my school of dance and observe the method. I have a desire to establish a dance village away from the din and bustle of Delhi. Money can be obtained from the cultural division of the United Nations and other international agencies. A proper location is needed. There is a place twelve miles away from the Qutub, in Haryana. If I can get twenty-five acres there, a dance village which can attract international students—boys and girls—can be built there. If you tell your friend Deshmukh and bring him to my dance school, this can be done. I have heard that you do a great deal of creative work in Bombay in the field of art. That is why I am seeking your help.' She extended her hand and gave him a handshake. Her eyes dripped with a friendly, intimate look. He saw in her eyes a look of triumph and knew that he had been defeated in his interview attempt.

He said, 'It is a very good idea. It will bring a good name to the country.'

'You must come to Delhi, stay put in your friend's house and see that this is done. Your flight and taxi fare are my responsibility.' Saying so she opened her bag and took out a wad of currency notes.

Though he protested, 'That's all right,' she thrust a bundle of notes into his hand.

Chapter 20

I

Four years since leaving the husband. No contact at all. Not even after the visit of the parents-in-law. Why didn't I write a letter after coming back? This question arose in the mind one day. What was there to write about? About the altercation with Mohanlal? He slapped me several times. After coming out with the recording machine, thinking of jumping into the ocean and finally deciding to pursue music even without him. The thought occurred, whether I shall write about this farmhouse and the training from Rajaram Tipnis for the last four years and what I had achieved because of these two things? But I have lost the right to write. It would come only if he gave it to me. After a week the idea flashed that he would not give it himself voluntarily, and I must take the first step myself. Why didn't he write, 'Madhu, in your madness for music you have become a victim for his hunger, you have confessed all the details to me honestly. We should not stay apart.' He has known for a whole year about my being here. He knows both, the addresses and the telephone number. If he doesn't come forward on his own and pardon me, how can I write? She stood without seeing a way out. Of late she couldn't sleep properly. She would wake up when the telephone rang, she would wake up with a start, thinking that it was a call from him. But she would become aware of the total silence of the house, the surrounding garden and all the hillocks to the right. If it was midnight here, it would be midday there. Since it was not winter, there would be a difference of only twelve and a half hours. There was no need to call only from the house. Was it possible that he had called by chance and after ringing a couple of times it had stopped? He may be trying again. She thought she would pick up the receiver the moment it rang. No matter how long she waited, it wouldn't ring. She would wonder. Was it an illusion what she heard? Or was it a dream? After a week she thought of writing a letter and the decision became firm. One day, she sat up and wrote. Wrote the whole day.

She mentioned all the main details after she crossed into the security section at the San Francisco International Airport including the call she made home and the message she left. As she kept on writing her desire to become a mother crept in. She wrote about that also and requesting that he should accept her she ended her letter. Please call or write a letter. I can stay in India for the three winter months and stay the rest of the time at Los Gatos. If programmes come up, at such times I can pay a visit to India. That is, only if the listeners accept me in public concerts. Even otherwise, I have now reached a stage where I can sing for my husband's pleasure. That is enough. I will sing only at home.

After posting the letter she started counting the days. It would take a week to reach. In case he was not in town, another three or four days. Would he reply the same day after reading the letter? Would he write or call? If his sympathy is aroused, he would call. He wrote so little. Those in America have lost their habit of writing. With this man, it was the computer or the phone.

A week passed. Everyday she waited for the phone to ring. She started staying close to the phone lest she shouldn't hear it thinking that her letter would be in the mailbox by the time he returned home in the evening and it would be seven in the morning here. Thinking that she wouldn't hear the phone if she slept soundly she would keep awake. Eight days passed. Nine. Ten. Twelve. Even if he had gone on tour, he would have come back today. She waited. Fifteen, sixteen, even after twenty days, no call. Now only a letter is the possibility. If he did not feel like responding immediately, it only meant that he had rejected her. A feeling of depression enveloped her which took away her enthusiasm in everything, even in music practice.

A month had elapsed. Though she had given up the hope of expecting a reply from him she hadn't stopped waiting for the phone to ring. When she was singing aloud she imagined the phone ringing and would suddenly stop. The sound of the phone ringing would have stopped. Though she made up her mind that this was only an illusion and should stop getting influenced by it. When she was not singing, the ringing sound would persist until she ran to the phone. She thought of calling herself and asking if her letter had reached, thereby the matter would be settled one way or the other. But what would happen if it happened not this way but the other. She put down the receiver which she had picked up. Four days passed that way.

One morning at ten, when she was practising Malakshmi came up the stairs and placed an envelope in front of her. Even by observing its length and width, the stamp and the 'Air-Mail' printed in a corner, it was clear that it was from America, yes, even the handwriting of the address was his. The pressure of the blood increased. She put down the tambura and picked up the envelope. Malakshmi went downstairs. Madhu's hand was shaking. Afraid to open the envelope. It was a bit heavy. It could contain ten or fifteen pages. If the letter was lengthy, she felt instinctively it would be a refusal. No need to open it. When the answer was known where was the need to open it? For a couple of minutes she sat silently. It was possible he might have soundly abused her in such a long letter. He might have finally pardoned her. How not to read the letter which she had received. Consoling herself this way she opened the letter.

Addressed as 'Madhumita'. With the question why, instead of calling her Madhu, he had used the full name, she started reading.

It is three weeks since I received your letter. I delayed because one should not reply to such an important, serious letter without thinking deeply about it. I am happy that your music is progressing without any hindrance. I earnestly wish you to gain even more mastery and become a great singer. When I parted from you, I drove home with the enthusiasm that my wife would come back mastering more ragas and would bring back the tapes with the lessons taught by the revered Guruji. I could listen to them and learn about the nuances of those ragas. A feeling of loneliness crept in as soon as I opened the door. Though I was going on my business trips now and then leaving you alone, the experience of how difficult it is to stay in a house without you even for a single day was assuaged on thinking that you had gone to acquire more music, gave me strength to enter the house. Heard your recorded voice. Expecting that there was some surprising happy news, I ran up and opened the envelope. It is useless describing now what happened to me immediately after reading it. Incessant inquisitiveness started torturing me after a week. I have not deceived anyone. Have not hated anyone. Why did this happen to me? Is there no basis of right and wrong for the happiness and sorrow that an individual experiences? Since childhood I have grown up loving and following principles and ideals. Father who was in the Air Force was being transferred regularly. Some of the places that he was transferred to, did not even have a school. He would not take his family to such places. He admitted me to the Ramakrishna Ashram School instead of the school to which the children of the Air Force officers were admitted. There I imbibed the ideals and principles of the ashram school. One shouldn't give room to mean tendencies like lies, hatred and envy. In that Ashram School, trust, discipline, truthfulness and such ideals were nourished and students were made to imbibe them steadfastly. I would dream about those ideals. Even at my young age I had lost my heart to music. When I was eighteen I heard for the first time the concert of Lakshman Dev Maharaj at Delhi. Though I did not know the name of the raga and its characteristics, it had transported me to an ideal world beyond my wildest imagination. I felt that moral and ethical values like compassion, forgiveness, seriousness, sacrifice, control of the inner and outer tendencies became clear. At the end, before Maharaj sang Bhairavi he spoke a few words about how music was the easy means and method of knowing god. What is god? An ideal. The realisation of god is the realisation of the ideals. In three hours that had passed, I had realised that. Like this, grew my feeling that there was no better means to realise those ideals except through music. As I grew up, throughout college education and higher studies in America that dream of the eighteen-year old not only matured, but the conviction that music was the vehicle to create that dream did not at all change. I have mentioned this to you several times. Still I am writing this again. Because without writing this the suitable beginning of this letter cannot be found.

With whom could I share my agony after you left me? When you were here the group of music lovers were my friends. Could I share with Mishra, Sardesai, Goel, Gupta, Murti, Kulkarni, anyone like that? Could I tell them that Madhumita had a physical relationship with her guru and when she got her conscience aroused that this was cheating, she left? All of them knew that you were going for music lessons. I carried on for some weeks that you were still going for the lessons. For some more weeks telling them that your mother was unwell. Then one day I just told them that there is greater convenience for her to pursue her music there than here. So she is not coming back in the near future. Thereafter no one asked me. In whom should I confide about my internal state? How could I tell my parents that the very girl I admired and married—a wife in whom the only thing to look for was music, did this to me? I started writing a diary as the only means through which I could give expression to my inner feelings. Not daily. But only when I found that I could not contain myself at all. It is very long. To be exact, it is one hundred and sixty-six pages. To a great extent there is a repetition of feelings, thoughts and emotions. Therefore I am going to quote a few paragraphs.

'I am now beginning to understand how false my impression was that there is no ideal wife greater than Madhumita in the whole world. I, who was applying practical principles in company matters, in marketing, why was I not able to come out of this emotional loyalty? Even before I saw the girl, I had been told that she sang well and was desirous of marrying a husband who would encourage her music even after marriage. I believed, that god had created this girl just for me. I went to see the girl not to see her good looks, her height and her physical build like objective standards. But to listen to how she sang. She had purity and clarity in her intonation of swaras. She had command over her voice. I surely felt that she had already achieved a good deal. A good family too. I gave my consent without consulting my parents and even before they saw the girl. Pitaji said on the phone that when I had consented and there was very little time, why waste a day for us to come and see the girl? Mother got angry on the same phone call and said that I did not even know how to respect the wishes of parents. On the evening of the wedding my aunt called me aside and told me, "Vikku, your mother is unhappy that this girl is not good enough in keeping with the beauty and status of your family. Don't you know in how many places she had identified so many very beautiful girls for you to marry? She is not ugly. But she is not beautiful to be shown off as a daughter-in-law. But your consent is important. After all, it is you who are going to live with her! Why I am telling you this is because

I wanted to tell you not to talk back to your mother as many newly married men do in an intoxicated manner believing that their wives are beautiful. Anyway you are taking your wife to America. Your mother will gradually reconcile herself to the situation. I will also console her. All women desire that their daughters-in-law must be beautiful." Now, looking at it from another angle, a new insight appears. My pride that no other Indian in the entire Silicon Valley had such an ideal wife as mine. Not pride, I had the satisfaction. Most of the Indian men staying here give an indication to the bride searchers that she should be a computer engineer. If she has done engineering in some other branch, after she comes here they get her trained in computers. They boast that their wives get such fat salaries. I have always felt that it is mean to expect the wife to earn. I had thought that the pride that my wife could sing so well was qualitatively superior and a thousand times better. In comparison to what god had given me by way of my earnings, even the earnings of my wife as an engineer would be very little indeed. It is not important for me. But my belief that being a musician is superior to the profession as an engineer was demolished.

'My belief that it is not possible to have a more ideal wife has been sinking since the day before yesterday. I felt like making a list about considering my wife as an ideal wife (1) the positive and (2) the negative aspects. Has there been a single incident in your married life which has irritated the wife? Has there been any harassment from the mother-in-law? Any pinpricks from the wives of the brothers? Does the husband send his earning to his parents? Has she managed any irksome problems like unmarried sisters-in-law, widowed sister of the husband, displaced homeless brothers of the husband, an irresponsible, jobless husband? Has she managed any such difficult situations? Parents who don't want even a single dollar from their son, with no sisters and brothers, a husband so well educated and earning so much money with an income which only one in a hundred get among the Indians in the Silicon Valley, such a lovely house, a household help like Maria who does every household chore for four hours a day—how many White Americans, let alone Indians will have in their employment? When no such chores were there, with a husband who allowed her to practise her music as she liked to her heart's content, how could there

be any chance for her sterling qualities to be tested? How did I develop this feeling blindly that in the entire Silicon Valley among the Indian families no woman was more virtuous than my wife? Except that she cheated her husband, I don't consider her a mean woman in other respects even now. But to consider her a noble person no evidence is available for me.

'I notice a change in me. I don't know how to reduce it to writing even up to this minute. My love of music is of the level of love. It is not a result of learning from anyone. It was a state which would engender noble and elevating thoughts. After she left and I read her diary-like letter I had not heard music. The day before yesterday without any forethought I put on the tape of Raga Kaushi-kanada sung by the Mishra Associates which was in my collection. I thought it was a bore. I took it out and played Bilaval by the same artists. It was equally boring. Formerly, what powerful feelings would be ignited by these same tapes! I thought that I would let it go at that and tried the music of four others. I tried to console myself that it wouldn't be proper to lose interest in music itself because the wife whom I trusted and the guru whose feet I used to touch with reverence cheated me. It wasn't possible. I am trying to pick some cassettes, both vocal and instrumental at random from my collection and tried to listen to them, I am familiar with those ragas and their movements. But I don't have any taste for them. With the intention of getting rid of the feeling of depression that was plaguing me and lighten my mood, thinking that I could find solace in music I listened to Raga Darbari which expresses sorrow. Nothing came through. In no raga of the cassette can I see the emotion of dignity. Raga Bairagi doesn't retain any feeling of non-attachment. The question frightens me, "What is left for me if I lose my ability to get inspired by music?"

'I have been thinking about this for the last fifteen days. I am thinking that majority of the people in the world are without any taste for music. Don't they have any interest in life? What is the kind of feeling that music creates? Does a raga throb with the same feeling in all listeners? Don't we respond to music according to our own mental state? This is a kind of psychological question. It is a question of provoking an emotional upsurge. Why hadn't I understood it so far?

'Artists are basically provocators of emotions. It is but natural that they are caught up in emotions. This rise and fall in the love affairs is clearly reflected in the lives of the Hollywood stars. Did I need to have this experience in order to understand it?

'The tendency of the body flows exceeding the limits of psychological inclination. For the last two weeks bodily needs have awoken. At times it is intense. Formerly when Madhumita went to her parents if such a thing had happened her memory would form in the imagination and tease me. But now it was only desire—neither her memory or image is entering my mind. No other woman comes to mind either. I never had a pre-marital experience. Certainly not extramarital relations. Even after this marriage has broken down, my mind is not going after any other woman. I know that most men who travel as much as I do indulge in intervals of happiness. It is a public secret that a man and a woman go out together for a business conference together stay in the same hotel and after dinner while having social drinks indulge in symbolic invitation "Let us talk further in my room." I haven't done so even once. Not that I didn't have an opportunity. Only moral fear. Not just when I was with the wife. Even later. A year after she left me I feel like doing such a thing.

'Last night I had invited Cathy home. An employee in the Intel company with whom we have business. Divorcee. Thirty-five years. She had asked smilingly, "Shall we go somewhere this weekend?" A bold woman. The kind who was not particular about the custom that such invitations come from a man and not from a woman. In such circumstances a colleague working in the same company shouldn't be invited. Everyone is cautious that there may be embarrassment. "Will you come to my place this Friday evening? You can return on Sunday evening." When I said this my voice was shaking.

"Really?"

"Really."

"Don't joke. Your wife is not in town?"

"No. She has gone to the home country."

"Give me the directions to your home."

'If Maria prepared the food for Saturday and Sunday on Friday itself and kept it, she wouldn't come back till Monday morning. So I had

decided that home was the right place. I was also doubtful whether she would come. Because she would say such things even for fun. Though I felt like calling her and ensuring it, I kept quiet because of a delicate feeling. She asked with her map in front of her, whether the route was correct. I said, "Yes, correct. You can even give me the directions."

'As soon as she arrived, I took her coat, put it on the hanger, took her small box and led her upstairs, I took her to the guest room and asked whether it was convenient. She looked at my face. She exhibited anger on her face. I didn't understand. I looked at her questioningly. "Vikram, did you invite me as a guest to sleep in a separate room?" I understood my mistake. I apologised. "Look, this is not the way lovers meet. As soon as I come you should seize me in an embrace and kiss me. Instead of any such thing you take my suitcase, put it in the room like a hotel usher and ask me if it is convenient. You are stupid, inexperienced," she said.

'Both your accusations are correct. Sorry. Saying so I approached her, embraced and kissed her, she half closed her eyes passionately and devoured me, engaging me in a long and deep kiss. The embrace was very pleasant. It got rid of a year-long numbness and made me happy. After dinner when we came up again she asked, "Vikram dear, our bedroom?"

"This is it," I answered.

"Where is your master bedroom? Aren't you going to show it to me?"

"It's there. I am not using it," I said.

"Come and show it to me." She took the lead. I followed her. She stood in the centre, turned all around and drawing an intoxicated breath said, "How tasteful!" Her face was registering admiration. She then embraced me and said, "Vikram, when there is such a beautiful master bedroom, why should we sleep in that guest room? Come, let's go and take a shower together. The shower room must also be equally beautiful." She walked up, took a peek inside and was happy, like a child, "Beautiful, inspiring!" My enthusiasm diminished even with the proposal of sleeping in that room. A sense of sin enveloped me. After the wife left and I had read her letter I had not slept in that room. I was sleeping in a room opposite the guest room.

I was feeling embarrassingly awkward to refuse when Cathy was asking. I was filled with the moral fear that I would be betraying Madhu on the same bed she had cheated me on. I said Cathy, not here. That bed is also big enough for two. She asked, "Why? This is the nuptial bed. Are you afraid of committing a sin if you allow another woman to lie on it?" The accusation that I was a man of double standards was implied in it. "Or, it is difficult to make up the bed as before after it is used. Are you afraid that the wife may find out after her return? Or is it an understanding that this bed will not be used when you are not with your wife?" Not only did my courage give way by her probing cross-examination. I was anxious that if I slept with this domineering woman I might experience defeat at the beginning itself.

"Cathy, let us go to bed a little late. I want to make you listen to some pieces of Indian classical music. Let's go to the music room." I took her hand and she came downstairs with me. I asked, "You must have heard some Indian music."

"I know the name of Ravishankar. That's all. Harrison's guru. Nothing more than that."

"Then it's even better, come." I sat her down, opened the drawer of cassettes and played Raga Darbari-kanada. "Listen to this at leisure, then tell me what you think." She started listening with attention. After ten minutes she signalled to me to stop it and said, "Do you call this classical music? It sounds like the moaning sound of an old-model truck going up a steep mountain. There is no composition or form or melody." She confirmed what I had been thinking. Then I played Malkauns and Bhoopali. None of these interested her. Then I played the same ragas on sitar and sarod in drita movement in jugalbandi competing with the tabla. "Yes, this I admire," she said, got up and enjoyed herself gyrating, moving her hips erotically. When I asked her to say what she liked, she answered, "Speed, movement and suggestiveness." She was not an un-initiate into music. She was the sort who would go to San Francisco when there was a good concert. The meaning in music is what we give to it. My belief, that what we give is dependent on how our head has been filled with our traditional shaping, became strengthened.

'Brought her up to the first floor guest room and begged her pardon. "Cathy, please excuse me. My mind is not at peace. I will sleep in a separate room."

'She stared at me. Her eyes were spitting fire. She said, "If you say excuse me, excuse is not generated. You ruined my weekend. Without being certain whether your state is that of the body or of the mind, you shouldn't invite a companion and put her to shame. Another friend of mine had invited me for the weekend. Trusting you, I told him that I was not free."

'My helplessness had made me shiver. Fearing that if I repeated my apology she might get even more angry, I went to my bedroom. I couldn't sleep for a long time. After inviting and antagonising her and its shame, the thought that the meaning of music is what we have inherited from our tradition filled my mind. It was the early hours of the morning when I slept. It was nine when I woke up. The door of the guest room was open. She was not there. Her portmanteau was not there. I came down, opened the door and looked out. Her car was not there either.

'I saw the full video cassette of her concert with her guru at Sunnyvale Temple. Now I am beginning to understand clearly the inner truth of the concert about which I was so proud that my wife could sing equal to her guru and she had made such good progress. During the singing, the looks that they were exchanging had not been only pertaining to music. They were the inner expressions of deep love between a couple who were floating in amorous love. Here also, the gestures and movements of a woman are more than that of a man in erotic play are quite clear. Or her emotional crescendo was greater than his. When she sang mat jaa *her uncontrollable weeping was not because of the emotion of Meera. I am now beginning to understand that it was because her lover-guru was leaving the morning after.*

'This morning I read again the pages she had left for me. She has begun to understand that she had cheated her husband after she came to know that soon after the concert he went to the Los Angeles concert and was making out with another girl. Otherwise she would have continued her two-timing sweet relationship! Anyway, whatever the reason, I respect her inner prompting that she should tell the truth to her husband.

'Madhumita, if I start quoting from the pages which I wrote for myself I can write quite a lot. Anyway, I have quoted the main points. You have expressed your desire to become a mother. I don't have a right to comment on your desire. I agreed immediately to your wish that we shouldn't have any children as it would come in the way of your pursuit of music. I neglected the fond wish of my mother and father to have a grandchild. I also gave up my desire to have a child. Then your music was paramount to you as well as me. You didn't have the eyes to see the intense longing of your husband and your in-laws. Now you desire motherhood. Quite unable to reach a decision regarding our marriage, on account of inner strength, I was keeping silent so far. Your letter has given me the impetus to come to a decision. I have no love left for music. There is no other reason for loving you. My attorney will send you a letter separately. If you sign it in the presence of a notary with his signature and seal in his presence, divorce will be granted without any delay. It is good for both of us to be free. I wish you a great future.'

Yours sincerely, Vikram Shah

Her spirit became still. The tambura lying in front of her and the birds which were chirping merrily away outside the bars of the window remained outside her notice. Emptiness filled her head, like the strumming of the strings of a tambura which was immersed in water. Intense anguish. She felt like collapsing. She did. Collapsing on her right side with her eyes closed seemed to give some sort of solace to her agony. After a long time her mind told her, that she hadn't expected this, that she had not thought that he was so hard, so cruel. It seems he respects my internal pressure to tell the truth. But he never forgets anything, never forgives anything. The thought, that she was also deceived in thinking that he was very generous, took shape in her silently.

ऽ

She didn't do anything the whole day. She didn't walk about in the garden in the evening. She didn't climb the hillock by the side of the garden. She just lay next to her tambura. When Malakshmi brought tea in the evening she said that she had a headache. She went to bed and slept soon. In the middle of the night when her sleep became light, as if she was waiting for it, she remembered that letter and she became fully awake. She thought of switching on the light and reading it once again. But she told herself when the main message had penetrated deep into the mind, so why bother reading it again? I had never boasted that I was beautiful. I hadn't sought his commendation. He has derided me by writing that I am not beautiful. She remembered the proverb that a discordant husband discerns stone in curd. He waited four years to say this; even that till I wrote him a letter. She changed sides. All the emotions of music are lies. Tied to the mind with tradition. She told herself, what else can one hear if one listens with anger? She switched on the light. The clock showed half past three in the morning. She remembered that of late she had not woken at this hour and practised. She got up from the bed, washed her face and came back. She tuned the tambura and started expatiating the swaras of Raga Kafi. Ah, what humility is there *ri ga ma ga ri sa*. There is that delicate feeling that I have given up everything, forgiven everything. She expanded on the same notes to get the feeling again and again. She felt that a raga does not have its own emotional structure and it has been tied to the head by tradition was a false concept and a decision made in anger. As she went on singing her idea became firm. After she expanded on the Raga Kafi and repeated it till five in the morning she felt drowsy. She put down the tambura and went to bed. Slept for an hour. After rolling about in the bed for a long time when she got up to wash her face she saw the reflection in the mirror. The question arose in her mind whether she was beautiful. She didn't consider herself beautiful, ugly neither. She remembered that she had never thought about it much. The comment by some woman that it was her good fortune to get such a stunningly handsome husband had reached her ears at the time of the marriage. Compared to the bridegroom she was not beautiful. She remembered she had thought when he had accepted me as beautiful why should I think about it? But now the memory that he had degraded her from the beautiful category made her sad. She looked into the mirror above the sink. After she came to this farmhouse and started practising, she was not even applying cream to her skin and was wearing ordinary saris. Remembering that she was not wearing any ornaments either, she told herself that looks, shape of the body and height are necessary for a dancer. Why does a singer need those? Her good looks are in the power of her voice. She recollected that she had told herself that beauty did lie in the pure swaras created by the voice. But somehow this day that explanation seemed inadequate. She went to her room, stood in front of the old tall looking glass, a dressing mirror, and looked at herself. She consoled herself that after the heart is broken, any woman, no matter how beautiful she was, she would look ugly to her man. She went downstairs, ate the suji, drank coffee that Malakshmi had kept and came up. She didn't get the mood to pursue music. She didn't feel like stretching herself on the bed or sit leaning on the chair. Not knowing what to do she just paced about in the lounge. Then she descended, wore her chappals and went out with her umbrella. Came to the gate of the garden and turned right. After walking for a furlong, she took a right turn and started climbing the hillock, under the sturdy, tall teak-wood trees, climbing by surrounding the boulders, stopping in the middle to take her breath now and again, she reached the top. The spot she would come to sometimes. A huge banyan tree with its branches widely spread. The leaves were fluttering to the strong wind at that height. When she sat on a stone in the shade, she remembered the names of the ragas and their characteristics that she had contemplated in that place. When she felt that this day the ragas had disappeared from her mind, she thought she should have brought that letter so that she could have read it again slowly. Even without reading it a second time, she remembered the main points. Yes, it is true that there was no situation where she had to make an adjustment with anyone on her husband's side. There was no sister-in-law, brother's wife, brother-in-law or the wives and children of any of them. The in-laws did not stay with them. They would not demand any money from their son. There were no household chores to be performed. This was also true. If instead of Vikram his parents or his mother's sister had searched for a bride, they wouldn't have chosen her. Vikram consented immediately. The others had no alternative but to agree. He gave me everything before I even asked. He has now questioned me, 'What have you given?' The question remained, what had I given except music that he liked, no, not even that, but the practice of music, couldn't think of an answer. The mind became sad. Five minutes. Afterwards there was a consolation that which rich family girl would take anything to her husband's house from a house which had servants, cooks and a driver. She consoled herself that at least she had given him happiness with her achievement in music. But when she thought about how she had been overcome by the pressure of the guru in yielding to him and betraying her husband, she broke down and the dam inside her burst and tears flooded. She wept in spasms as if to stop the wind emanating from the fluttering leaves of the banyan tree which had spread itself like an umbrella. Then she wiped her eyes with the edge of her sari and sat looking at the dry sticks of the tree fallen on the ground. After a long time, she thought, what is the value of your saying that you respect my inner urge for telling the truth? Is this the present you are giving me for my honesty when I could have easily carried on with both simultaneously as I had both the means and the opportunity to do so? She questioned in her mind what was the difference between him and ordinary men? She felt like going home and asking him the same question over the phone. She who was sitting, got up. The storm had become a gentle breeze. Remembering that one should be more careful while descending than while ascending, she picked her way slowly round the boulders. Leaving behind the shade of the trees and while opening the umbrella she confronted the question whether minds can be patched up and unified by question and argument. Supposing he said that she had got angry because her guru, soon after he left Los Gatos, had an affair with a White girl in New York and neglected her and this anger had taken the shape of honesty, what could she reply? By the time she reached the gate of the garden, even the courage to call had vanished.

She could sleep after she had her food and went to bed. Only for ten minutes. She woke up with a start. Then she couldn't manage to get back to sleep. Didn't feel like sitting with the tambura. Thus the night also passed. The cycle of wakefulness and sleep changed its pace. It was like asking her to sing to an unknown rhythmic time cycle. Waking up at some time. Sleeping at some other time. Just drowsiness. Not sleep. Every morning she would climb the hillock and sit there for two or three hours under the banyan tree. Only there could she find some relaxation of mind. One day, even while she was there, her neck suddenly dropped forward and she felt a heavy drowsiness as if she would fall down. She lay down on the same stone she was sitting on. She had never laid down there. Immediately she fell asleep. Deep sleep. In that sleep she dreamt a pure vocal dream; what am I good for except for music? She woke up suddenly at her own voice. She was used to hearing the movement of some raga in the middle of her sleep. But she had never heard words. Now this clear voice remained firmly in her memory. On waking up, lying down on a stone was giving her body ache. She sat up. Still, the question that stood in the memory began to be heard by the mind, as if it was actually being repeated. After sitting for a little while she came home. By the next day she herself found an answer which would trample down that question. Which professional does anything other than what pertains to his profession? Successful lawyers don't drive their own cars. The same with engineers. It brought a little comfort. But by evening it occurred that all these people were professionals not for professional fulfilment but in order to maintain their wives, children and dependents. But whom have I brought up? This counter question made the mind wither up.

But by the next day, certain questions arose. At my age, can I do garden work with a pickaxe like Waghe? Shall I sit washing the vessels? Shall I study computer engineering? She shook her head uttering 'nonsense'. She got up, tuning her tambura she looked at the clock and decided to sing Raga Durgaa. A raga which was very soft, full of emotion, something that appealed directly to the heart, simple, something which she had liked and something which she had practised. She remembered the feeling too. Is it possible for a raga to remain in memory without its accompanying emotion? Thinking like this she started singing. The emotion gave way before it was expanded. It lost its interest. What remained was only its dry technical mastery. She felt it was a bore singing it. She stopped. The fingers were playing on strings. After a little while she felt that even that was mechanical and she stopped that too. When she woke up during the night, the question whether her taste in music was also disappearing began to be heard deep down within her. She was frightened.

Not knowing what else to do in the morning, when she returned after spending a couple of hours on top of the hill, there was an envelope for her on the attic. It was the custom of Malakshmi to keep the mail there so that the mistress could see it immediately if she had gone out. On the left-hand side top corner it was printed Slater, Dickinson and Okinava, Solicitors, San Jose. It immediately flashed that these were the divorce papers. She took it, went upstairs and sat down on the chair. There was no need to open it. Thinking that the solicitor would have asked her to sign it and return it, she put it on her lap and sat for an hour. Then she looked at the watch. 11 am. It would be half past nine there in the evening. She thought whether she should ring up and tell him that the solicitor's envelope had arrived, she wouldn't open it and that she would not give him a divorce. She sat with that decision for half an hour. But she did not have the strength to go to the phone. Meanwhile Malakshmi gave a call from downstairs saying that the food was ready, it would get cold and would she come down for lunch? She remembered that she had not taken her shower yet. She got up and went down.

In the middle of that night she wondered what she would gain if she kept the letter without reading it. She got up and opened the envelope.

We trust you consent to the enclosed divorce document. If you sign at the space indicated in the presence of the notary with his seal and number, it would be possible for us to complete the formalities without delay.

A brief letter. The divorce statement said, 'Both of us, of our own free will, have separated for the last four years. Now we have decided to divorce without either party giving any compensation to the other. Since I am living in far away India and cannot come to the law-court at San Jose, indicating my consent for the divorce I have sent it signed in the presence of a Notary.'

She felt that there was no use calling. Her self-respect also came in the way. But she didn't feel like signing the document. Supposing she kept quiet. What happens then? Let him write asking me why I didn't send it. Or let him call me. Then I will reply, she decided.

But in the morning when she went to the top of the hillock and sat down, she guessed that even for the reason that she left this country four years ago and she had not responded, it would be enough ground for divorce. Or, if she opposed it saying that she left her husband after committing adultery was enough ground. She was afraid. In the hands of lawyers, even delicate feelings could be interpreted rudely as harlotry and argued. After all, in legal battle, this could become anything. She remembered that she had seen a signboard 'Notary' on every street in Bombay and that there would be hundreds of them near the courts. She got up immediately and walked home. She called asking for an autorickshaw to be sent, gave the address of her garden-home and picked up her passport to be shown for identification and got ready.

A week after she sent the divorce document, her mind achieved some sort of equilibrium. But she lost her interest in music. What was the use in creating new nuances of feeling and working intricate embroidery of subtle emotions on them? The world was not standing on emotions. Indifference took over, thinking that only musicians, music-lovers and other artists say that emotion itself is world. Sometimes she would get angry that all this happened because of that rascal Mohanlal. After a little while she would console herself thinking that if she got angry with him, it would again be giving prominence to music. The question as to what she should do alone in this garden-house began to trouble her. But where else should I go? Where else is there any life for me? She would console herself in thinking that though there wasn't much communication there were at least Waghe and Malakshmi.

Chapter 21

I

Mohanlal was also feeling that he was getting angry with everyone. He was losing all, one by one. Slapping Bhoopali, her going to Paranjape to give him a statement in anger. He remembered again and again how she realised her mistake and when she asked his forgiveness, his saying, 'Slut, after having done what you have, telling me that you will support me. I will beat you with an old shoe if you come to my flat.' He felt sad, for not having realised that, for her, coming to India at that age, learning music only for four years, it was not possible to master Indian classical music. The girl came with confidence in me. Having come here she learnt as much as possible. He thought, it would be good for her if a farewell concert by her was arranged in this city before she returned home. Suppose he told some music organisation. Which organisation? He contacted three of them. Everyone agreed. But none decided and called. When he called Wankhede, the secretary of the Santa Cruz Association, the third time, he said, 'Panditji, why hide it from you? Her scandal has been published only very recently in the newspapers. A number of letters from readers have also been received. The members of the organisation won't like it if a concert by her with your blessings is arranged. In fact it is even possible for the papers to make fun of the entire programme.' Stupid girl. Doesn't have the devotion that no matter how angry she got, she shouldn't speak publicly against the guru. After all she is not an Indian, his sympathy arose. No need for any organisation. What if he himself spent ten or twenty thousand rupees and arranged a concert? Let the press people make fun. I will speak in the same concert and tell them, yes, it is true I slapped her. Doesn't the guru who taught with such great interest have the right to slap a student if she didn't learn properly? Let the people themselves judge the merit of the press people who made a big noise about a girl who ran to the newspaper in great anger and when it had subsided had begged them not to publish it. He found a way out that he would expose Paranjape by publicising that he as a newspaper employee had misused the situation to help his cassette business and that is why he had turned against him as a rival. He thought this would be the right thing to do. Let her practise for a couple of weeks, before the concert with the accompanists Raja Ram Tipnis and Prabhu. He called her to ask her before the concert hall was booked. He asked, 'Why haven't you even called for a month?'

'How can I, when you said that you would hit me if I came?'

'So what? Why should you heed it? Aren't you a pupil?'

'Guruji, saying one thing and expecting to act contrary to it, I don't understand these things.'

'You should come no matter what the guru says. You would understand if you were an Indian. Let it be. I will arrange a concert by you. Solo performance for two hours. I will speak as your guru. You give me a dhoti and jubba as guru-dakshina and touch my feet. I will give you a tambura and bless you. I will arrange for a special training in three ragas with Tipnis and Prabhu for two weeks before the concert.'

'Is that so, Guruji, what a good man you are! I didn't understand that your anger was only a fleeting mood of love.' She became silent. There was no response even after waiting for a minute or two.

When he asked, 'Why are you silent?' he heard the sound of her crying in spasms. Saying, 'Hey, girlee, don't weep. I am coming to your flat right away.' He put the phone down, sealed the door, got down by the lift, took the first passing autorickshaw and entered her flat. They fell into each other's arms. Love surged forth in both of them. Without speaking a word and without exchanging glances, they entered the bedroom together. Calling him Guruji, she started weeping. His eyes too filled with tears.

After both the ecstacies met, mingled, boiled and became calm, she said, 'Guruji, do you know the extent of the damage the newspapermen have done to me? The American Consulate people who were defraying my scholarship, have read the entire rumpus in the newspapers. There is a section in the consulate which translates all the news pertaining to America in the newspapers of all the languages of this country. They know my entire affair published in all the three papers in Marathi, Hindi and English. Elenor Gild, the cultural attache of the consulate had called and got me over to the office. She asked me to explain all this. I explained the situation truthfully. She asked me, 'Can I ask your guru about this?'

'He is angry because I went to the newspaper office in a fury. If you ask him he might give you an angry answer,' I said.

'Does that woman understand art and music?'

'Very well.'

'Then I am going to invite her as the chief guest for your concert. When she listens to it, she will get all the answers, won't she?'

'Guruji, how kind you are!' She became emotional and embraced and kissed him.

The programme was a great success. The auditorium was full and was overflowing as her affair had been reported in the newspapers and curious people had thronged to listen to the same guru who would speak about her and listen to her singing directly. Mohanlal himself thought that he should have fixed up a larger auditorium. He did not mention Paranjape's name in his speech but he reminded that a certain journalist running a private cassette business in his wife's name had tried to knock off his cassette on Omkara for twenty-five thousand rupees and failed, which came in the way of his getting fifteen lakh rupees from the Globe Company, and because of this he had concocted scandals about him and spread it through yellow journalism—all this he recounted. Now, it is true that I hit this student for not learning properly. It is also true that she complained to this journalist. After her anger subsided though she begged him not to publish this, he published it adding all kinds of lies and not merely got it published in other newspapers but has manufactured readers' letters to the editor in various names and has perpetrated a rascality loafer's crime. Now after listening to the concert of this girl, you who have come to the concert as listeners and the journalists, if they are legitimate children of their parents, may you decide whether it is possible without punishment to attain her proficiency in four years? He finished. Then the listeners admired the singing of Lauren which followed and nodded their heads in approval, that it was a great achievement on the part of Lauren to have learnt so much in four years and for Mohanlal who had taught so much, so well. The Cultural Attaché presented bouquets to both the pupil and the teacher and congratulated them. The next day many papers wrote in praise of Lauren along with her photograph. Just a few newspapers reported all the details of Mohanlal's speech. A week later, two yellow rags printed concocted stories aimed at Paranjape. One particular paper, without mentioning his name wrote a twisted story with a title about a journalist who wanted to seduce a White girl and having failed, set out to take revenge. In the middle of it, it added a double-edged barb: 'A pupil can submit herself to her teacher. But where is the necessity for her to give herself to a journalist?'

5

Mohanlal felt happy on seeing the newspaper write-ups. He was happier when he saw the yellow rags. He thought that villain had descended to this level. Now I will show him. In every concert in Bombay, without mentioning his name I am going to drag that bastard in the mud and then I will start shadja. But by the next morning his mind became saddened. Paranjape had supported me from the beginning to establish myself in Bombay. When I was kicked out by Manohari Das and came to Bombay, he had given me publicity, accommodated me in Desai's farmhouse. I felt that to quarrel with him now was not proper. He had harmed Bhoopali by misusing the scandalous opportunity. He realised that when business intervenes all the goodness of man gets washed away. But why was he feeling this emptiness? Not interested in anything. The feeling that he had no friends in the entire city. When he tried, he could recall the names of a hundred music admirers. But when he touched the phone he didn't feel like talking to anyone. There was none in whom he could confide. Even Rajaram was good only for accompanying him and take the money and go. Unknown to me he would go to Panvel and teach her. Didn't tell me about it till I found out and asked him. What sort of friendship is this, he thought. Bhoopali had also gone back to her country. There was no interest in calling other women. They also had their own problems and restrictions. If it is a continuing relationship, they would also retain hope and desire. If I cultivate it when I want and discontinue it when I don't want it, they also will have no interest. Even if you invite them by calling them, they will begin with an angry retort why I had discontinued the relationship all these days. All of them will want to know whether he deceived them with his affair with the American girl. When he became aware that he had no one with whom he could share his turmoil, his emptiness increased. If he sat with the tambura there would be no mood. His voice itself had become dry. Not only the ragas but their very source of emotion had dried up. Whatever he sang was from the force of habit and memory, not with feeling.

Once he thought, why not give up singing and that seemed the only solution. How long could one keep singing? Why not just make enough money for livelihood and go away somewhere? But where? To whatever town he goes he would be alone. The thought that it would be good to join some club in Bombay itself; just go there at four in the afternoon, stay till ten in the evening playing cards, have a couple of pegs and come back. The idea gave him some solace. But, when he thought that even playing cards everyday would be boring and drinking wouldn't be enjoyable without suitable company, he felt he was unfit for anything.

He got an invitation from Nasik for a concert. The organisers came personally and placed two lakh rupees in front of him. He asked, 'It is the usual practice to pay half in advance and the other half before beginning the concert. You are paying me the full amount in advance. What will you do if I don't turn up and cheat you?'

'Even if you decide to cheat. Your music will not allow you,' they said.

Since such flattery was not new to him, he remained silent.

After the Nasik concert was over, he felt like going to Triambakeshwar. He remembered going there twenty-five years ago. Then the temple of Triambakeshwar and its lofty lingam had possessed his imagination beyond imagination. He longed to see them again. On returning, in order to go to the railway station or the taxi stand, he checked out of his hotel room and took up his leather bag and got into the car. Tipnis and Prabhu left by the morning train itself. After visiting the temple he felt like going to Brahmagiri, the source of the River Godavari. Asking the driver to wait, he walked to the foot of the hill with a guide and started climbing. He remembered climbing the Bilva and the Neela mountains at Hardwar when he was young. Steep steps hewn from the boulders. Little temples punctuating the path. Hundreds of pilgrims ascending and descending. A feeling of freedom on reaching the top and looking around. Not a very high summit but as far as the eye could peruse around it, no higher peak was there. He asked himself whether there was any other more propitious place than a mountain top to establish relationship with the sky. He looked around. The guide informed; on one side the dam on the River Vetaranaa which supplies water to Bombay; on the other side, the several ponds of Triambakeshwar—Kushavarta Teertha, Indra Teertha, Gautama Teertha, Viswanatha Teertha, Bil Teertha, Prayaga Teertha. He wandered about freely on top of the hill looking at the sky. When finally he came to the temple of Goumukhee Godavari, its priest recognised him. 'Aren't you Pandit Mohanlal, the singer?' It was pleasant being recognised here by someone, when he was alone in this lonely place, especially by the temple priest. 'I have heard your singing. I had gone to Nasik in the evening only for that. I have heard you in Bombay also. I am very fond of music.' Mohanlal felt even more happy. He sat talking to him. He felt hungry. The priest served him the sweet rice on a banana leaf which he had brought as an offering to the deity. After eating it, he felt sleepy. He lay down on the stone bench next to the temple. He slept soundly and happily.

When he opened his eyes on waking up, it seemed as if the blue sky above him was enveloping him like a blanket. A quiet and peaceful state. He felt that he was not lying on a stone slab but on a slice of the sky itself. He lay there for a little while. Then he got up and went to the source of the river and sat near it. He went to Brahmagiri, Shankara and Shivajataa from there. Again he sat on a boulder and started gazing up at the sky. He felt that he belonged to the sky, he must be conjoined to it and that he should never get down. Meanwhile the guide came there and said, 'Sir, it has been a long time. If we spend so much time with each customer how can we earn a living?' Mohanlal felt irritated. He told him that he would pay him double and asked him to sit at a distance silently. Mohanlal sat looking at the sky and the evening sun, he asked himself why he shouldn't stay right there during the night also. He went up to the priest and asked him. He replied, 'Panditji, there is no lodging facility here, no bed, no room. All of us go away to Triambakeshwar before five in the evening. No one stays here at night.' He thought for a while. Then he said that he would sleep on the stone slab itself. Stay alone. He was not afraid and he had a strong desire to spend the night there. The priest thought for a bit and said, 'It will be cold outside during night. There are wild animals as well. They say there is even a tiger around but nobody has seen it. Still, there is a rumour. No one stays here during night. That too, alone.'

The thought occurred to him if he could rent a room at Triambakeshwar for the night, come back here in the morning and return in the evening. But, the desire to stay there the night strengthened. 'Maharaj, so many pilgrims come here during the day. If there was a tiger, someday it must have attacked someone or the other. There will, of course be some jungle animals. Please don't lock up the doors. If it becomes necessary I will sleep inside and close the door. There is nothing valuable in the temple. Even if there is something, it will be my responsibility. I strongly feel that I must stay here for a couple of days. You know my guide. Please instruct him to go to Triambakeshwar and bring my small portmanteau from the car. I will pay him as much as you fix him up with.'

The priest asked, 'Have you come to formulate a new raga?'

'You may say so.'

The priest gave him the remaining cooked rice which he wanted to take home and said, 'This won't get spoiled tomorrow either. It has been cooked in ghee. You can bring drinking water in this container from the river source. Down there, you see, there is water in that pond. You can use that place for toilet and wash. When I come in the morning at nine I will bring some food. The specially cooked sweet rice will of course be there.'

३

Moonlight spread in the night like the swelling of milk, as if it was bringing the impurity inside it to the surface and extending purity to all other places. He was looking at the sky, sitting on the boulder.

When he looked down, the sheet of water of the Ketaki Dam was shining. He remembered the Mahadev temple on the banks of Narmada in the middle of Guru Raja Saheb's forest, and formulating the basic, foundational shruti, sitting on the pediment of the temple looking at the shining stream, way down below the precipice. What marvelous moments of gentle peace were those! He bowed down in the devotional recollection at the memory of Raja Saheb who was coming there to teach him the ragas of the night.

Where did that sublime music that was intensifying the gentle peace disappear now? He started thinking. Couldn't find an answer. In a little while he began to feel drowsy. It is not difficult for a musician to keep awake a whole night. Still, when sleep came striding in, he remembered that he hadn't had his tea. With the awareness that it wasn't possible to be awake even there without a cup of tea to sip three or four times, he decided that some tea leaves, some sugar and milk powder must be brought the next day. He was worried about what to do for a vessel to boil the tea and for fire? When he pondered that buying a stove, a bottle of kerosene and a box of matches and like this a whole new life would begin, the answer did flash to him that the music which was intensifying profound peace, had been caught in these worldly occupations and was withered. He yawned. When he was wondering whether to sleep on the stone slab outside or go inside, he heard a noise of thud-thud rushing towards him. When he turned in that direction he saw a creature like a crocodile rushing past him. His heart beat faster. He was afraid that he wouldn't have survived if it had rushed on to him. Slowly it occurred to him that here where there was no water or dam, it couldn't be a crocodile. I have seen crocodiles in rivers Narmada and Ganga. He understood that this was not an alligator but an iguana, yes it was an animal that inhabited in dry hilly regions. Could it be a tiger? But when he remembered that the priest had said that nobody had seen one, he also remembered that while climbing this hill, he had seen some cows grazing here and there. This was not a lone peak. It was a part of a whole range of hills. A tiger could be anywhere, somewhere there. It could even come here. During the day since pilgrims arrived in groups, it wouldn't come. During the night it might. But supposing it smelt a human from a distance and came. The thought scared him. He looked around. The stony rubble, the boulders on cliffs, small little trees, everything inlaid in moonlight were looking like shadows. Why can't one of those shadows be of a tiger? When it is out on hunt, it moves stealthily. Doesn't make a sound. Doesn't growl. He looked back sharply, thinking that it might be coming towards him from behind. He perspired. Felt ashamed. Am I such a coward he asked himself. When he remembered the thought of going into the temple closing the door and drawing the bolt from inside, he felt more ashamed. Why should he be afraid of a tiger? Because he would die. What would happen if he died? He started thinking. Couldn't find an answer. He felt that it was a very big question. Nobody would be affected by his death. Nobody would weep remembering him. Nobody would die in sorrow. Some music listeners would remember for a few days that he was a good singer and he died. For a dozen years they would talk about him among friends. After that, nothing. When he thought that, that was what his life was worth, he felt a sort of disillusionment. The mind became barren, contemplating on how he used to think that the primordial power of the universe would emanate in his singing and the power of Omkara would spring forth from his strumming the strings of tambura. He became aware that nobody would weep privately if he died. It made him light-hearted. A feeling of sadness also arose. He identified himself as Mohanlal, the man for whom there is nobody to weep. Millions of people would feel sad. Several newspapers would publish obituaries. But nobody would weep, he told himself again. He remembered, running away, being afraid to reveal his identity to Giridhar who released the deer into the tiger's lair. He had not been in a position to identify himself to Giridhar's sister, Poonam. Bakula had turned away. Kishan was angry that the money given to him was insufficient. Swarmohan was angry that he had not been paid in pound sterling. He hadn't even seen the face of Shrutimohini. Who would weep? The mind saddened—contracted. There was greater freedom if there was none to weep. He consoled himself that this gave courage to die. After some time he asked himself if he really desired to die? In a short while itself he felt he didn't. The answer that he was sitting there to test his courage and not with a desire to die, seemed satisfactory. It occurred to him that he could test himself further by staying there the night and lying down right on the same stone slab. Yes, he could recline but what would be the difference between sitting and reclining? The test would be not sitting fully awake consciously but sleeping nonchalantly even when there was a possibility of a tiger turning up. He thought of sleeping peacefully without having a nightmare. Thinking that this was the right thing to do he lay down on his back. The moonlight was beaming. The ears were tuned to hear the slightest rustle of leaves. The nose was searching for the tiger's smell. In a little while the moon was hiding behind black clouds. Darkness began to descend. He thought that at least now he could get into the temple, closing the door and lying down. But the real test was now. Hereafter, by going inside because it had become dark, what would be gained? He turned over to a side. He invoked sleep, closing his eyes because what would the difference be whether he kept them open or shut as it was pitch dark anyway? Couldn't get sleep. He tried again. After a little while the limbs relaxed. The expectation of sleep occurred. A lot of time elapsed in this expectation itself.

When he woke up in the morning, the sun was piercing his face. He opened his eyes slowly and looked around. He told himself when fully awake, that he had slept soundly without any anxiety. He opened his little kit, took out soap, brush, razor and a small mirror, took up the small vessel that the priest had given him, went down to the watershed, finished his toilet, came up and sat down. In a little while the priest came, asked, 'Did you compose a new raga? What have you named it?'

'A new raga doesn't take shape in a single night. After it is completely formulated, then comes the question of naming it. I want to stay for eight or ten days.'

'Please do. I will bring the food. Let me have a part in the punya in the discovery of a raga. Now have your food. I will leave some for the afternoon also. In the evening there will be the sweet rice prepared for the offering to the Lord. I have brought some light snacks in case you feel like eating during the day,' he said.

'Shastriji, I will dedicate all the punya of the formation of the raga to you by offering it through the spring water of the Godavari.' Shastriji felt happy.

By ten in the morning the pilgrims started arriving. He sat at a distance under a tree on a boulder. No one came that way. The mind opened up the capsule of memory and started ruminating bit by bit. Uncontrollable physical desire. Without thinking of the result. I cohabited with Chunni. It didn't even occur to me that she made love to fulfill her own desired objective. I thought if I married this girl Ramkumari from a distant village, my physical craving may be satisfied. But it never occurred to me that Ramkumari's educational standard was that of Chunni only and once that desire was quenched I would be just myself and she would remain herself. This woman Champa was smart and educated. A city-bred girl. Not that I was unaware of it but what the consequences would be if I married her hadn't crossed my mind at all and married. I never thought for how long an intense artistic living could go on with someone like Manohari who gave a combined pleasure of dance and song; when I thought seriously was after returning from Manohari. When I started enjoying pleasure, happiness, inspiration obtainable by them, but not being caught by or attached to any female student or admirer. But I did not realise that as a consequence nobody would remain in my old age, and memory began to be linked.

That night when he sat in the moonlight, the fear that had occurred the previous night didn't recur. Actually there was no tiger. With a feeling that even if there was one he had conquered its fear, he wandered about in the moonlight on the mound of Shivajataa Mandir. The top of the hill had become quite familiar as he had wandered there during the day. The moon appeared as if moving in vilambit in the background of white clouds scattered like a streak of loose cotton. It is said the moon moves and even the earth moves on its axis. If there was no cloud, the motion of the moon wouldn't be seen either. The musical parallel flashed that if there were no transitory emotions there would be no manifestation of a constant and dominant emotion. When he was standing there pondering about these, memory of Madhu came to mind. Poor girl. He remembered that even when she was single and had offered herself to him she had begged him to marry her. All the girls used to beg like this. They would be caught up in this idea that this was the ultimate love. Besides, she came from an affluent business family. If only he had lived with her permanently at least after she left her husband! He had this afterthought as a past possibility. But she decided all by herself without even consulting me. It seems the mandra-shadja of Raga Asavari confronted her face to face with truth. Asavari filled his mind. Without emanating any sound, he started humming to himself the shadja of madhya-saptaka. Gradually he descended to mandra. What if there was a sound. Could a tiger lurking in the mountain range hear it and knowing that there was a man around, could come round with silent stealthy steps? Let it come. I have got rid of its fear yesterday itself. He started singing aloud starting with madhyama-shadja and started descending to mandra. Yes, it is wonderful, this was a raga that truly opens and shows the innermost being. But he remembered that any raga when it touches mandra-shadja does the same thing. Thinking, let me experiment, he started descending to mandra in Raga Bageshree. He reached shadja and paused there. He experimented the same in Bhairav. He followed it up in Todi, the emotion becomes different but the inner conscience does open up in mandra-shadja. The swaras, the combination of dhaivata vadi and gandhara samvadi *saa, re, ma, pa, dha, saa* | *saa, ni, dha, pa, ma, ga, re, saa* these have created in her the feelings of devotion, disinterestedness in worldly matters and emotion of sadness and must have stimulated her to act like that. He remembered the circumstances—his slapping her for giving that letter to her husband without consulting her guru earlier and for cutting down the self-respect of Mohanlal, the guru.

In a short while he felt sleepy. The moon had not set yet. It was not even as late as last night. He came to the boulder where he had slept the previous night and sat on it. He thought he might catch a cold if he slept in the open everyday. He remembered that he hadn't even covered himself with the shawl he had brought in his bag last night. He went into the temple, struck a match and lighted the sacred lamp. He took out his shawl, spread it on the floor and closing the door, slept in warmth inside.

He woke up early in the morning. When he was attending to his toilet near the pond he remembered Hardwar. Even the very name of the Baba was Omkar Baba. The ashram too was being called Omkar Ashram. When he remembered that the swaras were being practiced by Baba as Omkara itself rather than with the sound of Aaa, and the memory of his having heard at Brindavan from the yogi at Haridas Mandir came to mind, and it was practiced by him at the bank of Narmada below the Mahadev mandir of Raja Saheb, he remembered that his singing asavari had its roots in the Omkar Ashram and wondered whether there was anything which he could call his own. Let it belong to anybody or let there be nothing as one's own. No matter where it had originated, the propagation of such profound raga had been made a tool of music business, the anger of Paranjape, the commercialisation, no, the prostitution of writing made him disgusted. In addition to teaching the mastery over swara-sadhana in Omkara, Baba used to teach every pupil the secret of oordhva-retas and adho-retas. Nobody used to practice that. He asked himself what his own path was, following the path of adho-retas and acquiring such name and fame? This question confronted him. But he couldn't find an answer.

He stayed for a week on top of the hill. Looking at the dream world that was created by moonlight till late into the night or gazing up at the bright stars; sitting in the shade of a sequestered tree during the day or lying down where the pilgrims would not venture or just sleeping was his routine. If I was staying on the peak for a week on the mountain range of the Himalayas, the Vindhyas or the Sahyadris once every three or six months, I would not have been caught up in this much of turmoil. He felt that after his air-travels started he missed looking at the hills and dales from the train window. On the eighth day before leaving, he put in front of the priest two thousand rupees and said, 'Please accept this.'

Looking at him for a minute the priest said, 'Panditji, I told you on the first day itself that I am your admirer, you are giving so much money for the food I was bringing you, aren't you?'

'No, no.' He waved his hand in embarrassment.

'Devotees place ten rupees as dakshina at the most in the aarati plate. You may give the same amount. But you have not performed puja at all.' He was even more embarrassed. 'Everyone doesn't worship the same way. Yours is Naada-puja—worship through music. Please tell me the name of the raga you formulated here.'

'Godavari.'

'That now is the appropriate name. When I come to your concert somewhere I will request you to sing this raga. Would you sing? I was about to ask you to sing it right here. But you don't have a tambura. No accompanists either. The raga might have formulated itself in your mind. But it has not yet taken final shape, has it, to be capable of singing in a concert?'

'Yes, yes.'

'Please come back. I will send a boy to carry your suitcase.' He brought a sixteen-year-old boy and told him, 'Carry the suitcase of the maestro to Triambakeshwar and come back. He will give you twenty-five rupees.' He applied holy kumkum tilak to the forehead of Mohanlal and took leave.

By the time the bus reached Nasik, his plan had changed. Bypassing the bus and taxi stand, he engaged an autorickshaw, went to the railway station and enquired the route and the timings for reaching Hardwar.

4

He felt very sad that for forty-six years he had not visited his birthplace and the Omkar Ashram which had introduced him to music. Perhaps no one in this place knows that Mohanlal was a native son! Had they known they would have at least invited him to give a concert. Why hadn't he himself come here at all? Until reaching Bombay, he learnt at Sagar and Chittarpur. After mother died there was no one related to him. But why didn't I go and at least see Baba? Why didn't I beg him to forgive me for having run away without telling anyone, request him to listen to his singing, he had learnt elsewhere, to listen and bless him. Why didn't I touch his feet and ask for his blessing and correct my mistakes in singing. He would certainly have looked upon me with affection. He thought that now there was no possibility of his still being alive. It was obvious that it no longer was the Hardwar of his time. Then it was a town of pedestrians and free boarding houses. Now there were hotels, taxis and a tourist centre.

He checked into a comfortable hotel, gave the washer man his clothes, had his shower, engaged a cycle-rickshaw and went to the Omkar Ashram. The rickshaw fellow didn't recognise the place as such. He couldn't understand when he was told that it was an ashram where music was taught. When Mohanlal offered to show him the way and proceeded, he lost his way in the midst of small crossroads and bridges. He instructed the rickshaw man to leave the river to his right and go out of town for two miles. But the town had grown so much that he felt he had gone too far out. When he told him that it was behind the Vilva mountain the rickshaw puller brought him back. He saw the dilapidated gate next to the signboard Omkar Ashram which had escaped his notice. The garden inside was bare with empty space. The area was strewn with debris. Further inside, the old building stood which had not received a white or colour wash. It looked as if no one was living there. Still he went up and knocked on the door. After a while, a boy of about twenty who looked like a student opened the door. What was gleaned from him was there no one was learning music. There were ten poor students who would cook their food. The president of the ashram Nanda Kishore Varma would come once a week to supervise. Mohanlal remembered the name Nanda Kishore Varma. When he was a student there was a trustee of the Omkar Ashram who was thirty or thirty-five. Though all the management was by Baba, the rules stipulated that there should be a board of management. Varma was a Gandhian. He wore khadi. He would help in getting the building painted. He couldn't remember anything more than that. He went inside the building and looked. Though it was old it was in a good condition. There were fifteen rooms; two courtyards. Kitchen. A large empty ground at the back. Two mango trees. He obtained the address of Varmaji and came out.

The eighty-year-old Varma was in his old house, khadi clad. Near the wall, there was the charka which had been placed in the middle. A mat spread on the floor to sit. He could recognise the face which he had seen forty-six years ago. 'Baba, pranaam. I am an old student of Omkar Ashram. Do you remember me? My name is Mohanlal. I have made music my profession.' When he bent down and touched Varmaji's feet, doubt registered on the face of the latter.

'I have heard that you are the number one singer of the entire Hindustan. Baba used to remember you and say, "He has become such a great singer. Can't he come voluntarily at least once to his mother institution, the ashram?" You went away without informing anyone. You might have felt ashamed to come back and show your face. At least now, it is good of you to have come. The ashram is lucky,' he said.

Mohanlal told him about the purpose of his visit. 'I am staying in Bombay. I have a very good income. I charge two lakh rupees for a concert. But my native place is Hardwar itself. I want to come back here and settle down. I am thinking of bringing up the ashram to a good state, admit five or six students by giving food and shelter to them and teaching them music at an advanced level. Thus the debt will be paid. I will bear the entire expense. No matter in what corner of Hindustan, the deserving students will be admitted here and taught. What do you say?'

'Really?'

'Please believe me.' He held his hand.

'Do you know what happened? Even when Baba was alive the number of children wanting to learn music declined. The word spread that Baba would call only devotional singing music. He also didn't change his opinion. After his death it became difficult to provide even two meals a day to the remaining students. After his demise they appointed me as the president of the trust. Such a huge place. A building that was still intact. A lot of influential big people, politicians and even ministers tried to knock off the place for themselves. They are still doing so. My only achievement has been to protect it from falling into the clutches of these sharks. This is an institution that Baba built for the promotion of music. It shouldn't be used for other purposes. For the present, in order to guard the premises, I have given rooms to ten poor college students. If you come and take over, my burden will be lifted. If you teach music without charging any fee and providing free food, lodging and clothes, Baba's soul will find peace. Please stay for a couple of days. I will talk to the rest of the trustees, they are also honest people. But like me they are also helpless.'

He stayed on for three days in Hardwar. Every evening he went to Har ki pauri and set afloat the aarati. He sat watching the aarati set sailing by the others. When he watched them floating almost motionlessly he would get the comparison of time, which though moving beneath, would become still when it rested on a swara. His memory was filling in with the recollection of how he was begging for a few paise at the same place, singing bhajans. Along with it the memory of his mother. He went to the spot where they had a shack when she was alive. What he expected had happened. All over that area, three storied flats had come up.

When he was returning by train, his mind was pleasant. An unexpected conducive situation had come about. He had come with the plan of buying a four-acre land on the outskirts of Hardwar in a calm and noiseless place, get a building built and run a Gurukul. Now the very ashram established by his first guru himself had come under his care. If he spent two or three lakhs, the entire building and compound could be built. The students would come if publicity was given that free music education would be imparted at Pandit Mohanlal's Gurukul and those desirous of learning at an advanced level may join. Those who invited me to concerts would invite me no matter where I stayed. The expenses of the ashram could be met with the earnings of two concerts annually. He felt satisfied that in six or seven years he would train up six or eight singers who would be good enough to propagate his name. No, he would not insist on strict celibacy as the Baba had done, but there should be no room for free-love. He was now sixty-five. Would it be possible for him to remain celebate at least from now on? He asked himself. If there was a necessity he could make some arrangement. It would be all right if he didn't live in the ashram itself. It would be convenient for everybody if he lived in a separate private house not too near nor too far from the ashram. He thought that if he was always in proximity to the students they might feel claustrophobic.

ड

When he enquired at the Hardwar railway station they said they would issue a ticket upto Bombay but they couldn't assure reservation till

Delhi. They said enquiry must be made only in Delhi. Remembering that even while coming here he had train journey from Nasik, he now bought a ticket only upto Delhi. After that he could fly to Bombay or if the necessity arose he could try even by train. Anyway, he thought he had to stay the night in some hotel at Delhi.

After the train started the mind began thinking about the arrangements to be undertaken at the Omkar Ashram. He decided that those ten college students who were there now could stay till they finished their studies but afterwards only music students would be taken. By the time he had gone half the distance, the memory of Manohari suddenly appeared. Hadn't four years elapsed since he had gone to Paris with her? He remembered that at the Paris Airport she had suddenly become aloof and had said, 'You arrange for your check-in. You and I have nothing to do with each other hereafter.' When he thought what a strange woman she was, he sympathised with her attitude thinking of how in spite of her delicate erotic advances, he had stayed in a separate room and naturally, how could she not be angry at such behaviour? I would feel the same way had I been rejected like that. When looking at the flower stalk of the sugarcane crop in the fields on either side of the running train and feeling comforted, it occurred to him that since he was going to stay in Delhi anyway, why shouldn't he look up Manohari? When he was thinking of calling her from the hotel he thought it would be difficult to console her on the phone if she got angry and so it would be better if he meet her face to face. She might reject me, abuse me. He found consolation, thinking what if she does? It will be all right if I don't mind it, that's all.

When he got into the taxi and reached her dance school it was half past eight. The watchman said, 'Madam was not in town. She has just returned today. She is at home.' It was twenty years since he had seen that house. In the meantime how much it must have changed! He got the phone number and the address from the watchman. He gave directions to the driver. When he came to the turning his memory became clear. He recognised the place.

When he rang the bell and saw the look of surprise on her face, he had expected it. 'I have come from Hardwar. The suitcase is in the taxi. Tell me if there is accommodation in your house. Otherwise I will stay in a hotel and come and meet you in the morning. I have no other work. I came because I wanted to meet you for I haven't seen you in a long time,' he said.

She couldn't think of an answer immediately. Confusion was writ large on her face. 'Why do you ask if there is space? Why didn't you ask if I was willing to accommodate you at my home?' He could smell the strong whiff of whiskey emanating from her mouth. He felt that her reflexes had dimmed.

'Both mean the same thing. Let's not argue in front of the taxi driver. Give me a straight answer,' he said.

'I am not giving any answer. He who is willing may come in with his suitcase,' she answered still angrily.

He sent away the taxi and came in with his suitcase. When he saw the photograph of Guruji hung on the wall decorated by a garland, he understood that he had passed away. Manohari sat on the divan where he used to sit usually. In front on the teapoy was a whiskey glass with a little left at the bottom. On the plate next to it were some munchies. He deposited his suitcase on the floor and sat on a chair. She sat just looking at him, as if she didn't know what to say—had nothing to say. He was also staring at her. After ten minutes she herself said, 'Will you have some?'

'I don't want,' he said.

She fell silent as if she had withdrawn into herself. Three minutes later she said, 'Have some. You can vomit the poison in your stomach. And afterwards you can escape by saying that you don't know what you said.' Though the composition of the sentences was all right, the speech was very slow and slurring and loosely hanging about.

He asked, 'How many pegs have you had?'

'I don't keep the bottle in front as it encourages to drink more. After I pour myself the drink I put the lid on and keep it away in the cupboard.'

'You enforced this discipline on Guruji also. I had seen it.'

She nodded. After sometime he said, 'I am hungry. Is there some food? Is there a hotel nearby? If it gets late I am afraid it may be closed.'

After a minute she said, 'At no time will there be no food in this house.'

He got up, went to the bath, took a shower and came back. By that time she had laid the table, with two plates and cups in the dining room. She served food. After eating, her mind cleared a bit. She cleared the table and asked, 'Where had you gone? You came so suddenly. What is the reason for your visit?'

'I had gone to Hardwar. With the intention of taking over the Omkar Ashram and settling there.'

Immediately she giggled noisily. He lifted his head and looked. She acted out the scene in what she said, 'Trailing long white hair. A saffron tunic. Face smeared with kumkum. To become Jai Mohanbaba?' He smiled when he saw her acting skill and ability which were so spontaneous. But then again she became serious. Her face was sleepy. He went to the sink and washed his hands. Without saying a word she picked up his suitcase and went up. He followed her. He was familiar, after all with the upstairs room. Placing the suitcase on the side of a big bed, she sank into the bed. After a couple of minutes she lay down. He was embarrassed. The drink was a little too much. She had collapsed. She will be all right after three or four hours. But where would he sleep? Of the two upstairs rooms, this was the only one with a good cot and bed. In the other there was only a divan. Was it her intention to bring up his suitcase, ask him to sleep here and go downstairs herself and sleep in the big bedroom there? Or did she come up with the intention of sleeping with him? But the door downstairs hadn't been secured. The lights hadn't been switched off. He went downstairs, bolted the door, switched off the lights and came up. He thought about leaving her here and sleeping on the divan in the other room. But he wondered whether she would be hurt when she woke up in the morning. He put away the suitcase, moved her towards the wall, lay down on the side, covered himself with a sheet and covered her also. She started snoring gently in her drunken stupor. The smell of whiskey. She was drunk even before he had arrived. Was she drinking so much everyday? He was worried thinking that it was not good for people who lived alone, to drink so much. He looked at her face in the street light which was penetrating through the window curtain. She looked so unprotected in her breathing. He felt compassion. He turned over and put his hand over her. It didn't come to her notice. She was just breathing heavily. In a little while he also slept.

When he woke up there was a feeling that the night had passed. It took him two minutes to become aware of where he was. The realisation that she was still lying by his side dawned even without touch. He felt she was awake. She spoke, 'I could make out that you were awake by your breathing itself.'

'How long have you been awake?'

'About half an hour or three-fourths of an hour.'

He held her hand. She stayed quiet without any reaction. After a minute he withdrew his hand. She was quiet. He said, 'I didn't know where to sleep. It was not my intention to make love to you when you were not conscious.' Even then she didn't speak. He sat up and said, 'I will go to that room and lie down on the divan.'

'Are you going out to insult me?' she held his hand.

'During the night...' he started to say. She continued, 'I remember vaguely. Your coming in a taxi. My serving you dinner. I din't invite you. You on your own came up carrying your suitcase didn't you?'

'Yes', he simply said.

'Why are you sitting? Lie down. It is still the wee hours of the morning.' She pulled him by his shoulders.

He put his hand on her forehead and asked, 'Do you drink so much everyday?'

'Just one peg.'

'Formerly you weren't drinking even that much. You would only give Guruji.'

'After he passed away, I felt like taking his quota also. Otherwise, how to remember him?'

'Why did you drink so much yesterday?'

'I came back from Hyderabad. After performing the obsequies for my mother. I felt like having a little more.'

It was something he knew twenty years ago: the mother and the daughter were not in touch with each other. She never forgave her daughter for marrying her guru. She had left Delhi and had gone away to Hyderabad with her son. Very recently there must have been a truce. He asked, 'When did you start talking to your mother again?'

'It never happened. I never knew that my mother was such an adamant person. She never forgave me for marrying a man old enough to be my grandfather. When she died, my brother called. By that time Guruji had passed away. I was also alone. I felt like going to the tenth-day obsequies. I went. After I came back yesterday the emptiness inside the house troubled me uncontrollably. I felt that if I did not drink a little more, I couldn't bear it.'

He was watching her face. Her eyes were gazing at the ceiling. Just in order to continue the conversation he asked, 'Had I come half an hour earlier, you wouldn't have drunk so much, would you?'

'Me?' Her eyes which were looking at the roof started searching for an answer. Even after two minutes, no answer was forthcoming. After that the tongue moved to say something; but immediately stopped. After a couple of minutes, 'If you had come before I was high I would have abused you in foul language in front of the taxi driver! And perhaps you would have gone away swearing that you would never see my face!'

Now he became serious. His mind got perturbed. He felt like getting up from the bed, drawing a chair, sitting at a distance and talking. But didn't feel like moving away. She was still looking up at the ceiling. Not even for a fraction of a second did she shoot a side glance at him. Her face was not showing stubbornness. The eyes were lacklustre. He was just watching her. After a long time compassion towards her arose in him. Pity dripped. He put his right hand on her body. She was still. He drew her towards him. She didn't move. He exercised all his strength and embraced her forcibly. She expressed disgust on her face as if chastising him. He further tightened his hold as if her chastisement didn't apply to him, drew her face to his chest and pressed it. She didn't resist. He stroked her head with his right hand. Suddenly she started weeping. He caressed the top of her head and her back. As the caress continued her weeping welled forth in spasms and her body started shivering. His chest was completely wet.

He asked, 'Your mother must have loved you very much.'

'She had kept me at a distance till death. I thought she was cruel. Cruelty is only a passing emotion. I now know that love was her essential feeling.' After saying this, her crying came under control. He was stroking her back. She slept again. In a little while he also fell asleep.

It was morning by the time he woke up, she had left her bed. By the time he got up and finished his toilet, shave and shower in the upstairs room and descended, she was in the kitchen. In the courtyard below on the wall above the divan, the photograph of Guruji had disappeared. In its place there was a picture of Lord Krishna. He didn't ask why she had changed it. After she gave him cornflakes, apple and tea and taking some herself she said, 'I will go to the dance-school for a couple of hours. You stay here and rest.'

He didn't feel like talking about his onward journey. It was a fortnight since he had left Bombay. Though he didn't have any definite programme organisers might be waiting. Still he agreed silently.

She returned quickly from the dance-school. 'Are you surprised that I came back so soon? You have come voluntarily without any effort or expense. Why not listen to some music? I thought. Came back. Let's go to the upstairs room. The cook will come here in a short while. There will be noise and smell of cooking.' She took out a tambura and giving it to him, said, 'Take it up. I will bring the tabla.' The floor of the room with the divan had been carpeted. She spread a thick chaddar on it, sat him on it and said, 'Sing a song imagining it is early morning. Something that brings about peace.' Saying so, she added, 'Yes, I brought the tabla. But I am not going to play. If I engage myself in it, the concentration with which I want to listen to the nuances of the raga and its delineation will be affected. Why do you need the support of the tabla? Besides, your rhythm and my rhythm do not cohere.'

He brought forth the swaras of Bairagi-Bhairav. In a little while she closed her eyes and started listening with total absorption. Her face became tranquil with peace that had been achieved by detachment and disinterestedness. A look of having achieved the attainment of the equanimity of the mind. He was expatiating the nuances of the pure swaras without the accompaniment and support of the tabla. The pristine purity of the meditative state would crystallise especially when he descended to the mandra. She didn't open her closed eyes. He understood what she wanted. He turned Bairagi-Bhairav itself into the Omkara style. This turned into the roaring sound from the sanctum sanctorum, which spreads pure and painless peace and tranquility, that emerges out of self analysis and self surrender, totally different from Asavari. He conceived the possibility of generating an Omkara alaap in this raga also. He started exploring the nooks and corners of the complementary connecting links and giving them a shape.

It was an hour and a quarter by the time when he finished. Though he stopped singing he didn't stop strumming the tambura. For a long time she sat with closed eyes. Then suddenly opened her eyes stood up and said, 'Don't stop the tambura. I will come back in a jiffy,' and bounded downstairs. When she came back in just a minute she had changed her sari and was wearing salwar kameez. In her right hand was the nupura belts. 'Don't stop the tambura. Give me the lehara lead in vilambit teen-taal in Bairagi-Bhairav itself. I feel like dancing a little.' She sat on the floor and tied the bell belts to both her feet. He gave the lead and indicated the saam with his right hand. She started dancing. But very quickly she started the gesticulating with her face and limbs. Giving expression to all the details of the meaningful emotions, she gave the visual representation as if the graceful acting was more important than the movements of dance. He was watching just her gesticulation of body and emotional representation and slow movement through dance and the delicate and sophisticated facial expressions. Then she danced for a little while.

After she stopped, she sat opposite him and said, 'I didn't start with the intention of acting out Bairagi-Bhairav. I felt like dancing something to your rendering of the raga. I tied my dance belts. Otherwise I wouldn't have been able to internalise the peace that was created by your raga.'

He was just watching her face. Two minutes later she went downstairs. Ten minutes passed. She brought biscuits, sliced apple, banana and a cup of tea in a tray, placed it in front of him and giving him the half peeled banana she asked, 'Do you have any programme in the near future?'

'No.'

'Then stay for at least a week. Whenever you come to Delhi hereafter don't stay in a hotel. Just speak out and say boldly that you are going to stay at Manohari's place. Why be afraid of anyone at all?'

He nodded his head in assent.

Chapter 22

I

One evening he came to the house at Borivali. Ramkumari was prepaing the spinach. He was not surprised at the look of wonder on her face when she saw him. He had not expected that there would be pleasant talk at this encounter; that she would have forgiven him; or that she would entertain camaraderie. He had come with the awareness that he was paying a visit here before leaving Bombay to allay his own guilty conscience. Without talking, he sat on the sofa. She was separating the sticky twigs from the leaves. Her hair was totally, like jute. The hair was still thick. He thought if she had dyed her hair she would look fifteen years younger, but not knowing how to begin the conversation, he was fumbling, she herself spoke, 'Have you come to ask me if I am not ashamed to come back to the house which is in your name?'

He remembered that when he had come the last time also, she had addressed him in the singular instead of the respectful plural usually used to address a husband. As if he had not noticed it he said, 'I don't understand what you're saying.'

'After you left, though I was paying the rent, you had mentioned, hadn't you, that your name was there as the tenant? You had distanced, hadn't you, my children from me by paying them money though I had given birth and had looked after them, brought them up? Not to have any obligation of you by staying in your house and not wanting to have any contact with children you gave me, I have gone to Dahisar Building, my own house. I do not reside here.' He didn't understand her. He just started staring at her. Lifting her face and looking up at him she said, 'Have you come to ask me why then I have come here? I didn't come here because I don't have a patch that belongs to me. When their mother was there, looking after them, they did not know her value. After I left who was there to cook for them? Who was there to sweep and clean the house and wash their clothes? The quarrels that broke out between brother and sister would never stop. Starvation. They came and apologised. I have come because of the call of the affection of a mother's heart. I am working in the house of the master for my livelihood and come here to serve them.'

He felt sorry that he didn't know any of this. Three years ago when he had called Bakula she had spoken angrily. It seemed she had called Avinash at Bangalore that her father had arranged for her engagement and had fixed up a marriage hall and had agreed to give away the bride himself. It seemed he had said that his wedding had taken place and had slammed the phone down. She had said that her father had ruined her life. After that he had called her once and said, even now you look for a boy. I will pay even if it is a dowry of five lakh rupees. I had said boys will agree if there is a dowry. 'What are you saying, Pitaji, if I say that we will pay dowry and make a proposal do you think I can find a boy? You must search and make the proposal. But no boy's relations will agree if you go about with the proposal. I don't want to marry, hiding anything. When I hid something once, the boy whom I had liked, I missed. Even if the marriage takes place, when once the truth is out, the whole life will be a bed of thorns. You didn't bring us up, you didn't stay with us. My mother has brought me up by working as a charwoman. Besides, recently, your escapades have appeared in the newspapers quite a lot. Even if you set about to search, no bridegroom's family will agree. No one from a good family will agree for the sake of five lakh rupees. They want a girl only from a respectable family. All in all I won't be able to get married. This is my fate. Sorry, this is my office. I can't talk much. There is no use in talking either.' That's what she had said. After that I haven't called her. He remembered that he didn't have the courage either. With this recollection he sank within himself. But he didn't show it. He felt like asking what Bakula did afterwards and whether she had done anything about it, but he was afraid that she might retaliate. He wondered whether Bakula had told her about her conversation with him. Deciding that it would be better if he never broached the subject, he came to the matter on hand.

'Look, I have decided to leave Bombay, establish a Gurukul Ashram at Hardwar and teach pupils free of cost. It is close to your place of birth also. We both come from the same region. Whatever has happened, has happened. No one can escape what is ordained. You also come with me. Let us live together. I will employ a cook. You can be happy. Anyway you are my lawfully wedded wife.'

She lifted her head and looked at him with fire in her eyes. Then she turned towards the spinach. A minute later she lifted her face and spoke as if she would stab him. 'For so many years I worked as a cook in someone else's house and brought up my children. Now you have come to tell me to be happy employing a cook myself? Have the priests instructed you that when you stay in a holy place, you should sleep only with your wife and not with whores and bitches? Have you come with a plan to separate me from my children at this stage and ruin them?'

He felt sorry that he hadn't thought about who would look after the children if he took her with him. He felt he shouldn't have made that proposal. But his mind didn't allow him to accept defeat. He said, 'She is thirty-five. He is thirty. They are old enough to look after themselves'

'If they had settled, they would look after themselves. Since you gave him two lakhs, he left his job, started a business and lost everything. I had to fall at the feet of Gore Saheb and beg to get him a job. This is the help you rendered.' Saying so, she picked up the tin plate with the sliced spinach, the wooden plank to cut the spinach and the knife and went to the kitchen. He, who was sitting on the sofa couldn't think of saying anything, not even the necessity of goodbye. He got up, wearing the chappals he had left at the door walked towards the steps. He started descending with the satisfaction that he had invited her and she had refused, and so it was not his fault.

ऽ

The next morning by ten, he went to Kurla. It was a flat he had seen twenty-five years ago. There was a big signboard which said Mohan Music Academy. Why did I come myself? I could have spoken on the phone. Even now shall I go back? The mind hesitated. Remembering his decision that everything should be settled once and for all, face to face, he pressed the doorbell. The door did not open. He waited.

After a while it did. The person standing there was Champa. The body had become even more corpulent. The same white complexion. Her black hair had been tied in a braid. He could immediately make out that she had dyed her hair profusely. Gold-rimmed glasses for the eyes, diamond earrings, gold chain for the neck and diamond-studded bangles. She was wearing a silk sari. Though nonplussed for a minute she recovered at once and said, 'Please come in.' In the hall there were the tamburas leaned against the wall. Two harmoniums. Two pairs of tablas. A thick bolster against the wall was proclaiming that it was the seat of a music guru. He felt that it was a regular school of music. There was also a sofa on one side. His own big photograph on the wall. After pointing to the sofa and saying, 'Please sit', she added 'there, or here at the seat of the guru. This is your own school, your own house.' For a moment he felt that she had won and he had lost, or she gave the impression of her having lost by making him win. He sat on the sofa. There didn't seem to be anyone else at home. She came up and sat next to him on the sofa half a foot away with the naturalness of a wife sitting next to her husband. Not a word of condemnation. No talk about why did you do this? Why were you away for so many years? No such unpleasant harangue. When he was hesitating what to say, she herself said, 'Shruti had called only yesterday. She is fine. She said, "Mom, I have good news to give you. Tell father also."'

'Where is she?' He asked before he realised that he had been drawn into conversation before knowing it.

'At New Jersey. Her husband also spoke. "I haven't seen Daddy at all. When you come next time to America on a programme both of you should stay in our town for a couple of months and conduct a workshop. He was not in India at the time of the wedding. Please convey my pranaams to him. He will be happy on hearing the news of his becoming a grandfather," he said.'

Now Mohanlal understood that he had been pulled into conversation in which she was an expert. He thought now she had become even more adept. Without uttering a single word, he turned to his right and looked at her face. As if it would be an embarrassment if she stopped talking, she continued, 'Swara also calls up every Sunday saying Mom, the name Swarmohan is a bit too long. It becomes difficult in this country for people who are intimate. My friends call me Mohan. It seems even in that country, it is common to address the son with the father's name. He said, send some more of daddy's cassettes. Caroline also loves our music. She says that you should come with daddy for three months and give me music lessons. Though she is an English girl, she has adjusted herself better than an Indian daughter-in-law.'

He was still watching her face. She couldn't think of anything more to say. He was struggling within himself to say what he had come to say. She herself said, 'Come, let's both go. Let us stay for a month with our son and two months at our daughter's and let us have a programme tour of America. It seems the weather will be nice at this time.'

Understanding that she would go on like this if he was silent, he said, 'I have come to a decision to leave Bombay and establish a Gurukul Ashram at Hardwar and settle down. Like a sanyasin. Anyhow there has been no relationship between us for twenty-five years. It is good if it is included in the document. Let's not get into any legal complications through litigation. If we present an application with mutual consent, we will get a divorce without delay.'

'Divorce,' she put both her hands against her ears as if she had heard something inauspicious. After half a minute she said, 'Don't know where you went from Nagpur. Afterwards the news came that you were staying with a dancer in Delhi, you ran away merely because I said that we should be firm with a deceitful contractor. Though it is so many years, I haven't done a single thing to diminish your good name. I have educated your children and have given them a life of their own. What is the basis now for your asking for a divorce?'

'It is not only because of the problem with the contractor that I left. I left you because you made a rumpus by swearing by the child in your womb that if I saw the face of my wife whom I had married in the divine presence at a temple, she who had a five-year-old daughter and another she was still carrying, it was because of that I left you.'

'Did I create a rumpus? How many wives can a man have?'

'Knowing that I already had one wife, you registered yours, wasn't it?'

'It was your duty to discontinue that after this was registered.'

'Was it my duty? It is only to complete that duty that I am asking for divorce now. There are documents to show that this flat was bought with my money, and the money I was giving you every month and that the deposit you have at the bank came from me. There is also evidence to prove that there has been no connection between us for twenty-five years. At the most, you can haggle about in a court of law. I will definitely get a divorce from you without paying you a single paisa', he said firmly.

'Where is the necessity that there must be a divorce? Come on, I will also come to your ashram at Hardwar. You need someone to look after you and to manage the affairs of the Ashram, don't you?'

'I know that you are a leech which attaches itself without the possibility of getting rid of it. You just sign the divorce document politely. Otherwise I will go to court. My name has already appeared in the newspapers enough number of times. Isn't Paranjape your father's protégé? I will ask the other newspaper people to publish all the divorce proceedings in detail,' he said and walked out.

When he called two days later her tone had changed. 'You have insisted on divorce. All the deposits you mentioned have been spent. Was it easy to bring up two children and bring them to this level? Will it bring you credit if you divorce and make your wife a destitute? Provide me with some means of livelihood.'

'Tell me in plain language what you are saying', he said.

'Anyway you are going as a sanyasin and establishing a gurukul. You have two flats in Bandra. You give them to me.'

He smiled within himself that this was a real blow. 'Shall I beg in Hardwar? If you turn avaricious, I will get all your possessions investigated,' he threatened. Finally, she demanded ten lakhs. After bargaining she agreed for five lakhs.

३

The morning after, he finished his transaction with Champa on the phone, after finishing his breakfast, he engaged a taxi and went to Panvel. Though he had heard the name he hadn't seen the place. After he made enquiries he found out that three kilometres away there was a farmhouse belonging to a lady from Bombay, a musician. On further inquiry he found out the way also. He stopped the taxi at the entrance of the garden and went in. A mango grove, teak trees which were growing in an enclosure, and number of other trees and at the centre a one-storey tiled house. The moment he saw it, he realised that it was more beautiful than the Omkar Ashram at Hardwar. When he approached the house a dog barked. A woman of about fifty came out and asked, 'Who is it?' 'I wanted to see Madhumita Bai. I have come from Bombay.' She brought an iron folding chair, opened it, placed it in the outer enclosure and said, 'Please sit here. I will call her,' and walked towards the right-hand corner of the garden. He also followed her. There were four newly-planted mango siblings. A woman was filling a plastic bucket with water from a hosepipe at a distance and watering the plants. She was wearing an ordinary cotton print sari and had covered her head to protect herself from the sun. He wondered if this was Madhumita. When the servant called out 'Madam', she turned her face and he could be sure it was her. She also looked at him. He was sure that she recognised him. The servant said, 'He has come from Bombay and he wants to see you.'

Madhumita was nonplussed for a minute. Then as if recovering, she said, 'Malakshmi, arrange two chairs under the big jackfruit tree. Give him some water. Then bring him tea and biscuits.'

She didn't speak until they came under the jackfruit tree. After they sat facing each other four feet apart in the shade, she transferred the edge of the sari covering her head on to her shoulder. To begin the conversation he asked, 'How is your music practice progressing?' She didn't answer. 'When will you start giving concerts?' he started again.

She looked at him fixedly without any embarrassment and asked, 'Please tell me the reason for your coming.'

'I have decided to leave Bombay, go to Hardwar and start a music gurukul. Before leaving I came to see you and enquire how your music practice was going.'

She continued to look at him as if his speech had made absolutely no impression on her mind. A minute later she said, 'I have given up music. It has no meaning whatsoever. I became convinced that instead of music, digging the ground, washing vessels or doing any other job was fruitful.'

'Really, what about art?' he raised his voice.

'It was about art that I was speaking,' she concluded. He didn't know what to say. Meanwhile Malakshmi brought a container full of water, two glasses and a light plastic tee poi and left. After pouring the water into both the glasses, holding up one she asked, 'Will you have some water, Panditji?' His mind also took in the mode of her address. Four years had passed. There was anger still. The explanation occurred to him that she would not address him 'Guruji'. He decided not to show anger. He was feeling thirsty. He drank the entire glass of water, put it on the tee poi and wiped his mouth with a handkerchief. She was not speaking. He understood the situation that if he asked anything she was only replying. Therefore he decided to do the talking himself. She was looking at him as if she would corner him. He was perturbed. Finally, he said what he wanted to say, 'I know you are angry. To err is human. You also know that to forgive is divine. Bombay itself is the birthplace of an evil mind. I have understood that by staying here I won't be able to achieve anything good. I must go to Hardwar, take over the ashram established by my guru, the noble Omkar Baba and settle down. I have decided to admit six or eight pupils, provide them shelter and food, teach them music and continue the music tradition.'

'With the intention of developing your own gharana?'

'My gharana?'

'Yes, you have your own style of singing. The pupils who continue it, develop it as a gharana of their guru. You have come to this decision. Haven't you? Otherwise your name will vanish along with you.'

He was surprised. 'I will swear on my tambura and say that I have never thought this way.'

'You haven't thought. But people like you never think about a gurukul ashram without reason. Tell me now that you simply don't have any such idea at all,' she asked challenging him.

It was difficult for him to answer her. Could it be this way too? He asked himself. A corner of his mind said 'yes'. He remembered the implication of Bakula telling him that no eligible man would marry a girl without a good family and that she was without such a background. He felt that the inside of his head was a vacuum. The crowing of the crow from the top of the jackfruit tree seemed like a voice from somewhere in the sky. He remembered that the crow was the vehicle of the God of Death himself.

In a short while, the household help brought some tea and biscuits. After drinking the tea he recovered a bit. His mind contemplated whether he had been made to sit under the tree because it was cool there or with the feeling that he should not be admitted into the house. He felt like asking whether he was so bad, not good enough to be invited into the house, but if he did ask that question it occurred to him immediately that it would be as if he would be suggesting it himself. She was just sitting there without even asking him politely whether she could give him some more tea. Realising that if he sat like that he would be just sitting there forever, he came out with exactly what he wanted to say, gazing at the tea pot, 'What has happened has happened. There is no use in raking up the old thing. My divorce has been settled. She has agreed to grant it without any objection. I have come to ask you to marry me if you consent. I don't know how much you have achieved now. No matter how proficient, the harmonium master won't have full command over the intricacies of singing. You will be my first pupil at Hardwar. Within a year's time I will make you number one singer in the entire country. After singing together in unison as a married couple I will establish your name and fame. After that you also teach at the gurukul. In course of time, everything will be yours. Everything will be ours, the ashram, the musical tradition, everything. The day after we are married, I will write out a will leaving the two flats at Bandra, whatever money or property of mine, entirely to you, as my heir. You will be the successor to my music. I will swear on my tambura that I will never look at any other woman.'

After saying this he just started gazing at the teapot. She was just looking at his downcast face. She became aware that she must reply and every moment she delayed, it would be tantamount to giving her consent. But she couldn't think of what to say and how to say it. He continued to look at the lid of the pot, lacking the courage to lift his face. A couple of minutes later the first sentence flashed forth and then the rest flowed on; 'Isn't it Champa Bai who had got the marriage registered that gave the consent for divorce? For the first wife whom you had married religiously at the temple doesn't have any records and doesn't have the divorce powers of a government court. How are you going to divorce her?'

'I invited her to Hardwar to run the family. She herself said she wouldn't come.'

'Even if she says she won't come, it won't be a divorce. Let it be. I have completely left off music. There is no meaning in it. No purpose, no fulfilment, you still believe that it has. That is a question of your belief. You think that you are fit to marry me, that is also a question of your self-esteem. The courage to invite me to develop and continue your gharana and to share your physical and musical connubiality, that courage is also born out of your complaisant self-esteem, isn't it?'

He didn't immediately understand fully what she said. He understood that what she said in essence was that he was morally inferior to her. Since he had the experience of meeting such admonitions, without losing courage, he looked up at her face. She stood up saying, 'Goodbye, I have work to do' and she walked away towards the plants she was watering. Lacking the strength to get up, he sat for a little while looking in her direction. The household help approached. She picked up the tea things and the teapoy. Realising that if he continued to sit there it would be a shame, he got up and started walking towards the garden gate through which he could see the waiting taxi.

४

His proposal engendered disgust in her. She became aware that fourteen years ago when she ardently hoped and desired for him to marry her, the background of that unethical unrighteousness of it hadn't been understood. She remembered, she had not seen Ramkumari then, and felt, that even if she had seen, then she was not capable of understanding. Bringing the pot which was full, by filtering the water by holding her right hand against the nozzle, she started pouring the water to the young mango tree.

After he visited, the question of what she should do in future became intensified. There was no problem for food and shelter; she had enough. But she had no work to do. How much of this gardening could she do? What was the use of it all? Looking up a job in Bombay was even more meaningless. While remembering that even in childhood the mind rejected everything in favour of music, all that happened all these years unwound itself like a spiral spring. She thought of rejecting and subduing that memory and tried to think of some other matter.

A week had passed, a phone call came from Guru Rajaram. 'How are you? How is the practice going?'

She felt like telling him the truth. She wanted to say that music was a meaningless activity and that she had given it up completely. For the moment she was practising it on her own. How long would she be able to ward him off like this? She became aware that one day, just like that, he might drop in. Why not tell him right now? When she was thinking thus Rajaram himself said, 'Look, there is something. I am embarrassed to discuss this with you. But I am telling you for your own good. Mohanlalji is leaving Bombay and is going to settle down at Hardwar, establishing an ashram. I told him firmly not to quit. But he has already decided, he was in the city for thirty-eight, thirty-nine years. His name was so inextricably associated with Bombay that he was identified as Bombay and Bombay was Mohanlalji himself. Shouldn't we organise a send-off celebration in his honour? He had some bad qualities; they are still there. True. Which human being doesn't have them? In artists, excesses are natural. The newspapermen exaggerated them and irritated him. The music organisations also followed in the same track. I have decided to arrange a send-off celebration. I have formed a committee of music lovers. I am not asking you to be on the committee. But give a generous donation for the expenses. I know you have been unjustly treated by him. No one else except me knows that. Still, I am asking you to donate. Because you are the one who should come up in the musical world. You wash away all bitter thoughts and memories. It is my ardent desire that you should fill the place vacated by Mohanlal. I will see to it that you do. What do you say?'

She didn't know how to answer. She felt it would be mean to reject the training which she had been given by a guru for four and a half years. If she told him at this point her abandoning music completely, it would be tantamount to refuse his request for donation. She said, 'Kaka, you know how I feel about him. But still, your word is sacred law for me. Please tell me the amount. I will send a cheque.'

'Ten thousand. Not just paying the money, you should also come to the programme. You should wash away all bitterness.'

'To whom should I address the cheque?' she asked.

Thinking that it would be best if she wrote it out and posted the cheque immediately avoiding the possibility of her mind rejecting it and forming a second thought, she took hold of the cheque book. While writing the amount, she remembered it was a donation honouring the word of Rajaram Kaka. Her fingers wrote 'Twenty-five thousand'.

The send-off function had been arranged at the playground of Ruyiya College. A big shamiana, a mat spread on the floor. Baithak seating arrangement so that any number of people could adjust and sit close together. Only for those who couldn't sit on the floor, a hundred foldable chairs on special request. It would be a whole-night concert and in order for the outside traffic noises to subside, it had been arranged at nine in the evening. It had been printed in the announcement itself that Pandit Mohanlal would sing a Khayal for the evening, one for midnight and one for the morning which he would sing in great detail and there would be two brief Chota-Khayals interspersing them. When Madhu saw that Gore Saheb's name was printed at the end as the President of the organising committee, she was upset how could he agree to be the chief of the felicitating committee knowing about Mohanlal's notoriety.

By the time she arrived, there were more people than she had expected. Since it was mentioned in the handbill itself that it would be the Indian style sitting, she thought she could sit quietly somewhere at the back since it was not important for her to listen to the music. She could also leave in the middle of the concert. She had decided that it was enough to show her face to Rajaram Kaka once to register that she had come. Since he himself would accompany on the harmonium it wouldn't be possible to see him in the middle. She enquired where she could meet him to finish with the formality at the beginning itself. A volunteer said that he was near the college portico. When she was going in that direction, suddenly she ran into Mohanlal. He stopped as soon as he saw her and said, 'So, you have also come.' His tone revealed surprise.

Her voice was changed with emotion. 'My Guru Rajaram Tipnis said that I must come without fail. So I have come.'

'It is not important who brought you here. Come and play the tambura. Lend support to me. If situation permits, let us sing together even.' His voice was also emotional. He was in a mood of excitement.

She was confused. Got angry. There was also the discretion not to show it. At the same time there was also stubbornness as to why she should listen to him. 'Panditji, I am not your student to play the tambura and sit behind you to sing together. Ours is not the same style of singing. I have developed singing in my own method. I am not even interested in your music.'

'Then why did you come?'

'I have told you that it is to oblige Guru Tipnis.'

'Whatever that is, sit in front of me in the gathering. I need inspiration to sing.'

Now her eyes spat fire. Her teeth gnashed. 'Mohanlalji, speak with respect. I don't belong to the class of women who provide you with inspiration.' Her voice notched up.

'I didn't say it because you are a great beauty. If a connoisseur is sitting in front the inspiration comes by itself to reveal one's best. You also know that the intricacies of music cannot be comprehended by ninety-five per cent of the audience. You can understand even the minutest nuance. Just come without talking any more and don't spoil my mood.' Saying so, he held her left shoulder firmly and started pushing her forward. She became aware that if she struggled to free herself, it would create a scene in front of the surrounding people. Without letting go of her, he led her forward straight to the front of the three-feet high platform and seated her firmly on the pedestal directly below the stage. The full house, the entire audience was looking. Then he himself ascended the platform, went in, brought a big leaning bolster, put it behind her saying, 'You should stay till the end' and went away. Her face perspired slightly. Feeling shy to look back at the audience, she sat with her head bent.

The programme began. Gore Saheb came to the stage stood up and took the mike in his hand. 'Pandit Mohanlalji is leaving Bombay and going to Hardwar. Hardwar is his native place. Besides, it is a holy place. It is the focal point where mother Ganga roars down from the mountain and starts flowing down silently on the level ground. It is the confluence of slow and silent melody of vilambit movement and the sound of abundance of tanas jumping down. He is going to run the Music Gurukul established by his revered teacher Sadhu Maharaj. On behalf of our Bombay music lovers we are giving a donation of three lakh rupees to that Gurukul.' The crowd clapped thunderously like the roar of the ocean. 'Mohanlalji is giving a free concert today to the music connoisseurs of the place of his career.' Claps. 'Therefore, I will tell you in advance that he is going to sing marvellously.' Claps again. 'Though he is leaving today, he will be visiting Bombay again and again. You also might have heard unfounded rumours that he is leaving Bombay in disgust. A great artist never bothers about such things. There is spiritual sanctity in Hardwar. There is the sanctity of pure-hearted music lovers in Bombay. Music needs both. We have all come to listen to music. No one should interfere with it either at the beginning, middle or at the end with their running commentary. Now I am giving the donation of three lakh rupees on behalf of all of you and I am garlanding him. Afterwards some others will be offering garlands. They insist that they must garland Mohanlalji. We cannot say strictly that it won't be permitted.' He finished his introduction. After that the people stood in a line on one side of the stage and offered garlands. Though no matter how briskly they moved and how quickly the photographers clicked and flashed away their cameras, it took a long time. Madhu counted. There were three hundred and thirty garlands.

After it was all over, the pile of garlands were cleared and the singer, accompanists and tambura players had taken their positions, Mohanlal bent towards the mike and said, 'You have all shown such affection. You have spoken affectionately. I will not express my love and gratitude in speech. Gore Saheb has been mentioning for a long time that singers should not lecture and make speeches. Gore Saheb himself had mentioned that there should be three lengthy Khayals representing the emotions of evening, midnight and early morning. Now it is already eleven. What shall I do? I shall leave out the evening raga.'

Many people from the audience cried out, 'Think that it is still evening and sing.' One of them shouted, 'Through your singing bring back the evening which is already past.' The entire gathering clapped. Madhu turned back and saw. She estimated that there were twelve to fifteen thousand people. Then it is Shuddha-Kalyan, Mohanlal announced in the mike and adjusted the pitch and tone of the shruti. Two girls were at the tambura strumming proudly. Tipnis and Prabhu were looking forward enthusiastically to give the support with their instruments, Madhu sat looking at the singer. The same swaras that she knew, the same uthaav.

ga ga
ga, re, saa, re, ga, pa ga dha paga, re, ga, re. saaresaa| ...

But the mood of the raga is not emanating. He has half closed his eyes. Is it to invoke the emotion or to hypnotise the audience into visually representing the emotion? He could not invoke the feeling. He was just moving through the swaras by sheer practice. That's all. Once, with half open eyes he looked at me. A stealthy look. She thought that he was an expert in the stealthy glances. She looked back. Ten to fifteen thousand people were eagerly waiting for the initial wave of the emotion, with humbly bent heads ready to be engulfed in the emotion. But the emotion was not welling forth. Mohanlal was struggling. Closing his eyes tightly he is searching for the pulse, looking inward. She looked at her wrist watch. Quarter of an hour had passed. The pulse was not found. Altogether, he let flow his look secretly in Madhu's direction five times. Not a straight look. A look that lacked any direct meaning. There was no warmth in the swaras. He took the tambura from the girl who was sitting to the right at his back and set the shruti as if there was something wrong with it. Then he turned to the left and suggested that she move closer. She moved forward. The *ma re* which he picked up again was an arid sound. Again he turned his eyeballs in my direction, repeatedly. He didn't understand the why and the wherefore of it. His eyeballs are rolling. They are struggling, with what or why is not being understood. She looked back. People are whispering among themselves. She ruminated, was it not, when there is the birth of mantric mesmerisation in music the audience sway enthralled? At that point, it was felt, he had stopped singing. The harmonium accompanist, who has to take it up when the singer stopped, and has to keep alive the movement of music had also stopped. She turned her face to the stage and looked. Mohanlal had bent down and was saying something to Rajaram in a whisper. He had also bent his neck and had brought his ear near Mohanlal's mouth. Only Prabhu at the tabla was continuing softly as if to demonstrate the movement of time. Tipnis got up leaving the harmonium and even while she was watching he got off the stage, approached her and whispered in her ear. 'Please come backstage. I must have a word with you.'

She was embarrassed. She spoke softly, 'I won't come to the stage. I will not join my voice with his. I won't strum the tambura.' It was heard by at least five or six people sitting by her side.

'It is not to ask you to accompany him by singing with him, no, not even to play the tambura. It is personal and private. Just get up and follow me. The entire gathering is watching.' She stood up. Climbing the platform and descending next to the corner curtain, she followed him. A little distance away, standing near the portico of the college he said, 'Somehow today, Mohanji is not getting the mood. If you move away from his immediate presence and disappear from his sight, he may get the mood. He has sent word through me to make you get up from there and send you away.'

'Kaka, he himself forced me, brought me, pushing me made me sit there bringing also the large bolster to lean on and said that if there was some music connoisseur in sight, there would be spontaneous inspiration to exhibit all the intricacies. Otherwise I would be sitting in some corner. Actually I didn't want to come at all. I came just to honour your wish.' In the middle of what she was saying he said, 'Let it be. Now he has stopped amidst the alaap. I must return quickly,' and ran back.

ढ

No matter what he did, he couldn't find the pulse of the raga. A raga familiar for fifty years and mastered for forty years. There is no guarantee that when the theory is perfectly understood, the emotion would arise. Recently this was happening. It seemed, as though the resolution which he had formulated two weeks ago of singing wonderfully well at the farewell concert of Bombay was failing. No, he must not accept defeat. Mohanlal was not running away from Bombay having been defeated. Fifteen thousand audience are sitting there ready to submit themselves to the mantric power of music. In one successful moment when the mantra spread they will be entrapped and absorbed. I know the pulse of the listeners. Who knows the Bombay audience better than I do? He must sing this Shuddha-Kalyan extensively and in such great detail that it would be entirely unprecedented anywhere, at any time. Yes, he must descend to the mandra. Kalyan in the Avarohana, plenty of opportunity while descending, plumbing and plunging into the mandra. Bhoopali while rising up and ascending from there, enthusiasm. That girl is straightforward. Never loses enthusiasm. No higgle-haggle and half-measures. She just left. What else would she do? When I have no mind to keep her here. No matter how enthusiastic, she cannot descend to mandra; she cannot make me descend. Only Kalyani has the strength to make me descend. The more the descent, the greater the depth reached at shadja, the more intense would be the vision of the raga: the words that I spoke, the words that I taught. It is then that the vision of truth flashes forth, she got it but she turned it against me so that it boomeranged. What she said was Asavari, Komala-Rishabha. It seems that it was the vision that made her tell the husband everything. She has sat before me, piercing me with her examining, condemning eyes. One should never sing, with an enemy seated in front. There should only be sensitivity and sympathy in front. Without the sympathetic and mild twinkle of the eyes that sprinkle sensitivity, how is it possible to sing? I committed a mistake, bringing her and making her sit here though she used brash and offending language. Mohanlalji, I am not your pupil, disciple to sit behind you and play the tambura. I am not even interested in your music. I told you that it was to honour the word of Tipnis. After all this, why did I still drag her and sat her in front of me, making her comfortable with a soft cushion? The subtleties of the swaras are not being realised. Only the memory of long practice. What can I descend to? What can be expanded? The people are losing their enthusiasm. They sense immediately whether it is giving a kick or not. After all it is only what I get that they too will get. There is no evidence and registration, how can you divorce her? I asked her to come to Hardwar. She herself said she wouldn't. Even if she says no, it doesn't become a divorce. Though the voice is descending to mandra, the base is not being formed. When it has not happened, the very descent to mandra-shadja is a lie. She is sitting there watching me. With the intention of ruining my programme. I did a mistake in making her sit in front of me. There is no meaning in music. No fulfilment either. You still believe that there is. It is a question of your self interest. The slut called me a bounder. Without my laying the foundation is she practising now? What she has achieved under the tutelage of a harmonium master, I will myself see one day or the other. The people are getting bored. I must succeed in my programme today. They are murmuring and muttering among themselves. They expect to get the same level of enjoyment in every concert. It is impossible if I don't send her out of my sight. How to do it? Would she go if I asked her to? I have the mike in front of me. If I tell her, the entire assembly will hear. She won't go. She will answer back. Yes, she is sitting there just to spoil the programme. Suppose I bring it to my mind that I and she have no relationship at all and close my eyes, but she becomes more personalised if I close my eyes. She pierces me with both her eyes with increased intensity. She is the pupil of Rajaram. She will certainly go if he tells her.

After she has left, she has become even more sharp and more piercing. It is easier to face her when she is face to face. I shouldn't have chosen this raga. I have already begun it. I am not getting the mood for it. Supposing I say I am going to sing some other raga? Don't the audience know that an artist is subject to moods, that too to Bombay listeners? If I have to conquer them, conquer them, con-quer them, c-o-n-q-u-e-r them... Suppose I start with the Omkara? They will wave their heads hypnotised, mad; they will close their eyes and become meditative. I have seen it in so many concerts. 'I am not getting the mood for Shuddha-Kalyan. For some time in the beginning I will sing Omkara. After I get the mood I will begin and sing another raga in great detail.' *Wah*! thunderous clapping like the roaring of the sea. Yes, it is coming, the mood is coming. He adjusted the tambura, gave it to the girl, closed his eyes and filled his ears with the reverbering sound of the tamburas. Yes, now I've got it. No more worry. Should rise to the taara first and then descend to mandra. He didn't open the eyes. The interior space was opening up. Now it doesn't matter if I open my eyes; there was the assurance that that pest had left. He opened his eyes. She wasn't there. The entire assembly was mesmerised—men, women, the young, the old, the youthful, the mature, all. He opened his eyes wide and observed the assembly. There, at a little distance, they are sitting, not in line but just one behind the other, front and back, jostling each other. There at a distance about thirty-five, a silk sari, diamond earrings, diamond nose-ring, definitely diamond bangles, ring, wrist-watch—yes it is she... What's her name? I have forgotten. It's better not to remember now. The concentration on the swara will be shattered. Yes, I remember. Hyderabad. Holding the tambura she moved closer than was necessary. The French perfume, along with memories of the morning... the concentration didn't return even after five minutes. Boredom, an experience of defeat. Struggle. I am an artist, a signer, this is a work of art, creating its mood and emotion is my only job. Just like she was conquered, the mind of the audience too must be conquered and made to melt, there should be the emotion of such self-surrender, full of yearning. The mood ought to come if you sing pausing and moving along the required speed on the subtleties of swaras. Thinking like this, he began to strengthen his willpower and resolved to take complete control over his singing. If it is possible to do so in a private group why can't it be possible in a public performance? He started singing, accepting the challenge. She. Yes, it was only she. She must have come reading about the concert programme in a newspaper. Or, how many women aren't there in Bombay who don't load themselves with silks and diamonds? No, he shouldn't look at her, yes he must bring singing under his control... his control... what is that noise? The mutterings in the assembly. There are two tamburas. The loudspeaker under his control, still the noise from the audience is being heard. The kind of disturbing sound which he had never heard in his forty years of singing experience. He got angry. Immediately he stopped singing. Indicating that the tambura must be stopped, he put his hand on both of them. The murmur was becoming loud. This was his very first experience. He brought his face towards the mike and said, 'Some people in the audience don't seem to be in a mood to listen to music today. If those people will go home, the others can listen without any impediment.' He felt like a teacher who had the right to admonish the audience and call them to order.

A man stood up from the middle of the gathering and said aloud, 'Don't say that we don't have the mood. Accept that you are not succeeding to bring on yourself the right mood.'

He raised his voice and asked, 'Can't you see that I am also struggling to get it?'

Meanwhile Gore Saheb ascended the platform. 'The listeners must kindly co-operate by exercising patience. Many a time the artists won't have the mood. It would be a little difficult at the beginning. This had never happened to Pandit Mohanlal. The mood will come in a little while.'

The man who had shouted from the audience asked, 'Gore Saheb, you are an advocate. Would it be possible for you, after accepting your fee to present a case if you say that you didn't get the proper mood in the court to argue, and you are not responsible for the failure of your case. Can you say it?'

Gore replied, 'Arguing in the court is one thing but creating art is quite another.'

By this time an old man sitting at the front stood up and took the mike in front of the harmonium accompanist, Tipnis. A khadi dhoti, khadi jubba. Bald head. Sharp eyes. Pointed nose. Many people recognised him—Triambak Purandhare. Gore also recognised him. A man well versed in literature and music. A Gandhian. He had retired as the Principal of Navodaya College. 'Mr. Advocate, it is true there is a difference between a lawyer's profession and a musician's. But before you go to the court, you must have completely prepared for the case. It takes eight or ten days to prepare for each case. You must sleep well the night before presenting the case, which means that you shouldn't spoil yourself by attending parties and such things. Such a discipline must be there for a singer also, mustn't it be there? Anyway he doesn't devise a new raga in a concert. He sings only the raga which his teacher has taught him and which he has practised and sung all those years. On some days the singing may be marvellous. On some days it may not come out so well. If there is discipline he can certainly sing not descending below a certain minimum level. In very recent times some artists are substituting the word mood for indiscipline and irresponsibility. The people also are deceiving themselves by believing it either by ignorance or because it is fashionable.'

After having said this much, Purandhare looked at Gore's face as if he was demanding an answer. Gore couldn't think of an answer. Some people sitting at the right clapped. As if an answer was found to express their reaction, the others also joined in and engaged themselves in clapping away.

Mr. Gore didn't know how to manage the situation. Neither did Purandhare. The audience who stopped clapping also didn't know what to do. When no solution was in sight and the atmosphere was tensing up moment by moment, Mohanlal said, 'I had not asked for this money. I came agreeing to give this concert free. All of you gave this cheque for three-lakh rupees through Gore Saheb as contribution to the ashram. I am returning this cheque. I will run my ashram by earning through my concerts. I don't want this disgraceful money.' He announced this with the mike to his mouth, took out the cheque from his pocket and held it in front of Gore.

'This was collected as donation to the ashram. There is no connection between this and your singing,' Gore stopped his hand.

Holding the mike to his mouth, Purandhare said, 'Pandit Mohanlalji is behaving angrily as if his ego has been hurt, what is the meaning of his words in saying that he will run the ashram with the money he earns from his own concerts?'

Mohanlal couldn't think of an answer. Meanwhile some twenty-thirty people got up from the middle of the assembly. A few more followed them. Another fifty or a hundred people. Yet more people. Finally everyone started getting up. Gore held the mike in his hand and said, 'Everyone, please sit down. Please consider this as the interval. Mohanlalji will begin his concert in ten minutes.' Though some people in the audience cried out 'Sit, sit down' the people who had got up didn't sit down. Seizing the mike from the hand of Gore, Mohanlal said, 'No, I won't sing. No artist will retain his mood after having been dishonoured this way.' Looking daggers at Purandhare, he threw the mike on the stage and walked away to the back of the stage.

7

Though Madhumita told herself that she had come to keep her word with Rajaram Kaka and he had seen her, that there was no more need to stay there, without knowing where to go at the middle of night she stood at the portico of the college. Though the loudspeakers were pointed in the other direction, she could hear what was transpiring on the stage. She thought that today music was betraying him and he had put the blame for it on her and had sent her out, but she wasn't angry. She felt unconcerned that it was his lot and asked herself why should she come under his purview by getting angry. What a beautiful raga Shuddha-Kalyan was. She remembered how he himself used to sing it delving into all its minute, intricate details laying bare thread by thread, layer by layer putting forth all its emotional content. Quite recently she told herself that she had also practised it. Rajaram Kaka had helped in refining it. She remembered that she had herself developed it in her own way. She thought, what a unique emotion would arise if the tranquil peace of Kalyan would form the base, for the enthusiasm of Bhoopali. The explanation that they would be the lamps of Bhoopali floating motionless on the quiet waters running calmly in the canal of Kalyan, seemed more relevant. She walked into the inner quadrangle of the college. The lights were still on. There was no sound of the mike. She sat on the steps humming to herself Shuddha-Kalyan without letting it out loudly from the throat. Wasn't aware of how much time had passed. She didn't even look at her wrist-watch. Suddenly she heard a noise in the outer pandal enclosure. Claps.

She thought the raga must have been over. In a little while the turmoil of the people. Many people were coming in this direction. They were speaking loudly among themselves. She wasn't able to get at the pros and cons of the argument. She must at once leave. She felt he might come this way during the interval. When she came out she saw that the programme was over. The people were arguing with each other. Some people said, 'Purandhare shouldn't have said that. The mood of Mohanlal would be all right.' Some others, 'What he said was right. Look at his arrogance. How he went away throwing the mike saying that he didn't want dishonourable money for his ashram. Shouldn't he have some respect for the audience?' Though she felt like staying there and asking someone about what had happened, she didn't feel enthusiastic about it. She didn't feel like plucking her mind away from Shuddha-Kalyan where it had immersed. After she came away from the college a couple of furlongs, the crowd became sparse. She looked at the watch. It was past midnight. Anyway it was not possible to go to Panvel at this time. She didn't feel like going to her brother's and waking them up. Suddenly she made up her mind – go to Rajaram Kaka's house, wake his wife Sonu Tai, Kaka would not yet have come back, let him be back or not, just sit in his practising chamber, take the tambura, adjust the shruti and sing to herself, to her heart's content; delve into the depths and expanse of Shuddha-Kalyan and lay it bare layer by layer slowly. The thought occurred, Mahim is quite close anyway, why not walk up? Though she thought of unruly scoundrels roaming about on the streets at this time of the night, she felt confident, they could do nothing. Both fear and caution disappeared in the mood of the raga.

Kaki opening the door with sleepy eyes said, 'He had said that the concert would go on all night. Did you come away in the middle?' 'I felt like singing to myself. Please open the music room.' Kaki said still half asleep, 'Sing closing the windows tight. It is midnight. The people from the neighbouring flats may object. Shall I give you some pohe and biscuits? There are bananas. There is milk in the fridge.' Saying, 'Nothing for me, please,' Madhu went into the room, closing not only the windows but the door also, she closed her eyes and tuned the tambura. By then the doorbell rang. She thought Kaka might have come. She didn't get up to find out.

Thinking that Kaka would push open the door of the room anyway, she prepared to tune the shadja. She heard the sound of the door open. It was Rajaram Kaka who walked in. Before he said anything, she said, 'Kaka, I feel like singing to myself for a long time. If you are sleepy, please go to bed.'

'Which raga?'

'Shuddha-Kalyan'

'I also feel like playing the instrument. Do this. You sing. You sing freely, independently, just as you want to. Don't think that I am the guru, that I will correct your mistakes and that I will show you the way. I will just support you. I won't take the lead. You are the singer. Main artist. I am an accompanist.' Saying so, he closed the door, drew his harmonium to himself and sat in front of her.

With the vision of the lamps of Bhoopali floating on the still, tranquil silently flowing canal of Kalyan, she closed her eyes and invoked the Shadja. The peaceful and graceful movement of the delicate swaras even without the external indication of beats of tabla was equal to the movement of the fish, which turning and turning many cycles of time beneath the water, invisible to the eyes, shows its nozzle once on the surface of the water. When the movement of that saam became clear she herself would get encouraged. Even the swara that moves mildly but majestically, has its own laya. A feeling of fulfilment suddenly flashed, that, without externalising the laya, inventing it internally was the secret of the form of a raga. She became even more introvert. What a variety of possibilities and opportunities are presenting themselves? Though there is the permission to use the tivra-madhyama in the descending movement while sliding into gandhara from panchama as in a meend, if it is concealed, and wriggled out, it is possible to enjoy the humble quietitude of Kalyan without relinquishing the fragrance of Bhoopali. This knowledge did bring comfort. The detailed searching of mandra, which is not in mere Bhoopali itself, can be integrated into the expansive details of Kalyan without giving up the inherent sweet exuberance of Bhoopali. Ah, when this mandra-shadja is attained there is the bliss of liberation in the primary pulsation. Myriad independent streams manifest themselves without breaking the bounds of the raga. If the madhyama and the nishada are used very sparingly, almost suggestively, if a dhaivata of lower even than that of the dhaivata of Bhoopali is used, what a delicious delicacy can be obtained! Rajaram Kaka is just following me. He is following me in the corrugations I am entering into and the basins of the streams I am creating. It has not been possible to follow all the crevices through the harmonium. When it was not possible, his face is breaking out into a smile of satisfaction. Today's my secrets are unexpected, it seems, they are misleading. Giving the impression of creating conflict as opposing tradition, then with buttery smoothness it is sliding into the primary mainstream of the raga. Kaka is getting excited. He is tiptoeing carefully to catch and combat its secrets. I myself didn't know that my imagination would soar with such independence. It is the—independence—freedom of mastering the shastra and transgressing it, and then the freedom of establishing that even the transgression itself was a part of shastra. Kaka is still excited. He seems to be confused and fumbling for the path by the raga and expanse of unimaginable and unexpected spheres. Joy of transgressing the borders is shining on the face. Joy broke out with the awareness that her swaras and imagination had never achieved such transgression of boundary. Knowledge dawned that only with such transgression the bliss of art will overflow. But the question arose, is it necessary to break the dam of life to make this overflow? While another question appeared that if we break the dam of life, how can art outburst and overflow, the finale of the raga manifested as if it was another unexpected flash which she could never have imagined. With the realisation that if it is further expanded it would turn into a circus, she flowed into the finale of shadja.

The fingers were still strumming the strings of the tambura. As if she had been absorbed into its mild tranquil melody she just sat looking at the ground. She didn't feel like looking at the accompanist with a questioning look to find out how it turned out. An inward feeling that she had found a meaning within herself. A fumbling. The awareness that if she didn't listen intently to this almost incomprehensible subtlety, it would escape. She closed her eyes. The voice of Kaka reached her ears. 'In another month I will arrange your debut concert in a big way. It was the end of music for

Mohanlalji today, you have the power to take the place vacated by him. Hereafter, there is no need for my lessons. You will grow still further through sadhana.'

She didn't speak. She was immersed in her inner search. The tambura was still vibrating. Suddenly weeping welled up within her and without even the knowledge of controlling it, it broke all barriers of her dam and surged forth in spasms.

Rajaram Kaka consoled her 'Madhu behen, you sang well. You have really become a great singer. Your efforts are crowned.'

'Kaka, I also feel that I sang well. But Vikram should have heard this. He left me. Doesn't matter. He has deprived himself from music. What meaning is left for him in life?' She lifted her face and looked at him, her eyes streaming with tears.

Glossary

Aalaap — From the root word *laab*. It means the expounding on speak or utterance.

Aavartana — From the root *vrit* meaning cycle. The prefix 'aa' in the word Aavartana means 'complete in all aspects'. So Aavartana means complete reiteration of specific notes or musical patterns.

Advaita — Non-duality, a philosophical position advocated by Shakaracharya.

Bol — A line or phrase of a composition; also, a beat or a set of beats on the table.

Cheez — An Urdu word, meaning thing or gift; in music used to refer to the *khayal* composition.

Dhaivata — The sixth note of the octave, from the root *dheya* meaning 'to concentrate'. The note is produced from the point which is also the centre for *dhyana* (concentration) in the body. It is also said that *dhaivata* is a note understandable only to the sensitive musical ear.

Gandaa/ Gandaa-puja — It is the formal initiation of an aspirant into Hindustaani music. *Gandaa* literally means tying a sacred thread on the right wrist of the aspirant. The student pays obeisance at the feet of the guru, whence he or she is formally enrolled as a pupil, and besides learning the art, avows to be faithful to the tradition and the master.

Gharana A school adhering to a particular style and tradition of Hindustani music. *Gharaanedaar* from *gharana*, refers to the traditional music or to a traditional musician (musician coming from a traditional music background—Agra, Gwalior, Jaipur, Bhendi Bazar, Rampur, Shan Chaurasia, Kirana, Indore etc.).

Laya Literally means to merge. Refers to tempo, the continuity of *maataras* (beats) with equal intervals (1. tempo in metered parts 2. timing in unmetered parts). *Layadaari* is the perfection of *laya* as well as *taal*. Medium tempo is referred to as Madhya laya and fast tempo as *drit laya*.

Lehara A tune of the duration of one cycle used as accompaniment to drum or solos.

Mandra Bass, the lower octave. The lower octave, or the lowest notes, the range varying from musician to musician.

Mantra/ Mantrakriya Mantra is a sacred hymn often related to the Vedic literature, and any activity carried out by chanting of mantra is called *mantrakriya*.

Meend A vocal expression in which an arch like movement takes place between two notes (connects two notes by a glide). It is very sweet by nature and the glide is one of the hallmarks of Hindustaani music. It is one of the major gamakas used in this school of music.

Nishaada The seventh note *ni*. It is so called because, according to *Ramayana*, Nishaad was a community living on the Avadh border in ancient times. Nishaad therefore refers to border and nishaad in the saptak is the border note.

Panchama	The fifth note *pa* (of the octave). There is also a raaga by this name.
Rishabha	Second note of the octave. The word comes from *rish* meaning to roar. The word Rishabha is used usually to refer to the bull. Before entering the temple of Shiva, one passes by Nandi the bull. Shadja or *sa* is supposed to be a representative of Shiva to enter the domain of Shadja, one has to pass through Rishabha.
Saadhana/ Saadhaka	Saadhana is spiritual-aesthetic practice; the practitioner is saadhaka.
Saam	The word meaning equal, refers to the state of equilibrium reached at saam. 'Saam' is the first beat of the beat cycle of any beat. Naturally, the first beat is emphasised or shown distinctively when one cycle is through.
Sama	Sama is the simultaneous commencement of the lyric and the rhythm, unlike the *ateeta* and the *anaagata*.
Sangeeta-shaastra	Nowadays though sangeeta literally means music, by definition vocal music, instrumental music and dance were together called Sangeeta–Geetam nrittam tathaa vaadyam trayam sangeetam ucyate, says Shaarngadeva in his *Sangeeta-ratnakara*. Sangeeta-shaastra refers to the treatises which have codified with great lot of details the theory and nuances of practice of these arts in a methodical manner.
Saptaka/ Sapta-swaras	Though having seven notes, it is essentially an octave with the first note appearing at the end again making it a set of eight, an identical rhythm pattern of 4+4.

Shadja The tonic, first note of the octave. It forms the basis for the identification of the rest of the saptak. Shat swaraah atra jaayante iti shadjah; the rest of the six notes have their origin here.

Shruti *Shru* meaning to hear, and *tin* meaning to use. Shruti is that which can be made audible to others. In music there are 22 identifiable shrutis in the saptak...the difference between shruti and swara is that the latter is essentially a pleasing shruti (microtonal variations).

Taal From the root *tal*, meaning 'base' or 'land' or 'foundation' of rhythm pattern, or 'palm'. The beats are shown by the tapping of one palm on the other.

Taana The word comes from the root *tan vistaare*, meaning 'to spread'; these can be short or extended; rhythmic way of expansion

Taara-saptaka Higher octave.

Taara-shadja First note of the higher octave.

Taraana A very popular form in Hindustani classical music, it is slowly fading. It contains Persian and Arabic phonemes like tom, nom, dir, dir, naa, naa yallallah, yallallom, dernaa, deem tadeem etc.

Tarab Helping (resounding) strings fixed below the main strings in the sitar, sur bahaar, vichitra veena, sarangee, sarod etc.

Vaadi Comes from *vad*, meaning to speak. Refers symbolically to the note which speaks for the raga. It has a dimensional value in the scale. For example:

1. Bhairav: saa, re, gaa, maa, paa, dhaa, nee, saa—re is samvaadi and dhaa is vaadi
2. Yaman: nee, re, gaa, maa paa, dhaa, nee, gaa—gaa is vaadi and nee is samvaadi

In other words any two equal bunches of three or four notes in the uttaraanga and poorvaanga and their pointed or speaking notes are considered as vaadi and samvaadi respectively

Vilambit — The slow tempo.